SHIRLEY CONRAN

Lace

The Complete Story

KU-156-117

PENGUIN BOOKS

PENGUIN BOOKS

Published by the Penguin Group
Penguin Books Ltd, 27 Wrights Lane, London W8 5TZ, England
Penguin Books USA Inc., 375 Hudson Street, New York, New York 10014, USA
Penguin Books Australia Ltd, Ringwood, Victoria, Australia
Penguin Books Canada Ltd, 10 Alcorn Avenue, Toronto, Ontario, Canada M4V 3B2
Penguin Books (NZ) Ltd, 182–190 Wairau Road, Auckland 10, New Zealand

Penguin Books Ltd, Registered Offices: Harmondsworth, Middlesex, England

~ CONTENTS ~

This book is for
my sons,
SEBASTIAN CONRAN and JASPER CONRAN,
with love

Lace

~ PRELUDE ~

Paris 1963

SCRAPE ... scrape ... scrape ... The cold, hard metal dug deep into the child's body. She forced her knuckles into her mouth and bit against the bone as hard as she could to fight pain with pain. She didn't dare scream. She just mumbled, 'Jesus, Jesus, Jesus,' as she bit her hand.

Tears ran down her cheeks and on to the paper pillow. Her body was trembling and clammy with cold sweat. Outside she could hear the cheerful noise of a busy Paris street, but in this small brown room there was no sound except the scraping and her mumbling and the occasional clink of steel against steel. She would count to ten and *then* she'd scream! Surely it couldn't go any higher, whatever he was pushing up inside her? It felt like a dagger, persistent, cold, merciless. She wanted to vomit, to faint, she wanted to die. She couldn't bear it to go on and on and on ...

The man was intent on what he was doing as she lay on the hard table, her knees forced high and apart by the steel surgical stirrups. It had been horrifying from the moment she entered this place, the dark brown room with the hard, high table in the middle. A line of silvery instruments and a few odd-shaped bowls lay on another table; there was a camp bed and a cloth screen in one corner of the room. A white-aproned woman had pointed to the screen and said, 'You can take off your clothes behind that.' Naked, she had shivered behind the screen, not wanting to leave its protection, but the woman had taken her briskly by the wrist and tugged her to the table in the centre of the room. She had been positioned on her back so that her narrow hips rested on the edge of the table, while her legs were pulled apart by the woman and lifted into the cold surgical stirrups. The shivering child felt unbearably humiliated as she gazed into the powerful overhead light.

There had been no anaesthetic. The man wore a crumpled green surgeon's gown. He had muttered some instruction to the woman

7

and then he had inserted two fingers into the child's vaginal canal; he held the cervix with his fingers as he placed his other hand on her abdomen to feel the size and position of her uterus. Then she was swabbed with antiseptic, and he pushed in a chill speculum shaped like a duck's bill, which kept the walls of the vagina apart and enabled him to see the opening of her uterus. The speculum didn't hurt, but it felt cold and menacing inside her small body. Other instruments were also inserted and then the pain started as the cervix was opened slowly with the stainless steel dilators until it was wide enough for the operation to start. The man picked up the curette – a metal loop on the end of a long thin handle – and the excavation began. The curette moved in and around the uterus, scraping the life out of her; it took only two minutes, but the time seemed endless to the suffering child.

The man worked quickly; occasionally he muttered to the woman who was helping him. Hardened though he was, he carefully avoided looking at the child's face; her little feet in the stirrups were reproach enough as he swiftly finished the job and removed each bloodied steel instrument.

As the uterus was emptied it gradually contracted back to its original size, but the child's body was jerked with agonizing cramps until the contractions stopped.

Now she was wailing like an animal, gasping as each new pain clawed her. The man abruptly left the room; the woman swabbed her; the cloying smell of antiseptic filled the air. 'Stop making such a noise,' hissed the woman. 'You'll feel fine in half an hour. Other girls don't make such a fuss. You should be grateful that he was trained as a real doctor. You haven't been messed up inside; he knows what he's doing, and he's fast. You don't know how lucky you are.' She helped the thin, thirteen-year-old girl off the table and on to the camp bed in the corner. The child's face was grey, and she shook uncontrollably as she lay under a blanket.

The woman gave her pills to swallow, then she sat and read a paperback romance. For half an hour there was no sound in the room except for the child's occasional stifled sob. Then the woman said, 'You can go now.' She helped the girl to dress, gave her two large sanitary towels to put in her pants, handed her a bottle of antibiotic tablets and said, 'Whatever happens, don't come back here. You're not likely to haemorrhage, but if you start bleeding,

8

call a doctor *immediately*. Now get home and stay in bed for twenty-four hours.' For one moment the woman's carefully controlled, impersonal toughness weakened. '*Pauvre petite!* Don't let him touch you for at least a couple of months.' Awkwardly she patted the child's shoulder and led her through the passage to the heavy front door.

The child paused outside on the stone steps, wincing in the sharp sunlight. Slowly, painfully, Lili walked along the boulevard until she came to a small café where she ordered a hot drink. She sat and sipped it, feeling the sun and the warm steam on her face as a jukebox pumped out the new Beatles hit, 'She Loves You'.

~ PART ONE ~

~ I ~

IT was a warm October evening in 1978 with the distant sky-scrapers sparkling in the dusk as Maxine glanced through the limousine window at the familiar New York skyline. She had chosen this route for that view. Now, in the discreet, hushed comfort of the Lincoln Continental, they stood stuck in traffic on the Triboro Bridge. Never mind, she told herself, there was plenty of time before the meeting. And the view was worth it – like diamonds sprinkled across the sky.

Her neatly folded sable coat lay beside the maroon crocodile jewel case. The nine maroon-leather suitcases – all stamped in gold with a tiny coronet and the initials M de C – were stacked beside the chauffeur or stowed in the trunk. Maxine travelled with very little fuss and at enormous expense, usually someone else's. She took absolutely no notice of luggage allowances; she would say, with a shrug of the shoulders, that she liked comfort; so one suitcase contained her pink silk sheets, her special down-filled pillow, and the baby's shawl, delicate as a cream lace cobweb, that she used instead of a bed-jacket.

Although most of the suitcases held clothes (beautifully packed between crisp sheets of tissue paper), one case was fitted as a small maroon-leather office; another carried a large medicine box packed with pills, creams, douches, ampoules, disposable syringes for her vitamin injections and the various suppositories that are considered normal treatment in France but frowned on by Anglo-Saxons. Maxine had once tried to buy syringes in Detroit – *mon Dieu*, could they not tell the difference between a drug addict and a French countess? One had to look after one's body, it was the only one you were going to get and you had to be careful what you put on it and in it. Maxine saw no reason to force terrible food on the stomach merely because it was suspended thirty-five thousand feet above sea level; all the other first-class passengers from Paris had munched their way through six overcooked courses, but Maxine had merely accepted a little caviar (no toast) and only one

13

glass of champagne (non-vintage, but Moët, she observed with approval before accepting it). From a burgundy suede tote bag she had then produced a small white plastic box that contained a small silver spoon, a pot of homemade yogurt and a large, juicy peach from her own hothouse.

Afterwards, while other passengers had read or dozed, Maxine had taken out her miniature tape recorder, her tiny gold pencil, and a large, cheap office duplicate book. The tape recorder was for instructions to her secretary, the office duplicate book was for notes, drafts and memos of telephone conversations; Maxine tore them off and sent them on their way, always retaining a copy of what she had written; then when she returned to France, her secretary filed the duplicates. Maxine was well organized in an unobtrusive way; she didn't believe in being *too* well organized and she couldn't stand bustle or hustle, but she could only operate when things were orderly; she liked order even more than she liked comfort.

When Madame la Comtesse booked a reservation for a business trip, the Plaza automatically booked a bilingual secretary for her. She sometimes travelled with her own secretary, but it was not always convenient to have the girl hanging round one's neck like a pair of skates. Also, as the girl had now been with Maxine for almost twenty-five years, she was able to keep an eye on things at home in Maxine's absence; from the condition of her sons and her grapes to the times when Monsieur le Comte returned home and with whom.

Mademoiselle Janine reported everything with devoted zeal. Since 1956, Mademoiselle Janine had worked hard for the Château de Chazalle and she shone in the reflected glory of Maxine's success. She had first worked for the de Chazalles twenty-two years ago, when Maxine was twenty-five and had opened the château as a historical hotel, museum and amusement park, before anybody (except the locals) had heard of de Chazalle champagne. Mademoiselle Janine had fussed around Maxine from the time her three sons were babies, and she would have found life intolerably dull without the family. Indeed, she had been with the de Chazalles for so long that she almost *felt* like one of the family. But not quite. They were – and always would be – separated by the invisible, unbreakable barriers of class.

Like New York, Maxine was glamorous and efficient, which was why she liked the quick pace of the city, liked the way that New Yorkers worked with neat, brisk speed whether they were serving hamburgers, heaving garbage off the sidewalk or squeezing fifty cents' worth of fresh orange juice for you on a sunny street corner. She appreciated these fast-thinking people, their tough humour, their crisp jokes, and privately thought that New Yorkers had all the *joie de vivre* of the French, without being nearly so rude. She also felt at home with New York women. She enjoyed observing, as if they were another species, those cool, polite, impeccable women executives as they operated under the merciless pressure of the grab for power, the lunge for money, the lusting after someone else's job. Like theirs, Maxine's self-discipline was colossal, but – at the age of forty-seven – her grasp of people-politics was even better. Had it not been so, she would not have been travelling to meet Lili.

That gold-digging slut!

But Maxine was undoubtedly intrigued by Lili's offer and it was partly her curiosity that had brought her all the way across the Atlantic. Again she wondered whether she would accept the job. She would have thought that Lili – who must be about twenty-eight years old by now – would never have wanted to see Maxine again. Maxine remembered that long-ago expression of startled pain in the flashing chestnut eyes of the troublemaker whom the press had nicknamed 'Tiger-Lili'.

She had been amazed to receive the telephone call, to hear that low, sensual voice sound so astonishingly humble, as Lili had asked Maxine to meet her in New York to decorate Lili's new duplex on Central Park South. Lili wanted her new home to be a showpiece, a conversation-stopper, and she knew that Maxine could supply the correct blend of erudite elegance and spirited style. The budget would be as large as was necessary, and of course all expenses for Maxine's trip to New York would be paid whether or not she decided to accept the commission.

There had been a pause, then Lili had added in a penitent voice, 'I would also like to feel that something no longer has such painful memories for you. For so many years I have lived unhappily with my conscience, and now I dearly wish to do whatever is necessary to be at peace with you.'

After this apology there had been a thoughtful pause, then the conversation had turned to Maxine's work. 'I understand you've just finished Shawborough Castle,' Lili had said, 'and I also heard about the stunning job you did for Dominique Fresanges – it must be wonderful to have a talent such as yours, to rescue historic houses from decay, to make so many homes beautiful and comfortable while they still remain a heritage for the world . . .'

It had been a long time since Maxine had enjoyed a holiday in New York by herself, so eventually she had agreed to make the journey. Lili had asked Maxine to tell nobody of the meeting until after it had taken place. 'You know the press won't leave me alone,' she had explained. And it was true. Not since Greta Garbo had there been an international movie star who so intrigued the public.

As the limousine started to crawl forward, Maxine glanced at her diamond wristwatch – there was plenty of time before the six-thirty meeting at the Pierre. Maxine was rarely impatient; she disliked being late, but assumed that everyone else would be. That was life today – undependable. If a situation could be improved, Maxine would generally do it with a slight, one-sided smile, a look that combined conspiratorial charm with a hint of menace. If a situation could *not* be improved, then she folded her hands in her lap and imperturbably accepted *la loi de Murphy*.

She happened to catch sight of herself in the back mirror of the limousine and leaned towards it, lifting her jaw above the cream lace jabot and poking it sideways at her reflection. It was only five weeks since the operation, but the tiny scars in front of her ears had already disappeared. Mr Wilson had done an excellent job and it had only cost a thousand pounds, including the anaesthetist and the London clinic bill. There was no tautness, no pulling at the mouth or eyes; she simply looked healthy, glowing and fifteen years younger – certainly not forty-seven. It was sensible to have it done when you were still young, so that nobody noticed, or, if they did, they couldn't pin you down; today you never saw an eye-bag on an actress over thirty, or on an actor, come to think of it. Nobody had noticed her absence; she had been out of the clinic in four days and had then spent ten days in Tunisia where she had lost seven pounds, a satisfying bonus. She simply could not understand why some people went all the way to Brazil and paid heaven knows what for their lifts.

Maxine was a firm believer in self-improvement, especially surgical. One *owes* it to oneself, was her justification; her teeth, eyes, nose, chin, breasts, all had been lifted or braced until Maxine was a mass of almost invisible stitches. Even so, she was no great beauty, but when she thought back to her childhood and remembered the prominent nose, the horselike teeth and her painful self-consciousness, she was grateful that years ago she had been persistently urged to do something about it.

It had not been necessary to do anything about her legs. They were exquisite; she stuck out one long pale limb, rotated an elegant ankle, smoothed the blue silk skirt of her suit, then opened the window and sniffed the air of Manhattan, oblivious to the strong carbon monoxide content at street level. She reacted to New York as she did to the champagne of her estate – with happy delight. Her eyes sparkled, she felt high and ebullient. It was good to be back, despite the traffic jam, in the city that made you feel as if every day was your birthday.

Judy Jordan looked like a tiny, blonde, exhausted Orphan Annie, although she was forty-five years old. In her Chloë brown velvet suit, and a fragile, cream silk blouse, she sat in the crowded bus as it crawled up Madison Avenue. Impatient by nature, she always took what came first, a bus or a cab. She had in fact recently been photographed by *People* in the amazing act of getting on a bus. This had given Judy a great deal of satisfaction, because there had been a long period in her life when she couldn't afford anything *but* a bus.

Suddenly she felt sad. As if she were touching a talisman, she fiddled with one of the matching rings she wore on her middle fingers, each one an exquisitely carved coral rosebud on a thick gold band. Apart from these she didn't much care for jewellery – her passion was for shoes. Her walk-in shoe closet contained row upon row of exquisitely handmade boots and shoes. Judy decided she might just celebrate tomorrow by going mad in Maud Frizon. Why not? Her partner had told her only this morning that they were worth nearly two million dollars *more* this year!

It was increasingly hard to remember life in her old studio on East 11th Street, from which she'd been evicted because she couldn't pay the rent. But Judy forced herself to remember those days. They made the present all the more pleasant by contrast.

There was another reason why Judy never wanted to forget what it felt like to be short of money in a big city. That was how a lot of her readers felt. They bought *VERVE!* for its optimism, its encouragement, its sensuality, and they looked on the magazine as a *friend*. The truth was that Judy travelled by bus because she wanted to stay in touch with her readers.

Reconciling the opposite sides of her public image was sometimes difficult. On the one hand, she liked to be seen as a warmhearted, straightforward, hard-working woman who'd been known to lunch off a street-corner hot dog, a working girl much like her readers. On the other hand, those same readers expected her to lead a glamorous social life, dress the way they dreamed of dressing, and be a celebrity herself. So, when Judy was not eating hot dogs she lunched at Lutèce, dieted at the Golden Door when necessary, and travelled constantly. Like New York, she set a brisk, optimistic pace. On those occasions when – suddenly – she plummeted into black loneliness, she gritted her teeth and bore it. Loneliness from time to time was the price of freedom, and freedom wasn't a stars and stripes Boy Scout idea, it was doing what you damn well wanted to do – all the time.

The doors of the bus hissed open, sucked in more passengers and hissed shut again. A sallow, middle-aged woman collapsed into the seat opposite Judy, settled her shopping bag on her knees, then suddenly groaned. 'I wish the buildings would go up in flames, then there'd be no more problems.' She said it again, then yelled it. No one in the bus took the slightest notice until the woman got off; then there was a general rustle of relief, a few smiles and shrugs – just another New York crazy who didn't care what anyone thought of her.

But that was also a sign of maturity, mused Judy. You became an adult when you stopped caring what other people thought about you and started to care what *you* thought about *them* ... was it a feature? she wondered professionally. She thought about a possible author, celebrities to interview, a quiz, and made a quick mental note to get one of the editors working on it. 'Are You Grown-up Yet?' Not a bad title. Not a bad *question*, either, she thought to herself, unable to answer it. She still felt as childlike inside as she looked on the outside, although she would never allow anyone to know it. Vulnerability was bad for business. Judy preferred her reputation as an *enfant terrible*, a baby tycoon, the lethal little lady publisher who had already come a long way and intended to go much farther. The image that Judy projected was that of a woman to be reckoned with – a woman who made you think ten per cent faster when you were with her, but also a woman with a weakness for pretty shoes.

She was making up for lost time. Until she was fifteen, Judy had worn only sensible black shoes.

Behind the lace curtains her family had been painfully poor. Her parents were devout Southern Baptists, greatly interested in sin and its avoidance. In order to avoid sin, Judy and her young brother Peter were never allowed to do anything on Sundays. They could sing in church but they weren't allowed to do so at home, they were not allowed to listen to the radio, because radio on Sunday was sinful: the big, elaborate, walnut radio, with the wooden sunray pattern over the speaker, was the focal point of the living room, but on Sundays, apart from cooking noises, the only sound in the house was the clatter of the old icebox that stood by the door to the back porch.

Naturally, smoking and drinking were sinful. Nevertheless, her Grandad, who lived with them, would disappear from time to time into the cellar for a drink from the bottle that he kept hidden behind the boiler; perhaps he justified it to himself as medicine. After his Sunday drink, Grandad always went to the back porch to his rocking chair, which creaked under his weight as he beamed at the apple tree at the end of the yard and waited for the hereafter. Judy's parents must have known about the whisky because you could smell the stuff on his breath; her mother's mouth would tighten, and she would give a tiny, delicate, disapproving sniff, but she never said anything. Grandad was supposedly a teetotaller.

The man in the plaid shirt seated across from Judy looked uneasy and lowered his eyes furtively to check his zipper. She looked away quickly – she must have been staring again. When she was lost in thought, her dark blue eyes glared through the big tortoiseshell frames with a ferocity that was as alarming as it was unintentional.

She wondered again what the purpose of this meeting with Lili was, and why the mystery?

First there had been the contrite telephone call – and God knows, Lili had every reason to sound contrite. Ultimately, of course, the bust-up with Lili had been good for Judy's public relations business, but that hadn't been Lili's intention that night in Chicago ... 'If you could find it in your heart to forgive me for the very bad way in which I behaved ...' Lili had pleaded, in that deep voice with the slight continental accent ... 'I was so ungrateful ... So very unprofessional ... I am ashamed when I think about it ...' In spite of herself, Judy had started to mellow; it wasn't just because of Lili's stardom or her magnetism, it was simply because Judy had enjoyed working with her. They really had been a terrific team until that night in Chicago.

Lili had said there was a special matter that she wished to discuss with Judy, 'something of a very confidential nature I should like to speak to you about personally'.

Judy didn't waste her time on anybody. Dozens of strange proposals were put to her each week, and most of them didn't get past her secretaries. But this was Lili, whose name had been linked to more celebrities than that of any other woman, Lili, whose waiflike beauty was a twentieth-century legend, Lili, who *never* gave interviews.

The last fact counted most with Judy. Lili was worth at least a thousand words for *VERVE!*, whatever happened at the meeting, so Judy agreed to it. Eager and charming as a child, Lili thanked her and asked her to keep their rendezvous a secret. Judy hadn't intended to tell anyone anyway. But she was intrigued; like herself, Lili had also succeeded in life fast, mysteriously and against the odds. She must be about twenty-eight or twenty-nine now, although she didn't look it.

Last month's telephone call had been followed by a confirming letter on thick, cream paper with the single word L I L I centrally engraved in navy Bodoni typeface; for some reason Lili had no last name.

What could she have in mind? Judy wondered. Backing? Surely not. Publishing? Not likely. Publicity? No longer necessary.

It was six-twenty and the traffic was still motionless, so Judy jumped off the bus and walked the last few blocks. She always liked to arrive on time.

*

The cab smelled of stale cigarette smoke, the back seat had been slashed and the guts were spilling out. It was also stuck in traffic on Madison Avenue, but the driver, a surly Puerto Rican, was mercifully silent until suddenly he barked, 'Where you from?'

'Cornwall,' said Pagan, who never thought of herself as English. She added, 'The warmest part of Britain,' and thought that wasn't saying much. Pagan's pallor was due to poor circulation, she had always suffered from cold weather, which was eleven months of the year at home. As a child she had hated to put her naked feet out of bed on winter mornings and hurriedly plunged her chilblains into sheepskin slippers. Her first frenzied love-hate relationship was with her warm but uncomfortable winter underclothes; the scratchy, cream wool combination suit that covered her from neck to ankle, with sagging sanitary trapdoor that unbuttoned at the back; the prickly, flannel Liberty bodice, a vestlike garment that ended at the stomach with long, dangling suspenders to hold up her thick woollen stockings.

When Pagan was a child, at seven every morning a little housemaid had scurried around Trelawney to light the stoves and the fires, which were banked down or turned off every freezing winter night at eleven p.m. no matter what time everyone went to bed. Smelly cylindrical oil stoves stood before the lace curtains of the bathrooms and minor bedrooms, open coal fires smouldered in the principal bedrooms and great, glowing logs were piled in the hall and drawing room, but the long hallway and bathrooms were always freezing, and the food from the home farm was lukewarm when it finally arrived on the manor table. The uneven flagstones in the dining room always felt cold, even in summer, even through Pagan's shoes; when she thought no one was looking, Pagan used to tuck up her feet under her bottom and away from the icy floor – but it was always noticed and she would be told sharply to 'sit up like a lady'.

However, the worst part of winter had been getting into bed under the cold heaviness of the linen sheets. Once beyond the heat range of the oil stove, Pagan's bones would ache and her body become gradually numb until sleep mercifully anaesthetized the dull pain.

At this memory, although it was hot for October, the forty-six-year-old Pagan shivered in her pink wool Jean Muir coat.

As usual, Pagan was staying at the Algonquin, where she felt oddly at home. The lobby had the slightly seedy, unwarrantedly superior air of a London club with its high-backed, shabby leather wing chairs and dim, parchment-shaded lights. Her room was small but surprisingly pretty after the calculated gloom of the lobby. A comfortable, pink velvet armchair stood on the grass-green carpet; artful lace scatter pillows, cunningly placed brass lamps, a few bird pictures in golden frames spoke of the skilful decorator's touch. The old-fashioned, newly smart brass bedstead reminded Pagan of the nursery at Trelawney and the dark-green-on-white trellis wallpaper swept her mind back to the conservatory where her grandfather used to read *The Times* every morning, surrounded by slumbering dogs, palms, ferns and tropical plants. The conservatory was heated by long, hot, brown tubes that writhed around the walls at floor level and burned your fingers if you touched them. It was easily the warmest, if not the *only* warm spot in that draughty mansion, especially when the wind was blowing straight off the sea, sweeping harshly over granite-grim cliffs to the rhododendron-encircled lawns. The conservatory was also a terrific place to hide from her mother; with a book and an apple, Pagan would slither like a lizard under jade fronds and jagged malachite spikes, concealed by yellow froth and spume-scent greens.

Pagan could hardly remember her father, who had been killed in a car crash when only twenty-six. Pagan, then three years old, had been left with a vague memory of a scratchy cheek and a scratchy, tweed-kneed lap. The only traces of her father were the row of silver trophy cups, which stood on the oak shelves in the study, for school swimming matches and county golf, faded sepia photographs of cricket teams, and a group of laughing people at a beach picnic.

After his death, until she was ten and had to go to school in London, Pagan and her mother made their home with Grandfather at Trelawney, where Pagan had been both spoiled and toughened. When she was three years old, she had been taken out into the bay and lowered over the side of the dinghy in Grandfather's arms to learn to swim. When she was thirteen months old she had been put on her first pony; the reins were placed in her baby hands and her grandfather walked her around the paddock every morning so that she would learn to ride before she was old enough to be frightened; she first hunted with Grandfather Trelawney when she was eight.

It was her grandfather who had taught Pagan courtesy. He listened politely and with genuine interest to everybody, whether it was one of his tenants, the village postman or his neighbour, Lord Tregerick; the people Grandfather couldn't stand were what he called 'the money chaps' – lawyers, bankers, accountants. Grandfather never looked at bills, he simply passed them on to his agent to be paid.

Pagan had always been surrounded by servants, many of whom were there because her grandfather hated to dismiss anyone. Somebody put Pagan's gloves on, somebody pulled her boots off, somebody brushed her hair at night, and somebody put her clothes away, so the little girl grew up to be compulsively untidy. Pagan always remembered the soft rustle of the housemaid's skirt as she carried brass cans of hot water to the bedroom in the early morning and stood them by the rose-patterned washbasin; the blissful warmth of the butler's pantry, where Briggs cleaned the silver and kept the flower-decorated Minton dinner service on shelves behind glass doors; the cosy warmth and fragrance of the big kitchen; the resigned, sour face of her grandfather's valet as he scratched the mud from Pagan's riding clothes in the brushing room.

Pagan seldom saw her mother, and when she did put in an appearance she was obviously bored. She hated the country; there was nowhere to go and nothing to do. Cornwall in the 1930s was hardly sophisticated and Pagan's mother certainly was. Short hair sleeked beetle-neat against heavy, dead-white makeup; the daily masterpiece, a scarlet glistening mouth, was painted over her real mouth, which was much thinner; red traces of Pagan's mother could be found on glasses, cups, towels and innumerable cigarette butts. Mrs Trelawney often went up to London, and when she came back, she brought her London friends down for the weekend. Pagan disliked them, but nevertheless, she picked up much of their Mayfair slang, and for the rest of her life her conversation was dotted with their dated, breathless exaggerations.

Now in 1978 Pagan still missed her grandfather and regretted that her husband had never met him – or stayed at Trelawney before it had been transformed. Not that her grandfather would have had anything in common with her husband, who was interested only in books and his work. He took no interest in Pagan's fundraising – although without the money she raised, he would have been unable to continue his research. Exasperated, she sometimes scolded him. When she did, he would hug her and say, 'Darling, I'm sorry white mice are so expensive.'

Pagan knew that he was proud of her work, though at first her forthright business methods had alarmed him. Sometimes she suspected they still did.

She always hated to leave her husband, but after his heart attack it was unwise for him to travel; he was better off at home with help close at hand, a semi-invalid, but still one of the wittiest, cleverest and most distinguished men in the world. Although neither of them spoke about it, the past sixteen years had been a very special bonus – but sixteen years of constant care to keep him alive and working would be triumphantly worth that effort if now, as seemed likely, he might at last succeed within the next ten years. The question that they never asked each other was whether he could *last* until then. That was why Pagan hated to leave her husband, even to discuss the possibility of a major donation to the Institute.

And from such an unexpected source.

In the scarf-scattered, gumboot-glutted, coat-choked, stone-paved passage of her cottage on the Trelawney estate, Pagan had answered the telephone and heard the low, husky voice of Lili herself. As casually as if she were suggesting meeting in the next village, Lili had asked Pagan to travel to America to meet her on a matter that was both urgent and confidential. Pagan had been astonished by the telephone call. International film stars weren't in the habit of phoning her out of the blue and she had never met Lili, though of course she'd heard about her. One could hardly avoid hearing about that romantic, talented, sad creature.

On the telephone, the film star had spoken in a quiet, serious voice. 'I've heard so much about your projects,' she said. 'I'm fascinated by the wonderful work your husband is doing and I'd like to discuss a way in which I might be of help.'

When Pagan had politely pressed Lili for further details, Lili had explained that her American accountant had suggested several possible ways in which Lili might contribute, some extending over several years, and he had suggested a preliminary meeting in New York with Lili's tax advisers. It sounded as if a really big contribution was going to be made and a very generous cheque had then been sent to Pagan to cover her first-class travel expenses.

Sitting in the stationary cab and listening to the driver swear in Spanish, Pagan wished that she didn't feel so utterly awful. The waving mahogany hair that fell to her shoulders always looked fine, but today her face was puffy, her blue eyes dull, her eyelids swollen, and she looked all of her forty-six years.

New York time is five hours earlier than London. Pagan had arrived the previous evening, and after only a few hours' sleep, she woke at two in the morning, which was breakfast time in Britain. She wasn't able to concentrate on her book and she hadn't been able to get to sleep again. She never took sleeping pills or any other medicine, not even aspirin.

She was too terrified of getting hooked again.

Sleek black skyscrapers loomed slightly darker than the sky. You don't know how many shades of black there are until you've been in fashion or the printing business, Kate thought, as she hurried along West 58th Street, slightly late as usual. When she left the office at six-ten the sky had been pale blue and cream, but now, at six-thirty, it was dark. For a moment Kate thought nostalgically of the long English autumn twilights, then she paused at Van Cleef & Arpels. The Empress Josephine's diamond coronation tiara sat in state in one window; Kate preferred it to the tiara in the other window, the more magnificent Russian Imperial diadem which had candy-sized emeralds set in a three-inch-thick blaze of diamonds. Again Kate wondered why she hadn't let Tom pull her through the revolving doors last Monday. Most men hadn't even *heard* of Van Cleef, let alone know where it was, let alone offer to do a little shopping there. 'Let's go get Josephine's tiara,' Tom had said, tugging at her hand, and when she shook her head he had still tried to pull her in, pointing out that emeralds went with anything. Why hadn't she wanted to accept an expensive present from him? After all, her birthday was next week: she would be forty-six years old and she didn't care a bit. She didn't need expensive reassurance; she had got what she had always wanted – a wonderful man and a wonderful job.

Now that she was a successful magazine editor, nobody would ever guess that for years Kate hadn't known what she wanted or where she was going, that she had felt as little in control of her life as a rag doll being tossed around in a washing machine. She felt she was being pushed around, all right, but she didn't know in which direction. 'Now, girl,' her father always said, 'remember you're as good as anyone, Kuthreen, remember that your dad's got the wherewithal and that's what *counts*. Nothing to stop you being *top* of the pile, and that's where your dad expects you to be, make no mistake about it.'

The 'wherewithal' had been the vast profits from the rows of identical small, squat red-brick houses that her father had built across central England. The 'wherewithal' had paid for better clothes, better cars, better holidays and a better home than her schoolmates', but it had *not* been what counted; if anything, the 'wherewithal' had been responsible for unspoken resentment from some of the other girls at her London day school. She had *never* felt that she was as good as any of them, and neither was she *top*. She always dreaded the arrival of the end-of-term reports, anticipating her father's rages, the punishments and – most alarming of all – her father's attempts to coach her: the more he shouted the less she could remember.

She had been a cowed girl. The anger that she had never dared to show had built up in layers of silent resentment. She knew she was a moral coward, but she was terrified that argument would rouse her father's anger. So, like her mother, Kate always said as little as possible or fled.

Once they knew her well, men were always surprised to discover how easily they could make Kate do exactly what they wanted without a word of complaint from her. But then, when they pushed her too far, she simply disappeared without a word of explanation.

As Kate couldn't stand her father when he was alive, she couldn't understand why, whenever one of her books hit the best-seller list, the wistful thought came unbidden into her head, 'Wish the old bugger could have seen *that*.' She couldn't understand why she wanted the ogre of her youth, dead these twenty years, to be proud of her; she couldn't understand her disappointment because her father had died before she discovered what she was top *at*, before she could shout, 'Daddy, Daddy, you bastard, I've made it!' Kate didn't take much notice of her success, and neither did her friends, most of whom dated from the days when she was unknown, but her dad would have relished it, he would have cut her pictures out of the newspapers, kept all her cuttings and alerted his buddies when she was about to be on television.

Certainly this new book sounded an easy winner, another potential best-seller. Lili's story – true or false – should hit the list a week before publication. She was beautiful, romantic, irresistibly fascinating, and the public lapped up every detail of her life; for instance, *how* many times had she read that Lili always wore white, whether it was satin or silk, tweed or cotton? And of course Lili was a woman with a past – and what a past!

Before Lili had reached international status, when she had still been just another continental B-film actress who stripped in every movie, Kate had once spent some time hanging around the set in a wet wood outside London and had subsequently written the first big story to treat the teenage Lili as a potential star. Kate had not heard from Lili since the interview, but the piece had been syndicated around the world, which is why, Kate supposed, she had been summoned to the Pierre. Today, all the stars wanted an 'as told to' autobiography. Nevertheless, she had been surprised when Lili had telephoned in person and asked to meet her secretly.

Kate hurried towards the Plaza, smelled hot bagels and damp autumn mist, passed a group of blank-faced, bald-headed women, swathed in silver fox and lace, spotlit in Bergdorf's window; stopped at the traffic light beyond which was a blue police car, with two cops inside, both as bald and blank as the plaster models in Bergdorf's. Kate crossed the street. Dark green, elegant awnings stretched from apartment building doors across the sidewalk to where bored chauffeurs sat in spotless dark cars. Kate nodded to the blue-uniformed doorman, who saluted her as she swung between the marble pillars of the Pierre Hotel, through the revolving doors and along the wide, cream corridor.

At the reception desk they phoned up to make sure she was expected. The guests standing beside her murmured in soft Italian, the groups beyond spoke Arabic and French. Kate couldn't hear a word of English. It reminded her of Cairo. The elevator took her to the seventeenth floor and as she walked along the hushed grey corridor to Suite 1701, Kate pulled the back of her mulberry jacket down and fluffed up the purple silk bow of her blouse.

Just before she reached it, the door was opened by a thin woman with grey hair that matched her dress. Beyond her, through the open door, Kate could see into a long cream room that overlooked Central Park. A waiter was setting out ice, tongs and small dishes of olives; the secretary beckoned him out, stood aside so that Kate could enter and then softly closed the door from the hall.

Kate gasped.

'Jesus!' said Judy.

'Wrong again,' said Kate, who could never resist a one-liner. Astonished, she stood in the doorway, trying to decide what this was all about. Judy and Pagan were sitting on a couple of apricot velvet couches placed at right angles to each other; at either end of the couches, huge vases of madonna lilies and imported apple blossoms stood on low, smoked-glass tables and beyond, to the right, in a beige velvet armchair, sat Maxine.

'What's this, a surprise reunion?' asked Kate.

Pagan fingered the delicate little green malachite butterfly that hung around her neck on a fine gold Cartier chain. Maxine said in a fast, low voice, 'We'd better be careful what we say.'

The atmosphere was tense. Kate did not have time to move over to the other women before the double doors at the far end of the room were flung open and in walked a small, gold-skinned young woman, wearing a white silk gown draped like an ancient Greek tunic.

Star quality radiated from Lili. A cloud of black, soft hair hung to her shoulders, swept back from an oval face with high, slanting cheekbones. Her small nose had a faintly predatory hook, her full lower lip was slightly too large, but when you looked at her you only noticed her eyes. They were huge shining chestnut eyes, thickly lashed, that glistened as if a crystal tear were about to fall from each one.

Tonight, however, Lili's eyes did not glisten. They glared. They projected rage and fury. For a moment the star stood silent as she surveyed the four older women: Kate in her mulberry suit by the door; Pagan in pink, sprawled across the apricot cushions;

Maxine poised, porcelain cup in one hand, the saucer held on her blue silk lap; Judy in brown velvet, on the edge of the sofa with shoulders hunched, hands under her chin, elbows on her knees, scowling right back at Lili.

Then Lili spoke.

'All right,' she said, 'which one of you bitches is my mother?'

2

'I FEEL sick,' muttered Kate, leaning back against the headboard and fastening a new lace bra over her adolescent breasts.

'Worth it,' said Pagan, as she licked her fingers. Wearing orange satin boxer shorts and a pink kimono, she sat cross-legged at the end of Kate's narrow bed and looked regretfully at the white cardboard box between the two teenage girls. One chocolate eclair remained.

'We'll save this for after supper. Now shall I paint your toenails purple to take your mind off throwing up?'

The English pupils always splurged their first week's allowance on cakes, lipstick and nail polish. They had been freed from strict schools in order to be transformed into cultured young ladies by this Swiss finishing school. After years of deprivation, followed by a postwar period in which even bread and potatoes were rationed, the girls thought Switzerland in 1948 was a paradise compared to shabby, tired Britain – a paradise of cream cakes, chocolate, snow and romance.

Pagan hunched over Kate's left foot. A myopic, pre-Raphaelite beauty, she usually stooped to minimize her height. She rarely wore her glasses, partly because she was vain and partly because she kept losing them.

Lolling back on the bed, bare left foot poised in mid-air, Kate looked over Pagan's head. She could see the snow-topped mountains of Gstaad, framed by the white lace curtains of her open bedroom window.

'Let's go into the forest before tea,' suggested Kate.

'Keep *still*, you idiot,' said Pagan. 'We were told to greet the new girl. We'll go after tea if she hasn't arrived. Poor thing, you've bagged the best armoire. There's hardly any hanging space in hers; she'll have to keep her stuff under the bed.'

Most of the bedrooms in l'Hirondelle finishing school were for three girls, but on the top floor, under the wooden eaves of the huge chalet, the rooms were smaller. Leading off Kate's bedroom for two was a tiny, pale blue attic, with a low, sloping pine ceiling and just enough space for one narrow blue bed, a small table and a chest. Pagan had grabbed it and she was so exasperatingly untidy that it was just as well she had a room to herself. Nothing could teach Pagan to be neat. She had been christened Jennifer, but as her nanny's constant cry was 'Pick it *up*, you little pagan,' or 'No tea until your room's tidy, you little pagan,' Jennifer eventually became known as 'Pagan', and the nickname stuck.

'I'm not going to waste such a lovely afternoon!' Kate jumped off the bed and pulled on a neat beige cashmere sweater and skirt. Pagan tugged a pair of old jodhpurs over the orange satin shorts and wriggled into a gigantic Fair Isle pullover, which she yanked in at the middle with a man's thick leather belt that almost went around her waist twice. They clattered down the wooden stairs two at a time, flung themselves out of the front door and half-walked, half-skipped along the steep path that led behind the school and up into the forest. After climbing about a mile over fallen pine needles, they found a notice stuck in the middle of the path that read '*Attention! Défense de passer.*'

'Probably means that the pass is defended by attentive game-keepers,' said Pagan, whose French was atrocious, and they continued to puff uphill until the path stopped in a grass clearing that ended abruptly on a cliff edge. Below they could see the brown chalets of Gstaad, encircled by the dark green forest, and beyond, a spectacular amphitheatre of mountains that were snow-topped even in midsummer.

'Yoohoo . . . oooo,' yelled Pagan through cupped hands. As the sound echoed back across the valley, she turned to Kate and said, 'They'll expect us to yodel properly by the time we get back to –'

She stopped abruptly. Suddenly they heard an answering cry, seemingly from beneath their feet. Then someone shouted, '*Au secours!*'

'That means "help",' Kate said earnestly.

'And it came from beyond the cliff. *Pourquoi secours?*' yelled Pagan.

The voice yelled '*Parce que* ... I'm stuck.'

'Are you English?' yelled Pagan, starting to stride forwards, but Kate yanked at her belt to stop her. They were about ten feet from the cliff edge and it might not be safe.

'No, American. Watch out. The cliff just gave way. We weren't even near the edge ... It just suddenly crumbled.'

'How many of you are there?'

'I'm the only one that fell. Nick jumped back and he's gone for help ... aaaah!' Both girls heard the sound of slithering earth and stones.

'Are you still there?'

'Yes, but there isn't much ledge left. Oh, God, I'm so frightened.'

'Don't look down!' said Pagan, lowering herself to the ground and starting to snake forwards. 'And don't shout any more ... Kate, I'm going to crawl to the edge and then you lie down behind me and hang on to my ankles.' Slowly Pagan wriggled to the point where the grass stopped abruptly. She peered carefully over the edge. About six feet below her, two dark blue eyes looked up, surrounded by fair, shaggy hair.

The girl was standing on a narrow ledge, arms outspread as she hugged the cliff face. 'Nick just couldn't reach me,' she said. 'He tried and tried. He took off his shirt and tried to pull me up with it but it tore, then the ledge started to crumble and so he ran to get a ladder. But the ledge keeps crumbling, there's not enough room to sit down now. I'm so frightened.'

At least a hundred feet below, the earth was starting to slide again. It made Pagan feel sick. 'Oh, crumbs,' she gasped. 'Oh, Lord, don't look down.' She tried to reach the girl with her hands but her outreached fingertips were about two feet from the up-stretched hands of the frightened girl below.

'Look, hang on just a bit longer,' called Pagan encouragingly, as she withdrew her head and wriggled back to Kate. She started to take off her sneakers and jodhpurs.

'These pants are tougher than the shirt,' she explained, as she tied the end of her jodhpur legs with a reef knot so that the garment

31

formed a circle; then she threaded her belt through it, pulling the buckle tight.

'For God's sake hang tight on to my ankles,' Pagan hissed to Kate, as she wriggled back to the cliff face and peered over it. Some earth crumbled away beneath her breasts and she felt even sicker as she dangled the jodhpurs down to the girl below. 'Can you get them over your head and under your arms like a lifebelt? *Don't look down!*'

Slowly Pagan lowered the makeshift lifebelt until it reached the girl's outstretched fingertips. 'Keep your hands together and try to wriggle the jodhpurs down under your arms ... slowly ... slowly ...'

Pagan wrapped the other end of the belt around her left hand and hung on to the end of it with her right hand. All the time she noticed little crumbs of earth were sliding down the sheer cliff face towards the red earth, snapped-off pine trees and roots that were piled so far below.

'Now hold on to the belt,' she said in what she hoped was a commanding voice. '*Slowly*, try to walk up the cliff, like a fly.'

'I can't. I *can't!*'

A chunk of earth fell from below the girl's left foot, leaving it dangling in space.

'If you fall, I'm not sure that I can hold you,' Pagan said. 'You'll probably break my wrist and pull me over, so don't *think* about what I say. Just *do* it, when I count to three.'

Kate was now lying behind Pagan with her arms hanging around Pagan's waist. 'Now, one, two, *three!*' Pagan said, as forcefully as she could.

Obediently, the thin little girl – thank God she was so small – leaned out and started to scramble up the mountain. As the belt jerked taut, Pagan felt an agonizing pain in her wrist and shoulder. She wondered whether she'd dislocated it, then the whole of her left arm was in agony as, inch by inch, the girl scrambled up.

The leather belt started to slip in Pagan's sweaty hand. She was gasping for breath as she slowly wriggled backwards, pulled by Kate.

Two dirty hands hanging on to the belt slowly appeared over the cliff face, followed by a frightened white face.

'Slowly,' gasped Pagan, 'slowly!' She thought she felt the

ground move beneath her and experienced a moment of cold terror. Then the little girl collapsed over the top of the cliff and Kate quickly pulled her up over it and back to safety as Pagan's bleeding fingers released the belt.

But before Pagan could stand up, the ground beneath her fell away and suddenly she was dangling from the waist, head downwards over the crumbling mountain. The ledge that the girl had been standing on had disappeared.

Kate grabbed Pagan, and together they fell backwards, panting and sobbing as they crawled to safety.

Not until they reached the pine trees and the little path did Pagan feel safe. Then her knees gave way and she collapsed. Anxiously, Kate bent over her.

Suddenly a look of alarm crossed the face of the girl Pagan had rescued. 'Oh, my,' she said, putting both hands to her temples, 'I'm going to be late. Oh, I dare not. Oh, I *must* go. Oh, dear, oh, thank you, oh, look, do you know the Chesa? Can you come there sometime so I can say . . . I mean, I can't thank you enough but . . . *I must go!*'

And she turned and half-ran, half-staggered down the path, then disappeared around the bend.

'What a cow!' Kate said. 'You saved her life and she just ran off! Oh, darling Pagan, your poor hands!' Pagan's legs were filthy and her hands were bleeding. As the jodhpurs and sneakers were still on the cliff edge, she was wearing only the Fair Isle sweater and the dirty orange satin shorts.

Suddenly, from the other side of the clearing, a group of labourers appeared carrying rope, a net and a ladder. A tall, thin young man, naked to the waist, ran in front of them, but he suddenly stopped dead, ran a hand through his floppy black hair and yelled, 'Christ, it's fallen!'

'The girl's all right, we got her up,' called Pagan from where she was sitting. 'Are you Nick?'

The young man came running over. His crooked nose was smeared with earth, his aquamarine eyes looked distraught. 'She's all right? Judy's *all right*? What happened? How? . . . You're *sure* she's all right? Where is she? . . . Oh, God, I've been through such hell . . .'

'So has Pagan,' Kate said indignantly. 'She leaned over the cliff and pulled your girl up – and then she rushed off when Pagan had just saved her life, saying that she didn't want to be late!'

'Well, if she's late again, she loses her job, you see. She's already been warned twice. Was she *all right* – not hurt, I mean?'

'*She* must be all right to rush off like that,' said Kate scornfully, 'but Pagan isn't all right. Look at her hands!'

'Stop making a fuss, Kate.' Pagan wobbled to her feet. She was as tall as the young man who had jumped to help her. 'I'll be perfectly fine after a bath.'

'Just let me tell the rescue team there's no longer a problem and I'll see you home,' said Nick, pushing his floppy black hair out of his eyes and turning to talk in rapid German to the group of men behind him. He turned back and put a supportive arm around Pagan's waist.

'I'm perfectly all right,' said Pagan weakly, wincing as he touched her left arm. 'Let's get out of here before more mountain disappears.'

'That's unlikely,' said Nick. 'The rescue team said they've been dynamiting part of the mountain away because after last winter's avalanches, a dangerous overhang was left. Unfortunately, that's what we were walking on ... They're finishing the work next week.'

'Who's that girl, the one who was *late*?' Kate's voice was heavily sarcastic.

'She's an exchange scholarship student from America and she hasn't any money, so she's working as a waitress at the Chesa,' Nick explained as slowly they moved down the path. 'I don't know how she does it all, she works so hard, and she never seems tired, she's always ... oh, terrific fun.'

Kate noticed that he blushed. 'Are you ... uh?'

'No, we're not, but I wish we were. She's got some fellow in Virginia. Jim.' There was a pause. Both girls looked sideways at Nick and decided that Jim must be pretty sensational.

'Are you a student, too?' Nick was obviously English.

'In a way. I'm a *stagiaire*. An exchange waiter at the Imperial.'

'What's an exchange waiter?'

'Well, my family is in the hotel business, so I'm learning hotel management.' He pulled Pagan's arm round his shoulder. 'I left school early and took the two-year course at Westminster Tech, then I was a waiter at the Savoy. I came out here on an exchange scheme; one of the Imperial waiters is taking my place in London.'

'What was it like at the Savoy?' Kate asked, round-eyed at the thought of working in such sophisticated surroundings.

'Hard work. Hot. The restaurant kitchen was above ground so we had windows, but the poor bastards in the grill kitchen worked in the basement and never saw the light of day. We cooked on red-hot, old coal ranges, and there was sawdust on the floor to soak up any spilled fat so you didn't slip on it. You sweated so much that you drank anything that came your way – water and milk as well as your beer allocation – you never stopped swigging liquid.'

'Why did you leave the Savoy?' Pagan asked, as they stopped on the path so that Nick could support her more firmly. Her arm was horribly painful, but Nick was taking her mind off it.

'To continue my course.' Nick staggered. Pagan was no light-weight. 'I'm staying here until the end of the winter season, then I'll be eighteen and have to do my National Service. I hate the whole idea of being in the bloody army, but there's no choice. Anyway, my father says it will teach me leadership, if nothing else. He's very keen on leadership.'

'Goodness, do waiters *need* leadership qualities?'

'No, but hotel managers do!'

'That's our school,' Kate said, pointing. 'Nearly there, Pagan, only a few steps more.' She and Nick were now almost totally supporting Pagan as the dirty little group staggered up to the front door.

Nick blushed, then said apologetically, 'Look, I know you think Judy was ungrateful but you've no idea how hard things are for her. She's here alone and she's only fifteen. Why don't we meet at the Chesa for tea on Sunday, then she can thank you properly as I'm sure she wants to . . . And – and, I'd like it too.' Pagan nodded as carefully he released his hold, said goodbye, then hurried down the street. She waited until he turned the corner, then gave a little groan and fell to the ground.

Pagan was propped up in bed eating the last chocolate eclair with her right hand; her left hand was bandaged and her arm was in a sling. Kate was painting her toes bright orange.

'I can't, *can't* bear it,' Pagan groaned.

Kate looked up anxiously. 'Is the pain still awful?'

'No, I can't feel a thing after that injection. What I can't bear is that Paul carried me upstairs and I never knew about it! You wouldn't lie to me, Kate; he really did pick me up in his strong arms and hold me to his manly chest and . . .'

'. . . No, he didn't,' said Kate. 'No normal man could carry *you* upstairs like that. He *staggered* up with you. I was afraid he might fall backwards on Matron and me.'

Pagan gave a voluptuous sigh of regret. Paul was the head-master's chauffeur and the unofficial school heartthrob. All the girls were fascinated by his olive face, his slanting black eyes, his sleek dark hair and his erect tight-buttocked bullfighter's stance.

'Tell me again what happened,' Pagan begged, as Kate dabbed Oriental Orange on her big toe.

'You were too heavy for me to drag out of the gutter so I rushed inside. Paul was leaning against the hall table with his arms crossed and his cap in one hand – waiting for old Chardin to appear, I suppose. As soon as I explained what had happened, he dashed outside, flung his cap on the pavement and put his arms around you – you made his uniform absolutely filthy, by the way – heaved you over his left shoulder in a sort of fireman's lift, with one arm around your back and the other around your orange satin bottom, then he carried you straight into Chardin's study without knock-ing and lowered you on to the sofa and knelt by you and lifted your eyelid and . . . I've already told you the next bit.'

'Again.'

'Then he felt under . . . he pulled your sweater up and yelled at me to fetch Matron and telephone for a doctor, but I was rooted to the ground.' Kate giggled. 'I suppose he was checking your heart-beat; he didn't seem to *notice* you weren't wearing a bra. Anyway, I rushed off and got Matron, and when we came in your sweater was down again and you were whispering, "Where am I?" just the way you're supposed to . . .'

Suddenly the door crashed open and the Swedish matron stomped in, followed by the school porter dragging an old pigskin suitcase. Behind him stood a plump girl wearing a navy coat. Her brown eyes looked anxious as she smiled. She had buck teeth.

Matron scowled. 'It's forbidden to sit on the beds. It's for-bidden to eat in your rooms. It's forbidden to apply nail polish anywhere except in the bathroom.' She turned on her heels and left.

'Bitch,' said Pagan. '*Parlez-vous anglais?*'

'A little, but I am French and come here to learn English,' the new girl said. 'I am Maxine Pascale.'

'But *nobody* learns English here. Or French, come to that,' exclaimed Pagan. 'You'll see. The English and American girls talk English, the South Americans speak Spanish, the Italians yell nonstop Italian and the Germans bark in German. *Nobody* speaks French, except one Greek girl, and that's because nobody else speaks Greek. *Mais nous pouvons practiquer sur vous.*' Pagan's French was atrocious, as if to prove she was right.

'No, I shall only speak English with you,' the new girl said firmly, with a smile. She lifted her suitcase on to the bed and started to unpack, carefully pulling out and smoothing the many sheets of crisp white tissue that lay between each garment. It was more like a trousseau than a set of schoolgirl's clothes, and as Maxine hung them up, the girls could see the Christian Dior label.

'I say, you must be rich!' gasped Pagan. 'They're divine!'

'No, I'm not rich,' Maxine said. 'But I *am* lucky. I have an aunt.'

And indeed, Maxine's Aunt Hortense, who had made a good but childless marriage, was a shrewd realist. In her opinion there was no point in spending money on a trousseau *after* one had landed a man. Chic clothes were needed to set a girl up so she could make the best possible marriage. It was an investment in a girl's future.

So she had swept Maxine and her mother into the Dior salon, and eventually – Maxine was not consulted – the two older women decided on a midnight-blue wool coat with two huge buttons that glowed like sapphires; next, they chose a cocktail dress in blue satin covered in black Chantilly lace and a simple blue wool town suit with an alternative pleated skirt *pour le weekend* in blue and cream tartan. They also picked an apricot wool dress that flared tactfully over Maxine's ample hips, and their final choice was a floor-length, strapless gown in pale-blue silk taffeta with a little matching jacket. All the waists were tightly nipped in, all the skirts were enormous; all the garments were exquisitely stitched and fitted. It had taken three weeks to make them, with five fittings each, and Maxine had felt faint when she heard that the price of the five outfits was 750,000 francs. She would never dare to wear them, she had thought.

The girls missed tea because – with a secret view to future borrowing – Kate was trying on every stitch that Maxine had brought with her, and even though Pagan couldn't try them on because her arm was in plaster of Paris, she hopped around, thrilled by the glamorous clothes. Maxine was impressed by Pagan's height, her hair and her exuberant high spirits. 'I say, Kate, *silver high heels!* Oh, Maxine, your feet are sparrow-size, dammit,' she cried. Kate burrowed into the suitcase, sending tissue paper flying. 'Look, Kate, that's a real crêpe de Chine blouse – and a lace nightgown! Y'know clothes are still rationed in England, Maxine. There's nothing so ravishing as these! Oh, how I *long* for something pretty!'

Not fooled by this, Maxine could see that Pagan was used to getting what she wanted. How strange that she should be a friend of Kate, who seemed so quiet and ordinary-looking, even mousy despite the purple toes. They were obviously fond of each other, and Maxine quickly found out that they had been together at school in London since they were ten. That was not the only reason that Kate and Pagan were friends. What the two girls had in common and what had brought them together originally was that they were both, in different ways, outsiders. Kate, because her father was so very obviously so very rich, and Pagan because she had been brought up to live a life that no longer existed. Her world of privilege had disappeared forever, together with the wrought-iron gates of the manor which – like the saucepans in the mining cottages – had been melted down to make guns in 1940.

Because her speech and her background were so different from the middle-class students at St Paul's, Pagan tended to sound arrogant without meaning to do so. And even in a school with few uniform rules, she dressed in a most peculiar fashion. No store-bought clothes ever fitted Pagan, who was five foot ten and boyish in build. During the war, when clothes were severely rationed and brides pooled their year's clothing coupons in order to buy one wedding dress for eight of them to wear, everyone in Britain wore their clothes until they fell to pieces and made new dresses out of old tablecloths, sheets and curtains.

Inspired by the general example, Pagan went up to the attic and unpacked the clothes of her dead father. First she wore his cashmere pullovers and his silk scarves with a pair of jodhpurs; then she purloined his silk shirts, which she belted and wore as dresses, and Mrs Hocken in the village turned a white-dotted navy silk Charvet dressing gown into 'a best dress' for Sunday. Then Pagan plundered some of the other older trunks in the attic: she was never able to get into her grandmother's tiny-waisted silk dress, but she wore lace blouses that were a hundred years old with similarly ancient skirts of bottle-green velvet or dark blue silk. Soon she acquired a reputation not only for eccentric opinions but also for eccentric clothes, but because of her height, her slimness and her wonderful mahogany hair, Pagan always looked carelessly marvellous.

L'Hirondelle supper gong was rung at seven-thirty. Reluctant to leave Maxine's wonderful wardrobe, but very hungry, the three girls joined the human stream of flying hair, bouncing breasts and perceptible underarm odour as all the pupils clattered downstairs to the dining room, where old portraits hung in heavy gilt frames and brass Dutch chandeliers were suspended from dark ceiling beams above long oak tables. Above the noise, Maxine asked about the school routine.

'Morning bell at seven, breakfast at seven-thirty, lessons from eight to twelve,' Pagan mumbled, as Kate cut her lamb chop into little pieces. 'Voluntary sport from two to four-thirty and after that, study time 'til six-thirty. Then supper and lights out at ten. No work over the weekend. Church optional. *Qu'est-ce que tu penses du nourriture de l'école?*'

'It is revolting,' said Maxine with deep sincerity, 'like your French.'

'Never mind, Monsieur Chardin told my mother that my accent was excellent,' said Pagan cheerfully. 'Would you please undo the top button of my pedal pushers, Kate ... Have you met the headmaster yet? No? Well, he's a common little creep. Obsequious and oily, you'll see. In London he stayed at Claridge's and I went along to visit him with Mama. He was wearing a canary pullover and a big-checked suit that no Englishman would be seen dead in, especially not in town. I noticed that he didn't even *read* my school reports. Just as well, since they were absolutely grim ... I got the feeling that Chardin was fishing for any pupils he could *get*. He's obviously in it just for the money, don't you think, Kate?'

Kate nodded. She was slowly eating a chocolate biscuit. She could make one biscuit last two hours, nibbling nonstop at a steady pace, like a rat at a corpse. Pagan said, adjusting her sling, 'I'm rather surprised my mother sent me here, except it *is* supposed to be the best school in Switzerland and my grandfather's paying the bill, not her.'

She wiped a bit of bread around her plate. 'Also, dammit, I certainly *need* polishing up. I mean, I'm not good at being tidy or wearing clothes or knowing what to say to people at parties or doing *any* of the things that grown-up girls do.'

Kate said, 'We've been here a week and so far we've hardly seen Chardin; his apartment is on the other side of the chalet and it has a different front door. He seems to live an entirely separate life from the school. I'm certain he has better meals than *we* do, because you can sometimes smell things like roast duck coming out of the kitchen. *Not* my idea of a headmaster!'

'A couple of Brazilian girls have already been here a year and they say he's got a fearful temper,' Pagan added. 'But there's only one thing he really *explodes* about, and that's if you get out of school at night. Apparently *he* has hysterics – and *you're* expelled!'

There was an awed silence. Being expelled was a fate worse than death. The shame would pursue you through your whole life.

After supper, half the school squeezed into Kate's bedroom to gaze at Maxine's wardrobe until lights out. Immediately after Matron's inspection to check that all girls were in and all lights were out, Pagan crept into the adjoining bedroom, clutching around her, like an overweight redskin, the bulky, feather-filled quilt that is the only covering on Swiss beds. Pagan climbed on to the end of Kate's bed and the three girls whispered until well after midnight. Maxine told them about her three younger brothers and sisters in Paris. Kate, who like Pagan was an only child, thought that a big family sounded like fun, but Maxine's school in Paris, on the other hand, didn't sound like fun at all.

'We also had hours and hours of homework at St Paul's,' said Pagan. 'Each assignment was supposed to take you only twenty minutes, and at the bottom of your work you were supposed to put how long it took you, so naturally everybody lied because they didn't want to look dumb. If your essay on Greek architecture took three hours, you put down twenty-five minutes. All Paulinas are liars, and they all have weak eyes because they do so much of their work by flashlight in bed.'

'My mother complained to the high mistress once,' said Kate, 'and she sat Mummy in a little low chair opposite her huge commanding throne and said in her low boom, "Of *course* Kate must not work in bed, she must work in her lunch hour or *leave* if she cannot keep up."'

'The high mistress was a huge, commanding figure. She moved like a ship. You couldn't believe she had legs,' said Pagan. 'She wore pince-nez and her hair in a grey bun and very old-fashioned orange sweaters with no bra; you could see but you didn't dare notice. Somebody described her as God in drag. She thundered at us in a low majestic voice. I once came second in a reading competition simply by mimicking her. I was afraid I'd get ticked off for insolence, but nobody *noticed*. They said I showed promise.'

'Why did your mother send you to that school if she was frightened of the headmistress?' asked Maxine.

'Not headmistress,' said Kate, '*high* mistress. I went because my father wanted me to have . . . the best.'

Kate's father had wanted her to have the sort of education he hadn't had himself. She had been sent to St Paul's because Kate's father had read that royalty went there. Kate's father always wanted the best, so Kate's mother always asked for it, even when shopping. When she was buying plums she would ask the grocer, 'Which are the best?' When she was buying chairs she would ask, 'Which are the best?' When she was buying a dress she could never decide which one suited her, so she always asked the assistant, 'Which is the best?' and naturally the assistant chose the most expensive, which was all right, because the more things cost, the better they were.

Kate's mother was also influenced by royalty, and dressed like the Queen. Kate's quiet, ladylike clothes came from Debenham & Freebody because the little Princesses' clothes were bought there and 'By Appointment to Her Majesty' was printed on their boxes. Kate hated the place, with its pillared, echoing marble halls and the ancient, exquisitely polite assistants, all gentlewomen who had known better days. She would have preferred to shop at Selfridges, like the other girls, for the cheap cotton copies of the New Look.

Kate's mother also had the best at their home, Greenways. The antiques were expensive, but somehow the ornately carved chairs, the brocade sofas and heavy-fringed, satin curtains failed to achieve the casual look of elegance of Pagan's mother's flat in Kensington, where the simple furniture had come up from their country house and every piece was interesting and well proportioned, if a bit battered. Some of the china was chipped, but if your family had been using it for a hundred and fifty years, it would be, wouldn't it?

Kate hated the smug perfection of Greenways. On either side of the drive, the trees and foliage were spotlit at night; Kate's father thought this looked stylish and set off the pillared porch. Inside, on the ground floor, the chairs, sofas and tables were too big, the lampshades and pictures too small; the dining room was panelled in plastic wood, and the chandelier consisted of a circle of fake candles with little fake parchment hats. Upstairs, the bedrooms were surprisingly stark. After all, nobody ever went upstairs except to sleep, so Kate's father saw no point in wasting money there.

Kate was driven to school in her father's Rolls-Royce. The chauffeured car set Kate apart from her classmates. *They* didn't have a different dress for each day of the week, and *they* travelled to school by bus or on the underground. Kate always made the chauffeur stop the Rolls at the end of the road and walked the rest of the way to school. This subterfuge was general knowledge, but her fellow schoolgirls thought it right and proper that she should avoid showing off; showing off was a major school crime.

Unfortunately, Kate's father showed off rather a lot. When her schoolfriends came to the house he would show them his cars and ask them to guess how much money he'd made last year or what he had bought last week. Afterwards, he would have a little chat with Kate and tell her which of her friends he preferred. Eventually Kate stopped asking people home. She started to spend her free time and eat her lunch with Pagan, who was also a loner because she was considered odd by the other girls. It was unusual

42

for a girl of Pagan's age from a decent family to be so careless of her appearance or to be so indifferent to what people thought about her. For her part, Pagan made it clear that she considered the conscientious, hardworking girls of St Paul's as boring as riding around a dusty London park instead of cantering over the Cornish moors, hair streaking behind her in the salty wind.

Kate's father showered invitations on Pagan and her mother – who was obviously 'top drawer' – and once he invited them on a cruise to Majorca (he pronounced the j as in jug), although the invitation was politely declined. Kate knew why her father liked Pagan's mother. Kate knew her father wanted a good marriage for her, perhaps even a title: he didn't know how he was going to manage it, but after all he had the wherewithal, and he could see that Pagan's mother knew the sort of people who had titles and she also knew 'the done thing'. The reason Kate had been sent to l'Hirondelle was because Pagan was going. If a Swiss finishing school was 'the done thing', then Kate had to do it.

Pagan teased Kate about her father's secret hopes. 'When you're a marchioness, you'd better not ask the way to the loo, you'd better say bathroom.'

'What does it matter, so long as it's clear where I want to go?' asked Kate crossly, but secretly she read Nancy Mitford's novels and learned what established you as 'U' (or Upper Class), as opposed to 'non-U'. Kate said 'writing paper', not 'notepaper', 'napkin', not 'serviette', and offered visitors 'a glass of sherry', not 'a sherry'. She also practised altering her accent to a clipped, yet languid, drawl, but she soon realized that it was hopeless. The upper classes *seemed* to speak the King's English, but in fact they spoke a secret language full of subtle references you could learn only in the cradle. In 'U' circles there was only one thing worse than not knowing these subtleties and that was *pretending* to know them, aping your betters. One little slip and this was apparent: all you had to do was to refer to the Royal Yacht Squadron as the Royal Yacht Club *once*, or hang family photographs on the walls instead of propping them on side-tables in silver frames from Asprey, and you were *doomed*.

Sometimes Kate stayed overnight with Pagan, who lived in Kensington, near St Paul's – although after that awful Friday she always found an excuse not to do so. For some reason Kate always felt guilty when she remembered that November week-end.

Pagan lived in an apartment on the top floor of a once-elegant, now slightly seedy house on Ennismore Gardens. They had been playing hockey all afternoon and Kate was sweaty, so she decided to take a bath while Pagan went out to do an errand for her mother. Kate was naked and about to step into the bath when the door opened and Pagan's mother entered, wrapped in a white terry robe. Somehow Kate knew her presence was not an accident and she was nervous. Instead of apologizing and backing out – as one would expect – Mrs Trelawney moved towards her, and Kate grabbed a towel as her hostess smiled, droplets of steam beading her scarlet lips. As she came closer, Kate could distinguish the aroma of gin.

'*What* lovely little breasts,' said Mrs Trelawney in a husky voice. 'A girl's body is so much more *delicate* than a boy's, don't you think? *Most* men don't appreciate that, of course. They don't appreciate the exquisite *tenderness* of the breasts, the nipples.'

Clutching her towel around her, Kate backed into the small space against the window, between the washbasin and the lavatory, where she was effectively trapped. 'I expect you've noticed . . .' and suddenly she reached out with one manicured hand and squeezed Kate's nipple.

Kate was frozen with horror, unable to move. To her bewilderment and mortification she felt a sharp thrill in her groin. She could see the pores of Mrs Trelawney's nose, the drooping, fleshy folds above her eyes, black-beaded with mascara. Then Mrs Trelawney closed in on her, clutching Kate with one hand while she tried to pull away the towel with the other. She bent down so Kate could see the white line where her hair was parted. Her tongue moved swiftly, like a snake's, towards Kate's nipple, while her fingers slipped into Kate's crotch with a strength that was at once painful and exciting. For a few moments Kate felt erotically hypnotized, then her knees buckled and she slid to the floor, pushing the woman away. Gasping, she brought one knee up to her chin and prepared to kick if Mrs Trelawney pounced again. Kate said nothing, but her eyes glittered with fear and anger.

Mrs Trelawney got the message. She seldom made a mistake, but when she did, she knew how to retreat.

44

Mrs Trelawney backed away. 'I'll leave you to bathe in peace,' she said in her soothing, perfect-hostess voice as if nothing had happened, and left the room.

Kate leaped into the bath and sat in it, shaking. She felt safe there and wouldn't come out until the water was cold. She spent the rest of the weekend trying to avoid being alone with Pagan's mother, and it was months before she could be persuaded to visit their home again. When she did, Mrs Trelawney behaved so normally that Kate was tempted to think she'd imagined the scene. Could she have been mistaken?

That unfortunate few minutes was destined to have a far-reaching effect on Kate's future love life, when in the passionate embrace of a man, she felt almost unbearable sexual excitement – and then fear, repulsion and shame.

~ 3 ~

THE noise of a piano, the chink of china, an occasional clear laugh sounded above the voices in the Great Hall of the Imperial. People had been drifting in since four o'clock for tea or cocktails: under the serene gaze of an oil-painted Madonna the bridge hostess was checking her list, and at the backgammon board the first dice rattled. In one corner Prince Aly Khan was earnestly whispering into the ear of a raven-haired South American girl. Beyond him, the young, slim Elizabeth Taylor reached for her fourth slice of sacher torte.

Surrounded by a small group of impassive henchmen, Aristotle Onassis swung through the swing doors, followed by a small, blonde young woman who clutched a pile of books under one arm. It was a fatal entrance for a girl who was trying to avoid being seen, because the heads of the concierge, the headwaiter and the maître d'hôtel all turned to make sure that one of the richest men in the world was being suitably attended. Behind him, Judy Jordan tried to look like a typical hotel guest as she headed for the elevator, walking rather fast and looking straight ahead as she approached the hall porter's desk. She wore a pleated tartan skirt,

45

a white sweater that buttoned down the back, white socks pulled to mid-calf, and saddle Oxfords that sank into the thick carpet. Nearly there. Fifteen more steps . . . ten . . . five . . . damn! A group of Arab bodyguards had suddenly appeared on either side of the elevator. Judy caught a glimpse of the neat, olive-skinned neck of a dark, slim young man who entered the elevator followed by an aide-de-camp in Western military uniform. For security reasons, nobody was allowed to travel in the elevator with Prince Abdullah or any other member of the Sydonian royal family, which kept two permanent suites at the Imperial while the eighteen-year-old Prince was at Le Mornay.

As Judy changed direction and headed for the stairs she felt a heavy hand on her shoulder. '*Fräulein*,' hissed the concierge, 'you have no business to be in the Great Hall; you are supposed to use the servants' staircase; you're not even permanent staff. This is the last warning you get before dismissal.'

'I'm sorry, but they kept us late at the language laboratory and I've got to change before going on duty at the Chesa. I was trying to save time.'

'No excuse is an excuse at the Imperial. Now get to the back-stairs.'

So instead of taking the elevator to the sixth floor, Judy had to plod up a hundred and twenty-two steps, then run the last two flights to the sloping attic under the roof that was sub-divided by thin partitions into shoebox cubicles for the staff.

She flung her books on the grey blanket and wriggled into the costume that she had to wear as a waitress in the Chesa coffee shop, which was attached to the hotel. Three more days until her free Sunday, she thought, as she pulled the drawstring of the embroidered white lace blouse, dived into the red dirndl skirt and tightened the strings of the black lace corselet. Still pulling the black laces, she ran to the end of the corridor, knocked at a door and without waiting for an answer rushed in.

Nick was lying on the iron bed. His white shirt-sleeves were rolled up, his black trouser legs were crossed and a toe poked through one of his grey socks. 'The year 1928 was almost as good as 1945,' he said. 'An exceptional vintage for Medoc, Graves, St Emilion and Pomerol, not quite so good for the dry white Bordeaux wines, but excellent for the Sauternes.' He threw his textbook down. 'Vintner's exam next Tuesday. Got time to test me on the vintages, Judy?'

'Not a hope, Nick. I'm late. I only looked in to ask if you could scrounge me something to eat from the kitchen in case I don't get a chance.'

'You're too young to starve,' he said, swinging his legs off the bed and sitting up. 'Promise to spend Sunday with me, and in my plastic-lined waiter's pockets I'll steal a meal that will last you three days.'

'It's a deal. I'll test you on the vintages then.'

'Okay. I'll drop into the Chesa later for a cup of coffee before going on duty. Anything to catch another glimpse of you.' She blew him a kiss in reply, then dashed out, heading for the hundred and twenty-two steps down to the coffee shop.

In spite of her abundant physical energy Judy felt very tired – in fact, she would have preferred to stay in bed on Sunday. This was only her fourth month in Switzerland but already she felt exhausted all the time. The hours of the Gstaad Language Laboratory were from eight in the morning until three-thirty in the afternoon and she did her homework in the hour allowed for lunch. Then until one in the morning, six days a week, she worked as a waitress at the Chesa coffee shop with only a short break for a snack. There were no union regulations in Switzerland, but no working permit problems either. She had been lucky to get the job. Pastor Hentzen had arranged it at the start of the summer season when the hotel had needed every pair of hands it could get. She had been taken on for a couple of months, then retained, at a wage far lower than any of the other waitresses. It was hardly enough to pay her laundry bill, but she got bed and board, which was all that mattered.

Maxine, Kate and Pagan were already sitting in the Chesa with a fourth girl who had been invited for one reason only – she had a brother at Le Mornay. However, Pagan had already decided half an hour ago that if Nigel was anything like his silly cow of a sister, there was no point in getting to know him.

'Daddy says it's really *changed* Nigel, he's made *unbelievably* good contacts.' Francesca droned on, 'Daddy says he looks upon the fees as a good investment because he wants Nigel to have an *international* outlook and at Le Mornay you only meet people with money and names. All the oil children go there, you know. It doesn't look like a school. It's in an old castle on Lac Leman.' She bit into a cream cake. 'They can go into Geneva or Lausanne on their evenings off, and they're allowed away for the weekend if their parents give permission.' Francesca took another *tête de nègre*. 'They have plenty of work to do, but they're not cooped in, like us Hirondelles. And of course the boys can come to the Saturday night dances. Every Saturday night during the winter a public dance is held in one of the hotels, you know, although Nigel only goes to the *smart* ones at the Imperial or the Palace.'

'We've never been to a dance,' Kate said. 'In fact, we can't dance.'

'Except for the polka and Highland fling – we learned those at school,' Pagan amended.

Boys, dances, grand hotels, it was all tremendously thrilling and alarming. Lucky, lucky Francesca to have an older brother, they thought.

'When are the Le Mornay boys coming here?'

'They're in Gstaad for three months, from January to March. Mummy says it's *so* well planned – after the Christmas holiday Nigel's trunk is simply sent to Gstaad instead of Roue.'

'That reminds me,' Pagan said, lying quickly, 'Matron asked me to tell you to go to the post office, Francesca. There's a parcel waiting there for you with three francs to pay on it.'

Francesca squealed in anticipation, paid her bill and rushed off.

'I couldn't stand much more of her,' Pagan said loudly.

'Neither could I,' said the tiny waitress. Pagan turned around and suddenly realized that the girl in the traditional Swiss costume was the girl she had rescued on the mountain. Her short blonde hair looked as if it had been hacked with a pair of kitchen scissors, which it had. Gravely she said, 'You saved my life . . .'

'. . . I'm glad you realize that!' snapped Kate.

'. . . and you've broken your arm!'

'No, only sprained the shoulder,' said Pagan. 'Are *you* all right?'

'Hardly a scratch, but I was really frightened. My knees wobbled for hours afterwards. I don't know what to say except thank you. I know I shouldn't have rushed off . . .'

'It's okay, Nick explained,' Pagan said.

'*You* may be all right,' Kate snapped, 'but Pagan wasn't. She fainted, and her poor hand as well as her shoulder were torn to bits. She was kept in bed for two days.'

'Shut up, Kate, what's the point of making her feel guilty? After all, she didn't fall off the cliff on purpose.'

'I didn't even fall off. The ground gave way beneath me. But I was almost more worried about being late on duty than ending up a corpse.'

'Well, let's forget it,' said Pagan, embarrassed. 'Hey, look who's arrived!'

She waved to Nick, who had just opened the heavy carved oaken door. He waved back, ducking his head to pass under a low beam, blackened by hundreds of years of smoke from the hearth. The Chesa was older than the rest of the hotel and had once been a seventeenth-century farmhouse, with walls as thick as an arm's length.

'I can't talk any more,' said Judy, 'but Nick and I are off on Sundays and we'd love to meet you properly – and thank you properly. And I've got something for you.'

She hastily refilled the cups with hot chocolate and dashed off with her tray as Nick gazed after her, clearly besotted.

The following Sunday afternoon the Chesa door burst open and a blast of cold air came in with Judy, followed by Nick. She was wearing her Sunday uniform of blue jeans rolled up to mid-calf, saddle Oxfords, white socks and an American navy pea-jacket. She looked around, then beamed when she saw the girls.

'Hi there!' she called. She presented Pagan with a large gift-wrapped box tied with white satin ribbon. Inside was a pair of scarlet knitted knee socks with leather soles. Pagan was delighted. 'They match my red silk sling,' she said, insisting that Kate put them on her immediately.

Maxine turned to Judy. 'Why did your parents send you to the language laboratory and not one of the finishing schools?'

'They didn't send me anywhere. I didn't tell them I was entering for the exchange scholarship, because I never thought I'd win it – and when I did my mom was furious. She thought that fifteen was too young to leave home and anyway she can't understand why I want to learn foreign languages, but our minister persuaded her that I ought to use the talent that the good Lord gave me,' she grinned. 'The pastor of the Lutheran church here is supposed to keep an eye on me. He seems to think I'm going to be an African missionary so I'll need French and German for the heathens of the Belgian Congo and East Africa.'

'And aren't you?' Maxine carefully smoothed the skirt of her best tangerine dress, which she was wearing because Nick was, after all, twenty-five per cent her date.

'No, I'm going to Paris,' said Judy in a firm voice.

'Alone? Will your parents let you go alone?'

'They won't know. I'll tell them when I get there after I've got a job. Otherwise they might say no,' Judy explained.

There was an awed silence from the three girls around the table who had never thought about the future, never planned further ahead than the next holiday. As in a child's colouring book, everything in the picture of their future life was clear and simple and the responsibility of someone else. Eternal bliss awaited each of them beyond the altar, and the only bit that hadn't been filled in was Prince Charming's face. To the Hirondelles, Judy's work sounded *real*, as opposed to chopping onions for the cookery mademoiselle or half-heartedly typing, 'Please believe in my most distinguished sentiments' at the bottom of a business letter copied from a textbook.

Eagerly, Kate questioned Judy about the language lab.

'Yes, the courses really *are* concentrated,' Judy answered, 'and it's just as well, because I've only got one year to learn fluent French and German. All the other students are in just as much of a hurry. They're all older than me, *really* old – some of them are over thirty! If they need an extra language for business, they fly into Gstaad from all over the world and sit all day in little booths with earphones. My German isn't yet good enough for conversation. I shouldn't really talk to Nick at all, I suppose. I should be practising German instead.'

Nick looked at her fondly. 'We hardly get any time to talk as it is. We only get to our bedrooms to sleep. I start at seven laying tables for breakfast, then we work in the restaurant straight through until three in the afternoon. Then there's a break until six-thirty and we're back in the restaurant until eleven. Unless there's a function, in which case we work until two in the morning and *still* get up at seven.'

'We're lucky to have such good sleeping quarters here,' Judy said. 'The student waiters who are on loan from the Lausanne Palace say that there it's five to a room under the roof, and at the Palace Saint Moritz I hear that the temporary staff have to sleep in the basement.'

'Goodness, I feel as if l'Hirondelle is a rest cure,' said Pagan, who rather enjoyed the slack tedium of the school routine – unlike Kate, who was exasperated by the laziness and boredom of the lessons.

After that meeting, Judy always saved a table at the Chesa for the girls on Wednesday afternoon when they each took two hours to drink one expensive cup of chocolate, and Nick took them all out for tea on Sunday afternoons when they ate their heads off.

Judy's obvious independence immediately fascinated the other three girls, who envied her energy, her stamina and her cheerfulness, not realizing that Judy had to push herself every morning to survive the drudgery of her day. Reluctantly, the girls followed their school timetable, but Judy set her own harsh timetable, and she stuck to it grimly. The Hirondelles were also intrigued by the forceful way that Judy spoke. She said exactly what she thought, whereas the three more privileged girls had been brought up to hide their feelings and not express their own wishes and opinions.

The girls quickly realized that while Nick was besotted with Judy to the exclusion of anyone else, here was the older brother they had all longed for – to admire them, to protect them, to tease them, to provide them with introductions to other boys and to pay for their outings. Nick was safe. He wasn't part of the sexual success-or-failure, scalp-collecting game, so the three Hirondelle girls instinctively developed a special way of flirting with Nick. They could be outrageously provocative with Nick with no fear of the consequences; they could practise their act with a safety net, as it were.

Nick was flattered and delighted with his new role as escort to three attractive but undemanding girls. Brought up in the stone-cold confines of the traditional British boarding school, a timid child, living in the country, he hadn't had much chance to meet girls, attractive or otherwise. But he had beautiful manners and once his blushing was under control, he was as proud as a pasha when escorting the four of them. Playing such an important part in what the other girls at l'Hirondelle enviously christened 'the Set' also meant that Nick soon lost the bashfulness of an only child and the agonized self-doubt of a British teenage male.

The girls knew that they would eventually meet other boys once the weekly dances started in mid-November, but despite Nick, they were sometimes restless and thirsty for adventure.

'Maybe we could sneak out the back door one night and go to some divine nightclub, somewhere like the Gringo,' Pagan said with a yawn one Sunday afternoon, after an enormous banana split.

Nick looked up sharply and brushed his black hair back from his face. 'You'd better be careful, you know. You'll get expelled if you're caught ... and there's something else.' He blushed. 'Something nasty. You know old Chardin's driver, Paul?'

'Yes, the chauffeur,' said Kate.

'No he's a *driver*,' Pagan corrected. 'Unless you're speaking French, a chauffeur is someone you hire for the evening. A driver is in your permanent employ.'

'Whatever you call it, you all know what I mean. Well, Chardin is a ... er ... homosexual and his ... er ... *friend* is Paul. I know it's true because Paul is also carrying on behind Chardin's back with one of the chefs at the Imperial.' He turned even pinker. 'The next bit is just a strong rumour, but I've heard it several times. You *all* know that what Chardin really loves is money.'

Everyone nodded.

'Well, it's rumoured around town that if a girl is caught outside the school with a boy, she's immediately expelled – unless her father pays hush money to avoid the disgrace. The girl might just have been out for a lark, nothing serious, but Chardin exaggerates to parents over the long-distance telephone. It's always her word against Chardin's, and the girl has to admit that she got out, so the parents usually believe the worst and pay up.'

'I can't believe it!'

'How do you know?'

'Do people realize he's homosexual?'

'All the waiters around here know that Chardin's queer,' said

Nick. 'For years he's had handsome male drivers when he doesn't need a driver at all. There's a bar at the back of town called Le Cous Cous – some pretty odd types hang out there – *I* wouldn't walk into the place, I can tell you!'

'But wouldn't he be afraid of being blackmailed?' Pagan asked.

'If the blackmail stories are true, then Chardin is playing a dangerous game, but it isn't as dangerous as it might seem. He picks his victims carefully. And there are plenty to choose from. You don't suppose for one minute that he couldn't *stop* girls from getting out at night if he wanted to, do you? The parents of the girl are always a long way off in another country, and they're rich. Chardin never asks for sums they can't easily afford. I believe the lowest rate is an extra year's tuition. On the whole, the parents can easily afford to pay their way out of a minor scandal, and because they're all from different countries, none of them are in touch with each other, so there's no danger of their meeting up.'

The girls hung on his words, fascinated by these awesome, wicked possibilities. 'So for heaven's sake be careful,' Nick continued. 'Just in case any of these rumours are true. I know it's gossip, but I *keep* hearing the same thing on the hotel grapevine. And that's not all. Some fellows say that Paul is bisexual.'

There was a pause while Nick explained what bisexual meant. By now he was blushing fiercely and wished he hadn't started, but he was also enjoying this flattering attention. 'It's said that if a very rich girl gets out at night and she's caught by Chardin, then she might be . . . deliberately *seduced* by Paul and photographed in . . . er . . . compromising positions. The barman at the Imperial told me that last year the father of one of the Brazilian girls had a few too many and started cursing Chardin. He said he'd flown over only because the headmaster was blackmailing him, and he couldn't go to the police because his daughter was involved and if the scandal leaked out, his wife would never forgive him . . . He had to protect the family name and his daughter's reputation or she'd never make a good marriage, and so forth . . . Then he said that he was never going to forgive his daughter for putting him in such a position, because he couldn't risk calling Chardin's bluff. There were photographs of his daughter with Paul.'

Nick smiled. 'They must have been pretty unusual pictures. He told the barman that he paid thirty-six thousand Swiss francs for them. Cash.'

For Pagan, Maxine and Kate, life at l'Hirondelle passed in a charming haze of sentimental naivety. Although disguised in the bodies of women, the pupils were still children. Exuding puppy-like exuberance and energy, they giggled and tittered, scampered and shrieked, and were, on the whole, rather silly. Lessons bored them, love fascinated them, passion was what they longed to study and their only ambition was to fall in love. There was a heady air of anticipation as they prepared to be – *women*! Hours were passed with magazine instructions and diagrams in one hand, costly tubes of make-up in the other, as girls decided whether their faces were oval, round or square. Much time was spent discussing, trying on and swapping clothes. All the girls yanked their waists in to minimal with wide elastic belts; they wore low ballet dancer's slippers, huge full skirts and pale pink or blue sweaters with a small strand of small pearls. The bras of the American girls divided their breasts into circular stitched cups that thrust sky-ward like twin ice cream cones. On their second Saturday, every new, non-American pupil rushed out and bought a French lace bra. After that, the girls endlessly compared their new bouncing breasts, measured them and worried about them. 'One of mine's larger than the other ...' 'Why are mine lower than yours ... ?' 'Serena's got *hairs* on her *nipples* ...' 'You can get more cleavage in the middle if you stuff socks down the side ...' 'I wish I had more ...' 'I wish I had less.'

Maxine tried hard to avoid mammary emphasis. She had large, rather low breasts, and she hadn't yet become accustomed to them. They still embarrassed her, so she pushed as much of them as possible under her armpits and gradually acquired a round-shouldered stoop. Nothing that the other girls said could convince Maxine that her splendid protuberances were an asset. She would turn scarlet as soon as she saw a group of workmen in the distance, knowing that when she drew level with them, the men's mes-merized eyes would follow her breasts as she passed. To comfort Maxine, her mother had told her that her *embonpoint* would disappear when she breast-fed her first baby, but the thought of carrying those footballs around for years until they were battened on by a baby that hadn't yet been conceived did nothing to console Maxine, who, when not wearing her expensive Dior clothes, hid under enormous, shapeless sweaters.

Maxine was wearing one of these short woollen shrouds as, one evening, she taught Kate to dance *un slow*. Humming 'Slow Boat to China', she grasped Kate as they solemnly shuffled around the narrow space between the two beds. 'It's better that there's no space, because that's how it feels in a nightclub,' explained Maxine, who had never been to one. None of the three girls had ever had a date with a boy, wouldn't know what to talk about if they did, desperately envied all the girls with older brothers and worried endlessly about where you put your nose when you were kissed.

They talked about such matters every night. After lights out, Pagan would creep from her room, clutching her heavy goose-feather quilt as a wrap, and sit cross-legged on the end of Kate's bed while they discussed all aspects of being a woman. Always it was unanimously agreed that they would dare *all* for true love, which would instantly be recognizable as such. Next, they decided what sort of man they were going to marry and sketched their personal Prince Charming to each other. They discussed what their wedding dress would look like, and then the honeymoon was described. In the cosy darkness they would draw deep breaths and discuss the fascinating mystery that none of them had yet encountered . . . sex. This was invariably romantic and never left you sleeping on the damp patch. They never imagined Prince Charming with an erection and certainly not wearing a rubber.

The universal lack of accurate sexual knowledge in the school was surprising, but all girls at l'Hirondelle lied in their teeth about their sexual experience – which, on the whole, was nil – in order to avoid looking unsophisticated. Hitherto, Kate and Pagan's only sexual experience had been furtively fantasizing about tampons. To date, neither of them had used tampons, but Pagan had stolen the brochure from her mother's box and she and Kate had pored over the perplexing illustrations.

None of them had explored, felt or seen the area between their legs. None of them had heard of masturbation or knew that they had already experienced it. The fourteen-year-old Maxine, bored and wriggling on a chair during Scripture class, thought she had

55

experienced religious ecstasy. Pagan, hunting on a borrowed mount with an unusually high-fronted saddle, had once felt exultant with what she thought was the divine thrill of the chase. Kate had always loved climbing ropes at gym class because of the lovely tickly sort of itch you got when, having pulled yourself up arm-over-arm, you slid down the rope with your legs crossed around it, thighs tensed and descent controlled by your feet acting as brakes. Once she'd had this feeling right at the top of the rope and had hung there swaying, blissfully frozen, unable to move and heedless of the cross, clipped voice of Miss Haydock, the instructress (who was used to girls being frozen on top of the ropes), telling Kate to come down immediately.

Maxine, being French and seventeen – a year older than Kate and Pagan – was their unquestioned and respected authority in sexual matters, especially as she had been *instructed*. Boys were all the same, Maxine's priest had explained, tomcats. They were only after one thing and you weren't to let them get it, because once they had got it, they despised you for letting them get it. Even if a boy swore that he loved you, after getting it he would spurn you (both privately and – worse – in public) because then, obviously, he wouldn't respect you any more. If a really serious boy really loved you, and tried to insist, well he was just testing you – the priest didn't say for what. In some mysterious way a man couldn't control himself, so if he went berserk with sexual passion, it was your fault for being so attractive, which was called 'leading him on'. This might easily lead to disaster, for then what would you tell your husband on your wedding night? Were you not to save yourself for your husband, the marriage would be a disaster from the start, and therefore your life would be ruined. Because the man could always tell.

It was strange that not one of the girls queried the sexual double standard. They accepted that a boy could be driven uncontrollably mad by passion, but it never crossed their minds that it was understandable if a girl felt the same way. They accepted that setting the sexual limit was the responsibility of the girl, not the boy; it was *her* job to control *his* lust. So girls would learn to chop off their own erotic urge, a behaviour pattern was formed, and after years of cutting off their natural feelings, many of these girls later found it difficult to proceed – or even be aroused – *beyond* that permitted sexual cut-off point. Their sexuality had been programmed and warped.

Maxine insisted that Italian girls saved themselves for their husbands and at the same time let a man go all the way by using an alternative route for the journey.

'Ugh! You're inventing it, you revolting creature,' said Pagan. 'Anyway, *how* can a man tell?'

'If he can't get his thing in, that's proof that you are a virgin,' said Maxine, 'unless you are very sportive, or ride on the horse or the bicycle or do gymnastics.'

Even if you had a serious beau who you thought might metamorphose into a fiancé, there were definite rules of sexual etiquette. Luckily, Maxine knew them all and shared her information after lights-out. 'Nothing on the first meeting – the rendezvous,' she said with authority, 'except a significant look when you say goodbye.' There was a pause while they all practised significant looks in the darkness.

'Then after the second meeting you would permit him to kiss you on the cheek. And the next time, a real kiss at the farewell.'

'French kiss, with the tongue?' asked Kate.

'Not until the fourth rendezvous.'

Maxine had to admit that she hadn't done it and hurried on to the fifth rendezvous, where, if the boy was serious, you might wish to go to the waist, a category that had two sub-divisions: over clothes and under them. Personally, Maxine would never permit either. She intended to be prudent until she was married.

A certain sort of girl allowed the man to go below the waist, in which case the two sub-divisions were (1) above and (2) below the underclothes, but with his thing firmly zipped up, you understand.

'But what *happens* under the underclothes?'

'The boy strokes the fur.' There was a further silence while in the dark they all furtively stroked their pubic hair and felt nothing.

The seventh stage of wickedness was letting the boy go all the way. Going all the way would be ecstasy, of course, but it would also be dreadfully dangerous.

Considering that every girl in l'Hirondelle was terrified of getting pregnant, it was surprising, when it came to the point, that they all felt a firm, almost religious conviction that pregnancy couldn't be inflicted upon them, especially not the first time. God wouldn't let it happen to you, and anyway, statistics proved it. Unless, of course, you touched ... the stuff. All the girls were terrified of semen. It only took one microscopic sperm, from all those millions, to get you pregnant and the damn things could stay alive for four days, invisibly creeping up your panty legs. So it was better to take no risks at all, and vital for the boy to take a precaution. But how revolting if he used the rubber thing!

'It's called a French lettuce,' said Pagan with authority.

'No, it's called a *capot anglais*,' corrected Maxine coldly.

Whatever it was called, it led to another etiquette problem. Did you look away while he was putting it on? Did you pretend not to notice? Or did you put it on before he arrived? In which case it would *prove* that he had not been carried away by your beauty, but that he'd really meant to do it all along. Anyway, how was it put on? 'I think they smooth it on when the thing is pointing upwards,' said Pagan, 'like a glove with only one finger.'

Not very romantic, they thought. But they had to admit it was better than being pregnant. Being pregnant was, well, inconceivable. Any unfortunate girls at whom fate pointed the finger had to sit in a scalding hot bath and drink a whole bottle of neat gin. A true friend would sit beside her in the steam to cheer her up, stop her fainting, drowning or making loud drunken noises that might be heard by Matron. Alternatively, you had to find a relatively large sum of money and visit an old woman in a back street, who would lay you out like a plucked chicken and pull your legs apart on her grubby kitchen table. Then, *without washing her hands*, she would push a knitting needle up you. If you were rich you could go to a private clinic and have an anaesthetic, and the knitting needle would be made of stainless steel and sterilized and everybody would pretend that you were having your appendix out.

Kate woke before the bell sounded and immediately realized that something odd had happened overnight. The street sounds were muffled and the room seemed unusually light. She dashed to open the window and push aside the lace curtain. The frost pressed white flowers against the glass. Barefoot in her blue nightgown, she leaned out. The trees were sprinkled with snow, the roofs of the chalets below were covered with thick white blankets that glistened in the early sun, the turrets of the Imperial Hotel shone white like a child's frosted birthday cake. Beyond the town, the pine forests looked ghostly, like grey lace.

Snow fell heavily for several nights and in a week the little town was transformed. The ski-rental shop hardly ever closed; skiers slid along the streets; children wrapped like bulky parcels pulled little coloured sleighs, the milk was delivered by dog sleigh and the local stable immediately brought out its magnificent horse-drawn sleighs. It was, at last, The Season.

Overnight a new elite appeared. Any man who could ski well was attractive, and any man who couldn't, wasn't. Men who had spent the summer being ignored as farm labourers and bricklayers suddenly became gods in the form of ski instructors. Every plumber's winter hope was to marry one of the heiresses from the finishing schools, consequently the girls were given preferential treatment in ski class and a great deal more attention than they deserved. The suntanned, lithe instructors, in their red wool hats and sweaters, captured every girlish heart as they coaxed, scolded and helped the stragglers, swooping back and forth with effortless grace that every girl envied, for to ski well was the ultimate social distinction.

Also worshipped, but from a greater distance, was the Swiss ski team, in training at Gstaad. The merits of the four team members and two reserves were endlessly discussed, but the team members themselves had time for nothing except training. They lived in a chalet on the edge of the town and were hardly ever seen. Which, of course, made them even more attractive.

One morning at breakfast, Pagan interrupted the now nonstop speculation as to what would happen next Saturday at the first dance of the season. She looked up from a rare letter from her mother. 'Guess what?' she asked. 'My mother knows Nick's father. I told her about him in my last letter and she thinks he might have been at Eton with my cousin Toby. She says that if his surname is Cliffe with an 'e', then he's Sir Walter Cliffe's son and he's going to inherit an enormous family hotel business.'

'It *can't* be the same or he would have mentioned it,' said Kate.

'If he's Sir Walter Cliffe's son then he certainly *wouldn't* have mentioned it,' Pagan said, adding for Maxine's benefit, 'It's British understatement, you see.'

Later, in the cloakroom of the Chesa, they told Judy, who said, 'No kidding! He's never said anything to *me* about it. I thought he was learning to be a waiter so he could *be* a waiter.' They went back to their table. Nick edged his way over to them through tightly packed tables. To the embarrassment of the other girls Judy immediately pounced on him.

'Is it true that you're going to inherit the Cliffe hotel business one day?'

Nick blushed. To give himself time to think he pushed his hair back from his face, then stammered, 'Well, yes – I'll have to *run* it, but it won't actually be mine; it's in a family trust. It'll be my job to look after it . . . for the family.'

'Does that mean you're rich?' Judy asked. There was a pause.

'I'm not poor,' Nick admitted unhappily, 'but I'm going to have a lot of responsibility.' With unusual firmness he added, 'Now d'you mind very much if we don't discuss it any more?'

Later, in the cloakroom, Maxine turned to Judy and beamed. 'Well, now you know about Nick, this will be the end of Jim in Virginia, I suppose?'

'Why?' asked Judy, astonished.

'Well, Nick is obviously mad about you. And it would be a very good proposition, no?' Maxine asked.

Judy laughed. 'Look I'm not sixteen yet. I don't intend to get married to *anyone* now, let alone a guy I'm not in love with. I promised my mother I wouldn't even go *out* with a boy while I was here, and it was only because of that that she allowed me to come. I think it was a sensible promise, and I'm going to keep it. I know it must seem crazy to you rich kids, but *I've* got to earn my living. It's hard keeping up with the French classes as well as the German ones, and working as a waitress doesn't make studying any easier. But I'll only get this one chance, so I'm grabbing it. There'll be men around for the rest of my life. They can wait.' She hesitated, then admitted, 'If you want to know the truth, I don't *have* any beau at home. Jim in Virginia doesn't exist. He's just a smoke screen that I tell other guys about if they get interested in me. It lets their vanity off the hook. Men hate being told no for no's sake.'

'But if you make a good marriage you won't *need* to work,' said Maxine, puzzled.

'Wanna bet?' said Judy.

That evening the school supper table buzzed with excited discussions as all the girls decided what to wear for the dance. Maxine had her blue silk strapless gown, with a puffed-sleeve bolero; Kate would wear her dull, Debenham's cream moiré dress with a sash and a modest heart-shaped neckline, filled in with a lace fichu. Maxine offered to recut the front in a daring low scoop, and her offer was immediately accepted, but that didn't solve the problem of what Pagan was to wear.

'It's no use. I can't go. I haven't got a long dress,' Pagan said gloomily.

'But you've got a full black taffeta skirt,' said Maxine, 'and your grandmother's white silk blouse. Suppose we buy a couple of metres of shocking pink taffeta and make a huge frill around the bottom of the skirt so that it reaches your ankles and pleat the leftover material around your midriff in a cummerbund, then unbutton the neckline of the blouse so that it's low?'

Pagan cheered up. In an odd way Maxine sounded just like old Mrs Hocken in the village, and Pagan liked nothing better than converting a garment into something for a totally different sort of occasion than the one for which it had been intended.

That evening Maxine chalked a new, daringly low scoop on the cream moiré, and Kate shut her eyes and crossed her fingers as the scissors bit into it. Then, on her knees, Maxine moved around Pagan, pinning newspaper to the bottom of her skirt to make a pattern for the frill. All over the school girls were trying on their dance dresses. Some of the continental girls wore an entrancing garment called a 'Merry Widow', which encased the wearer from armpit to suspendered thigh in black satin and lace. It was backed with steel strips as uncomfortable as the whalebone stays worn by Victorian women, but it was sexy.

All over the school girls without one wrote home by airmail, begging money for extra violin lessons . . .

The Imperial, with its fairytale towers and turrets, is one of the most beautiful hotels in the world. As the unheated green school

61

minibus drew up to the glittering glass porch, the pupils took off their unchic winter coats (few of them had evenings wraps) because it was better to freeze than look dowdy. Escorted by two harassed mademoiselles they trooped across red carpet under crystal chandeliers to the ballroom, where people were already sitting at small white candlelit tables. The girls sat down in the row of dark red banquettes that had been reserved for the school and ordered gin fizzes – the girls had to pay for their own drinks, and gin fizzes were supposed to last longest. Politely formal, Nick was one of the waiters who took their orders.

All the girls were nervous; they dreaded being asked to dance, they dreaded *not* being asked to dance, they dreaded dancing badly or stepping on their partner's toes. They pretended to ignore the stag line that was beginning to form at the far end of the room as they prepared for – possibly – their first major public humiliation. Pagan was glad she was sitting down so the boys couldn't see how tall she was. She was too tall for half the men in the room, although she couldn't imagine why they hated it – she didn't mind small *men*.

'I think I'll go to the ladies' room,' Kate said casually.

'No you *don't*,' said Pagan. 'One thing's certain, nobody's going to ask you to dance if you're in the ladies' room. Don't be in such a funk. Look at me! *That* will take our minds off this horrible ordeal. I'm terrified I'm going to step on this damned fuchsia frill and rip the whole thing off.'

The band struck up 'La Vie en Rose', there was a sudden scuffle and their table was surrounded by boys who all wanted to dance with ... *Kate!* Stunned, Kate accepted the invitation of the nearest one, who led her off for *un slow* as she thanked God for Maxine's lessons. Soon all three girls were on the dance floor, saved from the awful fate of being wallflowers.

At the end of the dance they were escorted back to their table, where their partners bowed and left them. Then, as the band struck up a samba, there was the same wild rush to ask Kate to dance. She couldn't believe it as she floated around the dance floor with a handsome, loose-limbed fellow called François, a student at Le Mornay.

François was – according to prescription – dark and handsome. In the arms of this loose-limbed fellow (so confident, even when reversing in the waltz), Kate wafted around the dance floor in a haze of joy as his masterful arm pulled her closer to his white starched shirt front, and her heart thumped as she felt his unfamiliar warmth against her breasts. The second dance was a rumba, which François did with all sorts of tricky variations. Before it had finished Kate suddenly flushed. This room's too hot, she thought, then she felt an unfamiliar sensation; a simultaneous wooziness of the head, a lurch in the stomach and a weakness in the knees. She thought, I'm going to *faint*, how odd it feels. But then she suddenly realized what was happening. This must be *it*, Kate realized, bursting with happiness as she mistook lust for love.

François had a smooth, well-practised line of small talk. As they floated around the floor, or as he bent her body back and forth against his in an increasingly close samba, he spoke very politely, as if they were having tea with his family. Kate found it was oddly erotic to feel his body hardening against hers (or was she imagining it, because he obviously hadn't noticed) as he suavely described the best forest walks, ski runs, guides, bars, hotels and ballrooms in the district.

Kate said very little. Her green eyes just looked up adoringly into his tanned face as François explained that there was one stumbling block to the Saturday night dances. After the dance was over, the girls from l'Hirondelle were forbidden to speak to the men they had met. On Saturday night you could cling to the man of your dreams through innumerable accordian renderings of 'La Vie en Rose', but should you meet him on the street on Sunday morning, you were meant to ignore him, to look straight through this potential love of your life.

From the headmaster's point of view, the girls were supposed to dance perfectly by the time they were shipped back to their parents. François explained that other inadequacies could be blamed on a girl's inherent inability, laziness, pubescent nervousness or premenstrual tension, but the parents got angry if their daughters couldn't dance. A good, cheap way of finding partners willing to teach them and getting the girls to practise their French was to allow pupils to attend public dances at the expense of their parents. However, Monsieur Chardin didn't trust a single one of the pubescent young women for whom he was responsible, and he wanted no irate grandparents-to-be on his doorstep demanding compensation or (even more difficult) identification. The easiest way to ensure his tranquillity and to keep his pupils safe was to lock them in every night, like chickens.

It was an invitation to trouble.

By midnight Kate felt like Cinderella. She was, in fact, too dazed to notice that when she went to the cloakroom none of the other girls spoke to her. They were not simply jealous of Kate's success. What made them angry was that they couldn't *understand* it. Kate looked so *ordinary*. 'I can't think what they see in her in that boring old dress,' sniffed one girl. 'It's not as if she's *pretty*. Thin hair – not even long – and those odd, green, hooded eyes.'

Kate had just had the first taste of a disbelieving jealousy that she would have to endure from women for the next thirty years. Because they could not understand why men were attracted to her, women thought that Kate was sly, that she had tricked them, that no man was safe with her. In fact they were wrong; Kate was safe with no man.

With a crash of cymbals the spotlight shone on the bandleader as he announced that the competition to elect 'Miss Gstaad' would take place after the next dance, during which the voting slips would be passed out to each table. 'Well, it's quite obvious who's going to enter it from our table,' beamed Pagan. 'Kate is the belle of the ball; she'd better be Miss Gstaad as well.'

'Don't be ridiculous,' said Kate. 'I'm not going to go up on that stage and make a fool of myself.'

'I *dare* you,' said Maxine. 'It's not serious, it's not Miss World, after all, it's only a little village hop.' She gave Kate a firm push, shoving her off the maroon velvet bench. 'Don't be so bloody British.'

Kate stood up. Reluctantly, she shuffled on to the dance floor and was pushed into line by the major-domo, who handed her a large card marked number 17. A couple of other finishing schools had also come to the ball, so there were about thirty girls in line on the dance floor, including a voluptuous Italian girl in a black velvet, strapless gown. Kate saw she had no chance of winning, but it was too late to back out. Slowly the girls formed a circle.

But Kate had reckoned without Nick, who walked over to the

waiter responsible for passing out the voting slips, gave him a smile that meant, 'I'll settle with you later,' shoved a handful of slips into his own pocket, dashed into the men's cloakroom and quickly scribbled '17' on all of them. Then he walked out and picked up the top hat that was to be passed around the tables to collect the voting slips. Simple.

The lights were lowered, and an erratic spotlight illuminated each competitor as she slowly walked up the steps that led to the platform, stood centre stage, beaming or looking embarrassed, held up her number and then walked down the steps.

Amid applause and wolf whistles the lights came up again as everyone dropped his voting slip in the hat that Nick held out to each table.

Each girl in the competition tried to look unconcerned. To them, the beauty contest wasn't a minor evening's diversion, decided upon by the bored-but-professionally-jolly major-domo; for each of them, it was their first taste of public sexual competition, and their hearts thumped and they found it hard to breathe until after the next samba when the major-domo stepped forward and announced that the new Miss Gstaad for 1948 was, Ladies, Lords and Gentlemen – number 17!

Kate shook her head in disbelief, Maxine flung her arms around her and hugged her, Pagan whooped with delight and a flock of knowing waiters lined her path to the little stage where, scarlet with surprise and pleasure, a pale blue sash that read 'Miss Gstaad 1948' was draped around her by the major-domo, who then popped a diamond tiara on her hair, presented her with two magnums of champagne and stood at her side in an avuncular pose as photographers' flashlights popped.

'We'll be having trouble with *that* one,' muttered one of the harassed mademoiselles who had been sent to escort the Hirondelle girls.

It was an accurate forecast.

~ 4 ~

BY the end of November nearly all the schoolgirls had steady boyfriends and had discovered that the little town was astonishingly full of places for secret meetings. They met behind the church, in stables and in barns, crouching in the backs of cars, in the back of the ski shop, in tearooms on the outskirts of town or on top of the ski runs. At the weekends the Eggli, the Wasserngrat, the Hornberg and the Wispile each had their quota of courting couples, as did the inns and cafés of nearby villages such as Saanen and Château d'Oex, which had already catered to generations of foreign finishing-school girls suffering from the symptoms of puppy love.

After a Saturday night spent with their hair twisted up in paper curlers and their faces covered in cream or dried mud to prevent wrinkles, the l'Hirondelles invariably headed for the Chesa. Their show of self-confidence barely hid their uncertainty and indecision. One remark or laugh could produce an instant, hateful blush – and it was doubly humiliating to be betrayed by one's own neck. Flirtatious and pert, conscious only of their appearance and their audience, the girls appeared not to notice the young men who were sitting at nearby tables, tilting their chairs back, impatient but resigned to all this feminine play-acting, as the girls pretended to ignore them.

Unexpectedly, for the first time in their lives, the girls had discovered they possessed a sort of power. Once she realized this, each girl felt a strange pride in being able to enslave a boy – or two or three, which made a girl twice or three times as powerful. None of them realized the strength or dangers of this sudden sexual power; they never realized that it could be black magic or white magic, depending on how you used or abused it. In 1948, sex appeal was *power*, the only power these girls were ever likely to get, and you used as much of it as you had as hard as you could and full blast! Naturally, the girls knew their own prim petting cut-off points, but it never once occurred to any of them that a man might find it difficult to switch off his own powerful urges at the moment when it suited the girl to do so. It never occurred to any of them that the power they had raised in the man was not only passion but, if thwarted, the power to rape or kill. The reactions of a frustrated man had never been explained to any of them.

Judy acted as postbox for all the adolescent lovers. For the first time since term started, dictionaries were thumbed, grammars consulted and Maxine was much in demand as a translator. Judy also passed messages about meeting places, which often depended on the weather. When she placed a bill or a paper-lace napkin on a table it might well be accompanied by a note that read, 'Sheila, Nursery slope ski lift at five', or *'Hélas! Gérard chéri, impossible cette semaine. Samedi prochain à trois heures, ton Isabel.'*

Occasionally, a girl was caught talking to a boy by one of the school staff and punished by being kept in school the following weekend, but Kate was the only girl who *kept* getting caught, first, because she was besotted with the dazzling François, and second, because she was at heart a straightforward girl, unaccustomed to being devious. When challenged by Matron, she admitted meeting François in the local church. A fortnight later a jealous classmate reported Kate's rendezvous with him in a stable and the following week a mademoiselle saw them drinking *Glühwein* on the Hornberg – a major offence. Kate was increasingly anxious until one weekend François told her he had booked a sitting room in a little *pension* on the edge of the town. He wanted to be alone with her in comfort, not crouching in straw, standing half-frozen in the snow or sitting on public exhibition in a café. He wished to talk to her in private because he had something important to say. *He's going to propose*, thought Kate.

So she followed him into a green-shuttered chalet, their boots clattering up the dark, wooden stairs. François unlocked a door and Kate stopped dead at the sight of the carved wooden double bed covered with a blue-and-white checked quilt. François gently pulled her to an armchair by the window and started to kiss her. Knees melting, Kate thought that perhaps he hadn't *noticed* the bed. Perhaps the bed was a mistake, perhaps he couldn't get a room without one.

She kicked her boots off as she felt his warm tongue licking her ear, then his lips were on the back of her neck and finally she lay in his arms, eyes almost closed and mouth half open.

'*Chérie*, we're going to have a wonderful life together,' François said, as he slowly undid each pearl button on her grey lace blouse and slid his hand inside it. Kate felt as if she were swimming under water in a slowed-down film as with gentle movements he pushed back her blouse, unhooked her bra and bent his lips to caress the pink tips of her nipples.

Then, naked from the waist up, she was lying languorously under the checked quilt and the wet tip of his tongue was warm in her other pink ear. She felt his hand under her skirt, a cunning, casual movement as if the hand was moving without the knowledge of its owner.

She shifted and tried to jerk her body up from the bed. François thrust her back. Quite hard. 'Cock tease,' he hissed. Under a sea of stiffened prickly petticoats Kate felt his grip on her thigh as he thrust his hand above her silk stocking top and then up the leg.

She tried to pull away from him. 'I never have, I don't know how to, please don't, I'll do anything if you won't.'

Oh, God, Kate thought, he'd undone his trousers and now she could feel his flesh throbbing against her soft inner thigh. Poised above her, François was looking at her as if he didn't know her, he was breathing hard, his eyes were glazed, intent, somehow uninvolved. 'I'll be careful then,' he muttered and to Kate's relief he withdrew his hand; but only so that he could roll sideways and strip his clothes off. He didn't seem to realize that his thing was showing. The lavender-pink penis reared up from its nest of black hair, balls wobbling beneath it. How *ugly* it was, Kate thought.

Kate tried to get up again, but he thrust her down on the bed then roughly pulled her breasts towards him, lunged his throbbing penis between them and started thrusting his body. Squashed beneath him, Kate felt bewildered, indignant, disbelieving. She couldn't breathe because of his weight on top of her. With a hoarse grunt François stiffened and shivered, his grip hardening painfully on her breasts. Then he collapsed on top of her and Kate felt a stickiness trickling over her collarbone and down her neck. She knew what it was and she didn't dare move in case some of the stuff got in the wrong place. She was terrified.

'You see, I told you I'd be careful, my darling,' François mumbled.

Kate didn't think he'd been careful at all. How *dare* he call her his darling? On the other hand, wasn't that just what she'd *wanted* half an hour ago? To *be* his darling? His passion for her must have been uncontrollably great.

Yes, that was it, she told herself. He loved her, that's why this had happened. It wasn't what she'd expected, it hadn't been romantic and wonderful, it had been messy and uncomfortable. But perhaps making love was like skiing, painful and hard for the first couple of times . . .

Anyway, now she'd let him go below the underclothes, stage two, so obviously he *had* to be the love of her life.

But, strangely, she felt like crying.

Two days later Kate discovered that the rest of the school wasn't speaking to her. They were ostracizing her. Smugly, theatrically, publicly, they made it clear that they despised her. 'What's the matter? What have I done?' Kate asked Pagan, who looked harassed.

'Oh, they think you've gone all the way with François. Pay no attention to the jealous bitches,' she said.

'But I *haven't*,' Kate said, wondering whether, in fact, she really *had*. Certainly the school thought so. Kate was puzzled by the hypocrisy of a world that condemned certain actions in public but practised or envied them in private; she had disobeyed the eleventh commandment: Thou shalt not be found out. And besides, she was being punished for being Miss Gstaad.

The following Sunday, Judy was waiting for Kate outside the Chesa, arms held across her chest and tucked in her armpits, stamping her boots in the snow to keep warm. 'Listen, Kate, that creep you're going out with has told the whole town that he's slept with Miss Gstaad. The barman at the Imperial told Nick and Nick came straight to me. We thought you ought to know.'

'I don't believe it,' said Kate, realizing at last how the school knew. She dashed to the *pension* to meet François, where François smoothly denied telling anyone. Kate believed him because she wanted to. She felt drained of energy, forlorn, bruised. She clung to François, let him undress her completely, clung to him shivering under the warm quilt as he stroked her body, as he pushed his hand beneath her buttocks, as he felt between her legs ... That hurt a bit as he wriggled his finger inside her. But Kate remained passive – she didn't know what was expected of her, but since she'd already been blamed for it, she might as well do it. She could feel the hard warmth and weight of François on her stomach, there was a second of suspense, then she gasped in pain. But soon they were moving together smoothly, as if they were dancing, and she began to feel a slight warmth and excitement. But before it developed into anything even approaching an orgasm, François stiffened with a gasp, then she felt a warm wetness as his erection subsided. He seemed pleased with himself, but Kate felt oddly disappointed, wobbly and stranded. Perhaps there was something wrong with her? Perhaps she was frigid?

It did not occur to her that François was at fault. Boys, she assumed, knew how to do these things. Perhaps she just needed more practice. She supposed that she'd get the hang of it in time.

'Two to come out, the black ones in front to be capped and I have to wear a brace at night for a bit,' reported Maxine that night in bed. 'He phoned Papa on the spot and Papa said go ahead. Not nearly as expensive as I thought, cheaper than my tangerine dress.'

'Well, now your hair,' said Pagan, huddled under her quilt in the moonlight. 'It grows too low on your forehead, like a Neanderthal woman ... I'm going to trim away a bit with my nail scissors and give you a lovely widow's peak. If you don't like it, you can loop your back hair over it, and if you *do* like it, you can have it done permanently by electrolysis.' She sprang off the bed and reached for Kate's little purple underarm razor. In the face of such assurance, Maxine allowed her hairline to be shaved away by the light of her pocket flashlight. Pagan looked slightly worried after she'd done it; Maxine looked terrible, as if she were being prepped for a lobotomy.

'Maybe if you plucked her eyebrows?' suggested Kate, so Pagan attacked Maxine's bushy eyebrows. Unfortunately, she plucked too much from the left side, then attempted to match up the right side and took too much of that away, so she returned to the left for further depilation until Maxine was left with two thin odd

70

horizontal question marks of hair under her lopsidedly shaven forehead.

Maxine looked in the mirror and burst into tears.

The following day Matron hurried her off to the hairdresser, and later that afternoon Maxine returned, beaming again. Her hairline had been properly trimmed, and the hairdresser had persuaded her to have her hair streaked and styled. Her braids had gone and in their place was a thick, blonde, shining mane.

'Now your weight,' Judy said firmly the following Sunday. 'Ten kilos. No more cakes. You're always saying you hate the school food, so it shouldn't be too difficult. You can buy seven hard-boiled eggs a week and have one for breakfast with black coffee, an orange and a slice of ham in your room at lunchtime, no tea break, and as little as possible for supper. And the footballs will slowly disappear.'

They didn't, but the rest of Maxine diminished at the rate of a kilo a week. Fascinated, the rest of the school watched her transformation. Some tried to emulate it, but they hadn't Maxine's determination and tenacity in the face of warm bread, fresh from the oven, with strawberry preserves for breakfast or the cream cakes and steaming chocolate of the five o'clock break.

When Maxine was no longer a size sixteen but a size fourteen heading for twelve, Judy examined her thoroughly, as one might a horse on auction, and nodded with satisfaction. Then she stepped back and said, 'The nose.'

Surprisingly, Maxine was worried that she might appear vain, that people would *notice*, that her mother would object, that it was sacrilegious to alter the nose God had given her.

'God didn't intend you to wear a bra either,' Judy said. 'It's up to you to help God a bit, you know, if you want to look as good as you can.'

After Christmas Maxine returned to school ten days late, with two black eyes and a perfect nose. 'What a performance,' she said, lifting her sunglasses to show her bruises. 'I nagged and I cried and I refused to go out, oh, you would have been proud of me, I behaved so badly and with such determination. I wheedled Aunt Hortense into paying for it, provided my parents consented.' She readjusted the sunglasses. 'The aunt didn't expect my parents to consent, but I kept telling them that they couldn't be so cruel as to refuse such an offer. I tell you, the whole of Christmas Day I was in tears. So eventually they agreed. It only took four days, and I needed the rest after that performance!'

Maxine's new nose and figure greatly increased her self-confidence, and she now concentrated on losing more weight. She ate and drank as little as possible, she was on skis as often as possible, every night and morning she would sit on the floor of her bedroom and roll her plump thighs away with a wooden kitchen rolling-pin. 'Ninety-eight ... ow, ninety-nine ... *il faut souffrir pour être mince*, ouch, a hundred. Pouf! Now where are my ski socks?'

'Surely you're not going to ski today?' Kate asked. 'It looks like an upended paperweight outside. It's a Sunday for staying by the fire.'

'I only lost half a kilo last week, look at my chart on the wall. Five more kilos to lose.'

Maxine trudged off to the ski lift. She had decided to try a longer, more advanced run so she caught the *gondelbahn* cable car to the top of the Wispile. The top of the mountain was grey and threatening with black clouds lacing the sky behind. Maxine shivered and looked at the signpost, a Christmas tree of coloured arrows nailed to the post that pointed to different ski runs. The yellow runs were easy, the red ones more difficult and the black runs were only for very experienced skiers.

Maxine, who had only been skiing for a couple of months, thought that the black track didn't look all that difficult – in fact it looked quite easy and much the prettiest. And so it was for the first two hundred yards, then the *piste* took a sharp turn to the left and Maxine found herself in a rutted ice path that fell steeply through the forest. For a moment she thought of climbing back, then she was going too fast and couldn't stop; her skis clattered over the ruts. She was frightened of wrapping herself around a tree; it hadn't occurred to her that there might be nobody else on the *piste*. She jerked over a bump, fir trees loomed, she floundered and fell.

She pulled herself to her feet, shot forwards – again too fast – on the corrugated ice track and fell again, bruising her hip. Although she was wearing two pairs of woollen mittens inside her ski gloves, she couldn't feel her numbed hands and her cheeks and forehead already ached with the cold. She pulled herself up again and for the next ten minutes she managed to ski slowly and carefully with a great deal of side-slipping. Then it started to snow, which limited visibility until she could only see a few yards in any direction; the *piste* was quickly covered by snow and she could see no arrows. As snowflakes fluttered down remorselessly, the lack of sound was eerie and she felt frightened.

Suddenly, a lone, black-clad skier with an orange-peaked cap shot past her. She waved her ski poles after him and shouted, but he didn't stop. Maxine groped her way onwards and downwards, following the direction the man had taken. She found herself alone on a steeply sloping field of icy bumps, but she didn't dare take it straight. She started to traverse it slowly. Each time she reached the edge of the field, she did a laborious kick turn and clumsily levered herself down a couple of feet. Her knees started to tremble with the effort but she zig-zagged on, all thought of style forgotten. She had just reached the bottom of the field when the man with the orange-peaked cap slipped gracefully past her.

'*Au secours,*' she shouted. '*Help!*' But the skier didn't seem to hear, so again Maxine followed in the direction that he had taken and soon found herself on the edge of the steepest slope she had ever been on.

She was terrified. She considered climbing back, but downhill, she reasoned, would be easier than uphill, so she took her skis off and dragged them behind her, kicking footholds with the heels of her ski boots, terrified lest she drop a ski, because it would undoubtedly shoot off down the glassy mountain and be lost forever. As perhaps she was herself . . .

Although she was heading downhill, she had a nasty feeling that she might be going the wrong way. It was now three hours since she had left the top of the mountain. She was soaking wet, she'd got snow down the back of her neck and could no longer even feel her feet. Cold, forlorn and frightened, she sat down to rest in the snow, worrying about frostbite and peering into the thick greyness all about her.

This time, because she wasn't skiing, she heard the orange-hatted skier descend, scrambled to her feet, waved and screamed at him.

'Stop, *stop*, please *stop*.'

He pulled up by her side.

'Could you please tell me the easiest way down?' Maxine asked anxiously.

He looked at her through yellow goggles and said in French, 'There *is* no easy way down. You're on the black run. Why did you pick the black, why not one of the easier runs?' He sounded exasperated. 'Look, you'd better follow me or you'll never get down. Put your skis on.'

Slowly Maxine inched her way after him down the hellish mountain. He would ski forwards then stop and wait, watching her as she jerked, slid and wobbled forwards, her new teeth gritting with determination as the grey obscurity started to thicken into darkness. Then suddenly her knees gave way and she collapsed into the snow. She gave a little sob.

'I'm afraid I can't go on. I've got to rest. I'm sorry, but I can't move anymore.'

The black skier's voice became gentle and persuasive as he urged her on. 'Come on,' he said, 'you're doing wonderfully well, we're nearly at the halfway station, it's just around the next bend, then you can ride on the *gondelbahn* back to the bottom!'

So they slowly inched forwards until Maxine fell again. She ached all over. 'I can't go on,' she muttered, then buried her face on her knees and rolled over in the snow, curled in a foetal position.

The skier sighed, unclipped his skis and stuck them upright in the snow. 'Here, let me rub you warmer,' he said. He rubbed each arm, then her back until she ached with the pain of it. Then he roughly rubbed her legs until she could feel them again and helped her stand.

Slowly, painfully, they progressed onwards. The halfway station wasn't around the next bend or the one after that. It was almost an hour before they turned around a bend and saw it. Maxine almost crawled into the station, but her rescuer said he was going to ski down the remainder of the *piste*. He would join her in the bar at the bottom, if she liked.

Effortlessly, he slipped downhill and away from her.

At the bottom of the ski lift Maxine, slightly recovered, headed for the near-by bar and staggered to the cloakroom. She took off her cap, goggles, scarf and extra sweaters, washed her face in warm water – oh the bliss of it – and fluffed out her hair as best she could. Then she clumped into the steamy pine-lined bar. Because no one was stupid enough to ski in such dangerous weather, the bar was empty except for a huge, husky black figure leaning against it, dangling an orange cap and yellow goggles.

'Hot buttered rum for you, I think, tea for me,' he said, as she smiled her newly irresistible grin. 'I must admit that I never expected to find a pretty girl under that collection of old horse blankets you were wearing.'

His bronzed face was ringed with neatly curling blond hair. Maxine took one look into the clear, blank blue eyes and fell in love with him on the spot.

The added bonus was that Maxine's saviour was a reserve on the Swiss ski team, and every girl in l'Hirondelle would have killed for a chance to meet any member of the team. *Wait* until she told them! she thought.

But she didn't tell them because Pierre Boursal sat with her, alone in the deserted bar, until it was time to go back to school for supper, then walked her back, carrying her skis, while Maxine prayed that he would ask to see her again, and by the time he did – not to ski, mind you, once was enough – he had become too important to her to boast about. She didn't even tell Kate or Pagan in case it was tempting fate. Or Kate or Pagan.

From then on, Maxine met Pierre whenever she could – after the last ski lift stopped, of course. Pierre had not intended to get involved with a girl. He took his training seriously. He didn't smoke, didn't drink and didn't intend to be distracted by women. Maxine's virtue was splendidly safe with him, thanks to his training, she thought, longing for him as they clung to each other on some tiny dance floor or she sat with his muscular arm around her waist in the darkest corner of some tearoom. At such times she clearly saw how very, very easy it would be to be wicked.

If only she ever got the chance.

The slalom race was due to start at ten o'clock that morning. Urged by Maxine, wearing her best yellow ski jacket and her beautiful silver fox hood, the girls were again on top of the Eggli. Shepherded by the sportsmaster, they had caught the little green bus from Gstaad, up the mountain to the funicular which carried the skiers even farther up. At times the dark green pines shuddered and snow fell silently from their branches.

Although it was early, the girls shared a mug of hot, red *Glühwein* as soon as they reached the summit restaurant, for they knew they would soon be numb with cold. Their sportsmaster explained again that ski racing was a combination of trained technique, superb physical fitness, the best equipment – and favourable weather conditions. On a grey day, when visibility was low, a skier would be able to see only a short way ahead. The hazy white sky would merge with the snow and it would be impossible to see where the track ended and the sky started, whether there was mountain ahead or a vertical drop. In bad conditions, luck was more important than when the weather was perfect, for the sunlight showed up uneven ground so that every bump, ridge, dip and rut was clearly defined by shadows on the snow.

When the girls left Gstaad that morning, the steep icy slopes had glistened in what had been the first sun of the week. But by the time they reached the summit, the sun had disappeared between low clouds and it had started to snow – not hard, but just enough to reduce visibility. The officials at the top of the slalom course decided to start the race twenty minutes early before the snow worsened.

The only sound on the muffled mountain was the crunch of snow under their skis as the girls glided down to the finishing post. On either side of the course a soft beige row of fencing leaned away from them and disappeared up the quiet white mountainside. The 300-yard course with a drop of 300 feet was staked out to the right of a clump of pine trees. Fifty pairs of coloured slalom poles had been driven into the snow to make fifty 'gates' at five metre intervals. This race, the Men's Slalom, was an individual event. Each skier would not only be competing against the other racers but against his own best time as he skied alone down the first course, then the adjoining course. The fastest aggregate time would decide the winner.

Pierre Boursal didn't think he had much chance of winning. There were thirty-seven starters, including three members of the team and the other reserve. However, one reserve would have to qualify for a team place, because the day before Leist had broken his collarbone in a car crash.

Suddenly impatient, Pierre thought why wait when he could ski? He went up in the funicular and streaked down the *piste*. More than anything else in the world he loved silently slipping downhill on skis, using only his body and earth's gravity to flick like a hawk over the magical white surface. For him, it was the ultimate physical exultation, that thrill of constant risk and deliberate danger when he allowed himself to go a little too fast and just out of control. He had first been put on skis when he was a tiny child and quickly discovered that it was the only way he could escape from his glamorous mother and her insufferable hordes of would-be lovers, crowding the smarter parts of Saint Moritz every year. Rather than be dragged along in the wake of that mob, Pierre used to take his skis and seek the solitude and purity of the snow at the top of a mountain, and hear in that celestial silence only the faint noise of his skis as he carved his own path through the virgin snow.

Pierre was not a good scholar and by the time he was thirteen, his only source of joy and satisfaction was skiing. Afterwards, carrying his skis through some village street, he loved to notice two responses from passers-by; sometimes he would see a little group staring up at his trail and hear them exclaim, 'Only a madman would attempt the Scharnfürts today,' or 'Did you see how fast his descent was?' Sometimes, in ski villages where he was known, Pierre would notice that he was being pointed at in the street, that men were muttering and turning their heads to look at him from the opposite sidewalk.

Only his mother and father were unaware that their son skied like a demon.

It was not until the president of the multinational company that was sponsoring the junior team congratulated Monsieur Boursal at a banker's dinner in Zurich on being the father of a future champion that Pierre's father realized his son was neither un-talented nor lazy – he was merely not interested in scholastic subjects.

Now, Pierre moved down the Eggli with perfect style and breakneck speed, skiing to the limit – and a little beyond. Un-limbering before the race, Pierre swung around the most difficult

77

bumps, then veered off the *piste* and into the deep virgin snow, leaning backwards so that his ski tips wouldn't catch the powder. The snow plumed up behind him, a silent diamond spray. He cut back on to the *piste*, then crouched low, elbows to knees, into a final *schuss* with skis flat and fast, head down and sticks tucked under his arms. His anxiety was forgotten. All he felt was the sheer physical sensation of his body, the snow and the heady, cold champagne-sparkle of the winter air at this high altitude.

Carrying his skis, Pierre walked up the side of the course, trying to memorize it, because competitors weren't allowed a trial run down. The right route would only become apparent when he was on it, flashing through the maze of bamboo poles. As he waited his turn, he would watch the skier before him, trying to work out the course from his movements. Total concentration was essential because the gates were pitched irregularly and often closely together; it was very easy to crash into a pole or miss a gate.

Today's course didn't look too difficult; two steep drops, both near the beginning of the descent, several sharp 'V' turns, one of which was almost immediately followed by an exceptionally tight twist that would have him straining uphill to reach it. That was the bastard to watch for.

Pierre reached the top of the course and waited with the other competitors, shuffling up towards the start, breath visible in the frozen air. He had drawn number 8, a good number because the track would be defined by the seven previous racers but wouldn't have developed the deep ruts that might catch the ski tips of the last few racers.

Now he was next. Pierre checked the red knitted headband that kept the hair out of his eyes and prevented his ears and forehead from freezing. He cleared his throat, spat in the snow, then stood at the top of the run. Tense, poised, flexing his shoulders and neck, impatiently he slid his skis backwards, forwards, backwards, waiting for the starter to touch his shoulder and his boot to start the timer.

Now!

As he leaped off, Pierre was conscious of a black, silent human hedge of spectators alongside the course. He swooped down, then took a sharp left turn above his first gate. Before he was through that gate, he would be preparing his crouching body for the next gate, and deciding where his turn would be for the gate after that. From the moment he started to train, his instructor had yelled at him to 'think two gates ahead', and 'faster, faster, *faster*'. He had been taught to start cautiously, get the feel of the course, then – as soon as he had his rhythm and momentum – to move as fast as he could without losing control.

He snaked sharply to his right through the gap, legs slightly apart for balance, crouching low, then transferred his weight on to his inner leg as he leaned into the mountain. With a scraping, skating motion his lower, outer leg pushed, pushed, *pushed* him around and on.

After the steep drop at the eighth gate his body began to adjust to the rhythm of his movements. Pierre felt the tension leave him and his heart pumped unusually loudly as excitement took over from anxiety. As each gate flicked past, there was a flash of relief.

Suddenly his skis shuddered, then rattled on the sharp dip to gate 14. Pierre fought to regain control. For a few terrifying seconds he hit black ice where the racers before him had scraped away the thin covering of powder snow. Almost immediately came the third steep drop. He swung to take an awkward gate on his left. His skis shuddered badly against the ice again and for a moment he lost control. Abruptly he stopped thinking two gates ahead and saw only the couple of bamboo sticks immediately in front of him, an impassive challenge.

He made a painful effort of will, lips tight and eyes bulging as he regained his mental control, then grimly swung through the next gate, his concentration once more two gates ahead, hardly noticing – as he swept past – a blue-jacketed casualty who was crawling to the side of the course.

This was a sneaky little tight turn. He had felt a gate pole shudder against his upper arm. Almost immediately came an even tighter turn on almost the same level. He quickly pushed himself upwards with his outer ski and felt his leg muscles quiver with the effort. It was going to be too much for his legs, he'd never make it.

He jerked to the left to avoid a pole that had fallen sideways and hadn't been straightened. He nearly missed the thirty-fourth gate and again his concentration faltered as he checked his speed and just missed a headlong crash into the pole. Shaken, his first reaction was to slow down, but his inherent determination urged him ahead and with the tenacity of a born champion, he skied even faster through the next ten gates.

Not *another* sharp drop? He thought, I'd like to get the bastard who laid out this course ... Surely, this must be the last one ... ?

Then suddenly Pierre could hear the encouraging rhythmic roars of the crowd. He knew they yelled in time to your turns if you were going especially well. He thought, I *mustn't* listen, I *must* concentrate.

Then, dear God, *no* – there was another steep drop ... Recklessly, Pierre used it as a springboard, and his whole body lunged forwards as he forced his skis onwards and summoned up his remaining energy to propel himself past the finishing post.

He suddenly felt euphoric. *Not* bad ...

After all the competitors had finished the first descent, Pierre led by 1·50 seconds. Fourteen of the thirty-seven starters had dropped out.

The second slalom was laid out beside the first course and speeds were usually faster because the racers had loosened up, but weather conditions had now worsened; it was cold and overcast with a deceptively gloomy light. Visibility was almost at the danger point and Pierre wondered whether the race would be cancelled. Please God, no, he prayed.

This time, at the end of his descent, he didn't feel euphoria, only tired anxiety. He thought his time was good, but was it good enough?

He skied over to the huge notice-board where the times were marked up, and stood by it, his back to the slalom course, as he watched the figures go up. Maxine kept away from him and held her breath. The course was claiming more than its fair share of victims; one had overshot the gate when taking a steep, icy drop. Then a pole hit another racer in the face, luckily resulting only in a slight concussion and a black eye. One racer caught his ski in an icy rut and took a tremendous tumble into the fence that guarded the course, scattering spectators as he broke his left leg in three places below the knee. Pierre held his breath hopefully and he couldn't help inwardly rejoicing when, three minutes later, his personal rival, Klaus Werner, neatly wrapped one ski around a pole and cartwheeled gracefully out of the race, uninjured.

Suddenly, number 8 went up on the board, with a time of 1·56 minutes. Maxine clambered through the snow to throw her arms around his neck, as she yelled, 'Pierre, you've won, you've won!'

And to her surprise, and his, he kissed her with a passion that took her breath away.

Pierre whispered, 'I've got to go with the team, darling. Meet you at the Chesa in half an hour.' Then he was surrounded by instructors, fans and fellow racers grinning and slapping him on the back.

Maxine waited for him at the Chesa. They were both too excited to eat, although they drank from the obligatory bottle of champagne. After half an hour, Pierre – who hardly ever drank – put his arm around her and said, 'Now we go to my room, eh?'

'Now?' said Maxine, doubtfully, longing to and yet afraid.

'Now.'

They clumped through the streets as congratulations were shouted at Pierre. How long did it take to do it? wondered Maxine as she slunk along at his side.

The ski team chalet was empty. They clattered up the wooden stairs in their heavy ski boots.

Pierre's room contained two narrow beds. He put the ashtray outside the door before locking it – the standard signal to the roommates.

Maxine wanted to leave but she also wanted to stay.

Pierre started to undress her quickly, kissing her whenever she started to say something. She wanted him to stop but she also wanted him to go on. Should she tell him she had never been below the waist?

He flashed a careless smile, expertly unsnapping her bra hooks with one hand. 'Don't worry, I have been in this situation *hundreds* of times.'

'Hundreds?' said Maxine, relieved, shocked and cross.

'Well, enough.' There was a struggle over her ski pants as she clutched them to her body, so Pierre started to pull off his own clothes. As he unzipped his trousers Maxine shut her eyes. Then she opened them, jumped on to the bed and hid her head under the quilt like an ostrich.

'Pierre, it's *daytime*. I'm shy. Anyone might look through the window.'

'We're three storeys above the ground,' he laughed, but obligingly he drew the lace curtains.

Suddenly he was lying naked beside her, gently prying her hands away from her face and kissing her naked breasts in a determined manner that Maxine found wildly exciting. Torn between embarrassment and ardour, she involuntarily twisted around towards Pierre's body, burying her head against his chest so that she couldn't see anything. Then she stiffened again. Now she could feel his muscular nakedness and smell his desire. And she could feel something else. Stealthily she pulled her hand away, but Pierre firmly took it and drew her hand gently downwards. Maxine tugged it back rather sharply. Softly, insistently, Pierre again pulled her hand downwards and clasped it over his flesh. Maxine decided to pretend that it wasn't her hand. She was terrified of doing something wrong, of hurting him. Did you bend it forwards? Did you rotate it? Could it snap off?

There was a loud knock on the wooden door. 'Monsieur Boursal! Photographers downstairs.'

They both froze. Pierre cursed and sat up crossly.

'Tell them . . . Tell them I'm asleep. Exhausted. Later.'

There was another pause, then footsteps clattered away down the corridor.

Pierre turned back to the matter at hand. Maxine was surprised that her stroking should have such an effect on him, should render him so helpless, that she was lying here under the warm quilt sending this man berserk just by gingerly touching his thing.

'Let's get those damned trousers off,' muttered Pierre as articles of Maxine's clothing went flying across the room from under the quilt.

She risked a furtive peep downwards and froze again. The size! But it was an impossibility, she would be cut in half! 'I'm frightened, I think we should stop,' she said, stopping. With a groan Pierre also stopped.

'You're right, you're too young,' he said reluctantly. Whereupon Maxine was furious and grabbed the thing again.

'I don't want to hurt you,' muttered Pierre, rolling on top of her nevertheless.

Then suddenly it wasn't so painful and the thing was *in* and they were moving together.

'Am I doing it right?' whispered Maxine, worried about the rhythm. It was a bit like doing the samba horizontally, Maxine thought, but should she be moving *with* him or in the opposite direction?

'Just don't think about it; don't worry about a thing,' he murmured in her ear. She lay there feeling waves of warmth lap over her. She felt a strange tingling all over her, then found herself instinctively responding to him.

Suddenly he started to move more frantically, with increased urgency. He arched his back, gave a strangled gasp as if in pain and collapsed on top of Maxine. For a moment she thought he had fainted, but after a few minutes he made a noise like a sleepy, contented puppy and then he dozed off.

All was well. Or was it? She felt a sense of relief that it was all *over*, that she had crossed a hurdle and was a real woman, but she also felt strange – exhausted, but wide awake; tense and uncomfortable. Pierre's arm lay under her back and she didn't dare move for fear of disturbing him. Slowly she inched down the bed until his arm was under her neck and she was hidden by the quilt. She felt lonely. She shut her eyes and wanted to cry.

Was that *all*? All they had speculated about and hoped for after lights out, all that had been hinted at in a hundred magazine romances? This damp patch of bloody sheet under her elbow, the unfamiliar, sweaty smell of bodies, the sour smell, this sticky stuff trickling over her thighs.

All she felt was a longing to be clean, lying in her own bed in her own room with the sun shining in the window through the lace curtains. What she wanted more than anything else in the world was a bath.

She must have done something wrong ... Or else he hadn't done something right.

'In training for some things, out of training for other things,' Pierre said as sleepily as he raised his head and looked at her. 'Oh, Maxine, you have the most wonderful breasts,' and with great concentration he pounced on them.

Soon Maxine felt more cheerful, then she was caught up in warm waves of delight. Her body started to move to his rhythm, she couldn't help it, she felt that she was melting into him, or was he melting into her? She stretched her hands around his body and pulled his hard strong buttocks against her. 'Please don't stop, please don't stop, please *don't stop*,' she gasped urgently. She felt poised like a frozen waterfall, then her body arched again and again and what she felt was an amazing pleasure, every bit as good as one had heard about – in fact, better.

The hammering on the door grew more frantic. Maxine woke with a start, felt the warm naked body next to hers, and jumped again.

'Maxie! Maxie!' She recognized the urgency in Pagan's voice. Stumbling out of bed, she felt her way through the unfamiliar moonlit room to the door, which she cautiously opened, shielding her naked body behind it.

Pagan stood there in her oversized green tweed coat. 'D'you realize it's nearly midnight? You said Pierre would bring you back before supper, but we didn't really worry until bedtime.'

'*Mon Dieu*,' gasped Maxine. 'I mean, sheet, then they know I'm missing!'

'No, when Matron did the lights-out round, Kate just said you were in the bathroom, then we waited until everyone had gone to bed and tossed a franc to see who'd come to look for you. I lost, so Kate crept off with her flashlight to the office and lifted the back door key off the hook and she's waiting to let us in again. Four fast knocks at the kitchen window is the signal. For heaven's sake, *hurry!*'

Trembling, Maxine scrambled into her ski clothes without waking Pierre. The two girls tiptoed along the passage, down the creaking wooden stairs and into the street. Without speaking, hands in their pockets, they ran clumsily through the snow as fast as they could, sometimes stumbling, sometimes skidding on an icy patch.

As they approached the dark bulk of the school chalet, the road was suddenly lit by the oncoming lights of a lone, slow car. Then the car stopped abruptly, and to their horror, the headlights were switched full on to them. As they drew level, a window slid down and a man leaned out. 'Well, well,' he said cheerily, 'been visiting the nightclubs?'

It was Paul, the headmaster's driver. 'Get in the back,' he said sharply. They scrambled in, then Paul turned and put one arm on the back seat as he grinned at the two white-faced girls who knew they faced expulsion.

'Why go back now? Why not come out with me to a *real* nightclub? I know one where you won't be recognized and you'll be safe with me.'

'No, it will only get us into worse trouble,' muttered Maxine, remembering what Nick had said about Paul. But Pagan's first thought was that if she went with Paul, he'd be a fellow conspirator; he wouldn't be able to tell Chardin. They wouldn't be expelled.

She summoned up her courage. 'Maxine had better go in as someone will be waiting for us. I'll come with you, but how will I get back?'

'I've got a key, of course.'

With an anxious backward look, Maxine slipped out of the car and ran through the snow to the back door. The blue Jaguar slid off through the snow.

But Paul didn't drive to a nightclub. He drove right through the town and then out the other side.

'Hey!' Pagan said, sitting upright, as they drew up at a lone chalet. 'Is *this* a nightclub?'

'No, it's my home,' Paul said, 'it's safer than a nightclub. We'll just have one drink, then I'll take you back to school.'

Pagan looked out of the car. She could no longer see the lights of Gstaad, and she had no idea where she was, so she obediently followed Paul into the little chalet and found herself in a surprisingly modern living room. There were groups of low, chrome-framed chairs; abstract pictures hung in huge silver frames; a lifesize marble statue of a male torso stood candle-white against the black walls.

Pagan blinked as astonishment overcame fatigue. Still in her coat, she stood silently in the middle of the room as Paul prepared a silver cocktail shaker. He shook it, poured the contents into a tumbler and handed it to Pagan. It smelled like soap and dry-cleaning fluid, though Paul said it was brandy and vodka with a dash of something special. Better keep friendly with him, Pagan thought – but the only way she was going to be able to drink the stuff was to hold her breath and knock it back. She did so. She spluttered, felt her legs grow weak, then passed out.

Pagan wished her stomach would keep still. She didn't think she'd ever be able to lift her head again. Carefully she opened her eyes. There was a shower of bright lights. She shut them again. She was dizzy; she was going to be sick; she seemed to have no control over her limbs. She felt cold steel on her wrist and heard a click . . . What *did* the man imagine he was doing?

Paul had handcuffed her to the bedpost.

'And now the other hand. Just so you don't do anything imprudent, miss.'

Pagan felt too weak to think. She shut her eyes again, and couldn't decide whether she felt worse with her eyes open or shut. She was freezing cold and *she had no clothes on*. She wished she understood what was happening . . . wished that Paul would leave her alone . . . What *was* the bloody man going to do?

'I'm just going to stroke you, that's all that will happen, then I'll take you back to school. You don't really want to get up now, do you? You don't really want to stop me, do you? You can't, can you? You *like* it, don't you?'

And Pagan *did* like the soothing, soft, catlike strokes on her breast, on her ribs, on her stomach. She tried opening her eyes again and saw that Paul was lying beside her, naked, on black sheets. His sleek head propped on one hand, an amused, detached smile on his face, Paul was stroking her with a black feather. She shut her eyes again. Then he slid softly off the bed and Pagan felt something else, a snaking sensation on her thighs.

She opened her eyes again and got a frontal view of her first erection. Paul's naked body was poised over her, legs apart, and, no, it just wasn't possible! He was gently tickling her thighs with a black leather whip. 'You have no choice, you have to do *exactly* as I say,' he whispered.

She shut her eyes again. It was all too much. How her head ached! There was a sudden flash, and Pagan suddenly came to her senses.

She had just been photographed.

After that, he did it to her and it wasn't painful at all. Revolting, but not painful.

Then he sat on the end of the bed and smoked some sort of herbal cigarette. That was the faint odour she'd smelled as she entered the chalet. Paul ignored Pagan until suddenly he turned towards her, started to giggle helplessly and stubbed the cigarette out on the sheets. This alarmed Pagan so much that she became alert. She had no idea of the time, but she had to get these handcuffs off, find her clothes and get back to school before this bloody man burned the house down.

'Paul, darling,' she said, '*please* undo me so I can go to the bathroom.' He crawled up on the bed and undid her handcuffs. Pagan groped her way into the living room, looking for her clothes. She started to pick them up, then peered into a bronze-ringed mirror over the bureau and saw her swollen face. Her eyes had almost disappeared; she must have been crying at some time.

She noticed that the top drawer of the bureau had been pulled half-open. The contents made her eyes snap wide open.

Quickly she put her hand in.

It was past dawn when Pagan crept up to her room.

'You look terrible. It's past five o'clock.'

'You smell awful, where did you go?'

'What happened?'

'We went to a bar and I drank too much; now *will* you kindly *piss off*?' Pagan growled. She rinsed her mouth with disinfectant, bathed her face and staggered into bed. She didn't go down to breakfast, and when Matron saw her swollen face and red-rimmed, dull eyes, a thermometer was immediately stuck in her mouth. Though Pagan's temperature was normal, she certainly looked as if she were developing something, so she was moved to the school infirmary for two days.

5

Ten days later the resilience of youth had triumphed. Pagan had managed to convince herself that she had wiped that revolting incident out of her mind and could pretend it had never happened.

Amazingly, the episode had not lowered her high spirits and one Sunday afternoon, sparkling with restless energy, she wheedled the other three into hiring the horse-drawn red sleigh for an hour.

Off clopped the horse over the snow-laced cobbles, the four girls huddled luxuriously under the ancient silver fox fur rugs. Jogging along to the jingle of the silver bells on the harness, they waved to passers-by as they drove through the fields outside the town and headed towards Saanen. When they stopped, the girls took turns sitting on the driver's seat, whip and reins in hand, as Pagan photographed them with her box Brownie.

Without thinking, Judy – who couldn't ride – flapped the reins and shrieked 'Giddy *yap*!' flicking the whip in the air. Unfortunately the leather thong caught the ear of the middle-aged mare. Startled, the horse reared. Judy dropped the whip in fright and clutched the driver's seat as the horse broke into a canter, swaying the heavy sleigh from one side of the track to the other. Kate and Maxine crouched in the back as they hurtled over the snow. Pagan and the driver were left behind, standing open-mouthed by the path.

For the first time in ten days Pagan really forgot that loathsome scene. She dropped her camera and dashed after the sleigh as it lurched from one side to the other of the snow-rutted path, the horse leaping ahead with unaccustomed speed.

As the sleigh passed a small group of skiers, one of the men caught at the reins, half-running, half-pulled along by the mare. Gradually, the horse slowed down, and by the time Pagan had puffed up to the sleigh, the skier was soothing the quivering horse, stroking her steaming neck and murmuring in a language that Pagan didn't understand.

'*How dare you!*' Pagan yelled to the frightened, white-faced Judy. 'How dare you hit that mare! How dare you make her rear and gallop on ice, you bloody idiot! Get in the back!' Her head was thrown back, her short, straight nose pointed imperiously, her nostrils flared with rage.

Still intent upon the condition of the horse, she took the reins from the stranger, said thank you almost without noticing him, and walked the horse back to the furious stable driver, who headed for home.

Outside the stable a man was waiting for them, a dark fellow wearing ski clothes and the arrogant air of a privileged servant. With a face devoid of expression except for a hint of hauteur, he approached Pagan and gave a slight bow.

'My master, His Royal Highness the Crown Prince Abdullah, wishes to invite you to meet him at the Imperial Hotel.'

'And I'm the Queen of China,' said Pagan, still furious and refusing to listen to Judy's apologies.

'Abdullah certainly *is* staying at the Imperial, Pagan,' Judy said. 'He's got two permanent suites there, while he's at school. I've never *seen* him, but this guy certainly looks like one of his Arab bodyguards.' Judy flung her pale blue scarf-end around her chin. 'Look, I must go, I'm due at the Chesa, but I'd consider that invitation. How often does royalty invite you to tea?' She ran off, hampered by her heavy boots.

Remembering her previous painful escapade with Paul, Pagan hung back. She didn't want to get involved in anything else outlandish.

'No harm in going along to the Great Hall,' the other two insisted. 'Oh, Pagan, *royalty*,' Kate added, as they followed the dark-faced man towards the Imperial.

In a corner of the Great Hall, wearing all-white ski clothes, sat Prince Abdullah, upright and impatient. Under winged eyebrows he had the watchful look of a hawk, the eyes of a man who is used to being obeyed. Without moving his head, his eyes followed the girls' approach, then he stood and said politely, '*So* good of you to come. Wonderful weather we're having, don't you think?' His English was clipped, with only the faintest trace of an accent.

The Prince waved a hand at the velvet chairs grouped around his table. They all sat down and talked about the weather, the hotel and the ski runs. The Prince's ramrod back, his arrogant, almost menacing calm proclaimed majesty but sat oddly on the shoulders of an eighteen-year-old boy. Pagan thought he would probably look more at home on an Arab horse than on that old green velvet hotel chair. She steered the conversation to horses and the Prince smiled for the first time.

From that moment, the other two girls might not have existed.

'Snap!' screamed Pagan, lying on her stomach on the polar bear rug, in front of the blazing log fire. She pulled the pile of playing cards towards her, as Abdullah, sitting cross-legged opposite her, grinned and shrugged his shoulders.

Prince Abdullah refused to go to the Chesa. He said he didn't like people staring at him and didn't want any *paparazzi* poking cameras in his face, but though he didn't say so, he considered the crowded tearoom a security risk. Pagan had at first refused to visit Abdullah's suite, but eventually, trusting his promise to 'behave himself', she agreed to spend Saturday afternoons lolling on the thick maroon carpet in Abdullah's private sitting room, talking about horses or teaching him nursery card games like 'racing demon' and 'snap'!

In private, Abdullah dropped his invisible cloak of majesty. It disappeared as soon as his bodyguards were dismissed with a curt nod of his head.

'I'm starting to think you cheat,' yawned Abdullah, who always cheated himself. His grin widened into a full-lipped smile showing white, even teeth.

As Abdullah twisted on to his side with an agile, catlike movement that was somehow lazily dangerous, there was a sharp crack from the adjoining room. With one bound, Abdullah was on his feet and as he moved, Pagan – still gathering up the playing cards – saw him pull a gleaming automatic pistol from beneath his purple sweater. He leaped to the bedroom door and kicked it open.

Except for the crack of the burning logs, the room was silent. With another catlike crouch, Abdullah jumped inside, his back to the door.

'No problem,' he called after a moment. 'Sorry, Pagan.'

She stood up and ran into the adjoining room. In contrast to the velvet, soft-carpeted luxury of the private sitting room, Abdullah's bedroom was totally bare – it wasn't even curtained – except for a double bed that stood in the centre of the room with a small low table beside it upon which stood a water carafe, a bottle of pills and another pistol.

Abdullah was standing beside the window wall, looking out. 'I think a tree just fell,' he said. 'I'm sorry I alarmed you, but I have to be careful.'

'But the bodyguards! . . .' gasped Pagan.

Abdullah shrugged. 'The price of a bodyguard is low. I'm in

the same position as the poorest beggar in my kingdom – if I don't look after myself, nobody else will.'

'What an odd room!' Pagan said, looking around it again.

'Arabs have an uneasy, love-hate relationship with comfort and luxury,' Abdullah said. 'Luxury softens a man, and if I'm to survive I can't afford to be soft. I have to keep my mind as tough and hard as my body.' Seemingly unperturbed, he looked at her with the steady gaze of a superbly self-confident male animal. He pushed the pistol back into his trouser band and pulled the purple sweater over it.

'Let's get on with our game,' Pagan said hastily, still round-eyed as she tugged him back into the sitting room. 'What were you afraid of ... what did you think was going to happen?' Pagan asked.

'Maybe a kidnap plot, maybe an assassination.' He shrugged his shoulders and looked slightly embarrassed. 'Would you care for some tea?' He pressed the bell.

'You don't *really* think you might be kidnapped?'

'The first kidnap attempt was before I was a year old. My nurse was stoned to death for her part in the plot. The next attempt was when I was seven years old. I had a bodyguard who pushed me under the bed, but they hauled me out, then stabbed him five times and left him for dead. But he didn't die immediately and managed to raise the alarm before the plotters got me out of the palace.' He gave a lazy grin as he looked at Pagan's incredulous face. 'The next attempt was when I was fourteen. We were returning from a hunting trip. I was in the first Land Rover. We were ambushed in a gully and I was shot twice in the arm and once in the chest before our second Land Rover arrived on the scene, with guards shooting in all directions. I was shot in the leg by one of our men, but I managed to kill one of my attackers.' Suddenly he looked ruthless. 'From then on I trusted no one. It wasn't difficult. My heart seemed to harden overnight. To risk trust is to risk death: it was that simple. And that was the last time I was careless. From then on, I always carried a gun, slept with a gun by my pillow, and drove with my own submachine gun on the seat next to me.'

There was a quiet knock at the door. Nick, wearing his waiter's uniform, opened the door. The respectful look on his face dropped for an instant when he saw Pagan lolling on the bearskin, then he resumed his waiter's mask. Abdullah ordered lemonade and tea, then, still not quite at ease, he padded nervously around the room.

'Stop prowling,' ordered Pagan.

'I have a restless spirit; if you never feel secure, then naturally you feel restless.'

Nick returned with a laden tray and gave Abdullah another look of servile insolence as he stiffly bent and placed the tray on a low table by the velvet couch. Pagan winked at Nick, who ignored her. He can't stand Abdullah, she thought. I wonder why?

Not by one muscle movement did Abdullah show that he had recognized Nick, but he had, and for one swift moment Abdullah remembered the most humiliating moment of his life.

The eight-foot-long green baize board that hung by the staircase had been the hub of school activity; on it was pinned much purple-stencilled information about special classes, outings, clubs and chapel together with the sports lists. Abdullah remembered his boyish exaltation when one morning on his way back to his room after school breakfast, he saw his name listed on the house team for Eton football. There it was in a handwritten scrawl – Abdullah. He was the only boy in the school without a surname. He was the only boy in the school without a friend.

Abdullah didn't understand why every boy – himself included – was of equal rank inside those ancient stone walls. To Abdullah, the centuries-old, traditional top-drawer British school was a hostile, incomprehensible world. Ignorant of the private language and rigid conventions of his schoolfellows, Abdullah did what was not done and said what – according to Eton etiquette – should not be said. But now, he had thought, all would be forgiven. *He was on the house team!* With a whoop of excitement he ran along the stone corridor to get his books for the next lesson.

Each pupil had his own small room with a scarred wooden table, two chairs, a narrow metal convertible bed, a bureau, and a chest in which he kept his sports gear. Abdullah's was pretty much the same as the other rooms with one exception: on his wall hung framed photographs of his father's yacht, his mother dressed for court, his father in ceremonial uniform being decorated by King George VI, a picture of Abdullah, aged thirteen, taking the salute from the Sydonian Palace Guard, and another picture of himself being kissed on the cheek by Rita Hayworth.

As Abdullah rummaged in his bureau for a missing Latin grammar, he heard voices that he recognized outside the door.

'Can you believe it? Look, Horton, the baboon's on the House Side.'

'No! Bugger me!!! Can't think why we even have to have him in Coleridge's. We certainly shouldn't have a dirty little wog representing us on the House Side. Couldn't they have kept him in the Sine?'

'I suppose he's not bad at dribbling, but he's always cornering and sneaking ...'

'Some nigger lover will put him up for Pop next ... Expect he'll get a record number of blackballs ... Black balls, ha, ha, ha! What colour balls do baboons have, royal purple, d'ye think?' There was a burst of hoarse laughter as a bell rang and the malicious voices drifted away from the notice-board.

Abdullah didn't dare face them. All three were members of Debate, so it was inconceivable that he should complain about them – he would only be laughed at. Abdullah's hands started to shake with impotent fury. Why should he care what that trash thought? They were destined merely to be farmers, soldiers or politicians, whereas he was destined to be a king, the leader of his people, beloved of many tribes, cheered by his men and his women.

Suddenly he took a deep breath ... Women! Those arrogant nonentities hadn't been instructed for three weeks by the *hakim* in Cairo ... Standing there, shaking with rage, his battered Latin grammar book in one hand, a sweet revenge occurred to Abdullah.

He decided that he would have their women.

Pagan left Abdullah's suite earlier than usual. Instead of leaving the Imperial, she took the elevator to the top floor and ran up the remaining stairs to Nick's room, to which, by now, the girls had all made giggling visits. She was in luck, because Nick had just come off duty. He answered her knock in his shirt-sleeves.

'Slumming?' he inquired coldly, as Pagan pecked him on the cheek.

'No, just wondering why you can't stand Abdullah. You can't

93

expect to have *all* the attention of all *four* of us, you know, especially when we know that you're besotted with Judy.' The springs sagged as she sat on his iron bedstead. Nick looked unhappy.

'Your private life is none of my business.'

'But what is it, Nick? Has Abdi already got a girl?'

'I've no idea. Anyway, it's none of my business, and I wouldn't tell you if I knew ... But ... we were at school together, and I promise you that bastard Abdullah is not what he seems. Of course *women* think he's irresistible. He's obviously attractive.'

'It's not only that,' said Pagan with a giggle, 'it's the stage props that are such fun. The bodyguards and the flowing robes and the fierce black moustaches and the ... er ... precautions.' She suddenly wondered if Abdullah was officially allowed to carry firearms in Switzerland. Presumably he travelled on a diplomatic passport and could do anything he pleased. She sighed. 'I can't *think* why I haven't fallen for him, but I haven't. He's fascinating, but I'm just not besotted, the way you are with Judy.'

'Well, you're bloody lucky, because Abdullah doesn't treat women like a gentleman, he *uses* them. I mean *he doesn't care about women*. Not the maids or chaps' sisters or even their mothers.'

'Nick! Surely you don't mean –?'

'What I mean is that he's oddly ... objective about women.' Nick didn't know how to say that Abdullah was calculating and deliberate in his attitude towards Western women. He used them. He learned from them. His lovemaking was to prove his power over them and their menfolk.

'Oh, Nick, he's wary about *everyone*, wary of being exploited or shot or whatever other things princes have to be wary of,' Pagan said, thinking Nick merely had a case of straightforward jealousy.

'And that combination of menace and charm is just what women find irresistible,' Nick said bitterly, and with a tinge of envy.

'Am I to understand that you think Abdi might deliberately play cat-and-mouse with me? Make me miserable?'

'Pagan, stop talking about silly sex games and listen to me. I'm very fond of all four of you, and you know how I feel about Judy. But I'm your *friend*. I wouldn't use any of you, and that's what Abdullah *does*. He has no respect, no understanding of chivalry and he's ... no gentleman.'

Pagan threw her head back and laughed. 'Darling Nick,' she said, 'you are an old auntie! In the future, I'll wear barbed wire instead of knicker elastic.'

What Pagan wanted to know – and what the whole school wanted to know – was whether Abdullah would invite her to the St Valentine's Day Ball. Abdullah was rarely seen in public, especially after he had hired the horse sleigh one Sunday afternoon and a street photographer took a picture of Pagan and the Prince together. The negative was swiftly sold to *Paris-Match*, and within twenty-four hours it had appeared in newspapers around the world.

Every two days an armful of long-stemmed red roses, with no card attached, arrived for Pagan. 'You said red roses were vulgar,' Kate said gleefully, and had a pillow thrown at her. After the third sheaf, Pagan was summoned to the headmaster's study and told that she could not accept any more flowers. Monsieur Chardin sounded unusually agitated. Half the gossip writers of Europe had been plaguing him. No doubt the publicity was good for the school, but he was obliged to display disapproval.

A few evenings later Pagan was called down to the headmaster's study again. She returned looking bemused. 'What happened?' asked Kate, lying on her bed, one foot in the air, having her toenails polished by Maxine.

'Telephone.'

'*Who?*' A telephone call was always an event in their lives.

'My cousin Caspar. He's our Ambassador in the Emirates. He said that he's heard I was seeing a great deal of Prince Abdullah and that I should be *most prudent*.' She giggled nervously. 'Caspar also said that in Sydon, women are regarded as possessions and once defiled they're discarded. In fact, they're sometimes stoned to death. Can you imagine?'

Maxine said, 'Bloody well keep still, Kate.'

Pagan flung herself on the other bed. 'So I asked what had defiled Arab women got to do with me?' She was wearing a tattered Victorian nightgown that was over a hundred years old and a pair of scarlet Turkish slippers with the toes turned up.

The other two sat up and nail polish dripped on Kate's ankles as Pagan continued. 'Old Caspar said that Abdi was pushed into power long before he was old enough, because his father is apparently very religious and a bit mad and lives in total seclusion. But Caspar said that although Abdi is very, very tough, he isn't nearly as sophisticated as he thinks he is, and not nearly well enough equipped to handle the twentieth century, and if he feels he's being laughed at or humiliated he can turn nasty.' She giggled. 'He went on and on about Abdullah really being two people – a Western-educated ruler who will negotiate diplomatically with Western politicians and a ruthless, immensely powerful Arab leader whose word is the law and whose instincts are violent, dangerous and medieval.'

She kicked off the Turkish slippers and jumped on the end of Kate's bed. Sitting cross-legged, she added, in an offhand manner, very fast, 'Caspar also told me that Abdullah is engaged to be married.'

'*What!*' Maxine, in her white nightgown, stopped climbing into bed. '*Who?*'

'To some Arab Princess who's only ten years old! Can you *believe*? They're going to be married when she's fifteen.' Pagan tried to sound unconcerned. Her voice broke and she said unsteadily, 'I hooted with laughter, so Caspar got cross and said he was going to phone Mama.'

Suddenly the lights went out, switched off as usual from the headmaster's apartment, and the moonlight, streaming through the lace curtains, cast a wreath of intertwined pale grey roses on Maxine's bed as she tossed back the sheets and rushed over to hug Pagan. 'Poor darling, poor darling! He is a bloody two-timer, a rat, a sheet.'

'If it's true, it sounds medieval,' exclaimed Kate.

'That's exactly Caspar's point. Abdi isn't like a rich Western teenager trying to behave like a man of the world. He's sort of . . . a ruthless very powerful desert hood.' She paused. 'I rather think that's what I find so fascinating.'

'But he's certainly not to be trusted!' Maxine said. 'But then of course *no* man should be trusted.'

'Cut out that sophisticated act,' Kate said. 'Who *can* you trust?'

'We can trust each other,' Maxine said firmly. So rather solemnly, they all sat on Kate's bed in the moonlight and promised lasting friendship.

'Through thick and thin,' Pagan said wildly, shaking her hands over her head like a bruised but victorious boxer.

'Thick and thin,' giggled Kate, '*especially* thin.' She prodded Maxine's still well-covered ribs.

'Sick and sin,' said Maxine, who, like all the French, pronounced 'th' as 's'.

'Well, yes, that too,' Kate said thoughtfully.

The next morning Pagan was called out of the classroom, where chunks of Lamartine were being analysed by Mademoiselle as, in their heads, the girls planned what to wear for the St Valentine's Day Ball and how to get more money from home, supposedly for needlework but really for cigarettes. The lessons were a farce, Kate thought crossly as she continued (under cover of her sheet of pink blotting paper) to hack out her initials with her nail scissors on the graffiti-covered wooden table. A nimbus of lethargy hung over the school-room, which smelled of chalk and underarm odour; the only noise was the squeak of chalk on a blackboard and the thump of the old upright piano upstairs; maddeningly, the unseen player kept faltering, making the same mistake, then starting again.

Pagan came back giggling from her telephone call and sat down demurely.

'What was that?' The harassed mademoiselle whipped around from the blackboard just too late to see Pagan, with the top of her wooden ruler, flip a note to Kate. Kate didn't send a note in reply because Pagan's little paper pellets never needed a reply. She only sent them to relieve her boredom. The note said, 'Getting ball-gown, whoopee!'

When class was finished, Pagan immediately rushed over with her news. 'Mama was quite agitated. She just tried to make me promise not to see Abdullah alone. I asked if she could please send me some decent clothes – which stopped her in her tracks, rather – but I explained that he might invite me to the St Valentine's Ball and she knows perfectly well I've nothing to wear. However, I thought I'd better make sure of a dress, so after *she'd* been cut off, I phoned Grandfather and asked him if he couldn't please see that I had a proper ballgown. In fact,' she added, a litttle ashamed, 'I hinted that if I wasn't sent a dress Abdi might cough up for one. Grandfather said he'd be happy to buy me a dress, but made me promise not to accept any presents from Abdi.'

A few days later a huge brown box was delivered by special messenger to Pagan. The whole school crowded behind her as she ran into the dining room, flung the box on one of the long empty tables, tore off the wrapping, plunged her arms into crisp layers of white tissue and drew out a beautiful cloud of pale grey net that sparkled with diamond droplets. It was a Norman Hartnell ball-gown with a heart-shaped neckline demurely high, but not impossibly so.

The whole school sighed longingly.

After her next meeting with Abdullah, Pagan returned somewhat more subdued. 'I asked whether he had a ten-year-old fiancée. He looked rather displeased and pointed his chin at me and said he did, but that it was entirely a matter of diplomacy and nothing to do with *us*. He was a bit odd for about ten minutes, then he went into his bedroom to make a telephone call and – can you imagine – about twenty minutes later there was a knock on the sitting room door and one of those grim bodyguards came in with a little man from the Cartier boutique. He handed Abdi a box and backed out of the door very fast. Then Abdi turned to me and gave me this blissful crimson velvet box lined with white satin, and in it, sparkling frantically at me, was an utterly divine diamond necklace. If I hadn't promised Grandfather, I'd have accepted it on the spot. So I told him I couldn't accept anything from him. I don't think he's used to people turning down diamond necklaces or saying no in general.'

On the following four occasions when Pagan turned up at teatime in Prince Abdullah's suite, he tried to give her gifts of jewellery. Always a crimson velvet case was produced, but Pagan would never so much as try on the emerald earrings, the tiara of golden birch leaves, the bracelet of aquamarine or the enormous uncut sapphire ring. But the only thing Pagan accepted, with her mother's permission, was Abdullah's offer of his grandfather's old riding cloak, which he made her reluctantly promise to wear to the ball, as a penance for not accepting his valuable gifts. Pagan wasn't sure that she wanted to wear a smelly old Arab horse blanket to the ball, but, she thought, she could take it off in the school bus before entering the Imperial.

*

The following night there was another small dance, this time at the town hall. The girls from l'Hirondelle, wearing clumsy *après-ski* boots and tweed overcoats over long dresses, carried drawstring cotton bags for their dancing shoes as they climbed on to the little green school bus. As usual, Mademoiselle counted each head as they got on, as she would again when they re-entered the bus to return after the dance.

Pagan had coaxed Maxine into lending her the pale-blue taffeta Christian Dior dress, although she couldn't shed the bolero because she couldn't pull the zipper completely up. Maxine had tacked up the hem a couple of inches to make it ankle-length for Pagan. As she and her partner whirled around the dance floor to the music of a gypsy band, Pagan was tapped on the shoulder by one of Abdullah's bodyguards, ill at ease in a Western dinner jacket that was at least two sizes too large for him. 'My master, the Crown Prince Abdullah, wishes to dance with you,' he said.

'Well, he'll have to wait,' said the Danish student who was dancing with Pagan, and moving his arm more firmly around her back, he started to dance again. The bodyguard took a swift step forwards and suddenly the Danish student was sprawled on the floor.

Pagan turned around indignantly and saw Abdullah standing in the doorway. Slowly, with a small smile, she moved over to him, propelled by his bodyguard's iron hand in the small of her back. Still smiling she said, 'May it please your Royal Highness to tell your thugs *never* to touch me again. And remember that I'm *not* one of your subjects. You don't own *me*, and I shall dance with whom I please.'

Suddenly she dropped her hauteur and said in a quiet voice, 'Oh, Abdi, why bother to humiliate Hans and draw attention to me?'

There was a pause, then Abdullah said stiffly, 'Most regrettable. My servant was over-zealous.'

'Oh stop talking like an Indian Raj phrasebook,' said Pagan crossly. 'Of *course* I want to be with you, but you really can't push people around as it suits you and expect them to *like* you. I hate it when you're suddenly imperious. This is just an ordinary dance, and if you didn't want to be treated in an ordinary manner, you shouldn't have come.' Wickedly she added, 'I hope you aren't going to be as bossy with your poor little ten-year-old fiancée.'

Abdullah's mouth tightened and his eyes blazed with anger. For a moment Pagan thought he might hit her, but instead he put his arm around her and they danced off in silence. Unseen by Abdullah, Pagan blew a kiss over his shoulder to Hans, who scowled back at her.

Suddenly, Pagan found that she was trembling as she leaned against Abdullah's muscular body – closer to him, suddenly more physically aware of him in that crowd of dancers than she had ever been when alone in his suite. Tonight, Pagan felt different, reckless, as she felt his warm breath on the side of her neck, then the tip of his tongue against it, erotic and inviting.

For the rest of the evening Pagan moved around the dance floor in an erotic trance. As the midnight curfew approached, Abdullah looked straight into her eyes and murmured persuasively, 'Come back with me and let me show you what love is. I'll make you feel as you've never felt before.'

'Mmmmm,' sighed Pagan, as his hand lightly touched the nape of her neck. 'How can you be so sure?'

'Because when I was sixteen I spent three weeks in Cairo with the *hakim* Khair al Saad, who taught me how to make love, to think only of your pleasure.'

'You had lessons in *love* for *three weeks*? You studied it, like geography?' Pagan was astounded, impressed, intrigued. She longed to ask what he had learned and how it was taught. Were there real live women or a blackboard and chalk, and what was the homework and what difference had it made? Instead, she simply blurted, 'How?'

He nibbled at her ear-lobe and purred, 'Come back to the Imperial and let me *show* you.'

Fascinated, Pagan couldn't stop staring into those self-assured black eyes. She found herself following Abdullah towards the main door. But then she remembered her cousin, her mother, the fiancée and the *paparazzi*, and stopping, she said with real regret, 'I can't, I simply *can't*, Abdi. Look, Mademoiselle is waving us all to the cloakroom.'

Aching with desire, Abdullah pulled her to him as Pagan tried to break away.

'*What do you expect a man to do?*' he growled. 'You arouse me and then you vanish into the night. In my country we have a name for such a woman.'

'Oh, in my country too.' Then Pagan couldn't resist adding, 'but after all, you *are* engaged to be married.'

Abdullah's black eyes blazed again, as an impatient Mademoiselle waved a beckoning finger at Pagan. Prince or no Prince, she wanted to get to her bed. Once more Abdullah pulled Pagan tight against his body and she felt his throbbing arousal. Then Abdullah turned on his heel and stalked angrily out of the room.

On the evening before the St Valentine's dance Kate burst into the bedroom. 'Pagan, you slut, you didn't clean the bath after you, there's a grubby ring around it.'

'But surely a bath is for cleaning *oneself*,' said Pagan, puzzled. 'One does not clean *it*.'

'One hasn't up to date, but one damn well will in the future,' said Kate. 'You really are the slut of the school.'

'*O rage, o désespoir.*' Pagan yelled hcr new curse words and threw a tattered exercise book at Kate. 'I'm sick to the withers with both of you. Kate's always criticizing and Maxine doesn't keep her promises.'

'I do keep my promises, you *beech*.'

'You *promised* to lend me ten francs.'

'*Merde*, I mean sheet, why don't you ask your rich little Prince for ten francs? He can afford it better than I.'

'Only because you spend all your money on diet food to get skinny for a stupid ski bum who likes skiing more than he likes you.' Pagan pounced on Maxine and pummelled her.

'Ow, *merde*, sheet, ferk, dammit, *bloody* beech.'

'Stop that sexy scuffling,' Kate cried. 'You know Matron already suspects that the whole school is a seething mass of lesbians. Ppppplease don't quarrel, I can't bear it. Pagan didn't mean what she said about Pierre. Of course he really loves you.'

'Of course he does. I know that, because of *it*,' Maxine said with dignity. She had wound up her hair in twists of toilet paper to curl it for the St Valentine's Ball on the following night. 'Especially because of the afterwards, that golden glow like fireworks dying in the sky.'

There was a pause, then Kate said timidly, 'Afterwards is the awful part for me. I feel so jittery and weepy and sort of apart from François.'

'*Mon Dieu*, I feel much *closer* to Pierre.' Maxine frowned thoughtfully at her hairbrush and speculated. 'Maybe you haven't done it *enough*. I didn't like it the first time with Pierre, but I didn't want to upset him so I said nothing. I wanted him to *stay* with me, that's all I felt at first.'

'That's the only thing I feel with François,' Kate worried. 'I've been doing it longer than you have, Maxine, but the last thing I feel is deep peace. When I really feel sexy and utterly marvellous and glowing is *before* we start. The afterwards is just a letdown. I mean you cling to someone for hours and hours on the dance floor, you can feel his body against yours, you can smell it, and you rock to the music, wrapped around each other, and every time he moves you almost swoon, and you finally go the whole way because you know that it will be *even better*. Then he puts the thing in you and suddenly everything goes flat. He's in seventh heaven and going wild, but I'm suddenly looking down on the scene from the ceiling and that marvellous, melting-knees feeling is gone. I want to hit him and cry.'

Perplexed, Maxine suggested, 'Maybe you should relax more, Kate. Maybe you worry too much about what you *should* be doing, instead of what you *feel* like doing. I always feel *wonderful* afterwards.'

'It must be because you're French,' Kate said, gloomily.

'Don't be silly,' said Pagan. 'Maybe François hasn't had enough practice, or maybe he's *never* been told what to do. When Abdullah was sixteen, he was sent to a special doctor to *learn* about love – for three weeks! Imagine! I didn't like to ask him if he was given tests or exams.'

There was a sudden, polite, interested silence. Pagan immediately said, 'You're *wrong* – we never have, and I'm not going to say another word.'

'How do we know that story isn't just an upmarket brand of old Arabic bullshit if you won't talk about the consumer tests?' demanded Kate. '*We're* coming out with our secret sexual experiences in the interests of further education, and if you won't join in, then you can't listen. This is *serious* for me. Maybe I'm a freak, I'm worried.'

There was another long pause, then Pagan said, 'Well, if you're a freak, then I am too, because I felt the same way as you did . . . But it wasn't with Abdi, it was with Paul, and *if you dare tell anyone, I'll kill you.*'

'So you *did*.'

'Yes,' said Pagan gloomily, 'and it was *beastly*. I think sex is over-rated.'

'I suspect it's addictive,' offered Maxine, 'like oysters.'

There was a bang on the door. 'I don't like *them* either. *Entrez!*'

The ancient porter carried in a huge box addressed to Pagan. The other two girls peered over her shoulder as she opened it. This time there was no tissue paper. The box was full of soft, dark Persian lamb. There was an awed silence as Pagan lifted it out and draped it around her shoulders and pulled the hood over her tangled mahogany hair. The wonderful cloak reached to the floor.

'Oh, Christ, I mean *mon Dieu*,' said Pagan, 'this isn't what Mama expected. I'll have to check with her or she'll give me hell.'

After the girls had each tried on the cloak, Pagan went to the telephone to call her mother. She came back half an hour later looking vexed.

'She says that as she agreed I could have it, I can keep it, but as the cloak is valuable, I can't wear it. I can wear it to the St Valentine's Ball because to do otherwise would be discourteous, but after that I'm not to be seen in it.'

'Well at least it will be warmer to wear at night than that rotten old bed quilt.'

So for the rest of her time at school, after lights-out, Pagan sat cross-legged on the end of Kate's bed, wrapped from head to toe in priceless Persian lamb.

~ 6 ~

MAXINE had dressed her frizzed hair up in a topknot for the dance; it had taken nearly two hours to skewer it into place so that it stayed up. Almost painfully excited, she immediately spotted Pierre.

Kate couldn't see François. In fact it had been over a week since she'd seen François. Judy had slipped her a note in which he explained that he had to cancel their rendezvous because his father insisted that he have extra ski coaching. Kate wished that his father wasn't so ambitious for François, but it was understood that skiing took priority over anything else. His father wanted him to try for the Swiss team. Kate shut her eyes to François' faults and wouldn't hear a word against him. She had gone All The Way because she was in love with him. Or was it the reverse? She wished she knew.

As Pierre moved purposefully towards Maxine, Kate suddenly saw François. He was seated between two plump, dark girls with identical heavy-lidded, somnolent eyes. Kate waved at him but François didn't seem to notice. Someone asked her to dance so she fox-trotted around the floor and waved as she passed his table, but again François didn't seem to see her.

At the end of the dance Judy slipped over to Kate's table. She was wearing a traditional Swiss costume with white blouse, tightly laced black corselet and voluminous scarlet skirt. 'I'll be glad to stop wearing this cuckoo-clock outfit – I can't stay long because I'm helping behind the bar. What's up, Kate?'

When Kate explained, Judy said, 'You've got two legs and a tongue in your head. Don't just sit there, go over to him and say hello.'

So Kate, a striking sight in her cream taffeta, the neckline of which was cut lower for every dance, went over to where François was sitting. He looked up and gave her a little frown.

'Ah, good evening, Kate. May I present Anna and Helena Stiarkoz?' Kate smiled at the two girls, who both inclined their heads towards her about one-eighth of an inch. One of them carefully fitted a cigarette into a long, gold holder and François snapped his lighter under it almost as a reflex movement.

Kate said, 'I'm sitting in that far corner, François.'

'So I noticed. I look forward to dancing with you later, perhaps.'

Bewildered, Kate recognized his note of dismissal and clumsily bumped her way back through the tables to her seat.

Later? ... Perhaps ... *This was the St Valentine's Day Ball!*

'What's wrong?' Maxine asked.

Kate couldn't speak. She was afraid she'd cry. An unbecoming dull flush crept up from her neck and over her face.

'Come to the cloakroom,' Maxine said quickly, tugging at her hand.

Once there, Kate burst into tears. 'I think perhaps you exaggerate,' Maxine said soothingly. 'Perhaps they are old friends of his. I'll go over and say hello. You wait here.'

So Maxine went over and greeted François. Again, he introduced the two girls and made it clear that he didn't wish to speak to Maxine.

Poor Kate, thought Maxine as she hurried back. Across the dimly lit room, Maxine saw Judy and jerked her head towards the cloakroom. Judy joined them a few minutes later. Maxine was saying, 'Kate, *chérie*, you must stop these tears. There must be some reason for his behaviour.' But even as she spoke, Maxine knew that there were indeed *two* reasons, one sitting on either side of François.

'Look, he's a rat and you're well rid of him,' said Judy, too inexperienced to know that a friend should never denigrate a jilted woman's lover. 'There are two things you can do,' Judy continued, taking Kate by the shoulders and shaking her. 'Either have a scene with him out there – which you will lose – or refuse to let him see that he's humiliated you. Men don't like weeping, snivelling, clinging women. You've simply *got* to summon up your pride. Get back in there smiling.'

'You mustn't let him know that he has hurt you,' Maxine agreed. 'You must deal with it properly and at the correct time when you face him with it so he can't avoid it.'

'Look, François has been having lunch at the Chesa all last week with those two Greek lumps,' said Judy. 'They're heiresses to a shipping fortune, and don't think that François doesn't know it. So you can either snivel on or be brave and not show that he's dumped you.'

Unfortunately, this conversation was overheard by another Hirondelle pupil who was in one of the toilet booths. She gleefully sped out to spread the whispered news. Miss Gstaad had received her come-uppance at last. When Kate emerged, freshly made-up, she instantly recognized that her humiliation was common knowledge. It brought out the Irish in Kate and she beckoned to the waiter. 'Nick, get me a double something,' she said, 'there's a darling.'

Nick, who also knew about the Greek twins, produced a forbidden double brandy. Kate choked and spluttered over her drink, then asked for another, but Nick wouldn't let her have one. However, he kept bringing her ridiculously colourful, non-alcoholic drinks full of sliced-up fruit, for which he paid, and he kept up a cheerful stream of chat that needed no reply. It comforted Nick to comfort Kate. He knew how she felt because that was how he felt about Judy whenever he had time to think. Why didn't Judy feel the force of his love? Why didn't it *force* her to love him? Why did she constantly refuse to treat him as anything but a friend? For both Nick and Kate, part of the pain of their love lay in not realizing that it was not the only love of their lives, but only the first love of their lives.

'Look, there's the bunch from Le Mornay,' Nick whispered to Kate, 'all waiting to fall in love with you.'

A group of dinner-jacketed adolescents had just come through the glass entrance doors. They were remarkably cosmopolitan, two Persians with arched dark eyebrows that met above their noses, a sallow Indian Rajah and a thin blond Scandinavian boy, who carried himself as if he were used to everyone else walking behind him. The group also included two current gems of Le Mornay – the immensely rich Hunter Baggs and Prince Saddrudin, the younger son of the Aga Khan.

As they sauntered over to their table, a sudden unmistakable hush fell – it was that moment of anticipation that always precedes the entrance of royalty. All heads turned towards the door where Prince Abdullah, the guest of honour, stood as stiffly as if he were reviewing a parade. Demure on his arm, Pagan floated down the steps in a cloud of sparkling, mist-grey tulle.

Kate now openly flirted with Nick, with whom she felt safe. At midnight pink-and-white balloons fell in a cloud from the ceiling and all the women guests were presented with golden heart-shaped powder compacts and a single long-stemmed pink rose. Silver streamers were hurled around the ballroom, and all formality was abandoned.

Kate could no longer bear the gaiety and headed for the cloakroom, but she was waylaid by Nick, who had been drinking although he was on duty. 'Look, we're both unhappy,' he whispered, 'Judy won't have anything to do with me except as a friend, and she won't even *talk* to me tonight. I'm so lonely and miserable. Kate, I need you,' he said simply. 'Come to my room, darling Kate.'

To her surprise, Kate considered it. She longed for the reassuring warmth of a man's arms after the pain of rejection. 'Well, I don't know,' she said, 'I mean, how do we fix it?'

'Be one of the first to be counted into the front of the school bus and then nip out the back door while Mademoiselle is still busy counting at the front. Get Pagan to let you in later.' Kate looked so forlorn and miserable that Nick risked a quick hug.

'All right, I'll try, but I can't promise. It depends on Pagan.'

She went back to discuss possibilities with Maxine, who was slightly tipsy after two glasses of champagne. 'Pierre wants me to stay, too,' she said, obviously longing to do so.

'Is he going to take you to the team chalet?'

'No, he's booked a room upstairs, just in case.'

Kate was impressed. 'Goodness, on the off chance. How expensive!'

'Well, why shouldn't we?' The two girls looked across at Pagan pretending to be a princess as she danced around the floor. 'You don't think Pagan will want to stay out?'

'I don't think she'd dare.' They signalled across the room to Pagan and again rushed to the cloakroom.

'*Stay?*' Pagan exclaimed. 'How can I possibly stay? Everyone would *know*. I'll let you in at five. But for heaven's sake, don't be late.'

At one o'clock Kate and Maxine climbed into the bus. They were just ahead of Pagan, who created a diversion by fussing loudly as she lifted her Hartnell skirts over the grimy steps and nearly managed to knock Mademoiselle into the gutter as Kate and Maxine slipped out the other door.

Kate fled back into the Imperial and up the backstairs, slowing down as she reached the sixth floor where Nick was waiting. They hurried down the passage to the servants' stairs. Once in the security of his room, he hugged her, then unbuttoned her bulky tweed coat. Kate perched gingerly on the edge of the bed, which creaked. Nick gently pulled her head against his chest and stroked her hair for a long time until he felt her relax against his body. Then he started to kiss her hair, then her cheeks, although he didn't touch her mouth. That was still his private measure of treachery. But later Kate reached up and pulled his lips down to hers and then, with a gasp, all thought was forgotten as he kissed her with all the pent-up ardour of his eighteen years and the accumulated anxiety and pain of the last eight months. That kiss seemed to last for half an hour. He couldn't bear to leave her mouth, he felt himself drowning in her fragrance and the soft feel of her body, warm through the increasingly creased cream taffeta.

Then the taffeta was thrown on the floor and he was softly kissing her breasts. 'Under the blankets,' he murmured, but oddly that was Kate's measure of treachery, so they lay in a tangle of half-shed clothes, limbs entwining, writhing, gradually discarding garments and inhibitions, until at last Nick lay, triumphantly naked, on top of Kate's yearning body.

But something wasn't quite right, thought Kate, as she slid one arm down Nick's body to caress him with her hand. It was as if he had done it already. As she touched him, Nick flinched, then kissed her with renewed ardour, moving himself away from her hand.

Ten minutes later Kate again felt for him, eager to caress him as François had shown her, anxious that she should not fail some unexplained test. She felt soft little pouches and limp flesh against the palm of her willing hand, which Nick again removed. They both felt embarrassed. They neither of them knew what to do next. In a frenzy of misery, they threw their arms around each other and cuddled tenderly, as friends, warm and comforted by each other's arms.

But they both felt sad.

Maxine crunched down the snow-covered, blue-shadowed street towards Kate, who was shivering under the street lamp. Without a word they held mittened hands, ran down the road to the back door and gently tapped on it.

The door was flung open by a wrathful Matron, fully dressed in her navy uniform. 'A fine pair you are,' she shouted, 'you should be ashamed of yourselves. You're to go to the headmaster's office immediately.'

Wearing a maroon silk dressing gown, Monsieur Chardin was pacing up and down in a rage. Pagan, wrapped in her shabby, camel's hair Jaeger dressing gown – cut on the lines of a monk's habit but yanked around her waist by a purple satin sash – was sitting pale and silent, nervously picking at the arms of her chair. She looked unhappy. She had been awakened at three o'clock that morning by Matron, whose white hair hung in a long plait over her dressing gown. Pagan's mother had been on the telephone – her grandfather had suffered a massive heart attack that afternoon, had collapsed in the stables and died shortly after midnight. Pagan was to return to England immediately.

As Matron passed through Kate's room to reach Pagan's inner room she had noticed that neither Kate nor Maxine was sleeping in her bed. Dazed by the news of her grandfather's death, Pagan nevertheless admitted nothing and – as if to indicate this to them – she looked up as the two girls were hustled into the study and said, 'Where *have* you been? To Gringo's?'

Now suddenly Kate and Maxine faced reality. Shivering in their overcoats in the unheated study, they trembled in front of Chardin, terrified of facing their parents. The soft, pink petals of Kate's wilting rose floated to the floor, leaving only the long, thorny stem in her hand.

Then Chardin exploded. He hurled every insult at them from ingratitude to whoredom, until he finished by pointing a chubby finger at Kate and shrieking, 'And *you*, you *putain*, you chase every pair of pants in town!'

At which the Irish in Kate rose again and she replied, 'So do you, Monsieur.'

There was a nasty silence, then Chardin said with venom, 'You will both be expelled from this school tomorrow.'

'No they won't,' said Pagan in a tired, oddly disinterested voice.

Chardin turned to her, 'And who are you, miss, to tell me what to do?'

'I am a friend of your friend, Paul. He took me to his house and showed me lots of photographs. I didn't think he'd miss them so I stole a few and left them with a friend in town. But here's one.'

She felt in her dressing gown pocket and produced a photograph of Paul in bed with the two little South African girls who had left so suddenly after Christmas. Pagan showed the photograph first to Matron, then to Chardin, then she put it back in her pocket and produced her trump card – a photograph of Monsieur Chardin himself, plump and naked as a baby, poised above the naked body of Paul.

'Happy snaps,' said Pagan with disinterested weariness. Yesterday this scene would have been dramatic and terrifying. Today, it was trivial compared to her grandfather's death. 'I can't help thinking that your scheme only works if you play one father at a time. If any father had seen photographs of more than one girl, it would have been apparent that you are in fact a cheap blackmailer, Monsieur Chardin, and that you deliberately set those girls up to be photographed with Paul. Anyway, he told me all about it.' Nobody spoke or moved. 'I think he said the going rate for fathers is six thousand francs every three months. I don't really know what to do about it, but if you take any action against Maxine and Kate, I'm going straight to the police with my story and the other photographs. So it's your decision, Monsieur Chardin.'

Chardin stood silent for a moment. Then smiled. In a forced voice, he said, 'Miss, you are no doubt overwrought because of your grandfather's sad death, therefore I shall take no notice of your ridiculous accusations. And because I do not want to bring disgrace upon my school, I will not punish these two foolish girls.'

He cleared his throat and paused to regain his authority. 'But I trust that they realize the seriousness of their folly. It is just lucky that none of your set is pregnant. Now get to bed, all of you.'

The exhausted, frightened girls stumbled off to bed, weak with relief. There was no need for further anxiety, they thought, as they wearily undressed.

But they were wrong, and so was the headmaster.

Because one of the set *was* pregnant.

~ PART TWO ~

∼ 7 ∼

CONSCIOUS of her shabby overcoat, Judy suddenly felt like a hick. She longed for the fragile, beautiful clothes, so artfully displayed in the windows of Paris, that Maxine pointed out, chattering nonstop until they reached the corner where Hermès stood. Timidly, they pushed through the glass door, whereupon Maxine adopted a haughty, nose-in-the-air attitude, examining the most expensive silken scarves and handbags in the world as if none of them was quite good enough for the two teenage girls. Intoxicated by the smell of rich leather, Judy bought a Hermès diary, a beautiful calfskin appointment book with its own gold pencil stuck in the side.

It made her feel a bit more French and a bit more grown-up. After all, she was now seventeen years old and she had been in Paris for two whole days. She was completely fascinated by the city, by the superb chestnut-lined boulevards, the glittering boutiques, the elegant, scented women, the wonderful mouth-watering restaurants and the cheerfully noisy apartment of Maxine's family, where Judy was staying for a week or two until she found a job and a place to live. She wasn't going to think about that yet; today she was going to pretend that she was able to lead the carefree, protected existence that Maxine, Pagan and Kate were able to lead. *One* day, Judy promised herself, she would live like that *always*, not just for a few days.

'Now for the Latin Quarter,' Maxine said. They hurried down the streets, still snow-covered in February, and clattered under the wrought-iron art nouveau lilies of the valley that decorated the entrance arch of the métro at Palais Royal. They plunged down the steps and past the fat old flower seller huddled on a stool, a grey shawl around her head. A blast of welcome heat carried upwards the fragrance of Gauloise cigarettes, yellowing news-papers, bad drains and garlic.

'We're late. I told Guy we'd meet him at twelve,' Maxine worried, as they emerged into daylight at the end of their journey.

'Not that he's likely to be on time, especially not for *me*. Ever since we were children he's been conscious of the fact that he's three years older than me. We only saw a lot of each other because our mothers were close friends at school, so he had to put up with me.'

She hurried along the Boulevard St Germain, tugging Judy with one scarlet glove; the American girl dawdled to peer down the winding streets that branched off the main boulevard.

'What sort of clothes does Guy make?' Judy asked.

'Mostly suits and blouses, with a few light coats.'

'Does he sew them himself?'

'No, no, he has a cutter and a seamstress. They work in one room and he sleeps in the room next to it. He'll soon have to look for an *atelier*, but they're unbelievably scarce if you have no key money – and Guy hasn't.'

'Then how does he pay the seamstress and the cutter?' asked Judy.

'His Papa refused to help him because he said that fashion was an occupation for *pédérastes*, so Guy got money from a few private clients. At the start he went to my mother and offered to dress her in four outfits a year for a modest annual advance payment. She accepted and sent him to her friends and *they* all signed up, even my Aunt Hortense.'

Judy was still bewildered by the thought of Maxine's Aunt Hortense, who was unlike any aunt she'd ever met – or any other adult, come to that. The previous evening Aunt Hortense had taken them to dine at Madame de George, an elegant meal that had transported Judy from Rossville forever, as she ate quails' eggs, artichokes, guinea fowl and a dessert that tasted like frozen brandy. After the sumptuous meal, the lights were lowered and the floor show began, with a *frou-frou* of pink ostrich plumes covering – just – the pudenda of a line of unusually beautiful showgirls, all tall, elegant, slim-hipped and high-breasted. Suddenly, Judy noticed their wide shoulders, biceps and muscular forearms. Her mouth fell open. She couldn't believe her eyes. She pinched Maxine and said, 'Are those ... er ... girls ... er ... *men*?'

'Yes,' Maxine giggled.

'I'm amazed that your aunt would bring us to such a place.'

'She wanted you to see something *oo la la*!' Maxine laughed.

'And this is the least naughty of the naughty Paris nightspots. Aunt Hortense likes to *épater les bourgeois* – she can't stand pompous people and she likes to shock the smug.'

'I'll never understand you Europeans.'

'Aha, but *we* understand *you*, we know what shocks you,' said Aunt Hortense. Her voice reminded Judy of gently drifting snow, raindrops splashing on an old stone fountain, the well-bred chink of china and weathered leather riding boots. Judy sensed that Aunt Hortense, while raising hell, would never raise her voice. She had a large, craggy face with a huge thrusting nose above a wide mouth drawn back in a permanent, deceptive smile, and her eyelids were painted emerald to match her emerald satin cocktail hat. She was tall, imperious and forbidding until she fixed you with her oddly enchanting wide smile.

Hurrying through the snowy streets, eventually the two girls reached the steam-misted glass walls of the café Deux Mágots, where they sat down at the only empty table and ordered hot lemon punch.

'*Merde*, I mean ferk, no one I recognize,' wailed Maxine. 'It's different in the evening. I once saw Simone de Beauvoir having a row with Jean-Paul Sartre. And I once saw Juliette Greco. She always wears a black sweater and pants – an odd wardrobe don't you think?'

'Saves making a decision in the morning,' said a small, wiry blond boy wearing a black sweater and pants. He sat down in the empty seat beside her. He looked like an unmasked cat burglar – small with a slightly hooked Roman nose, a wide sensual mouth and a shock of hemp-coloured hair. 'Heavens, the difference ... Your face, Maxine ... I would only recognize you from the rear. And you're so svelte that I could use you as a model.' He unwound the long black scarf from his neck and ordered three *croque-monsieur*, the fried ham and cheese sandwich that is the staple diet of French students.

'What's been happening to you?' Maxine inquired.

'I've been living here on the Left Bank in the Hôtel de Londres for over a year, being a master couturier, but nobody seems to have noticed.'

'How did you become a master couturier?' Judy asked, plunging right in. 'How did you get out of your *service militaire*?'

'I had TB when I was fourteen so the army didn't want me. Papa was furious, of course, but Mother was enchanted when I joined Jacques Fath because I no longer insisted on making dresses for *her*. She said it was so tedious being fitted by me – I stuck pins in her!' He giggled.

'*How* did you suddenly jump out of school and into the studio of a world-famous couturier?' Judy asked.

'Frankly, I got the job with Jacques Fath because my mother knew the head *vendeuse*. When I wasn't picking up pins, I spent every spare moment sketching the Fath clothes. As publicly as possible, you understand – I can draw wonderfully.' He blew a straw at Maxine.

'When my first year was up at Fath, they took me on as a studio sketch artist, and when my second year was up, I was promoted to designer's assistant. Not assistant to Fath himself, you understand, but to one of his menials.' He poured wine for all of them. 'My job was to translate Fath's sketches for the workrooms, then sort out the decisions until the *toile* was made, then look after every zipper and button until the garment was ready for the first model fitting. Naturally, we never had anything to do with the clients – the *vendeuses* dealt with them ... Maxine, you shouldn't eat *croque-monsieur* at such a rate if you want to keep this amazing new shape.'

'But how did you learn to make clothes?' Judy persisted. She wanted to know everything.

'Oh, I don't know, I just *did* it.' Guy shrugged his shoulders.

In spite of his careless pose as a newly hatched genius, the real secret of Guy Saint Simon's success – apart from his talent – was the obsessive interest in fashion that had led him to spend every spare moment with the Jacques Fath tailors and cutters, learning to cut with the skill that had evolved over generations and had been passed on – only by example – from man to man (the tailors were always men, the women worked as dressmakers).

'But you *can't* "just start",' objected Judy.

'Well, I made some *proper* suits for my mother and she wore them. I thought she was doing it just to please me, but then all her friends wanted to buy the same suits. So – *voilà!* – I was in business! Now tell me what *you* intend to do with yourselves.'

'I want to be an interior decorator and study in London,'

Maxine said, 'but I don't dare tell Papa yet so I'm going to try and get Aunt Hortense to intercede for me.'

'And I'm going to get a job here in Paris as an interpreter,' Judy added, sounding far more sure of herself than she was. She knew that the job competition in Paris was almost as fierce as the traffic, and that French working hours were long and poorly paid.

'Then she's going back to New York,' said Maxine gaily, 'to get a job in some glamorous international company where she can use her languages and eventually, of course, marry the boss!'

'Can we see your clothes, Guy?' Judy asked, wanting to change the conversation.

'But of course. You might both marry appalling old million-aires and become my best clients. But not today; I have to see my button-maker in ten minutes. Meet me after work tomorrow, six o'clock at the Hôtel de Londres. I'll take you to dinner at the Beaux Arts afterwards, because it's St Valentine's Day tomorrow and all the students will be having a terrific party ... What's wrong? ... Why are you both looking so odd? ... Have I said something to upset you?'

'No, no,' said Maxine hastily, 'it's just that we had a bit of trouble at school last year on St Valentine's Day. We ... er ... got back from a dance later than we should have done.'

'Well, you won't be bothered by such childish things anymore,' said Guy, waving for the bill and not noticing the girls' uneasy silence.

Outside, a weak winter sun was shining, the wind had dropped and it wasn't nearly so cold. The two girls drifted along the cobbled *quais*, by the stone parapets of the Seine, past the second-hand book carts and the dark green stalls.

'Does Guy like girls?' asked Judy as they walked over the Pont Royal. There had been something about the way he moved his hands.

'I don't know. Perhaps not, I've no idea. Either way, you mustn't fall for him, you know. I want to leave you with someone to look after you, someone to take the place of Nick – a brother, not a lover, for the moment. I don't want you to feel alone in Paris.'

'Can't I have both?'

'But of course, you won't be able to avoid it in Paris. Just wait until the spring when the chestnut trees are flowering. Look, there are already some flowers here in the Jardin des Tuileries.'

The girls hurried through the gardens, then turned left towards the Avenue Montaigne, becoming increasingly excited as they neared number 32, the salon of the greatest couturier in the world, Christian Dior.

A cloud of perfume enveloped them as they entered the pampered warmth. Aunt Hortense, whom they were to meet, was nowhere to be seen so they wandered around the boutique, fingering exquisite silk blouses in sugar-almond colours, eyeing the unbelievably fragile lingerie and stroking the suede gloves.

To Judy's relief she was ignored; but the *vendeuses* fluttered around Maxine, who was wearing her navy Dior overcoat, so she daringly decided to try on a couple of things. She put on a floor-length jackal coat, watched by an indulgent saleswoman who knew that this child had no intention of buying, but that nevertheless somebody had bought her clothes from Dior. Then she slipped on a white cotton nightgown trimmed with narrow green satin ribbon that cost the equivalent of her allowance for three months. She had just discarded it and purchased a pale blue lace garter belt – three weeks' allowance but worth it – when Aunt Hortense swept in and they went off to claim their reserved seats from the big antique reception desk.

Had Aunt Hortense not been a regular customer, the elegant receptionist would have courteously asked her name, address and telephone number, then written them in the big leather visitors' book; she would also have asked who suggested they visit the house of Dior. This procedure helped to sort out the spies and time-wasters from the genuine customers. Commercial spies rarely tried to get in after the opening of a collection because they had all the information they needed by the third day of the show, but smartly dressed women (sometimes genuine customers like cosmetic tycoon Helena Rubinstein) often visited the collection with a less well-dressed 'friend', who was really a dressmaker – and whose second-rate shoes, bag and gloves invariably proclaimed the fact.

'So comfortable here,' said Aunt Hortense, as they were seated in the pale grey salon in the front row of delicate gilt chairs, 'although I have never understood why men think women enjoy shopping. It is a painful ordeal that has to be endured in order to acquire new clothes. The pain comes in two parts – choosing the right garment, then making sure that it fits ... Oh, the arguments I've had with fitters! So I come to Christian Dior because I *dislike* shopping. One isn't demoralized at a couturier, as one is in a shop where they urge you to try on clothes that make you feel fat, awkward and ugly.'

'Or complain that you're not a stock size, in a way that makes you feel like a freak,' agreed Judy.

'Or intimidate you, so that you end up buying something expensive merely because you don't look as dreadful in it as the other things you tried on,' Maxine added.

'Quite so. It's easier to go to Dior. You pay more, but you never waste your money and you always look your best. Ha, here comes the first model!'

The audience concentrated keenly, like buyers at a horse auction, as each haughty, elegant model appeared, held a pose and then drifted back through the grey velvet curtains.

'How can that girl *possibly* have such a tiny waist?' Judy wondered, as a raven-haired model appeared in a pale grey flannel coat cinched with a wide silver-grey calf belt. 'Where does her food go?'

'If you remove the belt,' Aunt Hortense murmured, 'you'd find that there was no flannel underneath, only silk taffeta joining the top to the skirt. That's why her waist looks so tiny. But she shouldn't carry her furs so carefully. Pierre Balmain says that the trick to wearing mink is to look as though you're wearing a cloth coat, and the trick to wearing a cloth coat is to treat it as if it were as precious as mink.'

As always, the final item in the collection was a white bridal gown with a flutter of little lace frills frothing from the shoulder to form an eight-foot-long train. 'Excellent,' approved Aunt Hortense, 'a bride should always choose something with back interest for everyone to look at when she's kneeling at the altar. A wedding service is so boringly predictable. Now for my fittings.'

They moved to a dressing room where the silent fitter – silent because her mouth was full of pins – made minute alterations on an apricot silk dress with billowing gypsy violinist sleeves and a wasp waist. 'Three fittings for every garment,' grumbled Aunt Hortense, 'but it means a perfect fit, which is one of the main attractions of a couture garment.' She addressed herself to the fitter. 'It needs a little more room at the waist, don't you think? . . . You want to know why I chose this dress, Judy? Because it's fairly original but not outrageous. Only the very rich, the very beautiful or the truly creative can carry off really original clothes. I am not one of them. But I know what effect I wish to give, whereas most women want to look distinctive and indistinguishable, both at the same time, which is impossible.'

'That V neck doesn't plunge as low as the one in the show,' Maxine criticized.

'No, Monsieur Dior kindly agreed to a high neck. Before six-thirty and after forty-five one should never show an inch of skin.'

'It's very chic,' offered Judy, and was immediately contradicted.

'Very *elegant*, not very chic. Schiaparelli invented the word "chic" to mean eccentric and original. One can't be chic now and again. One either is or one isn't. I am not chic.'

But Aunt Hortense *was* a perfectionist. Energetic and tough enough to know what she wanted – and get it – she never spared anyone's feelings in order to achieve perfection. Always polite, she would return a dress, coat or hat to the workroom again and again until she considered it satisfactory. Nothing was ever better than satisfactory. Aunt Hortense did not have many clothes, but they were all made of the finest chiffon, the softest silk, the most subtle tweeds and supple furs. Apart from her Dior clothes, her outfits were different variations of one ensemble that she considered suitable for her age and style of life; this was a suit, a collarless jacket worn with an A-line or pleated skirt made from silk or wool, with a chiffon blouse in the same colour, and each outfit always had two hats, a small head-hugging one and a big-brimmed felt or straw. These simple outfits blazed with exquisite jewels. Although Aunt Hortense liked discretion in clothes she did not care for it in jewellery; she liked hunks of gold, heavy chains of platinum, chunks of emerald quartz spiked with diamonds, and long ropes of knobbly baroque pearls.

After the Dior show, Aunt Hortense took the girls for a cup of tea in the Plaza Athénée. The wide corridor was lined with clusters of little velvet armchairs and smelled of expensive scent, rich cigars and well-laundered Americans.

'What did you think of the show?' asked Aunt Hortense as the pastry trolley was wheeled up.

'It was very splendid,' Judy said, leaning back. She enjoyed being waited on more than could possibly be imagined by anyone who had never been a waitress. 'Very beautiful and very splendid, but I think that clothes should be practical, and those weren't. Even if I could afford them, I couldn't afford to look after them, so I shouldn't buy them however rich I was.' She put her fork into a meringue. 'Maxine, you needn't look as if I'm insulting the Virgin Mary. How do you hand-wash a dress with five yards of fabric in the skirt? How would you dry-clean that white crêpe ballgown? And how do you keep a cream suede coat clean?'

'Your American designers can't produce anything nearly so good as our Paris collections,' said Maxine indignantly. 'That's why they all come over *here* to buy.'

'Look, Maxine, I said the show was divine, but I also thought that for most women who haven't a lady's maid and endless credit at the cleaners, it was impractical. Your Aunt Hortense asked me what I thought and I'm telling her. I hope I'm going to be much too busy to spend half my life looking after my clothes.'

Aunt Hortense, sitting bolt upright on her little velvet chair, like a Saint Cyr cadet, said, 'Interesting and practical criticism. I would tell Monsieur Dior except, of course, he wouldn't take the slightest notice. There are only about eighteen thousand women in the world who are rich enough to afford couture clothes from Paris and they all seem to be queueing at his door, so he doesn't have to bother about the practical aspects of his collection. But Judy is quite right to say exactly what she thinks; I always do. When I was your age I was a timid little mouse – well, not little, but terrified of opening my mouth. Children were seen and not heard, you know, before the First World War.'

'The reason I always say what I think,' said Judy, 'is that I don't know how to talk any other way. I know Europeans think I'm ill-mannered, but I don't understand why.'

'You're tactless and you shout,' said Maxine, still annoyed by Judy's criticism of Dior.

'I shout sometimes when I get excited because I had to when

I was little or none of the bigger kids would have paid any attention to me.'

'Don't change,' advised Aunt Hortense. 'You think for yourself, you don't repeat other people's opinions. You are direct and expect other people to be. Perhaps your manner seems a little brusque to people who don't know you, perhaps it may even irritate or alarm them, but you will soon pick up the social graces now that you are no longer a child. Personally, I find you refreshingly straightforward, somewhat similar to myself, in fact. This charming naivety, this ruthless innocence I find fresh and appealing.'

She took a thoughtful sip of her tea. 'Losing your innocence has very little to do with virginity, you know. Loss of innocence comes when you have to deal with the real world by yourself, when you learn that the first rule of life is kill or be killed. So different from one's nursery stories.'

She picked out another crystallized violet. 'I realized this quite quickly during the war. It was only then, at the age of forty-two, that I learned what real life was like. The war was dreadful, but sometimes it was also exciting. I still miss the action. As Maxine knows, I prefer action to discussion. You shouldn't just sit and twiddle your thumbs and wait for something to happen in your life.'

'No,' said Judy eagerly. 'You have to make it happen!'

'Quite so. Oh, what fun we used to have in the middle of such horror and pain! Maurice, our chauffeur, was my *chef* in the Resistance and we worked on the railways.' In answer to Judy's unspoken query, she snapped her middle finger against her thumb. 'Blowing them up. Then we became part of an escape route – not so much fun, but even more dangerous.' Daintily, Aunt Hortense stirred her porcelain cup with a silver spoon.

'But where did you learn that?'

'Oh, I was never taught anything useful. But you pick things up very fast when you have to.'

'What do you wish you'd been taught?'

'I wish I'd been taught to expect change as a matter of course in everything including oneself. You will find that you're one person when you're seventeen, but by the time you're twenty-five you've developed into quite a different person with different aims, interests, attitudes, friends.' She paused, then shrugged her shoulders. 'Then ten years later you find you've changed again – and so it goes on. Finally, when you get to my age, people say you get set in your ways, but what they really mean is that you like having your own way. It is the beginning of the selfishness of old age.'

She paused and lifted the silver teapot. 'You two girls seem so much more adulterous than I was at your age. No? That's not the right word? Well, my English is rusting. Judy will be good practice for me.' Judy nodded, and Aunt Hortense continued. 'To me you both seem very grown-up. At sixteen I thought I knew nothing and it caused me great anxiety; at eighteen I thought I knew everything, then at thirty, I realized that I knew nothing – and possibly never would, which depressed me until I noticed that no one else knew anything either. Adultery implies a certain objectivity, restraint and wisdom, don't you think?'

'I don't think you mean adultery. That's other people's husbands committing intimacy.'

'Thank you, dear child, I meant adult behaviour. My point was that you don't necessarily grow more adult as you grown older.'

At first Judy thought Aunt Hortense a snob, but she quickly realized that Hortense was merely French and rich and old, that she was experienced and worth listening to and didn't give a damn for anyone's opinion. Judy was fascinated by her. She was so different from her mom, Judy thought with disloyalty. The thought made her feel guilty. She was still frightened by the spectre of Rossville, terrified of letting her life slip away like her mother without anyone noticing – not even herself. Unlike her mother, Judy didn't intend to spend her life being frightened of doing anything.

Her mother was unable to forget her memories of the thirties, when for two bad years her husband had been out of work. She had managed to pass this fear of being penniless on to Judy, who consequently thought about financial security the way other girls did about Prince Charming. Judy couldn't help noticing that her father had not turned out to be Prince Charming. Marriage was no guarantee of money and security, she knew that. She'd have to work long and hard before she could pull a large bill out of her alligator purse and hand it to a waiter without looking at the cheque as Aunt Hortense had just done.

Having cross-questioned Judy about her future plans, Aunt Hortense said thoughtfully, 'If you have nobody to look after you, please remember that I have nobody to look after. I am not as fierce as I look, and I remember very well what it was like to be seventeen, so telephone me if you need help. In fact, please telephone me anyway.'

Maurice drove the two girls back to Neuilly. Judy looked at his broad shoulders below the black peaked cap. 'Do you think intimacy was ever committed?' she whispered.

'With Aunt Hortense, who knows?' Maxine whispered back.

As the old Mercedes sped through the centre of Paris, Judy felt as if she were in heaven. Like many an American before her, she was already in love with Paris.

~ 8 ~

THE dusty foyer of the Hôtel de Londres had an air of minding its own business. Faded wallpaper peeled from the top of the walls and the baseboards were well kicked.

'Where is the elevator?' Maxine asked the receptionist.

'At the Ritz.' He jerked a thumb towards the staircase at the back of the hall. The girls walked past an exhausted palm tree that sagged in a copper pot, then climbed the creaking stairs to the fifth floor where at the end of a dim passage they found Guy's work-room. Small and low-ceilinged, far cleaner than the rest of the hotel, it overlooked a small courtyard. Silhouetted in front of the window, a woman crouched over a whirring sewing machine; shirt-sleeves rolled up, a man in a white apron was cutting into a length of mauve wool on a table that occupied most of the room. Bolts of fabric were stacked in a rack to the left of the door and on the right were two dressrails on wheels from which hung garments shrouded in white tissue paper.

'So now I show you,' said Guy, after introducing the girls to his cutter and seamstress, who were just about to leave at the end of their day. One by one, Guy took the clothes off the rail and carefully slid off the tissue. His designs were mainly suits or separates; sensuous silk jackets and skirts in misty rose and lavender were matched to pants in darker jersey; jewel-coloured velvet suits in garnet, topaz and sapphire could be worn with matching wool coats. The designs were simple, without boning or padding.

'These clothes should be worn with a lot of bold, gilt jewellery,' Guy explained, as the girls tried on the clothes and then admired themselves in the big mirror. 'I'm only doing one raincoat but in three different lengths; it's reversible. It can be worn over anything in the collection with or without a belt.' He produced a cinnamon gabardine raincoat with a purple wool lining. 'I would also like to do it in pewter grey lined with pale pink, but I can't afford to produce my designs in too many colours in my first collection.'

'I love nearly everything,' Judy said enthusiastically after she and Maxine in their petticoats – clothes-mad like all girls of their age – had spent half an hour trying on the garments. 'They're so easy to move in – easy to live in, as well, I should think. They feel as if you're wearing no clothes at all. You're not conscious of them.'

'What I'm trying to do is to produce clothes that make a woman look smart without making her feel uncomfortable. Did you notice that all my skirt bands are elasticized? And I insist that my models visit the bathroom in every single garment to make sure it's totally practical.'

Guy's comfortable clothes were very different from the exquisite but constricting ensembles that Judy had seen at Dior. Although Guy's look was casual, it was nevertheless elegant because of the clever cut and the beautiful fabrics he used.

He pulled a bolt of mauve silk from the rack, draped a length over Judy's bare shoulders and started to pin it. 'This isn't the way most designers work,' he mumbled through a mouthful of pins. 'Only Madame Grès cuts straight from the fabric and pins on to a live model.'

'Do your cutter and seamstress fit people?' asked Judy.

'Never! The fit is the *most important part* of a garment and *I* do it. I don't much like doing it, but I have nobody else who can.

Good fitters are born, not made, and in Paris we have the best fitters in the world. Keep still or I'll jab you. I can also make patterns and samples, cut, sew, fit and supervise a small workshop, but I'm primarily a designer and when I'm big enough I'll never do anything else, thank you.'

'What about selling?' asked Judy. 'Who sells your stuff?'

Guy looked worried. 'To date there has been no need for a *vendeuse* because my clients know me and they bring their friends. They think it's intriguing to come to this shabby place – they feel they're getting something cheap, which of course they *are*. Also they feel they are in on a new discovery, which I hope is true. Now, how do you like that, *ma chère*?' He stepped back and Judy moved carefully to the mirror. She was wearing the classically draped dress of a Grecian goddess.

'Oh, how I long for this!'

'When I'm richer, then we shall see. At the moment every sou I spend is vital.' He rapidly unpinned her and deftly caught the length of silk as it fell from her shoulders. 'Now can I offer you an aperitif?'

He opened the adjoining door that led to his bedroom, a strange contrast to the immaculate, severely practical room in which they stood. Guy's personal possessions – books, underwear, shoes – were piled on the end of the bed, which was the only semiempty space in a room crammed with half-draped tailor's dummies, metal clothes racks, bales of muslin and paper patterns. Guy pushed the heap of books and shoes farther down the bed and the three of them sat cross-legged on it, sipping white vermouth from one toothmug and two paper cups, as the girls listened to Guy's plans. He outlined his career and spread his life plan before them – almost as clear as the aerial view from the Arc de Triomphe had been yesterday, Judy thought wistfully as she said, 'You sound so confident.'

'Myself? I live in constant self-doubt, indecision and secret panic about my capability,' Guy said. He added gloomily, 'You have no idea what agony it is to decide whether a jacket should be double- or single-breasted – and such a decision is vital because I cannot afford to produce many garments, so it has to be the one or the other. And until I can afford an assistant, there is no one with whom to discuss *anything*. I tell you, it's lonely at the bottom.'

'I know what you mean,' said Judy. 'I'm going to miss Maxine dreadfully. I'll have no one to chat with, not even a room to live in as yet.'

'Why not move in here?' Guy suggested. 'It's the cheapest decent place I could find, only five hundred francs a night – that's about two dollars isn't it? The Left Bank is full of cheap rooming hotels for students, but *this* one is clean, and they bring you breakfast in bed, if you can afford it. When I had influenza I had three breakfasts a day sent up. And there's a telephone; they take messages if you tip that surly bastard in the hall once a month.'

'A wonderful idea,' Maxine said. 'Guy can keep an eye on you, and you can advise him on double or single breasts.'

On their way to dinner, they stopped at the hall desk where Maxine negotiated with the surly porter over monthly rates and got a fifteen per cent discount. Then they walked along the rue Bonaparte to the noisy Beaux Arts restaurant on the corner. Lifting her glass of wine, Judy felt much more settled. Now all she needed was a job.

Judy didn't feel so cheerful two days later when she went job hunting.

Armed with her Swiss diplomas, she was interviewed in a shabby employment office where she sat in line until her name was called. She was interrogated by a woman of uncertain age, with a typically French face – that combination of sallow skin, weary brown eyes and expensively gilded hair pulled back in a chignon. She spoke very fast and Judy stuttered when making her replies. At the end of the interview, the woman gave a long sniff to imply doubt, shrugged her shoulders to imply resignation, then pulled a large kitchen timer out of her drawer and gave Judy a typing test. In spite of the intimidating atmosphere, Judy passed. The woman gave another long sniff to imply surprise, shrugged her shoulders to imply that one never knows, made four telephone calls, handed Judy four address cards and sent her off to her first interview.

Having finally located the building, Judy took the cagelike elevator to an airless office where she was interviewed by a finicky little fat man who kept looking down and brushing his left sleeve as he asked his questions. After he turned her down, she went on to the next interview, and, in all, spent a week and a half visiting similar dingy offices. They were all painted grey or beige, smelled of dust and old biscuits and the desks were piled with overstuffed, crumpled, cream cardboard files. Finally, after being beaten down from the salary that the agency had quoted, Judy was accepted as a temporary secretary by a large, middle-aged fabric importer, with a face like a grey egg upon which had been painted a drooping black moustache. He dictated in French, but when necessary, Judy translated his letters into English or German before typing them, and struggled with the innumerable custom forms that were necessary to get tweed from Scotland and linen from Dublin to Paris, or to send silk from Lyons and lace from Valenciennes to New York. Her employer obviously regarded her as nothing more than a walking, talking, typing machine and made no effort to speak to her apart from a brief '*B'jour, mademoiselle*'.

'I wore your beautiful silk dress to a ball last night, and I danced every dance with a different young man – and I was bored limp,' Maxine said gloomily to her Aunt Hortense as they sat in the small, maple-wood panelled library of Aunt Hortense's Paris apartment. Maxine, who had sought the meeting, was tense but determined.

'I can't seem to talk about this to my parents without a fight. Anybody would think we were living in 1850, not 1950. Mama can't understand that I don't *want* to go to all the right parties and dance with all the right men, then marry one of them. I don't want to marry Pierre, the god of the ski-slopes, and then have a complete duplicate of the dull, comfortable life that my mother has led.'

Under her huge, green-brimmed straw hat, Aunt Hortense raised bushy eyebrows above her big bony nose and sniffed. Unlike Judy, Maxine was a bit frightened of her aunt, who now nodded without saying anything. Encouraged, Maxine continued. 'Of course I love my family, but I don't want to be part of that nursery life any longer. I want to get away from them. I want to have a life of my *own*. "You will have, if you marry the Boursal boy," says Mama.' She mimicked her mother's exasperated voice. 'Pierre has already spoken to Papa, you know, but when I visit his parents in that apartment on the Avenue George

V, I can't get out fast enough. It's claustrophobic and I feel trapped again. Although it's much grander than our home – white marble and a black maid – his mother leads exactly the same life as my mother, except that *she* does it in haute-couture clothes. I don't *want* to marry Pierre because I don't *want* that life.'

Angrily Maxine bit her thumbnail although there was little left to bite. 'And there's another more important reason. Pierre is really only interested in skiing, you know. I realize that sounds ridiculous and you're going to tell me that it will pass, but I think that with him, when it does pass, nothing else will take its place. He's rich and he likes to ski; he doesn't like to work and there's no reason why he should.' She looked up at her aunt pleadingly. 'But I couldn't stand being married to a rich ski bum, especially an *ageing* rich ski bum. So I'm going to refuse Pierre, and then I want to leave Paris for a bit. I know Paris. I've lived here all my life. I want to visit other places – London and Rome.'

Again Aunt Hortense nodded slowly in order to give herself time to think. At that age, many girls felt like Maxine, but the child was unusually impatient in this attempt to get what she wanted. In time, Maxine would learn to move slowly and carefully in order to get her own way, not to crash aggressively into a prerehearsed argument like this one. She would learn that, whoever she married.

'What exactly *do* you want?' Aunt Hortense asked.

'I want to go to London and learn to be an interior decorator, then come back to Paris and open my own concern. *You* are the one who started to educate my eye – shopping for clothes with you, shopping for antiques with you, going around museums with you. *You* have your own style. Now I want to develop one of my own. French designers are still doing the same thing that they've been doing since before the war. Stuffy, overdecorated, over-expensive interiors. This is not what I want to do.' She looked up from under her lashes. 'I'm going to ask Papa to let me study in London for two years. I want you to persuade him to let me go because I know I can't, and I know you can.'

Aunt Hortense nodded again as she tended to when she thought it prudent to say nothing.

Encouraged, Maxine continued. 'My friend Pagan says that the best London decorator is James Partridge, who's just done her mother's flat. She says he's got a marvellous understanding of colour and antiques and Pagan's already talked to him. She's asked if he could find a job for me.'

Aunt Hortense nodded again. It was not such a stupid idea. It was always useful if one married well. It would certainly improve the girl's eye and if she were making money, then she could hardly be spending it.

So she asked Maxine's parents to one of her smaller, grander dinner parties. She seated Maxine's father between a mildly famous, mildly flirtatious actress and a pretty little Countess who had been widowed the previous year and was rumoured not to be inconsolable. Maxine's father enjoyed himself hugely. After the meal, when her guests were sitting over brandy and coffee in the library, his sister drew him to one side and said, 'A little word with you, Louis, about my goddaughter. I feel that Maxine shouldn't waste any more time socializing in Paris. It's time that she continued her education.'

'Well, we rather assumed that she's going to marry the Boursal boy . . .'

'Oh, surely not, surely that's not what you want for your clever daughter? That blockhead? Why, the girl is hardly out of school and you want to marry her to a brainless idiot like that! No, I think that Maxine takes after you. She is clever, she shows a definite talent for the arts. It would be a good idea if she studied them seriously.'

'Well, perhaps you're right, Hortense,' said Maxine's father, who really didn't think it was important what Maxine did before she married provided it didn't cost him too much. 'I'll ask her mother to see what courses are available at the Beaux Arts.'

'Very wise of you, Louis. And there's one other small thing that should be attended to. Her English isn't nearly good enough – not nearly as good as yours. She speaks English the way Winston Churchill speaks French – *exécrable*! What I should most like to see for her is two years in London, studying with a really good decorator. One learns so much faster in practice than in theory, don't you think?'

'*London? Two years?* You must be mad, Hortense, her mother would never let her go. She's only nineteen, remember.'

'You've just implied that she's old enough to be married.

Besides she has friends in London. Oh, Louis, think what a joyless adolescence *we* had. She has such talent, your Maxine! Surely you wish to allow the poor child to spread her wings a little before she has to knuckle down to the serious and often tedious business of being a wife.'

There was a pause. 'And if I allowed her to go to London, to whom would she go?'

'The best decorator in London, of course,' said Aunt Hortense decisively, 'and that is Monsieur Partridge. I have no idea whether there's a free place in his office, and I don't know if he charges for apprentices, but I can telephone him tomorrow and find out. No! No! It would be a *pleasure* for me to attend to your wishes in this matter, Louis.'

She led him back to the library, quite pleased with herself. It was amazing how you could spoonfeed flattery to a grown man.

So in due course, after kissing Judy goodbye, Maxine caught the Golden Arrow to London. Kate and Pagan were waiting at Victoria Station. Kate had already rented a basement apartment in Chelsea for herself and Maxine. There were only two small, dark rooms, but it was in Walton Street, a charming little road of tiny nineteenth-century houses in Chelsea.

Every evening at six, Judy rushed from the depressing office back to her shabby, overblown-rose-patterned room at the Hôtel de Londres. The room overlooked an inner courtyard that was as full of life as a soap opera. Nobody ever seemed to draw the curtains, and beyond the other windows you could hear the fights, see the lovemaking and smell the cooking from the apartments on the opposite side.

As Guy's collection progressed, his own bedroom grew less habitable, so when he finished work he would climb two further flights of stairs to Judy's room for a glass of wine and sympathy. Sitting cross-legged on her pillow, she quickly learned about the world of French couture.

'One whole day wasted on fittings,' groaned Guy one evening, throwing himself on to the bottom of the bed. 'How I long to design for the boutique market!'

'What difference will that make?'

'Mass orders, *ma chère*. Mass manufacturing and *no* damned fittings. An haute-couture garment is made to order and has three sacred, time-wasting fittings, but boutique clothes are made in batches, in standard sizes, and are sold ready-to-wear. It's up to the customer or the store to alter them, if necessary.'

Judy leaned under her bed for the wine bottle and filled two small glasses. 'I thought you liked couture customers?'

'Only because I have to. Very few women can afford couture clothes. All of them are spoiled, and most of them are fickle. Hardly any women stick to one couture house, except the best dressed ones.' He sipped his wine very slowly, then continued. 'Celebrity clients often borrow ballgowns for a gala, then return them dirty, sometimes even torn, with never a word of thanks. *Zut!* I don't want to spend *my* life at the mercy of a few rich bitches who spend *their* life dressing for cocktails.' Suddenly he sat up and pointed under the washbasin. '*Nom d'un nom*, what is *that*?' Standing on a strip of linoleum was a wastepaper basket, and propped up in it in a nest of aluminium foil lay an upended electric iron.

'It's my stove. I've bought a little saucepan and I cook on the flat side of the iron. It's one of the new thermostatic ones – I set it at "linen" for boiling eggs or making toast and at "wool" for simmering stew.'

Guy rolled his eyes. 'A terrible fire hazard! You're lucky to be alive! You know the hotel doesn't allow cooking in the bedrooms. They'll throw you out.'

'I can't afford to eat at restaurants all the time, so I keep food in a suitcase under the bed.'

'You'll have mice and cockroaches.'

'No, it's all in a tin box.' She dragged the suitcase out to show him. 'Look, I'll boil you an egg.'

'Please don't.' Intrigued, in spite of his disapproval, Guy said, 'You Americans are undoubtedly ingenious. I see it in your fashion industry – you're ten years ahead of us in your manufacturing and marketing and in the way you specialize. In the States, a single firm doesn't offer its customers every sort of garment from skirts to ballgowns, as we do in France. A firm that makes skirts to retail between ten and twenty dollars won't know much about skirts that retail between forty and fifty dollars. One is more likely to make money in fashion if one specializes.'

Thinking of her own odious job, Judy sighed. 'There must be a lot of satisfaction in being a designer.'

There was a pause. 'Not really,' Guy said gloomily. He moved back and sat on the edge of the bed. 'I'm sorry, I am in a dark mood. It's *le cafard*. It is only because I'm tired and worried, and instead of getting on with the important work, I've been fiddling about all day, letting out a quarter of an inch here, taking in a quarter of an inch there.'

'You only feel depressed because you're exhausted and under pressure. You'll be in love with couture again tomorrow.'

'Yes, but I repeat, I don't want to spend my life working for a few rich women. I want to produce clothes that will make *thousands* of women feel marvellous.' He gave an exasperated sigh. 'Today, women want to look like themselves and I want to help them.' He snorted. 'Haute-couture is a dwindling market – every year there are fewer and fewer rich private customers.'

'Let me massage your back,' Judy said, turning from the window. 'It'll help you to unwind.'

He stood up wearily and started to unbutton his blue cotton shirt, still thinking aloud. 'Another disadvantage is that one's designs are always stolen by mass manufacturers from all over the world so one's virtually working for them, unpaid.'

Judy took the pillows off the bed, straightened the cover, spread a clean towel on it and rolled up her sleeves. Guy sat on the edge of the bed, kicked his shoes off and lay down.

'. . . But one doesn't make one's name in mass production, one makes it in haute-couture.' He lay face down on the bed and Judy started to work on his spine, pressing firmly with her thumbs, starting in the small of his back, as Guy continued to think aloud. As she worked on his shoulder muscles he could feel himself unwinding, breathing more deeply. 'Shall I tell you my plan?' he mumbled. 'I want to do something new, to specialize in high-quality mass production. My clothes won't be as expensive as haute-couture, but they won't be as cheap as most manufactured garments. My long-term ambition is to have a business that's halfway between the two, producing my own designs with my own label.'

Now her thumbs were on the back of his neck, firmly pressing the tension out of it. 'Mmmm, that feels better already . . . I want to make exquisite, ready-to-wear clothes that have the design, cut and fabric quality of an haute-couture garment, although the customer won't get personal fittings. The clothes will have to be carefully designed so that they're easy to alter to fit. I'm starting with a collection of separates, a lot in wool jersey ... aaah, that's wonderful.'

'Now, turn around and face the window,' Judy said, 'otherwise I can't get at your left side properly because the bed's against the wall. Listen, world tycoon, when will your suits be ready, and what will you do with them?'

'My sample stock will be ready in July. I'll hire a hotel suite and show the designs to stores and boutiques. The stores will order – with any luck – and the clothes will be made up by a little factory in Fauchon.'

Judy gave him a gentle slap on the back and said, 'You are now a new man.'

Guy stood up and put on his shirt. 'Thanks.' He leaned forward and ruffled the ragged fringe of her new street-urchin coiffure. 'Look, Judy, I'm *truly* sorry I've been in such a rotten mood, but the entire day has been unproductive. José, the seamstress, has been off for the whole week because she strained her wrist so we're behind schedule. I have to do so many jobs, even the damned deliveries.'

'I'm going to take you out to dinner,' Judy said.

'Judy, you're an angel, but it's not possible. I must do the bookkeeping before paying the wages tomorrow. It is the book-keeping that drives me the most crazy – it's only about an hour a week but somehow there never *is* an hour.'

'If you like, and if it's *really* only an hour a week, I'll do it for you,' Judy offered. 'You can pay me when you can afford it. I process orders and invoices at the office and I'll get Denise, our office bookkeeper, to show me whatever else is necessary. I could do it on Thursdays.'

'Angel! Shall I pay you in advance with a suit? The blue silk with the low V neck to the breasts? You can wear it in the evening with nothing underneath, just pearls.'

9

'KEEP still, and breathe in,' urged Judy, heaving on the zipper. 'Now for heaven's sake don't breathe out.'

One of the four models had let them down, so Guy was showing his first collection on only three girls. Voile curtains stirred in the slight breeze, but the July heat was still almost unendurable, even here in the Plaza Athénée. Guy was checking the accessories list and laying things out on the three trestle tables that had been set up by the hotel in place of the usual twin beds, which had been taken away for the day. Three hundred invitations had been sent out, but only thirty people were expected.

Having worked almost nonstop for the past four months, Guy was grey with fatigue and understandably tense. He was going to supervise the models. Judy, who had taken a week's vacation from her job, would usher guests to their seats and announce the models. Most of the important couture houses of Paris had already shown their collections; clothes were still pretty but uncomfortable, with voluminous skirts, boned waists and breasts squashed flat under jackets that were stiff with padded interlining; Guy's simple, comfortable clothes would certainly look different. Every evening, Judy had rushed to buy newspapers in order to read the reports of the collections that had been shown that day, and Guy anxiously telephoned around for backstage information.

First through the gilded double doors was Guy's mother with a group of friends, then, one by one, his private customers appeared. Aunt Hortense gave Judy a conspiratorial wink and whispered, 'You can get your order book out, I'm going to buy two outfits even if he's showing shrouds.' A couple of Guy's friends from the Jacques Fath studio also showed up, but none of the press appeared and only three of the buyers who had been invited from the smarter shops and stores of Paris.

The first model appeared from the hallway, wearing a garnet suit with a short, straight jacket and box-pleated skirt. She wore a black sailor hat on the back of her head and dragged the cinnamon raincoat. As if to an audience of thousands, she gave a radiant smile, advanced into the room with the gait of a nervous racehorse, then pirouetted very slowly. Because of the missing model, appearances were to be dragged out as long as possible in order to give the other girls time to change.

Once in the bedroom the model moved on the double. The seamstress held her second change ready to step into, the cutter snatched up the discarded clothes and Guy, standing by the door with his stopwatch to time each model's departure, held her accessories ready for her to grab.

At the end of the collection there was a round of polite applause, then champagne was handed around by a waiter who had strict instructions to keep the glasses full. Behind the scenes, Guy paid the models in cash, as was the custom, while his two helpers packed up the clothes. All the private customers gallantly placed orders. Guy's mother waited to see what nobody had ordered – a cream wool battledress-top suit that did not flatter a middle-aged figure – and then ordered it. Aunt Hortense bought the cinnamon raincoat, a saffron velvet jacket with a short skirt, a long skirt and matching chiffon blouse, but she declined the drainpipe pants. The private clients all left together, still trilling applause and encouragement.

As soon as the last one had gone, Guy slumped into a pale blue brocade armchair and buried his head in his hands. 'Not *one*, not *one* order, except from friends!'

Back in Judy's room at the Hôtel de Londres he slumped on the edge of the bed, staring in despair at the blowsy roses on the opposite wall. 'Lie down and I'll make you a cup of tea,' Judy said, gently pushing him back on the bed, but by the time the iron had boiled the water, Guy was already asleep. Judy took his shoes off and arranged him tidily on the bed as if he were dead or drunk, then lay down beside him. She, too, was exhausted. Alas, she thought, there wasn't going to be much invoice work . . .

The following day the telephone woke them in midmorning. It was José phoning from the downstairs workshop. The Galeries Lafayette boutique buyer wanted to know when Guy could show to them.

*

Five weeks later Guy bounced into Judy's room, jumped on the bed and leaped up and down on it, giving Indian war whoops. 'First my problem is failure, now it's success,' he shouted. 'We're completely sold out of the winter collection and I've had to turn down two million francs' worth of orders – that's eight thousand dollars, isn't it? The orders are *flooding* in! It's frightening because I haven't got enough money to finance a bigger turnover and I don't want to find myself in a liquidity crisis. My father says that's what generally happens if you expand too fast.'

'Since when has your vocabulary included such phrases as "liquidity crisis"? And stop jumping on that bed. The chambermaid hasn't reported my food suitcase but she couldn't avoid reporting a broken bed.'

Guy sat down and stayed seated on the end of the bed. 'My father has changed his tune. He's really being quite helpful. We went through the figures last night, and I think he was surprised to find I'm so businesslike – entirely due to you, of course ... Anyway, he says it's vital to make only a certain number of each design, and not to take more orders than I can afford to produce. I'm to tell latecomers that I'm very sorry but my production schedule is booked up. *And it is*! Put your suit on. I'm taking you to the Ritz for a glass of champagne.'

'Isn't there a better way of saying no?' Judy asked slowly, as she slipped into the pale blue silk suit – suitable for all seasons – that was her only decent dress. 'Isn't there some way that won't exasperate customers but will make them order faster next time? How about giving away a couple of suits to celebrities, on condition that they'll go around saying they're *mortified* that they weren't allowed to order more than two?' She pulled up the zipper. 'It could make your collection seem more select. Instead of trying to hide the fact that you can't finance your orders, *flaunt it*.'

'But I don't know any celebrities. And I can't afford to give away clothes. I haven't sweated for years to give presents to strangers.'

Judy quickly buttoned the jacket and snapped on a gilt dog collar. 'Guy, you have to pay something for publicity. Europeans *never* understand that! Nobody is going to blow your trumpet for free. Dammit, I wish you could afford to hire *me* full time!'

'As soon as I can afford it, you're hired, *mon chou*. Right now I need all my cash to buy you a drink at the Ritz. No, no, *not* the black patents, the cream pumps.'

In spite of her friendship with Guy, Judy missed Nick more than she cared to admit. Although he wrote to Judy every week, Nick's letters arrived irregularly, sometimes three in two days, sometimes none for a month. Judy's replies were similarly spaced, because she only wrote when she had something special to say. Then she would scrawl a few lines in green ink, just as if she were speaking to him, with a total disregard for grammar and punctuation. She wrote to Maxine, Kate and Pagan in the same way. The only person to whom she wrote regularly, neatly and once a week was her mother, and Judy hated doing it. Writing home was like doing homework. She couldn't write freely and she couldn't say anything about the fashion business that was her growing passion, for her mother would die of shock if she knew that Judy was involved in it.

By the end of August, Paris was sweltering and the very cobblestones of the streets seemed to melt in the heat. Still, it was probably even hotter in Malaya, thought Judy, as she saw a pale blue airmail envelope in her pigeonhole and eagerly ran towards it. Standing by the wilting palm tree in the hotel lobby she tore open the envelope and then gasped.

'Darling Judy,' wrote Maxine, 'I have some very bad news. At first we hoped it wasn't true, but we have checked with the War Office and there is no doubt. I don't know how to tell you, but Nick has been killed on duty ... in a Communist ambush in Malaya.'

Judy read the rest of the letter with her eyes but she didn't absorb the contents. Stunned, she moved mechanically up the seven flights of stairs to her room, carefully locked the door, ran over to the washbasin and threw up. Then she carefully cleaned the washbasin, took her shoes off, lay neatly in the middle of the bed and started to shiver in spite of the heat.

The concierge, the chambermaid and Guy were arguing in the passage.

'It's true, I haven't been able to get into her bedroom for two days; it's chained from the inside,' said the chambermaid. 'We should break the door down.'

'And she doesn't answer the telephone,' agreed the concierge. 'But the door is hinged from the inside – and to break the door down, well, I can't be responsible for damage.'

'I'll pay for the door,' said Guy, impatiently. 'We know she's in there, there's no sound, she's either ill or . . . I've been shouting out here for hour after hour. I'll break it down myself, if you won't!' Angrily, he threw his slight body against the door. '*Judy! Can you hear me?*'

'Maybe we should call an ambulance?' the chambermaid suggested.

'I should have done this yesterday,' Guy grunted, heaving his body against the door. 'How do we know she's alive after being locked in for two days with no sound from her?'

Suddenly, to his relief, they heard the scrape of metal as the chain was unhooked, then the door lock turned and the door slowly opened. Judy stood there in her stockinged feet and the crumpled clothes she'd been wearing for two days. She looked white and dazed.

'What's wrong? Are you ill? Why did you lock yourself in?' Guy asked, furious with her now that he could see that her wrists weren't slit and she wasn't in a coma.

They all crowded into the room. Guy pushed the concierge and the chambermaid out and slammed the door. Judy scowled at him. Then she felt tears fall on to her cheeks and suddenly she was able to cry.

Guy wrapped her in his arms and held her tightly to him. Blindly, she reached one hand out to the night table and handed him Maxine's letter. Guy read it over Judy's shoulder and softly stroked her hair until she was a little calmer. 'Get undressed and hop into bed,' he said gently. 'I'm going down to my room, but don't you dare lock this door again.' He was back within minutes with a large bottle of eau-de-cologne and half a litre of milk, which he warmed for her, carefully setting the iron to 'wool'.

'I feel so guilty, so dreadfully guilty about *everything*. I didn't love Nick, he loved me, and *now it's too late*,' Judy snuffled.

'You can't order love.'

139

'But I can't seem to love *any* man. I go out with a few guys, yes, but I can't seem to *love* anyone.'

'Judy, you're eighteen and you've told me before that you don't want to fall in love with a Frenchman. You said you didn't want to complicate your life at the moment.'

He stroked her hair again, and stayed with her until, in the soft grey twilight, she fell asleep.

In the dark Guy slipped the pale blue letter into his pocket. He felt like throttling Maxine. Why hadn't she telephoned him?

Twice in the night Judy woke in tears, and he stroked her hair and soothed her to sleep again. In the morning he lifted the phone and firmly ordered *café au lait* for two, with double croissants, much to the surprise of the chambermaid, who had thought he was the other way.

～ 10 ～

THE Saturday after Nick's death, Aunt Hortense telephoned and immediately sensed a difference in Judy. 'Are you ill, my child? Your voice sounds so flat and weary. I was hoping to swoop you off to Versailles.'

'I don't think so, thank you,' Judy said. 'I have some paper-work to do for Guy.'

Aunt Hortense immediately telephoned Guy and was told the true reason for Judy's apathy. She called Judy again and firmly said, 'I'm sending the car around for you straightaway, because I'd like to see you for half an hour if it's not inconvenient. I have a present for you.'

She rang off before Judy had time to think of an excuse.

Usually Judy loved to visit Aunt Hortense's beautiful old stone house with the lacework balconies, which stood on l'Isle de la Cité, the tiny island in the middle of the Seine that was the original city of Paris. But today she sat listless in the back of the Mercedes as it threaded its way through the cobbled streets, past street criers carrying big wicker baskets full of fresh butter and eggs, Romany gypsies trying to sell dried lavender or hand-carved wooden clothespins to the passers-by, the wigmaker's shop and the buttonmaker's shop. And when the car passed the shop full of young girls making funeral wreaths of violets and lilies and white roses, she started to sob again.

The setting sun was gilding the walls of Aunt Hortense's drawing room as she silently handed Judy a small green velvet box. Inside was an antique necklace of seed pearls.

'But why?' Judy asked. 'It's not my birthday. I can't accept . . .'

'Yes, you can,' said Aunt Hortense. 'I accepted them at your age for a much more wicked reason and I want you to have them. What would I do with them now? They are for the neck of a young girl. Let me show you how the clasp works. If you don't care for the ruby clasp, then you can choose another one from Cartier.'

Judy slowly fastened the necklace and then moved to a mirror. In the old, warped, silver surface, the pearls gleamed against her skin.

'Why have you given me this, Aunt Hortense?'

'To be direct, because you are miserable, because you have lost a friend and because you are unhappy in a boring job. I think we should perhaps try and find you another job.'

'Well, yes, almost *any* other job would be an improvement, but other offices seem pretty much the same.'

'I wasn't thinking of an office job. I thought you might like to be an assistant saleswoman at Christian Dior. The assistants are quite young you know.' Her emerald eyelids fluttered. 'I cannot promise you anything, you understand, but I have spoken to the *directrice* and she is willing to interview you. The pay will be terrible, of course – *if* you get a job – because the competition is fierce. I know you don't really approve of Monsieur Dior, but it is the house where I have the most, how do you say?'

'Clout?'

'Exactly. They know me there so they will interview you. But please don't offer your opinion of Monsieur Dior's work. And don't forget to use the servants' entrance, my child.'

'Aunt Hortense, you are so kind.'

'It is merely common sense. Something has to be done.'

'Maxine and I secretly call you Aunt Horse-Sense.'

'I know, *ma chère*. I have been called worse.'

So Judy visited Christian Dior again, this time entering by the employees' entrance, which was heavily guarded. She wore her blue silk suit and tried not to sound overqualified. The shrewd-looking woman who interviewed her wore a perfectly cut grey linen dress and her silver hair was swept up in a French knot. 'So you speak English, French and German?' she asked.

'And a little Spanish.'

'And you've been handling exports and secretarial work. Why don't you want an office job?'

'Because I want to learn to sell and I want to be with *people*. I've been working in a room by myself for nearly a year. Also I would do *anything* to work at Dior.'

'Most of the girls that come here say that. They want a job because they love fashion, but they don't realize what a hard job it is. It's physically very tiring.'

As the interview continued, the *directrice* became increasingly surprised by Judy's technical knowledge of fashion until she mentioned that she did bookkeeping for Guy Saint Simon.

'Aha, now I understand. A young man to watch. Of course, it is not difficult to get a little publicity at his age, but if it doesn't go to his head, if he stays small for the moment, if the buyers remain confident of his ability, quality, finish and – above all – his reliability, then he could go far.'

'He intends to.'

There was no vacancy at Dior, but her name was taken and in early December the personnel manager telephoned to say that one of their assistant salesgirls had contracted hepatitis. Did Judy want her job, on a temporary basis, until after the collections in February? Anything to get her foot in the door, Judy thought, and immediately accepted.

All chatter stopped as Judy timidly entered the saleswomen's room for the first time. It felt like her first day in high school. Terrifying. Like the other saleswomen, she was wearing a grey flannel dress that had been provided free by the house. Her first Dior! She was rapidly introduced to everyone by her boss, Annie, who then whisked her out to the salons. Annie grumbled incessantly about her feet and her commission, which she was always working out on a hypothetical basis in her little black notebook.

'*If* the Countess also takes it in black ... *if* the Ambassador's wife doesn't think it's too flamboyant ... *if* Zizi Jeanmaire likes the scarlet feathers.'

Most of the other assistants were older than Judy and got no commission, only a meagre salary. They were putting in a two-year stint before getting a job as first saleswomen in second-rank couture houses, after which their next step would be to become a first saleswoman in a first-rate house.

Judy was surprised to find what a large staff was necessary in order to operate the elegant, pale grey salons. The doorman, the scent-sprayer, the boutique salesgirls, the *directrice*, the salon sales force, the publicity department, the six models and the dresser were only the visible tip of the iceberg. The huge behind-the-scenes force included the quiet, awesome, pasty-faced Monsieur Dior himself and his assistants, his design staff (all men) and *their* assistants. Also the business manager, the buyers, the accountants, the secretaries, the tailors and cutters, the head fitters, the first and second sewing hands, the *midinettes*, the stock girls and so on, down to the delivery boys.

She quickly lost her respect for the refined salon saleswomen who, behind the scenes, were always bitching over new customers or the location of seats for old customers. She acquired a new respect for the seemingly humble head fitters, such as Madame Suzanne, who had pinned the apricot silk dress on Aunt Hortense. The fitters spent the whole day on their feet or their knees and often worked until nine in the evening – or even later, before a collection – carefully pinning clothes on weary, bad-tempered models. Each head fitter was responsible for a workshop with perhaps forty workers in it, all stitching busily as they gossiped, all wearing plain black skirts and sweaters with white blouses, except on St Catherine's Day when they all pinned on the yellow and green ribbons of their patron saint.

Behind the scenes was a constant, hurried feeling of pressure, but once through the doors that led to the quietly sumptuous salons, everyone's manner changed. Annie spoke in a calm, almost hushed voice; her manner was respectful; she was solicitous but never urged a sale; she never criticized a customer in any way, especially when invited to do so. The customer was always right. If anything was wrong, it was the colour, the cut, the fit or the lighting. But once back behind the swing doors, her exquisite tact vanished in a flash. 'The Countess must have put on ten pounds since her first fitting. Judee, where's my order book? You'd think an ambassadress would be able to make up her mind, without asking *me*, if cyclamen suited her. Judee, where is the list of tomorrow's fittings? That old Belgian bitch knows perfectly well that no alterations can be made to a design without the consent of Monsieur Dior. Why does every single customer think that she's the only one who wants her clothes by Christmas? Judee, what news from the workroom about number 22 in white satin for la Comtesse de Ribes?'

At the house of Dior the atmosphere became increasingly rushed and tense as the day of their big February collection drew near. Models hurried from their dressing rooms to the studios in white wrappers that kept their clothes clean and prevented anyone from seeing them until the press show. Monsieur Dior also insisted that all the studio staff wear white smocks in order to keep the clothes spotlessly clean. A hushed atmosphere surrounded the design studios, which looked like a cross between a modern church and an operating theatre; no white-walled corners were unlit, there were no shadows; the cream window shades were kept pulled down all day and all night in order to prevent spying from binoculars on the other side of the street; Monsieur Dior had his own room in which he was surrounded by paints, crayons, photographs and scraps of fabric, but the designers worked in the outer studio, their drawing boards grouped around a huge central cutting table, twenty feet long and ten feet across. The walls were lined with shelves and racks neatly piled with buttons, belts, bags, shoes and jewellery and roll upon roll of fabric samples. Normally, this was where the manufacturers' reps showed their wares and often hopefully left a bolt of cloth in case it caught some designer's fancy, because if Dior used a new fabric, the whole world wanted it.

During the dress rehearsal, there was a guard on every door. Christian Dior – 'The Master' – in an immaculate grey suit sat straddled on a chair, his arms folded over the chairback, his pale, ageing-cherub's face showing no sign of emotion or temperament – only weariness – as, gently and quietly, he scrutinized each model that passed before him and, together with his assistants, decided which jewellery and accessories were needed to complete each ensemble.

It was drizzling on Avenue Montaigne as Judy rushed to work. By eight a.m. crowds had already gathered outside the main door. Photographers with gear hanging from their shoulder straps jostled next to the two parked film trucks; the film crew shivered farther down the sidewalk. There was a crowd around the staff entrance and a bottleneck at the door, as security guards checked each person. Inside, there wasn't much talking; everyone was hurrying, their anxious faces preoccupied.

Chaos broke out as the front doors opened and the crowd heaved inside, clutching invitation cards like refugee passports. Pandemonium swept the reception desk as each card was checked and suspects were asked to show their official *chambre syndicale* stamped press cards with their photograph attached. Security men linked arms at the doors like police at a football game to keep the crowds out. Blasts of cold air swept up marble steps and crowds shrieked as the celebrities arrived: Princess Aly Khan, once Rita Hayworth, Gene Tierney glowering at her, and the Duchess of Windsor looking like a little governess.

The approved guests surged into the main salon, where every gilt chair was numbered. Nevertheless, reporters argued over seats; neither the *chambre syndicale* (the couturiers' association) nor the fashion houses knew the relative importance of foreign journalists and they were too arrogant to find out; journalists were dragged ten thousand kilometres to stay at the Plaza Athénée, then treated like pickpockets on the New York subway; there were angry arguments when high-powered, syndicated columnists found their seats – booked weeks beforehand – occupied by Little Rock newspaper reporters with six-week deadlines. The syndicated writers were prepared to struggle ruthlessly as they claimed their places, fighting with kamikaze desperation.

It was different in the front row, which was always reserved for film stars, *Vogue, Harper's Bazaar, Women's Wear Daily* ... 'Who's that little blonde? How did *she* get there?' someone asked Judy.

'That's Empress Miller, she's the new fashion writer for the

New York Clarion.' Judy had met Empress at one of Aunt Hortense's parties.

The mob behind the front row were quieter now, all notebooks ready. The miasma of a thousand new perfumes grew more sickly. It was getting hotter and it would be worse when the arc lights were turned on.

The lights went on and there was an immediate hush.

Behind the scenes Judy felt she was witnessing a kaleidoscope of hissed queries, anxious eyes, strained faces and general chaos in the model dressing rooms. Naked to the waist, stockings snapped to their girdles (no models wore panties because the line would show through the clothes), the young women sat before their mirrors. The shelves below were a jumble of coloured grease, half-empty pots, grubby sticks of makeup and stumps of lipsticks. The models stuck on immense eyelashes while hairdressers stabbed at their coiffures. Then the models were helped into their clothes by dressers – zippers zipped, snappers snapped and buttons buttoned. The head dresser checked that accessories were correct, hems straight, clothes properly pressed and immaculate.

Holding the accessories ready, Judy watched the models leave their *cabines*, ready to go. Timing was by stopwatch and military-precise. The presentation had been planned to contrast and counterpoint the colour, cut and line of the new collection, and the clothes were grouped so that the press could see a new line or colour develop. Judy had seen it all decided at the first rehearsal. Instructions were then transferred to the big pinboard outside the dressing rooms; rows of cards with each model's name and the number of garments were listed vertically in appearance order. That pinboard was the blueprint of the show: 22, 13, 71, 49, 32, etcetera; the numbers were not according to appearance but had been allocated to the garments months ago, when they were first designed.

The models were as nervous as greyhounds at the gate, fiddling with the necklaces that Judy clipped on them, pulling down jackets and smoothing their hair. There were six house models and eight free lancers – cinnamon-stick thin – had flown in from overseas; they were even skinnier than the Dior house models because it was essential that they fit every designer's clothes. They lived on Dexedrine and yogurt and frequently collapsed after the collections from exhaustion, malnutrition and stress.

The first model was announced by an oddly high, breathless voice. 'Peking, *numéro trois*, nombair sree.' The model wore Oriental makeup, her doe eyes lined with black crayon. The loose white linen jacket, straight black skirt and straw coolie hat were carefully calculated pointers to the theme of the whole collection – the Chinese influence. Pencils leaped, the working audience concentrated. Some journalists were incessant scribblers, but Empress Miller only noted, 'No change skirt length/Chinese/b & w coolie look/fluid/no stiffening/no padding/easy move/hats straw big brim/suits sailor navy & w/skirts pleated & flat.'

Journalists were allowed to take notes but not to write complete descriptions or to sketch. It was getting even hotter. A girl in a lynx coat collapsed and was swiftly carried out. A raven-haired house model in a scarlet strapless net formal gown noticed a journalist sketching; the model paused, touched her left earlobe and smiled directly at the journalist.

Annie pounced.

Sketches and notes were confiscated and the journalist's name put on the *syndicale* blacklist. Two other journalists were expelled later. Rage, threats, pleas, tears – all were useless.

An hour afterwards, in the dressing room, Judy heard a sudden roar of applause. Monsieur Dior, in an immaculate pale grey suit, his face glistening with heat and fatigue, had stepped forward to bow his thanks. Judy paused as she unfastened a gold necklace from a model wearing only a feather hat and garter belt. The head dresser visibly relaxed. 'Not so loud as '47 but louder than last July,' she pronounced. Slowly they all grinned; then Monsieur Dior appeared in the dressing rooms and an orgy of kissing started.

'I feel like a broken spring,' Judy said gloomily, five days later.

'Cheer up,' said Guy, who was lying on her bedroom floor with his bare feet propped on the bed. 'You always knew that your job at Dior was temporary.'

'Yes, but I *hoped* they'd keep me on.'

147

'You've still got a job until the end of February when Annie's assistant returns,' he pointed out, 'and you've got your grey flannel Dior dress, which would have cost over eight months' salary if you'd paid for it. If you're willing to go anywhere and do anything for the same pathetic salary as Dior paid you, you can work full time for me. The hotel says I can't continue working from here; they say it's not a sweat shop. So your first job is to find us two workrooms somewhere near here. No, don't kiss me while I'm drinking.'

Judy found an adequate, skylit studio two streets away from the hotel. She was now responsible for all nonmanufacturing work, saw clients, answered the telephone, did the bookkeeping and handled dispatch.

Guy designed, bought materials and supervised the workshop staff. The faithful José had now been joined by another seamstress; the new sewing hand's mother was a first hand at Nina Ricci so Marie had been trained since childhood to sew to a professional standard.

Judy was busier than she'd ever been, and happier. The buyers liked her because she didn't stand blankfaced, order book in hand, but talked and joked with them. She had a keen sense of the ridiculous and liked to make people laugh, even if she could only do it by making them laugh *at* her. A few people found this exuberance exhausting, and some found it difficult to accept her forthright attitude, for she was direct and said exactly what she thought. After watching her scold a buyer for not ordering one of their new jackets, Guy said, 'You might cultivate a little tact, Judy. Why can't you behave with the buyers as you do with Aunt Hortense's crowd – with a little more respect?' He was annoyed. 'I know you're just being straightforward, but the French do not understand it. They interpret you as "tough", which you aren't.'

'More's the pity,' said Judy, scowling at the clip of invoices marked 'overdue' that she held in her hand, 'and here is where I start. I'm going to be tough about payments. You can't afford to give these people credit. In the future they'll have to pay when they sign the order, and we won't process it until the cheque is in our account.'

'Selling on cash terms is a nice idea, but nobody in the garment business does it. I'll lose all my customers.'

'And a lot of bad debts,' said Judy. 'But cash was the way you started, remember? Your mother and all her Avenue George V friends paid in advance. If people want your stuff, why *shouldn't* they pay for it when they order it? Now is the time to find out whether they *really* want you – *before* you go bankrupt.'

Judy earnestly tried to look older than her age. She and Guy found their youth a grave disadvantage in business because nobody took the young seriously. 'I suppose it's just a nuisance to be endured,' Guy complained, 'like a breaking voice or General de Gaulle; in time it will pass.' In the meantime, Judy didn't wear teenage clothes; she grew her hair and wore it twisted up in an unbecoming French knot; she lived in her grey flannel Dior dress and wore big hornrimmed spectacles, hoping to project an air of age, distinction and respectability.

'*Ma chère*, you quite frighten me,' said Maxine. She had returned from her two years' training in London the day before and they were catching up on each other's news over breakfast in the Deux Magots. Maxine planned to ask her father for a loan to start a business.

A touch envious, Judy said, 'You're damn lucky to have a rich father.'

Maxine, dunking a croissant in her *café au lait*, said, 'Papa isn't rich; I couldn't have gone to Switzerland if Aunt Hortense hadn't paid. Papa is *comfortable*. I hope he'll guarantee a bank loan for me. I don't think he can afford to give me the money, but he'll still be taking a risk on me.' She took a large bite and flakes fell on the table as she mumbled, 'Guy is the one with a rich father.'

Judy put her cup down. She was astonished. 'Then why is Guy always so short of money?'

'First, because he wants to make it on his own and second, because, as you know, his papa disapproves of designers. He made it plain he wouldn't help Guy. So Guy wants to show his old man he can get along without him.'

Judy went straight back and asked Guy for a rise. Then they plunged into work for the July collection; they were showing a range of separates – jackets, skirts, pants and suits – each in three alternative colours, with one overcoat and one raincoat. Judy loved the colours of the new collection: subtle, seductive greys in pewter, silver, oyster and pearl blended with pale rose, burgundy, burnished chestnut, copper and bronze. Narrow toreador pants were worn with brilliant taffeta tops that had huge puffed sleeves. Judy's favourite was geranium taffeta worn with saffron velvet pants. Their smoke-grey overcoat, bias-cut like a cape, was also lined with geranium silk; the raincoat, of similar cut, was dark green gabardine lined in pink silk.

With this show Guy hoped to establish himself as a serious businessman, not just a young design prodigy playing at fashion. So this time they planned to present it in style, at the Plaza Athénée again, but with a professional stage manager in charge. It was expensive, but worth it.

For Guy, this collection was make or break.

～ II ～

FIVE days before the show, Guy burst into Judy's bedroom. Too tired to work for another minute, she had decided to have an early night before the inevitable last-minute rush of the show. She was leaning with her elbows on the window frame as a hot July breeze stirred the white lace curtains. The couple opposite had just started their nightly fight.

'They've been stolen! Everything's gone! Even the accessories! They've cleared every damn thing off the racks, six months' work has just *disappeared*! My whole collection has vanished from the workroom.'

'Have you told the police?' Judy demanded, after she realized he wasn't joking.

'Of course. Immediately. They sounded uninterested. Then I telephoned you, but the hotel phone was out of order so I ran around. Every damn thing has disappeared, but only clothes; what's odd is that the thieves didn't take my little silver coffee set or the typewriter or the bales of cloth or anything else valuable. Only the clothes.'

Together they ran back to the empty workshop. 'We'll have to get this door fixed tonight,' Judy said. 'We can't leave the cloth here for anyone to take.'

'I'll sleep here tonight,' Guy said wretchedly. Then the telephone rang and they both jumped. A man's voice asked for Judy.

Surprised, she took the receiver from Guy. 'Judy Jordan here.'

'If you want your clothes back by Friday it'll cost his dad eight million francs in cash,' the man said in French.

The line went dead. Judy looked at Guy. 'It's blackmail!' She repeated the man's message and added with awe, 'That's nearly twenty-nine thousand dollars they want.'

'How does he know we're showing on Friday?'

'Plenty of people know we're showing on Friday; everyone we've invited, in fact. Better call the *flics* again.'

They spent the rest of the evening with the police. Only Parisian police could appreciate the disaster that would result to a couturier from the absence of the forty-two missing garments that constituted Guy's entire collection. If he didn't show his clothes when the buyers were in Paris and buying, then he wouldn't get any orders for them. Apart from that, there was the question of Guy's prestige. Without doubt, all the important buyers and all the important press would be turning up at Guy's next show; Guy would look like a careless amateur to a group of important people with not a minute to waste during the fortnight of the collections. And—most important of all—there was the vital question of Guy's reliability. If he couldn't produce his own collection on time, then the buyers certainly wouldn't risk his being unable to deliver their orders on time. The rumour that he was 'unreliable' would be Guy's professional death knell.

Again and again, the police questioned Judy. Was mademoiselle sure that she had heard correctly? Could she describe the voice? Did either of them have any enemies? What was the business value of the collection, as opposed to the value of the clothes? And so on.

Eventually Judy and Guy returned to their hotel. A shopping bag hung on Judy's white china doorknob; inside was a geranium taffeta blouse slashed to ribbons. Horrified, she was holding the rags in her hand when the telephone by her bed rang.

'Got the red blouse? Good. Be at the café Rubis, by the meat market, at four tomorrow afternoon. They'll have a parcel for you.'

Two floors down, Guy had also found a shopping bag hanging on his door handle. Inside was a pair of saffron velvet pants roughly bisected.

'Do we tell the police?' asked Guy.

'Not yet,' Judy said, 'they'll only give us another hundred forms to fill in. Anyway, I think I'm their chief suspect. Let's try and get more information before we go back to the police. Let's try and analyse what little we know.'

Suddenly, she shook her head. 'Both telephone calls were for *me*. Why not you? Everyone knows when you're showing your collection, but very few people have heard of me or know where I live. Besides, I'm a foreigner – I can't describe a French telephone voice except to say whether it's a man, woman or child. So it must be someone we know! Someone in the workshop, or a buyer, a journalist perhaps, or even one of our suppliers ... Let's make a list of them from the order and delivery books and the press addresses.'

The next morning outside the workshop door was a parcel pencilled 'Judy'. It contained a topaz silk shirt ripped across the middle.

Guy was distraught. 'They're only showing us they're tough,' Judy reasoned. 'They won't cut up the whole collection or they won't have anything to sell to us. They've only destroyed two blouses and a pair of pants, not jackets. Maybe we'll have time to remake them. They're all made by Marie, aren't they?' She paused for a moment. 'Now that's interesting! Not *one* of these three garments was made by José. Perhaps someone who sews as exquisitely as José couldn't bear to slash her own work.'

Guy refused to believe that José, who had been with him since he started, would rob him. 'How about the cutter?' asked Judy, but Guy refused to believe that he could have been betrayed by any of his tiny staff, all of whom had seen how hard he worked, how much he worried and how careful he was not to be over-demanding of them.

Then Guy suddenly remembered, 'José's husband is a meat porter and the café Rubis is near the meat market! I once gave José a lift there to meet him. I took her in the delivery van. I don't suppose she'd remember.'

'Hardly a coincidence with the whole of Paris to choose from.'

At four o'clock that afternoon they walked into the café Rubis. As the door swung open, a blast of steamy noise hit them; violet neon lighting glared down from a ceiling supported by slim iron columns. Against a zinc bar leaned hennaed whores, bloodied, white-aproned butchers and meat porters with leather-bound wrists.

Without being requested, a plate of appetizers was put on the table before them – thick slices of aromatic spiced sausage, chunks of fresh ham and large green aspic cubes containing smoked tongue. For the next three hours they dawdled over black coffee, but nothing happened and no parcel was delivered. They grew increasingly anxious, nervous and depressed until Judy said, 'I'm going to telephone Aunt Hortense and ask her advice.'

Luckily Aunt Hortense was at home. Quickly, Judy told her story. There was a silence, then Aunt Hortense said, 'Wait until ten o'clock, then telephone me again and if nothing has happened, come around here.'

But at nine o'clock the waiter said, '*Vous-êtes Americaine, Mademoiselle Jordan? Téléphone.*'

She went to the phone booth at the back of the café, an upright, coffin-sized wooden box that smelled of old sweat and dead cigarettes. She grabbed the old-fashioned earpiece off the wall and crisply said, 'Judy Jordan.' *Concentrate*, she thought. Listen for the sound of his voice, write down the words as he speaks them. But there was no writing surface and one-handed she couldn't hold her notebook against the wall.

'Get the money tomorrow morning and put it in a plain white envelope, the sort that's used for letters. Then wait in your office. Make sure the money is unmarked because we'll check it. If you try any tricks with the cops, you won't hear from us until Thursday because we'll be busy with the shears.'

Judy left the foul-smelling booth and repeated the message to Guy. The voice had been fairly deep, a man's voice, a rough bark. She couldn't tell more, couldn't even guess if the voice was disguised.

'He said "shears", not "scissors"? Are you sure? Only workshop staff would do that,' said Guy, grim.

They hurried to Aunt Hortense's apartment. She was waiting

153

in the library and to their astonishment Maurice, the chauffeur, was sitting back in an armchair, legs comfortably crossed, sipping a whisky and soda. Guy and Judy both refused a drink. 'Then let's have some black coffee to keep us awake,' said Aunt Hortense. 'The staff have gone off for the night so I'll make it myself – the Nescafé, so practical.'

'I'll do it,' Judy said, and moved down the gloomy corridor that led to a kitchen.

When she returned with the tray of coffee, Judy was made to repeat her tale. Then Guy was asked to repeat the whole story, in case there was any slight difference that might provide a clue. After a thoughtful silence Aunt Hortense asked, 'Do you know where your staff live? Do they have the telephone? No? That's good. Let us visit this young seamstress, Marie, immediately. Guy can demonstrate agitation and pretend that he wishes to know how long it will take her to sew two replacement blouses and the pants. Any excuse will do; the point is to catch her by surprise at home.'

Marie, in a white cotton nightdress with her hair twisted up in curl papers, was indeed astonished by Guy's late call. She immediately asked him in and said she was prepared to sew, nonstop, all night until the replacement garments were finished.

'Cross her off the list,' said Guy, scrambling into the Mercedes. 'Now the cutter. I'll ask him if he's prepared to stay at the workshop tomorrow and work through the night.' Again, although it was now nearly midnight, Guy was invited in and the cutter immediately agreed to work throughout the following night.

'Cross him off the list. Now let's visit José.'

A clearly terrified José poked her head around the grey front door of her second-floor apartment. Guy asked if he could enter, but with agitation she demurred. At this hour she was not dressed so it was impossible, her husband was sleeping and she didn't want to disturb him, he had to get up early to be at the meat market by five in the morning. Guy said that he wanted her to try to remember whether any stranger had been in the workshop the previous week. José answered that the police had already asked her twice and she'd said that delivery boys and fabric salesmen were always in and out. Again Guy asked if he could come in, and again José refused, panic in her eyes. 'Tomorrow morning at the workshop I'll talk about anything you want but not now. It's too late. Not now, Monsieur Guy. I dare not wake him.'

Guy said good night, clumped off loudly down the passage, then tiptoed back and put his ear to the door crack. He could faintly hear low, staccato voices arguing. Furious, Guy felt sure that his clothes were inside the apartment and felt like breaking the door down. Shaking with rage and impotence, he walked around the block to the waiting Mercedes and reported to Aunt Hortense.

'What do you think, Maurice?' she asked.

'It's unlikely to be a buyer or a journalist or a supplier, Madame, it's too great a risk for a mere eight million francs. It's more likely to be someone with a low income – a delivery boy or a fabric salesman or one of the staff.'

'A delivery boy or a fabric salesman would never have said "shears",' Guy pointed out, 'but workshop staff never say any-thing else.' He hesitated. 'I once gave José a lift to the café Rubis. Her husband works in the meat market. If we are going to be negotiating in that café, he won't look out of place, because I expect he's always popping in and out, and even if somebody *did* notice him, I doubt they'd say anything to the *flics*; it's a tough sort of place.'

'But if the husband knows that you have taken José there he would be unlikely to use it.'

'I only dropped her outside; maybe she didn't mention it or maybe she's forgotten it. She's not a master brain, you know, and tonight she was terrified; she gabbled whatever came into her head first, she wouldn't let me in and she lied to me. She said her husband was asleep, but I heard them talking two minutes later. *Why* should she lie?'

'The fact that she lied, that she didn't let Guy inside, and that she goes to the café Rubis, which is a meat-market café, and that her husband is a meat porter apply to José and nobody else,' said Judy. 'Apart from that there is the odd coincidence that none of José's work has been ruined. She knows my name, she knows that I'm a foreigner, she must know that Guy's father is rich and she would certainly say "shears", not "scissors".'

'And what none of you saw except me,' added Guy, 'was how

terrified she was at the thought of letting me into her apartment tonight. She was gibbering with fright. I think she was terrified of me and even more terrified of her husband. But why should that be unless she's guilty?'

There was another thoughtful silence, then Aunt Hortense said, 'If we broke into their apartment when they weren't there, what would we have to lose if they were innocent? The police wouldn't prosecute unless José pressed charges, and in such circumstances I'm sure she would prefer the cost of a new front door and a large cash bribe by way of recompense. What is your opinion, Maurice?'

'I'm inclined to think she's guilty, Madame. I suggest a surprise attack at José's apartment, at the time of the arranged rendezvous to hand over the money. By ourselves, Madame. The police will not move fast enough.'

'Exactly my opinion. Oh, it's like old times! I'll drive the Mercedes as I used to. You and Guy can break in; you can hold off any attackers. Guy's job will be to get a window open, then throw the clothes out to Judy. She will be waiting on the sidewalk ready to stuff the clothes into garbage sacks and throw them into the Mercedes. If there's any trouble I'll drive off with the clothes and leave you to sort yourselves out. Wear low-heeled shoes, Judy, in case you have to run.' She turned to Guy. 'Maurice is very good at this sort of thing, but you *must* move fast. You'll only have five minutes, that's all you can count on. However, you'll be amazed at what you can do in five minutes.'

The next morning Judy and Guy went to the workshop as usual. While Guy played the part of a distraught designer, the staff started to work again. José – who really did look terrified – apologized to Guy for not letting him into her apartment the night before.

'Forget it, I shouldn't have come. I'd had a couple of drinks.'

Guy went to his bank where he obtained a few small bank notes, which he added to an envelope already full of plain white paper.

Back at the office, the sewing machines stopped whirring and everybody froze expectantly whenever the phone rang. The call came at midday, again for Judy.

'Be in front of the Odéon Cinema on the Champs Elysées at five minutes past five o'clock this evening. Come alone or we won't pick up. Face the photo stills display on the right-hand side of the cinema. Hold the money in a white letter-size envelope in your left hand down at your side. And do not move your head. The envelope will be taken from you. Don't move for five minutes after that.'

'How do we knew we'll get the clothes back?'

'We have no use for the clothes. Once we have the money, we'll send a message to tell you where we've stored the clothes.'

This was reported back to Aunt Hortense. 'Clever,' she said. 'The film probably ends at five, so there will be a crowd pouring out around Judy and their pickup will be in it. Judy would hardly feel the snatch and she certainly wouldn't be able to identify anyone. Of course, they have no intention of handing over the clothes; they're incriminating evidence. I expect they plan to dump them in the Seine. We had better plan the surprise attack.'

At a quarter to five that evening, Maurice parked the Mercedes two streets away from José's apartment and changed places with Aunt Hortense, who wore a navy coat, navy beret and enormous sunglasses. She turned to Guy, whose face was chalk-white, and cheerfully said, 'Justice depends on who is holding the scales. My dear, you have three things to remember. First, if you're caught by the police, say nothing, not even your name, just ask for my lawyer. Second, do *exactly* as Maurice says – he is in charge. Unless Maurice gives you an order, just do your own job and get out after five minutes. Ignore any fighting. With luck you'll hear me blow three blasts on my whistle when your time is up. And finally,' she added in a reasonable voice, 'remember that you're merely collecting your own property.' She put the car in gear with a crash as Maurice winced. 'We hit them at ten to five when they'll be most jumpy, when their thoughts will be at the Odéon.'

Upon reaching José's apartment building, Judy – also wearing sunglasses and a navy beret – jumped out of the car and stood on the pavement, a pile of garbage bags in her hands. Guy followed Maurice under the arch into the inner courtyard, up the stairs and along a dark, narrow corridor. Maurice looked around carefully, inspected the grubby, grey door, then put his ear to it. He felt the lock with the tips of his fingers and paused. He leaned casually against the wall opposite, lifted his left foot to the level of the lock, then gave it one vicious kick. The door flew open and Maurice charged in, flinging the door flat against the wall with his left arm, then throwing his back against it.

The shutters were down and the apartment was muggy and silent except for the noise of traffic outside. There was very little furniture – a flowered sofa and two armchairs, a standard lamp with a fake parchment shade, a sideboard, a few pictures of agonized saints hanging from the wall.

Maurice stuck his head out of the door and beckoned Guy in.

'You take the left room and I'll take the right.'

The right door led to a small, bare kitchen and a lavatory. The left door led to a large room containing a double bed with a crucifix hung above it, a small wardrobe, an ornate birds-eye maple dressing table with triple mirror and another fake parchment lamp, this one with maroon fringe. Leading off the bedroom was another smaller room. In the dim, shuttered light, Guy could see that it contained another small wardrobe, a kitchen chair and a single bed – upon which was piled his entire collection of clothes.

He gave a cry of triumph and wrestled open the shutters as Maurice dashed into the room.

Guy could see Judy two floors below and about fifteen feet away, anxiously looking up. He screamed at her. She heard immediately and dashed towards Guy's window. Aunt Hortense started up the motor and the Mercedes slowly followed Judy, then waited with the engine running.

Both men started hurling the clothes out of the window so they landed far too fast for Judy to stuff them into the bags. She wrenched open the near side door of the Mercedes and threw suits, dresses, hats and shoes into it as fast as she could pick them off the pavement. The few astonished passers-by watched motionless until Aunt Hortense gave three sharp whistle blasts. Judy jumped into the back of the car, throwing herself on top of the clothes, the two men ran out of the doorway and squeezed into the front seat of the Mercedes. Aunt Hortense stepped on the gas and took the first corner on two wheels, leaving a pink satin shoe and a green scarf fluttering on the pavement behind.

'Steady, Madame, steady!' Maurice said. 'We don't want a speeding ticket at this point.' But Aunt Hortense was enjoying herself. She drove at top speed to Guy's dry cleaner, where they left Judy with the clothes. Judy felt exultant as she never had before – she now knew the exhilaration of action. She had expected to be frightened but instead she had positively *enjoyed* it. And they had won.

'Nothing seems to be missing,' reported Guy, as Aunt Hortense drove to the workshop. 'Only the hat brims are wrecked.'

Aunt Hortense braked, then reluctantly yielded the wheel to Maurice. 'No need to mention anything to the police,' she said carelessly. 'They don't like breaking and entering. And they might want to keep the clothes as evidence. So why not let this remain yet another of their unsolved mysteries?'

Guy nodded, then raced upstairs, two at a time, hoping to catch José before she left for the night. The other two employees had already left and José was belting her beige raincoat. One look at Guy's face told her that she had been found out. Roughly he leaped across the room, caught hold of her wrist and dragged her to the telephone. 'If you don't want me to call the police, you'd better tell me why you did it and who helped you,' he said, tight-mouthed with fury.

'Let me go! You must be mad, Monsieur Guy, let me go. I'll scream.'

'Scream away – and someone will call the police.' She tried to free her wrist, tried to kick Guy, then jerked her head in despair towards the window as she and Guy fought. He panted, 'I'm not going to let you throw yourself out of the window, José, what good would that do? I don't want to hurt you, I only want to know what happened. I know it wasn't your idea. I know you didn't want to do it. We've got the clothes back. They were on the bed in the little bedroom in your apartment.'

Astonished, she stopped struggling and looked at him, frightened but wary. 'What good will it do me if you go to jail, José? I've got the clothes back. But I want to know what *happened*. If you tell me all I want to know, I *might* not tell the police. But if you don't come clean I'll call the *flics* straightaway, and that'll mean prison. So tell me the truth, José. It was your husband's idea, wasn't it?'

'I don't know what you mean.' There was a pause.

'We found the clothes in your apartment.'

José burst out, 'It *wasn't* my man.' She paused again and Guy jerked her towards the telephone. 'No! It was his pal André – he's a pickpocket. I've never liked him. My man would never have tried this by himself. Oh, Mother of God, what's going to happen to us now?'

'And who else helped you?'

'No one else! No! Put the phone down, Monsieur Guy! I'll tell you! There was no one else.'

'Was it this André who telephoned?'

'Yes, yes, it was André who phoned.'

'Liar!' He yanked at her wrist until she started to whimper again, but she still looked surly and wouldn't speak. 'André would not have said "shears". One more lie and I call the *flics*.'

She burst into tears again. Guy shook her shoulders but she only howled louder. However, when he picked up the telephone she stopped in midshriek and told him the rest of the story. It was very simple.

At five o'clock that afternoon, her husband had been waiting fifty yards from the cinema in the Champs Elysées because he hadn't trusted his pickpocket friend. Their plan was that after snatching the money both of them should dive into the métro, catch a train at random, get out and find a park. They would wait until dark, when there would be few people around, and then divide the money. José's husband then planned to post his share of the money addressed to himself, *poste restante*, at his local post office. When he felt safe, he would collect the money.

Guy could only whisper, he was so furious, so weak with rage. 'Get out,' he croaked, 'and never, never, never come around here again or I'll call the police immediately.'

José burst into fresh tears and fled.

Within twenty-four hours, the story of Guy's kidnapped and returned collection was known to the entire fashion trade of Paris, and although he denied the story to reporters, the intriguing tale drew many more journalists to his collection than might otherwise have seen it.

That collection established Guy as a serious designer to be watched, not just a rich brat dabbling in fashion. Judy suddenly found that dealing with the press was almost a full-time job.

The only person to publicize an accurate story of the theft was Empress Miller, who was so charming, so disarming, so unobtrusively efficient that she always found out the truth – which was why Judy was a little afraid of her.

～ 12 ～

THE next two years were breathlessly busy but packed with excitement. Success invariably involved money problems until Guy obtained support from an unexpected source – his bank manager. Having studied Guy's financial history and the profit and loss projections, his bank manager – unprompted – telephoned Guy's father and said that it seemed a pity to turn his back on a potential money-making business simply because it had been started by his own son. The result was that the bank agreed to back Guy, and his father – quite glad to be able to drop his dogmatic stance – guaranteed the loan. Nevertheless, Guy was still determined not to expand simply because he had enough orders to do so.

'I'm not interested in short-term turnover but in long-term stability,' he explained to Empress Miller, who was wedged into a creaking conical cane chair perched on three thin black metal legs. Their new, modern office not only had an elevator and a tiny reception area, it also had a picture-window view of the grey rooftops and chimney pots of Paris – now covered with January snow – and a louvred cupboard, inside which was fitted a compact little kitchen. Judy hovered with the coffee pot as Guy answered Empress Miller's questions. 'What I eventually want is to establish a small, good-quality ready-to-wear collection. There's no RTW fashion in Europe, as there is in the States, only cheap, manufactured garments. But on the other hand, in the States there are no name designers – which is why your manufacturers buy their designs from Paris. I want to combine the two operations.'

'Yes, that's quite a good idea, Guy.' Empress always praised with caution, although she did not hesitate to criticize in a manner that ranged from mildly ironic to downright acid. But she was always fair, and when she didn't like something, she explained exactly why.

Her neat blonde head bent over her notebook. 'How does it feel to be so successful when you're so young? To have come so far in only a couple of years?'

Guy wriggled on his purple canvas womb chair, suspended on a thin, black metal butterfly frame. 'That's the question that everybody asks me, but you might as well ask me what it's like to be a dog or a university student or a post office messenger. I am who I am, and there's no getting away from it, and I don't know what it's like to be different. I'm a fashion designer, just the way someone else is an accountant. I started young because it worked out that way and because I wasn't interested in anything else.' He looked reflectively at the orange ceiling. 'If you're going to do something really well, I suspect that it has to be to the exclusion of everything else. And I *haven't* been an overnight success. I'm twenty-six and I've been working hard in fashion for ten years. It's simply that people suddenly *realized* it overnight. I suspect that most overnight successes are the same.'

'Nevertheless, Wool International went out on a limb for you with your last collection.'

'And so did I for them. My entire collection was made from wool and nothing else.'

Not without some of the noisiest rows I have ever participated in, thought Judy, who had insisted on this publicity-attracting theme.

Empress raised her eyebrows in polite query and Guy explained. 'Wool jersey drapes well and is flattering to the figure – synthetic fabrics tend to be either too stiff or too limp.' He heaved himself out of the purple canvas sling, pulled a bolt of dark green wool from the rack, then deftly draped and pinned the fabric around Judy, an old favourite trick to demonstrate his point. 'See what I mean? And look at the colour – it glows, it has depth, because a natural fibre absorbs colour better than a synthetic.'

'Ow,' said Judy, 'a little less depth to the pins please.' Guy finished his work and stood back.

'See how that's going to *flow* as she walks?' The pinned material had taken the shape of a coat, flared at the back like a bullfighter's cloak. It was cut on the same lines as that mulberry coat he'd just finished for Maxine, hanging on the rail by the door, ready for them to take to her this evening. Judy was looking forward to a couple of peaceful days in the country, tramping the frozen, silent woods by day and lying in front of a crackling log fire in the evening.

'How does Pierre Mouton feel about wool?' Empress suddenly asked, looking him straight in the eye.

How did she know? Guy wondered. The Belgian manufacturer would never have told Empress of their plan, and the only other person who knew it was Judy. It had to be a factory leak. You couldn't keep a damned thing quiet in this industry, everybody knew everything within five minutes.

'The buzz is that you're producing a new RTW collection and it's being manufactured outside Brussels by Pierre Mouton. You'll show the RTW at the same time as you show your summer couture collection, then start selling the next day so that RTW garments will be selling before any couture customer can get her clothes fitted, let alone finished.' Empress never took her eyes off Guy's face. 'Of course this *might* turn out to be professional suicide on your part, because all your couture customers will be furious, but I can see that it could be a daring new way of linking RTW to couture designs. Do you agree?'

Guy stared at her. How *did* she know? No factory hand could possibly know that. They had calculated that the couture customers wouldn't be irritated by the RTW collection if they were offered first choice of the RTW garments. And the RTW wasn't a copy of the couture collection. He had designed two collections calculated to overlap, rather than have one a cheap copy of the other.

'Pierre Mouton has always bought from me,' Guy said, affecting calm, 'but you know that his factories aren't geared up to produce boutique-quality clothes.'

Empress looked at him sharply. 'You haven't answered my question.'

'If what you say were true, you know I couldn't answer it. Pierre Mouton is one of my best customers. That's all I'm prepared to say.'

'Well, that wraps it up,' Empress said gaily, snapped her notebook shut and turned to Judy. 'Now I'd *love* another cup of coffee. It's a joy to get a good cup of coffee in Paris. Sometimes I suspect that they're still making it out of ground acorns as they did during the war.'

'It's because the French are so stingy that they won't use enough coffee. The secret is simply to use twice as many beans as they do,' said Judy. She was happy to talk about anything to get the conversation away from Pierre Mouton. 'But you can't do anything about French milk,' she said. 'I don't think French cows have blood in their veins. I still sometimes *long* for a glass of real American milk. I still get homesick for silly little things like that, although I've now been away for six years.'

She got homesick for bigger things than milk. However long she lived in Paris, however much she loved it, she suspected that her character was too basically American to allow her to settle in Europe forever. She sometimes wondered if that was the reason why she never seemed to fall in love like every other woman in Paris. She didn't want to marry a European. She went out with the eligible Frenchmen that Aunt Hortense produced from time to time, but she never seemed to feel entirely at ease with them except for darling Guy. The rest were so damned suave. But that was another worry: she was certainly having a terrific time, but she didn't want to play second string to Guy all her life. What had happened to her own career?

After Empress left, Judy shook off the sudden wistful yearning that she always felt after a visit from an American journalist who knew that a cheerleader wasn't a political position and who knew the difference between a milkshake and a soda.

Judy shook her fist at Guy, 'I didn't say a word! *You* practically told her. She only had to put two and two together, and she must have heard something as well. You *must* have told someone, you *must* have hinted. I knew you wouldn't be able to keep your lip buttoned. Pillow talk, I suppose.'

'I swear I haven't said a word, you're the one who chatters to journalists the whole time.' He grabbed her wrist, they lost their balance and both fell noisily on to the purple canvas sofa, pummelling each other, shrieking and laughing, flinging cushions – a deliberately childish reaction to the strain, the carefully casual mood of the interview.

'What will the night cleaner think if she comes in?' giggled Judy, looking up at Guy's tousled head.

'She will be totally confused, decide that all the gossip she's heard about me is a dirty lie, then she'll buy a pair of black fishnet stockings and make a pass at me. You know it's in the French blood, mixing the romantic with the practical. I'll never have a moment's peace.' They were giggling at the idea of their enormous sixty-year-old cleaner pouncing on slight Guy when the telephone rang. Judy scrambled to answer it. Strange, someone telephoning the office at nearly nine o'clock at night.

But it was only three in the afternoon in Rossville. She heard her father's voice and was immediately apprehensive. It could only mean a disaster; her father would only make a long distance call in a cataclysmic emergency.

'Is that you, Judy?' There was a lot of echo on the line. 'I've got some real bad news. It's your mother. Can you hear, Judy? You'd better come home.'

At two in the morning they were still sitting in Aunt Hortense's chilly library, Judy in a red wool dressing gown, Aunt Hortense in a fragile, green lace negligée under a mink coat. The central heating had shut down at midnight.

'Your mother may well recover. A cerebral aneurysm is terrible, but not always fatal.'

'It's not only that. I feel so guilty. I've been away six years.'

'But you told me that you wrote every week. And you were working hard. You were doing something that your mother was going to be proud of.'

'Oh, she never said a word, she never complained or asked me to go home, but however good the excuses, I know I simply didn't *want* to go home. Paris is more fun than Rossville. The weeks just dissolved into each other, it was all so exciting, and I felt that going anywhere near Rossville would be ... an emotional trap. I was frightened that once I got back, she'd ask me to *stay* – and I was afraid I wouldn't be able to say no.'

'Judy, your mother and you may not have much in common, but from what you've told me she realizes that. I don't think that she would have tried to stop you doing anything. I can't see that she ever has. She obviously loves you, just as you love her in your own way. This emergency proves it – you can think of nothing but flying back to her.'

'Prompted by guilt. Knowing that I haven't flown back in six years.'

'Unfortunately, I don't know what it feels like to be a mother, but if you were my child I would give you a good shake. Guilt is boring and pointless. You are going home to see your mother who is sick. Kindly do not overdramatize the situation. You will have a happy time with her; then you will return to Paris with her blessing.'

But Judy didn't return to Paris. After an agonizing twelve weeks, during which her mother hung between life and death, she slowly opened her eyes and saw her only daughter at her bedside. She tried to smile and whispered with the urgency of the very ill, 'That's all I wanted. To see you once again.'

'Oh, thank God, Ma, thank God.' She clutched her mother's shoulder and knelt at the bedside, to bring her face close to her mother. 'What can I do, Ma? What can I do to make you happy? What do you want? What can I give you?'

There was a moment's silence, then that weak whisper. 'I've always thought how wonderful and brave it was of you, Judy, to go off and see new things . . . I never could . . . I was always afraid . . . you're so different. I want to get to know you, I'm so proud of you . . . I want to know you before I die . . . I want to spend time with you . . . Please. Stay near by a while. I know I mustn't keep you in Rossville, but please . . . stay in America.'

Without a moment's hesitation, Judy promised.

~ 13 ~

THE offices of most working publicity agents do not look as if they are waiting for the *House and Garden* photographer to arrive, and this one was no exception, Judy thought – in fact, it was almost as dingy as the office where she'd first worked in Paris. Outside the grimy window on her left, girls in flowered dresses on the sidewalks of New York were getting the first wolf whistles of spring; inside, opposite the window, was a row of chipped, grey filing cabinets, on top of which magazines were stacked almost to the ceiling. The wall in front of her was covered with lavishly dedicated photographs of people who had been showbiz celebrities five or ten years ago. Hanging in one corner was last year's calendar. Someone had stopped tearing off the leaves at April 5, 1954. In front of it was a grey metal desk stacked with old newspapers, more magazines and metal baskets full of old press releases. A tall, loose-limbed blonde woman, wearing a scarlet suit and ludicrously high-heeled black patent shoes, perched on one corner of it. She looked as if she belonged in a detective story.

'I guess very few people actually *decide* to be a press agent and study it in college,' said the blonde. 'You just suddenly find you're in it. I was a reporter until the paper folded. I was on unemployment when a friend told me that the Ice Follies was looking for an advance man. I said, "What's an advance man?" and the next week I was in Philadelphia, being one.' She dragged on her cigarette. 'Just why do you want to be in PR?'

'I've done some publicity work in France. I worked fairly closely in Paris with Wool International and they suggested I apply here for a job.'

Suggested, did they? Didn't this child realize that the head of WI in Paris had telephoned Lee & Sheldon to see if she could be fitted into the agency's New York office? And when the agency had hesitated, it had been pleasantly suggested to them that WI would like this unknown Miss Jordan to work on their account. Simultaneously, the agency president had received a phone call from Empress Miller herself, saying that she had worked closely with Miss Jordan, whose understanding of haute-couture was far greater than her years might suggest. Empress always underplayed things, but quite obviously this kid had friends. And although she was very young, her experience was certainly impressive. So why did she want an assistant's job? Why all this exasperating internal reshuffling just to fit in Miss Jordan?

But Judy knew she needed on-the-job experience before she could handle an account in a New York office. She didn't want to be an executive secretary; she wanted to bide her time while she sorted out her Seventh Avenue contacts and saw whether there was any chance of getting a job like the one she'd held with Guy. PR seemed a good way to mark time while looking around.

She had stayed in Rossville for seventeen weeks, until her mother recovered – as much as she was likely to; she would never regain the complete use of her left arm and her mouth still drooped a little.

Although Judy still felt guilty about having left home, she had now made peace with her mother and as much peace as she was ever likely to make with her father, who bragged in a rather touching manner about how Judy had 'flown all the way from Paris, France, *the very next day*.' A child's presence in time of crisis was a form of local prestige, based on the distance that the child had to travel and how fast the child covered it.

To Judy, the town felt as claustrophobic as ever. She knew everyone, their faces, their family, their outlook and their future. The men were uninteresting, the women walked around in shapeless winter coats or shapeless pastel prints. They could only talk about recipes, the weather, their children, their last pregnancy and the last pregnancies of all their friends. The people of whom they spoke rarely had a name. Instead, they were identified by the name of their parents and where they came from, as in, 'I hear Tom – Steven's boy – is going to marry Joan MacDaniel's girl,' or 'She's the MacDaniel girl who's marrying that fellow from Quantico.'

Again, Judy felt that she had to get out – and now it wasn't only for her own self-protection. She had to earn enough to pay for the therapist and her mother's enormous medical expenses, which her father's insurance had only partly covered. She wrote to Guy and her other French friends to tell them why she couldn't return to Paris, and she also sent a note to Empress Miller asking if she could suggest a suitable job in New York.

Guy replied with an immediate, extravagant telegram: DESOLATED LOSE MY RIGHT HAND STOP UNDERSTAND YOUR MOTIVES STOP REFUSE END RELATIONSHIP STOP HOPE YOUR NEW CONTACTS HELP ESTABLISH ME AMERICA STOP HURRY HURRY STOP ONE BILLION KISSES STOP GUY

Once in New York Judy rented a studio on East 11th Street, sent out three hundred resumés, and had telephone interviews with seventeen people, only three of whom wanted to see her when they heard she had had no previous experience in America. At times, thinking of her exciting job and the friends she had left in Paris, Judy's shoulders sagged; she felt alone and that she had thrown away a promising future for a sentimental promise.

Then she received a note from Empress Miller suggesting that she contact Lee & Sheldon, and a day later a letter suggesting the same thing arrived from Wool International in Paris.

'You realize you would have to do a lot of travelling?' asked the blonde in the scarlet suit. 'Basically you would assist me on the WI account. We forecast fashion trends to the press, send out news releases, prepare press kits with photographs and sketches and twice a year, after the Paris collections, we coordinate the wool models that WI has commissioned from French couturiers. We promote any wool copies that are being produced by American manufacturers and generally plug the message that wool is wonderful and they'd better buy more.' She swung an elegant nylon leg and lifted one eyebrow in query.

'I've handled all that,' said Judy. 'On a small scale, of course.'

'We also appear on TV and give talks on wool, illustrated by photographs and sketches. None of it is nearly as glamorous as it sounds, by the way, not even taking fashion editors to lunch.'

'I'm used to that,' Judy said with growing confidence.

The blonde shifted position, started to swing the other shapely leg and said, 'Press agents spend their careers explaining why their client is not an asshole. And mostly they are, of course.' She lit another cigarette. 'If you join us, we would want you to handle the truck shows. The models we buy from the Paris collections immediately tour the best stores in every important town in America. We would expect you to arrange the shows, book the models and then travel with them, looking after the girls and the clothes, carrying publicity materials, photographs, display cards, samples of the fabrics being used and inexpensive give-aways. You would be booked into a different town every day of the week for four weeks twice a year. D'you think you could stand it?'

'Try me.'

'Let's both try a martini.'

*

Judy had never worked so hard in her life. Her boss, Pat Rogers, was merciless. An ex-journalist, she was demanding; she expected everyone else to work as fast as she did and she was a superb trainer. Judy quickly realized that if a thing wasn't absolutely right it was *wrong* – nearly right was not good enough.

'The easy way to be a good press agent,' Pat told her, 'is to realize that you can't buy good coverage with a free lunch. You have to have a good story. This isn't Paris, kid. You have to fight for every inch of coverage because the competition is fierce.'

She leaned back, crossed her feet on the desk and tilted her chair. 'You're trading services. What a journalist wants is the facts and fast, and maybe in return he'll publicize your product; that's the basic deal. There are *very* few really good press agents and they're mostly ex-journalists, which is why they understand what's needed. An ex-journalist knows what *news* is. News is what nobody knew yesterday, and if a story isn't news, then it won't rate good news coverage, however interesting.'

One day Pat said, 'About time you learned to write, kid. Don't mess around with correspondence courses. Go sleep with a journalist for a couple of months. No? Well, clear the decks for Saturday, get the Kleenex out, come around to my apartment and I'll teach you. I am the Saturday School of Compressed Journalism, smallest of its kind in the world.'

After two Saturdays of crumpled paper and insults, Pat stretched and said, 'You've got the rough idea, kid. People either pick it up fast or not at all, mostly not at all. You're impatient, which helps; you're easily bored, which also helps; you'll never be Ernest Hemingway, but for straight factual reporting all you need is practice. Now let's have a martini.'

That September, Judy set off on her first tour, travelling two days ahead of the show to check arrangements and spread the news, just like the carnival advance men of years ago. She lugged suitcases full of advance material, straightened out the inevitable snarls in arrangements, flattered, soothed and sweet-talked her way around the country and from the moment that she staggered out of bed in the morning to the moment that she fell into the next one in the next town that night, she thought only of wool.

It was a tough and lonely life, but during the day she was too busy to care and at night she was too tired. Her life was spent rushing from airport to cheap hotel room to offices and TV studios, then back to the airport and on to the next airport. Her tiny budget didn't enable her to stay in good hotels. Try as she might, she couldn't stretch her personal travel allowance to cover her expenses as well as her food, and she couldn't get the accounts department even to discuss the matter, so she started cheating on her expenses, until Pat said that the executive vice-president had pointed out that her telephone bill was bigger than his, at which Judy exploded. She liked to eat; the accounts department never allowed for the speed with which she had to cover a town in one day, or for any deviation from her theoretical routine. She suggested that the next trip be handled not by her but by one of the junior accountants and they could see how *he* made out.

Pat said, 'I can see you enjoy shouting, but it's not the way to win an argument,' and went off to shout at the chief accountant, after which Judy's expenses were raised. It was still a lonely, dyspeptic life, but at least she ate.

And she produced results.

Less than six months later Judy was able to persuade Pat to fly Guy to New York to discuss a truck show. Pierre Mouton accompanied him to investigate the possibilities of selling in the United States. Guy's new collection of separates covered the blue segment of the spectrum from lavender to deep purple. The unconstricting clothes projected a pulled-together style that was easy to move in, made a woman feel as if she wasn't wearing anything and enabled her to look her best without feeling self-conscious. He had used only luxurious fabrics and refused to produce a really cheap line. 'One good suit is a better investment for a woman than three so-so suits,' he said firmly to Judy as they leaned against the boat rail.

From the green-gold water, Wall Street looked like strips of tickertape stretching towards the sky. 'This is the obligatory tourist's starter trip,' Judy had explained, 'down the Hudson River, past the Statue of Liberty, then up the East River to circle Manhattan. After that, I'm going to march you right around this city. You have no idea how I love it.'

'More than Paris?'

'Different.' Within a week of being in New York, Judy had decided that this marvellous, glittering, exhausting place was where she belonged and that she would never leave it. She felt personal and possessive about the city in a way she had never felt about Paris. 'I love New York and I'm starting to love my job; life isn't quite so hectic and it's a good deal more comfortable now that I travel with the show and not ahead of it.' She turned towards him, squinting into the late afternoon sun. 'Incidentally, Pat wants to meet us for dinner so we can discuss touring your next collection. I warn you, she wants you to travel with it – a genuine French Frenchman wiz faseenateeng accent. They'll keel over at the mere *sound* of you in Cleveland.'

'I wouldn't mind a free trip around the States.'

'Don't expect a vacation.' Judy turned her back to the water, leaned against the rail and wagged a finger at him. 'Certainly the trips look wonderful when you see the models being greeted at airports, with armfuls of cellophane-wrapped roses as they step into the limo, but that's all baloney. What really happens is that we arrive on the last night plane – six people and thirty-eight suitcases – and we're met by a truck at the airport. I drag them out of bed at dawn, then one model will zip off to do the TV breakfast show and the rest get ready for a store show where the entire fashion-conscious audience is wearing tired-looking trouser suits or limp raincoats. Then we're interviewed by every newspaper in town, and after that there's the afternoon store show, then TV again, then off to the airport. If you travel on in the evening you arrive too late to eat, and if you travel on the dawn plane there's no time to eat or drink anything anyway, except those packets of Nescafé in the hotel bedroom. I tell you, after a truck tour you need two days in bed with the telephone off the hook while your nerves and your stomach sort themselves out.'

She paused and watched the seagulls swoop over the grey water. 'It's a nonstop routine of packing and unpacking. The poor dresser has to get all the garments pressed before each show, then she has to lay out the accessories. They're real saints, those dressers!' she snorted. 'But the models are devils, and the sexual complications never end. We had two lesbians on the last trip, they couldn't keep their hands off each other, even on the catwalk ... Then there's the food problem. Of course the models are terrified of putting on weight and the really skinny ones are the worst – they're all either on some diet of dried seaweed and lime flowers, which they expect the hotel to stock, or else they order champagne and caviar and try to charge it to room service. We always tell the hotels that we won't pay extras, and the girls know it. Still, they sulk when they find that they either have to pay cash for the caviar or send it back.'

'So tell me more about these poor thin girls and their sexual complications. Surely they can't *all* be so tiresome.'

'I suppose that some of them are basically sweet girls, but they lead very insecure lives. They're totally exterior-oriented – they don't even enjoy their good looks because they constantly worry about losing them. *No* model thinks she's good-looking. Not surprising! They're constantly being auditioned, even the famous ones, for some assignment, and if twenty girls are auditioned, then nineteen will be turned down. They have to put up with endless rejection, and consequently they're very vulnerable.'

She pulled her cream knitted cap down to cover her ears. 'Some girls live on uppers to cut their appetite – so they're edgy and take offence at the slightest thing. Or else they can't sleep because we move on every night to a different hotel, so they take sleeping pills. Then I can't get them up in the morning.' She giggled. 'Of course, sometimes I can't get them up because they aren't *there* to get up. They'll have picked up some guy in the bar and disappeared. Just keeping the photographers off them is a full-time job.'

'You can't frighten me.' Guy tickled Judy's button nose. 'Of course I'll tour. We'll go together. You helped me to become a success in France. This time, Judy, I'm going to see that you stay a permanent part of the success! You won't escape from me so easily again . . . Unless you insist on wearing such ridiculous hats.'

He tugged off her cream knitted cap and threw it into the East River. 'That is the sort of thing my grandmother used to keep her boiled eggs warm. First thing tomorrow we buy you a beautiful fox fur hat from Saks. Only tiny babies wear that sort of knitted thing.'

Much to his surprise, Judy burst into tears.

~ PART THREE ~

14

THE frost hung white lace curtains outside the window.

Elizabeth hated to get up in the freezing winter. The sky was still dark and cold, a dim sprinkling of snow topped the apple trees and beech hedge around the garden. She wanted to stay safe and snug under the feather-filled quilt, luxuriating in the warmth as she listened to her family downstairs.

'You'll be late, Elizabeth,' shouted Maman from the bottom of the stairs.

Eyes still shut, the small child put her bare feet on the rug and stumbled to the foot of the carved wooden bed, where her clothes lay neatly folded on the red-lacquered lid of the blanket chest. Sleepily she fumbled into thick black tights, heavy, wool winter underwear, blue-checked frock, navy apron and then she sat on the rug to lace up her stout, stiff black boots. In 1955 this was the typical winter school uniform of a Swiss child.

She climbed on to the chair by the window, rubbed clear a chilled glass pane and peered out at the weather. There was no snow today, as light started to show above the jagged black mountains on the other side of the Alpine valley. Below her, dimly visible beyond the snow-encrusted wooden balcony of the chalet, was the garden. Underneath her window, the first floor balcony ran right around the chalet. Under the fish-scale tiles of the roof, an old prayer had been carved

GOD BLESS ALL WHO LIVE HERE
1751

The child jumped down from the window, clumped in clumsy boots across the wooden floor of the corridor and flung open the door. Her foster brother's small room faced the mountain, and very little light filtered through the ancient windowpanes.

'Get up, get up, lazybones.' She laughed. She flung herself on the patchwork quilt as an indignant head emerged from it. 'You haven't fetched the bread from the bakery.'

'Felix said he'd bring it up,' mumbled Roger, sleepily.

'I don't believe you. Felix is on late duty this week.'

Felix was the Hungarian head receptionist at the Hotel Rosat in Château d'Oex. In 1939, Felix had been dragged from his father's farm and conscripted into the Hungarian army, then he had been forced into the German army to fight the Russians on the Eastern front. After the fall of Budapest, Felix's division fled towards Germany, at which point Felix had managed to escape into Switzerland. Felix chopped the wood and did other jobs that were too heavy for a woman; in return, Maman did his washing and sewing.

'I tell you he's coming up early, he promised.' Elizabeth rushed off, her boots clattering down the wooden stairs to the kitchen, where they always sat and ate in winter to save fuel. Maman was heating chocolate in a saucepan on top of the green, enamelled stove.

'Roger hasn't got the bread for breakfast.'

'Well, it doesn't matter, Elizabeth, I'll just flick water across yesterday's loaf and reheat it in the oven. You won't be able to tell the difference, Miss Telltale.' Her foster mother's dark hair, still in a loose braid, not yet coiled in its neat daytime bun, hung down the back of her white flannel nightgown. Her red hands, skin flaking, placed a white pot of hot chocolate on the table.

Maman's husband had been killed on the Diablerets glacier eight years before. A ski guide, he had been leading a party across the glacier when they ran into bad weather. The party had been lost in the snow. Angelina Dassin was left with a small baby, which prevented her from working as a live-in maid as she had before her marriage. Almost penniless, she took the first job she was offered, scrubbing floors at the local hospital. In the evenings and on weekends she embroidered lace-trimmed white blouses for the tourist souvenir shop. For three years life had been very hard. Then she was asked to foster a baby girl who had been born at the hospital. The extra money meant that Angelina was able to stop her back-breaking cleaning job, stay cosily at home with two babies and concentrate on her embroidery.

Elizabeth was brought up as one of the Dassin family, but she was always told by Angelina that she had another mother, a *real* mother, and that one day – when she was older – her real mother would come and take her home. Those were her thoughts as every night Angelina softly sang '*Au clair de la lune, mon ami pierrot*' and other nursery rhymes as she rocked Elizabeth to sleep and the pines rustled outside in the dark garden.

In fact, Angelina knew little more than Elizabeth about this mythical mother. A monthly cheque came in an anonymous envelope from a bank in Gstaad. Angelina always began her laborious reports, '*Chère madame,*' hoping that by now the poor child was married, but the replies gave no information about the sender. There were merely questions about the child's progress that were duly answered in the next report.

At first Elizabeth imagined her real mother as a kind of angel in a lace nightgown. Every night after saying her prayers on the rag rug she would whisper: '*Bonne nuit, vraie maman.*' Then she hoped that her real mother was a fairy princess and the reason that she couldn't come to see Elizabeth was that she was sleeping in a forest glade until the fairy prince woke her with a kiss. How Elizabeth wished he'd hurry up! She hoped that the forest wasn't too damp and that there weren't any ants.

Roger teased her that *vraie maman* was a witch woman with long fingernails and no teeth or hair, but Elizabeth refused to believe him, and when she overheard, Angelina, for once, scolded Roger. Such unkindness to his sister when he knew that if it wasn't for her five hundred francs a month, Angelina would be on her knees with acres of wet ward floor in front of her instead of sitting in a warm kitchen and embroidering blue edelweiss around heart-shaped necklines.

'Roger said Felix is coming up early,' Elizabeth said, as she gulped her hot chocolate.

'Then I'd better dress quickly – hurry up, little one.' Almost in one movement, she twisted Elizabeth into her scarlet coat, guided her fingers into the gloves that were attached by a tape threaded through the sleeves, tugged on her red wool helmet, wound a thick scarf around her neck and kissed her goodbye.

Outside, Elizabeth stood on tiptoe at the top of the steps, hopefully searching for Felix. She shivered, her breath froze on her scarf, her eyes watered and ran with tears that immediately turned to ice. A piercing whistle echoed across the mountains as the blue train to Montreux swished along the track, steel-pointed plough in front to clear the early morning snow. Elizabeth heard the low lulling noise of the cows, the clanging milk pails and the clatter from the next door farm; she sniffed the straw and dung. Except for this farm, the Dassin chalet was the last one on the mountain track. Beyond and above it, dark pine forest stretched to the summit rocks, now covered in January snow; below the chalet, the garden fell away down the mountain slope towards the frozen river that divided the snow-covered valley. The white blanket was broken only by that winding black line and the sharp dark line of the railway.

Trudging up the mountain track from the village, she saw the bulky figure of Felix, a large basket over one arm. Shrieking greetings, the frail child slithered down the track to meet him. 'Felix, will you be here when I come back from school? Will you tell me stories? Will you mend my doll, her arm's hanging loose? Will you make me another igloo?'

'Yes, yes and yes, if you're not late for school.'

'Oh, I promise.'

The skinny little girl slithered and slid down the hard-packed snow track; she just managed to slip through the glass doors of the village schoolroom and dodge past the blackboard as Tante Gina rang the pewter handbell. The clock chimed seven-thirty as Elizabeth scrambled to her place on the splintered wooden bench that would feel harder and harder as the day wore on, until all the blue-apron-clad children perched upon it wriggled with numb discomfort.

After prayers, the whole school always chanted their multiplication table, '*Un fois deux, deux. Deux fois deux, quatre.*' Afterwards, as it was Wednesday, Elizabeth climbed the stairs to Tante Simone's sitting room for her special English lesson. She also had a special French lesson but that was on Friday.

Tante Simone's sitting room smelled of biscuit crumbs, mothballs, eau de cologne and old ladies. Dark brocade wallpaper was punctuated by the monochromatic serious stares of previous pupils. Below these photographs stood an old upright black piano, while the centre of the room was dominated by a round table covered with an ink-stained Indian shawl and surrounded by faded blue velvet chairs, a white lace antimacassar draped over each high back. On one of these chairs sat Elizabeth's favourite person.

Mademoiselle Sherwood-Smith taught Elizabeth to chant traditional nursery rhymes and brought her books about a rabbit called Peter, a bear called Rupert, and the battle-scarred bloody history of the English kings and queens. She helped Elizabeth to assemble the big jigsaw puzzle that was a map of England and played a fierce game of racing demon, which was how Elizabeth learned to count in English.

Elizabeth wasn't nearly so keen on her special French lesson. She had learned to talk in the lilting French Vaudois accent of the canton, which sounded a bit like cows in a barn, as the voice was always lowered in the middle of a sentence, then lifted upwards at the end of it in a gentle, musical moo. Mademoiselle Pachoud was much older than Mademoiselle Sherwood-Smith and she walked with a stick because of her bad leg. She was French from France, and she gave Elizabeth elocution lessons so that she should speak classic French, not a Swiss dialect. But after Elizabeth started to do this, the other children teased her.

They pounced on her again at midday as Elizabeth wound herself into her outdoor clothes before going home for the midday meal; one of the big girls snatched her balaclava helmet and tantalizingly dangled it just beyond her reach. Elizabeth, small for her age, jumped and jumped for it, until she was out of breath and scarlet-faced with exertion and suppressed tears.

'See, you're not so smart, skinny, in spite of your special lessons; no wonder nobody wants to be your special friend, you stuck-up show-off.'

Elizabeth jumped and grabbed again but the scarlet wool was jerked away. 'Think you're better than us but you're not. I heard my maman say that you're a *bastard. Skin*ny *lit*tle *bas*tard, *stuck-*up *skinny little bastard.*'

Two other girls took up the taunting cry and danced around Elizabeth, tweaking her long dark plaits, until suddenly the exasperated small child put her head down and butted one of her tormentors in the stomach. Caught off guard, the girl fell to the ground, shrieking, just as Mademoiselle Gina entered the cloakroom.

'She pushed me over, Elizabeth *pushed* me, Mam'selle.'

Mademoiselle Gina looked at Elizabeth, scarlet-faced, teeth

bared, leg drawn back, ready to kick. 'Shame on you, Elizabeth, go home immediately.'

Later, over their midday soup, Mademoiselle Gina spoke to her sister. 'More trouble with Elizabeth fighting again.'

'Oh, dear, you don't think they tease her?'

'Even if they do, there's no need for violence. There's plenty of teasing in the playground, but Elizabeth is the only child who uses her fists. She fights like a boy.'

'Well, her foster brother Roger is more of her friend than any of the girls; I expect he's taught her some rough tricks. It's a pity she seems so different from the other girls, somehow an outsider. They feel suspicious and ill at ease with her, that's why she's so difficult and that's why she has no close friends.'

'No excuses, Simone, the child is very touchy, always ready to suspect an insult and overhasty to avenge it. She shouldn't react so violently.'

'It's only when she thinks she's being unfairly treated that she loses control of herself; then she needs the action to get rid of her resentment. Five minutes later she's always calm again and, apart from that, she's a quiet pupil, very conscientious.'

'Yes, well, she can't afford to have such a hasty temper, no matter what the reason. Life is not going to be easy for that child . . .'

As Elizabeth ran home through the hushed snow, the cold calmed her turbulent feelings. Holding tight to the iron railing, she clambered, one foot at a time, up the high stone steps to the front door, which was above the winter snowline. She stood on tiptoe to bang the iron door knocker, then bent down to push open the letter box and sniff; diced potatoes with bacon and onion chopped into it. She always felt safe as soon as she was home.

Careful not to let the snow in, Angelina opened the door a crack. As usual, she was wearing a blue denim dress, blue apron, long shapeless black cardigan and black boots; she never wore makeup or jewellery apart from her wedding ring.

'Maman, what's a bastard? That's what they called me at school.'

Angelina looked harassed as Elizabeth stamped the snow off her boots. 'It's a silly name for people who haven't got a father.'

'But Roger hasn't got a father, is he a bastard as well?'

'You can both have a father if you want one.' Elizabeth glanced up, perplexed, as Angelina pulled her gently into the sewing room and shut the door.

'Shhh. It's still a big, big secret. But who would you *choose* for a father?'

'A fairy prince.'

'No, someone you know.'

'Not Roger, he's not old enough . . . I know – *Felix!*'

'Right!'

Long dark hair and fingertips touching the cobbles, Elizabeth hung upside down in a yellow, striped bathing suit, her skinny legs wound around the ropes of the trapeze. 'Now swing around and up to sit on the bar,' Felix said. 'Now, over again, Lili, as high up the ropes as you can get . . . Good.'

Since he had married Angelina, eighteen months ago, Felix had taught the two children some of the tricks that he had practised with his brother long ago in Hungary.

'Now a little trampoline work, Lili,' he ordered, pulling the little green trampoline on to the grass. As he put Elizabeth through her paces, the setting sun slowly touched the peaks of the far mountains with a flushed red glow. Angelina leaned over the balcony to call them to supper. In front of her, a cloud of cream butterflies fluttered around the mirabelle tree and a light sweet scent rose from the pink-and-blue sweet peas that grew against the wooden lattice under the balcony. She watched Elizabeth grasp the man's hands; her thin legs swiftly ran up his thigh, then his hip, then sprang on to his strong shoulders. There she wobbled until she gained her balance, let go of his hands and slowly stood upright with knees slightly bent and arms outstretched.

'Can I walk?' called Felix.

'Not yet, I'm not ready . . . Ow, Felix, you brute.'

'Stop talking and concentrate, Lili. I want to see a beautiful leap off my shoulders and on to the trampoline with feet together and no sloppy finish.'

Obediently, the small girl flew through the air, bounced on the green canvas twice and then bounced off on to the grass. She landed with her feet slightly apart. Drat! She saw Angelina above her and waved, then the child wandered off to the wooden swing under the balcony where she lazily pushed herself backward and forward as she sniffed the summer. The warm odour of earth, garden roses and pine trees in the forest rose to meet the pungent richness of the hay and liquid manure. Summer was a honey-warm smell, autumn smells were sharper and smokier; autumn was the sour smell of fallen apples stored in the cellar to make pink jelly and applesauce, hazelnuts collected from the forest, and piles of rotting pungent leaves at the bottom of the garden begging to be stomped on, kicked and scattered.

Felix carried the trampoline into the cellar. Then he and Elizabeth clattered up the flight of open wooden steps that led up to the kitchen and supper. Roger was already sitting at the table. He had been swimming in a forest stream and on his way home he had filled his cap with small, wild strawberries.

'Almost as good as in Hungary,' Felix said approvingly, after a delicious meal of river trout. This remark was always greeted with jeers, but tonight he added, 'Before the 1939 war, *every* Hungarian restaurant – no matter how grand – had to feature on its menu a meal for one pengö; that's one Swiss franc. So long as he had *one* pengö, theoretically any old tramp could go in and eat, no matter how dirty he was; by law the restauranteur was supposed to serve him.'

Elizabeth climbed on to his lap, as she always did after supper, curling up like a kitten.

'Tell us about Gundels,' begged Elizabeth, who loved hearing his stories about the gaiety and romance of prewar Hungary.

'Well, Lili, I was just a young waiter, but oh, we saw such food. Pressed boar's head in aspic, cold pike with beetroot sauce and cucumber salad, shredded marrow in dill sauce, thimble egg dumplings, smoked sausage, rich red goulash, Transylvanian goose and pancakes stuffed to bursting with fluffy orange curd, sultanas and chocolate sauce . . .'

'Don't tell us about the food, tell us about the children and the parties in the park,' demanded Elizabeth, banging an imperious little fist on his chest.

'Well, Lili, you know that the Gundel family with their ten naughty children lived over the restaurant, and the restaurant was surrounded by trees, with two huge black iron gates at the front.'

'Get on to the party in the park,' Elizabeth shrieked with excitement.

'Well, the first fifty tables formed the outdoor beer garden – although we mostly drank white wine – and then the next fifty tables were for more expensive meals, and then, at the back, you walked up eight shallow stone steps on to the terrace where vines trailed down from the roof, and *that* was where the aristocracy ate. The whole of Hungary ate together in that garden to the music of the brass band in the beer garden and a romantic gypsy band near the terrace.'

'Show us how the gypsies played, Felix,' she called excitedly.

'They wore wonderful, bright Hungarian costumes.' The big man stood up, carefully put Elizabeth on his chair, draped his scarlet napkin around his neck, picked two twin-sprigged cherries from the bowl on the table and hung one over each of his ears; then he tied his red spotted handkerchief around his head and started to hop slowly around the kitchen table, like a great black bear playing an imaginary fiddle.

Elizabeth shrieked again with delight.

'Can we play the best night ever, Felix, oh, please?'

Felix looked at Angelina and asked permission with raised eyebrows. She laughed and nodded, whereupon the little girl tore out of the kitchen and dashed back in her petticoat, carrying two strips of white sheet and a traditional wide, red laceup belt. 'Start, Felix, start,' she cried with excitement, as Angelina indulgently knotted the two lengths of cotton over her skinny shoulders.

'The best night ever,' Felix said, stroking his long, dark moustache, 'was one velvet evening in 1938 when King Zog of Albania became engaged to be married to a Hungarian aristocrat. Geraldine Apponyi was her name.' Angelina untied the little girl's plaits and softly fluffed up the long, dark hair. 'She was dark and beautiful,' Felix sang, 'and she was going to become Queen of Albania. They had a huge dinner party on the terrace and I served there from seven at night until seven in the morning.' Taking white roses from the bowl in the centre of the table, Angelina started to pin them in the child's hair, like a coronet, as Felix continued. 'There was music but no dancing, and there were gay, happy speeches all night.' As Angelina laced the belt around the child's slight middle, Elizabeth stood up, straight and grave, awed, and aware of all those eyes upon her.

'Was the little queen a bit frightened, Felix?'

'A bit bewildered, perhaps. But she looked stunning in a white dress with lace and diamonds sparkling in that thick, dark hair.'

Beneath her wreath of white roses the child's big, dark eyes dreamed in a sun-golden face. Serene, confident and very lovely, she raised her little forehead, then gave a regal nod.

'What did I eat, Felix?'

'I served you with a dish of creamed eggs, calf's brains and mushrooms, just an ordinary in-between-courses dish,' said Felix, suddenly an obsequious waiter, bending to offer an imaginary platter. 'I could hardly breathe. I couldn't take my eyes off that beautiful woman. She only helped herself to a teaspoonful of the food, by the way, not like the Archduchess Augusta – that was the Emperor Franz Joseph's daughter – she had a face like a bear and an appetite like a bear, and a laugh like a bear. And she smoked huge cigars, puff, puff, puff.'

Suddenly the little girl tugged the roses out of her hair, draped her scarlet napkin around her shoulders, twisted her hair up into a bun with her left hand, slumped back into her chair, grinned with her lips pulled over her teeth, nodded in a knowing fashion and with her right hand puffed an imaginary cigar. 'Puff, puff, puff like this, Felix?'

'To the life, Your Highness.'

'You spoil her,' Angelina laughed, but then he spoiled all of them. They had led such a quiet, sedate and orderly life until Felix crashed into it with this masculine strength, exuberance and noise.

'Bedtime,' Angelina said, reaching forward to unknot Elizabeth's robe.

'Maman, can I have a proper white dress, not an old sheet?'

'No, you'd only get it dirty, my little acrobat. When you're older you shall have a white dress, if you're good.'

'Am I as good as you were when you were a little boy, Felix?'

'On the trapeze, Lili, yes, but not quite so good on the trampoline. But when you go to Hungary in September you can practise with Uncle Sandor on the trampoline we used together as children, and by then I expect you to do a double somersault and land *with both feet together*.'

15

ELIZABETH hung out of the window and waved to the people she passed. Farmworkers in blue dungarees waved back from fields of high Indian corn, luxuriant tobacco leaves or nodding yellow sunflowers. Herdsmen on horseback flourished their whips above flocks of great white oxen, lazily chewing. Like a time machine, the olive train ran through a Hungarian countryside which had changed very little over the past two hundred years.

It all looked so pretty that Elizabeth couldn't understand why Felix wasn't his usual cheerful self. He sat with his head turned away from the railway corridor, biting his lip, silent and trembling. Though he looked out of the window, he didn't seem to see the flat golden fields of wheat or the lake where placid fishermen sat in flat-bottomed punts and willow trees trailed their branches in the water.

Angelina tugged at Elizabeth's cotton dress as they passed pale grey towers and battlements rising above the trees. 'We're nearly there, let me comb your hair ...'

At Sopron, Uncle Sandor was waiting for them on the platform, waving his whip in recognition. He was dark and fiercely handsome, like a gypsy, with even longer moustachios than his brother Felix. After bearhugs of welcome, they climbed on to the flat-bottomed, dusty red farm cart. An hour's ride lay ahead of them, through poplar-lined, shady roads that cut through field after field of ripening grapevines.

They reached the farmhouse as dusk fell over the low building. Vanilla-scented pink and white oleander bushes grew along the white-washed walls, long strings of dark red peppers were hung to dry outside the kitchen window, dogs barked as the wagon wheels creaked to a halt. Grandma Kovago rushed into the yard, wiping her hands on her white apron, then drew the children into the lamplit kitchen where thin, bent Grandpa Kovago, wearing a collarless open shirt and frayed black suit, waited to greet them.

On the wall opposite the kitchen door hung a tambourine, three old shotguns and several gilt-framed pictures in which crudely coloured saints rolled their eyes towards the ceiling. Two nineteenth-century sepia portraits of the Empress Elizabeth gazed seriously into the lamplight. The kitchen table was set with wooden platters and huge earthenware crocks of food. A sour smell of cheese, spices and rough wine hung over the low room. Black hams hung from the smoke-stained rafters, along with strings of sausages and ropes of dried mushrooms.

When the women were putting the children to bed and for the first time Felix found himself alone with his father, the old man's amiability was abruptly discarded.

'Why have you come back, Felix? How dare you take such a fearful risk – not only for yourself but for your wife and the children!'

Felix was silent. It had been a hard decision. Three months before, after receiving the smuggled message from his mother, he had sweated at the thought of the danger he was running into. As a war refugee, Felix hadn't been granted Swiss citizenship and was in no position to apply for a Hungarian passport. It would have been an insane risk for him even to go to the Hungarian consulate in Berne and make inquiries about the possibility of visiting his homeland. Not only had Felix fought against the Russians in the Hungarian army, but also in the German army. When Felix consulted the Hungarian anti-Communist exile group in Geneva they told him he could expect to be arrested at the frontier and sent to a labour camp for twenty years – if he was lucky!

But after some argument, the group eventually agreed to provide Felix with the necessary forged documentation, and it was agreed that he would cross the border with his Swiss wife and two Swiss children to strengthen his story of a family visit.

So far, in spite of his fright, the scheme had worked successfully. In the lamplit kitchen, he lifted his head and for the first time he addressed his father man-to-man, and not as an amiable son.

'You know why I've come back, Papa. Because Mama sent for me. Because you're ... not going to live forever ... And we all know it. I came back to see you both for the ... once more ... And

I came back because Mama wants me to get Sandor out. That's why I've come back, and that's what I'm going to do.'

'Does Angelina know?'

'No. Because she's safer not knowing.'

'Does Sandor know?'

'Not yet, for the same reason.'

There was a silence, then the old man sighed and said, 'You're a brave boy and I'm proud of you, but you're foolish, and your foolishness makes me angry because of the danger.'

For the next two weeks the children lived the pleasant, pastoral Hungarian life that had changed little since medieval days. They rode bareback, swam in the lake and gathered berries from the hedges to make jelly. In the brackish wet soil of the woods they picked thick, fat mushrooms beaded with dew and as big as a baby's fist.

They practised acrobatics on the trampoline that Uncle Sandor dragged out of the stable, and he tossed, caught and instructed the two children as they leaped and turned on the canvas. Lili's small, thin frame obeyed Sandor's every command, and she continued to sail through the air long after Roger had become bored and wandered off to the stables. The two children went for short walks with Grandpa Kovago or long walks through the forest with Uncle Sandor, who carried their lunch in a basket strapped to his back. One day they even went as far as the Austrian border, which lay northwest of their farm. As they sprawled on a hilltop, eating smoked sausage, Lili was a little disappointed. She had expected to see a thick red line wandering as far as the eye could see – as it did on the maps at school – but no red line led through the forests of pine that covered the hillside.

Wherever they looked outside the farm, rows of vines stretched to the horizon. They weren't waist height like Swiss vines, but were trained around twenty-foot-high poles, and they looked like rows of green-leafed wigwams. When harvesting started, Angelina worked in the fields with the other women pickers, propping a fifteen-foot-high ladder against the vines in order to reach the topmost branches. The burly male supervisor moved slowly along the lines, stooping with the weight of the big wooden container that was strapped to his back. As he passed each woman, he stopped while she tipped her bucket into the container on his back. When it was full, he climbed up the ladder that was propped against the open truck and leaned over so that the grapes fell from his container and over his head on to the golden, growing pile of fruit in the truck.

One evening Elizabeth triumphantly dashed up to Felix and threw her arms around him. 'I've been practising all day! I can do a backward somersault off the farmyard gate and on to the trampoline!'

'You *can*?'

'Well, I *almost* can.'

'Either you can or you can't, Lili. Stick to yes and no; can or can't; did or didn't; will or won't; good or bad. Everyone knows what black and white is, but grey can be anywhere in between, so stick to black and white, miss. Now, let's see that somersault.'

That evening the two brothers walked down to the local *csarda*, two miles distant, to meet the men they had known since boyhood. Walking back in the moonlight after a lot of gossip and far too much white wine, Sandor suddenly said, 'Felix, I must admit I thought you were a fool to have left Hungary, a fool to risk coming back – most of all, a fool to have left the farm to me. But now I'm not so sure.'

'Why not?' asked Felix, guardedly. 'Everything looks as good as it ever did, the grapes grow, the sun shines, the children play.'

'Felix, you've never been able to see more than what's under your nose.' Sandor stumbled. 'Nothing's wrong with God's weather, the trouble is man's tyranny. Under the surface, Felix, things in Hungary are getting worse. *You* haven't felt the fear in the cities. *You* don't notice that everyone is shabby and everything is in short supply. *You* don't notice that men have been taken off the farms to work in the new factories, so farms are producing less because now farming takes second place.'

Sandor stopped on the moonlit road and with an exaggerated, tipsy gesture, he started checking off on his fingers. 'Farming takes second place to the coal industry, the chemical industry, the bauxite and the dye industry. The Russians send raw materials here to be processed and manufactured in Hungary, then it's nearly all sent back to Russia and our workers have nothing to show for their work. All the farm produce is collected by the state and a lot of the food is sent out of the country, so there isn't much incentive for farmers to produce it in the first place – but if there isn't enough food to collect, then a farmer might suddenly be thrown into prison.'

'But who's to know, Sandor, if you sell a pig or a goose?'

'If you're caught selling one goose on the black market, you can get a seven-year sentence. What I'm telling you is that, slowly, we are becoming Russian slaves.'

They walked in silence along the moonlit road, then Sandor added, 'Janos the schoolmaster says that the newspapers and radio are censored and most of the new books and plays are just crude Soviet propaganda.'

'Nothing new about that, Sandor.'

'No, but Janos says that even the Communist intellectuals in Budapest have now started to criticize the harshness of the Russian system. See what I mean?' He stumbled again. 'Hungarian *Communists* are criticizing the Soviet Union.'

'Very healthy.'

'The Russians won't allow it. The secret police get more powerful every day.' He hung one arm around his brother's shoulder. 'Back in June, Miklos the blacksmith got drunk in the *csarda* one night and said more or less what I've just told you. Next afternoon the secret police turned up in a car, shoved Miklos into it and headed back towards Budapest.'

He suddenly stood still in the moonlight, remembering. 'Nobody knows what's happened to him, but someone said he was being taken to the *Avo* headquarters at Andrassy Street and everybody knows that number sixty Andrassy is where the *Avos* have their torture chambers, so we don't expect to see Miklos again. I tell you, if it wasn't for the farm and the old couple, I'd leave with you after the wine festival.'

Felix kept his plans to himself as they clumped along in the peaceful moonlight. He simply observed, 'Farmers never starve if they keep their mouths shut.'

Vendors wandered among the tents pitched around the *csarda* tempting the peasants to buy their strings of pork sausages, cakes and sweetmeats. Inside the tents, a brisk trade flourished in hats, dresses, ornaments, pots and pans, scythes and other agricultural implements. The evening before, the land around the *csarda* had been covered only with grass, but now it was jammed with brightly dressed peasants in their Sunday best, celebrating the *szuret*, today's wine festival. Some of the women wore as many as twenty-five petticoats under green or scarlet skirts that reached to the top of their soft, scarlet leather boots; their white organdy blouses were richly embroidered, and so were their little waistcoats.

Early that morning the women had made a huge wreath of grapes mixed with wild flowers and bound it with coloured ribbons. This wreath had been carried in state from the vineyards to the village, followed by a gypsy orchestra which fiddled merrily in front of the parade of vineyard workers. Jostling along in the happy, noisy procession, Elizabeth and Roger passed slowly through the town until they reached the *csarda*, where, like everybody else, they drank a glass of pale, golden wine before the feasting started. Then the gypsy leader flung his dark head back and very slowly drew his bow across the strings of his fiddle. One by one the other instruments joined in until the music grew louder and louder, faster and faster, more and more insistent. Soon boots were kicking, skirts whirling, arms twirling as dancers spun with uninhibited shouts of joy.

'No other nation can dance like Hungarians,' shouted Uncle Sandor, pulling Angelina up to dance. 'Dancing is in our blood and nothing can stop us.'

Very different from the quiet, staid Swiss, thought Elizabeth, her eyes as big as eggcups, as she watched the whirling skirts, the flying dark hair, the flashing eyes of the dancers.

'Come on, Lili, I'll show you how to dance,' cried Felix, grabbing her hand and running forward. In an open-necked, white shirt with huge billowing sleeves, a scarlet cummerbund, black open waistcoat and tight black trousers thrust into high scarlet leather boots, he looked wonderfully dashing. Felix tugged her towards the dancers, then suddenly stopped, hobbled a couple of steps, stopped again and winced.

'Damned if I can. My foot's throbbing. You'll have to wait for Sandor.'

So Lili stamped and whirled and twirled with Uncle Sandor,

while Felix limped to a bench, took off his right boot and winced as Angelina examined his foot. 'It was a mosquito bite that I scratched; now it's septic. Nothing to make a fuss about.'

He didn't want a mosquito bite to spoil the fun of the *szuret* so he painfully squeezed on his boot again, ignored his throbbing foot and contented himself with watching the dancers instead of joining in. But that evening Felix rode back to the farm with the women on the horse-drawn cart.

Angelina bathed his foot in the tin basin, while Grandma Kovago prepared the bread poultice. Grandfather ridiculed Angelina's suggestion of a doctor. The gnarled old man took the black pipe out of his mouth and laughed. 'For a mosquito bite?' The gold watchchain that looped across his little belly wobbled with mirth.

The next day Felix sat outside the kitchen door. Swathed in white linen, his foot was propped on a chair seat. But by evening his leg had started to throb and the following morning Felix could hardly walk.

Angelina insisted on consulting a doctor, so Sandor set off for Sopron on horseback. By evening when the doctor arrived, Felix was sweating, with a high temperature, unable to move without pain.

'Blood poisoning. He needs penicillin, not bread poultices,' growled the doctor, frowning over spectacles pulled halfway down his nose at the swollen, purple-red foot. 'You're going to be in bed for a couple of weeks at least. If you're lucky.'

So Angelina wrote a letter to Herr Pangloss, the manager of the Hotel Rosat, to say that Felix could not return until the end of October. But there was no cause for alarm. After all, it was merely a mosquito bite.

Early on the evening of Wednesday, 24 October 1956 (three weeks after Elizabeth and Roger should have been back at school in Switzerland), Uncle Sandor took his usual, two-mile evening walk to the *csarda* outside the village to meet Janos the schoolmaster for their usual drink, smoke and chat. The evenings were now cold so he wore his *bunda*, the traditional long embroidered sheepskin coat with fleece facing inward.

When he hadn't returned by ten o'clock, Grandma started to

grumble. 'Politics, politics, always talking senseless politics over too much wine.' At eleven o'clock they gave up waiting and were about to go to bed when the heavy kitchen door flew open and Sandor burst in, out of breath.

'The revolution has started! In Budapest! Quick, turn on the radio! The students have captured the radio station.' A flurry of scraping chairs and questions followed him as he strode over to the big, old-fashioned radio and tuned into Radio Budapest, which was playing recorded gypsy music of a markedly un-revolutionary nature.

Wakened by the noise, Elizabeth crept out of bed and peeped around the door. For once Felix ignored her as the grown-ups gathered around the wireless. Uncle Sandor burst out, 'The Russians have appointed Nagy as President of Hungary again, and martial law was proclaimed at nine o'clock this evening. We heard it on the radio at the *csarda*. Later they said that Nagy had asked the Russian troops to help restore order.'

There was a chorus of cries. 'Nagy is a patriot, he'd never do that.'

'Well, he did, I heard them say so.'

'Then the Russians must have forced him to do it.'

'Now sit down, Sandor, and tell it from the beginning. We're obviously going to hear nothing except music on this damned radio.'

'Perhaps we should return to Switzerland,' suggested Angelina, worried.

'You can't. The frontiers are closed and no one can leave without a Russian exit permit.'

Horrified, Angelina looked at Felix. He limped over, hugged her and said, 'There's no reason to be frightened, we're safe here. Put Lili to bed again and sit with her until she's asleep – and you go to bed as well, Mama. War is man's business.'

Apprehensive but obedient, the women disappeared, then Sandor said, 'Until your leg is better, Felix, you stay here and see they're safe. I'll leave you one rifle and take the other two with me to Budapest. They're broadcasting for food, so we'll start loading up the cart at dawn tomorrow. No, Papa, they're fighting for you and it's up to you to feed them. Janos and I are off to Budapest tomorrow.'

In spite of Grandma's anguished tears, Sandor creaked off early the following morning, the horse-drawn cart laden with food and looking like a harvest festival float as it jerked down the steep, frozen, muddy ruts of the farm track.

In the afternoon Grandfather walked into the village for news and didn't return until nightfall. 'The *Avos* in Budapest fired on an unarmed crowd of twenty thousand people that included children, women and old men,' he growled, 'and then they threw the bodies into the Danube.'

By Sunday, only five days after the fighting had started, the tired but triumphant voice of Prime Minister Nagy announced over the wireless that Khrushchev had agreed to withdraw the Soviet troops. Unbelievably, it looked as though the country really *had* liberated itself as Russian tanks started to rumble out of the devastated streets of Budapest and – for the first time in ten years – broadcasts and newspapers were uncensored.

But Grandpa was sceptical and suspicious. 'It's not like the Russians to give in so easily, they're up to something,' he insisted. 'When you're my age you, too, will mistrust bears who behave like lambs. The uprising must have surprised them – after all it surprised everyone – and they probably didn't think we Magyars had so much fight in us after so long.'

He lit his pipe, sucked at the stem and shook his head. 'You mark my words, the Russians are being meek just to stop the Western nations from joining the fight. Once the fuss and interest has died down, the bastards will be back here with their boots on our necks again.'

And Grandpa was right. On November first came the ominous news that hundreds of Soviet tanks were streaming over the border into Hungary. Thousands of Soviet troops had marched in and surrounded Budapest.

Every morning and evening at eight o'clock Grandpa rode into the village to wait at the post office at the hour when Sandor said he would try to telephone. 'No news yet, Mama,' he reported, 'except that refugees from the cities are streaming to the Austrian border and the Russian tanks are turning them back and shooting anyone who tries to escape. Not much fun trying to escape in this weather; bitter wind, heavy snow and worse to come.'

On the following Tuesday, on the evening of November sixth,

Sandor got a message through to the post office. 'Now don't get upset, Mama, but they were storming a Soviet tank and Sandor has been shot in the right arm and shoulder,' said Grandpa, not adding that Janos had been killed at the same time. 'The Russians are apparently pouring into Budapest. They're shelling buildings and shooting passers-by. There's also been heavy fighting in the other cities, but it's worst in Budapest and the Russians are in control of the city again. It's just like 1945, God help us.'

Grandpa continued sadly. 'Sandor says that the city is starving, the Freedom Fighters have run out of ammunition and medical supplies . . . Sandor's trying to get home, and then he thinks that we should all escape to Austria. The reprisals are going to be terrible, and any able-bodied adults might be shipped to Soviet labour camps.'

Felix said, 'For God's sake take the children somewhere else, Angelina.'

The children had been almost ignored all weekend, and finding the strain of adult anxiety irksome, they had kept out of the way. It was too cold to go outside and there wasn't yet enough snow for play, just a thin film over the hard earth. But now Uncle Sandor had been shot and all the grown-ups looked worried.

'Hang a lantern in the window and keep it lit all night in case Sandor turns up,' Grandpa ordered, then he turned to Felix and took his hands. 'My son, we're too old to leave. We were born here and we want to die here when the good Lord wills it. But the rest of you must leave as soon as Sandor returns. We did not raise our two sons for the benefit of the Russians.'

Unable to speak, Grandma could not take her sad, wrinkled eyes off Felix. She feared that she was seeing him for the last time.

The moon shone through the clouds, flooding the countryside with silver. The small group could see a hamlet and vineyards edged with trees as they hurried along a path between bare fields of silver snow. They wore dark, heavy overcoats, and the two children had cardboard identification labels tied around their necks, as did all escaping children, in case they were separated from the adults who accompanied them. Sandor's right arm was in a dark sling, which meant that he couldn't button his coat up to the neck and the cold wind hurt his chest. Felix walked with the help of an old shepherd's crook and carried the farm's only remaining rifle in his other hand.

It was two o'clock in the morning and they were nearing the frontier. The journey had not been difficult, mainly downhill through wooded land. Twice they had waded through icy, rushing streams over which Elizabeth had been carried on the shoulders of Felix, who was still limping badly and should not have been walking on his poisoned leg. They were heading for a path through the woods to the frontier that Sandor knew hadn't been fenced off. It ended at a barbed-wire fence. Beyond that fence lay half a kilometre of no-man's-land, then a second barbed-wire fence, which was the actual frontier. Both fences and no-man's-land were patrolled with guard dogs by the frontier police.

Paradoxically, the safe places to cross were often near the high, wooden lookout towers that punctuated the frontier and from which a single guard had a good view of all the surrounding land. These towers were undermanned and even, occasionally, empty. That was too much to hope for now, but if they crossed near one of the towers, they would be able to see what was happening and where the searchlights were probing.

Their plan was to wait in one spot until the dog patrol had passed and then make a dash for freedom. Ideally, Sandor hoped to reconnoitre the spot in moonlight, then wait to move until the moon had passed behind a cloud. He would also have preferred to have picked a cloudy night, but they had no choice: the longer they waited before escaping, the more dangerous it became.

Suddenly, they nearly walked into the first barbed-wire fence. It was almost invisible, about six feet high and with much longer, more vicious barbs than agricultural barbed-wire. Beyond it lay no-man's-land. The patchy snow was spattered over rough grass that sloped up a fairly steep bank. They couldn't see what lay on the other side.

Sandor touched his brother, and wordlessly pointed to the right. They skirted the trees until they came within sight of a wooden frontier tower. It seemed to be operated by one man who slowly rotated a single searchlight. The little group of five melted back into the trees. They had to get out of the scent range of the dogs and yet remain within earshot; luckily, the wind was blowing from the frontier into their faces. After the patrol had passed, they would move down to the fence and cut the bottom wires with their two pairs of clippers, blades carefully smeared with dirt so they didn't glint in the moonlight. They would move back into the shelter of the trees when the searchlight swept towards them, and having cut the wire, they would dash forward to escape as soon as it had passed. Roger would hang on to Sandor's coat and Elizabeth would hang on to Felix.

Sandor could no longer feel his cold feet. His arm, neck and chest were painful, but they weren't as dangerous as Felix's poisoned, painful, throbbing leg. Silently Sandor moved forward, alone, and waited under a fir tree. It shuddered noiselessly and sprinkled his shoulders with snow. Then he heard a distant crunch of boots, low growls and animal panting. He faded back into the trees to where the others were waiting and looked at his luminous watch. Two-twenty.

They stood there in the freezing cold until the patrol returned because they had to know how much time there was between each patrol. Angelina gently rubbed the faces of the children with her wool mittens to help their circulation.

Then they again heard low voices and again the panting of the dogs as the patrol returned. The wind was blowing from behind them, so Sandor waited to get a good view, when he could see the two-man patrol wearing overcoats and round Russian hats with earflaps. They carried automatic rifles.

Fifty minutes between patrols; that should be time enough.

He hurried back to the others and beckoned them forward. The moon was now hidden behind the clouds and it was difficult for them to see Sandor and follow his dim shape as he ran between the firs.

Angelina and the children waited under cover as the two brothers crept forward to the six-foot-high fence and started to cut the bottom wires. Clumsily using his left hand, Sandor started cutting the bottom wire while Felix worked on the wire above it.

The clippers seemed to make no impression on the wire. Then suddenly Felix held two slack strands instead of a taut one. Swiftly he started to cut the next wire. Panting, the men hacked fiercely, knowing that their lives depended on speed. When the searchlight swept towards them – as it did every twelve minutes – they dashed back into the cover of the trees.

The moment the searchlight had passed, they ran back again to work on the wire, cursing and panting with effort, until there was a soft scraping sound and it parted at last.

Bending low, the two men stumbled back through the snow to where the others stood and they all waited, hearts pounding, for the searchlight to pass.

A grey beam swung through the darkness, getting brighter as it approached them. It moved on, then grew grey again. Like sprinters in a race, they dashed forward, Angelina so frightened that she tried to blot everything out of her mind except the will to follow Felix.

The men held the bottom wires back as she and the children scrambled underneath. Then, in sodden boots and coats, they all ran clumsily up the escarpment.

Sandor could see that they were nearly at the top of the slope. Twenty metres ... Ten metres ... Felix was falling behind ... Five metres ... Then they clambered over the rise and started to scramble downhill, sweating with relief, gasping painfully for breath.

But the distance from the other side of the slope to the second wire fence was much farther than they had expected. It was the greater part of that half-kilometre band of no-man's-land, and the lower slopes were covered by boulders that were difficult to climb over, although convenient to hide behind. The little group separated and scrambled for cover behind the first boulders only a few seconds before the searchlight swept over it.

At that point, for the first time, Felix allowed himself to hope that they might make it. Again they scrambled to their feet and started to stagger forward over the uneven terrain.

Suddenly Felix faltered and felt dizzy. Feeling Elizabeth clutching trustingly at his greatcoat, he willed himself to keep going. Then to his horror he heard the dogs barking in the distance, picking up the scent.

Frantically summoning up what strength remained to him, Felix dragged Elizabeth along. He now had no idea where the others were. His only thought was to get to the second fence before his throbbing leg collapsed or the dogs caught up with them.

When he reached it, he nearly ran into the wire. It was a brute – higher than the first, and with more barbs. He couldn't see it as clearly as he had the other one, because now there was no moon. He touched it, then jerked back with a gasp.

The fence was electrified.

Trembling, panting hoarsely, Felix threw away his stick, carefully put his rifle on the ground and swiftly bent down to Elizabeth, whispering urgently.

'Lili, darling. You know that an acrobat must be obedient. Now I want you to stand on my shoulders and show me your best jump *ever*, over this fence. Don't land the way you do on the trampoline. Try to go limp as you land, try to land in a ball. Do a *bad* landing for Felix. Got that, darling? A *very* good, *very* high jump and a limp, curled-up landing. Then get straight up and run down the mountain and into the first house. Don't wait for me, my darling, and *don't look back!*'

He pulled her mittens off, to improve her grip. Uncomprehending but obedient, Lili climbed on to his shoulders. Slowly, concentrating, she straightened upright, then she took a deep breath, bent her knees a little, and soared over the fence as if it did not exist.

She landed, painfully, on all fours, in the thin snow on the other side.

As she picked herself up Lili heard baying dogs and hesitated. Then she heard Felix shout, 'Obedience, Lili! Run. *Run!*'

She started to run downhill, a small grey shadow against the snow.

Behind the barbed-wire fence, Felix picked up the rifle and crouched. In the dim light, he could hear the harsh panting breath, the throaty rasp of the big Alsatian before he could see it.

As the animal flung itself at Felix, he squeezed the trigger. The shot hit the animal in the shoulder in midspring, but it was too late for Felix to avoid its leap, which knocked him to the ground. With a savage growl – regardless of training instructions – the wounded, maddened animal attacked.

Felix was pinned to the ground by the heavy, writhing body. He smelled the panting, fetid animal breath on his face, then felt unendurable agony as the Alsatian tore his throat out.

~ PART FOUR ~

16

THE seventeen-year-old Maxine started work in London at Partridge, in the chaotic studio above the calm shop off Bond Street. Mr Partridge looked and dressed more like a City stockbroker than a famous designer. He projected a sort of charming helplessness that made people feel *they* had to do the work because *he* couldn't; this made his staff feel needed and wanted, rather than merely employed. He was a gentle, kind, learned man, but ruthlessly uncompromising about his work. His supreme virtues were an extraordinary sense of colour combined with exquisite tact and discretion.

After familiarizing herself with Partridge's library of samples, Maxine's work consisted mainly of running around. She collected paint samples from here, and delivered fabric samples there; she matched up this lemon silk to that lemon yellow satin swatch. It was quite extraordinary, she thought, that there were so many different fabrics and textures and that ninety-nine per cent of them were perfectly repulsive. Quickly she was promoted to doing paste-ups; this meant preparing sheets of cardboard upon which Maxine stuck square samples of all the paints, fabrics and finishes, together with photographs or drawings of all the other items that were to be used in an interior; she loved this job, which combined her gift for colour with her impeccable sense of clarity. She also became very good at writing specifications. Maxine's mind was as orderly as a filing cabinet, and her practical shrewdness was invaluable in the crises that invariably filled their days.

Within a few months, Mr Partridge discovered her passion for old furniture and sent her scouting around the more distant, dusty antique shops and little-known auction rooms, such as Austen of Peckham, where you could buy a mahogany Victorian fitted wardrobe – with a special place for opera hats – for a few pounds or, for a great many more, an *almost* Chippendale breakfront bureau-bookcase.

However, Maxine's favourite source of furniture was an

esoteric antique shop next to Lord Raglan's cream-tiled dairy in Pont Street. The shop was very quiet and dark. The shop owner was a charming, elderly man called Jack Reffold, who had a high, quavery voice, discerning taste and an unerring eye for proportion. In his shop Maxine found objects that she would never see elsewhere: the blue, feather-patterned breakfast china from Queen Victoria's yacht; a bridal doll's trousseau packed in a miniature portmanteau; a gory oil painting of the battle of Trafalgar. Most of his better pieces were sent straight to New York, but Maxine grew to be a steady customer, particularly for the simple, stripped-pine Victorian furniture that her grandmother would have thrown out as unfit for the servants.

One July evening, tired after work, Maxine walked back from Mayfair in the hazy golden sunset of a London summer. She took a route that led through the cream Grecian beauty of Belgrave Square and into Pont Street. They were working late at Reffold's, so Maxine stopped to drink a glass of sherry with Jack and his three amiable, aged assistants.

Maxine now knew a great deal about English and French furniture and the price that Americans were willing to pay for it. Jack Reffold had refined her taste and shown her what to look for, whether in a Sheraton chair or a Meissen fruit bowl. That evening he was fussing over an ornate Rockingham vase that displeased him.

'Just look at this *horror*, Maxine! Remember, always look for the *basic* shape – it *must* be good. *No* use piling decoration on a shape like *this*, which is basically *ill*-proportioned,' he said in his quivering, scolding voice. 'And it's *enormous*! *Never* buy big pieces of *anything*, darling girl, because they're *so* hard to resell.' He filled her glass and continued, '*So* many people now have *small* rooms, so they want *small* furniture, they *don't* want overornate pieces that are difficult to clean. Sir Hugh Casson *says* that if a thing's worth *having*, then it's worth dusting, but I don't suppose Sir Hugh *does* much dusting.'

Afterwards Maxine strolled home through the gilded evening, thinking how lovely life was. However, as she unlocked the red front door she could hear the sound of sobbing in the bedroom. She ran in. Kate was lying on one narrow bed with her head in Pagan's lap and they were both weeping. Pagan raised a blotchy red face and without a word she handed Maxine the evening newspaper. On the back page, a two-inch item read, 'The War Office has announced that the subaltern of the Green Howards killed last week by Communist terrorists in an ambush in Panang, Malaya, has been named as Nicholas Cliffe, son of Sir Walter Cliffe of Barton Court, Barton, Shropshire.'

Maxine couldn't believe her eyes. Death was not a part of her life. Elderly relatives disappeared, aged cats were taken away to be 'put to sleep', but it was not something that happened to you or your friends. She, too, burst into tears.

'Does Judy know?' she asked. There was a horrified silence – they all realized that their sense of loss was minor in comparison to what Judy would feel when she heard the news.

That night they cried themselves to sleep and wept nonstop for the next two days, as almost everything from coffee cups to crumpled pillows seemed to remind them of something about Nick. Surprisingly, it was Kate's father who halted their mournful apathy. He sat in their badly lit small front room and encouraged them to talk about Nick. After listening patiently he said, 'And how do you think this fine young man would want you all to behave when you heard that he'd passed on?' They all looked up inquiringly. 'Would he want you to sit around weeping? No, of course not, he'd want you to carry on living and remember the happy times you had together. Now, if a doodlebug had got me in the blitz, Kate, I'd have wanted you and your mother to have one good cry and then never again remember me with tears. I'd have wanted you both to feel happy when you remembered me.'

Eventually he enticed them out of the basement along to the Berkeley buttery for lunch, then as the sun was shining, he took them to look at the ducks in St James's Park, after which they felt much better. They didn't forget Nick, but they stopped drooping and snuffling when his name was mentioned.

Pagan and Kate, who were doing the London season, both introduced Maxine to the countless young men with whom they watched polo at Windsor, tennis at Wimbledon and racing at Ascot. When not at work, Maxine was rowed in punts on the Serpentine, wore picture hats to picture galleries or watched hours of incomprehensible cricket. She stayed in English country houses, where she observed the extraordinary way that British women dressed in the country: the headscarf knotted under the chin like Princess Elizabeth, the twin set that never fitted on the shoulders and stretched across the bosom, the stockings that wrinkled around the ankle, the baggy tweed skirt (covered with dog hairs), the identical beat-up crocodile handbag. Mystifyingly, clothes that were neat, well pressed and tidy were the mark of an outsider.

At times Maxine went to dances, but not often, because she had to be in her office by nine o'clock in the morning. The drawback to dances was that an Englishman expected you to spend the whole evening with him, to the exclusion of everyone else. Having been used to Switzerland and France where both sexes at a party cheerfully changed partners until midnight, Maxine found it tedious to dance, talk and stay with one man for the whole evening until the inevitable attempt to entice her into the back seat of his sports car. She did not much care for these young men in their bowler hats and Edwardian suits or their golf caps and tweed jackets on weekends: they dressed, spoke and behaved alike – they even thought alike.

Pagan and Kate loved the London social life, but Maxine quickly grew tired of it. She was already *une sérieuse*. She preferred what was called work to what others called fun. When Maxine returned to Paris, she was determined to persuade her father to spend her dowry money on the lease of one of the small antique shops in the rue Jacob. She would paint the whole place in soft olive green and import directly into France the sort of furniture she was buying from Jack Reffold – pieces that were not quite good enough to ship across the Atlantic. She would specialize in what the French called *le style anglais*, decoration generally based on an English, eighteenth-century interpretation of antique Indian or Chinese designs, teamed with simple Adam furniture or else with comfortably upholstered Georgian chairs and sofas, so different from the uncomfortable, buttoned-satin chairs upon which Maxine's mother's friends perched in their drawing rooms. The French took these ingredients and refined the details; they manufactured fringing and braid to match the curtains and bedcovers, they wove plain upholstery fabrics that picked up the colours in the chintz patterns. With these ingredients the decorative formula was easy: you picked your basic chintz pattern, which was used for the curtains and sofas and perhaps one chair; then you picked two distinct colours from the chintz pattern and matched them to plain fabrics that were used for the rest of the upholstery and any bedcovers; walls were covered with the chintz fabric or with wallpaper in the same pattern or else they were painted in a colour picked from the chintz pattern, only much paler.

By the time Maxine had finished her two-year apprenticeship in London, she could produce *le style anglais* overnight although she was careful never to let her clients know this. Clients overvalued time and undervalued talent and experience, she realized.

James Partridge offered her a permanent, paid job with him in London, but Maxine preferred to return to Paris and get on with her 'career', as she now secretly called her job. 'The difference between a career and a job,' Judy had once told her, 'is that a job gets you nowhere. If you plan a career, then a job should be a step towards a definite goal – when you accept a job you should know exactly when you intend to leave it.'

'Nonsense!' Maxine had said. 'Why don't you go and write a self-improvement book like Dale Carnegie?' But it wasn't bad advice, in fact, and with it in mind, she quit her job and went back to Paris where she found that Judy – instead of getting on with her own career after leaving Christian Dior – was busily helping Guy to establish his career in fashion design.

Maxine's father was delighted to see her again, proud of her English and even prouder of her new abilities. He quickly found that he enjoyed making plans with her for the simple reason that she made *sure* he enjoyed them. She treated him like a favourite customer. He was impressed with her new knowledge and seriousness, but appalled by her ignorance of accountancy.

'I don't know *why* you insisted on staying six months extra in Switzerland to take your business exams,' he said. 'No wonder you failed them! An absolute waste of money! Until you have been in business for a whole year, you will phone me every day, at ten in the morning, and let me know the most important thing that happened to you the day before. I never want to hear about *more* than one thing, and I never want to hear less. That will teach you to sort out your priorities. And I want to see your accounts every Saturday morning.'

To her father's surprise, Maxine, in fact, had a head for business. Within a month, she had a seven-year lease on number 391, rue Jacob. It had not been difficult to find a shop in this street lined with dusty antique shops that had not yet become smart, shops that were still badly painted and dingy, visited by dealers rather than tourists. Number 391 was narrow and dark, but it was very deep and the apartment above was included in the lease. For the time being Maxine sublet it to an old Polish professor of Latin. She renamed the shop Paradis, and immediately hired an assistant, since otherwise she would never be able to leave the premises without closing. Then she found an art student to work part-time in the back of the shop, doing what she had done in London for James Partridge. Her father chose Maxine's bookkeeper, a big-boned rather ugly woman called Christina, with a long, cow face and bovine brown eyes. The two women were always in the shop by 7:30 in the morning, and Maxine kept a folding deck chair in the little kitchen, so that she or Christina could stretch out and rest for half an hour if they were going to be working late in the evening.

On Saturdays her father taught Maxine how to plan a budget and how to draw up a liquidity forecast. He also taught her how to read a balance sheet, which was much easier and more interesting than she had expected. To his surprise, and hers, Maxine turned out to have a strong streak of frugality in her and an instinctive business sense.

After she had worked at Maxine's shop for six months, Christina presented Maxine with a request to become a partner, backed by a cash investment. Christina also had a father and she had also persuaded him that a business with an income would be a better investment than a cash dowry, especially as, at thirty-four, Christina was not entirely sure that she would ever need a dowry.

After a year Paradis began to get bigger jobs – not just a bathroom here and a kitchen there, but complete apartments, small offices, even one country house. Paradis specified everything from the door handles to the window frames, and although modern colours and lighting techniques were used, Maxine specialized in traditional design. Paradis now had two full-time designers as well as part-time assistants.

Every Monday morning, Maxine and Christina planned the next week's work and allocated the different jobs to their designers, and every Monday evening there was a short conference for all their part-time staff. This was held after the shop closed at six o'clock, and the meeting was always followed by supper at the Beaux Arts restaurant, always full of cheerful, noisy students eating hearty, traditional French food. Everybody enjoyed Monday evenings, because it was then that they felt the camaraderie, rather than the anxiety, of business; and they were able to relax and gossip with each other about the jobs.

By 1953, when Maxine was twenty-two, she had attained a small but definite success; the shop was beginning to show a profit. Her father was delighted, but Maxine's mother worried because she wasn't married and appeared to consider suitable suitors tiresome. 'It's so unnatural,' she wailed to Aunt Hortense, 'the child's not interested in any man unless he's a designer, or a client, or a potential client, or some grubby, bearded protégé who's still at the Beaux Arts.'

Hortense nodded sagely. 'I'll see what I can do,' she said.

A few months after this conversation, Aunt Hortense telephoned Maxine. 'Maxine, my dear,' she said. 'I have a client for you. The nephew of a friend of mine. This poor boy has just inherited a decrepit château near Epernay; apparently it's in utter chaos; nobody has lived in it since the war, and the poor man hasn't time to deal with the house – he has to take over an estate that has been shamefully neglected for the past fifteen years. I thought it would be an interesting project for you. So, my dear, if you are willing, I shall collect you at nine o'clock tomorrow morning and we shall drive to Chazalle. I believe there's also a vineyard attached to the estate – about seven hundred acres, also sadly neglected.'

The next morning Aunt Hortense collected Maxine, who wore her client-trapping outfit – a stunning peach linen suit with shoes of a slightly darker shade; her hair, a shoulder-length hank of heavy gold, was tied at the back of her head in a peach silk pussycat bow. They drove out of Paris towards Champagne. The de

Chazalle estate was thirteen kilometres south of Epernay, on the edge of the Côte des Blancs region that lay south of Epernay, between Vertus and Oger, to the west.

From just below the forest on the flat hill summit, vine-covered slopes stretched down to the golden haze of corn on the plains below. The Mercedes turned off the dusty country road through a pair of rusting, wrought-iron gates, one of them sagging from its hinges, and drove for half a kilometre up a neglected, weedy drive, past overgrown flower beds. Etched against the lavender sky was the dark, turreted silhouette of a splendid château. When they came closer they could see that it, too, was shuttered and forlorn. Several smashed tiles from the roof lay in the courtyard, Maxine noticed, as she and her aunt stepped up the chipped stone steps to the front door and pulled the rusting iron bell handle. Surprisingly they heard it clang down some distant corridor.

The door was opened by a tall, thin young man, wearing an old brown sweater. His face was small and lean, with fine bones, and his grey eyes had laughter lines at the corners. He looked surprised and pleased, as if someone had just given him an unexpected present. He bowed, kissed their hands and invited them inside. 'Everything is dusty, which is why I keep sneezing, but I've cleared a space in one of the salons and a village woman comes up to clean it. The place is in a terrible state.'

The shuttered hall was depressingly dark and bare. The filthy paint was peeling, cobwebs laced across the corners and one of the dividing doors had been smashed and was lying on the floor. German soldiers had been billeted at the château; the beautiful carved doors had been chipped and broken, initials had been hacked in the antique panelling and obscene messages scrawled on the walls. Most of the furniture had been used for firewood except for a few pieces bricked up in the attics by the *Kommandant*, who had hoped to liberate them for himself at a later date.

'Apart from this, there are only four other good châteaux still standing in this area. Montmort is first class, so's Brugny, but Mareuil is less impressive and I don't personally care for the design of Louvrois.' The Count had a slight stoop and a long neck. Occasionally, furtively, he turned towards Maxine. She thought to herself, He expected me to be older – he doesn't want to trust the job to someone so young – so look efficient. She started to make copious notes on the large pad of her clipboard.

Diffident and modest, Charles de Chazalle was attractive in his sheer helplessness. Whereas a more aggressive man might have considered Maxine too bossy, she was exactly what he needed and he admired her more as the day progressed. Maxine scribbled nonstop, and at the end of the afternoon she suggested a simple, but efficient, system for dealing with the chaos in which Charles had so suddenly found himself.

Not surprisingly, she got the job.

After that, almost every afternoon she would bump up the drive in her little white Renault van, a different Parisian expert at her side. First a surveyor and an architect, then an auctioneer, a roof expert, a drains expert, a furniture restorer and a picture valuer.

In due course all the experts made their reports, and every Friday night Maxine and Charles discussed the project over dinner in an eighteenth-century post inn at Epernay. As summer faded, there was local venison and wild boar and always the soft, white, tangy Boursault cheese; and of course they drank the local white wine, naturally dry and delicate with a slight taste of hazelnut.

Maxine might as well have been eating dry bread and water. Despite a great deal of discussion before giving their order, she was hardly ever aware of what she ate; she thought only of how she longed for him to like her.

Charles always enjoyed every mouthful of the meal. He didn't eat out much. He liked his quiet life in the country and didn't want to sparkle around Paris, prattling at smart dinner parties. During the day he worked hard, tending his neglected vineyards. On the whole he preferred to spend his evenings alone by the fire, stretching out his long, thin legs, reading or listening to music. Maxine amused and intrigued him, partly because she was *une sérieuse*.

'There's such a lot to be done,' he sighed, one Friday evening as they finished their meal. 'For a start, we aren't producing nearly enough wine at the moment. The average yield from each hectare should be about 5,600 litres of champagne.' He signalled for coffee. 'How do I know? Well, it's not *surprising* that I know a lot about the theory of the champagne business. After all, my family has lived here for centuries. But I've only been able to put my theories into practice since my father died.'

He paused as the waiter poured his glass of brandy, then laid the snifter sideways on the table to check the measure; it should almost spill, but not quite. 'Most Frenchmen want their sons to join the family firm, but my father was so anxious to demonstrate his independence that he didn't let me take any real part in the business. On the other hand, he wouldn't let me work for any other firm. This was very frustrating, because he was resolutely opposed to using new methods. I knew he couldn't live for long – he'd been badly tortured by the Gestapo in the war – so I never went against his wishes.'

Country restaurants closed early, and the Royale Champagne was emptying, but Charles continued to turn the empty brandy glass in both hands. 'I suppose it's natural that he should have felt nostalgic for the prewar days. He liked to pretend that *he* hadn't changed, that *nothing* had changed.' The bill was brought on a plate. He glanced at it (He *can't* have added it that fast, thought Maxine), signed it and continued. 'Unfortunately, his business methods were also old-fashioned. When I tried to discuss work with him, I was put firmly in my place. "There is plenty of time for you to alter things when I'm dead," my father used to say. Those were his wishes and I respected them, but now I intend to work as hard as possible to restore the de Chazalle firm.'

He hesitated, looked at Maxine and then said, 'Our champagne is no longer considered one of the very best, but I'm determined to change that.' As if expecting to be contradicted, he continued, speaking fast and rather defensively. 'It's not such an insane ambition; the Lansons were originally a tiny firm and their premises were virtually destroyed during the First World War, but the two sons – Victor and Henry – travelled all over the world in pursuit of orders and their success has been amazing.'

The waiter started to switch off the lights. Charles took the hint.

'Shall we go?' With concealed reluctance Maxine nodded, stood up and another waiter leaped to pull back her chair. Charles nodded good night and followed her towards the door, saying, 'I don't see why I shouldn't try what the Lansons did. They made their champagne world-famous in half a century that included two World Wars – *and* a long period of depression.'

Increasingly, they both secretly looked forward to Friday evenings and Maxine's return trips to Paris got later and later. She found it hard to leave Charles, who had started gently to tease her about her efficiency, and who could make her laugh at herself or at nothing at all. Charles could make her giggle as she had not done since she left school.

To other people he appeared quiet, reserved and almost dull, but not to Maxine. The power to make a woman laugh is a strong aphrodisiac, and she couldn't wait for Friday nights. She always felt excitement in the air as she dressed that morning; she always changed her mind at least three times and left her bedroom untidily strewn with clothes. Her mother cheered up wonderfully at these unusual signs. Indecision in one's wardrobe always meant a man.

And in the evening, as they sat over coffee and brandy at the Royale Champagne, she longed for Charles to touch her. But he didn't.

One Friday their conversation seemed to drag over the meal, there seemed to be a barrier of embarrassment between them. Maxine was acutely aware that, to her, Charles was no longer just a client, and she felt very self-conscious whatever she was doing, whether scratching her head with a pencil (a habit much deplored by her family) or eating and drinking with suddenly noisy swallows.

By the end of the following week, Maxine felt so agitated that she could hardly bear to stand next to Charles. That evening she had shown him a group of battered oil paintings, horse portraits that she had collected from different areas of the house and stacked in a corridor; they were very similar to the ones that Jack Reffold had started to sell to America. They were late for their dinner reservation at the hotel, but she had particularly wanted him to see them, as she wondered whether it was worth sending a couple over to Jack for appraisal.

'Why don't you come back after dinner?' Charles asked. 'We can decide then which ones to send to London.'

'I'll be too exhausted and I'll get back to Paris much too late and the van will probably weave all over the road on the return journey.'

'I'll drive you back,' Charles offered.

'It's too far, you won't get back to Epernay until dawn.' Privately, she thought he might never get back – the only thing she disliked about Charles was his reckless driving.

They continued their meal. Then, after the waiter poured their coffee, Charles leaned across the table and slowly, deliberately stroked her thick, newly corn-coloured hair. Maxine felt the shock waves on her scalp, in her breasts, in her groin. She couldn't breathe properly, she was panting as if at a high altitude. Charles let the strand of hair drop back into place, and a little moan left her lips. Charles noticed. 'These late journeys are too much of a strain for you,' he said. 'Why don't you simply move in with me?'

'Because my parents would have a fit!'

'They wouldn't if we were married,' Charles said, not taking his eyes off her face but lifting her left wrist to his mouth and, very softly, kissing the pale blue veins that led to her palm.

Maxine, who was always in command of a situation, who always knew exactly what she wanted to do, was speechless. She felt short of breath. She didn't dare move. She felt so weak that she didn't know whether she'd be able to walk out of the restaurant. She couldn't take her eyes off his face. He was not smiling for once; instead, he seemed oddly impassive.

After they left the restaurant, Charles drove back to the château at breakneck speed without saying a word. He grabbed Maxine's hand and – still without a word – tugged her after him as he leaped up the steps towards the main entrance, oblivious of nocturnal scents of warm earth and hot grass. He was conscious only of the tense, expectant, determined passion that passed like an electric current through their clasped hands.

Once inside the front door, Charles pulled Maxine to him and kissed her hard on the mouth, as with one hand he held her to him and with his other explored her body. Gently he traced the outline of her spine down to its base, then softly felt the shape of her buttocks. Crushing her against his body so that she could feel his mounting excitement, he slowly pulled up her skirt and she felt his hand on the naked flesh below her panties, then he slid his hand under the delicate lace. Maxine was shaking. She wanted him as she had never wanted anyone before, her knees were trembling and she didn't think that she could stand much longer. She felt him hard against her stomach as his fingers caressed her quivering white buttocks and firmly pulled her against his body.

With an effort, Charles pulled himself away, gave a great sigh of anticipation, heaved Maxine into his arms (she would never be as light as thistledown) and carried her up the curved staircase to the dusty, but magnificent, blue-brocaded state bedroom. Moonlight fell in silver shafts across the room as he gently laid her on the antique, silk bedcover, then fiercely tore his clothes off and fell upon her.

Maxine gasped with surprise. She had not expected the gentle, amiable, amusing Charles to be so masterful, so passionate, so skilful.

For the next four hours Maxine felt her body move and respond as she had never known it could. Afterwards, she didn't want to leave him. Naked, she clung to him, her tangled, damp yellow hair falling over her full, milky breasts. 'I don't want to go,' she whispered, with tears in her eyes, resisting as he gently, insistently tugged her off the bed and helped her to dress in the moonlight.

'Your parents will be concerned,' he said. 'I'm driving you back to Paris now, but I shall speak to your father in the morning.'

Stopping only in the hall to pick up the torn, white wisp of lace, they drove to Paris, speeding through the air in Charles' open, dark green Lagonda. They both exulted as the vintage sports car leaped through the mysterious night landscape. It seemed oddly silent, theirs alone. Clouds swept across the moon, then the night was velvet-black again, except for the golden track forged ahead of them by the headlights.

As they tore past black poplar trees, through dark tunnels of green gloom, they heard the odd, harsh animal noises of the night, so similar to the inarticulate, helpless sounds that had just been heard in the moonlit sheen of the blue brocade bedroom.

17

PAGAN couldn't come to the wedding, because she was in Egypt, but nothing could have kept Judy and Kate away. Kate's gift was a hunk of amethyst as a paperweight for Maxine's desk, and Judy brought a charming Steinberg etching of a nervous, blank-eyed bride clutching her gawky groom. Pagan sent a beautiful antique Damascan chest inlaid with a mother-of-pearl design.

Maxine and Charles were married at the *mairie* in Epernay almost a year after they had met. Maxine wore a pale-pink silk dress with a skirt that was layered like rose petals, and a large cream straw hat. She and Charles sat in two hard little chairs while the brief marriage ceremony was performed by the mayor, who wore his ceremonial red, white and blue sash. Then they signed the civil register, the French equivalent of signing a marriage contract. They were now officially married, and with their whole family swept off to the Royale Champagne for a lunch that lasted until six in the evening, when Maxine returned to Paris with her parents, as was the custom.

The church ceremony was held on the following day in the mellow, stone church at Epernay. A French bride normally had no matron-of-honour and no bridesmaids, but Maxine's two small girl cousins were to be *enfants d'honneur*, following her over the ancient stones.

Maxine had asked Kate to help her dress. In the hotel bedroom Kate laughed as she looked at Maxine, who was wearing only a froth of diaphanous veiling and skimpy, white satin underwear. Her clothes had been laid out on the bed. 'Really, Maxine, even your wedding dress is practical!' Kate picked up the cream silk calf-length coat. Designed by Raphael, it was tight-waisted, with a row of seed-pearl buttons stretching from the demure mandarin collar to the hem of the lavishly full skirt. For the wedding, the coat was worn over a strapless cream tulle ballgown, but later it could be worn by itself – as a coat or dress – to the races at Chantilly or almost any formal indoor occasion.

'Well, it's the prettiest dress I've ever had,' Maxine reasoned, 'so I don't want to wear it only once.'

For once Maxine didn't look efficient; in fact, she looked ethereal as she floated down the aisle between solemn stone columns. Beneath the hem of the long, full cream coat billowed a froth of cream tulle, and on her head Maxine wore a simple coronet of starlike flowers. As she passed Kate, the demure Maxine gave her a quick lascivious wink.

As soon as they returned from their honeymoon, Maxine was introduced to all the notable families of the district. Christina continued to run the day-to-day affairs of Paradis while Maxine made these important new contacts. Most of all, she enjoyed her visit to the house of Moët & Chandon, whose tradition of hospitality dated back to the Napoleonic era. Like Empress Josephine, the Tsar of Russia, the Emperor of Austria and the King of Prussia before her, Maxine was shown around the long, subterranean cellars to watch the making of champagne. They moved through dark vaults, grey and green with age, smelling of damp chalk, mould and sour wine. 'There are eighty miles of these cellars carved from the chalk soil under Epernay,' said Charles. He took Maxine's hand and scraped her nails on the crumbly surface of the cellar wall. 'You see? The whole of the champagne district is composed of this special chalk; it's *only* on this ground that the vines produce grapes with the unique champagne flavour. There's nowhere else in the world like it.'

By the end of the visit, Maxine thought that she'd heard quite enough about champagne for a bit, although she knew it might have been worse. She might have married a sheep farmer or a canning industry king or a railway coupling manufacturer, after all. As if reading her thoughts, Charles said, 'You needn't worry. I don't intend to become just another champagne bore. My business is part of my life and my heritage – in other words, it's my responsibility – but I'm not a city businessman. I'm a countryman. I like looking after my land and walking across it with my dogs, then in the evenings I like to read or listen to music – a quiet life.'

'And then at night,' said Maxine, 'you like to make love.'

'All the time I like to make love,' said Charles firmly.

217

The next day Charles suggested that Maxine should pay a visit to his headquarters and learn a little about champagne production. 'As the wife of the owner, you have to know these things,' he said, 'so now for a little homework. I'll try not to make it too dull, my darling.'

We're in for a boring morning, thought Maxine as, in her bedroom, she stepped into her Christian Dior going-away suit of primrose linen. It had a huge, knife-pleated skirt and a little, tight-waisted jacket that buttoned down the front and she looked charmingly demure in it. 'You look prim and proper, very ladylike,' said Charles approvingly, as he helped her into the Lagonda.

They screamed to a stop just outside Epernay in a stone courtyard and entered the ancient building that now served as an office. In the dim, empty entrance hall, as they climbed the worn stone steps to the laboratory, Charles explained, 'What a champagne house tries to do is to produce a wine that has *always* the same taste and quality. As the weather is always different and each harvest is different, one can only achieve this consistency by blending.' He paused to open a plain, white-painted door. 'You are now going to meet the most important person in any champagne manufacturer's firm: my blender.' He beckoned her in. 'You can't blend champagne by machine. A good house must have a good blender: the reputation of the entire firm depends upon his palate, eyes and nose.'

They entered a scrupulously clean laboratory: in front of a row of wooden chairs there stood a few spittoons. Several unmarked bottles stood on the central wooden table. 'No Smoking' signs hung on the wall. It was indeed extraordinarily dull so far, thought Maxine, as she was introduced to a pendulous-bellied man with a lugubrious face, the purple-red colour of a turkey cock's wattle.

The *chef de cave* solemnly offered them a glass of nonvintage champagne. Maxine thanked him with the grace and dignity that befitted her new position, and Charles then led her back down the stairs and along the black and white marble-tiled corridor towards the dim hall.

Suddenly he grabbed Maxine's wrist and pulled her into a dark recess under the staircase. He swiftly unbuttoned her primrose jacket, dipped both his hands into her lace bra and stopped her gasp of horror with his mouth. She felt his tongue pushing against hers. Then Charles pulled his head back and said in a normal voice, 'The first bottling generally takes place sometime after April and we add a little cane sugar to the blend to start a second fermentation.' He started to kiss her nipples. Maxine felt physically helpless, but as she groaned with reluctant pleasure, Charles suddenly withdrew his hands and buttoned her up as fast as a lady's maid.

Weak with desire, Maxine whispered, 'You mustn't, you really mustn't ... do that sort of thing.' But she didn't sound convincing.

Charles took her by one hand and led her down more stone steps, saying loudly, 'The second fermentation is when the champagne acquires its sparkle. That sparkle is really gas. Fermentation builds up an explosive pressure of gas. So a good cork is vital.'

Still speaking smoothly, he tugged her from the bottom of the staircase and into the shadows underneath it. Then he held her against his chest as, with his right hand, he felt under the primrose pleated skirt and tugged at her panties.

'Off!' he muttered.

'Charles! You must be *mad*, someone might *see*,' Maxine protested.

'Off!' Charles ordered, giving the lace a vicious tug. Nervously, Maxine wriggled out of them and tried to pick up the scrap of yellow lace, but Charles wouldn't let her bend down. 'I'm not having you turn into a prim little countess who worries about what people think all the time, like my sisters,' he said.

Then he froze as they heard footsteps approaching them. Maxine shut her eyes, and waited for the humiliation! The footsteps advanced and paused, then she heard a door open and bang. Charles released his grip. Maxine quickly bent down, picked up her panties and stuffed them into her linen shoulder bag. Without saying anything, Charles took her by the arm and hurried her towards the elevator at the back of the hall, saying in a normal voice, 'I hope you're going to be warm enough: I warned you yesterday that the cellars are cold. Shall I get a coat from the car?'

A youth in a white overall appeared behind them and sprang forward to open the iron grille of the two-person elevator.

'No, no, Charles, stop fussing,' Maxine said in a wobbly voice for the benefit of the respectful boy as he closed the grille shut behind them. Charles pressed a green button, the little lift started to jerk downwards and, as Maxine half-expected, his hand was under her skirt, his thumb moving in a steady rhythm against her flesh. The lift jerked downwards. Charles' other hand was clamped around her naked buttocks, the back of her skirt was caught up against the lift. She'd never get those creases out, Maxine thought, it took hours to iron. 'Until Dom Perignon came along in 1668, bottles were sealed with linen bungs dipped in olive oil, and of course this didn't provide a hermetic seal,' Charles explained gravely. Oh, God, she could think of nothing except his fingers. Now she'd risk humiliation rather than have him stop. Charles went on, as if he was having a conversation with his mother. 'Dom Perignon's *brilliant* idea was to wet a bit of cork to make it pliable, then ram it into the neck of the bottle.' Maxine jumped and quivered as he continued, 'The cork sealed the bottle and stopped the gas escaping.'

The elevator stopped with a swift, gentle shudder. Charles pulled back the iron grille. 'The pressure inside a bottle of champagne is about the same as the tyre pressure of a bus ... so you see how important the cork is.'

Maxine staggered out, smoothing down her skirt. Breathless and wobbly, she moved along the cellars, past thousands of bottles tilted neck downward in racks against the green-tinged chalk walls. Charles waved one hand towards the neat, lustrous rows, the little green soldiers of his empire. 'We leave the bottles of blended wine in cellars for a year or two, then they're put in these special racks so that the sediment from the wine drains down slowly on to the cork.'

'On to the cork,' echoed Maxine, in a dazed voice. A drip fell from the ceiling on to her cheek, then Charles tugged her by the wrist into one of the dim bottle-filled bays and again unbuttoned Maxine's jacket. This time she didn't protest.

'Yes,' said Charles gravely, 'on to the cork.' He pulled her back into the main passage and they walked down the long, wide cellar towards a row of silent men in navy sweaters and overalls, all working with their backs to Maxine as they swiftly twisted the bottles.

Maxine watched the bottles slowly move into the shining maw

of a steel machine. Somewhat to her disappointment, Charles was now behaving perfectly. But he moved her closer to the machine so that it hid their bodies from the workers beyond, who could only see their heads. Then Charles grabbed her hand and held it against him, so that Maxine could feel his mounting excitement. Maxine grasped him as Charles continued to talk in a normal voice. 'When the cork is removed, the frozen sediment comes out, clinging to it. Clever idea isn't it?' His body shuddered at the touch of her fingers as he droned on in the bored, sing-song voice of a tourist guide. 'After that, the wine is sniffed to check that it's still in good condition, and finally, as you'll see in the next bay, these men give it a sending-off dose – that's a tiny quantity of sweetened liqueur made from old wine and cane sugar . . .'

He gave a great contented sigh. After a moment, they moved to the next bay where Charles picked up a beaker of liqueur and gave it to Maxine to sniff. 'You don't add much if you want a *brut* wine, which is generally the best wine a firm makes,' he said. 'The liqueur content is increased, according to how sweet you want your wine to be – extra dry, dry, *demi-doux* and *doux*, which is disgustingly sweet and will never be served at my table.'

'*Our* table,' said Maxine as they moved on. She added, 'I think I could make a batch by myself now.'

'You haven't seen the last working bay. There it is ahead of us. This is where the bottles are recorked and we fit those little wire nozzles over the cork to keep them in place. After that we rest the bottles for a few years in those cellars at the far end, then we label them and send them off to customers.'

Maxine looked along the high-arched tunnel; either side was lined with deep bays stacked high with champagne, the black-green bottle bases facing towards them in an endless rich pattern. Suddenly, Charles tugged her into another deep bay. He pinned her shoulders against the chalk walls where they could be seen by anyone who happened to pass, but Maxine was now heedless of anything except her urgent need for Charles, and their sexual tension swiftly built up to a climax as violently explosive as the cork bursting from a bottle of champagne.

18

WITHIN three months of her marriage, Maxine found to her joy that she was pregnant. Unfortunately, she felt ill throughout her pregnancy, so all her plans for the château had to be postponed and she did the minimum work for Paradis. She thanked her lucky stars for the stolid, tough Christina, who continued to run the day-to-day aspects of their business. As Maxine grew larger and larger, she felt dull and sleepy. 'I thought I was going to have a wonderful complexion and be radiantly serene,' she shouted to Charles from her bathroom, 'not become bovine and lethargic. No, don't you *dare* come in, I'm heaving myself into this disgusting support corset. I think I'm going to give up clothes and just lie around in a negligée on a sofa like Madame Récamier for the next few months.'

In an easy birth, she had a son, Gérard. Happily she and Charles counted his toes and analysed his features. 'He's got *your* nose,' said Charles fondly.

'But *your* mouth,' Maxine added.

'And my hair, though not nearly enough,' said Charles, tenderly stroking the soft, pale, beige silken head.

'I had no idea that being a father would make me so happy,' Charles admitted four months later. He tugged at Maxine's cream lace negligée and softly kissed the base of her throat.

'Then you're going to be twice as happy, Charles.'

Suddenly alert, he sat up and looked at her questioningly. "Goodness. You don't mean ... but Gérard is only four months old!'

'Goodness had nothing to do with it,' said Maxine, slyly quoting Mae West.

This time the birth was extremely difficult. She was in labour for three agonizing days, at the end of which she gave birth to another son, whom they christened Oliver.

The birth left Maxine exhausted and depressed. Her stitches

were painful whenever she moved. She burst into tears over trivial matters and she snapped at Charles. As she knew perfectly well that she was a very lucky woman with no reason to feel sorry for herself, she felt secretly anxious about the melancholy that swamped her. Was there something wrong with her? Charles quietly spoke to the doctor about her tears and tantrums. She hadn't been as bad as this after the birth of Gérard. The doctor said that it would probably be a couple of months before she recovered fully from the birth. Could not her sister or her mother or a friend come and stay to cheer her up? Someone she'd known a long time and with whom she felt comfortable?

As soon as the doctor departed, Charles reached for the telephone. Pagan was still in Egypt, and there was no answer from Kate, but he got Judy on his first try. He explained the situation.

'I can't possibly drop everything and come immediately,' said Judy. 'I'm a hired hand, remember? But I'm due for a vacation, and anyway, I'll be over in Paris for the collections in two months' time. I could come for a couple of weeks before then, if you like.'

Maxine burst into tears when she heard of Judy's visit. She didn't want to see anyone. Harassed, Charles took his dogs for a long walk in the rain. *Women!* However, as the weeks passed, his wife slowly grew stronger and more cheerful and by the time Judy arrived, Maxine longed to see her again.

Every morning Judy ate breakfast in Maxine's blue silk bedroom, while Maxine lay back against lace-trimmed pillows beneath the billowing blue silken swags that fell from the gilded coronet fixed high above her head. In the morning they went for a short, brisk walk, pushing the two high baby carriages before them over the frozen ground of the park. In the afternoon they sat and chatted in the nursery.

From the moment Judy arrived, Maxine began to recover her spirits. She loved Judy's ability to go straight to the point. 'You sharpen my wits, Judy,' Maxine said, with admiration and a twinge of regret. 'You make me focus on what is *important*, as opposed to what is merely urgent. And you do this naturally, whereas I find it takes a great effort of will on my part. Every day when I get to my desk, I find it covered with problems. It's so tempting to avoid the big ones, and so much easier to occupy oneself with little difficulties.'

'That's because you're fat, idle and happily married,' said Judy.

'I'm all for marriage,' Maxine yawned. 'Why don't you try it?'

'Oh, because I don't like very young men or very old men: I like middle-aged men, but nobody will admit to being one.'

'No, seriously, Judy, haven't you got some special fellow? You never mention anyone, but surely . . .'

'I know plenty of men, Maxine, but I can't seem to get particularly *interested* in any of them, that's all. I go out on dates but I never seem to fall in love. I see other women do it all the time, but it just doesn't seem to happen to me. Anyway, I'm on the road so much that a serious love affair would be a geographical impossibility.'

'You don't think that perhaps you're frightened of giving yourself to a man?'

'Oh, shove it, Maxine. No, really, there *are* other things to life, you know . . . I'm only twenty-two! *Men* of my age don't go mooning around and worrying if they're not in love. I suspect that women overrate falling in love.'

'Only because you haven't yet!'

'If you don't shut up,' Judy said amiably, 'I shall feel obliged to throw this glass of champagne at you.' She raised her long-stemmed, tulip-shaped glass as the cold red sun touched the horizon. 'Incidentally, how come you don't have real champagne glasses?'

'That *is* a real champagne glass,' said Maxine, clasping her hands behind her head and leaning back against the buttoned crimson velvet of her chair. 'The traditional glass is not supposed to be wide and shallow. A wide glass prevents the concentration of the bouquet, and the wine goes flat more quickly because such a large surface of it is exposed to the air.' She yawned, stretched and scooped up the black cat that lay in front of the fire. 'You see, I now know every bloody thing there is to know about champagne.'

Judy stared into the blazing fire, glanced around the room and then looked at Maxine. 'You got it all, kid,' she said, grinning.

'And Heavens, I *work* for it!' Maxine suddenly looked harassed and the cat stiffened in surprise. 'It's damned hard work running a home, no matter what the size is. In fact, I think it's easier to run a business, because your business shows results. Nobody notices housework unless you don't to it, then they complain. And business hours are generally only eight hours a day, five days a week, while housekeeping is sixteen hours, every damn day of the year, if you're running a home with young children.' She sighed, 'Well, at least I no longer have any guilt about being a mother who goes out to work – although Charles' sisters never stop sniffing about it.'

She relaxed again and the cat settled down. 'Do you remember, after I had Gérard I also became a bit depressed for no apparent reason? Charles was working hard, running a house was no longer a novelty, I was no longer a young bride showing off ... I felt *guilty* because I was depressed. I thought it must mean that I was not maternal, that I was a bad mother, otherwise I would have been happy with baby, wouldn't I?'

An ironic smile shadowed her face. 'So I started to cheer myself up with little snacks between meals, not exactly in secret, but when nobody else was around, you understand ... You remember that chocolate is my great weakness? I used to nibble chocolate cakes and chocolate ice cream, drink hot chocolate with thick cream ... When I put on weight, I simply stopped standing on the scales, and then I became pregnant again so fast that I had a good excuse for getting ... well, I never used the word "fat" to myself, of course.'

She looked up, still stroking the cat on her lap. 'Then one day, walking along the street, I caught sight of myself in a shop window – and I didn't *recognize* myself! I tell you it was a real shock and I thought, heavens, I'll soon be as tubby as I was when I first went to Switzerland. That had been puppy fat and not difficult to shed, but after two babies, the doctor warned me it would be more difficult.'

The cat stretched her front paws and extended her little claws and dug them into Maxine's knee. She gave it a little slap and continued, 'So in order to take my mind off the diet he gave me, I went back to work at Paradis. I worked there every single day for a month, and by the end of the month, to my surprise I found that I was happy again! I hadn't had time to eat, or feel bored or sorry for myself.' She yawned. 'So when I've stopped feeding Oliver, I'm going back to work. I've argued the case with myself and the doctor and we've decided that it's better the babies don't have a twenty-four-hour-a-day, depressed, overweight, worried mother. Sixteen hours a day is enough time to spend at home.'

'You get top marks for sheer ingratitude,' Judy said. 'Here you are, twenty-four years old, with a marvellous husband, two adorable babies, a flourishing business, a title and a château. What *more* could you want?'

'Money,' said Maxine simply.

'But I thought you were rich!'

'That's the other reason I went back to work. Paradis pays for all our personal expenses, although the profits really ought to be going back into the business. Christina is getting angry about it, and I don't blame her. But what can I do? We're poor. It's almost our only income.'

She hesitated, and then in a rush she said, 'To tell you the truth, we probably can't afford to live here much longer. That's why I'm so glad to have you staying here now. Charles is as stubborn as a mule, he refuses to sell the château, but it's going to fall around our ears at any moment. He insists that one day the vineyards are going to show a profit, but the harvest is mortgaged to the hilt, so it won't make any difference if we have a good one, and we'll be in dreadful trouble if we *don't*. Papa is going to discuss the business with Charles this weekend. He's an exporter, so it might be possible for him to improve our foreign sales. But there's so much competition in the champagne industry, and nobody's ever *heard* of de Chazalle champagne. They buy from Moët or one of the other big firms.'

Judy said thoughtfully, 'You must forgive me if I point out that you have six indoor servants. That's not what I call poor.'

'Yes, but the two maids are essential to clean this vast place. Charles needs a secretary. The children need a nanny if I am to work. The four of them need a cook, and five servants need a butler to supervise them.'

Judy raised a sceptical eyebrow, lay back against her chair and looked into the hypnotic flames of the fire. 'Maxie, I *know* you're sitting on a gold mine. I can feel it. I just can't *quite* work out how you can make money, except that you've given me such a wonderful time here that I find myself thinking I would rather stay here than at the grandest hotel. This last month has been a dream. I've never enjoyed myself so much in my life. And I've never felt so comfortable and so happy. You're a very gifted hostess, Maxine. Wouldn't it be possible to run the château as a sort of hotel, perhaps not *exactly* a hotel, but the sort that's run for paying guests who would like to experience castle life exactly as if they were private guests? For, say, sixty dollars each a weekend, you could give people a *fantastic* time!'

Maxine sat up. It was a brilliant idea! Why hadn't she thought of it? It was very much like what she was doing already, in a small way; Charles' sisters already used the place as a rest home. And perhaps she might open a branch of the antique shop in the stables.

'I could help to arrange for publicity at the American end,' volunteered Judy. 'What you need is a steady flow of people from the States who want to enjoy the château experience. Perhaps you should start by asking some well-known Americans to stay free.'

'But I thought the idea was to make money,' Maxine objected.

'Yes, but if you invite a couple of Hollywood stars – they often visit Paris – you'll get terrific coverage in the American papers and then you'll be talked about. Word of mouth! Honestly, Maxine, I know this business. You mustn't think that PR is free; you mustn't make the same mistake as the rest of your goddamned compatriots. You pay for it, just as you do in advertising, only in a different way.'

Judy rolled her eyes in mock Gallic exasperation. 'It's riskier, because you can't control what publicity you're going to get, but if you've got a good, newsworthy product and the PR is handled efficiently, you get good coverage.'

'I'll speak to Papa this weekend,' said Maxine thoughtfully, '*before* he speaks to Charles about the vineyards.'

Charles was appalled by Judy's idea and made it clear that he wanted no part of it. He found it painfully distasteful to think of strangers in his family home. He realized that something had to be done to stop the château from falling down, but he was working as hard as he could to make the estate pay and to modernize it and he simply didn't have time for any other ventures. Eventually, however, he was worn down by Judy's enthusiastic insistence and Maxine's quiet determination. Vulnerable because of his exhaustion and anxiety, knowing that something had to be done, he agreed to let Maxine go ahead, provided she committed none of his meagre capital to the project – because there was simply none to spare.

Maxine was tremendously excited. She found it difficult to keep her mind on the practical aspects of the project because charming little side ideas kept popping unbidden into her mind. She was sure they could set up a little arcade of shops in that great useless stable block; she could franchise some of them the way Paris hotels did, and they could have a little shop to sell champagne by the bottle or by the crate.

When consulted, Maxine's father cautiously said that while he thought the idea had possibilities, he couldn't possibly finance such a venture himself. However, they might be able to get bank financing.

As soon as they started to draw up estimates, they realized that the restoration of the château would need far more money than they could gross by running it as a hotel. Maxine had heard that one or two English stately homes had been turned into historical entertainment areas for family outings, with museums and amusement arcades. She thought this sounded like a good possibility, but dared not mention it to Charles until she had researched her scheme; she could imagine his rage at the idea of turning the home of his ancestors into an amusement park.

After Judy had flown home, Maxine also left for a two-week trip, during which time she visited those châteaux of the Loire Valley that had been opened to the public. The interiors were almost empty and devoid of interest, except to the scholarly. She went to England and visited Longleat, an exquisite example of Elizabethan architecture, owned by the Marquess of Bath; she went to the beautiful and highly successful Woburn Abbey; then she trudged up to Derbyshire to see the Duke of Devonshire's Chatsworth in all its chilly splendour. She returned to Epernay with very decided ideas: in her own castle she did not want merely to present a tour of an old family home – she wanted to try to *evoke* history, using stage production techniques.

Maxine, her father and the estate accountant drew up a new set of figures for her ambitious project. Both men were dubious, but Maxine was determined that her scheme would be accurately assessed for financial viability. Then, filled with despair by the total figure, Maxine telephoned Judy. 'We're going to need around $177,000. I don't think it's going to be possible.'

'It's possible until it's proved impossible, so just look quietly confident and project assurance.'

Maxine had learned a lot since drawing up her first financial forecast to extend her antique shop. Now, with the help of her father and the estate accountant she set out her business proposition, and together the four of them – for Charles had reluctantly agreed to participate in the presentation – drove to Paris to discuss it with a merchant bank. They needed to borrow 33 million francs, and if they got it, they would need to achieve a turnover of 39 million francs a year to cover running costs and show a profit. With any luck, it would take them fifteen years to get out of debt. But if they didn't have any luck they would be homeless and out of work, for the entire estate was now pledged as collateral against loans, not to speak of a further guarantee from Maxine's father.

Understandably, Charles fought against this. 'I said that I would agree in principle, *provided* that none of my capital was needed!'

'This isn't capital. It's a matter of using all your unmortgaged assets as collateral for the loan.'

'But if it doesn't succeed we'll be bankrupt.'

'And if it *does* succeed you won't have to leave your family home. Your sons can grow up here as you did.'

Maxine won.

From the day the bank loan was taken up and the interest began to mount, there was not a moment to be wasted. Maxine hired a secretary, a neat competent girl with a tight mouth, and from that moment it was difficult to tell whether Mademoiselle Janine was running Maxine or Maxine was running Mademoiselle Janine.

Charles shuddered when he thought of what could go wrong. Maxine thought only of the work to be done; she woke up remembering what she had forgotten the day before, her life revolved around a series of lists and lists of lists, but she was exuberantly excited. Judy had already designed her letterhead; in traditional script it read simply:

During the months that followed, Maxine couldn't spend as much time with her babies as she would have wished, but no matter how busy she was, she always spent the afternoons with them. After they had gone to bed, Maxine worked far into the night – every night – as she took over the responsibility of the château as a business proposition and continued with the work that she had abandoned when she first became pregnant.

Apart from the relatively small area in which the family lived, many of the rooms and passages were still in a depressing chaos. Forgotten treasures stood next to worthless watercolour daubs by Charles's great-aunts; everything seemed to be dirty, covered with cobwebs and fly-droppings or nibbled by mice. The attic in the west turret was filled with oil paintings – horses and dogs, sheep and prize bulls, as well as other animals treasured by Charles's ancestors; unfortunately, they had been badly stored, and many of the paintings were torn and in need of repair. It was a daunting project.

Paradis designed and superintended the rebuilding and decoration work. Maxine picked a young Parisian designer to work with her on the exhibition and together they produced a plan. Maxine didn't want crowds shuffling in and out of beautiful rooms while a bored guide chanted at them. She wanted the tour to be an exciting, theatrical event. 'I want our guests to feel amazement and delight,' she told the designer, who had never before dealt with such an odd demand.

Their first job was to get an accurate plan of the second floor, and once that had been surveyed, their next step was to plan the tour. For a week they pored over the plans together, scribbling over them on tracing paper and chalking out different ideas for the tour route. Then the whole family moved to a rented house in Epernay and everything in the château was cleared out to go into storage for six months while the building restoration took place. Before it went through the door and into the furniture vans, each item was catalogued and photographed. Aware of the inexorable change in popular taste – and also that the throw-outs of one generation are the antiques of the next – Maxine had resolved to sell almost nothing. 'We have plenty of space,' she reasoned, 'so we will invest in storage. This sort of nineteenth-century picture and furniture is already selling well in America, so we will only get rid of the really big pieces, like all those armoires, which I can sell to cabinetmakers who will make fake period bookcases from them.'

Maxine examined every single piece of furniture herself. Her greatest discovery was when she spotted the gracefully curved legs and fine bronze mounts of a slender pair of Boulle commodes; the handles, set in rosettes of five acorns, were the same as the Mazarine commodes in the Louvre which had been made in 1709 for Louis XIV. Only one item was sold – a cylinder-topped desk with inlaid floral marquetry by Oeben, dated 1765. Maxine hated it on sight. She sold it to the Metropolitan Museum for five million francs, to the astonishment and admiration of her husband, and it paid for the plumbing.

Then the building contractors moved into the château and Charles found it difficult to decide whether they were rebuilding it or tearing it down.

'I cannot stand much more of this chaos!' he roared at Maxine one morning, waving his arms in the middle of the gutted main salon, where doors and windows were being unblocked and partitions were being destroyed in a welter of banging rubble and dust. Maxine was used to the chaos caused by such work and she did not see the apparent muddle but only what would shortly be the exquisitely restored salon. Linking her arm in his, she led him away to the next wing, where much of the reconstruction work had been completed. But here the noise and bustle was even worse as the whole wing was being scrubbed from top to bottom by professional cleaners with huge scrubbing machines for the floor, complicated, automated ladders and arm extenders for getting into places that were otherwise impossible to reach.

Charles bolted out of the nearest door and headed for the stable block where the dogs were kennelled, but his traditional house of peace had been invaded by yet another army of workmen. The interior of the stable block was being rebuilt as an arcade of charming, old-fashioned little shops, and would also contain a coffee bar, a restaurant and a free wine-tasting cellar.

Charles threw up his arms in Gallic despair as Maxine caught up with him and tugged his sleeve. 'Darling Charles, you've been so patient ... only a few more weeks, love ... let me show you the part that's finished – Ancestor Alley – it was completed yesterday!'

Ancestor Alley was their joke name for the History Walk on the first floor. The entire tour was electronically operated by a push-button system, with the human element introduced as extra, because Maxine wasn't sure how much human element she'd be able to rely on. Pencil-beam spotlights marked the darkened, crimson-roped route. Some of the small rooms had been completely blacked out and furnished with museum showcases of clear glass, cunningly lit by narrow beams of light, so that it looked as if the family treasures were floating in space.

One eight-foot-wide corridor was painted Chinese yellow and used as a gallery for the portraits of Charles' ancestors. Charles calmed down as he walked past the beautifully exhibited rows of de Chazalles who stretched back into history – seven-year-old Christian with a blue sash under his lace shirt was leading a donkey across the park in 1643; in 1679 Amélie de Chazalle smiled in a pale grey, low-cut moiré dress, with a parrot perched on her shoulder; in 1776 a group of seven little children (with two sets of twins) sat solemnly around the dining table eating grapes and walnuts, while their beringed and ringleted little mother fed almonds to her pet monkey.

'Poor things, they were all beheaded in the Revolution except for the youngest boy,' Charles suddenly heard his own recorded voice saying. 'He escaped to Geneva, disguised as a runaway lady's maid, somehow managed to marry an heiress, and their daughter married Henri Nestlé of the chocolate family.'

Charles' voice also welcomed the visitors in the entrance hall and, as they moved through the house, he recited his entire family history from the twelfth century to the present; translations in twelve languages were available. Other rooms had background music – Strauss waltzes, harpsichord music, the voice of a young boy soprano floating to the arched roof of the family chapel, and the faint, animated chatter of children, which could be heard in the old nursery.

Maxine had hoped to open the château to the public on the first of July, but as always there were problems with workmen, so they were unable to open until mid-August. On the opening day they all waited, tense with anticipation. Supposing nobody turned up? Expectantly, they all waited at their battle stations at nine o'clock in the morning. But nothing happened.

In the cobbled courtyard, between the stable block and the house, a charming, nineteenth-century carousel had been erected, with carved and gilded horses, dolphins, swans and mermaids for children to ride. Children could also be taken for rides on ponies or on a trip in the old yellow-lacquered, eighteenth-century state coach, which once again would lumber up and down the drive. There were going to be as many free shows as Maxine could devise, from carousel rides to champagne-tasting – anything that was necessary to make a success of the first day, not only to boost the morale of the staff, but also because the press might be there.

Nothing happened until ten-thirty in the morning. Then as the first three coaches approached the château (Charles immediately thought, We'll have to reinforce that drive), a small cheer broke out from the excited group that was waiting for them on the front steps. In an unprecedented gesture, Aunt Hortense snatched off her scarlet pillbox hat and threw it in the air. She had been more worried than any of them. Only she knew that it had been her last-minute, behind-the-scenes arguments that had convinced Maxine's father to take the plunge.

If it failed, he would never forgive her.

～ 19 ～

FROM the beginning Judy had had no trouble in getting publicity for the château, and nearly all the first paying guests were booked in from the United States. Maxine had also invited a handful of French celebrity friends, including Guy Saint Simon, now a well-known fashion designer, in order that the Americans would feel that they were getting their money's worth.

'They're obviously all enjoying themselves tremendously,' Guy commented after his first visit.

'Oh, yes, one or two have already booked up for a further visit,' said Maxine happily. To her surprise, she found that she loved entertaining these strangers – she found something interesting about most of them, and their enjoyment was infectious.

Painfully, Maxine rebuilt the crumbling fabric of Charles' family home and brought it to life again. Of course, it was not possible to please everybody. Charles' sisters were icily critical, but then they always found something to complain about. They thought it vulgar that a de Chazalle should have to work and that their home should be opened to strangers. 'Serves him right for marrying a bourgeoise,' said his elder sister. 'God knows what she'll think of next: strip shows in the drawing room or a zoo in the park.'

Both sisters refused to face the fact that without Maxine's work there would no longer *be* any château, and that without her encouragement and support, Charles would be in no position to establish the estate as one of the principal minor tourist attractions of the Champagne. Most of all the sisters deplored Maxine's vulgar American associate, the one who had flown over from New York for the opening, that young woman, Judy, who talked loudly and discussed money and business at meals.

Just before Judy flew back to America, Guy drove out to the château from Paris. It was the chef's evening off, and a cold meal had been left in the library. As she took a slice of ham, Judy felt an odd, schoolgirlish, conspiratorial atmosphere of suspense and smothered giggles, as if a secret was about to be revealed. Maybe they were going to give her a present? After all, opening the château had been her idea ... She took her plate and sat on the footstool in front of the log fire at Aunt Hortense's bony feet, the metatarsals bulging after a lifetime spent in too-high heels. It wasn't really cold enough for a fire but Maxine always kept one burning in the little library.

'Something's going on. What's up? What are you hiding from me?' Judy said suspiciously.

Aunt Hortense gave a smothered laugh and almost dropped her plate. Guy looked at Charles, who gave an odd grin – Charles now enjoyed Guy's company, although at first he had resented this dress-maker who had been in the nursery with Maxine and who consequently knew what she was thinking far better than her husband.

Now Guy nodded his head at Charles and turned to Judy. His face was serious. 'We want to discuss a business proposition with you, Judy. We want to suggest that you open your own office and handle our publicity in the States.'

Judy was astonished. 'That's very ... that's wonderfully flattering and very generous of you.'

'Not at all, it would be in *our* interest,' said Guy. 'I need my own PR in the States, and I've worked with you for years in Paris. You know my business.'

'And we are obviously going to rely on American visitors to the château,' added Maxine. 'So we need someone we can trust to handle us in America.'

'Don't think that the idea hasn't crossed my mind! But I'm far too young and I haven't any capital. Maxine, you know I need every cent I can save for mother's medical bills. I've no money.'

'We're paying other firms to do this work now,' Charles said. 'We might as well pay you. To be frank, I *also* thought you might be too young, but we *all* started young. You're nearly twenty-three, Judy. A woman of that age is not too young to be responsible for little children, so why not for a little business? You don't have to start immediately. We could plan for six months' time.'

Judy turned to Guy. 'Was this what was at the back of your mind when you first came to New York? Was this what you were hinting at on the East River?'

'Of course. You've helped us to start. Now we intend to help you.' He stood and raised his flute of champagne. 'To Judy!'

They all echoed his toast. And Judy cried.

Charles allocated nearly all his small publicity budget to PR, rather than to advertising. He quickly became intrigued by Judy's ideas, by her straightforward approach and the impressive results. At first he found it difficult to work with a woman who talked in such a brusque, forthright fashion: Charles was used to business conversations that were more circuitous and women who flattered men, but he realized to survive, new ideas were needed; he also realized that as Judy was starting her own business she would work as hard as she could on his account. Which she did.

It was not difficult to promote an account as glamorous as champagne; had Judy been trying to sell brushes or sensible walking shoes, she might have had a far more difficult time. From the beginning she pushed three linked words: '*Paris-Champagne-Maxine.*' She used Maxine rather than Charles because Charles hated publicity. Maxine understood it much better. She enjoyed being a professional celebrity. The second reason was that 'Maxine' was very similar to 'Maxim's', the name of the world-famous Parisian restaurant. When Judy devised a new letterhead that read '*Paris • Champagne • Maxine*', there was an immediate, reproachful protest from Maxim's restaurant, which felt that *they* were inextricably associated in the public's mind with Paris, and that the use of Madame la Comtesse's Christian name might confuse the public. But Judy – delighted – begged to disagree and refused to change the letterhead.

Maxine became increasingly well known as a French celebrity. She was always able to provide a quotable sentence, a joke or a shrewd comment when it was needed. Judy warned her never to talk in public about money, politics or religion and never to complain to the press about anything at all; when the odd spiteful article appeared, she was to ignore it. 'Yes, I know that there are boxes and boxes of splendid press cuttings,' said Maxine sadly, 'but unfortunately, it's only the bitchy ones that one pays any attention to – these are the only ones that upset me.'

'Well, you've got to learn to live with it,' Judy said firmly. 'I don't mind how loudly you voice your feelings in private as long as you don't *ever* try to get an apology out of a newspaper. Sue them or forget it.'

Judy also stressed that Maxine should always be beautifully dressed. Maxine did not find this instruction difficult to obey. As often as she could afford to, Maxine shopped at Christian Dior, although at first she could only afford a couple of outfits a year. After visiting Dior, Maxine would take a leisurely stroll up the rue du Faubourg St Honoré to choose a few boutique items and restock her lingerie drawers.

Maxine needed a great deal of underwear for a very private reason.

*

Charles was an affectionate and indulgent husband. After a certain amount of initial irritability, he let Maxine take over the organization of their lives and was both proud of and quietly amused by the way she did it. Once in a while he put his foot down, but this happened rarely. Most of the time she had her own way and was allowed to win their occasional arguments, but Charles liked her to remember that this was not because he was doting or henpecked, but simply because he chose to indulge her. He had a special way of reminding his wife of this.

Sometimes on formal occasions Charles would make Maxine gasp or blush or even forget what she meant to say. He could manage this by directing one meaningful look at her. It was a power that he had over her and he enjoyed it immensely, this ability to destroy her calm with that one look that, he knew, made her heart lurch and her groin moisten. Maxine knew exactly what the look meant.

One night, shortly after they were married, Charles had murmured, 'I don't want you to wear any underwear to the de la Fresange ball tonight. I want to know that if I care to feel you at *any time*, you will be ready for me.' Maxine thought he was joking, but during the course of the evening he danced her out of the ballroom and on to a dark corner of the terrace, then swiftly felt beneath the pale-pink net layers of her ballgown.

Maxine was wearing panties.

Charles ripped them off and flung them to the ground and then, with his left arm, he held her pressed against the stone balustrade. From the back they looked like any courting couple, but his fingers were feeling fiercely for her. She was terrified that they would be seen, that she was going to fall backward over the low stone balustrade as he pressed against her, but she could not resist Charles' rhythmic fingers. Quickly he undid his clothes and she felt him inside her body, demanding her with a selfish fierceness that she had never felt from him before. After he climaxed, he kissed her gently on the lips and said, 'Darling, in just a few matters, I expect to be obeyed by you without question.'

After that, upon occasion, he would casually ask Maxine not to wear underwear, particularly if they were going to a very formal function. When this happened he gave his driver the evening off, somewhat to the man's surprise. In the car, Charles' hand would search under Maxine's skirt and feel between her quivering white thighs to find out whether he had been obeyed. Once when he hadn't been (because Maxine wanted to see what would happen), he had stopped the car and roughly told Maxine to get out. There on the grass verge of the country road he made her wriggle out of her panties, then he threw the flimsy scrap of peach chiffon over the hedge, pulled Maxine into the back seat, put her over his knee and spanked her. He was not joking.

A few days later, after they had dined *à deux* at home, Charles took her by the hand and led her to the office that they shared. The deserted room was like a comfortable drawing room, although around it were spread typewriters, tape recorders and filing cabinets. In the middle of the room was a six-foot-square green leather-covered antique partners' desk, with drawers on both sides so that two people could work at the one desk.

Charles threw himself on to his office swivel chair.

'Get your clothes off,' he said softly, '*now*. I want to see you naked.'

'But the servants haven't gone to bed yet. Can't we go upstairs?'

'Now! Here!'

He watched with a slight smile as Maxine undressed, then he leaned forward and tugged roughly at her neat chignon so that the blonde hair tumbled forwards and over her heavy breasts. Then he pulled her on to his lap so that she sat astride him, facing him, nervous, puzzled and more than a little worried. He bent his lips to one full, blue-veined breast and sucked passionately until Maxine, arching her back so that her tangled straw hair fell towards the floor, no longer knew where she was or what she was doing. Then he lifted her buttocks and pulled her body gently on to his, starting to thrust inside her, until, as Maxine was about to climax, he murmured in her ear, 'Do you care if the servants hear?'

'No, no,' she gasped, 'don't stop, don't stop!'

'Do you care if anyone sees us?'

'No!'

On another moonlit night in the office, he again made her undress and sit on the edge of the great desk. He caressed her back with silken strokes, voluptuous and oddly objective; softly he ran his fingertips over her rounded belly, tasted her warm, musky female odour. Then he gently pushed her backwards so that she was quivering naked on the leather desk and the strands of blonde hair fell over the dictaphone as Charles bent his head and flicked his tongue over her pale body. Afterwards, when she lay still and gasping, he quickly tore his clothes off and mounted her on the desk. Then he tantalizingly stopped and said, 'You wouldn't *mind* if Mademoiselle Janine were to see what happens here out of office hours?'

'No! Oh, *please*, darling Charles, come back inside me.'

'You don't mind if she knows that Madame la Comtesse, so correct, so elegant, turns into an abandoned hussy if I simply slip my hand between her thighs?'

But Maxine was groaning too hard with pleasure to answer.

As Maxine became more and more famous in France, as she was courted and quoted and photographed with this or that celebrity, Charles loved to think that he could shatter her poise with a single glance. He would look hard at her, across a room full of impeccably dressed, important people, and he would have the immediate satisfaction of seeing Maxine give a little jump and blush.

Later that night he would tear off her frail nightgown – he rather liked to tear fragile, lace-covered garments off his wife – and say, '*That* was what the General wanted to do to you, wasn't it?' Or he would roughly grasp her breasts and bury his head between them muttering, 'Was *that* what you wanted from the Newman man?'

Maxine had never dreamed that married life would be so laced with hazard and surprise or that her lingerie bill would be so large.

She loved every dangerous moment of it.

Most of Maxine's married friends had been involved with other men, but Maxine had long ago decided to be faithful to her husband – an unusual decision for a Frenchwoman of her class. Maxine felt – hoped – that she did not need any added excitement in her life.

In spite of Charles' amiability, he turned out to be an exceedingly jealous husband, but only if he saw – or thought he saw –

that some particularly handsome man was interested in Maxine. He was not the sort of husband who checked her every movement.

With one exception.

In the winter of 1956, without warning, without mentioning her intentions to anyone and only leaving a brief message with Charles' secretary, Maxine suddenly went away for a week. Just before her little green MG disappeared, there had been much long-distance telephoning in the privacy of her boudoir – a room that she rarely used.

After seven days, Maxine returned looking white and haggard, distraught and tearful. She told a furious, worried Charles that she'd suddenly decided to see Colette Joyaux, an old school friend in Bordeaux who had suddenly been taken ill.

Her husband exploded with jealous rage. She couldn't even be bothered to *lie* to him with her usual efficiency. He sarcastically said that he found it hard to believe that a friend whom she rarely saw, who was little more than an acquaintance, in fact, should suddenly be stricken with an illness that required the presence of Maxine.

What was the illness? What was the name of Madame Joyaux's doctor and his telephone number? Why did Maxine leave without warning, but with a packed suitcase? Why had she packed her own suitcase instead of asking a maid to do it? Why hadn't she told him of Colette's illness before she left? Why had she telephoned during the morning when she knew that Charles was never in the Epernay office to say that she'd be away for a few days? Why hadn't she telephoned *once* in the morning or the evening when she might assume that he'd be at home?

Maxine tried to answer his angry barrage of questions. Clumsily she clambered out of one lie with an answer that immediately plunged her into another, but she stubbornly refused to give any explanation of her absence. She looked white and ill, and Charles had never seen her look so sad. She seemed not to care what Charles felt, thought or said. She didn't even bother to hide her indifference. Although she was physically present, Charles could see that her mind was miles away. With somebody else.

He strode out of her boudoir, charged down the circular staircase, jumped into his Lagonda and drove to Paris for a week, giving no details of his whereabouts to Maxine. After his departure she found that two photographs of Pierre Boursal had been taken from her school scrapbook and had been left, in torn-up shreds, on her dressing table.

When Charles returned after dinner one night, looking grim but smug, they had a fierce fight that ended roughly and happily in bed. The matter was never referred to again.

Charles had made his point and knew when to let well enough alone.

~ 20 ~

As soon as Elizabeth saw the dim lights in the valley below, in the safety of Austria, she felt lonely and anxious. She almost didn't want to reach those lights. Out of breath, the small, tired child paused to rub her chilled hands and then trudged on through the Austrian snow down a twisting path that led to Eisenstadt.

An hour later, she staggered up the steps of the first house she reached and wearily jumped to bang the door knocker. There was a sudden glare of light, a big man's silhouette, then she heard someone say, 'More soup, Helga, here's another one.' Dazed and silent, the child was only vaguely aware of a steamy kitchen and strange adults in nightclothes fussing around her. Then she went to sleep, wrapped in a blanket and huddled in an armchair.

The following day she was taken to the Eisenstadt refugee camp, a collection of bleak old army huts with a constant stream of people plodding from one to the other – some of the hundred and fifty thousand Hungarian refugees who surged over the border in 1956. Hastily recruited voluntary workers moved from hut to hut taking particulars of the forlorn, silent groups who wore overcoats with turned-up collars and clutched knobbly shopping bags, potato sacks or small attaché cases that held their only possessions.

An impatient, harassed, oily-faced woman who carried a clipboard asked Elizabeth her name. She spoke at first in broken

German and the bewildered child didn't understand what she was saying until she switched to French. 'Speak up, child! There's a string around your neck but no name tag on it. Was it torn off? I must have your name before your medical inspection.'

Eventually the child croaked, 'Lili.'

'Lili what?'

'*Quoi, s'il vous plaît, madame?*'

'Your family, what's the name of your family?'

'Da ... da ...' No, she was no longer called Dassin ... Lili sobbed 'Ko ... Ko ... *vago.*' The woman wrote '*Lily Vago (French-speaking) born 1949*' at the head of the sheet of paper and so, at the age of seven, Lili acquired her fourth surname – the name on her birth certificate, then Dassin, then Kovago, and now Vago. She was then handed a piece of soap and a piece of black bread and stood in a line of sad-eyed adults for her medical inspection. Lili felt a singing in her ears and, from far away, a chill stethoscope on her chest. 'It sounds like pneumonia. Shock and exposure. Take her over to the hospital hut. Next one, please.'

As soon as the child was well enough to travel, a refugee committee worker told her that she was being sent to a family in Paris. 'You're a very lucky little girl, Lili. We haven't been able to find homes for half the people in this camp.'

During the long, uncomfortable train journey, the child hardly said a word to the group of other anxious and exhausted refugees. When they arrived at the acrid smelling station they were met by another refugee committee worker, carrying the inevitable clipboard. She ticked them off her list, then took them to the waiting room where they sagged on hard benches as their lives were reassembled.

'Lili ... Lili Vago, there she is, over there, Madame Sardeau. Stand up and say hello, Lili. You're going to stay with Madame Sardeau, who has generously offered you a home.'

The couple who stood in front of Lili did not look generous. They were bundled up against the cold, their sharp noses and pinched mouths showing from behind their dark scarves.

Oddly formal, this middle-aged couple shook hands with the child. Then the woman said sharply, 'But we were expecting a much older girl. We asked for a girl of twelve to fourteen!'

Equally sharply the refugee committee worker said, 'Madame, in this situation, while we appreciate your hospitality and concern, one cannot order children as if the refugee camps were a department store.'

'No luggage? No passport?' the man asked.

'No papers tonight,' said the refugee committee worker in a tired voice. 'If you would just sign here, and here, and there, we'll expect you at the office tomorrow – anytime – to fill in the forms and complete the other formalities.'

The child walked out of the station to her new home and life with the Sardeaus. She sensed that something was wrong, that she disappointed and vexed them. In silence they caught the métro to Sablon, then hurried through darkened streets to an old-fashioned apartment building. The huge arched entrance to the inner courtyard was covered by a pair of black doors, big enough to let a wagonload of hay pass through. Lili followed her new parents, too tired to notice anything but the ache in her calves, the ache in her chest and the fog inside her head. They paused outside a door, then, as Monsieur Sardeau fished for his keys outside the apartment door, the child slid to the floor.

'Henri, you don't think they've given us one that has something wrong with her?' Madame Sardeau asked anxiously. 'We didn't agree to an invalid; we don't want doctor's bills; we want a strong girl who can do the housework.'

'Nevertheless, we'd better call a doctor tonight.' Monsieur Sardeau picked up the fragile little body. 'You put her to bed and I'll get Dutheil.'

Doctor Dutheil was sympathetic. 'There seems to be nothing basically wrong with her. Children are remarkably resilient. She's suffering from exhaustion, and from what she says, it sounds as if she's recently had pneumonia and hasn't fully recovered. She's also had a bad emotional shock and won't discuss it; that's also normal and understandable. She's not strong enough at this stage to relive the experience by talking about it, so please don't press her to say anything. Just leave her quietly in bed, give her good food, plenty of hot milk and keep her very quiet.'

He looked uncertainly at Madame Sardeau, but could not imagine her in the role of comforter. He took off his spectacles, wiped them with his handkerchief, paused and shrewdly said, 'You are a heroine, madame! You are a saint to have rescued this poor child! I will come and see her again tomorrow and until she has recovered, and there will be no charge for my visits. Pray allow me to make this contribution to your noble action.'

The following morning, Madame Sardeau buttoned herself into her black overcoat, bound a thick, rust scarf around her neck, stabbed her hat into place with two pins and set off for the refugee committee central office. She gave her name to the receptionist and waited in the small, crowded office. People hurried in and out; some were officials but some were obviously voluntary workers. After an interminable wait, she was shown into a cold little cubicle piled high with files of documents.

'You're not the one I saw at the station last night,' Madame Sardeau said to the small, harassed woman who faced her.

'No, Yvonne speaks Hungarian so she had to go to the station to meet a new batch that we weren't expecting. I'm sorry, madame, it is not our aim in life to inconvenience you, but everyone here suddenly has far more problems than usual. Now where is the child?'

'Ill in bed. Being attended daily by a doctor who says she must stay in bed for at least two weeks! Imagine the expense! What a way to start!'

'Oh, dear, we're supposed to get the details directly, because we must try to trace the child's parents. We'll do the best we can for the time being, but when she's recovered, you *must* bring her in to answer for herself. Now let's try to get these forms filled in.'

And thus the forms were filled in, stamped and returned to the file, which was then placed in the V drawer of the filing cabinet.

When Lili was well enough, she sat up in bed with a coarse shawl wrapped around her chest and pinned at her back. Anxiously she asked what had happened to Angelina and Felix and her foster brother Roger.

'The refugee committee is trying to locate them. When you're well enough we'll go to their office and they'll tell you what they can.'

'And does *vraie maman* know where I am?'

'Aren't Monsieur and Madame Vago your real parents?'

244

'No, Angelina is looking after me until I can join my real mother in another land and Felix is looking after her and also Roger, although Felix isn't Roger's *vrai* papa of course. And Felix is called *Ko*vago and I am really called Elizabeth, except I prefer Lili because that's what Felix calls me. Everyone calls me Lili in Hungary, it's only in Château d'Oex that they call me Elizabeth. I like Lili best and I like Hungary better than Switzerland, I think, only I wish I could speak Hungarian properly. I only know a few words.'

Was the child still delirious? Madame Sardeau wondered. Best to wait until tomorrow, until after the doctor's visit and then ask again.

The next day Madame Sardeau took the kitchen notebook and a pencil into Lili's bedroom and sorted out her story. 'So you were the foster child of Madame Kovago and lived in Switzerland and were on a visit to Hungary when the revolution broke out? And you do not know any details of your real mother?'

'Yes, yes, yes, no. Can I go back to sleep now?'

Over their evening meal, Madame Sardeau discussed the matter with her husband.

'It's not our responsibility to trace her family; it's up to the refugee committee,' she said. 'I'm not sure I believe such a muddled tale anyway. Doctor Dutheil said this afternoon that it's possible she's living in an imaginary world, in order to avoid the real one. He says it might be the only way she can face the sudden loss of her family.'

'In the meantime, my dear,' said Monsieur Sardeau, slicing into the crisp onion tart, 'perhaps I should write to the mayor of Château d'Oex to inquire whether there is – as the child says – a family living there called Vago or Kovago. After all, if they escaped, then they would obviously return to their home and if they have, then we can return the child and ask them for the financial compensation that is our moral right. On the other hand, if they haven't escaped, or if they've been killed, then the child might stand to inherit some property – the house perhaps. So I shall dictate a letter tomorrow morning.'

The winter of 1956–7 was bitterly cold in Paris. Doctor Dutheil would not allow Lili to leave the stuffy, overheated apartment until mid-February, when Madame Sardeau returned for the second time to the refugee committee office, this time accompanied by Lili. Again, they had a long wait in the small, freezing waiting room, although this time it was not crowded. Eventually, Madame Sardeau and Lili were interviewed by a voluntary worker whom she had not seen on her previous visit.

'Your name, darling?'

'Lili Kovago.'

Half an hour's harassed search followed, thirty minutes spent burrowing under beige piles of paper that covered the desk and the tops of the filing cabinets, until Madame Sardeau thought to say, 'Perhaps the file is under V for Vago; there was an initial mistake. Not my fault you understand.'

Indeed, the file was found under V. The interviewer then lost her spectacles and Madame Sardeau lost her temper. 'It is intolerable that I should be kept waiting, that the documents should twice have been lost.'

The interviewer looked more harassed. 'We have received no inquiries for a child of that name.'

'Idiot!' snapped Madame Sardeau. 'Inquiries would have been for a child called *Ko*vago or Dassin, which was the mother's previous name, and they would be filed under K or D.'

So the interviewer again burrowed into the filing cabinet, looking under K and under D, but there were no files labelled Kovago or Dassin.

'You waste my time in this chaos,' Madame Sardeau snapped. 'You waste your *own* time in this chaos. It is obviously a waste of time to sit here like an imbecile.' And she swept out, towing Lili in her wake.

The exhausted voluntary worker put Lili's file – still labelled Vago – back into the V cabinet. Nobody searching for Lili would be likely to look under V because there was no reason to do so. Lili was now literally lost in a sea of misplaced paper.

The next morning, after hearing an indignant account of his wife's visit to the refugee centre, Monseiur Sardeau dictated another letter, complaining to the president of the refugee committee. He received an apologetic, but otherwise uninformative, letter.

Six weeks after that, Monsieur Sardeau received a brief letter from the office of the mayor of Château d'Oex to say that, so far as he knew, there was no family called Vago in the town, but a Hungarian waiter called Kovago had lived in a rented chalet on the outskirts of the area. Unfortunately, he and his family had been on a visit to Hungary when the revolution broke out and the whole family had apparently been killed while attempting to escape.

The town archives held no further details.

'Don't think we're rich.' Madame Sardeau gave a dainty snort as she carried her shopping bags through the big doors and into the courtyard beyond. 'This apartment is rent-controlled; we were lucky, after the war.'

'Don't think we're rich' was a favourite Sardeau phrase. If Lili took an extra bit of bread or forgot to switch off the light in the old-fashioned, windowless toilet or asked for anything at all, this phrase came automatically to their lips.

The Sardeaus were childless. No tyrannical baby had ever shattered their sleep or their ornaments. They had never had so much as a cat to care for and clean up after, and they soon discovered that they didn't care for the responsibility of looking after a little girl. Their reason for offering to adopt an orphan had been practical – they had no one to care for them in their old age, to push a possible wheelchair, to attend a bedside or collect a pension. They had never been able to afford a servant, Madame was now getting on in years and needed help in the home, and, yes, perhaps they could use some company, for Monsieur worked in a government statistics office and after twenty-seven shared years they had exhausted their conversation.

But although the child was small and thin, although she wasn't nearly as strong as a fully grown worker, she ate as much as a maid would. Worse yet, unlike a maid, she was often not there when required because she was at school or dawdling over her homework. Certainly, for the moment, she did not justify the cost of her keep. And she couldn't be trusted; she told lies. The child obviously had bad blood; they hoped she was not Jewish.

A docile, obedient, pale-faced schoolchild, Lili had indeed started to tell little lies in self-defence, in order to have some time to herself in which to dream of what might have been. She lied about the time she left school and whether she'd been in the park – where she wasn't supposed to wander; whether she'd been to church; whether she'd done the dusting or finished the ironing. As the Sardeaus forced Lili's imagination along this grey path of self-preservation, she turned secretive, living a life of inner fantasy in which the lonely child was always adored and a scintillating heroine. Lili became increasingly subdued and withdrawn. Increasingly, she built up her mother's identity into a romantic mystery – because the alternative was to face her mother's brusque rejection.

The apartment on the seventh floor was small, dark, uncomfortable and spotlessly clean. Every ugly china knickknack had its preordained place, as Lili discovered when she dusted them daily. Lili lived in a cupboard-sized room off the dark kitchen that faced on to the inner courtyard.

Although her schoolwork at the lycée was hard, Lili soon realized that she preferred the cheerful, noisy school atmosphere to the claustrophobic, funeral-parlour atmosphere of the Sardeau home. Certainly, she had to work far harder at school than ever before.

Madame Sardeau had no intention of letting Lili have time off. In the holidays, she not only had to do all the light housework, but she also had to prepare the vegetables, wait on the table and do the ironing and sewing. Madame Sardeau soon discovered that Lili's stitching was exquisite and piled more work on the child. After all, she thought to herself, watching Lili slave away, the devil makes work for idle hands.

After two years Lili understood – possibly better than they did – that the Sardeaus regarded her as a poor investment, which unfortunately couldn't be liquidated in favour of something more promising. They were not unkind to the child; she was dressed, fed and given suitably improving gifts on anniversaries – a book on the lives of the saints, a sewing kit, a new vest – but the girl was never grateful.

Just before her ninth birthday, Madame showed her a newspaper picture of a huge-eyed, stick-limbed African orphan and said, 'See what we saved you from!'

Lili was silent for a long time, then she said, 'My mother wouldn't have let me starve.'

'You know perfectly well that your mother is dead.'

'My other mother would have come for me.'

Madame Sardeau lost her temper. 'You little liar, your fairytale stories of your other mother and sleighbells in the snow are just fantasy. The priest told me that many children have them, especially if their parents have to beat them for bad behaviour. You would do better to be more dutiful to *us*. You owe a duty to *us*. It is *we* who feed you, shelter you and spend money on you. Your mother and father are dead! Get *that* into your head.'

'But not my Kovago grandparents. They didn't come with us that night. When I'm old enough, I shall go back to them.'

'You ungrateful little idiot! Even if they're still alive, they are now behind the Iron Curtain. You will *never* see them again.'

Lili was silent, struggling with emotion and frustration. Then her anger and long-suppressed resentment surfaced and, with a glare of hatred, she spat at Madame Sardeau. There was a shocked moment of silence then – outraged – the woman yelled, 'Such guttersnipe manners merely betray your low origins! I shall report your behaviour to my husband this evening and he will discipline you. Now get in your room!'

Lili fled, tears falling down her school pinafore. Lying face down on her lumpy bed, she longed for Angelina, Felix and Roger. Now she had nothing. No brother, no grandma or grandpa, no uncle, no father. And instead of two mothers, she had none at all. How would her *vraie maman* even know that she was in Paris? How could she now know where to find her, when the time came?

Lili felt as if an unseen, vindictive spirit was punishing her, crushing her, in this joyless apartment. Although she was only nine, she knew that her childhood had passed and that she now had to mark time through the grey days that lay ahead until she was old enough to run away.

21

MAXINE worked almost nonstop for three years after the château opened. By 1959 she had discovered that business progress zig-zagged, with one step backward for every three steps forward. The staff of the Château de Chazalle were learning their jobs day by day and Maxine – who was in charge of them – found it hard to cope with business problems that were on a far larger scale than those to which she had been accustomed in the rue Jacob shop.

In the first year they had 92,000 visitors and they grossed 30·8 million francs. In other words, they suffered a loss. *O rage, o désespoir*, thought Maxine, grimly remembering Pagan's oft-repeated schoolgirl wail. More days were spent with accountants, there were more anxious visits to the bank and – worst of all – more borrowing, which brought more sleepless nights.

In the second year they had 121,000 visitors and grossed 48·4 million francs. Success!

But would it last?

In the third year over 174,000 people visited the château, and in the fourth year they passed the magic figure of 250,000 visitors.

Yes, *it was going to last*. But could Maxine? Guy, worried, privately told Charles that he thought she was like someone running too fast downhill, forced on by her own impetus and unable to stop. Charles agreed, and repeated his original, overall instruction to Maxine's executive secretary. Mademoiselle Janine was to keep as much work as possible away from Madame la Comtesse. She managed this so efficiently that eventually Maxine was able to delegate nearly everything except the weekly business meeting on Monday with the estate accountant, and her weekly Friday meeting in Paris with Christina to go over the design work.

Maxine no longer stayed at her desk until past midnight in order to clear it, only to be greeted by a new pile of mail the following morning. Instead of getting up at six in the morning, Maxine now had a leisurely breakfast in bed, went to her office at nine and had finished the serious business of the day by lunch-time. To her relief, she was able to see far more of her children; it was one of the advantages of living over the shop, she thought, as every cold afternoon she played in the firelit nursery with her two charming little boys and every warm afternoon they all romped around the park with the dogs. Maxine had never expected to find such simple happiness with her children, and sometimes, looking at her sons, she felt a sudden pang of guilt; she felt that perhaps she didn't deserve them, it was all too good to be true; she sometimes shivered as the thought crossed her mind that perhaps Fate was going to demand some dreadful penalty for her almost ruthless practicality and success.

Partly because of the huge success of the château, Paradis was also steadily building a reputation for rescuing and converting historic houses. After the Château de Chazalle had opened in a blaze of publicity that proved what Paradis could do, potential clients streamed into the office. Maxine had successfully restored twenty-six buildings to date.

Paradis converted historic buildings into showplaces for the public, into hotels or small apartments for several families to live in. It now employed four full-time designers. Although Maxine expected everybody to work hard, she saw to it that her designers enjoyed their jobs and frequent gales of laughter would issue from the main studio when she was working there; but Maxine still approved every scheme at the sketch stage before it was presented to a client. Nothing, no matter how minor, could escape her eye for detail.

Maxine was also irreplaceable in one other very important area. Sometimes the investment needed for the Paradis projects could be as high as fifty million francs, sometimes it was considerably less. Maxine's expertise lay in presenting a scheme to a possible source of finance. 'You go off with your eyes lit up, like a bull-fighter about to go into the ring,' observed Charles.

To Maxine, work was fun, but this was partly because she had never had a major setback.

Then, in spite of knowing that Charles would be furious, Maxine did something that she'd been secretly wanting to do for a long time. For years she had hated her breasts. They *hadn't* diminished when the boys were born, so one day, without telling Charles, she slipped anonymously into a hospital for breast reduction.

Maxine and her Dior *vendeuse* hoped that she would emerge with the silhouette of Audrey Hepburn, but although her breasts were resited four inches higher, they still remained ample. As always, the operation was very painful and Maxine was left with a semicircle of blanket stitches under each breast and another jagged little row from beneath the breast up to the nipple. They were ugly. They would never disappear.

Charles was furious. He had particularly *liked* her breasts. 'Why the hell didn't you tell me what you were going to do? You know that there's always some danger with a full anaesthetic!'

'Because I thought you might stop me.'

'Damn right! They're not *your* breasts, they're *our* breasts. How would *you* like it if *I* decided to have an inch or two snipped off?'

But on the whole, Maxine's life passed excitingly and successfully until she was nearly thirty years old, when two things happened – Maxine became pregnant again and Charles fell in love with another woman.

At first Maxine knew only of the first event and not the second. She was not pleased to be pregnant again. Two sons were enough. She had just got on top of her job again and for the first time in years she was enjoying her position. She felt in charge of what was happening, rather than just keeping up with the daily treadmill of work. Her organization was now highly efficient, and she was paying off the château bank loan much faster than anticipated.

Then one morning, as she handed Maxine her mail, Mademoiselle Janine said, 'I noticed that Madame de Fortuny was here again yesterday. For a copywriter, that one is certainly devoted to her job. She's always on the telephone to Monsieur le Comte, and I notice that she's on the list of guests for lunch today. Myself, I find that she always smells too strongly of carnations. Too much perfume can be overpowering.'

This was such an unusually long speech for Mademoiselle Janine that Maxine looked up sharply. What on earth was the girl talking about? Some copywriter's scent? Wasn't de Fortuny the woman who was working on the new champagne labels and literature? she wondered idly, then pushed the thought aside as she switched on her dictaphone and started to sort through the mail. Nevertheless, she took particular notice of pretty little Madame de Fortuny at the luncheon. She was wearing a new Chanel suit – *un vrai Chanel*, not a Wallis copy – in cream wool banded with narrow cream satin – impractical and extravagant. And Mademoiselle Janine was right, the woman *did* reek of carnations. Still, she was an intelligent and amusing guest, told particularly droll stories about her job and was generally charming to everybody.

Maxine's attention was abruptly distracted by the arrival of Sir Walter and Lady Cliffe. After Nick's memorial service, Maxine and Kate had several times visited his parents at their London home; sadly, Nick's mother clung to his friends – especially the last ones to have been with him – as a last link with her dead son.

After the other luncheon guests had departed to visit the champagne caves, Lady Cliffe asked to meet Maxine's children. As the two women sat in the sunny, yellow nursery, watching Gérard wrestling with Oliver, Lady Cliffe said wistfully, 'For me, the saddest thing is that I shall never have grandchildren.' She paused, then added, 'Of course Walter's also concerned that there's no one to inherit the title, so it will die out, but he'd already come to terms with that long before Nick died.' Maxine looked mystified. 'Because when Nick was fourteen, he caught mumps, complicated by orchitis. Twice we were told he wouldn't live, but then he recovered, although the medical specialists told us that Nick would never be able to have children.'

'Did Nick know?' Maxine asked, astonished.

'Yes, of course he had to be told, but I don't think he ever really accepted it – I think he always secretly hoped that somehow he would be cured.'

'Poor Nick. Just as well for Judy that she didn't want to marry him,' Maxine said to Charles that evening, as they were dressing for dinner. 'Although,' she added, 'I'm not all that keen on children at the moment.' She patted her heavily pregnant stomach.

Charles laughed. 'Patience,' he said, 'you haven't long to wait.' He bent and kissed the back of her neck and, as he did so, Maxine smelled the faint but unmistakable fragrance of carnations. She swept the thought to the back of her mind. After all, Charles had been with the woman for the whole day.

Two weeks later, Christina said casually to Maxine, 'I saw Monsieur Charles yesterday evening at Le Grand Véfour. I must say, Maxine, he gets handsomer every year in that pale, charming way.'

'At Le Grand Véfour? Are you sure?'

'Yes. With that woman from his advertising firm. Jack Reffold was over here with a new delivery and I thought I'd take him somewhere nice. Charles was at the other side of the restaurant. I waved to him, but I don't think he noticed me.' She bent over her work and chattered on about the latest consignment of furniture from Reffold's. Maxine felt as if someone had thrown a glass of cold water in her face. Her fingertips were tingling and she couldn't breathe properly. She knew what Christina was telling her, that she had chosen her words so the subject could be ignored if Maxine chose to do so. Maxine had spent the previous evening quietly at home eating supper on a tray, watching ballet on television, because Charles had to entertain a group of Canadian buyers. He would have to take them out on the town, probably the Folies Bergère, then perhaps to a nightclub, both of which, as he correctly said, would bore Maxine rigid . . .

Christina looked up. 'Are you all right, darling? Maybe you'd better lie down. Is the baby kicking? Poor darling. We all expect you to carry on as if nothing is happening, simply because you always do. Come and lie down on the deck chair in the back room.'

'No, no,' said Maxine faintly. She felt as if she were hearing herself from a great distance. She had to talk to someone about her suspicions. She would telephone Aunt Horse-Sense, as Judy always called her.

From the tone of Maxine's voice, so carefully casual, Aunt Hortense immediately knew that something serious had happened. 'Come around straightaway, dear child. You know I'm always here.'

Once inside her aunt's front door, Maxine burst into tears.

Aunt Hortense led her goddaughter to a chaise longue and held both Maxine's hands in hers.

'Now, what's the matter, is it Charles?'

'Yes,' whispered Maxine, 'how did you know?'

'Well, it *is* your third baby, my dear, and you *have* been married eight years. I cannot tell you what to do, my child, because I know no details and I do not *wish* to know them. Is Charles trying to deceive you? . . . Yes? . . . Good! In that case, what I caution you to do is to ignore the situation, if possible, until the emotions have calmed down. Now is not the time to have the showdown.'

Maxine nodded as her aunt continued, 'Charles is no doubt besotted with some lady, in which case he is not thinking logically. You, my child, are suspicious and jealous so you cannot see things calmly. So you must – at all costs – not provoke an argument while emotion, rather than common sense, is possessing your head and his.'

Maxine looked rather surly, but Aunt Hortense spoke firmly, as if Charles were merely a car that needed its engine tuned. 'You do not want to clash with Charles. You never know with men. He might run off with this lady merely as an act of defiance. Charles obviously loves you, otherwise he would not want to hide his alliance from you. Men who no longer love their wives don't bother to hide anything, you know.'

Maxine said sadly, 'She's beautiful and slim.'

'My poor child, it would be worse for you if she were *not* beautiful. Then you would worry endlessly as to what invisible magic she might possibly possess.' Aunt Hortense released Maxine's hands and pulled the bell to order coffee. 'At the moment her attraction is perfectly obvious – good looks combined with the novelty of a forbidden liaison.' She shrugged her shoulders. 'However much he loves you, Charles has grown *used* to you. It's a pity that brides are never warned that they will undoubtedly fall in love again with someone else, and so will their husbands. But sometimes life is too painful to explain to the young, and anyway, they would never believe it.'

She turned aside to give instructions to the manservant who had appeared. 'So leave Charles alone, my dear, and notice *nothing*. My child, you must behave like an angel.'

She took Maxine's hands in hers again. 'There is only one further thing that you should think about,' said Aunt Hortense gently, picking her words with care. 'A good husband is more important than a business. That is not to say that your business is *not* important. I'm saying that a good husband is much, much *more* important.'

So Maxine behaved like an angel and found it very difficult, as daily she became more tense and clumsy. Charles was frequently away from the château, and when he was present he seemed preoccupied. Sometimes Maxine would glance up and catch him looking at her with a frustrated, accusing stare that made her heart fall sickeningly.

She felt ruthlessly jealous and possessive. In her head she constantly checked Charles' timetable, although she dared not question him too sharply about his movements. She tried not to nag him – she didn't want him to feel that he was hemmed in to the point where he might be tempted to run away. Sometimes her mood abruptly switched and Maxine felt violently resentful of her husband's treachery, the smoothness with which he lied to her – day after day and month after month – seemingly untroubled by conscience. Maxine suffered terribly from the strain of playing a part, of hiding her pain from her husband, of lying to him, as he did to her.

Charles was supposedly in Lyons when their third son was born, a week before he was due and after a far easier birth than Maxine had expected. She clutched her baby to her and wanted to keep him by her all the time. The tiny Alexandre was her hope for the future, her link with her husband.

This time there was no possibility of Maxine's being pregnant four months after the birth. Four months after the birth Charles had still not returned to her bed from the *lit Napoléon* in his dressing room.

By 1963, Charles and Maxine had been estranged for three years and Maxine continued to ignore her husband's infidelity. Invariably, she was only able to do this by repressing her natural instincts and relying on the formal good manners that she had acquired from her strict French bourgeois upbringing. From time to time she fled to Aunt Hortense for reassurance and sympathy.

Maxine was still behaving like an angel, but she found it a great strain. She no longer slept well, her face was gaunt, and even when she switched on her confident little smile, her brown-fringed eyes betrayed her anxiety. Sometimes she snapped at her children and at her staff, because the only alternative was to burst into tears or scream. Maxine was suffering from the intolerable strain of living a false life, of playing a false part while she waited and waited and wished she could put back the clock. 'If only' became her favourite game.

If only the cobwebs of time could be swept away and they could return to that lovely warm summer before she was last pregnant.

If only she'd chosen a different advertising agency.

If only the agency hadn't assigned that homewrecker to the Chazalle account.

If only she were thinner, taller, younger, more enchanting.

If only Charles could see in her what he used to see!

Her self-confidence dissolved. She alternated between dull clothes that were too old for her and outré clothes that didn't suit her. Her *vendeuse* despaired and grumbled to her assistant, 'If Madame de Chazalle can't put up with the competition then she shouldn't have married an attractive man; it's too shaming to see one of my clients lose her dignity in front of the whole of Paris. She should give Monsieur le Comte a taste of his own medicine, there are plenty of attractive young men in Paris who would adore to pluck such a ripe peach.'

In May of 1963, Judy was staying at the château for a working weekend. Looking at Maxine's sad, mechanical smile, and think-ing of her busy but lonely life, Judy came to a sudden decision. Charles was her client but Maxine was her friend. She chose her moment carefully and the following morning, as Charles drove Judy to the champagne office, Judy said, 'Aren't you happy that both the businesses are doing so well?'

Charles nodded, absently.

'And aren't you proud of those three handsome boys of yours?'

Again he nodded casually.

'And isn't Maxine a wonderful hostess? Doesn't the whole of France know it?'

257

Another mechanical nod.

'And how much longer do you think she will stand this present situation, Charles? I think she's almost at the breaking point. I know divorce almost never happens in France, that husbands and wives have discreet affairs which never threaten their marriages. But Maxine loves *you*, she doesn't want some other man. So I think that eventually she won't be able to bear the duplicity of the life she's leading – and she'll leave you and live in Paris, preferring to live with loss than with pain. Then think what you'll lose, Charles.' Judy was extremely careful not to appeal to Charles' better instincts, but to his Gallic instinct for self-preservation. 'You'll lose your easy, comfortable life, you'll lose your children, you'll lose the hostess you're so proud of and who is such an asset to your business. And what will you have gained? That calculating little cow of a copywriter and a number one scandal.'

Judy turned to look at him. Outraged and silent, Charles concentrated on the road ahead. She continued.

'Oh, Charles, *nobody* can have everything they want. You're risking so much unhappiness for such a stupid reason. In God's name, what has happened to your well-known appreciation of family, comfort and money!'

Charles' hand tightened on the wheel and he said nothing. His first feeling was shock that Judy should discuss such a personal topic with him, and his second was fury that she had dared to do so. But by the time they reached the office, Charles was already starting to consider what she had said, to imagine life without Maxine.

A week after Judy's departure, Maxine was sitting at the white lace wrought-iron table under the copper beech tree beyond the terrace. She was keeping an eye on eight-year-old Gérard, who, with a set of yellow and orange building blocks, was building a fort on the grass for two-year-old Alexandre. Maxine was idly checking the guest list for a big party they were about to give to celebrate the newly modernized champagne company's first great vintage year.

Suddenly Charles appeared on the terrace. Maxine looked up. It was odd to see him in midafternoon.

258

Suddenly, as Charles moved towards her, her life seemed to lapse into slow motion. He looked so purposeful.

She waited, her heart pounding.

When he reached his wife, Charles bent down and kissed her ear.

The way he used to.

Maxine turned her head sharply and looked into his eyes. Seeing his expression she felt weak with hope and joy, then she sprang to her feet and into his arms, as her chair crashed backwards to the ground.

Charles hugged her tightly. Then he leaned over Maxine's shoulder, picked up her pen and crossed the name de Fortuny off the guest list. Maxine grabbed his hand and kissed it. She couldn't let go.

Some time later, Maxine lay back on her bed, her thick blonde hair streaming over the blue silk spread. It had not been the same mad, passionate frenzy as when they first made love – it had been better, a sensual, sexually charged and shared experience, in which wordlessly Charles had asked forgiveness and wordlessly Maxine had told him that it didn't matter, nothing mattered but *now*.

Charles murmured, 'Feel under the pillow.' Maxine felt beneath the cream lace and drew out a small, scarlet box.

'It's from Cartier! But it's not my birthday!'

'No, it's not for a birthday. It's forever,' said Charles, looking guilty. Inside the small velvet box was a blazing band of square-cut diamonds.

'You got the finger size right,' cried Maxine. Again Charles took her into his arms, murmuring fondly into her ear.

'You're not the only one in the family who is efficient,' Charles said. And he smiled at her – just the way he had when they first made love together.

～ PART FIVE ～

22

SOON after her grandfather's death, Pagan – who had immediately returned to England from her Swiss school – realized that her mother's protracted grief was not because he had died, but because he had died poor. His business affairs were in chaos. The big Cornish estate was in perfect order, but it didn't seem to belong to them. It belonged to the bank – everything was mortgaged to the hilt. When searched, the Queen Anne desk in the study revealed a moth-eaten rabbit's foot and an anonymous wedding ring in the secret drawer; other drawers contained only torn-out newspaper cuttings, a cigar box full of letters home written by Pagan's father when he'd been at Eton, a few heavily marked, ancient copies of *Horse & Hound* and a heap of yellowing letters and documents. There were no bills because bills were always automatically handed to the agent and paid immediately against the vast overdraft at the bank, guaranteed by the manor house.

The chaos took a long time to sort out. Just before Christmas 1949, Pagan and her mother visited the lawyers' office in St Austell.

They were given the bad news straight: there was no money. Couldn't they perhaps sell the house for use as an institution of some sort, a school, perhaps?

'Impossible,' said Pagan's mother. 'We only have twenty-three bedrooms.'

In gloomy silence the two women drove back towards the low, stone Tudor house. Pagan's mother went straight to her bedroom and telephoned London. Seventeen-year-old Pagan wandered through the house as if it had already been sold and she were saying goodbye. All over the house innumerable clocks softly ticked in different rhythms, all collected by the grandmother she had never known: marble clocks, bronze clocks, china and brass clocks, an indigo enamelled bedside clock, given to Pagan's grandmother by Queen Alexandra, glittering with rhinestones around the face. Every now and then the clocks rustled and chimed.

For a week, the two women mourned their loss. Pagan never cried in the house, only in the comfort of the woods, or on top of the granite cliff, sitting with her legs stuck out in front of her like a wooden doll. Then Selma came for the weekend.

By now Pagan's mother shared her London flat ('So lonely while you were away darling') with Selma, a severe-looking woman in her late fifties who lived on a meagre maintenance paid by an ex-husband who lived in Hull. Selma was a big-boned woman with cheekbones that curved down like scimitars and a rectangular mouth that also bent down above a stringy neck. She was not a woman that Pagan would have expected her mother to befriend; you couldn't imagine Selma in pearls and a little black dress. She was not chic, not at home in London society, but gruffly imperious when away from it.

One evening after Selma's departure, as the sea wind shook the windowpanes of the library, Pagan lolled against the desk, remembering the hands that last had touched the maroon-leather stationery-holder and the paperweight carved from a whale's tooth. Mrs Trelawney, sitting by the log fire, took a quick, neat sip from her glass of sherry and said, 'Do stop fiddling, Pagan, I want to talk to you seriously. About money. Selma thinks it would be possible to turn Trelawney into a health farm.'

'A *what*?'

'A place where people go to get thin. Selma once worked at one in the New Forest. Actually, they specialized in drying-out socially acceptable alcoholics. Selma says it wouldn't be very expensive to set up that sort of thing at Trelawney.'

'Mummy, you must be dotty if you're planning to entertain a bunch of alcoholics on the edge of a cliff,' was all Pagan said.

Shortly afterwards, Mrs Trelawney packed Pagan off to visit Kate at Greenways; it would cheer her up, she explained. 'It also got me out of the way,' Pagan told Kate, as they were walking the Scottie dogs over the common. 'I'll bet Selma moved in as soon as I'd moved out; they're both totally engrossed in this batty project.'

But Kate's father didn't think it was such a foolish idea and made Pagan explain it to him. 'It might work,' he said thought-fully, 'I can see the advantages.'

'The only advantage to me is that, as there's no money, I won't be able to be a debutante as planned,' said Pagan. 'It costs about two thousand pounds to do the London season, if you're going to give a dance, that is. Thank heaven Mama can't manage it. I don't fancy whooping around London from dusk to dawn in pink net ballgowns.'

Kate's father said nothing, but in due course he telephoned Mrs Trelawney and offered to sponsor Pagan's London season if Mrs Trelawney would also launch Kate into society. He intended to give his daughter the best possible chance to meet the right sort of man, by which he meant rich and, who knows, perhaps with a . . .

Pagan's mother was delighted at the idea of having a season at somebody else's expense.

'What your papa doesn't realize,' said Pagan to Kate one even-ing, as they sat on the floor in Pagan's London bedroom sipping mugs of cocoa, 'what he doesn't seem to understand is that we aren't aristocracy. We're only landed gentry, and I'm not even sure about that. There might not be any land left by now.'

'He doesn't care so long as I get married. Now, how many ballgowns d'you think we can manage on?'

The year 1950 provided an idyllic British summer. By the time Maxine arrived in London, Pagan and Kate were whirling in a scintillating social Catherine wheel. They were both presented at Court. You could only be presented to the King and Queen by a lady who had herself been presented (in this case, Mrs Tre-lawney), so the three of them – wearing elbow-length white kid gloves and silk dresses with the obligatory below-calf hem, high neckline and covered shoulders – sat for hours in the Mall in a chauffeur-driven Rolls Royce with a special X label on the wind-screen, as all the other cars containing all the other debutantes slowly inched up to Buckingham Palace, then crawled through the ornate black iron gates and into the courtyard. Once past the impressive stone columns of the front entrance, they queued in a red-carpeted antechamber until their name was called. Pagan might have been waiting for school tea, she was so unconcerned, but Kate felt very nervous as she mentally checked her curtsy. In a squad of about ten girls, she and Pagan had taken the necessary three curtsying lessons from the famous Madame Vacani.

Kate shot upright as her name was called. She was ushered into another red-carpeted antechamber – rather like a very wide corridor – in which the Royal Couple sat on a red-carpeted dais. One step forward on right foot, one step forward on left foot, right foot move to side, then swing left leg behind and *down* you go with your head bowed in front of His Majesty King George the Sixth. Straighten up, then right foot to the side, left foot across in front, right to the side in front and that got you in front of Queen Elizabeth, then repeat curtsy and move off to right . . .

Kate wobbled into a palatial, chandelier-hung room in which all the girls ate cucumber sandwiches with their tea and talked to each other in unusually subdued voices.

Every day there was a plethora of different entertainments. Months before, the dates of these occasions had been anxiously checked and coordinated with Betty Kenward, the pace setter of modern London. Mrs Kenward wrote 'Jennifer's Diary' in the *Tatler* and was the unofficial arbiter of the Season. Nobody dared offend Mrs Kenward: everybody wanted to appear in 'Jennifer's Diary'.

Kate and Pagan held endless lunches to entertain other debutantes and they always had tea at Gunter's or the Ritz or Brown's. They attended at least two cocktail parties a night, unless they were going to a private dinner before an important ball, when Pagan's mother would not allow them to attend a cocktail party because they might get 'overexcited'. After a month there were permanent bags under their eyes, but with the relentless stamina peculiar to a debutante, they managed on very little sleep and a ludicrous diet. By the end of the summer, neither girl could face another glass of champagne, another cucumber sandwich, another cold slice of ballet-slipper-pink salmon, another chicken glistening in mayonnaise, another vanilla ice cream or silver dish of strawberries.

They went to the races at Ascot and Goodwood, they watched rowing at Henley, yachting at Cowes and cricket at Lords; on none of these occasions did they pay much attention to the sport in question (except for tennis at Wimbledon) because, like most

266

of the other debutantes, they were busy checking each other's clothes with satisfaction or dismay. They went to the Oxford Commem-Balls and the Cambridge May Balls, when dignified and ancient college courtyards echoed to the swing music of Tommy Kinsman or someone else especially imported for the occasion. And on weekends the girls did the rounds of British country houses.

Kate's father footed all the bills, and Kate's mother kept well out of the way so that she didn't make fatally shaming mistakes, such as saying 'appointment' instead of 'engagement', or holding her knife so that the handle showed. Courtesy of Kate's father, Mrs Trelawney gave lobster lunches at her apartment for all her old friends, who were also launching *their* daughters. Meanwhile, Selma directed activities at Trelawney. She had been right. Converting Trelawney into a health farm wasn't going to involve much work. Lobster lunches were also available for beauty editors who might mention the new health farm in their columns, and bottles of vintage champagne were sent to gossip writers who might mention the girls. Pagan exasperated her mother by carelessly ignoring the gossip writers, while cultivating other friends that her mother thought unsuitable.

Both girls had a group of presentable escorts: smart young army officers, crow-dressed fledgling bankers, stockbrokers and insurance men from Lloyd's – all learning to be men-about-town, sometimes on a very limited income. Nice girls were careful not to order expensive dishes, it was back to the old gin fizz routine when you went to nightclubs after a dance (especially with the young army officers), and it was best not to take too much money in your handbag or it might be borrowed and not returned (especially by the young army officers).

As in Switzerland, purity was at a premium. All the debs pretended to adhere to severe propriety, but in reality there was much panting and gasping in taxis, much exploring under pink net and burrowing under pale blue twin sets. However, all the girls knew that too much passion would result in your name being bandied around the mess, around the clubs, even around the all-night Turkish baths in Jermyn Street, for none of the chaps liked That Sort of Girl in theory, although in fact, they all seemed to want one. How Far You Went was again endlessly discussed.

Pagan still insisted that she hadn't let Abdullah go too far. Well, not below the waist. Neither Kate nor Maxine believed her. 'What's the point of going to a love school for three weeks,' yawned Kate, 'if they don't teach you to get below the waist?'

During the summer of 1950, Kate was in the *Tatler* twice and Pagan was in seven times, twice with Prince Abdullah. Normally Pagan didn't seem to give a damn about anything or anybody; thirty per cent of her seemed to be absent. But when Abdullah was in London, she became excited and alive, and although she swore to Kate and Maxine that she wasn't in love with him, privately they agreed that this was a face-saver. Pagan rarely knew in advance when he was going to dash into the Dorchester for a day or two; sometimes the other girls saw him, sometimes they didn't. At this time Abdullah was obsessed by the possibility that he might be assassinated, and going out to dinner with him meant pretending to get into one car and then suddenly hopping into another one that swiftly drew up behind it at the kerb; it meant being told that you were going to one restaurant and then being ushered in to a quiet table at the back of a totally different one. 'Don't you think Abdi's a bit paranoid?' asked Kate. 'Don't you think it's a bit melodramatic, all this cloak-and-dagger stuff?'

Two days later, Abdullah's equerry climbed into his official staff car, turned the ignition on and the vehicle exploded. Bits of the car and bits of the equerry were flung all over Kensington Square in front of the house that had been rented for Abdullah's stay in London. After that, Maxine and Kate weren't so keen on acting as Pagan's unofficial ladies-in-waiting, and Pagan never again complained about unexpected changes of plan when she was with His Royal Highness.

Together with three hundred other guests, Abdullah came to Pagan and Kate's coming-out dance, held in the ballroom of the Hyde Park Hotel. Kate and Pagan shone with excitement, Pagan in white satin, embroidered with pale green lilies of the valley, Kate in primrose tulle. Naturally, they were the stars of the evening as they danced under the proud gaze of Kate's father, her mother – looking nervous in grey taffeta – and Mrs Trelawney, whose skinny, birdlike, dieted-to-the-bone body was sheathed in bronze silk, courtesy of Kate's father.

As she waltzed Kate suddenly stumbled: for one heart-lurch-

ing moment she watched as François, her Swiss seducer, sauntered into the ballroom, accompanied by a girl in a white lace
gown. Then Kate realized that the man *wasn't* François, although
he had the same sort of Cary Grant face, the same brown eyes and
quizzical mouth. However, this man was even better-looking
than François, taller and with broader shoulders. Kate couldn't
stop looking at him out of the corner of her eye. She longed to
meet him and yet at the same time she wanted to rush as far away
from him as possible. Casually, she asked who the dark fellow was
and was told that he was a banker's son named Robert Salter,
studying at Cambridge.

For the rest of the evening Kate felt an irresistible attraction,
and yet she couldn't bring herself to walk up and introduce
herself – although it was her dance.

But the following morning, an orange tree was delivered to
Walton Street. Attached to it was a note that said Kate had been
the star of a wonderful evening. It was signed Robert Salter.
Although he hadn't had a chance to dance with Kate, his girl had
told Robert that Kate was an only child, her father was very rich
and that they lived in a castle in Cornwall.

Robert started to shower Kate with gifts. He knew that he'd
have to buckle down to work in his father's bank when he returned to Cairo, where he had grown up knowing all the
pampered, eligible girls in that city. Better to choose a wife in
England, he thought, and, as he watched Kate swirling happily in
primrose net, he decided to have a try for her.

Though he discovered on their first date there was no castle, he
experienced, close up, Kate's invisible, oddly irresistible, sexual
allure. She wasn't nearly as good-looking as her friend but it was
Kate he desired, Kate who filled his dreams.

Kate told nobody about their meetings except her mother, who
she knew would keep her secret. Kate was dazed by Robert's
good looks and his masterful sophistication. 'He just seems more
grown-up than the Hooray-Henrys on the stag line,' she confided
one morning as she and her mother were getting ready for yet
another trip to Harrods for silver dancing shoes.

'I must admit that Robert knows how to treat a girl in public,
which is more than those Henrys do,' her mother agreed.

'There's nothing unusual about having lunch at the Savoy,'

Kate said wistfully, as she pulled on kid gloves, 'but when you go with Robert every waiter in the place flutters around you. With Robert it's always limousines at the door and great bunches of lilies from Constance Spry every morning, and jewelled trinkets from Asprey's in those regal purple boxes, delivered with a salute by an impressive uniformed chauffeur.'

She snapped open her purse and revealed a gold cigarette case and lighter, a matching compact, a platinum lipstick holder, a little jewelled pencil and a crocodile notecase. 'It isn't as if Daddy couldn't have bought these for me, but to be showered with gifts like this – well, it's like Christmas every day.'

'I hope you're being *sensible*,' said her mother, meaning prudent.

'Oh, yes,' Kate lied, snapping shut the purse.

23

AFTER Christmas, Pagan refused Kate's father's offer of skiing at Saint Moritz, cheerfully explaining, 'I'd rather break my leg falling off a horse, and no man born will ever be attracted by the sight of me on skis.' She stayed in Cornwall. Kate didn't want to leave Robert, so she stayed in the snug little basement apartment in Walton Street and idled the day away shopping or chatting on the telephone. She occasionally toyed with the idea of going to art school, and when this mood fell upon her she would wander off to the Victoria and Albert Museum to look at the Elizabethan jewellery or the Persian miniatures.

Maxine was surprised by the recent change in her flatmate. When not on the telephone or wandering around the Victoria and Albert Museum, Kate just lay on the carpet listening to records or else flopped on the sofa doing nothing for hours on end. Maxine couldn't comprehend how a person could spend the whole week doing nothing. Every Friday, Kate caught the train to Cambridge and reappeared on Monday, either looking wildly happy or in tears. However much she was questioned and teased, Kate refused to discuss these trips, but obviously there was a man involved – and obviously Kate didn't want her friends to meet him. It must be serious, therefore, Maxine concluded.

In the late spring the social round started again, and Kate became a little more animated, surrounded by her usual cluster of lovesick swains. But she spent Easter among the floodlit joys of Greenways, either in gales of tears or else writing letter after letter. In early summer, Kate was off again to Cambridge every weekend, but in July her interest in that ancient university town suddenly lapsed and letters with a Cairo postmark started arriving at Walton Street twice a week. 'If you don't tell me about him I'm going to open the next one,' said Maxine. '*Why* won't you tell us about him? I *know* why, because you want to marry him and you think that if you tell us he won't ask you.'

'Bitch.'

Then one September morning a radiant Kate burst into her bedroom, her dressing gown unbuttoned, an open letter in her hand. 'He *does*, he *does*, he *does* want to marry me. Robert . . . Kate Salter . . . Mrs Robert Salter . . . Mrs Salter.'

'You mean it's really *it* this time? I thought you were already engaged to be married to about fourteen men,' said Pagan, who was spending a few days in Walton Street while Maxine was working at a house in Wiltshire.

'Only if they leave the country; only if their ships are posted abroad or their regiments go to Malaya; and I only say maybe, it's practically a patriotic duty.'

'Yes. And look at all the scent you get and boatloads of brocade from Singapore.'

'Oh shut up! He's going to phone me this evening. Robert's going to phone! *Of course* I'm going to say yes. So now I can tell you. He's been reading economics at Cambridge, but his father's a banker in Cairo, and he's going back to work there. Just imagine! *Living in Egypt!* Pyramids, rose water and a great desert moon above the sail of a *felucca* on the Nile!'

Kate then produced a sheaf of photographs of a rather portentous-looking young fellow. In none of the photographs was he smiling, and in all of them he looked as if he were about to pronounce on something important. 'He looks *marv*ellous,' said Pagan politely. She wondered why Kate had been so secretive about Robert, he looked such a pompous old prodnose, not worth stealing, even if he was handsome as Cary Grant.

Kate sat by the telephone from six o'clock in the evening until two in the morning, when Robert got through. The line was faint and indistinct and Kate had to bellow. From the next room Pagan could clearly hear the conversation. '*Yes*, I love *you too*, oh, darling Robert, yes, yes...' This went on for about twenty minutes. Jolly good thing his father *is* a banker, thought Pagan. Then there was silence.

Pagan padded into the room to find Kate in tears. 'Cheer up, you're the first one of our set to get engaged, that's nothing to cry about. Remember the pyramids and the moonlight over the Nile. When's the wedding?'

'Not until summer. Robert has just started to work at his father's bank and he can't leave for a honeymoon as soon as he starts. Bad example, he says. But we can't wait *nine whole months*. He wants me to go out there. He said why don't I go with Mother, but honestly I don't think that would be much fun and she'd hate it.' Neither of them could imagine Kate's mother on the pyramids under a desert moon or floating down the Nile in a *felucca*.

'Why don't *you* come with me, Pagan?' Kate asked. 'If Dad stumps up for your fare.'

'Well, he certainly won't let you go to Cairo on your own.'

Babbling with joy after a sleepless night, Kate phoned her parents at seven in the morning. 'Thought something was up,' her father said, 'you haven't been home for weeks.'

Kate decided to fly out to Cairo immediately after Christmas. Just before they left, Kate returned from a shopping trip to find Pagan lying on the living room floor, exhausted by her determination not to cry. Kate already knew the reason. She had seen the headlines in the evening papers: '*Abdullah and Marilyn – Film Star Declares Love for Prince – Marilyn Says They'll Wed.*'

'Is it true, Pagan?'

'Don't know about the bloody "wed", but I've known about the love bit for some time.' She kicked the brass fender. 'I thought she was like the rest, you know. I mean there's always some busty wench in the background. Marilyn was just more famous than the rest.'

She hesitated. Pagan hated to confess humiliation. 'I know he's at the Dorchester. The happy couple were photographed in front of their damned fountain, so I've been telephoning all afternoon – using our secret code – but he won't take my calls. Utter hell.'

'Be reasonable, Pagan, he might be doing something else – ordering a destroyer, or having a cup of tea at Buckingham Palace.'

'No, Kate, I can tell by his secretary's voice – a certain nasty smoothness. I *know* the absolutely grim way he talks to anyone who's on the blacklist.' She sighed. 'It's easier for Abdi not to talk to me, so he won't. Frantically convenient, being royal.'

For days afterwards Pagan sat in her mother's apartment looking out over the leafy treetops of the square but seeing nothing. She didn't cry: she wouldn't see anyone: she wouldn't go to Cornwall and she wouldn't leave her bedroom. Her self-assurance had been shattered by Abdullah's behaviour and it was as if one of the guy-ropes holding her upright had been cut. He had deliberately broken their special bond of intimacy and trust and seemed to consider that their friendship – which Pagan had treasured – was at an end.

Pagan only roused herself from her lethargy when it was time to pack for their trip to Egypt.

Robert met them at the Cairo airport and Kate flew into his arms. As the three of them climbed into the back of his Cadillac, Pagan gave Robert a swift, sidelong look. He was certainly good-looking, but perhaps a bit *dull*?

But Cairo wasn't dull, it was a dusty, beige, hot, urban tumult. Camels and donkey carts trotted alongside swaying trams and automobiles. Pagan saw a tent pitched next to a modern apartment building, by a clump of trees. The skinny brown men on the sidewalks wore black skullcaps and what looked like crumpled pyjamas or white, vaguely biblical nightgowns. Fatter men were draped from head to toe in white sheets; hurrying women were shrouded to the eyes, downcast in dusty black. Fly-covered beggars hunched on the sidewalks, newsboys shrilled and sweet-meat vendors crouched, languidly wafting a flyswatter over their wares. Some shops sported neon signs, others were grimy with peeling, sun-faded paint. Any spare wall space was plastered with posters of General Naguib, the new military governor of Egypt.

*

Robert's widowed father's apartment hung above the city. High, cool, white rooms led into high, cool, white rooms. The servants, all male, wore white uniforms with a dark red fez, and had all been with the family for years. From the roof garden, the girls could gaze down upon the languid Nile as it wriggled through the desert on its way to the sea. Faintly from across the river they could hear the sounds of Cairo: the whine of traffic, ululations, klaxon shrieks; the *muezzin* calling the faithful to prayer over the P.A. system on top of every mosque. Above them, black kites swooped over the apartment buildings, the mosques, domes, tombs, the palaces and slums of the dusty city.

Soon Kate wore a marquise diamond engagement ring that she flashed as much as possible. She doted on Robert, repeated everything he said, followed him around like a faithful spaniel and was terrified of playing bridge with him in case she didn't bid correctly. Pagan thought this very bad for Robert, who was self-satisfied enough as it was.

Every night Kate nipped along the passage to Robert's bedroom where, to her sorrow, not much happened. Robert was out almost before he was in. She didn't even have time to feel frustrated. So she faked.

Apart from that drawback Kate loved the leisurely life of Cairo. In the afternoon the girls played tennis at the club, where all the British gathered, swam in the pool, then played bridge for very small stakes until it was time for dinner. There were dances or parties almost every night: once they went to a ball at the British Embassy, surrounded by traditional Britishers of the sort that look like film extras: peppery old colonels, balding diplomats, dowagers shrouded in black taffeta.

Sometimes they drove into the western desert for a picnic.

Naturally they visited the pyramids as soon as they could and were duly photographed on camels. Having discovered that horses were for hire, Pagan immediately mounted one of the depressed-looking nags and, much to its surprise, galloped off into the desert. When she returned, Robert was furious and said that never, *ever* were they to go anywhere alone. When he took them to the bazaar he warned them to stay very close to him. They sniffed the scent of goat, tanning hides, tobacco, mint tea, cheap jasmine and patchouli oil.

All the narrow, winding alleys looked exactly the same as the streets leading off them. Robert led the way and their driver walked immediately behind. Nonetheless, the girls were pinched and pummelled, as they threaded their way down through rows and rows of stalls and shops smaller than a European bathroom. Inside, they listened to the clack of Arabic and gazed at Persian carpets, delicate wood carvings, beautiful teak boxes inlaid with mother-of-pearl and ivory, high-piled bales of brilliantly coloured gauzes. Much to their initial embarrassment, Robert bought nothing at the bazaar without haggling.

Robert didn't talk about money, but he thought about it a lot. He was a human calculator; everything he did and spent was balanced in advance against possible return; he kept a little notebook in which, unknown to Kate, he recorded every penny he spent on her – the original orange tree; every bunch of roses; every generous tip at the Savoy.

Pagan had lots of beaux. She was making a determined effort to distract her mind from Abdullah by never giving herself time to think about him. In one frenetic burst of energy she decided they ought to learn Arabic and produced a suitable phrasebook. 'You can learn in only eighteen lessons,' she explained to Kate, 'and we can practise on the butler. If we turn up late, we can mutter *Kulli shayy fi yid Allah* (everything is in God's hands) . . . hey, listen to this. *Ma takhafush, ehna asakir inkelizi*, that's "do not be afraid, we are British soldiers." It's followed by *akhad el-kull we-addi lek bih wasl* – that means, "I will take everything and give you a receipt." No wonder the British Empire crumbled. This might be useful, *ma kuntish azunnek ragil gabih kide*. That's "I did not think you were such an untrustworthy man." Oh, dear . . .'

Pagan made sure she was occupied from morning until night, although there were many times when she lay on her back, tears dripping from the corner of her eyes and trickling on to her damp pillow. She couldn't sit still and she couldn't stand being alone. When Robert and Kate went off by themselves, she immediately picked up the telephone and organized an impromptu party on the terrace; the engaged couple would return to the clink of glasses and laughter as Pagan imitated a belly dancer or whirled on the roof garden in a satirical Highland reel. She quickly became one of the most sought-after girls in Cairo, and it was obvious that Robert's father, a sardonic man with eyes like small black pebbles, was intrigued by her exuberance. In contrast to most of the languid small-talking women of Cairo, Pagan played wild tennis, wild bridge, laughed and danced through the night, was never seen on a darkened balcony. She had more style than the rest of the women put together, he decided, watching her move along the terrace with her impatient, long-legged walk, half-stride, half-swoop. By contrast, Kate trotted adoringly behind Robert, agreed with everything he said – especially if she didn't understand it – and looked a little insipid.

Eventually, Robert's father took his son to one side and, without preamble, said, 'I've made a few inquiries in England and I don't know whether you realize it, but Pagan would be a far more suitable wife for you than Kate, you know. She's far better connected, and although there's no money, she owns a manor house in Cornwall.'

Robert looked astonished. 'That belongs to her mother, doesn't it? The health farm?'

'No, it belongs to Pagan. Her grandfather left it outright to her, and her mother pays her a token rent for the place. There's quite a lot of land with it. Poor Kate doesn't seem about to shine in society as your wife *should*. Have a think about it.'

When Robert's father said 'Have a think about it,' he was giving an order, as Robert well understood. None of his Cambridge contemporaries would have stood for such parental interference in their love life, but Robert was neither surprised nor resentful. If his father felt that interference was necessary, then it probably was; he and his father thought in a surprisingly similar way. Besides, Robert's future depended upon his father.

A few evenings later, under the green palms of the roof garden, the two men talked again. 'I've been thinking about what you said, Dad, and I see that perhaps you're right,' Robert said, as he slowly sipped his whisky and gazed at the dust-veiled citadel, a twelfth-century mountain fortress on the horizon. 'Perhaps I was unwise.'

His father was pleased. He wouldn't have to stop Robert's allowance and he wouldn't have to send both girls back to England.

'Well, of course, it leaves one in a slightly embarrassing position,' said his father, 'but I have a plan.'

The following weekend, both girls had been invited to Alexandria by a rich Levantine widow with a great reputation as a hostess. At the last minute, Robert announced he wouldn't be able to go. 'I've got a lot of work to catch up with after an unexpected rush this week,' he explained. He also made it clear that he did not want Kate to leave him, so eventually Pagan set off alone for Alexandria.

That evening Robert drove Kate out to the Auberge des Pyramides for dinner. They watched belly dancers gyrate in their oddly determined manner to the rhythmic tinkle and clash of the gold and silver coins that hung in ropes around their rotating rumps. Then Robert suggested they watch the moonlight falling on the pyramids, as lovers have done since travel brochures first were written.

When the car drew up before the famous and now familiar tombs there was no moon. Kate looked across the car expectantly, waiting to be pounced upon. Robert thought he might as well get it over with. Adopting a pained expression, he said, 'Darling, uh, I've been thinking a lot about *us* – and, darling, I hope this isn't going to hurt you dreadfully – but I don't think it's a very good idea.'

Kate didn't absorb what he was saying. 'What isn't a very good idea?'

'Us getting married, that is. You've been here two months now and I felt – almost as soon as you arrived – I felt that I'd made a mistake. Although at first I thought that I should go through with it.' He looked sideways at her.

She was stunned. 'You mean wait longer? To get married you mean?'

Slowly, firmly, Robert shook his head. 'I mean, call it off, darling.'

Kate was bewildered, disbelieving. 'What have I done? What's different? What's happened?'

'It's nothing that you've done or that I've done, darling, it's just that, well, the *chemistry* isn't there,' he said looking at her with rather theatrical regret, a touch reproachful almost.

Kate was stunned. She was also ashamed and humiliated. She didn't know what to say or do.

277

'I've already spoken about it to my father some time ago,' Robert continued with smooth sorrow, 'and he suggested that I wait until I was *quite* sure before talking to you about it. I know it's hard on a girl when a man changes his mind, but it's just as well I found out *before* we got married. Dad says he'll do anything he can to help. He was awfully decent about it, awfully thoughtful. He said you might find it humiliating to stay in Cairo when everybody knows that we're ... well, that we've both ... that I ... that I don't want ... that we're not ...' He didn't have to continue.

'I want to go home,' said Kate in a whisper. 'I want to go home as fast as possible.' Suddenly Kate longed to be with her mother, someone simple, loving and undemanding. She felt soiled, rejected.

The next morning Robert came to Kate's bedroom. Her face was white and she lay limp on the bed. Robert was calm but concerned, rather as if Kate had flu. He had no idea that it would be so easy. Once again, Dad had been right. 'Dad's been able to pull a few strings and he's arranged for you to fly back today if that's really what you wish,' he said, 'but there was only one seat on the plane, so perhaps it's just as well if you let Pagan stay here until the end of the week. After all, this isn't *her* fault ...'

Oh, he *does* know that I faked, thought Kate, he knows I'm frigid.

'And it won't look as odd as if you both suddenly disappeared. We don't want people to talk. Pagan can say her goodbyes and explain that you were suddenly called back on a personal matter.'

Home. Oh, God. Kate dreaded breaking this news to her father. She could already hear him – 'So you made a mess of it? Let him make a bloody fool of you! You went *all that way* just to be made a bloody fool of, eh? I hope you realize that everybody's going to think you're a bloody fool.'

All she could think about on the long plane journey back to Britain was how her father was going to take the news. Her dread of his reaction even outweighed the misery and shame she felt as a result of Robert's behaviour. And Kate was right.

Both her parents were standing waiting at the airport barrier, her mother looking sad and her father scowling. He barely said anything to Kate until they had climbed into the Rolls, when he slammed the glass panel shut so the chauffeur couldn't hear, turned to Kate and said, 'I hope you realize you've made a bloody fool of yourself!'

But for once Kate's mother stood up to him. 'Don't you dare say another word to that poor girl,' she said quite loudly.

And for the first time since she'd heard Robert's news, Kate burst into tears.

~ 24 ~

To her astonishment, Pagan returned from Alexandria to find that not only had Kate disappeared but that she had left no message. Robert was looking desolate. 'She's chucked me,' he said. He unclenched his fist to show the marquise diamond ring. 'She even insisted on giving me the ring back.'

Pagan gasped at it. 'I can't *believe* that Kate did that, it's not like her at all to be so hasty and unkind. Did you have a row?'

'No, it came as a total surprise. She just coolly told me over a drink that she'd decided the whole thing was a mistake and that she wanted to leave immediately.'

'And she didn't leave a letter for me?'

'No (sigh), and although I'm *deeply* hurt, I can't help thinking that if this is the way she behaves, then it's just as well she did so before we were married, rather than after.'

In fact, Kate had left a letter for Pagan, but Robert had opened it and read her painful, unhappy, accurate account of what had happened between them. He tore up the letter.

'And she didn't want me to go back to London with her?'

'No, she said she was sorry she had to hurt me, but she didn't want to spoil your holiday. She said that she had deliberately waited to tell me until you were out of the way.' He put his head in his hands and his shoulders shook. Pagan felt wildly embarrassed and walked to the edge of the terrace. She couldn't stand seeing men cry.

Robert's father thought it might be more tactful if Pagan didn't telephone England; Kate would telephone if she wished to do so.

It would perhaps be better to respect her wishes and leave her alone as she had asked. He thought that Pagan ought to wait for a letter from Kate before writing to her. So Pagan waited, but no letter arrived.

At the end of the week Pagan wrote to Kate as tactfully as possible telling Kate how upset Robert was and asking Kate to reconsider her decision. Robert offered to post the letter for her at the bank. After a bit, Pagan wrote more letters to Kate and one worried scrawl to Kate's mother, but she received no reply because, of course, instead of posting the letters, Robert tore them up. It never occurred to Pagan that when Robert offered to post her letters from his office – which meant that they would go by express courier – he did this in order to check her correspondence; and it certainly never occurred to Pagan that her letters were being destroyed. With calm ruthlessness, Robert also intercepted Kate's letters to Pagan and tore *them* up; this was a simple matter of getting up in the morning before Pagan, who was always served breakfast in bed.

At first, Pagan was puzzled by Kate's refusal to write to her or even to send a postcard acknowledging the letters that Pagan wrote in her large, generous, long-looped scrawl. Then Pagan felt hurt by Kate's neglect of her and – finally – she felt worried. As Pagan was totally straightforward and honest, she never dreamed that Robert would suppress her letters and trap her in a net of lies. When Pagan asked again whether she shouldn't perhaps telephone to make sure Kate was all right, Robert gave her a pained look and asked her whether it had occurred to her that Kate might be ashamed of herself? Otherwise, she would surely have replied to at least *one* of Pagan's letters.

From the moment Kate left, Robert made a determined play for Pagan, subtly supported by his father. Wherever they went they had the maximum of attention, the best service and the best seats; flowers were showered upon her, and whatever Pagan wanted, Pagan had. She appreciated these attentions and tried to forget Abdullah in this leisurely round of pleasure. Cairo was as heavily romantic as a magnolia blossom and she was being delightfully spoiled. Pagan couldn't think of anything that urgently needed her attention in England, unless it was to work as a shop assistant in Peter Jones' department store: she wasn't academically qualified, she wasn't trained to do any job, she was too tall to be an air hostess, she wasn't thin enough to be a model.

Not only was Pagan bewitched by the luxurious life of Cairo, but Robert-in-Cairo was a much more beguiling proposition than Robert-in-London, where there was plenty of competition from other men. Cairo lacked eligible young European bachelors and the few who found themselves in the city were fiercely fought over by hostesses and flattered in the most outrageous way. Women hung on Robert's every word and responded to every joke he made with tinkling laughter. Pagan started to look at Robert with more appreciative eyes.

Robert bided his time until one evening after they'd been to a Christmas dance at the Semiramis. The creamy moon hung like a lotus in the sky. He had ensured that Pagan's champagne glass was never empty, and she was definitely giggly as they drove home. She swayed slightly as they walked towards the elevator, and Robert put his arm around her in protective fashion as they waited.

'Merry Night! Happy Night! Good Christmas!' chortled Pagan, and it seemed the most natural thing in the world to kiss him good night. Then she went to her room, threw all her clothes on the floor, fell on the bed, and immediately went to sleep.

Farther along the passage Robert adjusted the Japanese kimono that he affected as a dressing gown, pulled the sash firmly into place, then moved purposefully into Pagan's bedroom.

Pagan woke up the next morning wondering, as many had before her, 'What *have* I done?'

Robert then concentrated all his attention on a classic, whirlwind courtship, with his benevolent father beaming in the background. He brought Pagan charming little gifts – dangling golden bell earrings, a square-cut purple amethyst as large as her thumb, a darling little pet monkey in a scarlet jacket that Pagan immediately took off the delightful little creature.

Two months later, somewhat to her surprise, Pagan and Robert were married at the British Embassy. Robert's father gave her a pale blue Rolls Royce as a wedding present.

Almost immediately after the wedding reception, the marriage started heading for the rocks.

*

Pagan had never been passionately interested in sex, so at first she merely thought that all Robert needed was a bit of practice. She was wrong. A couple of months after their marriage, she tentatively said, 'Could you possibly wait for me?' He immediately stiffened, said he didn't know what she meant and accused her of being frigid. Amiably, Pagan agreed that she might be. 'It's just that I haven't been so far,' she added. Robert turned purple with rage. Quoting the *Kinsey Report*, he said the average man took two and a half minutes to climax, which meant that she was getting thirty seconds *more* than average, didn't it?

Pagan longed to talk to somebody about it, but she felt too shy. She dearly wished she could talk to Kate to ask if it had been the same with her. Pagan wouldn't mind asking Kate, because she was too desperate to be embarrassed, and she thought that if Kate knew how agonized Pagan was, then Kate wouldn't mind talking about it. But Kate hadn't answered one of her letters.

In fact, Kate had written a violent letter to Pagan when she heard her friend had married Robert, but Robert spotted Kate's handwriting and fished the letter from the silver salver in the hall. Slitting it open with his forefinger, he gave a sniff as his eyes flew over the five pages of accusation in Kate's little, neat handwriting, every letter clear and separated, with no loops on the down strokes or any sort of flourish, and pain in every line. Robert put the letter in the inside pocket of his suit and later tore it up in his office.

That evening – wearing his pained look – he told Pagan that he'd had a short letter from Kate, saying that she hoped he could forgive her and let bygones be bygones, that she was now in love with a Twelfth Lancer called Jocelyn Ricketts and hoped soon to be a soldier's wife. Pagan eagerly asked to be shown the letter. Robert looked in his inside pocket and said dash, he seemed to have left it at the office, he'd bring it back tomorrow evening. The following evening he said, with irritation, that he'd forgotten the damn thing, and surely Pagan realized that he had more important things to think about than a couple of scrawled lines from a woman who'd hurt him so deeply.

Pagan never again asked to see the letter, but after a few days – although Robert had distinctly told her not to do so – she locked herself in her pale blue bathroom as soon as Robert had left for the office and booked a call to Walton Street. After a four-hour delay, her call was put through but there was no answer. All that Pagan heard was the little quiet hiccup of that old-fashioned heavy black telephone, thousands of miles away in London. She immediately booked another call and again there was a four-hour delay and again no answer; Pagan didn't dare book another call because Robert was due home, but she telephoned again on the following morning.

There was no reply from Walton Street.

On the third day Pagan booked a call to Kate's mother. This time there was only a two-hour delay and Kate's mother answered the phone herself on the fourth ring. Oddly stiff and formal, she said that Kate was staying in Scotland with friends. Yes, perfectly well. Yes, she and Mr Ryan were also perfectly well, thank you.

'D'you think you could get Kate to write to me, then, or telephone?' asked Pagan.

There was a pause. The line crackled. Then, in a rush, Mrs Ryan said, 'I don't think Kate ever wants to hear from you again. Or Robert. Kindly leave her alone.'

Then Mrs Ryan carefully put down the receiver with no intention of upsetting her Kate by telling her daughter that Pagan had telephoned to beg forgiveness. What a nerve the girl had!

By Pagan's first wedding anniversary, the *Kinsey Report* had been quoted at her so much that she thought perhaps she had better check if she *was* frigid. So she had an affair with her tennis coach, a cheerful Italian with good legs, gentle hands and a voluptuous appetite. They weren't in love, so for Pagan there was a strange, embarrassing, impersonal feeling about the relationship at first, but Alfonso was a skilful lover and he adored everything about women.

Alfonso was mysteriously unavailable at siesta time (when it was too hot to play tennis) but three months later Pagan found that there was a very good reason for this – a rich American widow, one of those overscented, plump, languid women of Cairo who wore tight black dresses from Paris with too much ostentatious jewellery and had their hairdressers call every morning. Alfonso beat the hairdresser to it, and his proposal of marriage was accepted. Although he suggested to Pagan that they continue

283

their liaison, she thought it would be too complicated, however exciting.

After that, she had a couple of young diplomats from the British Embassy, but they weren't at all like the tennis coach – they were tense, elaborately polite and not at all cuddly, not very different from Robert, in fact.

Robert had now started to complain that she was not only frigid but sterile. Considering his hostility, Pagan was surprised he still wanted to make love to her. 'Well, shall we have another *stab* at it?' he would suggest with a polite snarl, and poor Pagan was duly stabbed with what she privately called the marital *chippolata*, wearily wishing that Robert would stop touching her nipples as if he were turning up the volume.

Urged by Robert, who wanted a row of little Roberts, she eventually consulted a doctor, not only to check that her fallopian tubes were unobstructed, but because after Robert had made love to her, she felt a heavy turgid pain in her lower back, as if she were having a really nasty period. This sometimes lasted for hours, during which time Pagan would be tense and tearful, drop glasses, upset cups and ashtrays; she also started to suffer from insomnia. Not knowing that these were classic symptoms of a sexually aroused and then frustrated female, Pagan would eventually get up at four in the morning and slug herself to sleep with a blissful half-pint glass of neat vodka.

The doctor confirmed that there was no reason why she shouldn't conceive ('Keep practising,' he said jovially), and decided that her other physical symptoms were psychosomatic because of her concern at not being pregnant. When Pagan suggested to Robert that *his* potency should be checked, he puffed up with rage like an angry pigeon and flatly refused to take a sperm test on the grounds that it was undignified.

Outwardly, Pagan seemed exactly what Robert needed. A splendid-looking woman, a charming hostess and, as such, a business asset. But once she had acquired a wardrobe of rich clothes, once she knew all the people and had been to all their parties, Pagan started to long for the woods, the trees, the cliffs and the cold grey sea of Cornwall. Increasingly, she felt oppressed by the yellow dust of the lotus, by the rich, pointless life of Cairo, by her own rich, pointless life and by her rich, pointless husband. She couldn't stand the way that Robert kowtowed to his father, who now – for some unknown reason – didn't seem to care for Pagan. Pagan knew that Robert blamed her for their lack of children, but she didn't realize that both he and his father also silently blamed her for not having her own money. Unfairly, his father blamed Robert for having made a bad investment decision, conveniently forgetting that the marriage had been his own idea in the first place.

'More trouble over your bloody estate,' snarled Robert, one evening when he returned from the office. With a nod he accepted the whisky and soda that Mohamed silently proffered on a silver salver. 'My father's spent thousands of pounds on lawyers and yet they can't upset your bloody mother's trusteeship!'

He strode over to Pagan, sitting on a flowered chintz sofa on the balcony, and spat, 'The old girl's as tough as nails. That place belongs to you and she's got it for a song!'

Pagan yawned, then said in an offhand voice, 'Well, it doesn't matter darling, does it?' She stretched both arms up and moved along the sofa so that she was directly in the breeze stirred by the overhead fan. 'After all, *we* don't want to live there at the moment, and it gives Mama something to do, and she's earning her own living, you don't have to help support her.'

'... Typical of *you*!' yelled Robert. 'Just as Father says. You're totally careless about money ...'

'... *You're* totally under your bloody father's thumb ...'

'... At least my father doesn't exploit me ...'

And so another row started. Pagan realized by now that Robert didn't love her. She also had painful cause to know that he was a verbal bully as he repeatedly tried to grind her down with criticism.

Robert was finishing the job that Abdullah had started – the job of wrecking Pagan's spirit. Not only did he not love her, he really wasn't interested in her. Robert was interested in presenting himself to the world as a wise, just man; and to do this he prevaricated endlessly. He was never guilty of anything; in Robert's eyes Robert could do no wrong. If the facts indicated otherwise, then the facts had to be readjusted. Certainly, Robert would never be honest enough to admit to himself that he was a rotten lover and a sham, Pagan thought.

One night, after Robert had performed his marital duty for the usual three minutes, she told him so. Robert snapped on the bedside light and sat up, glowering at her. 'What exactly do you mean by saying that I'm a dishonest sham?'

Pagan realized she'd presented him with the perfect excuse for a row, but suddenly she didn't care.

'I mean that you're not only a selfish lover but you pretend not to be. *That's* deceitful and dishonest, when you turn over and go to sleep *knowing* that I'm churning inside, but pretending that you *don't* know. I loved you when we married and I didn't want to say anything to hurt you, and as a matter of fact I thought that all you needed was a tiny bit of practice. In fact, I thought we both probably did. If you were still the same as you were then, I wouldn't mention it, but you've got worse.'

Robert grew redder.

'At first I thought you were too tired, Robert. I thought it was the strain of your job, but then I saw that it was just old-fashioned laziness and selfishness. And there was something nastier; you didn't want to be *involved with me*. If you could press a button and have me disappear after you've come, you'd press it.'

Robert turned purple. 'You're the only woman who's ever complained – and that's because you're *impossibly demanding*!'

Pagan took a deep breath and said what she'd been rehearsing in her mind for months. 'Robert, I can masturbate to a climax in five minutes. I checked it with the kitchen egg-timer. *That's* how long it takes to arouse me if I'm not anxious or under pressure. Not much longer than you. But you don't bother to find out what makes me come. I've hinted for a long time and now I'm happy to tell you straight, as well as show you, so that you can't go on pretending that you don't know.'

'You castrating bitch!'

'No, I'm not. It's just that I'm not an acquiescent Betty Grable or whatever female fantasy you imagine you have in your arms, when it's only me. You'd *rather* fuck an imaginary Betty Grable than a real me, because she responds in exactly the way that suits you and gives no trouble. Good old Betty disappears at the touch of a button when you don't need her any longer, doesn't she? I can't compete with a myth, with an invisible, acquiescent pinup. I want reality and honesty. I want a real relationship with a real man.'

286

'You've got a filthy whore's mouth.'

'You've got a filthy schoolboy's mind. I expect my mother's generation would put it more daintily – they'd say you were insensitive or didn't understand a woman's needs or something – but for once, Robert, I'm speaking plainly because I want there to be no doubt about what I'm saying. I don't want you to double-think this conversation into something that suits you. I'm saying that I don't want to be used only for sex. I want to be loved. I want intimacy and sensuality and mutual concern. Not a quick stab, thank you!'

She thought that Robert was going to hit her, but he didn't; he merely glowered at her and stormed off to sleep in one of the other bedrooms. For three days he wore an air of righteousness and did not speak to his wife; then he returned to her bed and behaved as if their conversation had never taken place.

Pagan wept. She had hoped that after he'd simmered down, he might take some notice of what she had said. But he didn't.

And she never tried again.

∽ 25 ∽

THE glass doors of the sumptuously decorated penthouse suite of the Dorchester were thrown open. Although it was early June, it was a warm day for London.

Inside the powder-blue bedroom, on the vast, rumpled, lace bedspread, the twenty-three-year-old Abdullah lay naked across a woman's half-clothed body. He slid his hand into her crumpled white silk blouse and softly pulled out her other breast. The rosy tip quivered erect in his mouth as his lips pulled on the vulnerable flesh, harder and harder on the sensitive, delicate skin. Abruptly he released it.

'Don't stop, please don't stop!'

Delicately he ran the tip of his tongue over the little jutting peak, ran it swiftly back and forth, the nipple quivering again as his tongue softly circled around it. He gently took it in his mouth and again started to suck softly, pulling at the now deep-red areola. Abruptly he stopped again. A little cry, a gasp. Purring, he rubbed his silky, black moustache against the nipple, slippery with saliva; gently growling, he played delicately with it.

'Oh, that's unbearable, don't stop, darling.'

Softly he nipped it with his teeth, let go, then pounced again, surrounding the raspberry flesh with his sucking mouth. Again he darted his tongue over and around the soft, dark bud, drawing it gently, then with increased firmness between his moist lips, pulling, stretching taut the heavy cream breast, clasping it with both brown hands, sucking harder and harder, greedy and insistent.

'Darling, I can't stand it. I'm going to come.'

Abruptly, he stopped and pulled his gleaming brown body away, poised above her, his hand holding her wrists to the bed as she writhed in frustration, trying to reach up to him. 'You can't touch me,' he growled softly, 'you can see me, you can see what you want and you're not allowed to touch it, you can't have it . . . until I allow it.'

He shifted his position, lay beside her and taking her wrists in one hand he pressed them to the pillow above her head. Then his other hand slid down her body, felt beneath the crumpled skirt, slid over the stocking top and found her warm thigh. The hand slid over to her inner, quivering warmth, and felt soft, enfolding flesh on both sides as he lightly pressed his thumb against the moist, silken hair beneath it. The body beneath him writhed in ecstasy, oblivious to all but his hands and mouth.

'Now I'm going to undress you,' he purred, 'very slowly.' Abdullah always talked to his women, always softly told them what he was going to do, just before he did it. It was sometimes easier not to undress a woman completely to whom he was making love for the first time. There was then no time to recall a husband, to feel guilt as clothes were being removed, and besides, Abdullah sometimes liked the urgent feel of a half-clothed woman beneath his naked body, he liked to feel the sensuous slither of satin and silk, the fragility of lace beneath his fingers or, in a more tigerlike mood, to feel fine fabric tear beneath his hard hands.

The woman beneath him moaned again, 'How can you . . . why don't you . . . How can you *stand* it?' But Abdullah had been instructed in the sexual customs of the East, and those special, subtle practices had taught that there could be no deep satisfaction for a man, one who was no longer a boy, without *imsak*, the control of his own fierce passion.

For an instant Prince Abdullah's mind spun back seven years to 1947, to the cool inner courtyard of the old doctor's house in Cairo, where surrounded by lemon trees the fountain splashed under the arched, white colonnades that surrounded the courtyards. There he had lain on a vast, cushion-strewn, silken divan to be instructed in the arts of love and the special, subtle sexual practices of Arabia. He remembered the soft feel of the plump, brown thighs of his first girl, the silken curve of her knee under his hand, the ever-fascinating undulations of her dimpled backside, the soft feel of it beneath him and her conspiratorial giggle as, unable to contain himself, he thrust into her with frenzy, then climaxed with a harsh, triumphant cry.

Only once was he allowed to do this, by way of introduction to the girl who for the first week was to be his partner, mentor, tease, informer and judge. Gravely, over thimblesful of black coffee, the old *hakim* explained that regular sexual intercourse was necessary to keep a man fit and healthy, but the sexual act could either be a simple one of reproduction – no more complicated than that of a beast in a field – or it could be a subtle act of love, a discipline to be learned and practised, in order to achieve and appreciate the most sublime gift of Allah.

Abdullah remembered the air, heavy with sexual promise, that hung over those cool rooms, and the soft, ululating wail of Arab love songs, accompanied by the music of the flutes. He remembered the odour of those rooms, a sultry mixture of cinnamon and spices, *kef* and coffee, warm black hair and female musk, the scent of rose and jasmine, mingling with the fragrance of vanilla that wafted in from the tubs of white oleanders that stood on the turquoise-patterned tiles of the central courtyard.

That first week was a week of eagerness and exasperation as he was made to practise *imsak*, a word that roughly translated means 'to retain': Abdullah was taught that his whole aim should be to avoid losing control of his body, and that this was best and most pleasantly accomplished by concentrating his mind entirely on the woman. By the objective study and prolongation of the pleasure of his partner, a lover could stem and control his own tide until she had achieved a height of passion that left her dazed and unaware of her surroundings. Only once a day was the sixteen-year-old boy allowed to climax. By the end of the first week his body was bruised all over where plump little Fatima had sharply pinched him when she judged it necessary, but he could tell by her pouts, by the regret in her merry eyes, the sly look she gave him under her glossy lashes, that she was sorry to see him progress to the older, more experienced women in the second week, as their plump, soft hands guided him, as they murmured words of suggestion and lightly scratched their sharp almond nails upon his skin when he needed correction. Always, after the evening bath, when eunuchs poured silver pails of warm scented water between his thighs, a masseuse in white robes would bend over Abdullah's silken couch to stroke and knead, to soothe, refresh and once again stimulate every tingling muscle in his body.

It was only because of those weeks of unrelenting, skilled tuition that he could now make this blonde creature beneath his body attain the heights of pleasure that she was unlikely to know with a Western man. Few Western women had experienced such consideration as Abdullah could show, such lifting of mood from gentleness to passion to wild abandon and then softly back again. Abdullah loved the primitive, musky smells of women, and he knew their bodies and their needs as he knew his own; he seemed uncannily able to read a woman's mind and know exactly what she longed for at any given moment – everything she had ever secretly desired – and he was the Nijinsky of cunnilingus. Abdullah was completely, naturally uninhibited, and so his women felt equally abandoned, which was generally what made the difference between how they felt with their stiff British husbands and how they felt about the breathless sensuality of Abdullah's body which summoned up such erotic response to what he murmured in their ears. He well knew that speech was an important part of seduction.

Prince Abdullah did not find it difficult to use Western women as his means of revenge upon Western men; he loved women as some men love horses. In almost every female he found something to admire and desire; he loved their softness, their elusiveness, their laughter. He loved small girls and big, voluptuous ones, slim bodies and rounded chubby ones; he loved dark silky hair and short blonde curls; he loved little, firm, high breasts and low, voluptuous breasts like melons; he loved slim waists, but he also loved little rounded stomachs, big rounded buttocks and thighs like soft pillows. He loved the excitement that he could summon up in that delicious, warm, sensual flesh, to see some beauty writhing out of control at his command, responding in a frenzy to his light, sure touch, while Abdullah, by contrast, stayed in complete possession of himself and could remain so for hours. He gave many women that romantic bliss that as school-girls they had dreamed of; he gave a few women the sort of unrestrained passion of which they had never *dared* to dream. He captivated women with his fierce, proud face, his lean, well-exercised body, and his aura of sexuality, wild as that of a stallion. Added to which, by the time he left Sandhurst, Abdullah had the carriage and savoir faire of a much older man as well as the invisible assurance provided by money and power.

However, to be loved by Abdullah was not always a bed of roses, although great sheafs of roses were, in fact, sent three times a day to his current lady. Abdullah always made it clear to all his women that, although at that moment he was completely at her command, there could be no permanent future for her in his life. He would whisper this regretfully, with heartbreaking sorrow, as if he couldn't really bear to speak of it, but felt it only honourable to say before he bent again to the distraction of her snowy breasts. So no woman could say that he had in any way misled her, although he might easily exasperate, hurt or anger her when he suddenly disappeared. No woman could say he had deceived or jilted her, or dropped her or left her, because he never really had. He hated saying goodbye to a woman; he always liked to feel that he was joined to them by an invisible silken thread that he could, if necessary, gently tug. After being loved by Abdullah, no woman ever remembered him with anger or remorse – only with nostalgia, a slight smile or a sigh and a memory of having been magically charmed. It was as if he had just appeared one night for a brief moment. Then – equally suddenly – he wasn't there anymore and the wonderful nights were gone.

But the memories were unforgettable, if only because they

were unlikely to be repeated. Abdullah, murmuring soothing words of flattery and love, encouraged most women to behave in a more voluptuously agile manner than they had ever thought possible as he led them swiftly through an erotic crash course which culminated in his sensuous pièce de résistance. With silken cords he would bind the wrists of the more adventurous ones to the bedhead and then he would dip one golden hand – his skin wasn't very dark, just a permanent sun-bronzed tone – into the bowl of golden fish that always seemed to be at his bedside. Abdullah would quickly scoop out one little fish and swiftly push the wriggling creature into the girl. At this point, she generally stiffened and shrieked with surprise, but Abdullah threw his body on top of hers and held her hard against the mattress until she relaxed and was able to enjoy the strange erotic sensations as she felt the little fish move inside her warm body. As soon as the girl started to groan, with pleasure, Abdullah would slide down her body and – with great dexterity – he would languorously suck out the goldfish.

Now, as the present blonde writhed beneath Abdullah's body and her harsh little shrieks grew louder, his aide-de-camp was calling him through the ornate doors of the Dorchester Hotel. 'Your Highness, Sire. The telephone, Sire. The prime minister, Sire.'

Abdullah threw his head back and growled. Suliman was supposed to see that no telephones disturbed him, especially not in the late afternoon.

'An emergency, Your Highness.'

Quick as a cat, Abdullah was off the bed and, in an instinctive reflex action, had grabbed his gun before the woman on the bed realized what was happening. She lifted herself on her elbows, as Abdullah backed towards the telephone, carefully lifted the receiver and had a short conversation in guttural Arabic.

Abdullah carefully replaced the receiver. In the dim light of dusk, he looked alert, wary and very upset. Suddenly the woman on the bed realized that although he was scowling fiercely at her, he had forgotten that she was there.

'Your Highness,' she said, uncertainly. There hadn't been time to get on first-name terms.

He blinked and looked thoughtful. 'Not Your Highness,' he said, 'Your Majesty.'

Damn, the tousled blonde thought as Abdullah strode naked to the door. Damn, damn, *damn*!

26

PAGAN was sitting up in bed and drinking her morning mango juice, when Robert threw the morning newspaper at her and said, 'That wog boyfriend of yours is now in the hot seat.' The headline read, *Young Warrior King Ascends Throne*.

Pagan said nothing until Robert had left for the office, then she went to the cocktail cabinet, took out a bottle of vodka and climbed back into bed with it. In 1954, after three years of marriage, her relationship with her husband had become one of polite, cold hate. Pagan was no longer such a good business asset. In fact, she was carelessly drunk quite a lot of the time.

The next morning, Pagan woke to see Robert, his head propped on one arm, looking at her from the next pillow with such venom that she felt frightened. Suddenly she realized that she'd always been a little frightened of him. She faced the truth – she had made a dreadful mistake; she'd married a pompous ass with an imposing exterior. Inflated by his own self-importance, Robert was as empty on the inside as a blown-up carnival balloon.

'You're thinking about that black bastard as usual, *aren't* you?' Robert threw the sheets back from the bed with cold fury and, still glaring at her with hate, roughly yanked at the shoulder strap of her topaz silk nightgown. As Pagan flinched away from him, Robert gave a strange little hiss, tore the silk from her breasts and raped her.

She cried out as she tried to push him away from her, but his fingers only dug harder into her breasts. Afterwards, she saw a look of satisfaction on his face, of power and cruelty. She realized he had enjoyed hurting her and would do so again. He had become her intimate enemy.

After he had left the room to saunter to the terrace for his impeccably served breakfast, Pagan staggered into the bathroom. Silk strips fluttered from her body, and in the mirror she saw fingermarks on her breasts. Shuddering, she ran a warm bath and lowered herself into the water. With a wet hand she carefully lifted the telephone and dialled the airport.

Leaving behind her pale blue Rolls – later much regretted for its trade-in value – Pagan caught the next plane to London.

Pagan's mother was appalled, but not surprised, to see her daughter. A cablegram had arrived for Pagan the day before and Mrs Trelawney had opened it, thinking her daughter still in Egypt.

INTEND TO IMMEDIATELY DIVORCE YOU STOP
GROUNDS DESERTION STOP ALIMONY NOT
FORTHCOMING FOLLOWING YOUR DISGRACEFUL
BEHAVIOUR STOP PLEASE ACKNOWLEDGE ROBERT
SALTER

Pagan scowled as she read it. 'He makes it sound as if I'd been sacked for incompetence.'

'Do you mind explaining what happened?'

'Darling Ma, couldn't we have a drink first? It's been eight hours on the train you know.' Pagan's mother sniffed, took a step closer and sniffed again. 'Yes, I know, I had a nip or two on the train. Medicinal. And consoling. So *cold* here after Cairo. And I was a tiny bit disappointed that you didn't meet me at the airport. Didn't you get my cable?'

'Yes, darling, but I could hardly just disappear and leave Selma on her own for two days; one has one's responsibilities. And after all, you're not a child, you only had to take a cab from the airport to Paddington Station. How long do you think you'll be here?'

'Darling, I've come *home. Here.* Trelawney is my home. I'm going to stay here in blissful Cornwall.'

There was a pause, then her mother walked towards a wall-hung corner cupboard. 'I think we both need a drink.'

She poured two glasses of Amontillado sherry. 'We're full at the moment,' she said, after a moment of silence. 'There isn't a spare guest bedroom, but one of the servants' bedrooms is vacant. It's on the top floor of the east wing.'

'You mean that utterly grim *attic*?'

'Well, darling, you must admit your arrival is unexpected. We didn't know you were coming and we're fully booked up three months in advance; doing quite well since the new hydrotherapy tank was installed. Goodness, you finished that quickly, darling, are you sure you want another?'

Pagan was intrigued by the change in her mother. She and Selma wore crisp, white uniforms and called themselves the Executive Director and the Dietetic Consultant. They spoke in low, soothing murmurs, even when no one else was present. Mrs Trelawney wore no makeup, sported a large pair of tortoiseshell spectacles, and had taken up yoga.

After four nights, during which Pagan slept in a small servant's bedroom, Mrs Trelawney said, 'I've talked things over with Selma and when it's free we're prepared to let you have one of the guest rooms – the housekeeper's old room I thought. But you'll have to behave. You know what I mean. No drink, darling. Not *one*, tiny, hidden bottle. You know I can't risk it.'

Pagan no longer wanted to live at Trelawney, where strangers in dressing gowns drifted down the overheated passages or sipped weak tea in the conservatory. She had decided to move into a gamekeeper's abandoned cottage about a mile from the house. It nestled in a dip in the woods surrounded by golden azalea bushes. Mrs Trelawney had intended to convert the old cottage into a luxury annexe suite, but when she said, 'Impossible, darling, I'm afraid' Pagan looked at her coldly and said, 'Darling, please remember that Trelawney belongs to *me*.'

The grey stone cottage was furnished with some castoffs from the big house, and Mrs Hocken came once a week to clean up. 'What you want is a bit of company, Miss Pagan,' she offered one morning, leaning on her broom. 'A nice cat or a dog. Mrs Tregerick was telling me since her Jim passed on there's not a body to exercise their dog, a sheep dog 'tis, no harm in having a look at 'un.'

Buster was black and white, shaggy and the size of an armchair. Together they kept the cottage in a state of chaos – it smelled permanently of wet dog. Every day Buster took Pagan for a walk, nearly pulling her arm out of its socket as he strained at the leash. Buster meant that Pagan didn't stay alone in the cottage all day, sprawled on her chintz-covered lump of a sofa whose sagging springs creaked as she reached for the vodka bottle.

She felt bitter and frightened – a failure. How and where had she gone so wrong? Could someone else have made Robert happy? Should she have tried longer, harder? It took more energy than she could muster to think it over again and what was the point? It would all end badly anyway. Better to stay home with her darling Buster and her vodka and blot out the loveless mess.

One morning Mrs Trelawney walked over to the cottage to find Pagan sitting on the kitchen floor wearing gum boots and a pair of old riding breeches and nothing else. She had been eating baked beans laced with vodka out of the dog bowl and could barely manage to lift the spoon to her mouth. She flung the spoon at her mother.

'Pagan! Pull yourself together!'

'People only say that when you can't.'

Pagan's mother suggested she might like to talk with the clinic doctor, who was able to help people with unfortunate addiction problems.

'It's a bit bloody late to start being interested in *me*,' Pagan shouted.

Pagan had arrived in Britain with only a hundred and fifty-six pounds cash, all that had remained in her account at the Ottoman Bank. After two months in Britain, this had been reduced to seventeen shillings and four pence, so Pagan decided to tackle her mother about funds. She waited until evening to walk up to Trelawney: after six o'clock her mother had no reason to give that sharp, meaningful sniff.

Mrs Trelawney was checking diet sheets at her desk in the study. 'Won't be five minutes, darling,' she murmured, peering over her tortoiseshell rims. 'Help yourself to . . .' But Pagan was already pouring a gin and tonic.

'Darling, haven't you any *dresses*? Since you arrived I've only seen you in gum boots and jeans.'

'Well, Ma, it's such a divine change from Cairo. Wearing clothes *there* was practically a full-time career, one was always having to change. Frantically boring. Anyway, I haven't any money to spend on clothes, which is what I'd like to talk to you about.'

'You mean you expect *me* to support you?'

'I don't see how else I can be supported, for the moment.'

'A pity you didn't consider that before you left your husband.'

'Ma, do you really want to know why I left so suddenly?'

'That's a personal matter between you and Robert.'

'But do you want to know?'

'No.'

Mrs Trelawney didn't want to be involved, she never had.

'But I must have something to live on, and my only asset is Trelawney.'

'No need to ram that down my throat, darling. If it hadn't been for Selma we'd have had to sell it.'

'But now that you're doing very well, surely you could let me have a small allowance? After all, you'd have to pay rent to somebody else if you moved the health clinic. I'm willing to work if I can find somebody to bloody well hire me, but what can I do? I've no saleable abilities. You never trained me to earn my own living. I'm useless.'

'I don't think you should have another drink, darling. If you'd only stop, we could perhaps give you a job in the hydrotherapy department.'

'Pointing a hose at fat old men?'

'You can be so incredibly vulgar at times.'

'What exactly *is* the position of the estate – or should I ask that solicitor in St Austell?'

'By all means do so, but I can tell you myself. As your trustee I leased Trelawney to the health clinic on a full repairing lease for fifty years at a rental that amounts to the yearly interest on the loans secured by the estate. It's already been explained to your husband's lawyers. They plagued the life out of me for months as soon as you were married.'

'Eh? Could you say that again please . . .' Her mother did so. 'Does that mean that when I'm sixty-eight I will *still* have Grandfather's debt around my neck although you will have been raking in the profits for half a century? What happens if you die tomorrow?'

Her mother looked into the fire. 'Selma and I have drawn up identical wills. We both own fifty per cent of the shares in the clinic, and upon the death of either shareholder the surviving shareholder may purchase the shares at par value. I saw no reason to mention that to Robert's lawyers – they were unpleasantly aggressive – but I suppose *you* ought to know now.'

'You mean that if you died, then Selma would get the lease of Trelawney?'

'Darling, I wasn't trained to earn my living, either. When Grandfather died I had to accept the business proposition that Selma put to me. Of course, now that I've had five years' experience, I could run the place by myself, but don't you remember the state I was in at the time? And it's a full repairing lease. You'll get the place back in perfect condition, which will increase the value.'

'Doesn't sound as if that's a bonus. Grandfather always kept it in perfect condition.'

'I do wish you wouldn't raise your voice, the patients might hear. To be quite frank, the other directors and I have already discussed the possibility of paying you a small allowance.'

'Who are the other directors?'

'Selma and her accountant. *Our* accountant.'

'And what did they say?'

'Mr Hillshaw thought we *might* manage three pounds a week.'

'Four. Plus the running costs and upkeep of the cottage.'

'Certainly *not* the running costs.'

'Then I'll go to St Austell tomorrow.'

'Oh, all right then. But no telephone bills.'

'No telephone, darling.'

～ 27 ～

BOTH men were sweating in the heat of the helicopter cabin. A thousand feet below, their own shadow bobbed ahead of them over the south Sydonian desert. Flying high over Sydon you could see to the north the narrow, green plain, split by the twisting silver ribbon of the river as it slithered west to the Red Sea from its source high in the magnificent mountain peaks of the eastern hills. Beyond the mountains, farther to the east, the implacable beige monotony of the desert was broken only by the roofs of Fenza.

Abdullah took the helicopter up a bit higher. He always felt happy and unfettered in the air, free from fear in a way that he could never be on earth. Both he and Suliman had learned to fly while they were at Sandhurst, and Abdullah had later qualified as a helicopter pilot. A helicopter was the ideal means for moving around his country swiftly and in relative secrecy.

They were flying south, away from Semira, his capital city. The old city stood on the north bank and upon its summit stood the Royal Palace, which overlooked closely packed, dazzling, white-domed rooftops, the narrow lanes between them and the small *souk* in the middle. All week there had been a sense of foreboding in the *souk*; the market had been unusually subdued, full of sullen, worried faces and the bark of sudden argument. Troublemakers were at work again, with all their usual slogans. Abdullah reflected that it was perhaps a mixed blessing to send young people abroad to be educated; they returned with impractical, radical ideas, loosely described as 'progressive', and talked of establishing a so-called people's republic where no one would ever again fear or want or work.

The previous evening the King had granted an urgently requested audience to the United States Ambassador. Together they had strolled under vine-covered trellises, along walks planted with low herbs, where no eavesdropping was possible.

The Ambassador had warned the King that another attempt to kill him could be expected within two days and that the plot was apparently planned at a very high level. Neither man was surprised. During the previous year, the young ruler of Sydon had made it clear that he intended to make many changes, that he intended to root out the cynical corruption and lethargy with which his country was run. Unfortunately, the older politicians did not wish the old ways to be changed and the Western-educated students wanted radical changes that included ousting the King. Trouble was only to be expected.

Ostensibly, the helicopter was flying south along the brilliant azure line of the sea, towards the southern border and royal seashore palace of Dinada, that beautiful steel-and-glass building designed by Philip Johnson for Abdullah's father. But suddenly the helicopter dipped and turned seventy degrees off course to the east, heading inland over the desert that composed seventy per cent of Sydon.

Within ten minutes they spotted the low, black goathide tent and a small group of tethered camels. The helicopter landed a hundred yards away from the animals, in order to alarm them as little as possible.

One young officer of the Desert Patrol and two officers of the First Armoured Regiment ran towards the helicopter and stood at the salute outside the circumference of the great blades. His gun drawn, Suliman waited until the blades were still and then jumped down.

'Salam Alaikum.'

'Alaikum a Salam.'

After the traditional greeting, the men bowed to their king, who entered the low tent, quickly sat cross-legged and motioned to the others to do likewise. There was a pause, then the usual exchange of extravagant compliments and declarations of devotion. Suliman, who had grown up with two of the officers, nodded to them.

'Your Majesty, it is said that the life of Your Sacred Majesty is in danger. This we know, for one of us was approached by a senior officer and promised higher rank if total unquestioning obedience was promised for the next few days.'

He paused and looked, as if for confirmation, to his two brother officers. 'Fortunes are being offered in bribes to the army, this we also know.' The other officers nodded, black eyes harsh above beak noses.

'And we have been warned that the First Armoured Regiment will shortly be ordered to leave on a long march, a secret night exercise.' There was another pause, and again the speaker looked around, as if for support, before he continued. 'Your Majesty, we fear we shall be ordered to surround the capital and bar all exits.

'If such a thing were allowed to happen, in the confusion either a civil war might start in Sydon or an outside power, such as those dogs, the Saudis, might quickly gain control of Semira, then the radio station and thus the whole country.'

He drew a final deep breath. 'We suspect there are traitors at all points in the army. We even doubt the loyalty of those who command us, and we wish to receive our orders directly from Your Majesty.'

Except for the harsh desert wind, there was silence as all four men waited for Abdullah to speak. Conscious of the dangers risked by these men in approaching Suliman to set up the meeting, Abdullah lifted his chin. Even when sitting cross-legged in olive fatigues, he had great presence and radiated tough energy. He said firmly, 'Remember, O my brothers, that I was appointed by Allah to lead you!' He lifted his left hand and slowly pointed at each man in turn. 'All of you remember the personal oath you swore to me when I became your leader. Our entire nation will applaud your action when they hear of it.'

He folded his arms across his chest and slightly raised his voice. 'Justice is on our side! Now we will move swiftly without mercy to wipe this menace from our land!'

There was a pause, then each man reaffirmed his loyalty, after which they discussed possible plots, suspected plotters and dates for their execution.

It was decided that all three officers would accept any offer made by the plotters and would then try to warn Suliman, by telephone or in person.

The meeting took less than a quarter of an hour.

In the darkness, small waves slapped against the hull of the sixty-foot cabin cruiser, hove-to three miles offshore and north of Semira harbour. Leaning over the bridge and straining his ears, the Greek captain could just hear the muffled oars of the two inflatable dinghies. Then he glimpsed the occasional phosphorescent flash, the occasional herring-silver glitter of their bubbling wake, as one by one the dinghies pulled away from the rope ladder that dangled from the main deck to the waterline. Even so far out, they dared not risk the noise of the outboard engines. Lucky there was no moon. Under cover of darkness, without being seen or heard, both dinghies should be able to make the harbour and nose in among the fishing boats lined up against the northern quay. They ought to be able to be there before dawn.

The captain squinted through his night glasses at the town. It seemed quiet and peaceful. There were a few lights around the port, although not many at this late hour. The dinghies had taken enough stuff aboard to blow the whole harbour to bits. Thank God it was out of his hold at last. There didn't seem to have been any new developments since yesterday afternoon when, at the seashore palace of Dinada, he had been ordered to cast off at twenty minutes' notice. His Majesty had dashed aboard with his bodyguard and ordered him to set off at full speed on a north-westerly course – final destination Cairo.

As soon as they were out of sight of shore and darkness had fallen, they had doused all lights, gone about and then, steering by compass, headed north through the night towards Semira.

Eight of Abdullah's armed guards were now in the lead boat. The best of the soldiers were with His Majesty in the second boat. Nobody knew who, how many, or whether in fact anyone awaited them at the harbour rendezvous.

The previous afternoon, one of Suliman's contact officers in the First Armoured Regiment had telephoned Suliman at Dinada Palace and suggested a hunting trip to shoot partridge in the desert; he had offered to set off immediately by car for Dinada with a few friends. Suliman had his answer ready. He would prefer to go fishing. He would meet his friend just before dawn at Semira harbour, between the low customs shed and the harbour-master's office.

'Impossible, I have already agreed to a hunting trip.'

'Then arrange for other friends to meet my fishermen.'

Suliman had then reported to Abdullah that it sounded as if a force of armoured cars was about to leave Semira barracks for the Dinada Palace, in order to kill him.

Neither King Abdullah nor Suliman had any means of knowing whether the young officer would have had time to arrange the 'fishing trip' and whether a party of loyalist fighters would await them at the harbour, but both men knew that after their flight from Dinada they would never again see the young officer responsible for it. His telephone call to the palace from the barracks would have been logged automatically and he would automatically be killed upon suspicion of being an informer.

They were now close to the shoreline; there were only two hundred metres between the lead dinghy and the harbour mouth. Now they could smell the small port odours – diesel oil, rope, sailcloth, tar, rotting fish, urine, iodine.

A low whistle through the darkness and their oars were raised. Under their own momentum the boats slid into the treacle-black harbour, turned to port and nosed quietly in among the fishing boats. As they docked, a barefoot sailor from each dinghy heaved himself up on to the stone quay and lashed the painter to a metal bollard. Another low whistle and the sailors helped the soldiers to scramble up, then the men and their burdens became part of the black night.

Behind the dark bulk of the customs sheds stood two armoured cars, each containing a driver and an officer. Silently the soldiers crammed into the two vehicles, leaving one on guard with the extra guns and ammunition for which there was not enough space in the cars. 'To the barracks,' Abdullah commanded.

Tense and silent, safety catches released, the grim band drove slowly away from the harbour and threaded its way through the winding, unlit streets that led to the northern gates; massive, iron-studded, ten-foot-high wood slabs, they were set into the six-foot-thick stone walls that surrounded the old town. As usual at night, a sentry stood on duty, and as they approached he lifted his gun and challenged them.

The officer leaned out. 'We wish you to open the gates and stand aside for His Majesty King Abdullah.'

'Tonight we have orders not to open the gates,' said the sentry, uncertain.

'Soldiers,' Abdullah commanded. 'It is I, your King. Advance so you may see that it is indeed your King who wishes to pass.'

Slowly the sentry moved forward, still uncertain, and peered into the car. He immediately stiffened to the salute upon recognizing Abdullah's impassive face, the dark eyes staring through him, then he ran to unbar the gates, shouting to the sentry on the other side to do likewise.

After they had pushed the heavy gates back against the walls and secured them, two of Abdullah's men jumped out to replace the sentries, who were silently motioned into the second car. Both vehicles shot forward towards the Semira barracks.

Light was just dawning as the two vehicles sped towards the main entrance of the low, brick-built barracks. Already trucks were lumbering slowly from the huge inner barrack square, out through the three arched exits. Abdullah's two vehicles jerked to a stop outside the first gate. All doors were thrown open and all occupants of the cars, except Abdullah and one driver, sprang to the ground, their guns at the ready. The two officers marched briskly up to the surprised sentries and halted the stream of trucks to allow Abdullah's car to drive into the courtyard.

The car stopped against the inner wall and Abdullah's escort immediately surrounded the car, while their King leaped on to the roof of the vehicle. Wearing the impressive scarlet *kaffiyeh* of the Palace Guard, he looked a brave and fierce figure as he announced that he, their rightful King, had come to lead his men against all traitors.

There was a burst of cheering as swarthy soldiers ran to his car and surrounded it. Fierce, black-bearded, hawk-nosed faces were upturned to his: delighted shouts rang out: scimitars were flourished. It was at least five minutes before Abdullah could quell the roars of delight and continue with his speech.

'All army personnel are to obey my orders only, issued from my mouth alone and not passed through officers or NCOs,' he shouted. 'No one is to leave the barracks until disloyal officers have been arrested! I now declare a state of emergency, during which my army – led by me – will assume sole control of the country.'

After further shouts of support, Abdullah continued, 'Parliament will be dissolved and the Constitution suspended until order prevails in our land! All political meetings are banned and from tonight there will be a dawn-to-dusk curfew throughout the land. Until further notice, no political speakers will be allowed on the radio.' More cries of approval. After which, Abdullah roared, 'Any rioting crowds will be immediately dispersed by mounted troops with tear gas, and anyone who erects barricades or tries to stone my troops from rooftops will be shot on sight!'

Half an hour after entering the barracks, Abdullah was able to hold a staff conference, after ordering his entire army to remain in barracks or camp and expect a visit from the King. Nearly all the plotters were senior officers; very few NCOs and no rank and file seemed to have been involved. To Abdullah's lasting bitterness, the plot had been engineered by the commander-in-chief of the army and included not only two other generals, but also three members of his Inner Council of Five, including the new prime minister. This was a greater blow than he had expected.

That afternoon, at the Royal Palace of Semira, the King summoned a meeting of the remaining two members of the Inner Council as well as all army officers above the rank of major. The murmur of voices in the great cool hall was hushed as the throb, throb, throb of the drums was heard outside.

Suddenly, King Abdullah appeared in the arched doorway. This was a very different figure from the fierce, scarlet-cloaked soldier-leader who had stood on the roof of the car that morning, legs astride, brandishing a scimitar that flashed in the rays of the rising sun. Wearing an immaculate white ceremonial uniform with gold epaulettes, Abdullah moved slowly forward, a ruler rather than a leader.

Two men stood silent on the topmost terrace of the palace, looking down over the white rooftops of Sydon. The sun, a blood-red ball, was sinking below the horizon; above the dark sea, the sky was streaked with orange and yellow. Suliman risked a respectful grin. 'That went well, Sire.'

'Yes, I rather thought it did. Would you please arrange to have the former prime minister executed in about three days' time, and also any of the other political plotters who haven't already fled to Syria, where they will no doubt continue to conspire against me.'

'It is wise to take all possible precautions, Sire.'

Abdullah watched the sun disappear and the sky fade. He reached a decision. 'That reminds me, will you please invite El Gawali here as fast as possible. To arrange the marriage. I can't put it off any longer. I need sons.'

28

CHRIST, what a noise! She wouldn't answer the door! . . .

Pagan decided to ignore the door knocker and then whoever it was would go away. She was about to put her head under the pillow when she heard a female voice singing, 'Happy birthday to you! Happy birthday to you!' The knocker was being thumped in rhythm with the song. *Christ* her head . . . surely . . . Could that be *Kate's* voice?

Pagan opened her eyes, sat up, shut her eyes again, staggered out of bed, opened her eyes, picked her dressing gown off the floor, tried to put it on, couldn't find the sleeves, threw it down, pulled the bed quilt around her, then carefully felt her way down the stairs and opened the door. Above a sheaf of sunny, yellow daffodils, she saw Kate's smiling face.

Kate stopped smiling when she saw Pagan's red-rimmed eyes, her puffy face and shaggy hair. She stepped forward and hugged Pagan as hard as she could. God, the smell of her breath . . .

'Come inside quickly, it's cold. Why were you singing?'

'Because it's almost your birthday.'

'Is it?' said Pagan indifferently. 'When *is* the twenty-seventh? Good God, I'll be thirty . . . I think it's thirty; if this is 1962 I'll be thirty.' She led Kate down the stone-flagged passage into the sitting room. 'That means I've been living down here for over eight years. Seems only yesterday I moved in . . . Thank you, I'll stick them in a vase . . . How did you know I was here?' She wasn't sure she wanted to see Kate, now removing the smart, khaki tweed jacket of her Mary Quant trouser suit.

Kate glanced at the sofa covered with dog hair and sat on a wooden Windsor chair. 'I met that woman Phillippa last week. You remember, the big, bossy one with the fuzzy red hair that we used to play bridge with in Cairo? She told me about your divorce so I phoned your mother straightaway.'

For years Kate had blamed Pagan for stealing her fiancé. But Phillippa had told Kate the gossip that most of Cairo society had known for years and thought Kate knew – the Byzantine subterfuge by which Robert had parted the two friends. It was Robert who had been traitorous, not Pagan. Now that Kate was happily married, she had immediately responded with remorse and guilt to the fact that she had been tricked into losing her childhood friend.

'I saw Phillippa about a week ago and I came as soon as I could, darling. I thought I'd surprise you. You were quite right to divorce Robert. He was my idea of a prize shit.'

'You might have told me.'

There was an uneasy pause and then Kate burst into tears. 'I can't bear to see you like this.'

'Don't *you* start,' said Pagan. 'I'm perfectly happy ... I don't spray tears all over the place like you and Maxine ... d'you remember, it was always either giggles or sobs? Can't think why women cry so much ... I'll see if there's any tea.'

She went to the kitchen, had a quick nip from the vodka bottle and eventually produced a tray of ill-assorted china with some old ginger biscuits and marmalade.

They chatted about nothing much for ten minutes, then Kate asked gently, 'Why have you hidden yourself away like this, Pagan? Why don't any of your old friends in London know that you're here?'

'Because I didn't *tell* them, darling ... I simply didn't want to see anybody after that three-parties-a-night life in Cairo.' She gave a sad laugh. 'I felt so ashamed of myself and Mama was obviously ashamed of me as well ... Nobody of our school year has been divorced.' She poured tea from a blue tin teapot. 'I just wanted to hide from people ... A few chums got in touch with Mama, or wrote to me suggesting a visit, but I never answered the letters ... The fact is, I never knew how I would react to anyone,' she sighed. 'I looked normal on the outside but inside my feelings were bubbling. If anybody spoke to me in a kind voice, I wanted to crumple up and cry. Idiotic, wasn't it? ... I used to get a lump in my throat and couldn't answer them back. So I avoided talking by avoiding people. I only spoke to the villagers when it couldn't be helped and I dashed upstairs and hid when I heard the postman's bicycle bell.' She added milk to the cup with a shaking hand.

Kate was stunned by the change in Pagan. How had that confident, vibrant creature changed into this confused, nervous wreck? Her speech was rambling and disconnected.

'Don't you see *anyone*, Pagan?' she asked.

Pagan shrugged her shoulders. 'I've become a bit of a hermit, except for occasionally seeing Mama ... One day I heard Mama explain to one of her patients that I was a recluse and that's why I talk to myself. That gave me a laugh.' She handed a cracked pink cup to Kate. 'Matter of fact I've never understood what's wrong with talking to yourself; your jokes are always laughed at ... you

307

always win your arguments ... it demonstrates a happy degree of self-acceptance.' She sipped from her earthenware mug. 'You don't have to finish that biscuit, it's about six months old ... Don't think I was unhappy. I had Buster for company and every day for the first six months I woke up and, oh, it was just utter bliss to see that Robert wasn't there on the next pillow. I'm comfortable enough here, listening to the radio and reading. I'm afraid it's not very tidy at the moment because Mrs Hocken broke her ankle falling over a puppy, so she hasn't cleaned for a couple of months.'

'Don't you still ride?'

'Well, I keep meaning to get a horse, but I always put it off until next week, like everything else. Mama sold the horses and the stables are now massage booths and a gymnasium ... More tea?'

She held out another ginger biscuit to Buster but dropped it. There was a moment's silence. Then Pagan said, 'Oh, dear, why weren't we sent into this life with an instruction manual? My trouble is that I don't seem to learn from my mistakes. I don't just *repeat* my mistakes, I make *new* ones ... When I look back, I suppose everything started to go wrong in Switzerland. Since then, everything I got involved with looked wonderful to begin with and ended in disaster ... Now I'm just permanently tired. Tired of everything. Tired of failure. Tired of life. So, I retired.'

She put her hands behind her head and gazed up at the ceiling. Kate quickly slipped her ginger biscuit into her handbag. There was another pause, then Pagan said, 'That's enough of me. You've now heard everything that I've done here for the last eight years. Nothing ... Unlike old Maxine. I sometimes see photographs of her in newspapers – not that I often read them, I just listen to the nine o'clock news and thank God that none of it is about me ... Amazing how old Maxine's sort of zoomed into being a glamour puss. One of the movers and shakers as they say ... Suppose the rest of us could be described as the shaken and the still shaking.'

Pagan stretched her arms and yawned. 'Now what's happened to *you* in the last ten years, Kate?'

'I was heartbroken over Robert,' Kate said, and sipped her tea, 'although it seems ludicrous now. After that, I went out on the same old round with anyone who asked me – anything rather than stay at home. It was parties, parties, parties until I met darling Toby. Then after we were married we had a far more quiet life.' She took another sip. 'But let's not talk about me this evening.' She finished her lukewarm tea and put down the cup. 'How about walking up to Trelawney? It's such a lovely day. The woods are full of bluebells.'

'No need to be in such a hurry,' Pagan said, picking up the tea tray. 'If you wait long enough to clean the car it always rains. Old Arabic proverb.' She carried the tray towards the kitchen and the vodka bottle that had been quickly hidden under a tea cosy. Whoever he was, Kate's husband could obviously afford Gucci shoes and a Hermès handbag, Pagan noticed.

While Pagan was banging away in the kitchen, Kate surveyed the living room – books piled on the floor, old newspapers piled on the chairs, half-empty teacups, a table covered with ring marks and cigarette scars, overflowing ashtrays, dog hair everywhere. Her first thought was to clean up Pagan and then the cottage; it could be a charming little home. Kate's second thought was to see Pagan's mother before taking any action. Why hadn't *she* done anything? The bloody woman was supposed to specialize in drunks, wasn't she?

They walked up the path through the woods, admiring the bluebells as they went. Past a mass of dark green rhododendrons, they crossed the steel cattle grid that supposedly stopped the deer from getting on to the main road. They climbed slightly uphill, over a muddy field of buttercups and then across the well-trimmed lawn that surrounded the beautiful stone house. In front of the conservatory was a ten-foot-high, curved, see-through, plastic shelter. 'The new, heated outdoor swimming pool,' Pagan explained. They walked through the conservatory, now filled with glistening chrome – the bicycles and huge mechanical rubber belts for massaging the buttocks. Once past the rows of pink-faced guests, cycling hard to nowhere, they went into the hall and climbed the six-foot-wide, purple-carpeted stairs that led to Pagan's mother's study.

Mrs Trelawney looked up from her desk, over her hornrimmed glasses. 'Nice to see you, Kate,' she said, as if she'd last seen Kate yesterday. 'You haven't changed a bit.' With neat movements she removed her glasses, folded them and placed them in a crocodile case. They shook hands; the marmoreal temperature of Mrs Trelawney's hand matched her welcome. She rang a bell and they drank lapsang suchong from rose-decorated Minton china. Then Kate was shown around Trelawney.

After her tour Kate managed to steer Mrs Trelawney to one side. 'I can only stay down here for a week,' she said in a low voice that, nonetheless, conveyed her fury. 'I want to tidy up Pagan and the cottage as soon as possible. I'm sure you can let me have a couple of your cleaners tomorrow; I'd also like to take all the treatments that you offer, and I want Pagan to take them with me. Perhaps you could give me the bill for both of us.'

'Frightfully kind of you,' Mrs Trelawney said in a polite voice, as if she were commenting on the view, 'but do please be my guest on the machines. I'm afraid that treatments might be a little difficult to arrange because the appointment book is already full.'

'Well, cancel a few,' Kate said coldly, and went back to join Pagan by the swimming pool.

They drove into St Austell in Kate's silver Karmann Ghia. First, Kate bought food: meat, cheese, fruit, Bath Oliver biscuits, pickled onions, two tins of pâté de foie gras, a box of homemade flapjacks, a honeycomb, clotted cream, black cherry jam, stone-ground bread, some Bendicks Bittermints and (because they were so pretty) a little bottle of crystallized violets. She also bought a new set of pots and pans, some buttercup yellow towels, flowered sheets and scented soap for the bathroom. Pagan protested but Kate firmly said, 'Birthday present,' as she scribbled another cheque for a couple of yellow-striped reclining chairs for the garden. Finally, she took Pagan to Jaeger and bought her a lavender cashmere sweater and matching tweed skirt with plenty of hem to let down; then she chose another sweater and skirt in sage green.

Pagan had been fidgety since pub opening time at eleven-thirty in the morning, but Kate didn't let her friend out of her sight. In order to avoid alcohol, Kate decided not to have lunch at a hotel or a pub, so she bought a couple of steaming onion-and-meat-filled Cornish pasties, which they ate in the car. Pagan shivered as she dusted the crumbs from her skirt.

'Why are you wearing that mackintosh and not a coat,' asked Kate, 'when you know how quickly the weather turns nasty down here? ... I suppose you *do* possess a coat?'

'Well, I *did* have one,' Pagan said, 'but I left it somewhere. One didn't need a heavy coat in Cairo.'

'Your mother was wearing a *mink* jacket this morning.'

'Well, if she gave me something like that I'd lose it,' Pagan said. 'You know how untidy I am.' She was not convincing.

Suddenly Kate remembered. 'Whatever happened to Abdullah's cloak?'

'My God, I bet it's still in the attic. She never let me wear it, you know,' said Pagan brightening. 'Didn't want me to lose my reputation!' She hooted with laughter and cheered up.

They drove back to Trelawney. 'If it's still there,' Pagan's mother said vaguely, 'it'll probably be in one of the cardboard boxes in the east wing attic. You'll see about forty boxes labelled "clothes".'

After looking through half the dusty cardboard boxes, Pagan gave a shout of triumph and pulled out glistening folds of black Persian lamb. 'Oh, heavens, moth!'

And indeed the beautiful soft black folds were bald in patches. 'But it is wearable,' said Kate, 'it's warm and I'll get it recut for you in the summer. *Next* birthday present.'

That evening they lay on the rug in front of the fire, as they used to when they were schoolgirls, and talked. 'Looking back,' Kate mused, 'I can't think what either of us saw in Robert. He was such a stuffed shirt behind that young-Cary-Grant mask. That awful, rigid, public school mould – all his lot, those Hooray-Henrys, were terrified of putting a foot out of line. I mean you can't imagine Robert saying piss off in public, can you?'

Pagan thought not. 'I can't think how you ever fell for him, Kate. *I* really fell in love with Egypt, not Robert,' she said dreamily. 'It was so warm, so ancient and mysterious. You know I don't really like parties, but I *loved* the attention, I loved being the belle of Cairo, it was so soothing after the pain of ... well, it stopped me thinking about Abdi.'

'In one way Robert was a bit like Abdi,' Kate added thoughtfully. 'Unlike the Hooray-Henrys, Robert used to be very good at supplying your every want – and even wants you never knew you had. Then, just when you got used to having everything supplied – as if it were Christmas every day – he would disappear to Cairo and it would all stop so suddenly that you missed it dreadfully.'

She paused, then added, 'And another thing, Robert didn't try to get you into bed like all the other scalpers. Robert always wanted to stop when you wanted to stop.'

'With good reason!' hooted Pagan, and they both giggled until it hurt, as they hadn't done since their schooldays.

'What about sex?' Kate asked curiously. 'What have you done about that for the last few years?'

Pagan sighed. 'Once I had a little fling with one of the patients ... I'd been to see Mama and he followed me back to the cottage. We had a jolly old time for a couple of days. He went back pissed to the gills – I've never seen Mama so furious. I was not to interfere with her patients/bread and butter/reputation/life, etcetera. Very unnerving.

'A couple of months later, I imported a hitchhiker, one of those irresistible blond hunks. That lasted for about four days and then, when he thought I'd gone for a walk, I caught him yanking open the drawers of my desk. I got the feeling he was looking for money, but I always keep cash in the toe of my spare gum boots, so I tiptoed away, then crashed in. I told him my mother was coming to stay for a few days, so he'd have to leave. He asked for money for the train ticket to London and was pretty nasty when I wouldn't give it to him ... anyway, I thought that maybe the next pickup would strangle me, hack me up neatly with the bread knife, pack me in a suitcase and dump me in the left-luggage at St Austell station and nobody would miss me for days. So I decided to forgo the pleasure. You know sex has never really been that important to me. There's always masturbation, but really after a bit I didn't bother. I didn't seem to need it.'

The following morning when two stout cleaning ladies appeared, Kate shooed Pagan out for a walk with Buster. Four hours later the cottage was clean and tidy, food lined the cupboards, a fire was burning in the sitting room grate, and Kate had planted a little basket with primroses. Exhausted, Kate thought she would open some of the pâté when Pagan got back.

But Pagan was already back. Kate found her after the cleaners had left, when she went to get more logs for the fire. Pagan was lying asleep on the floor of the woodshed with two Guinness bottles at her side and an empty hip flask in her hand. Chill with horror, Kate shook her awake. 'Darling, darling you'll catch your death out here. Come in and have a hot bath.'

She helped Pagan stumble into the kitchen, then ran a bath for her. Pagan's eyes were half-closed and she was beaming as Kate washed her face. 'Nanny, Nanny, mind the shope doesn't go in my eyes,' she gurgled, before slipping under the water.

Pagan was an amiable drunk, but a heavy one. By the time she had been dried and lugged to bed with a hot water bottle under the patchwork quilt, Kate was exhausted and very worried. She had something to eat and then, at six in the evening, she took a cup of black coffee up to Pagan's bedroom.

'*Why do you get drunk?*' she burst out crossly. 'When did it start?'

Pagan scowled; she had a headache; she felt queasy; she felt without energy or interest. Nonetheless, she sensed that it was now or never. She had never admitted to herself or anyone else that she was a drunk. But now she did.

'In Cairo,' she said eventually. 'That's when it started. A couple of drinks made those endless evenings with the same stuffy people a bit more bearable. And drink would blot out the reality of having to go home with Robert afterwards. Then in the mornings Robert liked to start the day with a quarrel; he enjoyed a row, the way some people enjoy tennis or Canasta. Whatever I'd done, it was always because I was lazy and useless and stupid. He was very convincing.' She gave a tired sigh. 'I used to stay in bed until he'd left for the office . . . then I'd numb the memory by sloshing some vodka into the fresh mango juice.' She felt for Kate's hand. 'I never meant to get drunk when I had a drink. I still don't, I never feel I *need* it, I just feel, "why *not*?" And then I have another, then just a little one, then another and another, until I can't remember how many.' She held the hand tight. 'In Cairo we never once mentioned it, but I *know* Robert knew about my drinking. He once let slip that he knew I'd been sick in the

313

night because I'd left the seat up, so he *must* have known.' She shivered.

'I mean, normal wives aren't sick in the night, are they? Of course, what he wanted was a wife who was sick in the morning, but there I was, labelled "frigid" and "barren". Nothing like spiked mango juice for that particular condition, and I knew why Robert didn't want to talk about the booze. He didn't want to feel gruesomely guilty about it.'

'But it's eight years since you left Robert!'

'Then my sense of inadequacy is eight years old ... I thought I'd feel better as soon as I left him, that the depression would be wiped away as soon as I got back to England. But it wasn't.' She paused and plucked at the patchwork quilt. 'I felt a sudden gulf of gloom when I left Cairo, because I knew I'd burned my boats. I stupidly expected Mama to meet me when I went through customs at London airport ... I hadn't seen her for two years, but I always wrote to her every week and I'd cabled her to say that I was coming back.'

Another pause and this time the quilt was carefully smoothed. 'But she wasn't there.' Kate squeezed her hand sympathetically. 'So I waited and waited until suddenly, standing there in the middle of the arrivals lounge, I completely lost my nerve. It's difficult to explain, but suddenly I wasn't certain of anything; I couldn't have told you the time, I felt so unsure and incapable. And then I suddenly felt *terrified* of being on my own.'

She gulped and paused for a moment. 'Odd, because I'd never been close to Mama, so why did the roof suddenly fall in when she didn't meet me at the airport?' Kate gripped the hand tighter in silent sympathy and Pagan continued. 'I suppose that was the first time I realized I was alone in life and it was a moment of stark terror. As a wife I'd been a failure, as a daughter I wasn't worth meeting at the airport and as a mother I really was a nonstarter, as we all knew ... Darling, I think my hand's going to turn blue if you hold it any harder.'

There was another long pause. 'Then I found I had hardly any money and that bitch, Selma, was totally in control of my mother. She really adores the old cow. That hurt.' For a moment Kate thought she was going to see Pagan in tears. 'I just had a feeling of futile emptiness, a flat sensation that nothing – *nothing* – lay ahead.

'Then the feeling tilted, it became steeper and steeper and I felt as if I were running too fast downhill and couldn't stop. There was a black hole at the bottom. It got worse and worse.' She clutched Kate's hands until Kate winced. 'It made me panic, and when I panicked I drank. I didn't need an excuse to die, I needed an excuse to live, and I almost ran out of excuses. If I woke up in the night I felt suicidal, but if I drank, I didn't wake up in the night. So I drank. Drink blotted out the depression; it made me feel like a real person, like the person I was and the person I might have been. When I was drunk I didn't feel like a failure.'

'Slower, slower,' said Kate, alarmed by this sudden agitation.

Pagan took no notice and continued as if speaking to herself. 'When I was small I used to hide from my nanny and escape into a fantasy world where my real friends lived; animals who talked and wore aprons and slippers and had teapots. Life became a bit like that again. Reality was too fearful, so I blotted it out. Once I fell into the bath when I was drunk and knocked myself out. I woke up in the bath with all my clothes on and my head hurting like hell. Luckily there wasn't any water in the bath or I might have drowned.'

'Oh, Pagan,' Kate said, 'I can only be with you a few days. Darling, won't you please, please try? Can't you stay in bed all the time and I'll look after you? Living alone here could be positively dangerous.'

'Yes,' agreed Pagan. 'I once passed out on the sofa with a cigarette in my hand and my book caught fire. Luckily it only made a mess of the book. But I *did* manage to stop smoking, and I don't drive a car; even when I'm pissed, I'm not very dangerous on a bicycle.'

'Pagan, there must be someone. Isn't there *anyone* who can help you? A local doctor? The vicar? They obviously all know you're an alc – That you drink.'

'Nobody knows. I'm *very* careful. I bury the bottles. I'm very careful in the village ... Oh, you're right, Kate, I don't suppose I've really fooled anyone. But I'm *not* an alcoholic. You're not to say that. Alcoholics are old down-and-out tramps who sleep in city doorways at night. *I* like getting drunk. There's a difference.'

'Pagan, how can you be so stupid? What does it matter what

315

you call it? You're wrecking your life. Can't you go to a doctor in London?'

'I'll tell you what I'll do, Kate. While you're here I honestly will *try* not to drink. And if I lie or cheat, I'll tell you afterwards. I can't offer more than that.'

For the rest of the evening Pagan was restless and twitchy, drank innumerable cups of tea, and only picked at Kate's cheese omelette. The next day they walked up to Trelawney where Pagan not only had a massage, a facial and a manicure, but had her hair styled and her eyebrows plucked.

Her hands started to shake that evening. Her teeth chattered, and then her whole body started to shiver. Kate put her to bed again, spooned chicken broth into her, and crooned as if to a sick child.

'For heaven's sake,' Pagan muttered weakly, 'stop *henning* around me. This is what you wanted, isn't it?'

Wrapped in a coverlet, Kate spent the night in an armchair in Pagan's room. Neither of them slept much. Kate wanted to talk to a doctor, but Pagan made her promise not to. 'Everyone around here knew Grandfather. I know I'm a disgrace to the Trelawneys, but I don't want everyone else to know.'

The next morning Kate went to see Pagan's mother. She wasted no words. 'You *must* know that Pagan's a drunk. Why haven't you taken her to a specialist or to some hospital or organization that can help her?'

'I can't see that Pagan's condition is any business of yours, Kate. Or mine,' Mrs Trelawney said in her well-bred, don't-touch-me voice. 'Pagan is a grown woman. She's thirty years old. As a matter of fact, when I suggested she see a therapist she said she could never see the word "therapist" without stopping after the "the".'

'But why didn't you *insist*?'

'Because there's nothing *wrong* with her. It's just that she *drinks* too much. There's nothing wrong with her head. All she needs is self-discipline. Psychiatrists are for the mentally ill and there's no mental illness in our family.'

'You mean that you refuse to face the possibility of mental illness in your family.'

'If there was anything I could do, then I would have done it, because, quite candidly, it's such a bad advertisement for the clinic. I've spoken to our doctor about her on several occasions, and Pagan has seen him, but the fact is that she's seemingly bent on self-destruction and I can't make her do anything about it. I never could.'

'You never tried,' Kate snapped, storming out of the room.

After a second sleepless night, Pagan's teeth were chattering and her body shook. Kate figured that when her body needed sleep, Pagan would sleep. Until then it didn't matter much whether or not Pagan slept. It wasn't as if she had any urgent appointments.

For three days Pagan trembled and was unable to sleep. She couldn't walk or stand without help. On the fourth night Pagan still couldn't sleep and retched horribly, but at dawn she suddenly calmed down and fell into a doze.

'I'm proud of you,' Kate said gently as she dipped strips of bread into a boiled egg and fed them to Pagan in bed.

'Oh, darling, so am I. No I can't force anymore down. I never dreamed that stopping would be so absolutely grim, I had no idea that I was so dependent on the bloody stuff.'

Kate worried that when she returned to London Pagan would return to her drinking. Pagan wasn't as worried as Kate. 'You see, darling, for the first time I really *want* to stop. After all, what's the alternative? Do I continue to knock back cooking sherry for the next twenty years?'

'We'll put in a telephone and I'll ring you every day. At least you'll be able to phone me if you get in a panic. There's one thing I want you to promise me. That you won't be ashamed of telling me that you ... if you can't make it.'

'No, I've already said that if I lie to you, I'll own up afterwards,' said Pagan.

Kate went off, though not very hopefully. Until the telephone was installed she sent a telegram or a short letter to the cottage every day. She also telephoned Alcoholics Anonymous, but was told they could be of no use unless Pagan approached them of her own free will.

~ 29 ~

THOUGH Pagan continued to feel exhausted, the increased comfort of the cottage cheered her up. Mrs Hocken cleaned the cottage twice a week. Pagan started to clear up the overgrown garden, for she wanted to keep herself occupied and out of the house. She went for a long walk every morning and would continue to do so until she felt strong enough to start riding again. They had both agreed that when she was again confident on a horse, Pagan might get some horsy sort of job that she would enjoy, even if she didn't earn much.

Wrapped against the wind in her ankle-length, Persian lamb cloak, Pagan walked with Buster to a weather-beaten wooden bench on top of the cliff. There she would sit in the sun, calmed by the waves slapping far below.

But one morning, as the spring wind tore at her cloak and she slowly climbed the rise, she could see that someone was already sitting on her bench. As she approached, she could make out that the figure was a man – a black figure hunched against the grey sky.

Pagan stumped up to the summit of the cliff. She muttered a brusque 'Good morning', then sat down on one end of the bench and pulled her cloak around her. She felt the raw wind on her face. The water was pale grey at the horizon and grey where it dashed against the cliffs beneath her, but the rest of the sea was black.

'Do you come here often?' her neighbour asked amiably.

'Yes,' she said curtly. There was silence for another ten minutes. When the wind flung the water against the base of the cliff, Pagan could feel the tremor under her feet. The grey sky was now laced with lavender streaks, in fact, there was likely to be a storm.

'Nice day,' the stranger said.

She turned and looked at him. 'It's my birthday.'

'Do I congratulate you?'

'No.'

'Well, have a humbug.' He produced a paper bag from his pocket and offered her one of the sticky peppermints. She'd never seen him before. He wasn't local and he couldn't be at the clinic with that bag of candy. 'May I offer you a glass of champagne in celebration?'

There was a long silence. Then Pagan fell.

'You mean you've got a bottle *here*?'

'No, but I'm staying at the Golden Lion in the village. I should think they'd have some. Are you staying in the village?'

'Not really.' Pagan hesitated, not liking to say that he was on her land.

They walked back through the woods to the saloon bar of the Golden Lion. 'Mornin', Miss Pagan,' the landlord said, 'not often we see *you* here.'

The low, empty room smelled of yesterday's beer and cigarettes. Behind the bar a row of gleaming bottles hung upside down, awaiting just one word from Pagan. There was only one bottle of champagne in the cellar. It was very old and much too sweet, but as they drank it on the upright oak settle by the fire, Pagan could feel the relaxation seep through her body.

The stranger's name was Christopher Swann, and he was staying at the Golden Lion in order to finish a book. 'It's not the sort of book that anyone's likely to buy to pass away the weekend. I'm a biochemist and a virologist; the book's an account of some experimental work. A group of us are trying to prevent cancer; we're trying to discover suitable vaccinations. My lab is working on a vaccine against hepatitis B, which is strongly linked to cancer of the liver.'

'Vaccination? Like a smallpox shot?'

'That was the most important shot of all.'

'Did a biochemist invent it?'

'No, a country doctor called Edward Jenner. Around 1796 he noticed that dairymaids didn't seem to catch smallpox, but many of them caught cowpox, which was a relatively mild infection. So Jenner thought that perhaps if everyone had a mild attack of cowpox, then they wouldn't catch smallpox. He checked his antibody theory by vaccinating an eight-year-old boy on the arm with pus that had been drawn from an infected pustule on a dairymaid who had cowpox.'

Halfway through her second glass of champagne, after Pagan had listened to the stranger's fascinating conversation for nearly an hour, she invited him to supper. 'It won't be an elaborate meal,' she warned, aware that she had nothing in the cupboard except a tin of pâté de foie gras and a jar of crystallized violets. He offered to escort her home, but she refused. 'I'll meet you here this evening at six o'clock and take you home.'

Suddenly energetic and hopeful, she flew off to Mrs Hocken.

'Darling Mrs Hocken, will you please, please help me? Will you clean out the cottage with me today instead of Friday? I'm having a visitor!'

Since Kate had left, not much cooking had been done at the cottage, and there was nothing in the refrigerator except half a jar of mayonnaise and a large bottle of vitamin pills. Pagan cycled back to the village and bought some thick veal chops, potatoes to bake in their jackets, salad and fresh Cheddar cheese. She also bought two bottles of wine.

She was very careful while her visitor was there; only filled her glass an inch at a time, waited until his glass was empty before refilling hers, and didn't open the second bottle of wine since he didn't seem to want anymore.

But after he'd left, she immediately drank the remaining bottle and woke up at four in the morning, still in the armchair, frozen and with an aching head. She burst into tears and smashed the bottle into the fireplace, where it scattered the still-warm ashes.

Next morning she suffered terribly from self-accusation but had a clear head. While lying in her bath, she considered what to do with the bottles at the back of the woodshed that she'd hidden from Kate. She considered throwing them over the cliff. She considered having a swig right there.

She dressed, piled the bottles into her big straw shopping basket, lugged them into the wood and buried them under a pile of bracken. Then she went home and looked up 'biochemistry' in her dictionary.

Christopher worked in the early morning and the afternoon. For the next three mornings, Pagan met him at the bench on the cliff. They roamed the woods and the beaches and climbed over the granite rocks above the sea line at the base of the cliffs. Together, they were soaked by salt spray, splashed on the beaches by waves that broke on the sand farther up than they expected; they slipped on slime and seaweed, then walked back to hot Cornish pasties and half a pint of bitter at the Golden Lion.

Every evening, Christopher came to supper at the cottage. Mrs Hocken was bribed, cajoled and flattered to act as Pagan's private cook. She provided soups, casseroles, pastries, even a steak-and-kidney pie with Christopher's initials in golden-brown pastry.

Every evening Pagan built a roaring fire, put classical music on the gramophone, and then they talked far into the night. She found to her surprise that, although she didn't understand it all, she was fascinated by what Christopher said as he talked about his work. Watching the firelight flicker over his face, once Pagan was so absorbed by his presence that she forgot Mrs Hocken's cottage pie warming in the oven. It was burned black.

Pagan tried to drink only one glass of beer in the mornings, and in the evening she restricted herself to one glass of wine by pouring the rest of the bottle into Christopher's glass as fast as she could. 'Are you trying to get me drunk, then take advantage of me?' he half-joked on their fourth evening together.

'I don't like to drink too much,' she muttered.

But the following morning, Pagan found herself scrabbling in the wet bracken, trying desperately to remember where she had buried the bottles. When she couldn't find them, she burst into tears. Looking again, she found her treasure trove, snatched off a cork and remembered no more until hours later, when she woke up stiff and damp. It wasn't the first time she'd blacked out, but it was the first time she cared. She only had fourteen days before Christopher would return to London.

She staggered back to the cottage, took an icy shower, then walked to the clinic to make two telephone calls. First she called the Golden Lion and left a message for Christopher that though she hadn't been able to see him this morning, she would expect him for supper as usual. Then she phoned Kate and confessed.

'But can't you see him without having a drink?' asked Kate. 'Plenty of people do.'

'But *I* can't, I *can't* stop. It's so shaming. I'd have to explain . . . I can't, I can't,' Pagan cried miserably. 'Keep sending the telegraphs and I'll keep on trying to drink as little as possible. But I can't stop, it would look odd to him.'

'Might look odder if you don't stop,' Kate said.

On the seventh evening, Pagan and Christopher were soaked by a sudden squall on the way through the woods to the cottage. Pagan thought she looked terrific with her hair plastered wet against her head, striding through the rain. It was an old trick of hers to suggest a walk in the rain, and besides Pagan really loved the physical sensation of getting soaked.

In the kitchen they pulled off their wet shoes and socks and shrugged off their soggy tweed jackets. The fire had gone out in the sitting room, and Christopher bent down to relight it as Pagan rubbed her purple hands. 'The only way I'm going to get warm again is by having a bath.' She ran upstairs and turned on the water, recklessly pouring in far too much hyacinth oil from one of Kate's bottles.

Fragrant steam filled the bathroom. 'We need a Boy Scout,' Christopher called up the stairs. 'I can't get this fire going.'

Pagan poked her head around the door. 'The wood's a bit damp. Try the firelighters in the cupboard on the right of the fireplace.'

She had just submerged in the blissfully hot water when he shouted up, 'There aren't any left in the box.'

'Well, there's a new box in the kitchen, it's on the ... I can't remember ... Wait a minute, I'll get them.' Snatching off her bath-cap, she wrapped her new yellow robe around her, padded down the steep stairs, and found the box of firelighters under the sink. 'Might as well do it while I'm here. I understand its temperamental ways.'

She knelt down to poke the firelighter under the wooden kindling and then leaned forward as she lit a match. As she did so, her dressing gown gaped open and revealed one pointed breast. Christopher leaned forward and cupped it firmly in his hand.

For a moment Pagan didn't move. There was a *whoosh* as the paper caught fire. She turned her head, her hair dripping, and the buttercup robe fell back from her naked shoulders. Then his mouth was on hers and they collapsed on the moss-green carpet.

Christopher's hand felt swiftly for her other breast. She felt his body as he tugged at her robe, pulled it open, felt between her slippery wet thighs. He softly explored her until her whole being

322

seemed to leap towards him as he slid his body on top of hers.

He pushed steadily inside her and she gasped as their bodies started to move, both driven by his hard rhythmic thrusts. His hands held her breasts firmly and Pagan felt as though she were flying as she yielded to this insistent strength. Seagulls swooped in her head, the tides sucked in and out, she felt the pull and depth of the sea, the sweet drowning of fulfilment.

Afterwards they lay together on the carpet, neither wanting to leave the other's body, neither speaking. Finally, Christopher murmured, 'Fire's gone out again. How about a bath?' Leaving her wet robe and his clothes strewn over the living room, they slowly mounted the narrow staircase outside the kitchen. He stood her in the warm bath and soaped her all over, his hands sliding down her body, following the soap as he explored every part of her. Then he took the hand spray that fitted over the taps, and she felt the warm sting of water caressing every inch of her body. She felt as if she were coming alive again.

Christopher hopped into the bath and they rocked together languorously in the warm scented water. Then Christopher lay back against the porcelain, and Pagan sat upon him as his hands tickled her erect pink nipples. She could feel him high inside her, as he thrust against the core of her. She wanted him to stay there forever, joined to her. Then she felt his pent-up energy inside her. He pulled her down to him and a wave of warm water swept over the bathroom floor as they laughed together in the hyacinth-scented steam.

He dried her in front of the bedroom fire, fondled her with Kate's soft yellow towels. In the dim light he embraced her, wrapped his arms hungrily around her. Then he slowly pushed Pagan backwards on to the patchwork quilt and gently spread-eagled her limbs. 'I want to get to know you,' he said softly. He knelt at the foot of the bed and started to stroke the sole of her left foot. Gently, teasingly, he kissed her toes and slowly licked between each one, drawing each toe into his mouth as he stroked her legs with a butterfly touch. Pagan swooned into semiawareness, conscious only of the voluptuous sensations that were flooding her body.

'My right foot's about to march in protest,' she murmured.

'Tell it we've got the whole night,' Christopher said, busy

323

tickling the back of her knee. When his fingertips, feather-light, reached up from her knee to her inner thigh, Pagan pushed them away.

'Don't. I'm horribly fat there, darling, it embarrasses me, don't touch it.'

'*All* women think their thighs are too fat. Shall I tell you something? Men adore plump thighs. They don't *like* stringy, boyish muscles there. Men love that soft, yielding flesh of your inner thigh.' He nibbled it gently. 'For most men there's nothing more erotic than slowly sliding their hand over the taut top of a nylon stocking, past the garter, feeling the warm satin-smooth flesh, then that softer warmth, that inner promise. Lace underwear feels harsh and scratchy against the voluptuous softness of a woman's inner thigh. Look, feel for yourself.' He grabbed Pagan's fingertips and, with them, he gently stroked her thigh then slowly brushed her fingers over her inner leg. 'There, see? Soft, baby flesh.' He made love to each leg and then each arm, and when Pagan tried to pull him to her, he pushed her firmly back upon the quilt, saying, 'Later.'

By the time his mouth had reached her navel, she was only conscious of the response of her body to his skilled touch. She made small, birdlike sighs, her pleasure became almost unbearable. She reached out one arm to touch his shoulder and tried again to pull him to her but was firmly pushed back on the bed. She started to stroke the grey hair on his chest, but her hand was gently laid by her side. 'Please don't interrupt my work,' he mumbled as his tongue reached her armpit. She felt as if she were about to faint from the tickling pleasure.

Then he was inside her again, and she felt as if the brass bedstead were slowly whirling up towards the ceiling. She was soaring ecstatically, about to fly through the sky. His thrusts were slow and insistent until the moment when she gave the wild shriek of a gull as it soars to heaven; then she felt his excitement mount as he thrust fiercely into her until, with a harsh cry, he climaxed.

They lay still and silent, warm together in the little bedroom.

30

PAGAN'S mother couldn't believe her ears. 'What do you mean? You're going to get married? To *whom*?' She looked at her happy, animated daughter, glowing as only physical passion can make a woman glow. Mrs Trelawney was even more astonished when she heard that she was about to become the mother-in-law of Sir Christopher Swann, the distinguished Director of the Anglo-American Cancer Research Institute.

Kate wasn't so thrilled. 'Are you going to tell him or *not*?' she asked Pagan in the cloakroom of La Popote, a small restaurant in Walton Street, where they were dining.

'Not *yet*,' said Pagan.

'Is it fair?'

'I don't care.'

'He's so much older than you,' said Kate doubtfully, 'and Pagan, he's so big and bald. Dammit, he's an *old* man! How can you marry an *old* man?'

'Darling, he's forty-nine, old is ninety. He says he's been bald since he was thirty. It's quite sexy, you know, that shiny, hard top. If you think what it's like to have the back of your neck stroked, then that's what it's like up there, he says.' She leaned forward to peer in the mirror as she dabbed her lipstick. 'And he's big but not *fat*; I mean, I promise you, darling, I've seen him as nature intended. That's all muscle.' She screwed back her lipstick. 'Do you like this new pale pink? . . . So do I. Want to try it? . . . You must admit he looks a bit like Peter Lawford, apart from the hair, that is. And don't you love that amused look in his eyes as if he can read your innermost thoughts! It turns my knees to jelly.'

'I can see you're in love with him,' said Kate, deciding that the pale pink lipstick didn't suit her, 'so it really doesn't matter what other people don't see in him.'

'And there's another thing. He is *the* most marvellous lover. Maybe it's because he's been doing it for so long, darling, maybe that's one of the advantages of old age. But all I can say is that for the last two weeks we've hardly been out of bed. I don't have any *time* to think about booze. He knows so much about me now, he can keep me out of my skull with delight for hours and hours.'

Kate was impressed. She had always wanted to know what a great lover did.

'Christopher says that he's never met a woman who's the same as another woman. He says we all like different things, we all – oh – *respond* in a different way, and the most important thing for a man is to get a woman to tell him what exactly she likes and wants.'

'But I should die of embarrassment. If Toby asks what I like most, I always say everything.'

'Christopher says that most women say everything, darling, but it's just being frightfully tactful. He says it's nearly always difficult to get them to talk because they're so madly shy of saying what they want or else they're afraid it's hrrrevolting, as Maxine used to say.'

She had started to tug a comb through her hair. 'It's wonderful. It's not that we get into seventy-nine different positions or that he can keep it up for hours, it's just that it's so *intimate*. Once I got over that hurdle of false modesty and was able to shut my eyes and blush in the dark and talk to him truthfully, it was such a relief. For years I'd been lying because I thought I was a freak, because the magic wand left me cold, and now Christopher has proved that I'm not a freak . . . I'll tell you what he does.'

'Careful, there's someone else coming in. You can't spout this filth in front of strangers.'

'I'll tell you when we get back from our honeymoon, only in the interests of education, mind. We're getting married in three weeks, at the chapel at Trelawney. You *will* come, won't you? You'll *never guess* where we're going for our honeymoon. Indianapolis! Christopher has to lecture at something called St Vincent's. He says I can lie in bed and recover while he's earning our keep. Then, thank God, we're going on to California and afterwards back to New York. I'll telephone you with all the filthy details when we get back at the end of June.'

'Well, be careful what you order from room service,' said Kate.

326

'I'm going to stick to beer, nothing but beer, and drink it out of little wine glasses. But I'm definitely going to stop drinking when we get back.'

Only Kate and Mrs Trelawney were present at the wedding in the sixteenth-century chapel in the hollow below the bluebell wood. Pagan wore a pink wool Chanel suit encrusted with gold chains and gilt buttons with lions' heads on them. With it she wore a navy silk blouse with a pussycat bow, a navy Breton straw hat and matching slingback shoes. She looks electrically happy, as if she could hardly bear to get out of bed long enough to get married, thought Kate as Pagan strode down the aisle on her husband's arm to the traditional triumphant burst of Mendelssohn, played rather jerkily on the organ by Mrs Hocken's sister.

But by the end of September, Kate still hadn't heard from Pagan.

It was mid-October before Pagan telephoned Kate.

'That was a long honeymoon.'

'Well, something happened, something utterly terrifying. On our first night in New York I woke up to hear odd strangled gasps. When I turned on the light, Christopher was purple and his eyes were staring and his arms were thrashing around. So I grabbed the phone, and the doctor arrived so fast you'd have thought he was waiting in room service. He gave Christopher a horse-size injection in his chest and I was shooed out of the way. Then they took Christopher off to the hospital in an ambulance. It was a massive heart attack. He was in the hospital for three months – thank God we had medical insurance.'

'I can't believe it,' Kate gasped. 'Where are you?'

'I'm in Christopher's apartment – I mean our apartment. It's in Onslow Gardens. Can you come around, darling? We got home last night. I've only just unpacked and I feel so utterly depressed. Christopher's in bed, and I have to be so bloody cheerful all the time. It's absolutely grim.'

Kate cancelled her luncheon appointment and drove straight to Onslow Gardens. Pagan's big sitting room was really an avocado-coloured library with books covering the walls from floor to ceiling. There were Persian rugs, tan leather sofas, brass lamps with blue-green glass shades, and a big bay window that looked out over the elm trees in the gardens.

'How long will it be before Christopher gets better?' Kate asked tentatively.

'Well, the doctors don't exactly look at it that way,' Pagan said glumly, sipping from a large mug of coffee. 'They treat heart failure by correcting the imbalance between the supply and demand of the blood and by removing all the accumulated excess fluids in the patient's body.'

'Eh? What does that *mean*?' Kate asked, completely mystified.

'It means that Christopher has to have a lot of rest – mental and physical. He isn't allowed to work for too long. And he has to diet, because being overweight puts so much strain on the cardio-vascular system. He isn't supposed to eat salt because he mustn't retain fluid, and he takes diuretic pills to make him pee a lot. In and out of the loo all day. He's also had to give up smoking. But the really awful thing is no sex.'

'For how long?'

'Forever.'

'*How awful!* But I suppose he can . . . pay attention to you.'

'No – it might excite him.'

'But the doctors can't be serious! How does Christopher feel about it?'

'Rather selfish. He doesn't want to die. As a matter of fact, I feel the same way.'

Now I'll *never* find out what a really great lover does, Kate thought. It would be too unkind to ask. Oh *damn*!

Kate immediately realized the danger of Pagan's depression. 'If he needs looking after, then you simply *must* stop drinking. Even beer in little wine glasses. Suppose he had an attack when you were bombed?'

'I've thought about it,' said Pagan dully. 'I know I've got to stop and I know it's not going to be easy. I lived here with Christopher for a month before we were married and I can't *tell* you how unbearably fast I got hooked again. I tried to fight the yearning, but it beat me within days.' She heaved a noisy sigh. 'As soon as Christopher had left for the laboratory I used to set the alarm clock for four p.m., then grab the cooking sherry and sip until I passed out or was sick. The alarm clock always jerked me

328

awake, and then I'd have at least a couple of hours to pull myself together with a cold shower, eau-de-cologne and aspirin. It was ghastly. I only seemed to do it when I was alone, never at week-ends. Perhaps I would slink out to the kitchen for an occasional swig, but somehow the dreaded craving wasn't too strong at weekends. Look, I want that address from you again, I've lost it. That list of AA places.'

'It will be no use unless you tell Christopher. Do you want me to tell Christopher for you?'

'No. I'll tell him as soon as he's got over the journey. Let's get this bloody phone call over.'

The following Thursday she went to her first Alcoholics Anonymous meeting, leaving Kate with Christopher and two sheets of typed emergency instructions.

'It was grim,' Pagan told her later. 'Tough. No pissing about. You felt they were all desperately serious, all there for a purpose. We all had that fatal interest in common. We met in the crypt of St Martin's-in-the-Fields, you know that church in Trafalgar Square, and we sat drinking tea and eating biscuits. They smoked a lot, after a couple of hours you'd have thought the room was full of sea fog. There were lots more men than women and a couple of them were quite shabby – they looked as if they might be just out of prison or something.'

'So what *happened*?' demanded Kate.

'Someone started off by saying that willpower was about as effective a cure for alcohol addiction as it is for cancer. If your system can tolerate ethyl alcohol, then alcohol can give you harmless pleasure, the way it does for you, Kate. But if you can't tolerate it, like me, you gradually become *dependent* on alcohol. I tell you, it was oddly cheering to know that I was merely addicted, not just an old soak.'

She was lolling on the hearthrug, cuddling the sheepdog, Buster, who had been out in the rain and smelled like a damp blanket. 'It's amazing that the government allows the stuff to be plugged on TV when they know that drink is the third highest *killer* in the country.'

'Did anyone talk to you?'

'Nobody asked me anything, I just sat, watched and listened. One thing I learned – you just try not to drink for one day at a time.' Pagan paused. For the first time she felt hopeful and not hopelessly weak-willed. 'And you're never cured. Once you're an alcoholic, you're *always* an alcoholic, just as a diabetic is still a diabetic, although he controls his illness with insulin.' She was high on hope.

'Pagan, you're too damn enthusiastic about it,' Kate said. 'It worries me. You're not to talk to Christopher until you're calm. Otherwise, he won't realize that you're serious.'

But Christopher did. 'Oh, I guessed just before we were married,' he said. 'There seemed no other reason for the reek of mouthwash on your breath every night when I came home, so I marked the bottles – not the ones in the drinks cabinet, I knew you'd be too crafty to take those. I marked the cooking stuff in the kitchen. I was waiting for you to tell me. I hoped I could help you.'

When he was able to return to work, Christopher took Pagan to the laboratory to meet his associates. 'I've told everyone to explain things to you in words of one syllable,' he murmured, kissing Pagan on the ear just before they got out of the car.

She was shown around the lab building as if she were visiting royalty, but the scientists might as well have been speaking Swahili for all she understood of her two-hour tour. She gazed at the machines, at the computers, at the racks of glass containers where human cancer cells were growing in tissue that would be used in the preparation of the cancer vaccine. Then she asked the least unnerving of the lab technicians to lunch on the following Sunday, because she was determined to understand Christopher's work, if she could. She'd get this black-bearded Peter to explain it to her.

In the car, on their way home, Christopher said, 'Look, if you're really interested, Pagan, why don't you help us to raise money? I think you'd be good at it. Perhaps Kate could help you.'

'Not Kate,' said Pagan thoughtfully, 'but Judy might.'

A few months later Pagan accompanied Christopher to New York, where he was giving a lecture at the Sloan-Kettering Institute. For the first time in thirteen years she saw Judy. They rushed to hug each other in the oak-panelled gloom of the Algonquin lobby.

'But Pagan, you look exactly the same, except you don't wear glasses any more. Contacts?'

'Yes. *You* look extremely different, darling. You always looked a child, but now you look a *rich* child.' Pagan eyed the blonde-streaked, geometric Vidal Sassoon haircut flopping over one eye and the creamy, raw-silk safari suit, worn with vanilla suede pumps.

'This is one of my working outfits – Guy's, of course. Must look like a success if you want to be a success. Pagan, that's the first thing you've got to remember when I get around to giving you the concentrated course in public relations that you talked about on the telephone.'

'I asked Kate to tell you and Maxine the truth about what had happened to me. It's all right, you don't have to order Coke just because I'm here ... Kate saved my life. And as soon as she told Maxine where I was, Max insisted that Christopher and I come over to stay with them. She was simply terrific. It was as if we'd last met a week ago. Now you've offered to show me how to help publicize the Research Institute. You're all being wonderful friends – I simply don't deserve it after ignoring you for all these years. It makes me feel even more ashamed.'

'Listen,' Judy said, 'guilt is the most useless bit of baggage. You don't want to clutter your head with it. It can't do any good and it only makes you feel awful.' She offered an olive to Pagan and grinned. 'Real friends aren't people you joke and have a drink with. You don't need to see *real* friends, you just know that they're there when you need them. We formed our own little support system, remember, back in Gstaad? Through sick and sin, as Maxine used to say.'

She firmly interlaced her fingers. 'Like *that*, we're interlinked, we're our own best safety net, so don't you forget it. Now keep your ears open and prepare for instruction.'

As usual Judy was bubbling over with ideas. Pagan took notes and hoped that she'd be able to sort them out later. Her head was spinning.

Pagan went back to London and set to work. At first she was

so embarrassed by the idea of telephoning strangers that she had to lock herself in her bedroom, and she blushed before dialling the numbers. But her background and fact sheets were fresh and interesting, her determination was formidable, and picking up her old network, she found that she knew a few rich people and quite a lot of influential ones. One person led to another. Pagan quickly discovered the charms and rewards of work. Every fortnight she wrote a report to Judy, who returned two closely typed pages of criticism and suggestions.

Pagan started by writing an article for her old school magazine in which she asked for money and helpers. She sweated over this for four days and worried about it for weeks afterwards, but she was delighted by the positive response. She found herself with £43·20 and two part-time assistants. Since drawing attention to the Research Unit was as important as raising money for it, Pagan started a pyramid letter. 'Please send me £2·00 and pass on a copy of this letter to two friends. Don't break the chain – it's a lifesaver.' This brought in £4,068 – far more than she had expected.

Some months later Pagan was standing in a small private room at the Savoy, hoping that her pale grey velvet suit with silver fox at the wrists wasn't too formal for the buffet luncheon she was about to give for twenty influential journalists. It was an expensive way to start, but she wanted nothing to be skimped at her first press party. She couldn't help feeling anxious. She wanted to be able to provide the right information for each journalist rather than give general information to a crowd. She had not invited medical journalists, who were informed on the subject, only mass-circulation writers. Nobody present wrote for less than a million readers.

Much to her relief the women were not particularly tough or aggressive. Most seemed to know each other and chatted quietly until Christopher started to speak. Then they jabbed at notebooks and asked questions that were ruthlessly to the point.

'My wife has specifically asked me to use simple language,' Christopher began, 'because when I first explained my work to her, she didn't understand a word I said. I hope that I won't oversimplify – later I shall be delighted to be as technical as you wish. First I'll give you a few facts, but I'd like to start answering questions from you as quickly as possible. I'm here to tell you about the work that we're doing at the Anglo-American Cancer Research Institute. I'm also here to ask you to help us raise money to continue with our work. Already one in three cancer victims recovers: we want to improve that figure.'

His small audience looked politely interested until, at the end of his short speech, Christopher announced, 'In our South London laboratory we have produced a very crude form of vaccine, which I shall refer to as Vaccine X; I am sorry if that makes it sound a bit like a washing powder. We cannot speak with certainty until our findings have been checked, but Vaccine X seems to stimulate the body's defence forces to attack and beat off the viral invader and prevent the formation of those particular cancer cells.'

Now they were sitting up and taking notice. 'In a recent experiment we took two groups of mice and injected one group with Vaccine X. We then implanted tumour cells that are associated with the virus in all the mice. After two months the tumours in the treated mice had either not grown or had disappeared completely, while the untreated batch of mice all showed considerably enlarged tumours.'

There was a burst of questions and a rustle of notebooks. Pagan felt she was off to a good start.

PART SIX

31

LILI stared longingly at the burning Atlanta skyline, at Vivien Leigh shooting a soldier with rape written all over his face, at Olivia de Havilland in a crinoline and at all the other colour posters in front of the cinema. Although she was now thirteen, Lili had only been to the movies twice. She bit her lower lip and thrust her hands deeper into the pockets of her raincoat, wondering how she could manage to get in.

'Have you seen it?'

She turned to see a young man grinning at her. He was blondish, tall and at least twenty-four. 'No, but doesn't it look wonderful? Have you seen it?'

'No,' he lied. 'Look, why don't we see it together? I'm all alone in Paris.'

Lili hesitated. She wasn't even supposed to be on the Champs Elysées that afternoon, but Madame Sardeau was away on her annual visit to her mother in Normandy, and Lili had invented an extra maths lesson for the benefit of Monsieur Sardeau, who wouldn't notice her absence anyway, since he was at his office. Monsieur Sardeau was a boring little pedagogue, but he had long ago stopped lecturing, correcting and reprimanding Lili – or, indeed, taking any notice at all of her – because the child's well-formed breasts and her gawky, sprawling legs aroused in him a physical response that at times he was afraid his wife might notice. He had once gasped Lili's name aloud as he imagined himself lying between those slim, firm thighs, when in fact he was writhing upon the bony body of his wife, clutching at the sagging breasts of Madame Sardeau. He'd managed to convince her that he hadn't said anything, that she had merely heard a voluptuous gasp of pleasure, but he couldn't risk trouble so close to home. Conscious of the danger, he prudently avoided Lili whenever possible.

Lili gazed up at the young man who had just spoken to her. He looked a bit like Leslie Howard gazing down at her from that photograph; he had the same limpid look. He sounded foreign as well.

She'd never get another chance.

'Yes, please,' she said. It was as easy as that. They moved past the box office into the darkness, into the previous century and the Civil War.

When the lights went up for the entr'acte, Lili was still in a state of romantic ecstasy. 'Isn't Scarlett beautiful?'

'Not more than you,' the young man said.

Lili's face was no longer childish. A tangle of dark hair was held back from her face by a velvet hairband; she had huge brown eyes that seemed to radiate a very adult sensuality; but what gave her face its most arresting quality was the elegant, slightly hooked little nose above lips so voluptuously chiselled that they might have been carved by Michelangelo. At thirteen, her figure was no longer childish. Her legs were still a trifle thin, but her body had filled out and her breasts were well developed – perhaps, in fact, *too* developed. Sometimes she thought that Monsieur Sardeau was furtively looking at them, and when they walked out of church on Sunday, his hand always grasped her upper arm, his knuckles quivering unnecessarily hard against her breast.

Lili's new friend bought her an ice cream, and she learned that his name was Alastair and he lived in New York. It was clear that he thought Lili older than she was, because he didn't treat her like a schoolgirl.

The lights dimmed again and Alastair reached over and took her fingertips. His hand felt warm and firm and almost unbearably thrilling, not like Monsieur Sardeau's furtive hand, which frightened her. Lili felt a shortness of breath, an eerie excitement, as if the fine down on her arms was standing on end like a cat's. She felt a dreamy yearning to have this stranger stroke more than just the inside of her palm and the back of her wrist.

As they shuffled out with the dark, swaying mob that moved towards the exit, Alastair asked, 'Would you like something to eat?'

Lili tossed her hair, summoned up her courage and said yes. They splashed through the drizzle to a restaurant, and by the end of the meal Alastair knew a good deal about Lili, although she had learned nothing about him. Towards the end of the meal Lili suddenly became anxious. It was nearly eleven o'clock – she had never been out so late before, she explained.

Without argument he snapped his fingers for the cheque and took her home. As the taxi splashed towards home, Alastair put one finger under her chin and gently turned her eager, anxious face towards him. Then, just like Rhett Butler, he bent over and kissed her. Trembling with this new tingling feeling, thirsty for love and warmth, Lili put her arms around Alastair's neck and lifted her head. By the time the taxi splashed to a halt, she was in love.

Creeping up the staircase, she trembled for a different reason, terrified of her reception, never imagining that she might be able to reach her room without being challenged. But Monsieur Sardeau hadn't yet returned; he had no intention of staying at home on the rare occasions when his wife was absent for a fortnight.

Lili now got up at five in the morning in order to do the sewing that ought to occupy her summer afternoons, because Alastair now occupied those hours. Never again did she dare stay out so late in the evening, but his working hours seemed conveniently elastic, so at midday Lili always ran to meet him in a café for lunch and afterwards, holding hands, they would wander along the trees in the Bois de Boulogne, stroll among the exquisitely dressed children in the Parc Monceau, take a *bâteau mouche* on the Seine or window-shop.

'Why don't you let me buy you a decent dress? I've only seen you in one sweater and one blouse since we met, and always that same navy skirt.'

'Oh, I couldn't let you buy me anything! Madame would see it.'

'Well, what about these little red suede shoes?'

'No, I couldn't hide them, they'd want to know where I got the money.' But in the stone arcade of the rue de Rivoli, Alastair bought her a heart-shaped locket on a fine gold chain that she could hide under her mattress. He'd never met such a trusting, affectionate, undemanding girl; even the youngest ones were usually after something, especially once they knew who he was. Then there were always demands for jewellery, money, sometimes even marriage. Skinner, his mother's attorney, handled them if things became difficult, particularly if a father turned nasty. Lili suited him admirably, and, as yet, few people knew him in Paris.

In the taxi Lili threw her arms around him and thanked him for the locket, affectionate as a puppy. But when they got out in the shadow of the Eiffel Tower, she looked up and asked in surprise, 'Where are we going?'

'To have a drink, kitten, in this hotel. I often come here.'

Behind the desk, a bored, fat concierge was knitting a grey tube that might have been a sock or a sleeve. Alastair passed her a note, and she slapped down a key. 'Number nineteen. First floor. You'll have to pay extra if you stay longer than two hours.'

Lili followed Alastair up the stairs: he usually took her to much smarter places. 'Is it a floor show? Why did you have to pay?' she asked.

Number 19 was a dim shuttered room containing a large bed with a faded pattern of pink shepherdesses on the counterpane, a collapsible tin bidet and a washbasin. Lili looked uneasy.

'I wanted to be alone with you, kitten.'

'But there's a bed.'

'It's difficult to find a hotel room without a bed, kitten. Now, let me put your new locket around your neck.' He lifted her hair and kissed the nape of her neck, then slid his hands under her arms and over her breasts, feeling for the nipples under her thin blouse, then slowly unfastened the small rose buttons down the front.

At the mercy of her innocence, of the newly roused passion stirring in her body and her longing for love, Lili offered little resistance. Soon, to her surprise, she lay naked among the pink shepherdesses, mesmerized by Alastair's easy air of assurance and his swift, practised hands as he stroked her quivering stomach, teased her silky pubic hair and murmured, 'Now, kitten, what's your real age, hmm? Let's pretend you're only ten years old and I'm your schoolteacher, so you have to do every-thing I say.'

He bent his head and gently bit the tip of her nipple. 'Because if you *don't*, you'll be punished. I'll have to telephone Madame

Sardeau and tell her what a naughty girl you've been, and you wouldn't want that, would you?'

Lili stiffened with fear. 'Don't worry, I was only joking, kitten,' he said. 'Now lie back and relax, because I'm going to make you feel wonderful.'

He slid his hand between her thighs and stretched out on the bed beside her. His fingers danced, probed, burrowed insistently between her legs. He kissed her on the mouth, hard. Then he suddenly thrust his fingers into her body, and, as it jerked in pain, his body jerked in ecstasy. 'Keep quiet you little fool, stop that noise,' he whispered. He played his trump card, saved against this. 'It's because I love you, Lili. This is grown-up love, kitten.'

'But it hurts,' she whimpered.

'I'll kiss it better,' he promised, and gently kissed her nipples, her breasts and her face, shedding his clothes as he did. Then he slid on top of her and inside her body. It happened so quickly that Lili, bewildered by her conflicting emotions, hardly even knew what was happening. She realized only that she ached again, then ached unbearably as Alastair straddled her small body, shuddered in his climax, then rolled off to lie beside her, exhausted.

Later he mumbled, 'That was wonderful, kitten, let's have you in your school clothes next time.' After a bit he started to stroke her pink breasts again, then the rest of her body, until it stopped shaking. Softly he spoke words of love. She wanted him to love her, didn't she? Slowly, patiently – thinking of the following afternoon – he won her confidence again, soothed her with his stroking, reassured her with words of love, hypnotized her with his self-confidence, terrified her with veiled threats of love withdrawn, of telephone calls to Madame Sardeau.

Then he relieved himself in the washbasin, dressed and left the room, while Lili washed in the bidet. She was thinking that if he loved her, he shouldn't have brought her here. But if he *didn't* love her, he wouldn't *want* to, surely? He had done it because he loved her.

After a few minutes Alastair returned and sat on the edge of the bed. He pulled her on to his lap and produced a packet of pills. 'Now I want you to take one of these every day. See, the instructions are on the label.'

'Why?'

'So that you don't have a baby. It's the new pill. Promise you'll take it.'

'Why can't we get married and have a baby?'

'Because you're too young, that's why, kitten. Later on, if you're good, when you've passed your exams, then we'll see.'

After that there were no more trips up the river, no more strolling under the trees. Almost every weekday during that hot summer, from three to five o'clock, a frightened, timid Lili met Alastair at the hotel. When Madame Sardeau returned, Lili explained that as it had been so hot she had taken her basket of sewing to the shady park every afternoon. Madame's *chemises de nuit* were exquisitely sewn and the child certainly looked as pale as milk, so perhaps the park was a good idea, provided she was back in good time to prepare the evening meal.

The early September sun crept down the opposite side of the courtyard as Lili retched for the fifth morning in succession. Panic stricken, she crept back to her bed. She had no knowledge of gynaecology, but she knew what early morning sickness meant. Too exhausted and worried to get up, let alone sew, she heard Madame Sardeau calling her. 'Lili, Lili, wherever has that child got to, why isn't the coffee on? So! Still in bed at seven o'clock!' But the child didn't look well, she seemed hardly able to lift her head and the black rings around her eyes were darkening. Perhaps she'd better call the doctor, although of course he would charge for a visit. Better see if a day in bed would cure her. There was no point in paying for a doctor unless she was really ill.

The waves of nausea passed and by midday, Lili no longer felt ill. She was merely panic-stricken. After taking Alastair's pills for three days, she had stopped, because they made her feel sick. She hadn't told him this because she was afraid he'd be cross with her.

She *had* to get out of bed. Alastair would be waiting for her at the Pam-Pam Café. Luckily, it was one of Madame Sardeau's afternoons for bridge.

When she confessed her fears to Alastair, his usually languid face hardened. Suddenly he didn't look at all like Leslie Howard.

'I might have *known* it! You stupid little *bitches* are all the same! ... Are you *sure*?'

'I haven't seen a doctor, but I've been sick all this week.'

'Well, it's your own damn fault. You're not going to pin anything on me. You don't know where I'm staying, nobody's seen us together, and for all I know you're sleeping with half the men in Paris ... Oh, God, *don't* start crying!' He thought for a moment; it was better not to frighten her. He didn't know how old Lili was, but she was certainly under the age of consent. Skinner might not be able to swing *that* with the French police. Though the French were tolerant about these things as a rule ...

'Can't we go to the hotel?'

'No, we can't. For God's sake stop snivelling and let me think.' Thank God she didn't know his real name. He must have been crazy, out of his mind, to pick her up! Still, it was too late now. He had to get out of this immediately before anyone could pin it on him. Of course, there was the hotel receptionist, but she'd keep her mouth shut for a few thousand francs. An idea occurred to him. He thrust his hand into his trouser pocket and pulled out fifty thousand francs, not much, about a hundred and eighty dollars, but it was all the cash he had on him.

'For Christ's sake, stop crying, Lili, or I'll walk out of this place. Look, this is what you must do. Take this money and go to a doctor to make sure that you're really pregnant – I've no idea what he'll charge, but this is bound to cover it. If you *aren't* pregnant, then there's been a lot of fuss about nothing. If you *are*, then go straight to the concierge at the hotel and she'll arrange for you to see someone who'll fix you up. I'll see that the bill is paid. Do it as fast as you can – *and don't tell anyone*.' He threw a note on the table to cover their bill and stood up.

'Don't go, Alastair, please don't leave me, when I love you so.'

'If you love me, you'll do exactly as I say. You'll obey me or I'll never see you again.'

'When shall I see you? When?' Now she was too frightened to cry.

'I'll see you here in two weeks.' He patted her shoulder. 'Cheer up! If you're a good girl and obedient, we can forget all this unpleasantness. Now do you *promise* to do as I say?'

'Oh, I promise, but you will come back again, won't you?'

'Of course, kitten,' he said soothingly, and he bent to kiss her wet cheek, with no intention of ever seeing her again.

He had gone before Lili ever thought of asking which doctor

343

she should visit. She sat staring at the pile of notes, then stuffed them in her raincoat pocket and walked to the hotel. She hung around outside, not wanting to go in, but eventually she approached the fat, knitting fingers behind the desk.

'I was told you could help me.' The woman's eyes immediately dropped to Lili's stomach.

'How long?'

Lili turned red and looked hard at the brass bell on the counter-top. 'I don't know.'

'When were you last due?'

'About three weeks ago. But I haven't seen a doctor yet.'

'Just as well. Sit on that chair and wait a minute.' Bare feet stuck into carpet slippers, she shuffled to the telephone booth at the back of the hall. Lili could not hear her low conversation. Then she shuffled back and said, 'Did he give you any money?'

'Yes!' She pulled out the bundle of notes and put them on the counter. The woman's fat fingers flew through them, counting.

'That's not going to get you far. You need another hundred thousand francs, tell him.'

'But that's all he gave me. I can't get any more. He said he'd see that the bill was paid.'

'That's what they all say, but the fact is, this sort of business is strictly cash in advance. Can't your family help?' Lili's frightened face grew terrified. 'Well, can't you borrow from a friend?'

None of Lili's schoolmates had ever *seen* a hundred thousand francs, let alone owned it or lent it. Slowly she shook her head.

'Tell you what,' said the concierge, speculatively. 'I know a photographer who might pay you to model for him. Three thousand francs an hour, less my commission, would that suit you?'

Lili nodded hopefully. She would have agreed to anything. The old woman shuffled off again to the phone box and when she returned she scribbled an address on the desk pad. 'Serge will see you right away, dear. Here's the address. It's just down the street; he's in the attic.'

~ 32 ~

SERGE, once a famous fashion photographer, had grown fat, bored, lazy and old, in that order. He had flourished in the traditional world of haute-couture and did not understand the unconventional, relaxed fashions of the sixties. The fashion magazines had dropped him, then his advertising accounts had dwindled, and he'd been almost totally out of work until he started selling nude photos. They were not the sort of models he was used to, of course. You'd never find Bettina or Ali or Fiona or Suzy stooping to that sort of thing. Most of the girls wouldn't so much as touch an *underwear* shot until recently, and you used to practically pay danger money to get them into a swimsuit, but these new, untidy models had no style and no shame. He'd always photographed women in the nude, of course, it was one of his pleasures, but he'd never thought of selling the photographs until one little tart stuck his close-up of her nipple into her portfolio, after which, for a while, his pictures of naked women were suddenly fashionable. You could seldom make out at first glance which part of the body it was, but the effect was original and often startlingly erotic. Anyway, they sold.

Serge's eyes narrowed speculatively as he looked at Lili, then he gave her a slow smile. 'Come in,' he said. 'Don't mind my judo suit, I always wear it in the studio. A glass of wine? No, well – there's the changing room, get 'em off, darling.'

'Get what off?'

'Your clothes, darling. What else would I pay three thousand francs an hour for? And from what I hear it won't be the first time, darling, but don't worry, there's nothing I haven't seen before. Look, there's proof.'

He waved a pudgy hand towards an enormous black felt pin-board, covered with nude photographs – and very good ones, for Serge loved women and was an excellent photographer.

Lili picked her way past the ten-foot-wide rolls of pink, blue and green backdrop paper, past a vast white hanging sheet and an even bigger black one, past two groups of what looked like silver umbrellas on sticks and a forest of studio lights. She went into the small dressing room, where odd coloured pots of grease, terra-cotta covered sponges, crumpled Kleenex, dusty little brushes, flimsy chiffon scarves and hair curlers stood on the makeup counter, above which blazed a row of naked light bulbs.

Lili stood there, not moving or thinking, numbed, for five minutes. 'I haven't got all day, cherub.' The voice outside was cheerful, but held an underlying menace. Quickly she undressed. The curtains were pulled aside and Serge looked through. 'Good, you're ready. Out here, please.'

He had set up the camera and lights in front of the black backdrop. 'These days I don't bother with an assistant, unless I'm on an assignment. Now, just stand straight with your back to camera, cherub.' Click! 'Now turn sideways.' Click! 'Chin up a bit.' Click! Click! 'Now face me, that's a good girl.' Click! Click! Click!

'There that's over, wasn't too bad was it? I'll develop them now and let you know tomorrow if I can use you.'

Lili was relieved. It had been about as erotic and frightening as having a passport photograph taken. Serge thought that it was a long time since he had seen such a pretty little cunt. Mind you, he told himself, she'd need a bit of work on her, but he wouldn't mind betting that she'd look even better on the contacts. In the meantime, he had no intention of frightening her. If he played his cards carefully, she was worth a fortune to him.

At her afternoon photographic sessions with Serge, Lili quickly discovered that more was expected of her than simply stripping and standing in the nude while Serge clicked his Rolleiflex. That first sitting had clearly shown him her potential. Studying the contact prints through a magnifying glass, marking with a red chinagraph the ones he wanted to enlarge, Serge had realized that the child was even better than he'd thought. She had a rare naivety, combined with a catch-your-breath eroticism of which she seemed totally unaware. The face had a pure, hopeful quality that was impossible to simulate, yet that mouth showed more than a hint of sensuality. She was a dream girl.

Serge knew he'd have to play her carefully. Kindness was the thing; fatherly kindness would reassure the little creature, then he'd add a light touch of authority. Lead her into it very gently, give her something to do in the first shots so that she didn't have time to think. Pay her a bit in advance, get her to sign an IOU, then, if necessary, threaten her with it. He'd have to watch out for those ribs and the gawky long legs – he'd have preferred plumper thighs squeezing that dark little bush – but the breasts were perfection. She was jailbait, but she was money in the bank.

When Lili turned up for the second afternoon sitting she found Serge waiting in the traditional photographers' costume of jeans and black sweater, with a thick leather belt that more or less squeezed his stomach into place. He had bought a frosted chocolate layer cake for Lili, while he himself sipped a tumblerful of red wine and seemed in no hurry to start.

Then he picked up his camera and said, 'Tell you what, cherub, I'd like to start off with some casual shots; just as you are in that cotton frock, sitting on the old velvet chair.'

He'd already positioned his lights before she arrived, and now he switched on soft, enticing, rhythmic dance music.

'Now cut another piece of cake, darling, it's all for you . . . Hold it . . . Turn your head slowly to camera . . . No, only your head, cherub . . . Now smile . . . That's *great*, kid. I can see you're going to be good. Now perhaps we'll try it with a couple of buttons undone . . . Would you mind? . . . Terrific . . . Keep looking to camera . . . A couple more buttons . . . Now lean over to the left and take a big bite.'

Carefully, Lili leaned to the left, then just as she was about to bite, the piece of chocolate cake disintegrated in her hand. She burst into peals of laughter as she turned her head to Serge and . . . Click!

Serge worked with two cameras. When he'd finished both rolls he vanished into the darkroom to change the film and came out, brisk and impersonal as a dentist. 'Now let's have you in a bikini. You'll find some in the top drawer of the chest in the dressing room. Pick whichever you like.'

Lili had longed for a bikini and needed little prompting. She finally reappeared in a white lace one that made Serge catch his breath as he turned on his wind machine. 'Now, flower, I want you to stand with your legs apart, hair streaming backwards in the studio breeze, and tilt this bottle of soda to your lips, hold it and smile . . . That's my girl, you're really catching on.'

Half an hour later, Lili was no longer nervous. 'Now let's try it with just the pants,' Serge said casually, fiddling with his light meter. Lili looked anxious.

'Do I have to?'

'Why, yes – if you want the money, flower. And anyway, no one will know except us.'

'But what are these pictures *for*? Are they for a magazine or something?'

'Now why ever should you think that? It's art. Just take your bra off, darling.' Lili was dubious, but unwilling to argue about the unformed, uneasy suspicions that Serge so smoothly wiped from her subconscious. She unhooked and stood there, looking anxious, hands held over her breasts.

'That's great, flower. No, don't smile, just like that.' Click! Herb Alpert continued to play cheerfully, reassuringly in the background. 'Now sit on the chair hugging your knees up to your . . .

'That's *terrific*, bud . . . And kneel with your hands clasped behind your head. Now I want you to put on a pair of stockings.' He produced a pair of thick, black stockings and schoolgirl shoes. Lili didn't think they looked very artistic, but obediently she smoothed them on to her legs. Combined with the white lace panties they emphasized her frail, young vulnerability, the innocence contradicted by her heavy, grown-up pink-nippled breasts.

The following day Serge took her out on the roof and photographed her against the Parisian chimney pots in her cotton frock, until she relaxed, until she *trusted* him. He'd throw that roll away. He wouldn't even bother to develop it. Then he tossed her an exquisite peach chiffon negligée and said, 'Now let's try this on.'

When she reappeared he put his head to one side, gave a small, disapproving frown and said authoritatively. 'Those pants ruin the mood. Just slip them off, flower, that's a good girl.' He turned away and adjusted his camera settings, then looked around. '*Just slip them off*, I said.' The light menace was unmistakable.

Shivering slightly in the weak September sunlight, Lili slipped them off and Serge got some wonderfully erotic shots of those big still pubescent breasts that topped her gawky adolescent body, seen through a thin veil of peach chiffon – which sometimes gaped open without Lili realizing it – against the slate roofs, chimney pots and pigeons of the Paris skyline. Serge was pleased. 'Tomorrow we'll go to a quiet little spot in the Bois de Boulogne,' he said. 'We'll shoot the next lot with trees and grass.'

Lili didn't want to continue with the sittings. Once away from the reassuring presence of Serge, she felt ashamed. She blushed and groaned to herself as she hurried home. She wouldn't go to the studio again.

But every morning she woke, head swimming with nausea, and as she ran down the corridor to the lavatory, she knew she had to continue the sessions. Just to harden her resolve, Serge presented her with some prints of her first sitting. Lili hid them under the mattress with her gold locket. She wanted to tear them up, but she also wanted to keep them. She *did* look very pretty in the pictures.

Madame Sardeau occasionally shouted at her, 'You've got to finish my winter nightgowns before the lycée starts,' but she didn't pay much attention to Lili, and she had more than night-gowns on her mind. Her husband now often worked late at the office. There had been odd telephone calls, and when she answered, the line went dead. His manner was strange, and not once since she returned from Normandy had he bothered her at night. It was odd.

Lili saw no money for her work. Serge paid it directly to the concierge and to give him due credit, he didn't cheat Lili of a sou. But the concierge would not arrange the operation until Lili had all the money, so she continued to model until she was three months pregnant.

Lili sat in the small steaming café, not wanting to get up and walk again. Her legs felt weak and her body felt as raw and painful as her thoughts. Until it was time to prepare supper, the café was a halfway house of cheerful, normal life, poised between that horrible experience this afternoon and the depression which, as always, she would feel when she approached the dark Sardeau front door.

She could not forget the humiliating *pain* of the operation, on top of the painful humiliation of Alastair's disappearance. She had thought he loved her. Was it *so* dreadful not to have taken those pills? Would it have been *so* dreadful to have had a baby instead of an abortion?

She dragged herself up the stairs to the seventh floor and rang the bell – she wasn't allowed a key. The door flew open and Madame Sardeau stood there, like a black, shrieking crow. In her hand was Lili's gold locket and the contact prints that had been hidden under her mattress.

'*What's this filth*? So *this* is what you were doing when I thought you were in the park! *This* is what you get up to when my back is turned! *This* is the way you show your gratitude, you slut!'

Lili backed away, terrified, retreating backwards down the stairs as the furious woman continued to shriek at her. From below a voice shouted up the dusty stairwell, 'Less noise up there.'

Lili stumbled backwards and nearly fell, clutching the stair rail to save herself. 'You filthy little bitch, it's easy to see where you come from – the gutter! Just as we thought, you lewd little whore! After all we've done for . . .'

Lili turned and fled, away from those dreadful words, back to Serge's studio, and threw herself, weeping, against his plump chest.

'Hmm, so the old trout found out, did she?' he said calmly. 'Well, I'm not surprised, but it's a pity, flower.'

He was not surprised because he had telephoned Madame Sardeau anonymously and suggested that she look under Lili's mattress . . . He wasn't about to lose her now that the abortion was done. Serge wrapped Lili in a rug, laid her on the studio couch and heated some milk for her.

'It was today, wasn't it?' he asked.

Huddled in the rug, Lili sobbed and nodded.

'Well, you'd better just lie there until you feel better, then we'll decide what to do.' He softly stroked her black, tangled hair until she fell asleep. From Lili's chatter, Serge now knew a lot about the Sardeaus. She wouldn't go back. He'd got her! There was no risk of losing her now, not after they'd found out so abruptly. She wouldn't be the first teenage runaway to disappear in Paris; there was unlikely to be a fuss if they couldn't find her. She could hole up with him and hide for a bit – he had no girl living with him at the moment to complicate matters. Lili was nearly fourteen; with makeup she could pass as an eighteen-year-old. Sweep the fringe away from her forehead, give her a lipstick, some new clothes and high heels, and she'd never resemble any photographs the police might be given. And if they *did* pick her up, well, he hadn't molested her, had he?

Serge had just returned from a visit to an advertising agency. His new portfolio contained only shots of Lili. Lili lying flushed and sleepy on a tousled bed, half-hidden by a lace shawl; Lili with her hair in braids, running naked through high, out-of-focus grass; Lili, in a straw hat and skimpy shorts, pushing a bicycle along a woodland path; a back view of Lili's little haunches as she twined jasmine in her hair before a bedroom mirror that reflected her voluptuous breasts.

The art editor had pushed up his heavy black-rimmed glasses, snapped out of his boredom and reached for the phone. 'Sorry to disturb you T J,' he said, 'but you know that tyre calendar we're considering for next Christmas? Well, I think I've got something here.'

An exquisitely tailored account executive hurried in, flipped through the portfolio in silence, then looked through it again with more attention. 'They're good,' he said, 'but these are only of one girl.'

'Well, of course we'd have other girls, but the *mood* is exactly what I'm after, something *different* from the usual tits and ass stuff, that quality of innocence, that feeling of eternal summer, that nostalgia and the counterpoint of exuberant *joie de vivre*.'

'Yes, yes, they're certainly sexy. Okay, he can have a shot at the dummy. But I want it fast, and we've got to have at least two other girls. And one has to be a blonde.'

Serge draped another blanket over Lili and quietly moved out of the studio into the next-door room where he lived, ate and fucked. He reached for his black address book, threw himself on the unmade bed and lifted the telephone. 'That you, Teresa? Got a nice job for you, flower.'

For the rest of the week, Lili stayed hidden in Serge's loft as she regained her strength and her spirits. He had gone shopping and returned with an armful of flowers, two Beatles records, a Victorian-style lace nightdress, an organdy-petal bonnet with white satin streamers, a see-through black string vest, some steak and a shopping bag crammed with bonbons and sugary food. After a day or two Lili lost her quivering fear of the Sardeaus, and Serge firmly encouraged her to regard that part of her life as over. She had run away, the sensible little creature. Now she was going to be treated as a grown-up and have fun. 'Next week Teresa will take you on a shopping trip and buy some pretty clothes,' Serge promised.

While Lili rested he worked hard with Teresa, a twenty-year-old model who wore her hair in blonde braids and tried hard to look fourteen. During the day she posed for margarine and soup advertisements, and in the evening she liked to go to expensive restaurants with old men. Young men bored her: she liked a sugar daddy with whom she could play at being a child. Teresa was a high-class call girl.

After a trip to the Galeries Lafayette, Lili returned with a pair of Jules-et-Jim tweed knickerbockers with a matching Jackie Coogan golfing cap; a white *broderie anglaise* cape that fell from her shoulders to five inches above the knee in layer upon layer of white frills; three dresses the colour of sugared almonds, each with a matching pair of high-heeled pumps; her first handbag and a coat of white rabbit fur. Her hair had been restyled and back-combed into a bouffant, Bardotlike, sexy tangle. All thought of returning to school, all thought of the Sardeaus, all thoughts of the past and the future flew from Lili's mind and she lived only in the voluptuous present. Her new friends laughed and chatted with her as she was coaxed into posing – naked – in the fur coat, then lay on the studio bed with Teresa, both wearing lace briefs and nothing else.

Sometimes they went out in the evening with Teresa's man friend, who was in the scrap metal business, and when they did, Teresa adopted a childlike voice and spoke of herself in the third person. 'Teresa wants to go to Fouquet's,' she pouted. 'Albert is a *horrid* man if he doesn't take Teresa somewhere pretty and Teresa won't talk to him.'

She always got her own way, then immediately stopped pouting and said, 'Oh, Albert is so *good* to little Teresa; she's going to sit on his knee and love him all night.'

'Christ, not in Fouquet's again,' groaned Serge. 'Don't you *ever* wear panties?'

When Teresa was working with Lili, the older girl was not petulant and childish, but friendly, shrewd and willing to pass on the wisdom of the hotel room. She gave Lili the benefit of her experience – shrewd bits of advice and sad little ways of avoiding humiliation.

'Never meet a man in a bar, Lili, always the bar of a restaurant or in a café.' Obediently she sat for Serge with one leg up on a kitchen table and hitched her skirt up so that her bare ass could be seen. 'Always take enough money to pay for yourself in case he doesn't turn up, then you simply order another drink or have your meal; no restaurant charges much for an omelette.'

At Serge's instruction, Teresa lay back on the wooden table while Lili unbuttoned her blouse and leaned over. 'This okay, Serge? If he doesn't turn up, you don't feel humiliated and if he's late, well, you're behaving as if you're used to expensive places. Ouch, Lili, that fucking hurt, keep your teeth to yourself.'

Serge moved them over to a wooden kitchen chair. Teresa stood behind and Lili knelt on it, clutching adoringly at Teresa's open kimono. She continued her advice. 'Always try to go to restaurants where you've been before, so they get to know you, and always tip well in the cloakroom.'

Serge didn't like the pose so they dropped it. Back to the kitchen table. One leg up again, but this time frontal. '... And never go out in the evening with more money than you need for one meal and your fare home, because then nobody can borrow from you.'

Both girls were directed to stand facing each other ... Closer ... Closer ... Touching.

Lili was told to drop her kimono. 'When you're in St Tropez,' Teresa continued, 'never pretend you're staying at an expensive hotel, because they'll quickly find out that you aren't. Always arrange to meet at Senequier, and if anyone asks where you're staying, say it's a little hotel that's *peaceful* and cheap. Rich men always respect that, and they're not to know you're sharing one room with four other girls.'

'Stop talking and let's get down to work seriously, you two. I want Lili to brush your hair from behind as you lean backwards over this wicker chair, Teresa, that'll lift those old tits of yours.'

When he was confident that no official search was being made for Lili, Serge briskly pursued his next step, which was to lure her into his bed.

One evening, after working late with a series of nightgown shots on the studio bed, Serge leaned over to give Lili the light, fatherly kiss on her forehead that usually meant that work was finished for the day. But this time he snuggled up beside her and muttered, 'Serge wants a cuddle.'

Suddenly wary, Lili stiffened. But soon she heard his heavy breathing, and finally she also drifted to sleep. Then Serge raised his head, quickly stripped and got under the sheets. In the middle of the night Lili woke up, drowsy, to feel a moist stroking of her clitoris in a slow, steady rhythm. Half asleep, she stretched languorously until her body quivered. Her narrow pelvis arched away from the bed and she shuddered to her first climax.

She lay panting, astonished, guilty, fearful, bewildered, as Serge heaved himself up, started to lick her eyelids, took her little hand in his and guided it firmly down his heavy hairy torso.

Docile and inexperienced, Lili had no idea how shrewdly she was being exploited.

Teresa and Serge seemed so sure of themselves, so sophisticated.

Teresa found Lili curiously appealing, she couldn't help being touched by the younger girl's awed admiration and teased her about it. 'But I've never had a proper girl friend before,' said Lili seriously, 'not someone who really likes me. When I was at school in Switzerland the other girls called me stuck-up because I had extra lessons and their mamas wouldn't let them play with me because I had no papa. When I was at school in Neuilly, there wasn't much time to get to know girls in school, and I wasn't allowed to see anyone outside school because Madame Sardeau said it would interfere with my work ... No, she meant housework ... So you see, it's wonderful to have a real, grown-up girl friend.'

Teresa felt uneasy. 'You'll soon have plenty of men friends, judging by the looks you get on the street.'

'I know what you mean, but I can't understand *why* they look at me like that.'

'It's something in your eyes,' Teresa grudgingly said. That evening Lili spent two hours locked in the bathroom, earnestly looking at her eyes in the mirror and trying to see something in them. But she just saw eyes. She was lucky about the lashes, but plenty of people had big dark eyes and long glossy lashes without inciting the extraordinary reaction that Lili got from the average man in the street. No, she didn't see *how* it could be the eyes. But she'd give it a try. So the next time she went for a walk, wearing a cherry-red velvet suit with a nipped-in waist, she looked straight at the first man she met, straight into his eyes, then blinked in a misty way and slowly gave a little smile. Immediately she saw his everyday lust turn into helpless fascination. It is the eyes, Lili thought exultantly. She didn't know why, but they worked like magic.

Serge spoiled and mesmerized Lili; he was expansive and charming when Lili was obedient, sharp and threatening if she didn't do as he said. 'Do you want the police to know where you are? Do you want them to know you had an illegal operation? Want to be in prison? Do you want to go back to the Sardeaus?' he growled one spring afternoon shortly after the calendar had been completed.

'Oh no, Serge, please don't. No more.'

'Then get on that bed with Teresa, dear, and let's have no more whining.'

Lili no longer felt humiliated and shamed by posing naked. The other two were so matter-of-fact about it, as were the other girls who occasionally modelled for Serge. They thought no more of stripping off their clothes than they did of kicking off their shoes. And the girls *all* slept with men. Teresa said it showed you were no longer a schoolgirl.

But this was different. This was a film. There was a movie camera and there were other men in the studio, men she didn't know. Scowling, Lili shed her cherry-red cotton wrapper and jumped on the double bed that had been pulled to the centre of

355

the studio and was now banked by lights. Serge switched on beguiling music, climbed up to the overhead camera platform and started directing Lili. She was stiff and awkward. Eventually, he said, 'Okay, take a break,' and moved to the bed where Lili crouched, arms around her knees.

'You're too tense, flower. Tell you what, put your wrapper on again and I'll get you some warm milk with a shot of rum in it. That'll relax you, bud.'

He slipped into the grubby kitchen, crushed three Mandrax sedative tablets, stirred them into hot milk and then poured rum and sugar in it. With an avuncular beam he carried it out and offered it to Lili. 'And if you don't feel better after that, flower, we'll stop,' he said.

After her drink, Lili felt drowsy and unresisting. 'Pinch her, Teresa, don't let her go to sleep. Now let's have some action, you two. Okay, Teresa, start on her tits.' Lili now sprawled limp on the bed; Teresa gently tugged at the red sash of her wrap and eased it away from her body. Then she started to stroke Lili's breasts. Dimly aware, Lili wriggled and tried to push her away, with arms that suddenly felt limp and boneless, but Teresa held Lili's hands back against the bed and bent her mouth towards Lili's left breast.

'That's great. Now you get in there, Carl.' A husky man who'd been leaning against the wall took off his leather belt, then stripped off denim battle jacket and jeans and walked towards the bed. 'Easy, Carl, take it easy. I want it almost as if the film's being slowed down. Just slither on to that bed behind Teresa, think dirty thoughts as fast as you can and let's see that hard-on. Okay, now you can stroke her ass.'

Serge was sweating, he'd never expected to find it so exciting. Shit, if it weren't for the rest of the crew, which was costing Christ knows how much an hour, he'd be in there getting his share. 'Let's have a little more action, get your mouth off Lili's bush, Teresa, and let's see Carl go down on her. No, don't stop, Teresa, your turn will come, we've got another twenty fucking minutes of film. Now you can slide around to Carl and give him head. Don't you *dare* come, Carl, recite the alphabet backwards or something. Now sit up slowly. Let's have your hands on Teresa's head. That's nice, very nice, stay with it. Now pull,

Teresa, we want to see what he's made of. Oh very nice, now Carl, I want you to slowly turn around, then lam it into Lili for all you're worth.'

Lili shrieked, her drugged face, panic-stricken, to camera. 'Nice, very nice, that'll have them creaming their jeans,' Serge purred.

After that, a weary quality was noticeable in Lili's pictures, an awareness of evil, a tired acceptance of it.

After all, where else could she go? What else could she do? As Serge endlessly reminded her, she had no qualifications, she was only fit to be a hooker or a shop assistant, and she couldn't get a job because she had no previous experience. She gnawed her little finger, knowing that what Serge said was true. But when Serge wasn't making her do these humiliating things, he was kind, gave her anything she wanted – bonbons, film magazines, records, high-heeled shoes, new clothes. He took her to the cinema, to restaurants and to parties, although she didn't much care for the parties. She didn't like the interested, slightly contemptuous, sidelong looks that the men gave her; she was glad Serge never left her alone. He saw that she never left his side for a minute; he wasn't bad to her and at least she didn't have to get out of bed at five in the morning to sew someone else's nightgowns.

Lili never thought about the past, as she enjoyed the new comforts of the present – and she tried never to think about the future. Now she was glad that *vraie maman* could never find her; when she conjured up that particular daydream, or when she caught herself remembering Angelina or Felix, she had to face the fact that she was ashamed of her present life. But how else could she live?

She started to develop a protective shell, to pretend she didn't care, that she didn't mind making these disgusting, shameful movies; only thus could she bear to lie naked on satin sheets with calculating strange men and hard-faced women of assorted age and colour, in front of other strangers on the periphery of the set. She seemed wearily prepared to accept any degradation, although she'd once – suddenly – become hysterical when Serge brought an Alsatian dog into the studio.

Once again, Lili remembered that cold, dim journey through

the snow and the slush, those dreadful growls and the one thin scream that turned into a gurgle. So Lili clung to Serge, shrieking, 'No! No! Felix, Felix, help me!' Her body shook and her teeth chattered and she was no use for the rest of the day.

Regretfully, Serge decided that he couldn't introduce animals into the act after all. He had to content himself with films of Lili chained to obviously papier-mâché dungeon walls, Lili being whipped by muscular bald boxers or manacled by monocled parodies of Englishmen, Lili kneeling to lick the cock of anyone Serge chose.

He felt not one twinge of jealousy or pity for the girl. He looked upon her as he would a clever pet monkey – she did her tricks and he saw to it that she had a comfortable life. He'd got her to sign a five-year contract with Sergio Productions – not that it was legal, mind, because she was underage, but she'd never find that out. Sergio Productions charged a steep price for slick, professionally made porn films, but Lili saw none of the money. On paper she was paid 400,000 francs a year by Sergio Productions, which was about as much as a secretary earned, but Serge deducted fifteen per cent as his agent's fee, thirty per cent for his fee as her manager, and thirty per cent for providing food, clothes and accommodation, which didn't leave much for Lili.

In the deep, dark velvet depths of a club cinema off the Champs Elysées, one man whispered to another, 'Who's the dark girl? She's new, isn't she? Serge's girl? She's too good for *this* crap. She deserves *better* crap. I'll phone him tomorrow.'

The following week, Serge summoned Teresa to the big basement that he now used as a studio. More care than usual had gone into the arrangement of the simple set; the focal point was a deep, old-fashioned, white enamel bathtub that stood on claw feet in the middle of a group of indoor palm trees. A hose filled the tub with warm water, which was then heavily squirted with liquid detergent, until foam hung dripping over the side in frothy stalactites. Banks of lights were switched on. 'Silence,' said Serge, then 'Action.'

Lili did what she usually did. She had developed the trick of disassociating herself from her body. She *willed* herself to feel that her skin was as irrelevant to her real self as old overalls, and therefore displaying it was no worse than displaying old overalls. The real Lili floated up and away from those grubby, alien hands that touched her flesh. She looked down on the scene from above, distant and uninvolved in the distasteful proceedings; or she dealt with the humiliation and protected her wispy sense of self-esteem by simply imagining herself elsewhere.

After such sessions Lili would be remote and silent, she would hardly speak until she had returned to the apartment and had a long soak in a warm tub of water in a darkened bathroom where slowly her body and soul were reunited. Lili always believed firmly in her future, sure of an eventual happy ending, because she had read so many of the romantic trash magazines that Madame Sardeau read every week. She therefore knew the traditional ending to these tales. She was an orphan, wasn't she? She was being exploited, wasn't she? She was going through tough times, wasn't she, like all those heroines? That meant she was currently at about the middle of chapter four of her life, and about six chapters away from the man of her dreams and eternal happiness. In the meantime, she had to put up with the standard soap opera plot.

'Action!' said Serge again, impatiently.

Slowly Lili slipped off her white rabbit fur coat, then stepped naked into the foam. Carefully she soaped her breasts, running her fingers slowly over her slippery flesh. Then Teresa stepped forward, wearing a man's shirt unbuttoned to the waist. She leaned over the back of the bath and started to soap Lili's body with long, sensuous strokes. 'Right, Teresa, now sit behind her on the edge of the bath, one leg on either side of her, more in the water Lili, now *splash*, I want Teresa's shirt soaked, I want to see those nipples press against it. Now slither in behind her, Teresa. Christ, there's water all over the fucking floor. Now, you little darlings, I want the normal action, yeah, that's nice, oh, very nice. For Christ's sake, Lili, look as if you're enjoying it, you know we'll just go on shooting until you do, that's better, now move in very slowly, Ben, I want you sitting on the back of the bath, legs in the water, cock standing at attention.'

Blue-black muscles shining, Ben appeared through the palms. 'Get out of the bath, Teresa, I want you standing behind him.

Now, Ben, lean over and grab Lili under the armpits, slowly, slowly, you're relishing the thoughts of what you're about to do, now turn her around. I want a close-up of your hands running over her ass and in the crack. Lili, could you please show a bit more interest. Let's have some sinuous writhing or you'll be fucking sorry. That's nice, *very* nice . . . Now, Lili, kneel down in the water as Ben stands up. We're tracking into this shot. Now purse those rosebud lips, Lili, and in it goes, smoothly. For Christ's sake, you little bitch, try and look as if it's your favourite flavour lollipop, that's better. Now slowly pull her up, Ben, settle your ass on the back of the bath and use that prick with imagination, *slower*, you black bastard.'

He shot the scene three times before Ben's penis went on strike. It wasn't as juicy as their usual stuff, but that was for a carefully calculated reason. Serge wanted the attention focused on Lili, rather than the action. He didn't want it too dirty, he wanted a *pretty* fuck. It was going exactly as he had hoped it would, like a routine whisky or bathsalts commercial, but with nothing left to the imagination or subliminal interpretation.

He knew he couldn't shoot a proper film test, but he'd be willing to bet his new Mercedes this would get the big boys interested – especially after that call from Zimmer. He was after bigger game than blue movies. He wanted to make Lili a star. Vadim had done it with Bardot, so Serge was doing his fucking best to get Lili discovered. He'd already arranged for her to have a walk-on part in the Christopher Lee sci-fi that Trianon was shooting at Versailles; she'd only be an extra, a spaceship soldierette, but she'd get the feeling of a proper set, ready for the big chance if it came.

Not if, he told himself, *when*.

Shortly before her fifteenth birthday, Lili made her first legitimate appearance on celluloid under a green, greasy film of Leichner, with her hair hidden by a silver, cardboard helmet.

The bus picked her up at five a.m. It was filled with sleepy, silent figures huddled in overcoats. They drove out of Paris, through Versailles and into the forest beyond; the bus pulled off the road, jerked down a rutted track and stopped in a large clearing where several trucks and trailers were parked. The passengers climbed out of the bus and stumped off in silence towards the nearest truck. As Lili hesitated on the steps of the bus, a thin young fellow in a white yachting cap said, 'Better grab your coffee while you can.'

'Where does one find coffee?'

'This your first day? Come with me.' He dug his hands into the pockets of his navy pea jacket, and they walked through damp grass towards the truck. Just before they reached it, the rear door flew open and a caterer started handing out coffee and croissants. 'This should wake you up.' He handed her a paper cup. 'For some unknown reason, the coffee's always good. You an extra? One of the spaceship crew? I'm one of the gypsies that see it crash into the clearing. Got any lines?'

'No.'

'I've got three. *A part!* My first, which is why I'm so cheerful.' He beamed. 'Also, I like being awake when everyone's half asleep and huddled around the coffee truck, sun barely up, birds singing, nobody around.'

'I *hate* getting up early. Why did we have to get up so early when shooting doesn't start until eight-thirty?'

'All motion picture people get up early; *everyone* has to be *ready* for eight-thirty and, believe it or not, it can take three hours to get them all ready.'

'You don't sound French.'

'I'm not. My mother was from Los Angeles, but both my parents were killed in a car crash when I was five. I was brought up by my French grandmother. I'm called Simon Pont.'

'I'm Lili, and I lost my parents when I was seven.'

'Tough, ain't it? Lili what?'

'Lili nothing. Just Lili.' She didn't explain that after having four family names by the time she was barely seven, she had decided that in the future she would just call herself 'Lili'.

'But where are the stars? Where are Christopher Lee and Mademoiselle Collins?' Lili asked hopefully, as she chewed the last ragged end of her croissant and they moved over to look at the call sheet.

'The stars stay in their trailers, which are *sacred*. Positively no entry allowed, nobody ever goes into a trailer if he isn't supposed to. There are trailers for the director, wardrobe, makeup and the stars, and everyone else has to manage without one as best they can.'

'Where's the director?'

'Staying in his trailer until we're ready to go. The writer, the set designer and the press agent won't turn up until around eight-thirty, lucky bastards.'

'Now I know everything I need to know about a movie set.'

'Everything except where the makeup truck is, which is where you should be at this moment. Look, there's your name on the call sheet – "Makeup six-thirty." You'd better run; I tell you, makeup can be *bitches*. You don't want little piggy eyes with bags beneath them, do you?'

She saw Simon again at lunch break, when he fetched their sandwiches from the trailer. He spread his jacket on the grass and together they sat on it. He bit into the crusty roll with teeth that were unusually small, white and far apart, like a child's teeth. 'Look at that idiot driving a Mercedes down the track at that speed.'

'It's Serge, my manager – the man I live with.'

'Oh, well, I'll be off then.' He didn't seem surprised or disappointed.

The following month saw publication of the tyre calendar. The calendar itself was an annual event, always expensively produced by a famous photographer and a prominent art director: the editions were collected like antiquarian books. The 1964 calendar, which starred Lili, was an overnight sensation. Every art editor and designer had to have one, every truck driver leered at Lili, every schoolboy lusted after her, and many of their fathers did as well. Within two weeks the calendar was sold out, and copies changed hands at eight times the list price. The print order for the second printing was a quarter of a million, and it disappeared as fast as the first one.

Almost overnight Lili was not only famous, but notorious. She couldn't move in Paris without being recognized.

Lili found one of the advantages of having such a low sense of self-esteem was that it wasn't difficult to ignore her growing public image as a tough, sexy, knowing little slut.

Serge taught her to tell journalists, in a whisper, that she was an orphan; orphans had good publicity value, he said. They were sad and appealing. Lili was to stop this crazy-sounding nonsense about her mysterious 'Mama', because it confused her pitch and, anyway, he didn't want a hundred crazy bag ladies turning up claiming to be Lili's mother and trying to grab half her income.

Most of Lili's early pictures were resold, and her blue movies changed hands at a price that made Serge's income almost an embarrassment. He huddled with lawyers and accountants, discussing the tax advantages of Andorra, Jersey or Monaco; of being offshore in the Cayman Islands or the Bahamas; of starting a company in Panama or Mexico; of having money paid to Dutch lawyers to lodge in numbered Swiss accounts, or Swiss lawyers in a group-participation company that fronted for big movie stars.

The pros, cons and percentages of these schemes were never discussed with Lili, because she owned none of the properties. She was under contract to Sergio Productions, so Serge owned her. All that Lili got were the sly looks, the leers and the gossip. She couldn't cope with any of it, so she greeted everyone with a suspicious stare.

What else could she do?

33

SHORTLY after Pagan's third wedding anniversary, on a warm spring day in 1965, Kate and Pagan were playing a nursery card game in the garden. 'Buster doesn't like being in London much,' said Pagan, as she shuffled the cards. 'Still misses Cornwall, poor darling. So do I, come to that.' They started to play. 'Did I tell you that Christopher got tough with Mama? They both sat in the library talking in quiet, polite, nasty voices – *snap*! Blast, you're fast – and the upshot was that we all trooped along to the solicitor ın St Austell – *snap*! Blast you – Christopher said he should never have allowed my guardian to lease my property to herself, although I don't suppose for one minute that was how she put it to the poor old bugger. He seemed to think that she was running the place on my behalf and he didn't even know about – *snap*! – oh you know, her will. She'd had that drawn up by some smart crook in London – blast, too fast for me! – So for ten pounds, I purchased an option to – *snap*! Oh, you cow – purchase Ma's shares in the health farm at par upon her death, and for another ten pounds – *snap*! Bugger! – I purchased an option to purchase Selma's shares in the health farm at current valuation upon her death. Missed again, dammit. Get that? What it means is that Selma – *snap*! Thank you! – can't get her claws on Trelawney if Mama kicks the bucket, and that I get it all back in – *snap*! – the end if I outlive them, plus the health farm.'

'That's nice – *snap*!' shrieked Kate. 'Thanks, a splendid pile of hearts and diamonds.'

'Oh, you cow, you've won!' said Pagan. 'Well, I hope it's put you in a good temper because I want you to help me in a delicate matter.'

'What is it this time?' Kate asked.

'I've worked out two things,' Pagan explained, 'for both of which I need your aid. Firstly, I love Christopher more than drink, and secondly I love him so much that I couldn't bear it if he were to die. And you know that he might at any minute, and I'd be left with nothing of him. There would be nothing left of Christopher. So I want his child. Even if it kills him, I want his child.'

'Can't you get ... er ... artificial insemination?'

'Certainly not! I can't bear the idea of anything unnatural. I want our child to be conceived as an act of love, even if it's the last one we ever share.'

Kate was awed by the ruthlessness of Pagan's reasoning. 'In spite of what the doctor said?'

'In spite of what the doctor said, darling. So I want you to help me to seduce Christopher, because I know he'll never agree.' Kate was speechless with astonishment. 'What I want you to do is the opposite of birth control. I want you to help me work out the dangerous time – my *unsafe* period. Then I want you to double-check with me, because my arithmetic is abysmal and I know I'm only going to get one chance.'

'Suppose one chance isn't enough?'

'It was before, remember? Only once in Switzerland was enough to produce that darling little thing.'

'Let's not talk about it or I'll start crying.' They both sighed.

'I've been to the family planning clinic,' Pagan continued. 'I've got a chart and a special thermometer and I'm going to take my temperature every morning, but I want *you* to keep the chart so that Christopher doesn't accidentally find it: I'd be sure to leave the damn thing on the mantelpiece one morning. When my temperature dips slightly that means it's just before ovulation. After ovulation it rises several tenths of a degree and then stays there until I get the curse. So when my temperature goes down is the time for *action*! The clinic people said that I'd better check my pattern for a couple of months before settling down to strenuous nightlife.'

Though Kate was scandalized by the idea, Pagan eventually talked her into it. Each morning after Christopher had gone to the lab Pagan telephoned her temperature to Kate. For the first two months there didn't seem to be any difference, but on the third month there was no doubt – the temperature dipped.

On the propitious day of the fourth month, when the moon was in the correct quarter and the thermometer had definitely wobbled, Pagan, calculating and steady as a tiger, set about seducing her lawfully wedded husband.

The next morning she reported to Kate. 'Darling, I rushed out to Fortnum's and bought some smoked salmon, a game pie, some country blackberries. I'd turned up the heating and when he got home I was sitting in that pink, gauze Arab shift with nothing on underneath. I'd already opened a bottle of Haut Brion '59, and as soon as he sat down I handed him a huge mint julep. Neat bourbon with chopped mint, crushed in melted sugar. Oh, it smelled divine! "Do you think it's strong enough?" I asked him. "Because you know I can't tell." Darling, it was six eggcupsful of neat bourbon, but you don't notice because of the minty sugar. The rest was easy. Mind you, it was too quick to be fun and I can't *tell* you how livid he was afterwards, except, of course, he dared not get too angry in case his blood pressure went up.'

Amazingly, she *was* pregnant. Once he'd got over his initial fury and was used to the idea, Christopher was hugely pleased. Pagan said that she wanted a daughter, 'a dear little girl with big brown eyes,' she said, nestling in his lap, though she was much too large for it. Her husband laughed.

'Well, you're not going to get one, my darling.'

'Why not?'

'Because we both have blue eyes and it's genetically impossible for two perfectly blue-eyed parents to have a brown-eyed child.'

'What do you mean, genetically impossible?'

He pulled her against him and started to stroke her mahogany hair. 'In the nucleus of every human cell are two sets of genes – one for each parent – and in an embryo they form the blueprint that determines the inherited characteristics of the baby.'

With one finger he traced her bronze, winged eyebrow. 'Now when you come to the genes for eye colour, you *only* get a blue-eyed child if the genes of *both* parents are for blue. The gene for blue eyes is what we call "recessive", which means that a person with only *one* gene for brown eyes and one gene for blue will always have brown eyes, not blue ones. And it also means that two perfectly blue-eyed parents can *only* produce a blue-eyed child. It is impossible for two perfectly blue-eyed parents to have a brown-eyed child.'

'What about hazel eyes?'

'Of course, there are degrees of eye colour. You can get greenish-blue or hazelish-brown, and there's a very slight possibility of a throwback to some brown-eyed ancestor, although it's very unlikely. But this *never* happens when the colour is definite in both parents.' He stretched over and kissed the other winged, bronzed eyebrow. 'You can't expect two clearly blue-eyed individuals to produce a clearly brown-eyed offspring, because it's genetically impossible.' Pagan shut her eyes and snuggled up against his chest. 'So because we've *both* got blue eyes, we have only blue genes to give our child. You're going to have a blue-eyed baby, my darling. And I hope she'll be an exact replica of you.'

The child, Sophia, was born in the summer of 1966. Surprisingly, Pagan was a perfect mother. Her carelessness and untidiness vanished overnight. This amazed Kate until one day, while she watched Pagan play pussycat on the floor with Sophia, Kate realized that Pagan treated her daughter as she treated her animals – with more care than she did adult human beings.

Naturally, Kate was asked to be godmother. 'Now, listen, darling,' Pagan said, 'this is *serious*. I don't want to have any more disasters in my life. I want you to be the sort of godmother that she can run away to. I want her always to see you as her ally, always on *her* side, whether or not she deserves it. To be frank, darling, I want what I *didn't* have when I needed it.'

Kate nodded gravely.

She gave Sophia a string of iridescent baroque pearls. Predictably, Pagan said, 'I'd better wear them, they'll lose the lustre if they aren't worn against warm skin. No point in keeping them in the bank.'

Though her alcoholic phase now seemed like an impossible dream, Pagan still went nearly every week to her AA meeting. By now she realized that they had better be part of her life forever – if she wanted to avoid yet another fatal mistake.

~ PART SEVEN ~

～ 34 ～

IN the spring of 1956, it had been four years since Kate had fled
from Cairo. After her return, she had spent the first week weeping, conscious of her father's tight-lipped disappointment and
indignant fury. Kate felt she had to get away from home, to get
away from him. She had to think of an excuse for staying in
Walton Street. She didn't want to be tied down by a full-time job,
so she decided to become a free-lance translator. Kate's French
wasn't good enough – neither she nor Pagan nor any other pupil
had learned much at l'Hirondelle – so Kate signed up for an
intensive course at the Berlitz School in Oxford Street and fled
the opulent, fake Georgian bricks of Greenways back to her old
apartment in the genuine little Georgian cottage in Walton Street.

She found her work easy. She was quick and accurate, and she
got as many translations as she could handle from a French
literary agent in Motcomb Street so she could juggle her working
hours to suit her private life. Although her father gave her an
allowance, within six months of starting work Kate could have
managed without it.

She tried to blot Robert out of her mind. Once more she started
to see old friends, and she quickly learned that, if she felt depressed, she should never stay indoors or alone. So she would go
for a walk, moving around London by herself as she had never
been allowed to when a child. She mingled with the crowds of
young, untidy foreigners who lounged around the base of the
statue in Piccadilly Circus. She liked to sit among the stone lions
and fountains of Trafalgar Square, then visit the National
Gallery, where she would sit for hours in the calm peace of the
Monet water lily room.

Since leaving Cairo, Kate felt that some part of her had been
cut off. Partly because she was an only child and partly as a result
of her father's verbal violence, she had always felt timid, tentative
and lonely, but now she felt an added sense of loss and didn't
understand it.

What had she lost? Not her virginity; that had gone long before she met Robert – and anyway, it hadn't been the melodramatic event that it was cracked up to be. She no longer wept over Robert, although it had been painful to hear that he had married Pagan.

But that was over – long ago – and it wasn't as if there weren't other men around to distract her. Kate knew lots of nice fellows, and as a matter of fact she was never out of love – a fortnight here, half an hour there, a five-minute passion for some unknown man on the top of a bus. She knew she was sensual, knew she loved to touch a man's body, to feel a man touch *her*. She found something to hunger after in almost every man she met. What she *didn't* know, but badly wanted to know, was why the only two men she had ever really cared about had dumped her.

Why?

Kate told herself she had been obedient, faithful, loyal, trusting and truthful. Well, almost always. So what was wrong with her? *Why* had she been kicked in the teeth?

'Why?' She asked Maxine, who was on a buying trip to London. They were sitting on the purple rag rug, drinking cocoa in front of the lavender gas flames.

'Maybe you give too quickly?' Maxine suggested. 'No, of course I don't mean your body, stupid. But maybe you are too eager for love – too quick to be affectionate, too clinging, too claustrophobic.' She blew on the drink to cool it. 'More than anyone else I know, Kate, you need love. One can see that. So when you think you have found it, you are all over the man, like a puppy.' She put the tip of her tongue in her drink and quickly withdrew it. 'Perhaps you should be more reticent, more elusive. Men value what is difficult to get. But with François, I remember, you threw yourself at him, threw yourself in front of him like a doormat with "welcome" printed on it. So, as we say in France, he wiped his feet on you.'

'But I was being emotionally honest,' Kate said.

'And you paid heavily for this pleasant self-indulgence and lack of self-discipline,' said Maxine, with Gallic cynicism. 'If you are difficult to pursue, if you make a man think and worry and invest a lot of his time and effort in pursuing you, then he will – of course – justify these efforts to himself by deciding that you are unusually worthwhile and desirable.'

'Deliberately playing hard to get is nasty psychological exploitation,' said Kate, '*and* it's phony.'

Maxine shrugged her shoulders. 'Then call it something else.' She blew again on the hot cocoa. 'I feel you lack discrimination. I see you with some real creeps.'

'That still doesn't explain why I have this sense of loss. I mean, I hardly ever think about those two bastards who dumped me. Thank heaven, I don't want either of them. But I want to identify this sense of loss. If it's not them, what is it?'

Maxine took a cautious sip. 'Kate, you may laugh, but I think what you have lost is your trust. You don't really trust people anymore. No, you *do* trust me; maybe it is only *men* you don't trust?'

Kate had been conditioned to love bastards. Without knowing or realizing it, she had duplicated in adult life the pattern she had learned at her daddy's knee: Kate was hooked on rejection. When men started to criticize her, she always fell in love with them. And when she fell in love with them, she fell into bed with them. And when she went to bed with them, she never climaxed. And she never dared to tell them. So Kate faked.

But Kate was always frightened that the man would guess. She was afraid he would leave her if he thought she was frigid. As Kate was terrified of rejection, she never had an honest relationship with a lover. Untrusting and nervous in her obsessive search for Mr Wrong, she felt so insecure that as soon as there seemed to be even a remote possibility that he might abandon her, Kate immediately left him or pushed him out of her life.

Though she was tense and defensive in her most intimate relationships, it wasn't obvious unless you were in bed with Kate. Fully clothed, her aura of intense sexuality attracted hordes of admiring men. Kate didn't see herself as attractive: since apparently she had been unattractive to the men she had loved, she became haunted by the feeling that no worthwhile man could ever really love her.

But she had to check.

The classic one-night-stand man only wants to get involved if he thinks the woman doesn't; the classic one-night-stand woman is hopefully, unsuccessfully searching for Prince Charming and feeling forever guilty about it. Many women imagine that promiscuity brings conquests and pleasures. This may be so with a man – the sort of man who wants to try every biscuit in the tin – but unlike a man, a woman is rarely promiscuous if she has a wonderful love at home. A promiscuous man is afraid he might be *missing* something. A promiscuous woman is *seeking* something and – sadly – not finding it.

So there Kate was, a classic case of potential nymphomania, until New Year's Eve at the 1956 Chelsea Arts Ball where, among the balloons and the streamers, among the real and the bogus painters, Kate met her first Design Man. Toby was a twenty-eight-year-old architect who specialized in hospital design, and had just been made the youngest partner of his firm. Toby introduced Kate to the haute-Bohemian circles in which he moved, and Kate found his friends a refreshing change from officers of the Household Brigade and budding stockbrokers. In fact, she was fascinated by the Design Men. They were so world-weary, scornful of everything that wasn't perfectly proportioned or that they hadn't thought of first. They held up a cocktail and squinted at the proportions of the glass before sipping the drink, and they could only eat from plain white china.

'The first night I slept with Toby,' Kate happily told Maxine (who had, of course, heard the intimate bits earlier), 'he took three, black cotton cushions off the tangerine cotton mattress – which was on the black-painted floor – and put them on the black leather sling chair.' Sitting in front of the fireplace, Kate pulled her knees up and put her arms around them, then said in a dreamy voice, 'There was no other furniture in the room.' She rested her head on her knees and continued, 'Then he went behind the kitchen bar, stood on a stool, took two quilts from an overhead cupboard, bent down and pulled out two black pillows from under the sink, then threw the whole pile on to the mattress.'

She heaved a long, sexy sigh. 'After that he took off his jeans and lay there reading *Design* by the light of one of those chrome caterpillars that wriggle out of the wall, as if they were trying to read over your shoulder. Then he glanced up and criticized my panties.'

'Super,' Maxine said politely, but to herself she thought, Oh, dear, another bastard.

Kate was hopelessly dominated by Toby, who told her how to

dress, look, think, feel, behave. When he criticized her in front of Maxine for being sloppy, clumsy and inefficient, Kate not only believed him, but to Maxine's surprise actually promised she'd try hard to do better.

Kate adored Toby's self-confidence and shared his high opinion of himself. She was still a happy, grovelling doormat, thought Maxine, although she had to admit that Toby was quick-witted and entertaining, if not particularly handsome; he was obviously clever and passionately interested in his work; he took the trouble to explain it to Maxine as they all sat on the pale beech floor listening to the delicate, lacelike intricacy of a harpsichord toccata.

'The drawback to hospital design is that it's often very frustrating,' Toby told Maxine, as he mixed a Campari in a plain glass. 'You haven't got *one* client – there's a whole bunch of them. Doctors who won't bother to read plans properly, head nurses, the Regional Hospital Boards *and* the Ministry of Health.'

He held the glass of red liquid to the light. Wonderful colour! 'The boards and the ministries are old-fashioned; they have pre-conceived ideas and they won't listen to new ones. They tell me to "economize", when they're really suggesting that I design over-crowded wards.'

'It sounds extremely complex,' said Maxine politely. At last a friend of Kate with some sense, thought Toby.

Kate listened adoringly. She loved to hear Toby talk about his work, loved to visit his calm, all-white office with the tilted desks and the vast blueprints. Unlike the doctors, she had quickly learned to read them.

But Kate didn't dare let Toby move into Walton Street, because her father would have exploded with rage. 'Then I suppose we'll have to get married,' Toby said ungraciously, and once again Kate's eyes sparkled.

Kate Harrington. Mrs Toby Harrington. Mrs Harrington.

This time there was no marquise diamond – in fact, Kate only just managed to get a wedding ring at all, because Toby thought they were bourgeois, if not a primitive token of possession. However, he was reluctantly persuaded to buy a secondhand gold band with a worn heart pattern winding around it. The previous owner must have been a very worried woman, because all the hearts were worn away on the right side from nervous twisting.

Toby's widowed mother came up from Essex for the wedding. Major Hartley-Harrington's widow was a big, brusque woman, with muscular legs and a nose she could look down. Although she wore navy silk, you sensed that mentally she wore tweeds and was worrying whether the dogs were all right in her absence. She said remarkably little, and during the dreary register office ceremony, she kept sniffing and hitching her fur stole up around her shoulders, obviously under no illusion that she was acquiring a daughter.

She mellowed a little over luncheon at the Connaught, but due to the wine, rather than any growing affection for her new daughter-in-law. At the end of the first course, Kate's father, who had been struggling to talk to Toby's mother for half an hour and knew a tough nut when he saw one, banged the side of his glass with his knife and said he wasn't a speechmaker, that young people's lives were their own affair, that he realized things were done differently today – which was not to say that they were done better – but that two people couldn't really live together in a dark hole, so he had bought the house in Walton Street as a wedding present.

Kate flung her arms around him and wept for joy.

After that announcement the wedding group relaxed, and happy laughter actually accompanied the bride and groom as they flew off for their honeymoon in Milan, where the Triennale Exposition was in progress. Toby could criticize any international award-winning designs that weren't quite up to his standards.

At first they were happy.

Kate's old basement apartment was gutted, painted white, covered with cork pinboard and transformed into Toby's office. It was always full of his friends; they came pouring in to be fed, often without warning, and to talk about their work before, during and after meals.

Kate loved it.

The ground floor of the little Walton Street house was also gutted. All walls, ceilings and window frames were painted dull chocolate, the floors were covered with white vinyl tiles – which showed every footprint – a rash of spotlights appeared, and the balustrades were removed from the staircase. On one side of the 'living environment', a ten-foot run of kitchen units was installed, hidden by a sliding screen of louvered pine, so that you had to heave the heavy screen back ten feet if you wanted to get a teaspoon. The wall opposite the kitchen unit was hung with shelves that supported books, drinks, visually acceptable flowers (such as a bunch of daisies in a jam jar or one long-stemmed rose in a chemist's beaker) and Toby's collection of battered Victorian toys. Toby himself had designed the metal chairs. Some looked like tractor seats, and some were made of criss-crossed wire. 'Ass traps,' muttered Kate's father, thinking how bloody bare the place looked; when her parents visited, Kate hid the priapic African carvings and the privately printed Aubrey Beardsley engravings.

In the evenings Kate worked hard and happily as a hostess, entertaining Toby's clients, his useful contacts, architectural journalists and the other designers who were working on Toby's projects. Kate loved learning to cook for them. After a couple of standard bride's-dinner-party disasters (a casserole burned black, a salted ham she'd forgotten to soak overnight before cooking) she discovered Elizabeth David's cookbooks, and from that moment on, only the breakfast boiled eggs were served without garlic. For a Christmas present she asked Toby for a hand-operated salt grinder and a jar of *confit d'oie* from Fortnum's. She served the preserved goose to her parents on Boxing Day. It was greasy, thought her mother, but this odd food phase will pass fast enough when she has a baby.

As he kissed Kate on the doorstep, her father bravely said, 'Usually I don't like mucked-up foreign food, but I must say that was *very nice*, girl.'

They were the last words Kate heard him say.

35

THE next day, Kate's father managed to give himself a mild electric shock while changing a lightbulb in the loggia, fell backwards off the ladder on to the flagstone floor and broke his neck. He was dead when Kate's mother found him.

Kate cried for a week and couldn't really understand why, for she had resented his rages and his tyranny. She would never forget the quivering, nail-biting fear of her childhood.

She was silent and strained after the funeral until the end of the month when, to Toby's relief, Maxine came to stay. Kate poured herself a Campari, sat cross-legged on the green and blue, long-haired ryja rug from Finland and burst into tears.

'It was the last thing I expected, Maxie – to feel depressed when the old bugger passed away. But I feel terribly tired and completely lacking in self-confidence. It's as if I were a school-girl again!' She took a swig of Campari. 'His death was such a horrible mixture of farce and tragedy. When I got to Greenways there he was, lying on a couch in the hall as if he were having a nap, stone-dead in his blue-striped pyjamas and clutching an arum lily. Someone had put makeup on his face, his cheeks were bright peach, and they had tied a handkerchief over his head and under his chin to hold his jaws together before rigor mortis set in.'

Kate took another large gulp, looked at the Campari with distaste, got up and poured herself a Scotch. She wanted 'a proper drink', as her father would have said. 'If he could see himself, he'd die of shame, I thought, and it was only then that I realized that he *was* dead. That was the only point at which my mother nearly broke down. Apart from that she was bloody marvellous, brisk and cheerful at the funeral, just as he would have wanted her to behave at his last appearance.'

Kate now started to snivel, looking sad and stunned. 'Mummy kept saying if a bomb had got him in the Blitz he would have wanted us to feel happy when we thought of him.'

She sniffed again. 'He obviously hadn't expected to die at fifty-five. His papers were in such a mess that it took me a whole day just to find his medical card.'

'Poor baby,' said Maxine, and gave her a big hug. 'You'll feel better soon.'

But instead, Kate had a row with her father's lawyer on the following day. 'Now, remember, Mummy,' Kate cautioned before they entered his office, 'for heaven's sake, don't be over-awed by him.'

The two women were shown into a small Gray's Inn office filled with shelves of red-leatherbound legal books, and to her surprise the normally timid Kate – feeling furious on behalf of her dead father – coldly reviewed the situation.

'Last month, Mr Stiggins, the day after my father died, you seemed to know very little about my father's assets. You told my mother then she would be unable to lay her hands on any money at all for some time.'

Stiggins nodded. 'Now; there is no need for you ladies to be anxious. As you have seen from the will, the late Mr Ryan's entire estate is contained in a trust fund for his widow, which will, upon her demise, be inherited by her only issue, Mrs Harrington. It's just a question of waiting for probate. A few months . . . Perhaps a year.'

He tapped his fingertips together. 'The late Mr Ryan named me personally as one trustee. The other trustee is his former partner, Mr Jellaby – who, as you know, has unfortunately been in the hospital for the past two months after a stroke.'

Portentously he continued, 'Consequently, I am currently responsible for the late Mr Ryan's investments, and after much deliberation and discussion with this firm's stockbroker, I have decided to sell all the shares. After death-duties have been paid, the remaining money will be invested in the British Widows Fund, which is a safe unit trust company.'

'What's a unit trust company?' asked Kate, aghast that apparently such financial decisions could be taken without her mother even being consulted.

'A company with expert advisers that invests its funds in the stock market. It is, I might say, a very *cautious* company. Naturally, I cannot allow risks to be taken . . .'

Kate didn't understand much of what followed, but she was determined to inform herself about the stock market.

The first thing she discovered was that British Widows was so 'safe' that it paid minimal interest.

'I can't help thinking that Stiggins must be getting a cut somewhere,' Kate muttered to herself, grimly determined to keep checking on British Widows.

She bought a child's exercise book and started to take notes on the stock market.

Two months later, Kate had another interest.

She was pregnant.

She was delighted. She rushed out and bought a wicker cot, an antique brass bed, some nineteenth-century Randolph Caldecott nursery rhyme prints and a large, traditional pram, like the ones the royal nannies push. Toby loathed it, especially as it blocked their narrow hall.

Her mother returned from an expedition to Bond Street with a pile of minute lace garments that had been hand-stitched by French nuns. Mrs Ryan was cheerfully living on a steadily increasing overdraft, for which the bank was charging her interest at two per cent above the normal rate because the loan was unsecured. She had decided to sell Greenways. It was too big for her. She was going to buy a country cottage in the Cotswolds and live there with her sister.

Kate was still absorbed by Toby's work, fascinated by his theories and his missionary zeal. On her next visit, Maxine, amazed, watched Kate pounding a pestle in an ancient marble mortar as they all three lounged around the kitchen end of the living environment. That morning, for two hours after her arrival, Maxine had listened to Kate pouring out her heart, her hopes and her happiness. Kate now seemed a new person, a person in her own right, a person of some importance. She no longer looked quiet and worried. She wore a self-confident smile and a canary maternity smock made from upholstery linen that she'd bought from Harrods furniture department – although she hadn't confessed that to Toby, because Harrods was terribly unvisual.

Maxine admired every hand-smocked, lace trimmed item in the layette and then listened to Kate's plans, as they both sat on the tangerine linoleum of the newly decorated Visual Nursery and watched the mobiles stir in a slight breeze from the window. As Kate babbled on, Maxine suddenly realized that her friend longed for a totally unworried love relationship. Maxine herself knew that the charm of having babies is that Mother is in charge: she is the boss and she calls the shots. At last.

For the following six hours Kate questioned Maxine nonstop about pregnancy, upon which, as usual, Maxine (being one step ahead) was the authority. They endlessly discussed how much it hurt, whether you called them pains or contractions, and what it *really* felt like. 'Shitting a football,' said Maxine in French with unusual vulgarity but much feeling. All the other mothers she'd known when she was pregnant had soft-pedalled this aspect to Maxine and she still felt angry about it. They discussed whether Kate should attend the new natural childbirth trust classes in Seymour Street, how much bigger your breasts become, whether they sag afterwards, how long it takes to get back to normal down below, whether you would still be the same circumference *there* and what you did about stretch marks.

At this point Toby came back from a visit to the Design Centre and suggested that they all have a drink. As they carefully walked down the bannisterless staircase, Maxine reckoned that, more than any pregnant woman she'd ever encountered, Kate *needed* this baby. Toby didn't seem nearly as interested as Kate in the baby, and whenever Kate mentioned hospitals (she was booked into St George's), Toby immediately started talking about cross-infection and Florence Nightingale. Toby was devoted to the theories of Florence, the famous nineteenth-century nurse: he had a daguerreotype of her hanging in his office, and he spoke as if the famous lady with the lamp were still alive.

'She talks such a lot of *sense*,' said Toby, meaning that he shared her views. '*She* says that patients should be the first concern of a hospital, although the first concern of any damn hospital is their damn medical routine. They wake you up to give you a sleeping pill and put you to bed at tea time, because that's when it suits the nurses' timetable.'

Toby was pouring himself a Campari, as carefully as if he were splitting the atom. 'Medical men don't seem to realize that a patient isn't an experimental dummy or a corpse to be dissected. They don't seem to realize that a patient is a frightened human being.'

'Watch out! He's getting on to the subject of ward sizes,' said Kate. 'Now where did I put the pine nuts? Oh, you're eating them. Hand them over!'

She waved her long, narrow, tapering hands at Toby. When talking, Kate used her hands a lot. She would flutter one like a fan, or bend her elbows to her waist and, with both hands, slowly make graceful, expanding motions away from her body. Now she waved the pestle in mock threat at Toby, who mock-dodged, then continued, unabashed. 'Well, ward sizes are much more important to an illness than patients realize. Of course, nurses like open wards – except when they're ill themselves – because they feel they can keep an eye on everyone.'

'Toby, Maxine's come for dinner, not a lecture.'

Kate touched a button and the blender shrieked, drowning conversation for a few minutes. Kate tested her mixture, added more salt and pepper and said, '*Tsatsiki*, a cold Greek soup for a change. Taste it, darling.'

She held out a spoonful to Toby, who waved it aside and continued to lecture Maxine, who accepted a pale-green spoonful and nodded approvingly (thinking it had too much garlic) as she listened stupefied to Toby droning on.

When Kate was seven months pregnant, her father's former partner died, so Stiggins was left the sole trustee of her father's will. Kate consulted her stock market exercise book and found that in the previous six months British Widows had fallen by eight and a half per cent, more than the rest of the market, and there was a huge lawyer's bill to pay for settling her father's affairs. Kate telephoned the Law Society and found that nothing could be done to get the Ryan money out of British Widows until Kate's mother was willing formally to accuse the trustee solicitor of gross negligence. This complaint would have to be made through another solicitor, and it might be difficult to get a solicitor to take on a case that meant suing a colleague.

'Oh, I couldn't *possibly* change my lawyer, dearest,' said Kate's mother, aghast. 'I could never look your father's lawyer in the face again.'

*

That night Kate woke with bad, cramping pains and found that she was lying on a sheet that was wet and soggy with her own blood. Toby rushed her to St George's Hospital where, four hours afterwards, he was told that she had lost her baby.

Later, Toby sat by his wife's bed and comforted her, held her hand for hours as she lay weak and speechless, brought her a bowl of blue hyacinths and was quietly advised by the doctor to get her pregnant again as quickly as possible.

He did so.

Again Kate lost her baby.

Three years later, on 6 May 1960, when Anthony Armstrong-Jones married HRH the Princess Margaret, Toby went to the wedding at Westminster Abbey, saw the royal bride walk gravely down the aisle in her billowing white satin Norman Hartnell gown, then saw her grave demeanour change to happy exuberance at the Buckingham Palace reception afterwards.

Kate didn't go because, although she also knew Tony, she was again in the hospital, recovering from her third miscarriage.

Passing through London on her way to New York, Maxine visited her. Kate lay alone in a very small, very high green cell. A tangle of pipes wound around the walls like serpents. 'Poor baby.' Maxine thrust an armful of daffodils at Kate, then blushing, she realized she'd said the wrong thing. 'What goes *wrong*, my darling?'

Kate sighed and nothing was heard except the grumble of water-pipes. 'The first two were miscarriages at the twenty-eighth and twenty-seventh week, but this one was at the thirty-second week, and it was born dead.' She pulled a face. 'I can't explain how tough it is, how *depressing*. You get the contractions and it hurts like hell and you feel what it's like to be in labour, and all the time you know that there's only going to be a poor little dead body at the end of it.'

'But isn't there some warning? Couldn't you lie down and stop its starting?'

'The first time I started to bleed when I was asleep and *then* got pains and lost the baby. At the hospital they blithely quoted statistics as if they were batting averages. "Cheer up, one in six pregnancies ends in a miscarriage, try again." But I *knew* they were lying to be kind. I knew nearly all those miscarriages would have been before the fourteenth week . . .'

She sniffed the sour, spring-scented yellow flowers. 'No vases left, I'm afraid, darling. I asked this morning. There are never any bloody vases in hospitals.'

'Damn, I forgot. Should have brought you a plant.' Maxine put the flowers in the washbasin as Kate continued.

'The second time was worse. I didn't even have time to get to the hospital. D'you know that if you miscarry you're supposed to keep the foetus and the afterbirth and put it in a clean kitchen bowl or plastic bag and take it to the hospital so that the lab can analyse it and tell you why you miscarried? Neither did I, so it was lucky that the doctor got to me in time.'

'Yes, but *why* do you miscarry?'

'Don't think I haven't asked that. The first time they said that the foetus had detached itself from the placenta, and the second time they said I had a weak cervix because it dilated too early. So I had some treatment for it. But I had exactly the same trouble again this time. Now they're going to give me a D-and-C to clean my uterus out.'

There was a pause, then she added, 'The doctors have quite nicely suggested that we shouldn't bother to try again.'

She lay with her hands limp on top of the sheet and she sounded almost indifferent, but in fact Kate had taken the news very badly – worse than most women, said the doctors, who suggested to Toby that they consider adoption, whereupon Kate had become hysterical and said that he was *never*, *never*, *never* to suggest such a thing again.

'Don't overreact so,' Toby said soothingly. 'It's just because you've never *considered* adoption.'

'I have, I have. Oh, God, yes, I have.' Kate became even more frantic, until a nurse rustled in with a syringe and pushed Toby out.

Kate went home weak, exhausted and unutterably sad.

Toby couldn't understand why she felt such depth of loss, such misery. It wasn't as if she had even held the child that she had just lost. She couldn't talk to anyone, she wanted to be alone, but at the same time she didn't want to *be* alone, and she cried for days.

Toby was comforting, but he couldn't be around much because he was finishing a big job near Swindon – ironically, a children's convalescent home.

It made Kate sad to see her breasts go back to normal size and feel her stomach grow floppy again, when only the month before it had felt hard and firm. She felt again what she had felt at her father's funeral – an odd sense of loss and bewilderment.

What had she done wrong?

She must have done *something* wrong! Why else this perpetual disappointment when she only wanted normal human happiness? Other people had it, why was *she* being punished? Why couldn't she feel, even for a brief moment, that she was a complete woman? Kate distracted herself from her sense of emptiness with a determined round of business entertaining and the more frivolous ambience of the Chelsea set. Her little house was only five minutes' walk from the King's Road, and at least three evenings a week, Kate and Toby would drop in for a drink at the Markham Arms, the elaborate Edwardian pub that stood next to Mary Quant's little shop, Bazaar.

Bazaar was a sort of nonstop, free-drinks cocktail party, to which the prettiest girls in London dragged their husbands and their lovers. As Bazaar had only one minuscule dressing room, the girls all had to try on the clothes in the middle of the shop, where every passer-by could gaze through the plate glass and enjoy the view.

Suddenly, Chelsea seemed to have sprung into fashion as Britain's San Francisco or Left Bank. As its cellars, espresso coffee bars, beat joints, clothes and 'fab' girls were internationally publicized, the little London borough ceased to be a geographical location and became synonymous with a way of living and dressing. Kate loved the excitement that throbbed from the artery of the King's Road into fashion, design and show business; she adored the new clothes and wore skimpy, high-waisted, grey flannel tunics with white knee socks over a scarlet leotard with scarlet vinyl boots. She wore plum and ginger outfits with swashbuckling black leather coats and fur hats as large as those of the sentries outside Buckingham Palace. Outwardly, she looked a Chelsea girl, a dishy bird, challenging, confident, leather-booted and black-stockinged, in the vanguard of the youthquake, which was establishing the fact that the second half of the twentieth century belonged to the young (or so they thought) as they went about the business of trend-setting.

Kate was a little in awe of Mary Quant, a small, redheaded girl who was terrifyingly silent most of the time. She and the other dishy birds, the Chelsea girls, seemed shatteringly sophisticated and *with it*. Beside them, Kate felt hopelessly unbrilliant and untalented. Oh, to have been at art school! Oh, to be able, like Mary, not only to invent but to *wear* with aplomb the Look of the Moment whether it was the Lolita Look, the Schoolgirl Look, the Leather Look or the Wet-Weather Look with yellow plastic skirt and fisherman's sou'wester.

Kate tried. She bleached her hair and had it cut in a sex-kitten tangle of curls and black-rimmed her eyes above pale-pink lip-stick (worn over a white base) and she felt utterly forlorn and unbelonging. She thought of joining Chelsea Art School and learning to paint, she timidly told Toby one evening, as they hurried through a drizzle to the Markham Arms. Toby dug his hands deeper into the pockets of his hair duffle coat, which he wore over black drainpipe trousers and sweater (he dressed like Audrey Hepburn), frowned at his beige suede boots, and said, quite kindly, that he didn't really think Kate had what it *took*.

Then Kate heard that Pagan was back in England and had been for a long time. Kate and Maxine both had heard rumours that Pagan's marriage had broken up. They had both written to her in Cairo and also care of Trelawney and neither of them had received a reply. Kate had heard that Pagan was living in Beirut and vaguely imagined her in baggy pink trousers, munching Turkish delight on a pile of silken cushions. Maxine was far too absorbed in her own marriage and her business to try to track down Pagan, especially if *she* didn't want to keep in touch. If Pagan wanted to see Maxine, well, Pagan knew where she could find her.

Then, one evening, at an art gallery opening, Kate met – and instantly recognized – Phillippa, the long-nosed, ginger-frizzed bridge player, whom Kate hadn't seen since her visit to Cairo. Phillippa was the sort of person who made a life's work of keeping up with people, never allowing them to escape her inexorable

United Nations Christmas cards. She told Kate that Robert had divorced Pagan ages ago and that Pagan had returned to England and buried herself in the country. 'Nobody was surprised when they split up,' added Phillippa. 'Robert was always impossible – that dirty trick he played on you both was absolutely standard behaviour for old Robert.'

'What dirty trick?' Kate was puzzled.

'But surely you know . . . ?' Kate's surprise grew into indignation, then fury, as Phillippa told her how Robert had deliberately separated Pagan and Kate so long ago – and that the whole of Cairo knew of it: you couldn't keep a secret from the servants east of Gibraltar.

Kate instantly guessed that Pagan would be at Trelawney, and suddenly she longed to see her friend again. She longed for the comfortable, noncompetitive companionship of Pagan. Perched on the plastic, inflatable, see-through armchairs that Toby had designed for the art gallery, Kate thought it was like suddenly yearning for a comfy old armchair instead of this tortured balloon she was sitting in.

She would telephone Trelawney tomorrow.

Kate returned from her visit to Pagan's cottage feeling loving and protective and with an object for her thwarted maternal instincts to focus on. She proceeded to spend a fortune on telegrams and was as anxious as any worried mother during Pagan's brief and dizzy courtship. After her marriage, when Pagan came to live in London, Kate found to her joy and relief that their friendship was still as strong as if they had never been separated by miles and years of bitterness. They immediately resumed their odd half-sentence, no-verb, one-word, shorthand conversations, unintelligible to their husbands or to anyone else who hadn't known them for twenty years.

36

JUDY'S phone rang at three in the morning. Sleepily she fumbled for it.

'Did I wake you up?' asked a charming, solicitous male voice. 'Yes.'

'*Good*! Because you *need* to wake up. This is Tom Schwartz of Empire Studios. You've just had the nerve to make a public announcement about one of our major new film purchases for 1963 without so much as *consulting* Empire. Yes, I'm referring to the Joe Savvy deal. Didn't it occur to you that a major studio might like to handle its own news? Or were you expecting thanks for saving us the trouble? Perhaps I underestimate your influence? Does Walter Winchell always consult you first?'

'Look, buster,' Judy said in a sleepy voice, 'you wanna fight, that's fine with me. The most maddening way to end a fight is by slamming the phone down, which is what I'm about to do. I'll come around to your place tomorrow around ten and let you shout at me for exactly seventeen and a half minutes, because it certainly was inconsiderate of me. I'll be wearing sackcloth; you bring the ashes.'

She slammed the phone down, took it off the hook and sank back to sleep.

'Would I have *intentionally* upset someone as important as you, Mr Schwartz?'

For seventeen minutes they had screamed at each other with increasing enjoyment in Tom's elegant office.

'As I've already indicated, I don't give a shit. But if you really want to make amends, you can start by putting your glasses back on your nose so you can at least see the top of my desk. I've seen pictures of you with that little French guy and you were wearing glasses in all of them. A woman who wears glasses for a photograph can't see without 'em.'

Judy fished her enormous, black-rimmed goggle glasses out of her purse, stuck them on her nose, sat up and threw him a hopeful smile. If she deliberately made herself vulnerable, people generally forgave her. But Tom was used to being wooed by ravishing starlets of both sexes. 'Cut it out,' he said. 'Let's stop wasting time.'

After they'd been working together for two months, Tom took her to lunch at Côte Basque and said, 'You're good.'

'I know.'

'I'm good.'

'I know. Together we'd make a great team.'

'Then why not?' Tom leaned over the table and covered her hand with his.

'Then take your hands off me. If you're really serious, you're the one man I'll never go to bed with.'

'With you a little hand goes a long way,' Tom said sourly. 'D'you say that to every man who asks you out to a meal?'

'Oh yes, I always make it clear that it's not because I'm ungrateful for the hamburger. I'm frank, but polite.'

'Then I might as well give up and tell you what we *can* do together. I want to quit my job, work with you and expand your office into a small coast-to-coast public relations business.'

'You *did* say small?'

'Yes. Headquarters in New York and tie-ups with other advertising and PR firms in every major city.'

'What would *they* get out of it?'

'Money. An affiliated office in New York. I've spent the best years of my life touring temperamental film stars for Empire and I know how to do it – which means that the local offices would meet interesting personalities as a change from handling detergent accounts.' Tom signalled for another bottle of Perrier water. 'I want to aim for one-shots as well as permanent clients. I want people to turn to us when their own publicity department is overloaded, or when a star needs special attention; Empire could certainly subcontract to us, if they don't feel too sore when I leave.'

'Why should a star agree to be handled by us?'

'If you try and book a tour from New York, it's mostly wasted effort, because it's impossible for one office to keep in touch with

389

what's happening to the media all over America. But local offices are always up-to-date. They know which guy in town has the most influence.'

'Why me?' Judy asked.

'I've been looking around for someone. You can do it.'

'Would I have to drop any of my present clients?'

'No. They'll be the base we build on.'

'Will I have to put up any money?'

'A little, sure. We'll need money for decent offices and a staff.'

'Then the answer is no, because I haven't any money.'

'I could maybe guarantee a bank loan for you.'

There must be something honest about my face, thought Judy. 'Where would *you* get the money from?'

'I've been investing ten per cent of my income in the stock market since I was nineteen years old.'

'I think the answer still has to be no. I've only just gotten *out* of hock to the bank, and I kind of like sleeping at nights.'

Three years of running her own business had meant three years of constant financial anxiety for Judy. Naturally, she knew how to handle publicity, but apart from doing Guy's simple book-keeping, Judy had never had anything to do with the business world, and it had been a great shock to find that there were people in this world who didn't pay their bills – because they couldn't or wouldn't or never intended to pay in the first place. Twice, Judy had been evicted from her studio apartment for nonpayment of rent. On the first occasion the money she owed had been paid by her former boss, Pat Rogers, who had remained a firm friend. On the second occasion, Pat insisted that Judy hire a new accountant; then she guaranteed Judy a sizeable bank loan and quietly slipped her a couple of minor accounts – a floor polish, and a young, aspiring singer named Joe Savvy.

'No one's going to sack me for disloyalty,' Pat reassured Judy, 'because I've just been offered a job writing features for *Harper's*, so I'm moving back into journalism at the speed of sound.'

Remembering her struggles to repay Pat's loan, Judy shook her head and said, 'No, Tom, I can't join you. I simply haven't the capital.'

'Look, if you prefer, *I'll* lend you the money, Judy.'

'Why should I put up half the money when I've got the clients

390

and you haven't?' A brazen navy-blue gaze flashed at Tom. 'Why can't you just buy my goodwill for, say, twenty thousand dollars?'

'You're joking, of course.' He settled back. She was going to say yes.

They haggled through the vichyssoise and the grilled sole, and eventually, over the honey mousse, they agreed that Tom would buy her goodwill for seven thousand dollars and invest a further four thousand dollars in the new business.

'But we can't continue to trade under your name alone,' Tom said.

'What do you want to call it?'

'How about Local American Creative Enterprise?'

'It's a bit of a mouthful ...'

'Not if you use the initials.'

'L-A-C-E. Neat.'

Even before they'd organized their national network, LACE was showing a profit. 'But I can't understand *why*!' Judy complained one evening in her office, as she and Tom went over the previous month's figures. She had just returned from a thirteen-week tour of the country, during which she had finally decided on the publicity offices she wanted to work with and had come to terms with them. Now she bit her thumb thoughtfully. 'I've still got the same clients and our running expenses have gone up, but suddenly it's paying off. *Why?*'

'Put it down to logic and my twelve formative, predatory years in the motion picture industry,' yawned Tom. 'It's nearly ten. Let's pack it in and go home.'

'I hope you invested your teenage savings in Bell,' said Judy, picking a telephone bill from the top of the pile and holding it at arm's length. 'That would have proved logical.'

Tom yawned again. 'Nobody really operates on logic, especially not a woman. Logic is merely the ability to rationalize what she's going to do anyway.'

'And in a man?'

'Man isn't a rational being either, he's irrationally controlled by fear.'

'Is that why we're succeeding? Because you terrify people?'

'Because I'm prepared to be ruthless, sure. If people don't see you're prepared to be ruthless, they'll take advantage of you. You used to let them, I don't allow it. That's what's different.'

'And your new budgeting system doesn't hurt.'

Tom insisted that fees be billed in advance and paid within thirty days. They didn't lift a telephone until the contract was signed *and* the money was deposited in their account, and they never did two minutes' worth of work after a contract expired.

Tom's responsibilities were to make sure that the business paid off, to run the office and to look after their regular clients. Judy's responsibility was to bring in the business, handle the major one-shot campaigns and supervise their local agencies. Judy also handled the creative work, planning the campaigns, working with writers and designers, which was the part she liked best. Once the general campaign had been mapped out and the design work was underway, Judy sent the proposed plan to her regional directors, who executed the campaign locally. A lot of calls were needed between LACE and the RDs – a twenty-five-city tour needed six hundred phone calls before the tour was over. But the client only made one single call – to LACE.

It was a ridiculously simple idea. And because of that, it worked brilliantly.

~ 37 ~

KATE still faked. Not always, because she could climax with very little trouble if she lay on top for long enough and wriggled herself into position, but that didn't always seem to happen and when it didn't, if Kate couldn't sleep, she would nip into the bathroom and quickly satisfy herself.

But after she and Toby had been married for six years, something horrible happened – and continued to happen for some time.

On a hot August night, Kate lay in bed reading a newspaper account of Marilyn Monroe's sad, tawdry death. 'Oh, dear, she was so lovable and funny.' Two teardrops of sympathy wobbled on her lashes and caught Toby's attention.

'She was beautiful, too ... What long eyelashes you have, Kate.'

'Yes Toby, but colourless. If I didn't wear mascara, you wouldn't be able to see them.'

'Would *my* eyelashes be longer if *I* put mascara on them?'

'I expect so ... darling, it says here that poor Marilyn's feet were dirty and the scarlet polish on her toes was chipped. Oh, how sad!'

Toby disappeared into the bathroom and emerged about ten minutes later. Casually, Kate looked up, then did a horrified double take. '*Toby!*' Toby was crudely and completely made-up, like a raddled old dim-eyed dowager.

Kate said, 'Oh, do take it off, Toby!'

But Toby smiled oddly, looked at her steadily and said, in a disturbing, high, brittle voice (a bit like Pagan's mother), 'No, I want to make love like this.'

So they did.

She didn't mention it the next day, but that evening Toby, having had rather a lot of brandy after the *quiche aux épinards*, said sarcastically, 'I don't think spinach tart is one of your stronger points, darling,' and proceeded upstairs.

When Kate went up to bed with indefinable fear in her heart, she found him lying on their Astrid Sampe turquoise-striped bedspread simpering at the ceiling. His face was fully made-up and he was wearing her fragile, white lace nightgown.

She said, 'Now come off it, Toby, I've had enough of this. Please stop it. Please cut it out.'

But Toby sat up, pouted and said in an odd, little-girl voice. '*Why* can't Toby have nice things like you do?' He pulled her on to the bed beside him and murmured, 'Toby *loves* looking pretty, Toby *loves* dressing up like this, but promise it's a secret between us, between two girl friends? A *very* important secret.'

He didn't take long. It was all over in ten minutes, but it took Kate twenty-four hours to pull herself together again.

And then it happened again, and Kate had another twenty-four hours of the shakes. Inexorably, night after night, Toby 'dressed-up', as he put it.

Within a fortnight, Kate was white and taut from lack of sleep and anxiety, but Toby was blooming. On the following

Wednesday he came back from Harrods with a size 48 sheer black swans-down-trimmed négligé and matching décolleté night-gown.

'I told the assistant it was for my mother,' he said, smoothing it over his lean hips. On Friday night he lashed himself into black garters and fishnet stockings and a frilly black padded bra that he'd bought on Shaftesbury Avenue. On Saturday evening he wore a red satin, wasp-waisted corselet and high-heeled pink pom-pom mules. ('They didn't have my shoe size at Harrods, so I got these backless things, but they're still too small.')

Kate found the situation as macabre and unreal as her father's funeral. The rouged cheeks, ever so carefully shaded peach, seemed to symbolize death. And once again – she was bewildered; what Kate couldn't understand was the *suddenness* of Toby's transformation. He had never given her the slightest hint, had always been so severely practical. He had never so much as worn a frilled shirt to a party, never indicated in any way that he preferred his balls veiled by lace, never by word or deed indicated that he was not a normal heterosexual. Kate had never for one moment suspected that what Toby *really* wanted in bed was this gruesome farce. One week she had had a husband and the next week she had this horror.

She could not understand what was in his mind, could not understand his odd, trancelike state when he was wearing women's clothes. What made it even more confusing was that Toby wore two sorts of female clothing, he seemed to want to pretend to be two different types of women, so poor Kate never knew from one night to the next whether she would find herself in bed with a 1930s lascivious, black-satin, sophisticated woman-of-the-world, or a demure, white-pantied, schoolgirl virgin. When Toby wore stockings and high heels his muscular, stringy calves somehow stuck out sideways below the knees, oddly bandy, not like a woman's but, yes, they *were* like one woman's legs. That night Kate had the nightmarish sensation that the person pant-ing on top of her was her mother-in-law, Major Hartley-Harrington's widow.

Toby refused to discuss the situation, and during the day he seemed to be a different person – that is to say, his normal self. But at night he couldn't wait to get upstairs, sometimes dragging

Kate by the wrists in a steel grip. His eyes glittered strangely in his masklike makeup: Kate thought he looked like a novelette villain. 'You've been reading too much Barbara Cartland,' she told herself. But there was no other way to describe that relentless, breathlessly excited, glassy-eyed expression on Toby's face. Kate didn't understand what was happening and she didn't know what to do.

What *had* she done wrong? Why had this terrible thing happened so suddenly? Was Toby homosexual? If so, why did he make love to *her*? Why should she be so *frightened* of him if he was turning into a homosexual? Lots of their friends were queer and they didn't terrify her as Toby now did. What was terrifying wasn't the makeup or the drag, the padded lace bras, that monstrous red satin corselet or the way he tried to strap his balls away between his legs (no wonder when he wore high heels he walked so oddly). No, what was so chilling was Toby's mincing, simpering, obviously totally sincere mimicry of what he thought a woman was – deep down – really like. It was a travesty, an insult to her sex, and that was what Kate, who had never heard the word 'transvestite', found so shocking.

She forced a scene and Toby threatened to leave.

Kate gave way.

She forced another scene and Toby gently reminded her that she was a thirty-year-old barren bitch, and would she shut the fuck up. 'Oh, aim so sorry, dahling, don't cray, let's kiss and make up, hmmmm? Just a teensy little *kiss*,' he said. And he bent over her and lifted her chin up to his heavily lipsticked mouth. Every pore on his face seemed magnified, as Mrs Trelawney's scalp had been magnified, as the black wiry hair had sprung from her white scalp on that horrible bathroom evening when Kate was still a schoolgirl. Now she saw in similar, horrid, clarified detail the magenta grease that smeared the fleshy cracks in Toby's mouth and clogged the shaven bristles on his upper lip. He still wasn't very good at putting on lipstick.

As her anguish and shame increased, she still hoped every evening that it wouldn't happen that night, that Toby's fixation would disappear as swiftly as it had arrived. Kate longed to confide in someone, to have Toby's behaviour explained away, to be reassured, to hear that everybody did it, that such things were part of a normal phase of a man's development. But she knew they weren't, and there was nobody to whom she felt she could unburden her embarrassing story.

When she suggested talking to their doctor, Toby went white and glared at her, compressed his magenta lips, then sprang at her and twisted her arm behind her back until she feared he was going to dislocate it. Then he violently shoved her down the small flight of stairs that led off their bedroom to the bathroom. Sprawled on the floor with Toby straddled over her in his black fishnets, hands on hips and eyes blazing, Kate promised that she wouldn't tell their doctor or anyone else. Anyway, who would believe her? she wondered hopelessly as she gazed up at lust in action.

'If you *do*,' said Toby coldly, in his normal, masculine voice, 'I shall simply deny it. There's nothing to prove these clothes are worn by me; after all, they're in your bureau.' He heaved pleasurably at the black lace of his corset. He needs a shrink, Kate thought, but she knew she would never dare suggest it.

But she also knew she couldn't stand it. She had to get away from London, away from Toby. Increasingly, Kate felt depressed by Toby's sexual behaviour, which disgusted and bewildered her. She hadn't mentioned it to Pagan at the cottage because Pagan obviously had too many problems of her own to cope with, but when Pagan returned from her honeymoon with glowing descriptions of New York (despite the ordeal of Christopher's heart attack) and an invitation from Judy, Kate decided to go and spend a month there. She wanted to run away and forget her misery for a few weeks.

During the war, when Kate was seven, she had found an orange in her Christmas stocking when nobody in Britain had seen oranges for years. Her father had bought it for a vast sum from a sailor in a pub. Kate could hardly remember what an orange was; like bananas and ice cream, they no longer existed. But obviously Santa Claus did. She'd been having doubts, but the orange proved it. Carefully she sniffed the fruit, dug her nails in the skin, peeled it in one long length; then she took a whole day to eat it, sucking each segment carefully, savouring the fragrant juice that spurted into her mouth. After that she nibbled all the peel and made it last for a week.

To Kate, New York wasn't the Big Apple, it was the Wonderful Orange. She knew London, Paris and Cairo and had expected New York to be another, similar, big city. But New York was like nothing she'd ever imagined. Out of her bedroom window she blew kisses to the city like a child.

Judy made a great fuss over her, gave a party for her, spoiled her, told everybody how wonderful Kate was and suddenly she came to life again. The glittering sparkle and excitement of the city simultaneously soothed and exhilarated her. It was like that shot in the arm they'd given her in the hospital, it made her feel that she could do anything – and made her want to do *something*.

The night before Kate left for London, she decided to tell Judy about Toby's dressing-up. She told Judy the whole story, finally finishing by yelling at her, 'I can't stand it much longer, so *what can I do?*'

After a moment of silence, Kate started crying.

'D'you still do that? Still cry all the time?' asked Judy absent-mindedly, as she thought hard.

'It's a fu ... fu ... fu ... form of self-expression. I lu ... lu ... *like* crying. It lets people know how I feel and it makes *me* feel better.'

'Well, kiddo, get your crying finished and then concentrate. Because I think you should head straight for a psychotherapist when you get back to London.'

'You think there's something wrong with me?'

'No, relax! I merely think that you should discuss the situation with someone who knows what he's talking about. Because you don't, and I don't, and it doesn't sound as if Toby does.'

So when Kate returned to London she visited a psychiatrist in Harley Street. He sat with his hands on his chin in a sage velvet wing chair on one side of the fireplace, while she sat on the other, reporting to him twice a week. The doctor first established that Kate *had* clearly told Toby she hated the 'dressing-up', then suggested that she do so again. Once more Kate hit the bathroom floor. The doctor wrote to Toby and asked to see him about 'a matter that is gravely disturbing your wife'.

Toby flew into a rage as soon as he opened the letter. 'You've told him our secret. I *know* you have. I thought we agreed that it was going to be a secret?'

'It's not my secret – it's your secret,' Kate shouted.

Eventually, Toby agreed to visit the psychiatrist, who later reported to Kate. 'Naturally,' he said, 'I cannot tell you what your husband and I discussed, but he's defiant; my prognosis is not optimistic, in fact, the reverse.'

'What does that mean?'

'I think he will continue this pattern and that he will increasingly take risks. Soon he may wear female clothes *outside* your home. He will take his bra to the office in his briefcase and wear women's underwear under his trousers.'

'What do other wives do?'

'Most don't put up with it, so their husbands visit prostitutes, taking their drag with them. That's one of the things that whores are for.' Another pause, then he said very gently, 'I think you may have to make a decision. Accept it or leave him.'

It took Kate another month of nightly argument and nightly capitulation to the muscular, glassy-eyed virgin or the wide-shouldered, weirdly padded, sophisticated lady before she decided she couldn't stand the dressing-up for the rest of her life. Even if he didn't do it, she would know that it was what he really wanted.

So after a battle over the house – which was in Kate's name – Toby left her, taking the silver, the priapic sculpture, the wire chairs and the more valuable old brass scientific instruments. When Kate miserably visited a divorce lawyer and told him the whole embarrassing story, she was told, to her astonishment, that she'd be unlikely to get a divorce on the obvious grounds.

'You say that he hasn't paraded in these garments before anyone but you?'

'Not to my knowledge. Well, he wouldn't, would he?'

'Then, unfortunately, we have no proof of this distressing conduct. If we had, it would count as mental cruelty, but that's extremely difficult to prove. I don't advise it. I think he must be asked to provide proof of adultery.'

'But I don't think he's committed it.'

'These things can be arranged.'

Toby agreed to provide evidence of adultery, provided that Kate would legally agree never to claim maintenance from him. 'As a matter of fact, I don't think we *could* claim maintenance for you,' said her solicitor and then sighed. 'This is *such* a complicated case.'

'What's complicated about it?'

'Well, you own the house; most women own nothing.'

Telling Pagan, Kate said, 'It costs seven shillings and sixpence for a licence to tie the knot and thousands of pounds to sever it. D'you think that marriage was invented by lawyers?'

When Kate and Toby split up, Kate suffered a violent reaction against pureness of line and the innate structure of an object. Instead, she went in for pink, frilled, gingham curtains, flowered chintz and bird prints. She reconverted the basement back into an apartment and let it at a rental that paid for all the basic overheads of the house. But she was suddenly left without an income once again, so she advertised for translating work in *The Times*.

All their visual friends were astonished that Kate and Toby should separate. Toby wasn't easy, but hell, who was? He had a perfect eye for proportion and was certainly heading for success, had just been appointed to his first committee. As she couldn't tell them what the trouble was, Kate poured her overburdened, indignant heart on to paper and posted it to Judy. From her letters, Judy sensed Kate's depression and wrote back that she was worried in case free-lance translating at home would be too lonely an occupation at the moment, when she thought Kate should be getting out of the house and meeting new people.

'Why don't you try writing in English for a change?' Judy suggested. 'You've been translating books and articles for years now; you and Toby seem to know a lot of journalists, so why not ask one of them to help you? Write a couple of articles about design and designers and get somebody to look at them. Just take a deep breath and telephone all those feature editors on Fleet Street. They can't eat you, they can only say no.'

So Kate telephoned, and all the feature editors said, 'What ideas have you got?'

'When?'

'Now.'

'Oh.'

'Submit a couple of ideas in writing and we'll let you know.'

So she did, but nobody seemed to want them. Then, at a party, she met the art editor of *House Beautiful* and she started to write captions for the magazine. She was paid very little but was glad of the chance to learn to write as a professional. After six months she submitted a few more ideas to Fleet Street and was commissioned to write two of them – a piece about pop art in the home and another about a new firm that had invented a way to reproduce very convincing 'antique' statues in reconstituted stone, complete with lichen stains. After that she got the hang of what was news. Anything that anyone had already read wasn't, no matter how interesting. Kate then interviewed a couple of designers in their homes and again the articles were printed. So she sent in more ideas, each one just three lines on a single sheet of paper, with her name on the top.

Then, one evening, Judy telephoned and said that she had arranged for Kate to interview one of her clients, a once fairly famous ballerina, now over the hill, who was heading for London.

'*What?*' Kate squeaked with horror. 'You wouldn't *dare!*'

'Why not give it a try?' New York sounded faint, a million miles away. There was a transatlantic hiss, then Judy shouted, '*I'll kill you if you don't, after I've fixed it.*'

'I'll kill you if you *do*,' yelled Kate, 'and she'll kill both of us.'

'No, she won't. Remember that Joujou knows nothing about London or anyone in it. Or anything else. And as a matter of fact she's quite fun.'

'Well, what would I do? How would I go about it?'

'Just ring the Ritz and make an appointment with her secretary. I've told her you work for the *Globe*.'

'*But I don't!*'

'Then avoid saying that you do. But they're expecting you to telephone and for Chrissake act cool. Don't let Joujou guess it's your first interview. She thinks you're a top magazine writer, and I've seen enough top magazine writers to know that you could be.'

'*But I can't!*'

'Where are your British guts? The Dunkirk spirit? The anatomical area that we Americans label your backbone? Stop dithering and just get on with it, Kate. What's so terrible about failing, anyway? Not that you *will*, Kate.'

Judy's bark sounded faint, but Kate could hear that it would be infinitely less alarming for her to face Joujou than to face Judy if she didn't. After another expensive pause, Kate capitulated.

Wearing a pale-pink, moon-girl, thigh-length Courrèges tunic dress with shiny white vinyl boots, Kate sat on the edge of Joujou's bed, notebook open. She felt breathless, dizzy and apprehensive. Now more of a TV glamour personality than a ballerina, Joujou had beautifully streaked blonde hair and very good skin: she had looked thirty-five for twenty years. The picture of domesticity, she sat demurely in a persimmon brocade armchair, glasses at the end of her nose, delicately dipping into a little sewing kit. She was mending some love beads that had been torn off in a brawl the night before.

The bed was littered with diamonds and date-stamped photographs of jewellery. 'I have to have photos because it's a rule in the States that you've got to prove you've taken them out when you bring them back,' explained Joujou. She nipped into the bathroom, shed her caftan for a towel, returned, swept Kate, the diamonds and the photos off the bed and slid on to it herself. A masseuse started to attack Joujou's right calf. Without being asked, Joujou disclosed that the secret of life was not to look too thin or too young and never to nag. 'Every man I meet who wants to marry me says, "Joujou, I used to love my wife, but she nags me so, and after a day at the office I can't take it anymore." Ze *ozzer* zing zat men love is to enjoy their meals, so they can't stand women who are dieting under their noses. And a woman can't be too thin if she wants a good face, so she has to choose. I am eating my ass off, but carefully.'

Joujou recalled occasions only by the dress she had worn. What happened when she met General de Gaulle? 'Oh, I wore my brown lace.' How did she like to spend her day? 'Shopping. Always. Me and clothes, it is a love affair. I have brought twenty-eight feet with me,' she said, jumping up from the bed and shunting Kate into her dressing room. Exquisite garments hung on coat hangers from a twenty-eight-foot length of clothes rail.

'Not much when I travel. I prefer to be chic, not showy,' explained Joujou, 'I buy everything from Christian Dior, my favourite dressmaker. What size? I'm size eight, dahleeng. Well, maybe size nine, no, to be honest, I'm a ten.' She held matchless,

pale-grey chinchilla in front of her towel. 'I have the most beautiful clothes in the world. That's why I work, to pay for them. But
because of the work I don't have enough time to shop. I don't
have time to try them on, you see.' She cast a speculative look at
Kate. 'You should never go alone to shop, you know. They
persuade you into buying things that are bad for a big ass – I have
a big ass and so do you swidhart, never mind, the men love it.'

Another speculative glance, then Joujou said in an offhand
voice, 'You are lucky, you are my size.'

Kate looked surprised. 'But I'm a size twelve, and only that
with difficulty,' she said.

Joujou looked carefully at her. 'Well, try some of my clothes.'

She was right. They were the same size. 'Now we can buy some
more clothes for me and *you* can try them on,' explained Joujou.
She immediately phoned the Christian Dior boutique and asked
them to send around a selection of 'appearance clothes'. Kate
struggled in and out of them in the sweltering hot bedroom, while
Joujou lay back on the bed, having her cellulite massaged away,
and bought the lot.

Then the phone rang again. Joujou listened and then said
coldly into the mouthpiece, 'I've *never* had a facelift. I started to
sue that columnist Suzy for a million dollars because, of course,
I've never had anything lifted, but who the hell has time for a
lawsuit?' She crashed down the telephone receiver and gave a
loud snort.

Kate instinctively recognized a good wrap-up line and shut
her notebook. Judy had warned her not to stay too long. She
waved her thanks to Joujou, dodged past two hairdressers and out
into Piccadilly. The roar of London's traffic was peaceful compared to Joujou's bedroom.

~ 38 ~

LILI lay slumped on the slimy, seaweed-covered rocks. Her legs
and arms were bleeding, her wet hair was dripping over her
shoulders and what remained of her pink dress concealed very

little of her nubile, seventeen-year-old body. Against the blue Aegean sea she looked exhausted, but not quite exhausted enough.

'Cut,' said Zimmer, 'and watch that eye, Lili.' Lili's left eye squinted slightly when she was tired.

'I'd like to try one more take before the sun gets too hot, please,' said Zimmer. 'Remember that you're nearly dead; you can hardly move, you've just survived a shipwreck.'

Please. That summed up the difference between Serge and Zimmer, she thought. Zimmer didn't treat you like a lump of meat. He was always courteous, encouraging, thoughtful no matter what was going wrong on the set – and something was, of course, always going wrong. If Zimmer stopped to work out whose fault it was, the argument would be endless and they'd never get started, so he just smiled the tight, little smile that was his danger signal – a gentle nodding of the head that indicated a sort of internal prayer, 'God give me strength to deal with this situation.'

Zimmer's polite consideration was a carefully acquired working habit, especially useful when working with women. He knew very few men who were really kind to women unless it was part of their job. But the way to get the best performance out of a woman, whether it was in the kitchen, the bedroom or on the set, was to praise and reassure while still remaining authoritative.

It was important to remember that an actress probably had no self-confidence, however cool she looked, so her confidence had to be built up. In a word, he had to give her the maximum possible attention. The average woman needed twenty-five hours a day of it, and if she could get a bit more, she'd try for it; but in return for that you would get the average woman's maximum performance.

There was a great difference between handling men and handling women. Women tried harder. Zimmer had seen women slumped and exhausted because they'd been up since five in the morning and it was now eight in the evening and they had to come to life again in front of the camera. And they could do it every time because, though they lacked the physical stamina of men, they had terrific reserves of determination. The actresses who succeeded were the ones who had a little luck and tapped that extra determination – but they all lacked confidence, poor cows, and they all needed reassurance. Zimmer doubted whether there was one really *happy* actress in the world. The responsibility and the sheer hard physical work finished them: by the time women were starring, they were terrified of losing their looks; once they reached the top and realized the insecurity, they could never believe they had made it. They always felt – and rightly – that they were walking a tightrope.

Lili was determined, she was a worker and she was a beauty, but she'd end up like the rest of them. That much he knew.

'Cut. Okay, print it. That's all until three o'clock, kids. When you've freshened up, Lili, would you mind coming to my trailer please? I want to discuss the beach scene with you.'

For nearly two weeks the cast and crew had been stationed ten kilometres outside Athens and Lili had yet to play one scene decently dressed. Still, it was a change to wear *any* clothes. Tying the sash of her blue cotton kimono, wet hair flopping down her back, Lili flung herself into a canvas chair in the shade of a silver-grey olive tree. She looked down over the little sandy beach. Aquamarine water lapped over the rocks off the cove. At the back of the beach, where sand mingled with scrub, some fifty people were gathered around cars and trailers. Carrying scripts and clipboards, wearing floppy cotton hats and sunglasses, gleaming with suntan oil, they moved slowly about their business. Lili could see Stan Valance arguing with Zimmer. The ageing American actor's face was lean as a skull – she'd never come across anyone who was on so strict a diet: the man never ate anything except *biltong* – thin shreds of dried beef that he had specially imported from South America. He chewed it like tobacco.

He had a remote manner and didn't waste an atom of energy talking to anyone on the set except Zimmer.

At three o'clock they shot the beach scene. Lili played a rich, spoiled, turn-of-the-century cruise passenger, and Stan Valance played the stoker who had just hauled her to shore from the shipwreck.

'Take your hands off me!' she spat at him, as he painfully

dragged her out of the water by her armpits. She jerked her wet arms away from Stan's lean grasp and lay, exhausted, in the foam. 'I can swim perfectly well,' she panted. 'I could have made it on my own!'

She tried to stand, then a look of surprise came over Lili's face as she found that her trembling arms wouldn't support her body, and her head fell forward on to the wet sand. Wordless, gasping for breath, Stan grabbed her hands and tried to pull her clear of the water. With difficulty, Lili lifted her face and through gritted teeth said, 'Don't you *dare* touch me!'

Her voice made it clear that Stan was a servant and a man, and that she wore only the wet, torn shreds of her nightgown. With those five words, Lili managed simultaneously to convey exhaustion, indomitable, spirited arrogance, and shocked, virginal modesty. She also looked extremely sexy.

'Cut!'

Later, in the darkness, Zimmer and Stan Valance were watching the rushes.

Suddenly Stan leaned forward and said: 'Shit, the cunt can *act*!'

The following morning Valance waited until Serge was out of the way and then ambled over to Lili's chair under the olive tree. He didn't waste words. 'I knew Marilyn, kid, and I've worked with them all, Joan Crawford, Vivien, Liz, you name it, and I'm telling you – don't sell yourself short. You've got what it takes ... The way I used to.'

'You really think so?' she looked up eagerly, her eyes shining.

'Sure thing. Whatever you're doing, it works. So don't let anyone change it. And don't take any shit.'

He means Serge, Lili thought, as Valance sauntered away. Serge never left her for a moment when she was off the set. This was just as well, because Lili needed Serge. She needed him because of her notoriety and her own reaction to that notoriety. Success had made Lili feel that she was merely a property that anyone could exploit or sneer at; success had made Lili feel humiliated. She could no longer shelter behind anonymity; sometimes she felt that everyone had seen the famous calendar and those horrible films. People looked at her nervously – women with unconcealed envy, men with a hard appraising stare. Lili grew increasingly paranoid. She could no longer buy a bunch of flowers from a street vendor without wondering whether he'd seen that calendar, wondering whether he knew what she looked like naked, wondering whether he'd recognized her, whether she had lubricated his dreams.

Eventually, she avoided such small human contacts; she rarely walked in the streets. She ordered what she wanted by telephone or asked Serge's new secretary to get it for her. Her insolent self-assurance was merely a pose to hide her uncertainty. When she was with people she didn't know, her manner was abrupt, awkward, rude. Often she would say something foolish, immediately regret it, then, to cover her embarrassment, say something worse.

Her mistakes were gleefully repeated around Paris and printed in the gossip columns – often inaccurately – which only increased her fear of people. Time and again her trust proved mistaken; people were nice to her only because they wanted something – and suddenly so many of them wanted something! Her autograph, her photo, her telephone number, buttons from her coat, hair torn from her head, interviews ... Strangers whispered that they had wonderful ideas for her; well-dressed, charming women invited her to endorse sweaters or deodorants, even a vibrator. Swift-talking, plausible men tried to get her to sign papers without reading them or tried to get her into bed, certain that she would agree. ('Well, darling, what difference could just one more make?')

Serge, with his easy self-assurance, found Lili easy to exploit and naturally did whatever he could to increase her lack of identity and consequent dependence upon him.

Serge's new secretary opened Lili's mail and answered the telephone. Lili herself stayed all day in the smart white-and-glass apartment that Serge had bought in the rue François I. She stayed there alone. Serge wouldn't even allow her a kitten because of his hay fever. He now wore Cerruti suits and was always out, too busy to be with Lili, huddled with advertising men or businessmen or directors or lawyers – cold-eyed men in dark suits with briefcases who looked at Lili with tight smiles and eyes that remained carefully blank. She was not a person to them. She was a deal to be made, an asset to be handled with care, 'meat on the hoof', as one agent said. Handling Lili was a major job.

Serge was no longer as indulgent with her. Lili was now safely tied up so he didn't have to bother with her needs or problems; his secretary got Lili everything she needed within a certain budget (Serge didn't want her spending a fortune on Yves Saint Laurent), and frankly, Lili bored him now. She was nearly eighteen, but an ignorant little bitch – it was lucky the school inspectors had never caught up with him – and if it weren't for the money he would have dumped her long ago. A man could get tired of even the most luscious pair of tits, especially when they belonged to an uneducated, unsophisticated little girl, who whined for attention like a kid.

Slowly, Lili felt Serge's growing lack of interest in her. She didn't understand – she didn't *want* to understand – the reasons, but it was obvious that she exasperated him and he no longer wanted her around. On the other hand he wouldn't let her set foot outside the front door without him.

Lili was puzzled and anxious. If she didn't *belong* with Serge, then she belonged nowhere, she had no place in the world. For nearly five years, Serge had told her what to do, what to say, what to wear, how to behave. Lili was terrified that he might tell her to go, as he sometimes hinted he would if she wasn't obedient.

'And just remember you were *nothing*,' Serge would snarl, snapping his fingers under her nose, '*nothing* before I found you. And without me you'd be nothing again!'

Q was premiered in Paris just before Lili's eighteenth birthday, and in spite of the fact that it was a low-budget film with a meagre publicity allowance, the movie was an immediate hit. At the premiere Lili smiled triumphantly at the flashguns, her head held high as she posed in a cream silk tuxedo, matching pants and a see-through, cream voile shirt, which demonstrated her new star status while by no means hiding the reasons for it.

After fighting their way through the crowds to return to their hired limousines, the stars, the director, the producer, the backers and the show's press agent headed for Chez Lipp, where theatre custom ordained that you should wait amid the engraved mirrors, the gilt and the red velvet for the next day's first editions – and the reviews.

Since the budget didn't run to the large chunk of extra money that Stan Valance demanded to attend the premiere, Lili got most of the attention. Escorted by Zimmer, still wearing his tight, grim little grin, Lili smiled, while the police formed a cordon around her until she was able to scramble into the limousine.

'You must practise getting in and out of cars slowly,' Zimmer commented. 'Always move *slowly* in public. If you want to be a great star, you need more than good looks and talent, you must have style and class; you should always look in public as if you were being helped out of a Rolls, not running for a bus.'

As the limousine nosed out of the crowd, Zimmer turned to Lili, his face alternately shadowed and lit by street lamps. 'Lili, I want to tell you two things, one of which is none of my business,' he said. 'I was surprised to find how good you really are. You've got a natural instinct for the camera. You respond to it as if you were in love with the damned thing. And you listen to direction, you really *listen* to what I'm saying. You don't just wait until I'm finished and then tell me what *you* feel should be done. You've got the makings of a good actress, Lili. Provided you work with good directors.'

He rested his left arm along the back seat and was silent for a moment, then he continued: 'I can't help wondering if poor Serge knows the difference between a good director and a second-rate one. A second-rate director will spot the obvious things about you, but he'll probably miss the wistfulness, the fragile charm, that hopeful trust that you project. But those are the magic qualities that will keep you a star, Lili.'

As the limousine crossed the Pont de la Concorde Zimmer sighed. 'Now we come to the part that's none of my fucking business,' he said. 'Christ knows why I'm telling you this, because I'm careful not to get involved in other people's lives, but do you know that we paid you a fee of twenty thousand dollars, to a Zurich bank? Of course we had to pay a lot more to get Valance, but we needed an international name. Now, I can't help wondering how much of that money you're going to see? Christ, Lili, why don't you get *away* from him? You don't *need* the bastard.'

'Yes, I do,' Lili said, suddenly sad. 'I'm afraid without him. That's why I need him. He's the only ... family ... I've got.'

'That's why you cling to him – for security. But you'll never get security from Serge,' Zimmer said. 'Look, it's only natural to be afraid. You're still in your teens. You've been through rough times. But you'll never develop into anything until you get away from him. He *wants* to keep you dependent on him. That way, you'll be frightened to leave.' He patted her shoulder, and sighed again as they drew up outside the Lipp brasserie.

Outside there were more flashguns, more photographers, a little burst of spontaneous applause from the other diners as they slowly moved to their table, where champagne was waiting in a silver bucket and a huge bouquet of lilies was surrounded by telegrams.

With a bow, Zimmer handed the bouquet to Lili, saying, 'From tonight, Lili, you will be famous.'

'I wish I felt famous inside,' she said in a perplexed voice, as she hugged the lilies. 'Inside I just feel worried.'

'That's understandable after the tension,' Zimmer said fondly, 'and you're anxious about the newspaper reviews. You'll soon get over that. Just remember, you're going to be a *star*. I don't need to see the reviews to know that. You wouldn't remember Elizabeth Berner, but she had a fragile charm with heart-rending appeal. You found yourself holding your breath as you watched this vulnerable little waif on the screen. She had the sweet sadness of a rose petal fluttering to the ground. And you have that same delicate quality, Lili.'

'I'm no rose petal,' Lili said.

For the past three months, Lili had listened very carefully to what Zimmer said – in fact, she'd got into the habit of trusting him. So after the party, Lili pondered his advice. Twenty thousand dollars was a fortune – it would buy her a house of her own, maybe even a little car. Then she could learn to drive. Serge wouldn't let her drive his new Mercedes.

In the chill grey dawn, as they undressed, she casually asked Serge, 'How much money did they pay for me to make *Q*?'

'Jesus, what a question to ask at this hour! You're going to be

409

the toast of Paris today after those reviews, and all you can think about is money!'

'Yes, but how much?'

'It all depends on whether you're talking net or gross, and *you* don't even know what the fucking words mean, Lili.'

'What I would *like* to know is the *total* sum that Zimmer paid to you. That's gross, isn't it?'

'Christ, it's six o'clock in the morning, Lili! Don't I do enough for you? Aren't I even allowed to sleep now? *Get to bed* or I'll beat the daylights out of you. We've got to be on a plane to London tomorrow evening, and you start shooting the day after, so sleep while you can. You look after your side of the business and I'll look after mine!'

'Serge I want to *know*. Did they pay twenty thousand dollars?'

The flat of his hand hit the side of her head. Systematically, Serge hit her so there would be no bruising, but he didn't hold back. He put all his considerable strength into each blow.

Lili fell to her knees. Seeing her on all fours, sobbing with fear and humiliation, Serge couldn't resist a kick in the ribs as he snarled, 'All you got going for you, kid, is me and those boobs. You lose me, you're nobody.'

When she opened her eyes it was nearly midday and she was in bed. Her head felt as if it would burst apart. Along the passage she could hear Serge chatting with his secretary. It was no use, there was nothing she could do. She was now as frightened of living with him as she was of living without him. There seemed only one way out. She staggered out of bed towards the fluttering lace curtains of the open window.

~ 39 ~

JOUJOU was the first article that Kate sold to the *Globe*. Kate's tongue-in-cheek interview was given half a page, and the *Globe* immediately asked her for more articles. Kate started to free-lance for the newspaper, aware that when Scotty, the feature editor, phoned with an assignment, she had to drop whatever she was doing and run. When Scotty asked her for ideas he expected six good ones within half an hour and if following up one of them meant sitting up all night, then that was what she did.

What Kate at first thought to be the brusque, unfriendly atmosphere of the vast, cream-painted, windowless editorial floor of the *Globe* turned out to be one of concentration against the constant noise of typewriter fire, teletype clatter, telephone chatter and the pressure of deadlines.

As Kate had no training or experience, Fleet Street life was tough for her. Everybody was working against a deadline and there was no time to explain things to a beginner; either you were right or you were out, and anyway beginners weren't supposed to start on Fleet Street. Kate learned by listening to the other desks to cultivate a good telephone voice. She learned to keep her notebook always within reach, never to alter a quotation and to check, check and check again.

Scotty was unusually kind as well as fast, funny and deadly serious. Kate was devoted to him. Once, when he found her rewriting an article for the ninth time, he patted her shoulder and said, 'Nobody's piece is ever perfect. Just try to get it as good as possible under the circumstances and then sling it in. And remember it's *not* your piece – it's a team product and you're only the beginning of the chain.' Again he started to chew his horribly maimed pencil.

Kate knew that she was lucky. In her first year on Fleet Street she often worked from eight in the morning until eleven at night because she hadn't yet discovered how to take shortcuts. She loved the calm, fast world of daily papers, she loved the excitement, the knife-edge deadlines, and she loved working for the engaging, humorous Scotty, who protected her, encouraged her, egged her on and ruthlessly cut her copy.

One spring morning in 1966, Kate was called to Scotty's panelled office. Against the right wall, at chest height, stood a ten-foot-long sloping shelf upon which the newspaper layouts could be spread. Scotty never sat at his impressive mahogany desk, he always lolled by the board, scribbling, or propped himself against the board as he talked. A stream of feature writers was always shuffling in and out, lining up if there were others ahead of them.

That morning the *Globe* had run Kate's interview with an Israeli tank commander, General Nakte Nir. Talking to this hero in the lounge of his modest London hotel, Kate quickly realized that someone must have put her name on the wrong press list. Nonetheless, the article had turned out well – she was coming along very fast.

'Sit down a moment, Kate,' Scotty said. 'The editor liked your piece this morning.' He gave her an odd look. 'D'you faint at the sight of blood? Have you ever slept in the open? Could you leave home for a month? D'you want a permanent job on the *Globe*? We're thinking of sending you to Sydon.'

'But there's a war going on!'

'Shrewd girl, very observant. We've already got a couple of reporters there, but we want something different from the stories they're sending back. We can get all that stuff from the wire; we want a few unusual feature articles.'

'But I've never . . . Yes, Scotty, of course. When?'

'There's a flight this evening. Five p.m. check-in at Heathrow. Change at Rome. Don't take too much gear, travel light, just pen and clipboard. Remember we don't want *any* woman's page stuff. We're not sending you out for the woman's angle. The editor is sending you out because we want background material from someone with a fresh eye. And don't forget to fill in your expenses properly,' he said. 'I'm sick of rewriting them for you.'

Kate hurried to Gamage's in Holborn and bought a pair of sneakers, a groundsheet, a backpack and a water bottle that could be slung from a waist belt. There wasn't time to buy anything else, in fact, there was just enough to telephone her mother and ask her to look after the house. Then there was an exasperating wait for her visa at the Sydon consulate in South Kensington. Luckily, it was only five minutes from home, where she had ten minutes to pack before catching a cab to the airport.

The plane landed a couple of hours before dawn, then there was a six-hour drive in the battered little airport bus to Fenza, where the *Globe* had reserved a room for Kate. It was not very clean, and there was no hot water. Nevertheless, Kate fell on to the hard bed and slept until noon when, following the hall porter's directions, she headed for the press centre, in the bar of the converted Majestic Hotel.

It was the first time Kate had been in a city at war, unless you counted the London blitz, and she'd never been in the centre of London during a heavy raid. But Fenza, near the front line, was a city that had already had the heart torn out of it. It was almost deserted – looters were shot on sight and anyone who could flee had fled. It was impossible to drive because of the debris that blocked the streets: walking was dangerous because a wall might topple on you at any minute.

Kate hurried through the blackened exhausted town. Defying gravity, wrecked buildings leaned drunkenly over the forlorn rubble-filled streets. A bed hung, the ludicrously striped mattress still on it, from the wrecked upper storey of a house that had no front, patterned wallpaper hanging in strips from the broken walls.

Kate smelled the heavy odour of charcoal from burned wood beams and window frames as she picked her way around piles of sandbags, ragged heaps of bricks and plaster, hurried past a broken-spoked bicycle that lay in the road among fragments of smashed furniture, past a burned-out car, and finally past a gutted truck lying black belly up on the sidewalk outside the semiderelict Majestic Hotel.

The next day she was up at four o'clock because the bus left at five. To Kate's astonishment, large buses were used to take the press corps up to the front, as if they were on a church outing. Under clear blue skies, it was hot as they bumped into the beige desert. The grit quickly got everywhere. Kate could feel it in her head, in her hair and eyes, under her eyelids, down her bra and in her pubic hair; she itched everywhere.

Kate's neighbour in the cigarette-stinking, dusty bus said, 'What's happening here isn't just one lot of Arabs fighting another lot of Arabs; it's really the Americans playing Sydon against the Russians playing the Saudis; all the equipment that's been captured was manufactured in Russia.'

The weary-looking man in fatigues who sat on Kate's other side explained, 'Sydon's only a little country, but it's got those southern oil fields and that's what everyone wants, so any excuse will do to invade the place. Officially, Moscow has refused to interfere in the battle for the oil fields, but that's mainly because the Kremlin doesn't want to provide a pretext for an American initiative in the area.'

The man sitting in front of Kate clearly thought that the *Globe* was mad to send her. 'I suppose they haven't sent the fashion editor or the gardening editor out with you?' He growled. 'War isn't the game they seem to think it is . . . *bang, bang*, you're dead, then get up for nursery tea.' He twisted around to glare at her. 'It's dirty and bloody disgusting.'

He gave her a cold look of disapproval and then added, 'Somebody should tell your editor that the Sydonian men won't let their women go to war because of the rape and mutilation. You don't want a hand grenade stuffed up your er . . . or suddenly find that your breasts are being cut off. And if you're a correspondent, you've got no protection whatsoever. No correspondent ever carries a gun.'

They jolted on in silence.

The distant thunder changed to a nonstop, ear-splitting crack as the bus bumped closer to the front line through a harsh giant wasteland of ankle-deep dust and faded, grey-green scrub. Heavy fighting had scattered the desert with damaged tanks, twisted wrecks that once were jeeps and burned-out trucks stuck head-first in deep sand drifts. The gunfire noise was painful.

As they got out of the bus, a bomb hit a Sydonian field gun and another hit a truck that must have been carrying ammunition, for it began to explode by itself, a stream of noisy stars. Planes flashed overhead, the ground shuddered and heaved with the concussion of the blast. Under heavy shell fire, upended, sparkling orange chandeliers streaked to the ground around them.

The front line straggled, it hid, it stopped. It was a series of little, dusty, khaki groups moving forward while other little groups tried to stop them, as men crept or dashed, bent double, from bush to bush, moving forward yard by yard. Corpses dotted the sand, flung down as if they were sunbathing with their clothes on. There was a stink of rotting flesh – although the Sydonians removed their dead every evening, they left the enemy corpses where they lay.

The sharp, acrid stink of cordite hurt Kate's nostrils and her throat. The flames and hellish cries frightened her ears and eyes. It was difficult to see. Kate crawled forward on her hands and knees through a pepper-coloured mist, peering through it to the thick ochre fog beyond, hazily striped by billowing plumes of black smoke from burning tanks and overturned trucks. She was terrified.

Two weeks later Kate had changed. Instead of being nervous, tense and anxious, she was simply too busy to be neurotic or afraid. She was on her own for the first time in her life. There was no one to tell her what to do, no one to criticize her, no one from whom to seek approval. Kate alone had to decide what to do and how to do it, and survival, as well as success, depended upon her decisions.

Kate found this situation curiously exhilarating. She was thirty-four years old and she felt fifty, but the concentration that was necessary to do her job blotted out all the feelings, even the constant exhaustion. Kate now easily understood how war photographers took what civilians called 'crazy risks'. They probably didn't notice them; there wasn't time.

The press corps weren't at all what Kate had expected. A serious, exhausted air hung over them at the Majestic bar, everyone looked under strain and nobody got drunk. There simply wasn't time. No one made passes at her; they were all too busy and too tired. Like them, Kate became wary, furtive and untrusting, guarding a possible lead as if it were a map of Treasure Island. Like theirs, her head never stopped thinking, speculating, plotting, interviewing, translating, drafting copy and sending it off. She set off at dawn, never knowing whether she would get a story, and thought herself lucky if she'd dispatched one by ten at night.

She concentrated on reporting the effects of war on human beings, perhaps in a town that was being bombarded, perhaps from the battlefield, using her interpreter – Ali, a twelve-year-old boy who had been to missionary school and pretended to be a lot older than he was and know a lot more than he did – who trotted along behind his white woman like a devoted dog.

'Where King, Ali?' she said sharply one evening, as they stood in front of the Majestic. 'Much, much money for Ali if Missus see

King.' What Kate most wanted was an interview with Abdullah, and she didn't realize that this was impossible because nobody had told her that the King didn't give exclusive interviews, only an occasional press conference.

For two days there had been a lull in the fighting. After initially being taken by surprise, the Sydonian army had forced the Saudis back east, towards the border between their two countries. They had pulled back behind a line of low hills that lay between the front line, now thirty kilometres east of Fenza, and the border, which was another forty kilometres beyond it. For two days, nobody had known the whereabouts of King Abdullah. He had been at the front line leading his troops, but now he seemed to have vanished.

'King in the eastern hills with the Hakem tribe.' Ali beamed. 'Now, money please, Missus.'

'But the eastern hills are behind the enemy line.'

'Yes, Missus, but enemy still in Sydon.'

'How do you know, Ali? I'm not going to pay you until I know it's true.' It was one of the rumours floating about, but Kate wasn't paying for rumours.

'I take Missus there,' offered Ali.

'How can you? We haven't got a car, and we can't take a jeep farther than the front line because the Saudis would immediately fire on it!'

'Jeep to front line like last time, then hire the camel of my cousin,' said Ali airily.

Camels! thought Kate. They might not fire on a woman and a boy and a couple of camels ... What was an expense account for, she thought, and started to argue with Ali about the cost of a jeep and two camels.

The next day it took two hours to get to the front in the fly-ridden, buzzing, shimmering, sandy heat, along a track marked by empty gas cans, past which their outrageously expensive jeep jerked, bumped, bucked and bounced. Kate hung on to the wheel with both hands, binoculars bouncing painfully against her breasts. Her stomach had been upset since the day she arrived, and now she felt as if she was going to be sick as well, as they passed burned, blackened corpses, twisted like overdone kippers. They bumped past a hut for collecting the dead, then the field hospital that lay ahead of it. At the hospital, a doctor and two orderlies were kneeling to attend to the wounded, and flies hung in a black-peppered cloud over men who lay silent, near dead, or screaming in agony. There was a sickening stench of flesh and blood as their jeep lurched past.

Finally, Ali pointed to what had once been a small hut and was now a crumbling heap of rubble with a few gaping holes. Bullet scars on the dirty white walls testified to close fighting. The green, tattered shred of the Sydonian flag still hung from one wall.

'Here?' said Kate, incredulous. 'Missus see no camels here!'

'Here wait for cousin,' said Ali firmly, so Kate stopped the jeep. For a moment she didn't move, so great was the relief after the shaking jeep, then she climbed down and walked towards the hut, followed by Ali. Two Sydonian soldiers smoking cigarettes leaned against the broken entrance. She waved and they all grinned at each other, then Kate climbed over the rubble and went to where she saw a third soldier lying on his stomach, keeping watch through a gaping hole in the wall of the hut.

Suddenly Kate's gut rumbled again and she shot out of the semi-ruin. Oh, the humiliation! It was the water, the other reporters said, but she couldn't clean her teeth in beer. Wet with sweat, she didn't care that Ali was trotting along behind her as she scrambled for shelter behind a little heap of rubble and squatted to relieve herself. Then, unbelieving, she saw the sand flicking up in spurts around her as hot, jagged shrapnel fragments flew through the air. A ping on her helmet made her flinch, and she wanted to fling herself down and hide. She held both hands over her helmet, crouched lower and groaned.

Suddenly the hut in front of her seemed slowly to collapse to the left. Kate yanked at her jeans and, zipping up, ran back to what was left of the hut.

The three jolly soldiers at whom she had been waving were just empty bodies. One lay spread-eagled on his back, disinterested eyes staring at her, his stomach spilling red, glistening snakes.

Frozen with horror, Kate heard noises and shouting from beyond the hut. She was terrified, but in a quick instinctive movement, she crouched and grabbed an assault rifle from the hand of one of the corpses. She had to untangle it from his limp arm. Just get the gun and then crawl up over the rubble, keeping your head down, she thought. Christ, I hope what's left of these walls isn't going to cave in. She carefully checked to see that the weapon was cocked.

She heard scrabbling sounds from the other side of the rubble and suddenly her backside felt naked and vulnerable. Oh, Christ, suppose someone came around the back and shot her up the ass.

Now she could hear heavy breathing, gasps and a grunt as someone scrambled up the rubble in front of her. Then, like a khaki egg, slowly, the rounded top of a helmet appeared. Fraction by fraction it rose, then a dirt-streaked brown forehead appeared over the broken bricks. Kate saw two young, surprised black eyes under heavy eyebrows as she gently squeezed the trigger.

The face exploded into a carmine hole, then disappeared. She heard noises on the rubble outside. Oh, God, was that more of them, she wondered, or was that the one she'd just shot? She waited, tensed and grim, ready to shoot again.

But the enemy hadn't expected to find anyone alive in the ruin, and the two remaining soldiers swiftly scrambled back towards their own line.

Kate heard nothing. She lay, waiting, unable to take her eyes off the top of the rubble, oblivious to the fact that she was lying on top of the soft, warm shreds of a body. Then, from behind, she heard Ali call softly in his singsong voice, 'Missus, Missus! Bad man all run away!' He stumbled towards her.

Kate was shaking. His eyes. He'd looked right into her eyes and then she'd shot him. For nine months his mother had carried him; for years she had cared for him and loved him; and now in ten seconds Kate had just destroyed somebody's son Those surprised eyes had looked into hers and she'd just squeezed. No doubt he would have shot her first if he'd had the chance, but Kate knew she had just taken a life and found it a terrible thing to think about. She sat staring into the rubble, agonized, ashamed of what she'd done, sternly reasoning with herself (Be sensible, it was him or you), then weeping as she thought of his family and then of Nick.

Ali fidgeted behind her, not understanding why she was upset. 'She one good Missus, she kill Saudi soldier!'

Two hours later, much to Kate's surprise, they saw three

specks on the southern horizon that in due course turned out to be a very old man riding a mangy camel and leading two more. Much money changed hands – three hundred and twenty dinar, which was enough to buy camels, rather than hire them. More money was offered, but the old man refused to accompany them. He hissed at the camels to couch them, helped Kate on to the carpet-covered leather saddle, and hissed again for the camels to rise. Then he handed a thorn stick to Ali, nodded and remounted his own camel, which started to lurch south again.

'What did he say?' Kate asked Ali.

'He say camels back here in one day or Missus pay more money. He say Western machines no good for desert, camel still goodest. Camel eat very little, only drink once in five days, carry big loads.'

'You're sure you know where you're going, Ali?'

'Yes, yes, to the hills, Missus.'

They lurched off under the hot sun. At first Kate thought she was going to be seasick; she'd never be able to stand it, this awful, heaving gait, but after ten minutes she found it quite soothingly similar to a rocking chair.

It got hotter and hotter as they made their leisurely way over sand, thorn bushes and withered, grey grass, heading for the low smudge of hills now visible on the horizon.

As dusk fell they reached the lower slopes and shortly afterwards found themselves lurching along the bottom of a small boulder-strewn ravine. 'Now Missus in eastern hills.' Ali beamed. 'Now Missus find King.'

'No. Ali take Missus to King,' said Kate sharply.

Ali stopped beaming and looked rather frightened. 'Ali know King in hills, but Ali not know where belong in hills.'

'But, Ali, you said you would take me to the King's camp!'

'No, no, Ali say Ali take Missus to eastern hills.' Ali now looked sulky.

Kate was aghast. The trip had taken far longer than she had expected, it was too late to turn back, Ali obviously had no idea where he was and they were behind the enemy lines.

'Couch my camel please, Ali. We'd better stop here for the night. It's so dark I can hardly see you.'

Ali hissed at Kate's camel, which took no notice of him and continued to amble along the rocky bottom of the ravine.

'Ali, stop this damn camel!'

Suddenly, there was a slither, a click, and shadowy figures sprang out of the darkness. One of them tugged the camel reins away from Kate and she found herself looking into the muzzle of a submachine gun.

Through sobs, Ali answered in Arabic the questions that were spat at him from the darkness. His hands were tied behind his back and he was roped to Kate, whose hands were also bound. There was a muttered discussion and then, still roped together, they were roughly prodded over the ravine and then along a narrow path that led upwards, then downwards until Kate lost all sense of direction.

Suddenly, they turned around a bend in the hillside and moved downwards into a shallow, bowl-like area covered with low, black goatskin tents. After a muttered discussion outside the tents, Kate and Ali were roughly shoved inside by their captors, and Kate, to her astonishment, found herself pushed on to her knees in front of a man she knew. Although she had never seen him wearing white desert robes, Kate couldn't mistake that lean, hard face.

'Suliman Hakem!' she said, astonished.

Her first feeling was relief that they weren't in enemy hands, swiftly followed by the sharp realization that Suliman was never more than two steps away from Abdullah.

'What are you doing here?' Suliman asked sharply, in English. So he also recognized her, Kate thought.

'I'm a newspaper correspondent. I was looking for King Abdullah, because . . . I have a private message for him.'

'How do we know that you are not spies?'

'If someone could untie my hands, I'll get my press pass out of my pocket.'

Kate's hands were not untied, but a man emptied her pockets and Suliman Hakem studied her press pass.

'How do I know this isn't a forgery?'

'If you'd only get a copy of the *Globe*, you'd see my printed copy and by-line and my photograph,' said Kate, thinking that a nearby newsstand was rather unlikely.

Suliman barked a few guttural words. Their hands were untied and they were pulled to their feet. 'You'll be returned to Fenza at dawn, under escort,' Suliman said shortly. 'Your camels and the boy will be cared for. Think yourself lucky that the sentry didn't shoot you.'

As he strode out of the tent in his flowing robes, Kate found it hard to believe that this man had attended one of the world's smartest boys' schools and that he had been trained at Sandhurst.

A moment later Suliman swept back into the tent. 'You will be guarded all the time you are in this camp. Now you will wash and eat.'

By herself, Kate was led to a small tent and a guard was posted at the opening. A bowl of water and a cloth were brought to her, followed by a boy in a white robe who carried a tin jug of water and a tin tray piled with rice and chunks of roast lamb. Kate suddenly realized how hungry she was, as she sat cross-legged in the carpeted tent, eating the food with her fingers. Through the slit, Kate could see the moon casting black shadows over the silver sand, and beyond the flames of a campfire she could see the necks and swaying heads of a camel herd silhouetted against the sky.

After she had finished her food, two more guards suddenly appeared, wearing white flowing robes and red, black-banded headdresses; each man carried a rifle in his hand and a curved scimitar at his side. They said nothing, but jerked their heads towards the tent slit. Kate rose and followed them into the night, past yellow circles of light around campfires that cast shadows up into the lean faces of the shaggy-haired men who surrounded them.

She was led into a tent thirty feet long. Richly patterned carpets had been laid on the desert sand and heaped with tasselled cushions upon which, alert and straightbacked, sat King Abdullah. He gestured to the guards and they withdrew, leaving Abdullah and Kate alone.

Self-assured as ever, Abdullah's watchful eyes moved warily, arrogantly. His tawny skin was stretched tight over the bone, his winged black eyebrows rose above a nose that curved like a falcon's over his wide mouth. He looked at her and said in a deep voice: 'How the hell did *you* get here, Kate?'

She told him as quickly as she could, thinking that he looked older, grey and tired, which wasn't surprising.

'You're very lucky,' Abdullah commented shortly, when she had finished. 'And so am I, to tell you the truth. The damned Saudis haven't made a move for the past few days, so all we're doing is waiting for them, and that's a boring business. A surprise visitor is very welcome ... Although you're not looking quite your usual soignée self, Kate.' He grinned at Kate's dirty khaki jacket and trousers, her grubby sneakers and her tousled hair.

'You realize, of course, that this is a private and personal visit,' Abdullah continued. 'I can't discuss the war or politics or there would be trouble from the press corps. You may describe this place vaguely and say that I am firmly confident and looking forward to victory. And we will, of course, check your copy.' Then, looking out into the night, he casually asked, 'How is Pagan?'

Kate told him all her news, including the fact that Pagan was expecting and that the baby was due in a few months. Abdullah gave a curiously grim smile. 'Yes, I knew about that.'

There was an uneasy pause. 'How old are *your* children?' Kate asked.

'Mustapha is four and looks just like me. He's a naughty little devil, always up to some wicked trick – lots of guts.' There was another pause. 'Of course, I'm sorry I haven't more sons.' He corrected himself: '*Legitimate* sons. After all, I've been married ten years. But I'm lucky to have Mustapha. My wife had a miscarriage shortly after we were married, followed by a still-born daughter the following year. Then in 1957 she had a premature son who died two weeks after he was born.' He scowled.

Kate could only stare at him, remembering her own miscarriages.

'Then nothing happened for four years. In fact, I thought of taking a second wife – as a Moslem, you know, I'm allowed four wives. I realize that in the West this would be thought barbaric: your menfolk prefer several wives in succession instead of simultaneously, as we are allowed in the East. Anyway, I eventually took my wife to a clinic in Lausanne where they found she had a malfunction in the fallopian tubes. Fifteen months after the operation, she gave me a son, an heir.'

Abdullah suddenly remembered that as the child was placed in his arms, it gave a lusty yell, and much to Abdullah's surprise, he felt a flood of warmth, a choking feeling in his throat. Instinctively, at that moment, he had known that he would do anything for this imperious, tiny creature. The baby's crumpled face had turned from white to pink to an odd lavender shade as it cried. Abdullah had roared with laughter, hugged the tiny creature to him, gently kissed the soft black down on the top of the fragile head, and for the first time in his life, he felt love.

'Now I pray to Allah to send me more sons,' Abdullah continued. 'I visit Serah's quarters regularly. She's had another checkup at the clinic and apparently there's no reason why she shouldn't have more children. But she hasn't ... Anyway, let's stop talking like a couple of midwives!'

So Mustapha is the only person on earth that Abdullah really loves, Kate thought.

'What exactly are you doing out here, Abdullah?' Kate asked.

'You'd better say that it's one of my routine visits to the Hakem tribe,' he said. 'I'm going to tell you nothing of value to the enemy. But I regularly visit the more important sheikhs. We recruit our toughest soldiers from the desert tribes, not from the cities.' He gestured towards the tent opening. 'Tonight those men will sleep on the sand protected only by their cloaks. Bedouins are tough, they scorn comfort, they have only contempt for the outside world and its mechanical marvels.'

'Except for pistols, rifles and transistor radios,' commented Kate.

'Agreed, but they like to live with the minimum of possessions. A family might have a couple of camels, perhaps a few goats, a tent, a rug, knives, leather buckets and a rope. That's all they need and all they want.' He grunted. 'I promise you, Kate, I often wish I could spend my whole life among tough, simple men like these, in the desert.' He looked across at her and grinned. 'Now you'd better get back to your tent. You know what a fearful reputation I have, and you're going to have a tough day tomorrow.'

Kate didn't realize that she had achieved the impossible – which apparently included riding a camel through a minefield – until the following evening after she had been returned by jeep to

Fenza. As she walked into the Majestic bar, the other journalists clapped quietly. Just as well nobody told me it was impossible, thought Kate, or I'd never have tried to do it.

She started her article 'A Day of War' with a description of the battlefield after the fighting had finished. '*A sea of white papers fluttered over the ochre sand. Even before the vultures could get at them, Arab scavengers had looted the dead bodies, ripped off the watches and torn through the wallets, looking for money. Pay books and other documents had been thrown out on the sand. Love letters that yesterday were precious, photographs of girls, wives, children, parents – all smiling up at no one.*'

Scotty was delighted with her copy. 'I *said* we'd get something different from her and she comes up with an exclusive on the bloody King!' He turned to his secretary. 'Send her a cable straightaway. *Congratulations Abdullah Scoop Big Kiss Scotty Globe.*' He continued to read Kate's copy. 'Jesus! I didn't tell her to kill anyone! Better rewrite it in the third person. Correspondents aren't supposed to carry weapons. Maybe we'd better recall her before she gets into trouble.'

The article was syndicated worldwide. It told a receptive audience, quite simply, that war was about killing people.

～ 40 ～

WHEN she returned to England, Kate found herself something of a curiosity, if not a minor celebrity. Christ, she looks awful; she's lost a lot of weight, thought Scotty, and gave her a two-week leave. She decided to spend it in New York with Judy.

Judy had now started to publicize books and celebrities, as well as fashion, and she had obviously prospered in the past couple of years. Kate looked around the airy living room of Judy's new apartment, which hung high over East 57th Street: that Bokhara rug must have set her back about seven thousand dollars, she thought. Opposite her, Judy leaned back with her arms behind her head in a bronze upholstered chair with curving serpent arms, the wood inlaid with ivory. She said, 'The next thing you've got

424

to do, Kate, is a book. You've achieved a certain fame, but it won't last long unless you keep it going. A book is always good for prestige, if not always for the bank account. Did you keep a diary during the war? And all your notes? Well, turn it into a book – something slim – say around sixty thousand words. You stay in bed tomorrow and write the synopsis, then I can look at it when I get back in the evening ... *Of course*, you can write a synopsis! Sit down right now and write three simple sentences saying what the book is going to be about.'

After a moment's thought, Kate fished a notebook out of her cigar-brown Gucci tote bag, did as Judy said, then tore off the page and handed it to her.

Judy beamed. 'Great. Now just expand those three sentences into a synopsis and split it up into chapters. And I'll let you practise being a famous author by taking you to supper.'

Kate had the talent all right, thought Judy, but she couldn't seem to channel it by herself. She needed someone to give her that push *up* instead of the push *down* that the men in her life seemed to have given her, although Judy had to admit that Kate sat up and begged to be kicked in the teeth. Still, she seemed a lot more positive than on her previous visit.

The following evening Judy fiddled around with Kate's synopsis, altered the pagination slightly and then said, 'Fine. This I can promote. We'll call it *One Woman's War*.' She pulled a little gift-wrapped parcel from her purse and tossed it to Kate. 'A present.' Kate caught it with one hand, opened the Tiffany box and saw a two-inch-square navy-blue leather case, inside which was a small square, golden, navy-blue enamelled alarm clock.

'That's so you can start writing the book the morning after you get back to London.'

'But I don't have time,' protested Kate, 'and my job takes all my energy.'

'Set that thing for five in the morning, fix yourself a cup of instant coffee and type for two hours before going to the office *every single day* ... No, not when you get back at night, because you'll be stale ... All right, all right, you can have Sundays off. But if you knock out a thousand words a day you'll have finished it, allowing for the rewrite, in about four months.'

*

425

Starting a book wasn't easy, because upon Kate's return to Britain Scotty worked her hard. One morning she answered his summons to find him standing in front of his work shelf, scowling as he groped around with one hand for his heavy, black-framed glasses; he never wore them for reading or writing, but he couldn't think without them. In intensely cerebral moments he polished them, so when you saw Scotty whip his glasses off his nose, fish out his grubby handkerchief and start to rub his glasses, then you knew that he was about to say something that would shake you.

'I want you to stop being a bloody celebrity and get down to interview work again. I don't want you typecast in khaki battle jacket. Go and see this woman who's just been found not guilty of murdering her transvestite husband. Seven hundred words.'

Aghast Kate looked at Scotty. 'I *can't*.'

'Why not?' Scotty turned his attention to the page in front of him. Kate supposed that she had no real reason for not covering the story – it might even help to get it out of her system.

Kate's book was published in June 1967. There were simultaneous editions in Britain and in the United States, where Judy was going to promote it.

Kate turned up late one night at Judy's apartment in New York. She headed for the tub and disappeared in a warm fog of Chamade, snorting, 'Those swine at the airport! When I told them they'd lost my special television wardrobe, they merely handed me a form to fill in and then presented me with a toothbrush and two pairs of paper panties. Not really enough for "Today".'

'Oh, I don't know,' said Judy, pulling a notebook from the pocket of her purple Courrèges pants suit as Kate submerged completely and lewd-sounding bubbles rose from the tub. When the dripping head reappeared, Judy started to scribble a list. 'While we're making life miserable for those incompetents at Kennedy, let's buy you some stuff for the road. We'll go shopping tomorrow, and remember, the less you buy the better. A couple of lightweight dresses for the South and for evenings: one good suit with at least seven blouses because you won't have time to wash one out every night. Make sure they're polyester, not silk, so you can hand-wash them in the hotel basin. And get some junk jewellery and scarves. Margot Fonteyn tours with hardly any baggage, just one black suit. In between interviews, she sits in the back of the limo, turns the collar up or down, undoes a couple of buttons, pulls some pearls or a scarf out of her tote bag and manages six entirely different looks in one day.'

There was an anguished cry from the tub. 'Are you trying to make me feel inferior before I start? I am not a prima ballerina. I'm here to talk about a war. People won't expect me to look like a fashion plate.'

'Yes, they will,' said Judy earnestly. 'All those women are going to remember what you wear. If you can't get your act together, why should they listen to you?' She shook more Chamade into the tub and added, 'As for feeling inferior, wait until you get out West to the body-beautiful belt – perfectly capped smiles and twenty-four-hour immaculate hairstyles. We don't want confidence to melt at that point, do we?'

Kate scowled and slicked her hair back, reaching for the shampoo. Judy squinted at her. 'Hold your hair back again. At least when your hair is wet we can see what you look like. Kenneth can cut it tomorrow. Tell him to get the hair off your face so that we can see those green tiger eyes.' She dodged a wet sponge. 'Christ, it's just like being back at school. You should also take one comfortable pair of low pumps and a large box of Band-Aids. On tour you have to look after your feet like an infantry man.'

'Anything else?'

'Vitamin pills, some eyedrops if you don't want bloodshot eyes after long flights, and a stick of men's deodorant. Those studios can get really sweaty.'

'Well, you needn't bother to get my suitcase back from Mombasa or wherever it's gone,' said Kate clambering out, 'because there's nothing like that in it. I brought rather stately, royal-tour-type clothes. I'm glad I lost them.'

'What you've got to realize,' Judy said, handing her a towel, 'is that you've really got to make a constant effort to look good for every goddamn minute of this tour.' Kate scowled, and Judy yelled, 'It costs a minimum of two hundred bucks a day to keep you on the road, so you better look like a million dollars.'

427

On 5 June Kate left on tour. At home, Judy suddenly stopped brewing her breakfast coffee and turned up the radio. 'Lightning attack by Israel caused severe Arab losses and capture of territory, mainly from Egypt and Jordan.'

It was the first radio report of what turned out to be the Israeli-Egyptian Six Day War.

Judy immediately realized that *One Woman's War* was going to be a best-seller.

'Just to bring you down to earth,' scowled Scotty, when Kate returned to London, 'let's see how you tackle a tits-and-ass story.' So Kate was sent to interview a continental teenage starlet who was making a film in Britain, an updated fairy story that was being shot in the New Forest, Hampshire.

At first light, Kate was waiting on the set in the cold, damp forest clearing, heavily wrapped up against the weather, sniffing the autumn reek of wet leaves. A yellow trailer was parked under the trees, and suddenly, in the doorway, stood the most ravishing little creature Kate had ever seen. Lili's hands were pushed deep into a dark fur coat with upturned collar, under which she wore picturesque rags that had been carefully slashed to show as much of her body as possible.

Kate caught her breath – Lili really was exquisite. She had flawless olive skin, huge dark eyes, an almost perfect profile. Even Lili's back view was entrancing, thought Kate. When she threw off the fur coat, ready for action, a black, silk curtain of hair hung down past her ribs, stopping just above the tiny waist. Her exquisitely modelled buttocks and satin thighs were visible under those ridiculous rags as she walked towards the clearing. A fawn-like innocence emanated from her, as if she might melt at any moment into the misty forest behind her.

On the set, Kate hadn't expected to feel anything except cold, but she was awestruck by the quietly magical quality that seemed to radiate from Lili as she moved, barefoot and graceful, through the forest.

They had very nearly finished the movie, which was well over schedule and budget. Everyone except Lili seemed to be strained, bad-tempered and bitchy. The director was only speaking to the cameraman through his assistant, and most of the company were not speaking to each other at all. In between takes, wardrobe rushed forward with a bowl of hot water in which Lili put her frozen feet until the company was ready for the next take.

Later, in the trailer, Kate interviewed Lili, who spoke good English. Serge had insisted that she learn to speak fluent English and ride a horse – both important, he said, to a movie career. Lili was composed and quiet when answering questions about her acting.

'How do you start to interpret a role?' Kate began.

'Oh, I don't think of it that way, not at all. I just read the part over and over again, until I know how I would behave if I were that character. I ... brood over it ... until it's obvious how that character behaves, and then suddenly, I feel that I *am* that character, and the character then becomes more real to me than my real self. I've always playacted this way since I was a little girl, so it's not difficult for me.'

Lili looked wary when Kate started to question her about her notoriety and asked if she enjoyed being in the limelight. 'Of course not, but this thing is part of my job, so I do it,' Lili said, speaking accurately but with a heavy French accent.

'I hate these unpleasant things that are printed about me. I cannot bear what the newspapers say – always I am in bed with this man or that man. They just write lies. I would never get any sleep if I slept with all the men I am supposed to.'

'You mean you *don't* enjoy being a celebrity?' Kate asked. 'You don't enjoy heads turning in restaurants, people recognizing you at airports, kids asking for your autograph, all that stuff?'

'If you think that is enjoyable, it is only because you have not experienced it,' Lili said in an earnest voice.

She became a little agitated as Kate started to probe into her private life and ask questions about her first public appearances. Kate had taken Lili's cuttings envelope out of the *Globe* library, and finally she produced early photographs of Lili in the notorious see-through communion dress.

'You can't expect to do this sort of thing and get good publicity.'

'Those photographs were taken when I was thirteen; I did as I was told. I expect *you* did, when you were thirteen.'

'But why did your parents allow it?'

'I'm an orphan, I ran away from my foster parents because ...

they beat me,' Lili said, as Serge had taught her. Then suddenly she added, 'As a matter of fact, I was pushed into it . . .' And for the first time, she found herself describing that first long-ago photo session in Serge's Paris studio.

As Lili spoke, Kate saw the helpless girl-child, saw how easy it must have been to exploit her timid vulnerability. She sensed that while Lili seemed surrounded by care and attention, in fact, she was only getting it from people who were making money off her.

'But don't you have any friends?'

'Not me, I don't have time.' Lili sounded resigned. 'But Serge knows *lots* of people.'

The last thing Kate had expected to feel for a sexpot starlet was affection and pity.

'Get cracking, I want that piece in by five o'clock,' said Scotty. Kate sat down, hashed it out and handed it in with half an hour to spare. Scotty quickly scanned her copy, then gave an exasperated groan. 'I can't use this in the page three slot! This hearts and flowers stuff won't sell newspapers.' He read aloud: ' "Strangely insecure and unsure of herself . . . quivering like a deer ready to dart back into the forest . . ." For God's sake, Kate! Let's see your notes.'

He looked at them and grunted. 'Give this stuff to Bruce, he's just got time to do a rewrite. He can do this stuff in his sleep!'

The article started, ' "*Always I am in bed with this man or that man*," said Miss Muck, known to the porn trade as Lili.' It was a scathing attack; contemptuous and – apart from the starting sentence – more or less accurate. Unfortunately, it was accidentally printed under Kate's by-line.

'Nice,' said Scotty. 'A real killer.'

Kate hit the roof. 'Why was it run under my by-line?'

Scotty shrugged his shoulders. 'You know these things sometimes happen on a daily.'

'See what happens if you're interviewed without me?' Serge sneered angrily. 'This English cunt tied you up in knots! You can't do a goddamn thing properly by yourself, whether it's giving an interview or jumping out of the window!'

'I didn't jump!'

'No, but you were going to in Paris if I hadn't come in and grabbed you from behind.'

Serge threw the newspaper to the floor of their hotel bedroom and poured himself another whisky. 'Why can't they give you a full ice bucket? Even at the goddamn Dorchester!'

He stood looking out over the treetops of Hyde Park, watching the wet traffic slowly pass in the lamplight beneath him, ghostlike in the light London fog.

'You know your problem, Lili? You're fucking stupid. You don't even know who you are unless I'm around to remind you.'

'No,' said Lili sadly, thinking of *vraie maman*, 'I don't know who I am.'

'Well, you'll never be able to stand on your own feet unless you find out, and until that day – you *need* me baby! In the meantime, just remember that you're now a high-class act, so start behaving like one!' He picked up the crumpled copy of the *Globe*. 'You *must* have said it, it *sounds* like you, "always I am in bed with this man or that man", Christ, you stupid bitch!'

'She's left out parts of what I said. I didn't mean it that way. We were talking for over an hour in the evening and I find it so tiring suddenly to talk English all the time.'

'But all this about the see-through communion dress! You sound like something from the gutter, a crude little whore.'

'Well, aren't I?' Lili was getting exasperated.

'What's the point of staying in the best places, buying you the best clothes, angling all the publicity to your acting, if you let some smart bitch of a journalist say that you're just a cheap pair of tits?'

Serge looked at her in disgust and drained his glass. 'Even if it's true,' he said, 'it's bad for business.'

By 1968 'Swinging London' was in full swing. Fashion was suddenly one vast fancy dress party. The miniskirt had given reality to lustful, commuter dreams. Women dressed as tattered gypsies, Indian squaws with leather forehead bands and frizzy hair, fantasy female cowboys with fringed buckskin hot pants, wagon-train settlers in patchwork or as flower-sprigged, straw-hatted milkmaids. Laura Ashley made a fortune. Carnaby Street was fantasy land, where once-staid British businessmen now bought their tight-assed bell-bottoms, velvet three-piece suits, flowered shirts, rainbow sweaters, high-heeled boots, necklaces and even handbags.

London was a boom town and the stock market was soaring. Kate had eventually persuaded her mother's lawyer to change stockbrokers, her persuasion having consisted of a list of share comparisons over the previous ten years and a threat to take the matter to court on the grounds of gross negligence. Having had to study the figures herself, Kate finally became intrigued by them and decided that she might as well play the stock market on her own. She borrowed from her bank, using her house as collateral, took a quick, lucky plunge into the Australian nickel market with Western Mining and found that she had made more than two years' salary in one month.

After that, Kate had no time to think about anything except her work because Scotty gave her a new job. On the theory that nobody does much on Sundays and therefore there isn't always much news on Mondays – which meant a dull paper – Scotty gave Kate a new section to edit, called 'Life & Style'. It was intended to cover the whole frenetic new scene and the people who were making it. Kate knew little about editing, but she had now been working for Scotty for five years and she took to it quickly, working far into the night, arguing with Scotty over the content, the photographs and the articles. She no longer had time to leave the office during the day. She sat in a small, windowless cubicle behind a large desk with five telephones in front of her. Her secretary and three assistants were located in further little cubicles, opening off the corridor. Kate planned, argued, listened and gave briefings. She cut copy and dealt with crises and problems.

'Life & Style' was a success from the first day it was published. Advertisers lined up, the section was immediately copied by all the *Globe*'s rivals and women wrote to L + S in droves.

'You've hit on a winning formula,' Scotty told her one night. 'It's about time you had a night on the town. Me, too.' He reached into an inside pocket of his jacket. 'Hunter Baggs has just bought a vast house in Campden Hill and he's giving a party tonight. I can't find it, but the invitation promised a fantastic housewarming or something like that. Why don't I take you?'

So they ate supper at San Freddiano and arrived at the party around eleven that evening. Lights beamed from uncurtained windows, cars swarmed around a pillared porch and the noise was like being on a battlefield again.

Once inside the door, Kate blinked. It wasn't a fantastic party, it was a fancy-dress party – but a bizarre one. Several showgirls wore pigtails, short gym suits, frilly panties, black stockings and garters. A nun wore a long black habit that was slit to the thigh, revealing fishnet stockings and frilly red satin garters as she danced with a youth who wore only a golden G string and a halo around his sprayed golden curls.

A lethal champagne cocktail was being served from a big silver punch bowl by their host, who was dressed as Count Dracula, immaculate in tuxedo, red-lined cloak and vampire teeth. He said, 'Hello and welcome, darlings.'

'Hunter, what *is* this?' Scotty asked.

'Don't you read your invitations, darling?' asked Baggs pleasantly. 'It said "Dress as your own favourite sexual fantasy," and as you see almost everyone has.'

He waved a hand around the entrance hall.

Kate looked around. Two lady SS officers danced together wearing black peaked hats, black shirts, black tights and jackboots. There seemed to be a great many black leather garments, whips, see-through plastic macs and the odd brandished dildo. A few men wore an old grey mackintosh, sockless shoes and a furtive look. A couple of devils danced with two black bunny girls in thigh-high satin swimsuits with little white cotton tails.

'Why don't you go upstairs?' suggested Baggs. 'There's a poker room, a roulette room, a blackjack game and a blue-movie room with a water bed.'

A tall, familiar figure dressed as a schoolgirl whirled past Kate, and – feeling slightly sick – Kate saw that it was her former husband, Toby.

Kate said to Scotty, 'I think I'll give it a miss and turn in early.'

As she walked towards the entrance she almost collided with a beautiful girl in a white lace catsuit who was angrily saying to her escort, 'No, sorry – I have to put up with this sort of thing in my work, but I'm damned if I see why I should do it in my free time!' She tossed her luxuriant dark hair, which fell to her waist from a demure white lace cap tied under her chin with a satin bow.

'That's Lili!' The whisper ran around the huge hall, 'That's Lili, that's Lili.' The girl in white walked out into the night.

~ PART EIGHT ~

～41～

'I'm surprised that you ever *managed* to lure a man in here,' Maxine sniffed, 'or that any man manages to find his way *out* of this mess. You're a closet magpie, Judy! You've never been able to throw anything away. You're a thirty-five-year-old pack rat, that's what!'

'Well, I guess that's because it was a long time before I *had* anything to throw away! And please remember that my bedroom is also my *working* area. This is where I read, brood and scheme, as well as sleep. It's where I make my money, Maxine!'

'You always realized that money was important, Judy. It took the rest of us longer to learn.'

Maxine stood up and opened the doors to the two walk-in closets that separated the bedroom from the living room. One of them was entirely full of shoes and the closet looked like a jewel box.

Judy said, 'Real protection isn't a man – it's money! That's what gives you the power to do good, the power to be bad, the power to stay or to leave.'

Maxine peered at shoe shelves, which were lined in crimson moiré taffeta. 'Most women prefer not to think about money. They think that dealing with money is tedious.'

'Not so tedious as being without it, and only if you haven't been taught how to handle it,' Judy replied sharply. 'We should *all* have been taught how to earn it, how to make it, how to multiply it, how to *keep* it! But women are merely taught how to spend it. And when there's trouble, few women have any money, *that* I have noticed.'

Maxine agreed. 'When a couple split up, the woman gets possession of the children, but the man gets possession of the money. Of course that is exactly when a woman realizes the importance of the stuff.'

She examined the scarlet shelves – different ones for low pumps, for high pumps, for delicate sandals, for low-heeled boots and for the rows of high-heeled boots in tinted suede, supple as gloves.

'Having money isn't important, but *not* having money is vital,' Judy added.

'You may know a lot about money, *ma chère*, but you don't know much about the trappings of wealth.' Maxine looked around the room again. Nobody was allowed in Judy's bedroom to tidy up, so it was in a permanent state of chaos. The two bedside tables were covered by stacks of magazines, yellowing newspapers, books and legal pads. All the other flat surfaces, including the window ledge, were piled high with antique tinware, souvenir ashtrays, unframed paintings, last year's New Year's cards loudly hailing 1968, and fading Mexican paper flowers.

'Most people never get beyond the living room,' Judy apologized.

Maxine sniffed, picked up one of the legal pads and sat on the edge of the bed. 'A little organization is needed, *ma chère*. No, I promise I won't throw anything out, but we put it all in different places. Now you don't need three guest bedrooms, do you?'

'Well, yes, I do. That's one of the reasons Tom wanted me to get a bigger apartment: this is our entertainment base; we put up a lot of people from out of town – our regional directors – and sometimes they overlap.'

'Why not try having only two guest bedrooms and a study with a convertible sofa? I'll make a list now and we'll go to Blooming-dale's tomorrow before I go on tour. At least your closets are tidy and your clothes are cared for.'

'Yes. Francetta doesn't care much for scrubbing floors, but she's a marvellous maid, and her husband does the heavy work on his day off.'

Maxine picked up a lavender silk pump with a single feather curling across the instep. 'Handmade in Florence, I see. Your business seems to be doing as well as ours. Isn't it wonderful to sleep at night? Sixty-six was an even better vintage than '64 – which was the year that really put us on our feet.'

'Oh, this money doesn't only come from LACE, it's the result of Tom's speculation. I have terrible anxiety attacks about it, and as a matter of fact I *can't* sleep at night. It's different for Tom – he can be objective about it, but I *can't*.

'I've tried and tried to live with it,' she continued, 'because Tom seems to need the thrills and suspense of speculation the way some people need to ski down mountains or climb up them. He says he needs the adrenalin charge.'

'Good heavens, you mean Tom is a gambler?'

'I say he is and he says he isn't. He says that every business move is a calculated risk, but gambling is for idiots who believe in luck. Oh, no, he disapproves of gamblers.'

'Then in what way does he speculate with such danger? Has he always done it?'

'No, because his wife couldn't stand it. Hell, a lot of people invest on Wall Street, Maxine, it might *not* be dangerous. I just don't know. But what he does goes against everything I've been brought up to believe in. Not being in debt, always saving a little ... My mother thinks the two most obscene words in the English language are "credit card".'

'But I couldn't move around Europe without a credit card!'

'My mother doesn't move around Europe.' Judy moved to the window and looked down over the park. 'To tell you the truth, it scares the hell out of me.'

'... Remember what Edward G. Robinson's Renoirs fetched?' Tom had asked in the quiet of their office the previous night. 'No, I'm not buying Impressionist paintings because it's too late for that. But the point is that if you buy the best there's always *someone* who will buy it, if you need to sell. The best is always in short supply ... Anyway, I hope so, because we have just acquired a T'ang horse. Yes, an eighth-century Chinese ceramic horse about eighteen inches high, sort of earth-coloured ... No, you can't, it's in the bank vault ... It's acting as part collateral for the loan that helped to buy it. For God's sake, what's the difference in principle between buying that horse and the office building mortgage, or the land near Houston? Except that we can't rent a T'ang horse out for grazing?'

As Judy saw it, LACE was the puny, endangered base that all this borrowing rested upon, and however much Tom stabbed his index finger at the balance sheet, she couldn't fight her childhood indoctrination to the point of seeing their increasing wealth as reality. LACE was a real business, the rest was just figures on paper. She remembered the fight they'd had when the LACE bank loan crossed the half-million-dollar mark and Tom had merely said, 'Grow up, Judy, no business or fortune can be started today without getting into debt – and it's only the first fifty thousand that's hard to borrow.'

But what worried Judy most were Tom's commodity speculations. In the last few years he had staked their hard-earned profits first on cocoa, then on sugar, while Judy lay awake nights wondering whether they were going to be stuck with a warehouse full of the stuff. As a matter of fact, Tom also occasionally lay awake at night, because he'd started to buy on margin and that was very different from his more cautious stock market investments. But he was lucky and prices moved up – cocoa by twelve per cent and sugar by nineteen per cent – within a month of his buying. With the profit, he went short on cotton and long on cocoa again, and lost on cocoa and made a killing on cotton. By the time he plunged into soy beans, he no longer took much notice of what he called Judy's 'irrational fears' and made a profit of thirteen per cent within six weeks of his purchase. After that, he mainly speculated in cocoa and sugar, on the whole with great success.

Judy explained all this to Maxine and added, 'He wasn't like that to begin with. A couple of times during our first business year we weren't able to meet the rent payments, so Tom always took his figures along to the landlord before the payment was due, and he never got thrown out, as I did. *That* I could understand, but at the end of our second year – when he bought cocoa on margin and it paid off – d'you know what he did? He bought our office building, using the cocoa profit as a down payment! From that moment I felt strangled by the debt around our necks.' Judy sighed. 'The worst part is that I can't talk to anyone about it. You must remember that it's a secret, Maxine.'

'Once you tell a secret to another person it no longer is a secret,' Maxine pointed out. 'Is this apartment paid for?'

'Yes, I *insisted* on that, and to my surprise Tom didn't make a fuss. He just sniffed and said my useless ethics were expensive. I *cannot* understand how this perfectly rational man, who is marvellously good at a job I understand, can be so insane when it comes to money. Or why he gets so exasperated when I tell him, especially when he loses on some deal and thousands of dollars disappear overnight. After our last fight I thought we'd have to stop working together.'

Thoughtfully, Maxine stroked the lavender silk shoe; then she said, 'You're thirty-five, you own a smart apartment and you've got a well-paid, enjoyable job. I should forget the rest and let Tom do as he wants.'

So Judy shut up, but she didn't stop worrying.

Three weeks later, Maxine returned from her promotional tour across the country.

'A true friend is someone who confesses that she weighs more than you do,' Judy said, watching Maxine stand on the scales in the guest bathroom.

'Especially if she doesn't,' Maxine agreed. 'Can it be possible that I've put on eight pounds in three weeks on tour?'

'People either gain a lot of weight or lose a lot. Now put your robe on and come into the living room. I've brought your press clippings back from the office.'

They moved into the cream-walled, double-cube living room. The ornately carved, low, dark opium beds stood on three sides of a vast *sang de boeuf* marble table. Zebra skins lay on the dark hardwood floor and an antique, red-and-black painted Persian screen zig-zagged across one corner. Two elaborate Louis XV gilt mirrors hung on either side of the marble fireplace and on the opposite wall was a growing collection of Steinberg drawings.

Maxine rushed to a pink file that lay on one of the opium beds, then stretched back against mauve and blue silk cushions as she skimmed through the newspaper clippings. She hadn't seen them because she had left each city before her interviews were printed.

'Not bad, not bad. This column in *Time* with the little picture is delightful. It was so good of you to telephone every night, Judy. It was always an anxious time, not knowing whether or not one was succeeding, and it was also lonely. I almost wished that I'd taken my secretary.'

'When you've finished admiring your press clippings, come and see how the bedrooms have been altered while you've been away. I told the decorator to do exactly as you said.'

Judy's bedroom now looked luxurious and peaceful. Wild silk drapes covered the window wall and a rich red-fox spread had been flung over the velvet brown bed. On one side of it was a control panel for TV, stereo, radio, telephones and drapes. Two large, low rosewood chests now stood on either side of Judy's bed to hold all the work clutter. There was only one picture in the room, a Manchu noble, inscrutably lifesize, in a seventeenth-century Chinese silk painting that hung opposite the vast bed. Apart from the bed, the only other piece of furniture in the room was a chaise longue upholstered in red-tinged chintz. The same chintz had been used for the couches in the adjoining room, which was now furnished as a study. The walls had been completely covered by bookshelves and painted deep raspberry. Judy's collection of odd objects, when spaced upon the shelves, could suddenly be seen as a collection of antique toys and other esoteric memorabilia. A Victorian rolltop wooden desk stood in front of the window.

'I love this dark red,' Judy said.

'I've just used it in Guy's new offices. He's got more competition now, since Saint Laurent started his own salon, hence the revamp.'

The two women moved back into Judy's bedroom where she started quickly to undress and change for the evening. 'Guy needn't worry about competition. Nobody can compete with his suits,' Judy commented, as she unzipped her exquisitely cut, scarlet pants suit and stepped out of it. 'I've practically lived in this for the past few weeks. When did you last see him?'

'Oh, I haven't seen him for months, but not seeing each other doesn't seem to alter our relationship. It's the same with Pagan and Kate, we never write, we don't see each other for months, but when we meet we just pick up where we left off.'

'Friendship expands to fill the space available.' Judy pulled on a flesh-coloured bodystocking.

'In a way, yes. Friendship can wax and wane and disappear like the moon – then rise and wax fat again at some later date . . .' She clasped her hands behind her head. 'I mean *real* friendship.'

'My idea of a real friend was your Aunt Hortense.' Judy hitched up the bodystocking shoulder straps. 'I can't imagine her wearing these clothes, can you?'

'On the contrary, she'd have looked wonderful in a trouser suit. Oh dear, the last time I saw her before her stroke was when she was playing under the beech tree with Alexandre – he must have been two years old that summer – and she was wearing a green chiffon blouse. He'd managed to undo a couple of buttons and was solemnly stuffing daisies down her cleavage. She looked unusually untidy and unusually happy, and that is how I like to remember her.'

The two women were silent as Judy wriggled into a thigh-length skimpy, black crochet dress.

'*Ma chère*, you look as though you're wearing nothing underneath. These new short fashions make us all look like showgirls in the miniskirt and the high boots. No wonder men love it. Is it for some special man that you want to look as if you wear no lingerie?'

'No, no special man.' She clipped on a pair of sunburst diamond earrings. 'We're dining with Tom and an editor from *Newsweek* ... You know I never seem to fall in love like other women.'

'Hurry up!' Tom yelled from the living room a couple of days later. 'Move it, Judy.' He poked his head around the bedroom door. 'You can't be late at your own reception, especially not when the Nixons are guests of honour.'

'Sorry. Maxine got stuck with a late takeoff to Tokyo.' Vigorously towelling her hair, Judy zipped up her black velvet dress then quickly brushed her hair.

'Why don't you ever use makeup?' He had sauntered into the bedroom, hands in pockets.

'Because I either look like a clown or a raddled twelve-year-old, even after a lesson from Way Bandy. How's that?'

'Jailbait. Incidentally, why did the cancer people choose the Carlyle?'

'They didn't, I did. The security's excellent and their staff is very tightly screened. We've lost Martin Luther King and Bobby Kennedy this year, and with Nixon coming tonight I couldn't be more nervous.'

'Sure. It's a new account, as well, and your friend Pagan moved it our way. But they know you're good, honey, you don't have to worry.'

But all evening, Judy felt as jumpy as a cat, especially when she realized that she was being watched by a tall, dark-haired man.

443

He leaned against the wall with his hands in his pockets and said, 'You look wicked and wonderful,' as she hurried past.

'So does Mount Everest.' She smiled tightly. He was definitely not Security. She ignored him for the rest of the evening, except once, when she felt his eyes upon her back, turned, and sure enough there he was, calmly gazing at her from under heavy eyelids. To Judy's amazement she started to blush; hastily she looked away from him, down at the floor. Then with an effort, because they trembled and yet felt weighted, she slowly lifted her eyelids. Steadily he looked back at her without moving and she felt as if she were naked before him. She felt helpless, her breath unsteady, her face flushed. With an almost painful effort, she turned away, furious with herself ... There was something familiar about his face, although she couldn't place him. That bumpy forehead with the slight frown, the wide mouth and attractive, crooked teeth, that slow smile ... Now he was talking to another man, making fast, impatient movements, jerking his head to flick the dark hair back out of his eyes, stabbing the air with his index finger.

Got it!

It was Griffin Lowe of Orbit Publishing. He hadn't been on her list, but someone high on it must have brought him. Briskly she moved over towards him. 'It's Mr Lowe, isn't it? Can I introduce you to anyone?'

'No, thanks. I came with the Javitses but I don't think I'm staying. It's my second day with contact lenses, and they're fighting back. Why don't we split and have dinner?'

'Because I'm working.'

'No need to, if I say you're not.'

'I'm sorry, but no.' Judy walked away with just a hint of rudeness. She didn't need that kind of rich man's power play and didn't appreciate it one bit.

She was the last to leave. After settling the details of the bill with Luigi, she stood under the awning and was about to ask for a cab when a maroon Rolls Royce drew up and the back door opened. 'An offer you can't refuse. A lift home, with no strings. We know the address.'

She laughed and climbed into the back, which was fitted out like a small living room and smelled discreetly of real leather.

She didn't ask him in and he didn't suggest it. The car simply drove off into the night and Judy headed for a hot tub, rather sorry not to have had the opportunity to turn down Griffin Lowe again ...

～ 42 ～

THAT was the last she heard of him for six weeks, then he telephoned at seven-thirty on a Monday morning to ask her to dinner on the evening of her choice. She said, 'You must be crazy! Is this business? Because it certainly isn't pleasure.'

'Look, I *know* you get up early. It's whatever you care to make it. Sure, I use PR firms.'

'Okay, how about Le Chantilly at seven this evening.'

She wasn't surprised to find Griffin Lowe an interesting and entertaining companion. Of course she had ordered his clippings file sent up to her office, but everyone in the media world knew about Griffin. His publishing empire included a great deal of profitable trash, but also one or two of the best magazines in America. Everyone knew that Griffin was a tough, clever bastard who didn't care what anybody thought of him, which was just as well; they knew he could bring off brilliant, surprising business coups. They knew he had his own sense of rough justice, and that he was a forty-five-year-old, well-known womanizer. Oh, yes, and they knew he was married, with three children – or was it four?

Griffin Lowe sat across the velvet banquette from Judy and they ate lobster bisque, roast lamb with watercress salad followed by caramelized, sliced oranges. Then as they sipped their coffee, Griffin gently took her hand under the table and Judy almost died of shock. Was this not 1968, when the up-to-date standard approach was 'Hello, do you feel like a fuck?' And was she not a thirty-five-year-old figure of emerging womanhood, strong, direct and adult? So was she *really* experiencing that old familiar feeling in the pit of the stomach as if she were back in school again?

Yes.

They sat there for over an hour just holding hands and saying nothing. Judy didn't move out of the restaurant, she floated. After the driver had helped her into the waiting car, Griffin murmured, 'You must be wondering if this is my standard approach. I just felt happy holding your hand, so I didn't want to stop. Now d'you want this to go any further or not?'

'Well, perhaps just to the elbow.' He leaned over and took her in his arms. Judy suddenly felt his mouth pressed on hers, his arms crushing her body, his breath on her cheek, his fingers in her hair.

She couldn't remember getting out of the car and into her apartment. She only knew that her hands were shaking as Griffin slowly unzipped her black velvet dress and it fell to the floor of the living room. He pulled her to him and again she felt his mouth on hers, his firm square hands sliding gently down to the small of her back, pressing her body against him until her knees shook so that she could no longer stand. Then he gently pulled off her sheer black pantyhose and laid her, still trembling, on the yielding soft cushions of the couch.

Shivering with pleasure she yielded to his touch, his fingers, his mouth. Then he, too, was naked and she could smell and feel the warmth of him against her.

He lifted her in his arms. He put her down on the silk sheets of her bed, then, savouring each moment, they abandoned themselves to slow, sensual lovemaking.

He licked her secret places. He tried to lick her ear, but Judy jerked her head away – she couldn't bear that warm messy wetness. But of course sex *was* messy, so she gave in, surrendering to pleasure. He checked where else she liked to be licked, and they found it was almost everywhere. Then suddenly he grew fierce and so did she and they had a little wrestling match to see who got on top and he allowed Judy to win, but somehow they fell off the bed and on to the red-fox spread and then she felt his fingers inside her, after which he rimmed her rather noisily and she didn't mind the warm messy wetness, not one bit. Then she twisted her body until he was powerless beneath her, or so it pleased them to pretend. She moved against him, driving him to the same frenzy that he'd made her feel ten minutes before, then she pushed him back against the cinnamon silk pillows, then

446

leaned back and grabbed his ankles. She felt his strength inside her, his hard, hairy thighs beneath her ass, his fingers driving her wild.

She woke early, happy, and calm. Suddenly remembering the night, she jerked her head around and saw his winged black eyebrows. She felt an odd, new sensation. *She didn't want him to wake up.* When he woke up, he would leave. Immediately she felt suspicious of this new vulnerability. She suddenly felt possessive. Reminding herself that her bedmate was a well-known woman-izer, Judy slid out of bed, put on her dressing gown and fixed breakfast.

Griffin Lowe opened one eye, reached out one arm and tugged at her pink lace gown, then he pulled her down on the bed and murmured how he'd like to start the day, and it wasn't with breakfast. So she slid on top of him again and once more they melted into each other, her slight body on his strong, lusty one.

At last he said gently, 'I told Carter to bring the car around at eight, so I'll have to go soon. But I'll be back.'

Then he showered and suddenly he was gone, leaving her breathless, incapable of thought, incapable of work, incapable of doing anything except to relive in her imagination every minute since she'd met him.

Suddenly it occurred to her that this new sensation wasn't merely carnal desire or passion. For the first time, at the age of thirty-five, she correctly suspected that she was falling in love.

Unsummoned, Griffin now drifted into Judy's thoughts when she least expected it, catching her off-guard during conferences and meetings. She wasted a lot of time gazing dreamily into space, thinking of his skin, the way the back of his neck joined his broad shoulders, the soft hair on his forearms, the shape of his hands, the scar on his left hand (Why? There were so many things to ask him), the warmth of his body. Griffin even knew how to undress erotically, that slow loosening of the tie as he looked steadily at her, removing his socks before his pants to avoid that ridiculous, vaudeville view of hairy legs between shirt and socks.

In a rosewood drawer by her bed she kept a pale blue shirt that he'd worn, and when he wasn't there, she pressed it to her face and inhaled the musky odour of his body.

Griffin immediately hired LACE for one of his new companies, pointing out that it would give them a reason to be together, which it did. Judy was surprised by his relaxed business methods. He didn't waste energy looking dynamic; at times he seemed almost idle. He would sit at a meeting in a gentle, almost apologetic manner, rubbing the side of his nose with his left index finger as he questioned, commented, queried and encouraged other people, probing for every detail. Then he would sum up the entire meeting in three minutes. When Griffin Lowe went to a meeting, whether it was a formal one in his grey suede-panelled conference room or a casual discussion with feet on the desk, everyone present seemed to think fifteen per cent faster and better. It was one of the things that Judy and he had in common.

He and Judy saw each other three times a week. At first they were discreet, but increasingly they became reckless. His wife must surely know, Judy reasoned, and so did Griffin. 'She won't say anything, she never does,' he told Judy and she winced. She hated to think of herself as one more of Griffin's affairs.

There was a long silence.

'That was a very *shitty* thing to say,' she said, and she was only half-joking. She wanted to hurt him, the way those three words had just hurt and humiliated her. '*She never does*.'

They'd had lunch at her apartment – smoked trout and half a bottle of Pouilly Fumée at the bedside – then Griffin showered, dressed and was now about to leave.

'*Very* shitty . . .' Judy repeated, turning to him with a wicked gleam in her blue eyes. 'So I'm going to punish you so that you never hurt or humiliate me again.'

Griffin went along with it – he could have kicked himself for saying those three words – as she led him by the hand back to the rumpled bed and shoved him down on it. With a forced laugh – he was late for his next appointment – Griffin put a lazy arm up to pull her down against his chest, but she caught his wrist and said, 'I'm going to tie you to the bed; then I'm going to have my way with you. I'm going to punish you so that you will never, never be shitty and thoughtless with me again.'

448

She bit his forefinger hard enough to make Griffin jump with pain and surprise. Then she pulled off her maroon-silk dressing gown sash and swiftly tied his right arm to the headboard.

He tried to protest in a playful voice, going along with the game. He recognized the real pain behind her teasing tone of voice, and he also recognized that he wasn't going to make his next appointment. As she reached for his other wrist and wrapped a red silk scarf around it, he said in a resigned voice, 'Aren't you going to undress me first?'

'I'll take off your shoes,' Judy offered, yanking off his handmade Italian loafers and then tying his ankles to the bed with his beige silk socks, so that he was spread-eagled.

'Oh, no,' Griffin said in a high falsetto. 'No, no, no! *Not* Gestapo-style correction, *not* ... the whip, *not* torture, *not* the studded leather belt with the cruel brass buckle and the vicious stiletto heels and the swastika armband!' Groaning between laughs, he didn't mind playing a masochist for once.

'Worse,' said Judy, disappearing into the kitchen and then appearing naked in the doorway with a pair of shears in her hand. As she headed for the bed, still with that wicked glint in her eye, Griffin nervously said, 'Okay Judy, I'm *sorry*. Now let's quit fooling around. This ridiculous horseplay has gone far enough, and I'm late as it is.'

'Oh, but I haven't *started*, so I'm certainly not going to stop,' she said. And before Griffin realized what she was doing she'd slashed through the jacket of his handmade suit.

'*Judy!*' He tried to jerk himself upright but found, to his surprise, that he really couldn't move. She started to snip through his silk shirt, imported the previous month from Jermyn Street.

'Judy! *What* are you playing at? *You* gave me this shirt only yesterday. Remember?'

'A mistake,' said Judy calmly, carefully cutting into his left trouser bottom and slicing up, roughly, towards his groin. 'You really did hurt my feelings, just then, so I'm afraid I'll have to upset your life the way you're upsetting mine.'

Griffin started to simmer. He wouldn't have minded if it were a Saturday, but he had a busy afternoon ahead, and after all, they'd just ...

'You did come, didn't you?'

'Shut up. As a matter of fact, I think I'll make sure that you *can't* talk.'

She put the shears down, picked up her tights, stuffed them in his mouth and gagged him with his tan silk tie. Then she carefully slashed up the other trouser leg and yanked away the debris of grey flannel. For one second Griffin worried as the shears were flourished in the air and then slashed towards his boxer shorts. He started to give muffled yells for mercy. Whatever she was playing at, it seemed the correct way to react.

'I'm going to punish you so that you *never do it again*,' Judy said softly. 'I'm going to make you sorry! I'm going to make you suffer! There's a law against what I'd *really* like to do to you at this moment!' As she bent towards his cock, to his embarrassment, Griffin felt himself stiffen. She curled her tongue and flicked it at his flesh with butterfly strokes. Griffin groaned with pleasure, whereupon Judy stopped. She scrambled off the bed and again headed for the kitchen, reappearing with a bottle of olive oil. She said in a conversational voice, 'You really should be more considerate, Griffin.'

Kneeling on the bed beside him, she tipped the whole bottle over him, and the oil ran off his body and on to the sheets. Judy moved to the bottom of the bed and started to massage his left foot, carefully starting with the big toe and kneading hard under the instep, then going all the way up his leg with hard, oily strokes. He thought, She's going to suck me off; that's what this is leading up to. But she didn't. She stopped short of that point and started to rub his right foot, then expertly massaged his entire body until her hands were kneading the big muscles on either side of Griffin's neck. Occasionally she brushed the tips of her nipples across his chest as her thumbs pushed rhythmically towards his ears.

'*Now* you should be limp and acquiescent,' she said thoughtfully. Then she crouched over Griffin's oil-slick body and with the tip of her tongue *just* licked his stiff cock with little cat-licking-the-cream sort of licks, after which she knelt astride him and carefully stroked her clitoris with his cock, taking no notice whatsoever of Griffin, in fact, treating him as a sexual object to bring herself to orgasm. Griffin was spread-eagled on the bed and she was sitting on top of him, so there wasn't much that he could do about it. A muffled groan escaped his lips. By now he was slightly purple in the face and highly excited as Judy very carefully knelt astride his hips and put just the tip of his cock inside her, then quickly lifted her body so that it almost slipped out. After a few minutes of this teasing, she suddenly pushed it right in, and ground her body against his. Then, just as suddenly, she jumped off him.

There was a muffled yell of fury from Griffin.

'No! I'm going to fix myself a highball!'

She padded away, leaving Griffin jerking at his bonds, and returned with a large Scotch-on-the-rocks. She took a swig and rolled it around her tongue like mouthwash. Then she stretched out beside Griffin, took two ice cubes in her mouth and bent down again. He gave a muffled yelp, because the stinging sensation was totally different from the normal inside of somebody's mouth; instead of being warm and soft and wet it felt freezing and dangerously lumpy.

Judy sucked away until the ice in her mouth had melted and Griffin had lost his erection. Then she curled her forefinger inside him and wriggled around a bit, feeling for his prostate, and when she found it she pushed against it until Griffin quickly jerked to a climax.

She stood up and poured the rest of the highball over his head – the bed was now covered in a revolting mixture of olive oil and melting ice – then she nipped out to the icebox. Saying, 'This always looks so *humorous* on film,' she returned with a lemon meringue pie, which she carefully ground in Griffin's face. She pulled the tinfoil base away, stood up and surveyed the scene.

'My *God*, what a mess!' she said disapprovingly, then turned on her heel and headed for the shower.

Ten minutes later she reappeared, immaculately dressed in a buttercup, sleeveless, short linen tunic with matching pumps. 'I've got an appointment, Griffin, so I have to go now,' Judy said in a polite voice. Then she picked the shears off the floor and placed them on the bed, about a foot from Griffin's head. He tried to yell his indignation at her, but only muffled sounds came through the gag in his mouth as he struggled furiously.

'*You* were in the Boy Scouts, Griffin, you work it out,' she said, and walked out of the apartment.

Griffin couldn't believe it. He couldn't believe that she'd really left him. He couldn't believe that he wasn't able to free himself. He jerked and struggled with his ridiculous silken bindings, gradually getting very cold on the unpleasantly sticky, damp bed, which stank of Scotch.

Eventually he found that by curling his right hand carefully around, he was able to pick at the knot of the dressing gown sash. It took him about half an hour, but then with one bound he was free – and telephoning Carter to bring around a fresh set of clothes.

Griffin was furious.

But he was also impressed. He – Griffin Lowe, the big-dealer, the lover and leaver, who kept his women neatly organized in a private emotional filing system which never overlapped with office hours or impinged on his domestic comfort – had been faced with a situation that his power, charm and savoir faire were unable to resolve. There had been real fury behind what Judy did – and she hadn't weakened. She had also demonstrated the physical power she had over Griffin. She understood his body so well that she had kept him at the point of orgasm for an hour and a half, teasing him almost beyond endurance until his nerves were raw.

He had been humbled, if not humiliated.

From that moment, the pattern of their relationship shifted, and Griffin treated Judy with a great deal more care and respect, not because he was afraid of her, but because she had done exactly what she said she would do – she had punished him!

But Griffin knew that he had to risk her pain and fury once more. He knew he had to spell their future out to her – it was only fair. One evening, a week after she'd tied him up and slashed his clothes off, they both lay naked on her bed, in the soft, final rays of the setting sun. They were both voluptuously tired after making love, and Griffin didn't really want to talk, but he knew he had to. He held her hand hard, knowing that he had to make it clear to her, knowing that it was going to hurt her. Eventually, he simply said, 'Delia knows I'd never leave her or the kids, Judy.

I've fought too hard for what I've got to dump my family or to hurt them.' There was a long silence. He felt ill at ease and Judy looked so closed off and remote that he slid off the bed and padded, naked, to the kitchen, returning with a bottle of Dom Perignon in one hand.

'I can't think why she puts up with you,' Judy said.

'Delia knows there's an odd kind of security about a man who's always falling in love.'

Judy projected anger as he untwisted the wire and eased out the champagne cork with his thumbs. He had to be straight with her. 'Fact one, Judy – I meet a lot of beautiful women and I enjoy them. Fact two – I also have a family. For me these are two entirely different areas of interest, and I hope you realize this.'

She stretched one arm from the tousled, cinnamon silk sheets and took the glass of champagne he offered. 'I mean, Judy, I'm *underlining* it. I don't want to hurt you and I don't want you to get any wrong ideas, but I want you to understand *I will never, never leave my wife*. It would hurt her too much and I could never live with myself afterwards.'

There was a long pause.

'That's what they all say.' Judy carefully tipped her glass over his head. 'And anyway, who asked you? A long time ago, I decided I was never going to marry. I didn't see the point of making unrealistic promises I wasn't sure that I or anyone else could keep.'

Griffin put down the champagne bottle and headed for the bathroom. At least she hadn't smashed it over his head. And he *had* – finally and clearly – said it.

Judy continued in a dreamy voice: 'I keep telling myself that I shouldn't *want* to marry you and I don't think I really do. It's just that I hate your being married to somebody *else*.' She raised her voice so that, in the bathroom, he could still hear what she was saying. 'I don't want to be *dependent* for my happiness on someone else, and I can't help feeling that way.'

Griffin padded back, and she thought how handsome he looked as he stood in the doorway towelling his hair. He tried a tentative grin.

'Goddamn it, Griffin, *listen*, please. I've always valued my independence, but now I notice in myself a sudden painful urge to tell you *everything*, Griffin, every secret of my life.'

She looked up at the ceiling. 'Now I know that you don't feel that way about me, because men *don't*. And suddenly *I want to be with you all the time*. But intellectually I know I don't *want* that.' She thumped the bedspread with her small fists. There was a short silence. Suddenly she sat up and he couldn't help looking at her small rosy nipples. He threw the towel to the floor, moved towards her and bent to her breasts, but she pushed him aside.

'Griffin, I want to keep my own privacy. If you laugh at this, I'll kill you, but I want to be alone, quite often.'

She slid down the bed again and pulled the covers up to her neck. 'Even if you *can't* keep your eyes off my tits.'

He sat on the edge of the bed and said seriously, 'Why? Why do you want to be alone quite often?'

'Because so many people are frightened of solitude, instead of valuing it. I was, once – and I never want to be like that again.'

Slowly she pulled herself up to a sitting position against the pillows and said, 'There's a world of difference between being alone and being lonely.'

He looked sceptical. She hesitated, then added, 'Sure, it's sometimes lonely to come home at night after a hard day's work to a dark, empty apartment. But I'd rather be down in the dumps occasionally than trapped with someone I don't really want to be with.'

She scowled. 'And I don't want to play that part in some man's life.' She clasped her hands behind her head and her nipples again tilted upwards. 'Are you listening to me, Griffin? Once upon a time if a man told me he was lonely I used to melt with sympathy. But now I run a mile.'

'Sounds as if you want to have your cake and eat it.'

'Neatly put, for a cake.'

Laughing, he lunged at her.

On her next trip to New York, Maxine was charmed by Griffin. 'At last our lives seem to be sorting themselves out,' she said, as she stood in Judy's kitchen, arranging an armful of arum lilies and pink roses that she'd brought in with her. 'No, thank you, Francetta, I like doing the flowers. Pagan and I are happily

454

married, with babies as well as jobs. Kate's happily divorced and a successful writer. And *at last* you've fallen in love.'

Reflectively, she sniffed the rounded, pale pink tip of a rosebud. 'We all hoped it would be Nick, then we all hoped it would be someone nice.' She finished the vase and stood back to admire it. 'And then we didn't care *who* it was, so long as he made you happy. Darling, what's all this Dom Perignon in your refrigerator? . . . Well, tell Griffin you prefer *our* champagne. And now listen, because I have a little surprise for you.'

~ 43 ~

LONDON life and the afternoon traffic were totally disrupted, and Pagan and Judy were one of the reasons for it. Outside the gates of Buckingham Palace stood a very smart line of women in large, flowered, floppy hats and men in pale grey top hats and black suits. They were the honoured guests of HM the Queen at the annual Royal Garden party. Pagan saw Kate, who had just been nominated woman of the year by the Association of Professional Women, so Pagan waved her invitation in the thick, cream envelope with the dark red, royal crest stamped on the back. It listed the time as four to six p.m., but you could enter through the magic gates at three-fifteen p.m. and a lot of people seemed to want to do it. Kate wore a cream Tuffin and Foale crêpe suit with a flounced jacket, Pagan wore a trumpet-shaped silk dress with leg o'mutton sleeves in Jean Muir's latest pink and grey art-nouveau pattern, and Judy looked unusually demure in a lemon linen suit from Guy's summer collection, with slightly darker shoes and a big-brimmed straw hat.

The best part was walking past the scarlet-coated sentry, through the big black curlicued gates beyond the barriers that held back summer tourists. Once inside the gates the three of them walked across the gravel and under the arch of the quietly elegant, pale grey facade. Then they were in the inner courtyard and climbing the wide, red-carpeted stairs to the Queen's own doorstep.

'It certainly was a surprise, Pagan. I still can't believe I'm actually *inside* Buckingham Palace,' said Judy. 'And I still can't understand how you fixed it.'

'Nobody can fix Buckingham Palace,' said Pagan. 'Christopher suggested about a year ago that you might be welcome, because of the voluntary work you'd done for cancer research.'

They found Maxine, the guest of the French Ambassador, in the main drawing room, which was decorated in gold and scarlet, like the entrance hall, and lined with glass cabinets containing priceless porcelain. Looking unmistakably Parisienne in light green chiffon, Maxine winked and moved towards them. The four women greeted each other in an unusually subdued manner.

'Let's go outside in the sun,' suggested Kate, so they moved on to the balustraded terrace that runs across the back of the palace. Beyond the vast lawn was a lake, and beyond the lake was a wood. It was difficult to believe this garden was hidden in the middle of London, it was like being in the country. On a circular bandstand the Band of the Royal Marines was thumping out a selection from *Oklahoma!* as they'd done for the last twenty years. On the left of the balustraded terrace was the green-and-white-striped tea tent. Waitresses in pearl-buttoned black silk dresses already bustled around small circular tables set with cakes and teacups. Over to the right of the terrace was the small red-carpeted royal tea tent, with sumptuously gilded Regency chairs and a golden tea urn on the table.

Everyone looked happy as they strolled over the lawn. It was like being at a favourite cousin's wedding, but with no drunken uncles. Half the women were dressed like the Queen and the other half were dressed like Princess Anne. One guest wore black goggle sunglasses with a topless, shocking-pink sheath; among the white kid gloves and the rose-trimmed straw hats she stood out like someone from another planet. Considering that 1969 was the year when fancy dress was fashionable, it was odd to see nobody dressed as a flower child, no wealthy gypsies, no outrageously embroidered Afghans, no buckskin-fringed Indians or other ethnic oddities, although there were quite a lot of expensive-looking milkmaids, romantically ruffled by Laura Ashley.

Towards four o'clock everyone suddenly moved towards the

terrace as the band struck up the anthem, then everybody froze to attention. A small figure in turquoise stood out from the group that had appeared on the terrace, and the Beefeaters leaped into action in a surprisingly sprightly manner to clear the royal path.

The Queen wasn't in turquoise – that turned out to be a lady-in-waiting. HM wore a red silk dress over a cream petticoat that the wind revealed quite often. She and Pagan were the only women who wore low-heeled shoes, but then it was Her lawn. Under a big-brimmed red straw hat, Her Majesty's face was pale, neat and animated as she talked to guests whom the ushers beckoned forward at random, as she slowly moved towards her tea tent. Red-liveried footmen with white stockings served as Her Majesty chatted to the diplomatic corps.

It was a perfect Edwardian tea: white-iced layer cake, pale-orange layer cake, chocolate cake, plates of bread and butter thin as vellum, cucumber rounds covered with cream cheese and minced gherkin. No liquor was served, but there was plenty of iced coffee, tea and fresh orange juice.

'A neat place to have a reunion,' said Judy from beneath the brim of her huge straw hat. 'None of us expected *this* twenty years ago.' She waved a hand at the resplendent scene as they sat at a table.

'We never expected *any* of the things that happened to us,' said Kate, smoothing her cream lace ruffles as she sat down. 'And we never got any of the things that we *did* expect, like Prince Charming.'

They talked nonstop, with much infectious giggling, of children, husbands, lovers, houses, friends, enemies and all the paraphernalia of being alive. Then, more thoughtfully, they drifted into a grown-up version of the way they used to talk in the moonlight, after lights-out at school, as they discussed what they wished they'd been taught.

'To earn my own living,' Pagan said firmly.

'To handle my own financial affairs,' Kate said, thinking of how her father's estate had been mismanaged.

'To realize that we were going to run into trouble,' Maxine said thoughtfully. 'You cannot expect to skip through life with a princess-and-the-pea attitude, hoping to find no lump under the bedclothes. The bed is always lumpy.'

457

Judy said, 'I wish we hadn't picked up the idea that you were a failure if you didn't have a man because then you would be without status and protection.'

'We picked up that idea from our mothers as well as our fathers,' Kate pointed out. 'It was our mothers who brought us up to be dependent and lazy where it matters most – in the head.'

'I suppose we can't blame our parents for not teaching us things that they didn't know themselves,' Maxine argued. 'They did the best they could.'

Judy said, 'That was the problem. Somehow you got this feeling that a dependent woman *was* feminine and an independent woman *wasn't* feminine, that it was unfeminine to be responsible for yourself.'

Kate agreed. 'I might have avoided a lot of the problems I ran into if only I'd had the self-confidence to think for myself instead of relying on other people's opinions.' They stood up and wandered over the lawn towards the lake and the rose garden beyond as Kate continued, 'From birth we were all wrapped up in warm lace shawls and it's very tempting not to struggle out of them, to stay snuggled up in the lace and let someone else run the world for you. But these shawls are spiderwebs of false security . . .'

'Which is worse than no security,' Maxine interjected, 'because they make you so damned vulnerable when you find that your lace shawl has been whipped away by Fate, leaving you naked and defenceless.'

Judy nodded in agreement, thinking that it would be nice to pick a rose to send to her mother.

But it was a very small rose garden.

44

SHORTLY after Judy returned to New York, Tom put his head around her door. 'We've landed our first dirty movie. Empire Studios has bought that French film, *Q*. The title's a pun, remember? It means "ass" in French. Lili stars, and we're going

458

to tour her. We have to think up something special because her English isn't so great. Okay if you handle it?'

'Sure. Maybe we could tie in with the Jewellery Federation's Year of the Emerald launch. How would Lili like to tour in two million dollars' worth of emeralds? That's pretty special!'

Judy set up the tour for early January, which was always the dead season: nothing much was happening, everyone was at home in front of the TV. She decided to travel with Lili because Lili was definitely difficult and the emeralds could easily attract trouble. Anyway, it was time Judy visited the boonies.

After delays from the Legion of Decency and innumerable Bible Belt organizations, *Q* was released just before Lili's twentieth birthday, and after Christmas she flew to the States to promote it. Serge had come ahead of her. He wanted to talk to a few people on the Coast. Surprisingly, he didn't meet Lili when she flew in, but the press agent waiting at the airport told her that Serge had been feeling ill, he'd see Lili by the hotel pool. Lili let him see that she wasn't pleased. A likely story, she thought – probably a hangover. Or some girl. It was too bad, she'd just travelled halfway around the world to meet him and he couldn't even be bothered to turn up at the airport.

She sulked until they reached Beverly Hills.

Lili found Serge lying on a yellow daybed, on the sunny side of the aquamarine rectangle. Opposite him was a row of lemon-and-white tented cabanas. A few children were jumping off the diving board at one end, but apart from that nobody seemed to be swimming – none of the women had the sort of hair that got wet, their hairstyles were all immaculate and twenty years out of date and several women even wore diamond jewellery with their swimsuits. Serge looked up at Lili and waved a languid hand. 'God, I feel terrible,' he moaned.

She forced herself to look concerned, solicitous, bent over to kiss his cheek. 'What's wrong, Serge?'

He groaned again peevishly, scratched his hairy belly, lifted his sunglasses and said, 'Liver. The hotel doctor says I need a rest. Christ, I can't tell you how terrible I feel.'

'Why aren't you in bed then?' She still didn't believe him, didn't even believe he'd seen a doctor; it was simply too damn comfortable lying here in the sun, with palm trees waving beyond the high pink walls. He had some chick here, hidden away. 'What's that you're drinking?'

'Fucking orange juice, with nothing in it – doctor's orders.'

'May I?' She sipped his drink. It really was plain orange juice. Maybe he really *was* ill.

'You want some juice or something, Lili?'

'No, no thanks, but maybe something to eat. Has this doctor given you any medicine? How long are you likely to be ill? We're supposed to start on Thursday, you know.'

'Yeah, I've been worrying about it.' While Serge heaved his body off his couch and wrapped himself in a lemon towelling robe, Lili took another look around the pool. Middle-aged men in sunglasses were reading *Variety*. A couple of dark-brown old men, wearing heavy gold necklaces, were simultaneously smoking cigars, playing backgammon and talking on the telephone.

'I didn't expect Hollywood to be like this. These people look so ordinary, just like any families at a resort.' What sort of hotel had Serge picked? Where were the stars? Lili was disappointed.

As Serge started to amble towards the café tables at one end of the pool, a pale, exquisite creature with waist-length golden curls appeared on the steps that led down from the hotel. She wore a burgundy one-piece swimsuit, burgundy high-heeled sandals and burgundy toenails. As gently and carefully as if she were tending a sick child, she devoted herself to rubbing oil on the chest of her escort, a tiny gnarled gnome with a head like a brown-speckled egg.

'That's not a starlet. That's a whore,' Serge said, reading Lili's thoughts. 'They have *wonderful* ones out here, sweetheart. She's seen more hotel rooms than a Gideon Bible distributor. Now come on, if you want lunch.'

They moved up to one of the white banquettes, sat down and ordered Caesar salads. Serge picked morosely at his lunch.

'The fact is, Lili, the doctor's forbidden me to tour with you. I have to stay here, maybe move into a clinic, take tests –'

'*I don't believe you!*' Lili's fork crashed to the table and she leaned towards him, raging in a low voice, so that the waiter couldn't hear. After that *Globe* article written by Kate, Lili was terrified of seeing journalists without Serge. 'I'm going to see this doctor for myself.' Except that there was no point, she thought. Serge would have fixed him. She'd guessed right the first time. He'd found some bitch. Her velvet brown eyes glared. 'You've got a girl here somewhere!' Her voice was low, fast, and angry. Serge knew she was building up to an explosion. 'This is all I need, no protection on tour because my so-called manager is resting up in Hollywood, that well-known health resort.' She glared at him. 'You're pushing me off on tour so you can screw some other bitch in comfort on *my* money.'

'For Christ's sake, Lili, do we have to have a scene before you've been here five minutes? Even if they don't speak French, they can hear that we're having a fight. Keep your fucking voice down and use your fucking brains.'

Three young men slumped into the banquette on their other side and ordered three black coffees and a telephone. 'Think about it,' Serge urged. 'I never allowed you to see one goddamn reporter on your own after that English bitch fouled you up, did I? So is it likely that I'd suddenly push you off on a goddamn important, expensive four-week tour all by yourself? My financial future is just as much at stake as yours is.'

'That's true.' But somehow it didn't feel right. 'You're not telling me everything. Something's wrong. You're being evasive, I can *feel* it.'

'Lili, darling, when I get you alone in our little pink bungalow, I'll knock your fucking teeth in if you don't shut up,' Serge said. 'I'm feeling like death; in fact, I may be dying and you have to start a scene.' He was starting to feel self-righteous, because for once she was wrong. 'There is *no* other chick here – and if there was I couldn't do much about it. I feel so sick I can hardly raise my goddamn head, let alone anything else.' Serge pushed his salad away. 'You can speak to the doctor yourself, when he calls tomorrow. Incidentally, I've also asked him to give you a quick physical – I thought it might be a good idea to check that you're really fit before you start this tour. And don't worry, you're *not* going alone. The president of the P R firm that arranged the tour is going to travel with you, and I'll telephone you every night . . . Now could I *please* have a little sympathy?'

He certainly didn't look well. In fact, he looked terrible. Lili leaned forward, contrite, and patted his hand.

461

Serge *was* ill. The truth was that he had syphilis. A couple of days before, he'd noticed two swollen lumps in his groin and then he found a small blister under his foreskin. Fuck, he'd thought, and phoned the doctor, because you didn't kid around with that, it could rot your brain, paralyse you, eat your nose away, even kill you.

The doctor had given him the usual caution about warning all sexual partners (which Serge ignored), and prescribed an immediate course of penicillin injections, which is why Serge had to stay in one place and dump the one-town-a-day tour.

Thank God he hadn't touched Lili for some time, Serge thought. But the doctor said she still had to have a physical. She'd be surprised when she found that the physical included a vaginal examination, but he'd let the doctor handle that one – he was getting paid enough for being discreet.

If Lili was clean, there'd be no need to say anything to her. He didn't want to upset her before she went on tour. But Serge was worried about that. He didn't like sending his bank account off on her own.

So Lili arrived alone at Kennedy, huddled in an ankle-length black fox coat, a cloud of black hair around the pale, feline face. Tired after her night flight, she hardly spoke to Judy on the trip to the Pierre, where two bodyguards and a security man from the Jewellery Federation were waiting for her. They all moved to the manager's office, where the door was locked, then the safe was unlocked. A big, flat, dark-green leather case was brought out and put on the manager's desk, then unlocked. Everyone looked at Lili. She moved forward, slowly swung the lid back, and they all caught their breaths.

Inside, on dark-green velvet, to celebrate the Year of the Emerald, lay a magnificent bracelet of blazing emeralds encrusted with diamonds, an emerald and diamond brooch, a pair of green stud earrings, a pair of heavy, chandelier earrings and two matching finger rings – both square-cut emeralds – banded with diamonds. But the pièce de résistance was a magnificent emerald necklace.

Slowly, with both hands, Lili picked it up and held it to her white throat. Her fatigue fell away as she looked in the mirror at the green fire that flashed against her breast.

'It does tricks,' said Judy, 'let me show you.' She picked up a silver diadem, and hooked the necklace over the top spikes, converting it into a tiara. Gently she lifted it on to Lili's head. Lili seemed to grow six inches, as regal as a Snow Queen.

'That will do nicely,' said Judy. 'We'll photograph you in that after you've freshened up. Sorry about the rush, but we need pictures right away for the press kits. There's a hairdresser waiting in your suite.'

By five o'clock that evening, the big reception room was hazy with cigarette smoke and buzzing with journalists flipping through their dark-green press kits. They quieted down as Judy stood on the dais to introduce Lili, then looked expectantly towards the door, outside which Lili was slowly counting to ten before making her entrance.

Suddenly, she was in the room, head thrown back, chin high, in a white satin evening dress that was a perfect background for the emeralds that shone from her hair, her throat, her ears, her wrists.

She gave a slow, gentle smile, then walked over to Judy, green fire flashing, her satin dress like a moonbeam. She's got class, Judy thought with satisfaction, she looks like a princess, not the two-bit stripper they'd expected. What a contrast to those wet rags she wore in the movie! And why not, Judy thought. She'd had Guy Saint Simon design the entire tour wardrobe.

All over America, hotel detectives were waiting for them and the police had been alerted. After the 'Today' show and other TV and some newspaper interviews in New York, they flew to Seattle, then down to Houston, Dallas and Atlanta, then north again to Philadelphia, Boston, Cleveland, Baltimore and Detroit, followed by Los Angeles, Cincinnati and Pittsburgh, where Lili was mobbed at the airport and they quickly decided to switch hotels. To Lili, the cities were a bewildering blur of hotel suites, heavily guarded cars, planes, tape recorders, cameras and questions. She had to concentrate to catch the often fast-spoken queries in the strange accents; sometimes her own answers exasperated her; sometimes she fumbled for words; but the press was amiable and the coverage was fantastic.

Merv Griffin was affable. Phil Donahue was lovable. Mike Douglas gave Lili an easy ride on what a poor orphan felt like when wearing two million dollars' worth of emeralds: he jokingly concluded that the emeralds were almost an inconvenience for any normal happy woman – too much trouble, too much of a responsibility. Johnny Carson took to Lili on sight and managed to cover her career truthfully, but sympathetically, without making the sordid parts sound terrible, as if they were some kind of obstacle course Lili had bravely circumvented in order to reach her true destiny – the spotlight of fame and the flashing green fire of those emeralds.

Nevertheless, Lili felt that she was repeating herself too frequently as she tried, haltingly, to give different answers to the same questions repeated over and over again by different mouths in front of different microphones. She rarely left her hotel and ate her evening meal in her suite. Sometimes she switched on the television, but she was generally asleep before the programme ended.

In spite of the luxury and care that surrounded her, by Monday of the fourth week she was red-eyed, depressed, exhausted and sneezing in the biting cold January wind of Chicago.

'Cheer up, you're on your last week,' consoled Judy. The kid had been no trouble up to now. Quiet, almost limp in fact, although she came to life miraculously as soon as she saw a camera. 'You've done very well so far. *Everybody* is exhausted and disoriented after three weeks on the road. They've *all* said the same thing over and over. Tell you what, if you really feel too ill to do it, I'll cancel everything for the afternoon. The only really important spot is Soapy Finnegan this evening. After that we'll tuck you into bed and leave you alone with a couple of aspirin.'

Soapy Finnegan was a smiling, self-opinionated Irishman with a double ration of blarney and a treble quota of charm that was carefully beamed at his audience of respectable, suburban matrons. Soapy knew their reaction to his every word, innuendo and gesture; he could almost see them all out there, feet up, coffee cup in hand, comfortably watching their good friend Soapy, who shared their values and their viewpoint, who wanted the same sort of things that they wanted, a quiet life with no problems, who enjoyed the same simple family pleasures that they did. They were not to know that Soapy Finnegan wore a girdle under his suit, had just had his second facelift and was obsessed by constipation remedies, especially enemas applied by young male nurses.

Waiting to be cued by the floor manager, Lili willed herself not to sit down on the offered chair. If she sat down she'd never get up. She only had to do this one little show, then she could collapse into bed and they'd get her a doctor. Her forehead was burning, her head throbbed and her ears felt muffled. Certainly, she couldn't go on tomorrow.

Later she was to wish that she had not struggled on that evening, as Soapy Finnegan mercilessly slaughtered her on the altar of respectability. He had been charmingly solicitous to her in the green room, so Lili was unprepared when he suddenly started to attack her, raised his voice in a loud, fast, judgemental monologue, hurled questions at her as if she were being cross-examined and then answered them himself, not giving Lili time to speak. After a long tirade, he suddenly switched away from the camera and turned to the bewildered Lili.

'*How* exactly would you describe yourself?'

'Why, as an actress.'

'You wouldn't describe yourself as a *woman* who *exposed* herself when hardly out of *school* to whichever *gentleman* was willing to *pay* for this doubtful *pleasure*?' His voice became louder, faster. In the producer's box Judy sprang to her feet. She could see what was coming. The self-righteous voice continued to accuse Lili. '*Flaunting your body for a string of emeralds!*'

Judy ran along the passage that led to the studio. Lili could never handle this alone.

But she could. Bewildered by the loud stream of accusations, trying to answer, groping for the English words, stuttering, Lili was at first afraid that she was going to burst into tears. But she'd cried enough in private. So far she'd always managed to conceal her true feelings in public – that had been her only protection – and her secret pride. So why cry for this bastard? Almost without thinking, she concealed her emotion with anger and action as she sprang to her feet and tore the emeralds from her ears. 'They're not my emeralds,' she said in a low voice. 'I've had enough of you and I've had enough of them. I *knew* they were unlucky. Emeralds are always unlucky!'

She tugged the bracelets from her wrists, then with both hands she yanked at the necklace, breaking the safety clasp and scratching the back of her neck. '*You* keep them,' she cried, throwing the jewels into the plump lap of the astounded Soapy Finnegan. '*You* see what it feels like to be paraded like a circus animal.' Hardly knowing what she was doing, knowing only that she had to escape, Lili ran from the cameras and past her bodyguards at the studio door and bumped into Judy, who was rushing down the passage in the opposite direction.

'Please, Lili, go back, we'll go on together. *Please*, *please*.'

Lili pushed her away and glared at her.

'Lili, I'm on *your* side. You can't afford to lose your temper.'

Lili continued to glare.

Judy's own temper flared up. 'So why should people always be nice? You should have shut up and smiled, or looked *dignified*, for Chrissake, then you might have got some audience sympathy. Now you've behaved like a stupid street brat, which is exactly how he described you. *And you called the emeralds unlucky! Twice!* That'll be all over America within hours.'

She beckoned to the hovering bodyguards. 'Let's get back to your dressing room, Lili. Christ, I can't decide whether to phone the Jewellery Federation and apologize or quietly slit my throat.'

Or yours, she thought, as she hurried Lili down the corridor, waving people away, still muttering. 'I can't *believe* you let him get to you so easily; it's so goddamn *unprofessional*, Lili. Can you imagine Jane Fonda or Liza Minnelli behaving like this? Or any reputable actress? Oh, God, where can I get a jeweller at this hour to mend that necklace before we leave tomorrow?'

'I leave now,' said Lili, in an offhand voice, as they entered her dressing room. 'No more tour.'

'You *can't* go off in midtour,' said Judy, aghast.

'Yes, yes, indeed, I *can*. Oh, I forgot these.' And she tugged the rings from her fingers, carefully placed them on the makeup counter, grabbed up her coat and walked out.

Back at the hotel, Lili threw a few clothes into a suitcase and put a call through to Serge. He wasn't in his bungalow.

She telephoned him again when she reached O'Hare, but there was still no reply.

So, head throbbing, she sat and waited two hours for a plane to Los Angeles and peace.

Serge was astounded to see a bedraggled Lili appear in his room in the middle of the night. He sat up in bed. He was alone. They both noticed that. 'What the hell's happening? You're supposed to be on tour for another week.' He squinted sleepy eyes against the sudden light. 'Where's that PR woman? Stop crying, cherub, come to papa.'

Lili flung herself into his arms. Serge terrified her, Serge depressed her, and Serge physically abused her, but nevertheless Lili basically felt safe with him.

'She's st . . . st . . . still at Chicago. I telephoned you from the ho . . . ho . . . hotel, then I telephoned again when I re . . . re . . . reached the airport, they paged you but y . . . y . . . you weren't there so I wai . . . wai . . . waited at O'Hare and c . . . c . . . caught the next plane to L.A.' She burst into tears again.

'There, there, cherub, calm down. Whatever's happened, Serge will fix it. There, there. There.' He stroked her hair until the sobs turned to sniffs, then he pulled her around and kissed her. 'Now tell Serge, cherub.'

There was a pause, then Lili said, 'The first part was fine. The reception in New York was fine; they gave me a very easy time.' She paused again. 'The woman from the agency was nice and friendly. But we did so *many* shows a day and my English just wasn't up to it.' She sneezed. 'It's such a relief to be talking French to you again. And to talk without being guarded.' She coughed hard. 'And always in English, you see, and very fast. Then I caught a virus, so the hotel doctor, in Michigan I think it was, gave me pills, but they made me sleepy and stupid. My head felt like a big balloon stuffed with cotton.'

Lili grabbed another tissue as she started to sneeze again. 'By yesterday evening I also had a throbbing headache, so I took some different pills; otherwise I swear I don't think I could have moved.'

She pulled her shoes off, then her clothes, dropping them in a heap by the side of the bed. 'And after all that, this loathsome little swine said these revolting things to me in front of thousands of people – what a filthy whore I was, a shocking example to the youth of America . . .'

Serge thought even with her nose and eyes streaming, even when she had totally lost her cool, Lili naked was nevertheless one terrific sight. And much to his surprise, he'd missed her. It was like finding that you missed a dog you were used to kicking.

'I felt as if I were being cross-examined in a murder case.'

'There, there, petal,' soothed Serge, one arm comfortingly around her.

Serge telephoned Judy in Chicago and sorrowfully explained that Lili had a fever, a temperature of 102 degrees and was under doctor's orders not to be disturbed. He hoped she'd be better in a couple of days. Maybe he shouldn't have let her go on tour, poor kid. She'd had a hectic year, she was really too tired, and now she'd caught the flu.

But Lili didn't recover after a couple of days. She had worked nonstop under pressure for months, she had been coaxed, wheedled and pushed beyond her powers of endurance by Serge. Two weeks later, Lili still lay in bed, listless. She didn't seem to hear Serge, she wept silent tears if anyone spoke to her, she didn't want to eat or drink or read or watch television. She just lay in bed, limp as a rag doll.

'We'd better transfer her to a private clinic,' the doctor said. 'She's suffering from what you could call exhaustion or a clinical depression – that's how this condition is generally described when the sufferer is a celebrity. But I'm afraid she's heading for a serious nervous breakdown.'

There was a pause.

Serge looked worried.

'When will she be able to work again?' he asked.

～ 45 ～

CAP Camerat is a rocky headland on the French Riviera, half an hour's drive from St Tropez. A white lighthouse on the tip of the cliff warns ships to keep their distance. Beyond it, clinging tenaciously to the steep mountainside, is a newly built cluster of villas constructed of naked brick, exposed concrete and unadorned wood. These dwellings are furnished in what the French call 'contemporary' style, with conical wickerwork chairs that look incapable of supporting a round human bottom, tables inset with handmade ceramic tiles and messy splashes of violent colour.

In the spring of 1970, Serge borrowed one of these villas from a bachelor friend so that Lili could recuperate in the warm air of the Mediterranean. He was glad to have her off his hands for a month. She seemed to have no energy, no stamina, and dissolved into tears whenever he suggested a little work.

Since her breakdown, the twenty-year-old Lili had lost her self-confidence and nerve. At the age of twenty, she was now frightened of being with strangers and terrified of being alone. Serge found her easier to manipulate when she was obedient and listless, but he also knew that she had lost the strange vitality she used to possess when facing the camera.

For the moment, Lili's magic had gone. The face was the same, the body the same, but she had no life in her. Lili had had little to do with normal people; her sort of success inevitably attracted gapers, con men, and sexual exploiters. Women were always on their guard against Lili; they mistrusted her, and they were jealous of her because of the mesmeric effect she had on men. So she had no close girl friends to coax her back to vitality. Serge had tried everything. He soothed the little bitch, flattered her, fucked her silly, frightened her, even roughed her up a couple of times. Two films had been cancelled – it was bloody lucky he was covered by the medical clause – and he'd lost a lucrative poster contract. She hadn't earned a penny for him in the last six months, and she was costing him a fortune in medical fees.

The doctor had recommended plenty of sun and a quiet life – no parties, no late nights, and even . . . no Serge. So he had hired a nurse to look after her. Someone he could trust. Serge promised himself he'd be on the first plane to Nice if there was the slightest sign of another man sniffing about. He'd given the nurse an immense bonus for keeping Lili under constant surveillance, and just to make sure of AC as well as DC, he'd picked the ugliest bitch on the nursing agency's books.

Lili sensed that she was being spied on, but she didn't care. She just wanted to be left alone. Nevertheless, she cheered up as soon

469

as she and the nurse were driven beyond the palm trees of Nice airport under the Mediterranean sun.

From inside the house, the view of the sea was almost obscured by a mass of green vegetation that hung over the glass doors from the roof above: the light that filtered through was dim and green. But outside on the patio in the brilliant, Provençal sunlight, standing in a writhing, dark green jungle dotted with tenacious pink geraniums and watching little white yachts slowly move over the dark blue sea under a pale blue sky, Lili stretched her arms up to the sun. At last she felt alone, unpressured and at peace.

Few of the neighbouring villas were occupied so early in the year, so Lili was able to wander about the village unrecognized. Every morning she sunbathed naked on her private beach, although the water was still too cold for swimming.

One morning, just as she was about to climb back up the winding, rock path to the house for lunch, she felt a shadow fall across her body. Opening her eyes, she was alarmed to see a black, rubber-clad figure leaning over her.

'Lili! I thought I recognized you!' said Zimmer, who had been spearfishing in the bay.

Lili was delighted to see him, and Zimmer was obviously just as pleased to see her. 'I'm staying in the next bay; I shut myself up for a month to write a screenplay. You're the first woman I've seen for weeks. I leave on Monday, which means I'm not going to see much of you because I've promised to lunch with the Fouriers tomorrow.' He looked at her. He'd heard she was ill and had had to cancel a couple of things, but she seemed fine now. 'Their parties are always terrific. Why don't you come with me?'

'I don't want to see people.'

'Wear a *yashmak* and talk to me alone,' Zimmer said. 'Serge can't object if you're with me.'

Lili had never been anywhere so exotic as the Fourier place. Monsieur Fourier was a rich Belgian in the transport business. To offset the toughness of his work, he surrounded himself with opulent luxury, which included an art collection consisting mostly of nudes. His pornography was covered by a veil of respectability: all his art was either virtuously antique or else the product of famous sculptors and painters. The oak door was flanked by a couple of naked ladies desperately clutching their slipped marble draperies; the vast room beyond was hung with Russell Flint watercolours – gypsy women in various alluring states of undress. A maroon-leather visitors' book lay open upon the entrance table, next to which lay a plaster cast of Madame Fourier when newly married – to be exact, it was a hand-tinted replica of her buttocks, which had, at the time, been heavily smeared with Vaseline before being slathered with plaster of Paris.

Life-size stone nymphs lined the path that led through the garden to the swimming pool, at one end of which a frenzied stone orgy was in permanent progress. Beyond the pool stood three Corinthian columned Greek temples, and under the central pediment a more sedate party was in progress: turbaned Indian servants proffered drinks, including five different sorts of freshly squeezed fruits for anyone who didn't want whisky or champagne, as well as a profusion of bite-size hot pastry shells filled with seafood.

When Lili appeared between the Greek columns, wearing a flesh-coloured chiffon bikini, there was a slight but noticeable lull in the talk. She settled on to a purple, cotton-covered couch. A pink-turbaned Indian bowed as he offered her caviar from one silver salver, cold lobster and a dish of little crabs from another. Suddenly, Lili felt hungry again.

Zimmer propped himself up on one elbow. 'Look who's just arrived,' he murmured. 'Stiarkoz with La Divina, making her usual late entrance.'

All eyes flickered towards the avenue of cyprus, down which a small, silver-haired man slowly walked towards the pool. Beside him was La Divina, looking exactly as she did on all her record albums, with her magnificent head thrown back. La Divina managed to carry off a big nose, a big mouth and a big head: enormous quantities of coarse, black hair made her look a little top-heavy and her heavily made-up doe eyes glittered. She was a tough prima donna who for many years – at least four of them before his wife died – had openly been the mistress of Jo Stiarkoz.

Now, as she moved slowly forward, her quivering, upthrust breasts threatened to break loose from her low-cut gown of mantis-green gauze. She no longer sang in opera but her voice was still superb. All over the world people waited all night to get into one of her concerts, while managers shuddered at the thought of the trouble she caused. Their hostess fluttered forward to greet her latest guests, as the turbaned Indians offered platters of fresh salmon dressed with fennel.

Shortly afterwards Madame Fourier clapped her hands and suggested that they all have lunch.

'I thought that *was* lunch,' groaned Zimmer. 'I've already eaten too much,' he added. 'D'you want to meet Stiarkoz? He's an incredibly rich, Greek shipowner with a wonderful art collection, a really nice old boy.'

～ 46 ～

SWINGING in the hammock on the geranium-scented patio, Lili could hear the nurse arguing at the front door. Presently she appeared with a golden antique birdcage in one hand. Inside it was a white cockatoo. 'I don't know where we're going to put *this* – the saints alone know what it eats!' The beautiful bird looked at Lili with bright topaz eyes. Delighted, Lili jumped off the hammock, pulling up the yellow strings of her bikini top.

'No card?'

'No. And the delivery boy didn't know who sent it.'

Half an hour later, while Lili was still playing with the cockatoo, a camellia tree arrived. Hanging from one leafy branch was a small packet wrapped in pale blue silk and tied with fine gold chain.

'Feel how heavy this thin chain is,' the nurse said. 'D'you think it could be *real* gold?'

Inside the pale blue silk package was a white seashell in which nestled a huge, square-cut aquamarine pendant on an almost-invisible gold chain.

'It's the colour of the Aegean,' Lili cried, running to a mirror in the living room and clasping it around her neck. In the greenish light she saw the pale blue rays flashing from her throat.

The telephone rang. 'Hello, Zimmer. Did you by any chance

send me a bird in a cage or anything else this morning? . . . Hang on a minute, that's the doorbell again.'

This time a pale blue beach buggy awaited her signature on the receipt. On the driver's seat lay a thick, cream envelope addressed simply to 'Lili'. Inside was a card across which was neatly penned, 'Shall we say Senequier this evening at eight?'

Lili tore back to the telephone. 'No, it's not me,' Zimmer said. 'It's either Fourier or Jo Stiarkoz. I'd bet on Stiarkoz. Fourier would merely have sent you a diamond brooch. Stiarkoz has more style. Now that I think about it, why *hasn't* Fourier sent you a diamond-studded something? You must be losing your touch, Lili.'

'Maybe he thinks you and I are having a scene?'

Zimmer giggled. 'Not me, darling, that they know. I'll drive you into St Tropez this evening, then you can say you were with me if Serge hears about it.'

Lili shivered. Serge would beat her mercilessly if he suspected she were flirting with anyone. Once he had actually cracked her rib. Particularly since her American tour, he had seen that she was never left unguarded.

That evening Zimmer drove the buggy into St Tropez. Lili had dressed with unusual care; she wore a white silk blazer and a finely pleated skirt that matched; besides that she wore nothing, no blouse, underwear or jewellery, except for the glowing aquamarine that settled at the base of her throat.

St Tropez looked like a lavish film set. Where trawlers and fishing smacks had once anchored, the harbour was now crowded with expensive white yachts. The quay was a solid line of smart boutiques and casual but expensive restaurants; under the famous orange awning of Senequier, the beautiful people who sipped aperitifs were better dressed than the patrons of the Ritz bar in Paris. Threading her way to the table that Zimmer had reserved, Lili reflected that the women looked straight out of the pages of last week's *Elle*; not one pair of white jeans had cost less than a thousand francs, not one of these beautifully tousled women had taken less than two hours to dress.

At exactly eight o'clock Zimmer winked at Lili. 'I was right, there's Stiarkoz getting out of his Rolls Royce. I wonder what conjuring tricks he's planning for the cocktail hour. Perhaps he'll pull a string of pearls out of his ears?'

He stood up and waved to Stiarkoz, who bowed slightly and moved to their table. He was a well-cared-for man of sixty, with thick silver eyebrows that hung over alert eyes. His lower lip protruded under his upper and curled up at the left corner, giving him a permanent look of amused belligerence. Stiarkoz was a careful man. He never signed his name to any document, whether a cheque or a love letter, because he did not like to commit himself. But he made up his mind fast, especially when he wanted something. And he wanted Lili.

Although Lili did not sense the seriousness of his interest, it was immediately apparent to Zimmer. Stiarkoz did not seem surprised to see Zimmer and made no effort to get rid of him; he obviously didn't want to alarm Lili. He wasn't going to make a crude grab at her. This was an exploratory meeting.

They ate a leisurely dinner by candlelight. Stiarkoz didn't ask Lili personal questions, but he sought her opinion on everything they discussed and listened carefully to her answers. As Zimmer described the making of *Q*, Lili felt less self-conscious, and she even started to laugh as he recounted an incident when a huge polystyrene rock had bounced off her head. Stiarkoz seemed pleased that both of them had so obviously enjoyed their visit to his country. 'All Greeks love Greece,' he said, 'especially the ones who live in London, Paris, New York and Monte Carlo.'

Zimmer's next film was also going to be shot outside Athens. 'It's not just another sex epic,' he explained, tongue-in-cheek. 'It's a modern Greek tragedy played against a background of the international shipping business, a fight to the death between two shipowners who both want to marry the same beautiful girl, the daughter of a third Greek shipowner. Her father forces her to choose the richer man, rather than the handsome younger one who only owns one cargo boat.'

'Brute,' said Lili.

'Not at all,' said Stiarkoz. 'Many Greek shipping marriages are arranged. Marriage is considered too serious a family matter to be decided by love. So is money.'

'Are all big shipowners Greek?' Lili asked. 'It always sounds like such a clannish business.' She sipped champagne as Stiarkoz took out a brown leather cigar case and selected one of the five cigars in it.

'Most of the world's commercial shipping is controlled by Greeks.' He sniffed the cigar. 'Out of a total dead weight tonnage of about fifty-two million, Onassis controls about four million and Niarchos about five million, apart from his shipyards.' Gently he slid the band from his Monte Cristo Number 2. 'Which leaves about forty-three million tons belonging to a small group of people that you never read about in the gossip columns, people like the Paterases and the Hadjipaterases, the Colocotronises, and the Lemoses; usually all intermarried.'

He leaned back and took out a tiny gold cigar cutter. Lili looked at it. 'Once this belonged to my great-grandfather,' Stiarkoz said.

'Was he a shipowner?'

'Eventually. But he started as a barefoot sailor, trading around the Greek islands.'

'A simple sailor?'

Stiarkoz smiled. 'Powerful Greek shipowners are never simple. They are highly complex men with a minimum amount of sociability and a maximum of egocentricity. Other people usually can't stand them.' Again he grinned at her.

Two expensively dressed girls approached their table. The redhead wore a sea-green lace see-through catsuit, her companion wore three blonde hairpieces above a red and white, diagonally striped minidress that barely covered her bottom. Stiarkoz put his cigar down, politely stood up and greeted them, but didn't introduce them to his companions. When they moved on, he again sat down. 'The husband of the lady in green is an arms dealer and has the mooring next to mine in Monte Carlo. I didn't think you would have much in common.'

At this moment a waiter hurried up to Stiarkoz with a telephone. He excused himself for a moment, picking up the receiver. 'Well, what's the present price of bauxite? No, no, on the Chicago exchange ... Well find out ...' He called for another telephone, dialled and said, 'Get Amsterdam on the telex and check the bauxite price.

'This won't take a moment, forgive me,' he apologized to Lili. 'Well, *make* them ... Well, hire another Lear jet ... Dammit, don't bother me with details, hire two ... Now, what are the bauxite figures? ... Fine, buy six hundred and fifty thousand from Chicago.'

The two telephones were removed from the table and Jo smiled at Lili.

'Finish about the shipowners,' she said. 'What do they do with all that money?'

He turned towards her in his chair. 'If you were to ask these men *why* they are amassing all their wealth and what they're going to do with it, they simply wouldn't be able to give you an answer. You'd be surprised to see how poorly they live, particularly the women of shipowners.'

'What about love?' asked Lili.

'They're interested in sex, of course, but again in their own special way. For the normal person, sex doesn't exist in a vacuum. But if a Greek shipowner meets a woman and likes her, then he wants sex with her straightaway. *Immediately!*' He shrugged his shoulders. 'Just as they can't make friends, they find it difficult to approach a woman, and afterwards they don't know what to do with that woman, which I think is appalling.'

'They sound like lousy lovers.'

'Certainly there's a lot of divorce, but a major reason for that is because the women always think they're marrying a husband and then they wake up to find they've married a business.'

'Don't they ever think about anything except business?'

Stiarkoz reflected. 'After their fiftieth birthday, they seem to wake up – *suddenly* – and realize that there's not much time left. It's exactly at this moment that they feel panic and get into those messy situations with mistresses, divorces and remarriages. That's when they start to look pathetic. Their end is often positively tragic, because they eventually realize that business is not the only thing in life. Then they realize all they've missed.'

The following day Lili lurched up and down the coastal road in the beach buggy, then played in the shade with her cockatoo. She was excited but wary, for the nurse had persistently questioned her about her anonymous gifts and was clearly suspicious about Lili's evening out with Zimmer.

After an evening swim off the rocks, Lili showered and changed into gold Grecian sandals and a white silk, ankle-length sheath under which she wore nothing.

At eight o'clock a chauffeur-driven Rolls appeared. The nurse looked surprised, then worried. 'Where are you going? I *must* know where you're going!' She caught hold of Lili's fragile wrist. 'You're ill, you mustn't go out alone.'

Lili quickly twisted her arm away and slid into the back seat. Speeding through the fragrance of the warm pine trees, Lili felt the excitement of an obedient child who suddenly defies its nurse-maid and, as the evening breeze lifted her dark hair, she started to sing the 'Marseillaise'.

This time Jo Stiarkoz was waiting at a discreet table in the rear of the café. She was not physically attracted to this small, quiet Greek, but she was enjoying her defiance and she felt he was no threat. He would, of course, make a pass at her, but she felt it was unlikely that he would pursue it if she made it clear that she wasn't interested.

To Lili's surprise, Stiarkoz made no attempt to touch her. He didn't try to detain her after they had finished dinner, although it was barely past eleven o'clock.

'I know you've been ill,' he said, 'so I don't expect you want a late night.'

They drove back to Cap Camerat through a silent landscape. Stiarkoz knew that he was no longer young, and he had never been handsome. But a man who has made billions is generally an interesting man, provided he talks about subjects that interest him. Jo wanted Lili to feel at ease with him. He knew that any man who got the chance probably made a pass at Lili, so he wasn't going to try. He wanted her to wonder why he didn't.

And he wanted her to wonder what it would be like if he did.

The following morning Lili went down to the beach at ten o'clock and swam ten metres to a small speedboat that was waiting to carry her to the *Minerva*. The bay wasn't deep enough for the huge yacht to come in close to shore.

As she was helped up to the white deck, Lili suddenly felt as free as a seagull. Strength flooded back into her body. As Stiarkoz showed her over the vessel, she again found herself humming the defiant tune of the 'Marseillaise', the rallying song of the French Revolution.

According to Stiarkoz, she was a small boat—no swimming pool and only one helicopter. But the *Minerva* could sail across the

Atlantic, if Lili wished. She could cruise anywhere in the world.

He had ordered a cabin to be prepared for Lili's use. The rosewood-panelled stateroom was somewhat larger than Lili's bedroom at the villa; two sea-blue bathrooms led off it, both with the regulation dolphin gold-plated fittings, both stocked with expensive toilet articles, Christian Dior perfumes and a complete, unopened range of Estée Lauder makeup. The walk-in closet contained a stock of scarlet dress boxes from Joy, the most exclusive beachwear shop in Monte Carlo. Six new swimsuits, six new beach wraps and six couture evening dresses hung from a rail. On the bed lay a huge Christian Dior box, inside which was a cream silk, lace-trimmed négligé, delicate and beautiful as an antique christening robe. 'In case you wished to change or rest,' explained Stiarkoz with a wave of his hand.

They lay on deckbeds on the main deck sipping champagne under the blue awning. They were not entirely alone – a secretary and two aides moved discreetly in and out of the forward cabin and from behind the door Lili could hear the impersonal clatter of a telex. Two stewards attended them on deck, along with a large, silent sailor with a mole on his left cheek, who followed Stiarkoz everywhere. 'Socrates, my bodyguard,' Stiarkoz explained.

All day they stayed at sea, swimming from the boat or lying in the sun. Jo asked no questions about Lili's background or her work. (In fact, the evening after he met her, one of his shore secretaries had handed him a hair-raising dossier on her.) Jo skilfully chatted with Lili; he instinctively sensed her mood and tailored his conversation to suit it. She is the the most sensational woman I have ever seen, he thought. She is young enough to be my granddaughter and I do not give a damn. I am about to make a public fool of myself and I do not give a damn. I am only afraid that she will make a fool of me, and if she does, then life will not be worth living. Jo knew he wasn't being prudent; he wondered why he put his private life at risk, but Lili's presence drove all prudence from his head.

In a daffodil bikini she was sitting on the edge of a chair with one foot up on the seat and her head thrown back, as she held the last spear of asparagus above her mouth and sucked at the tip. She looked as natural and unaffected as a charming little animal, totally unaware of anything except the sun, the sea and her own laughter.

Jo watched the butter sauce running down her chin. He thought, she is a beautiful, sensual, ignorant, uncultivated little savage. Why don't I just give her dinner this evening, say goodbye nicely, send her home in the Rolls and never see her again? But what he said was, 'Do you want more, Lili?'

At dusk they docked in the glittering port of Monaco. The castellated towers of the royal palace topped The Rock to the left of the harbour. Beyond it rose the town, pink and white layers against the lavender mountains. As they slid into harbour, the sky turned from aquamarine to violet, to purple, then to velvet black and strings of fairy lights lit up the town.

Because of the heat, the roof was open in the grill room of the Hôtel de Paris. They ate quail stuffed with white grapes, after which they strolled down the hill to the harbour, discreetly followed by the Rolls.

Jo asked if Lili would care to stay the night on board the *Minerva*.

Immediately wary, Lili explained that she had to sleep at the villa, since Serge telephoned every morning. Jo immediately said that she should be driven back at eleven that evening. He made no attempt to dissuade her.

On the darkened deck of the *Minerva* they sat listening contentedly to Strauss waltzes from the stereo. The odour of seaweed wafted from the cliffs beyond the harbour and mingled with the fragrance of Jo's cigar. Blue smoke trembled on the still night air.

Suddenly there was a scuffle at the end of the gangway. Lili heard her name yelled by a voice that she recognized only too well. Suddenly afraid, she jerked upright. Stiarkoz slowly stood up, looking neither unsettled nor surprised. He put an arm around Lili's shoulder, touching her for the first time. 'There's no need to be frightened.'

'Lili, Lili! I know you're there, you bitch, I can *see* you.' Serge was lurching up the gangway towards her. Jo tightened his arm around her shoulder.

'Don't break his fingers, Socrates, just hold him.' Socrates moved surprisingly swiftly out of the shadows of the quay and

Serge's arms were jerked up behind him. Stiarkoz, moving towards him, took a puff of his cigar.

'My friend, I regret my lack of hospitality. Why are you here?'

'Because you've got my woman, you Greek bastard. When I heard she was with *you*, I caught the next plane to Nice. What do you think you're doing with that old goat, you stupid bitch?' he yelled at Lili.

Jo turned to Lili. 'Are you his woman?'

'Yes . . . No. I don't know.' Lili burst into tears.

'Well, do you *want* to be his woman?'

'Oh no, no, no! But he protects me. I haven't anybody except Serge.'

Stiarkoz put his arm around her and turned to Serge. 'I'm afraid she prefers the old goat. So would you please get off my ship before I have you arrested.'

He spoke softly in Greek. Socrates tightened his grip and Serge screamed. 'Aaaagh! You bastard. You oily Greek bastard. Aaaaah!' Socrates had grasped Serge around the waist from the rear, lifting his feet off the ground, and was carrying him backwards down the gangway.

'A perfect suplex,' murmured Stiarkoz. He turned his back on the struggling man, put his hand under Lili's elbow, and guided her towards the saloon. 'I think we will spend the night at sea.' He reached for the ivory intercom.

Just after midnight, the *Minerva* slowly moved out of the harbour. Standing in the stern, Lili and Jo watched the golden outline of the town etched against the black sky in a billion golden pinpricks. As the town receded, Jo threw his cigar butt into the phosphorescent wake of the *Minerva*.

'You mustn't worry,' he said. 'You mustn't feel trapped. I don't want you to feel that you are moving out of one cage and into another. For the moment you are my guest. Later, when you feel strong enough, we can discuss your future. If you have signed any contracts, they can be renegotiated. That's what lawyers are for. You have nothing to worry about.' He broke off for a moment, then continued, 'You are a very lovely young woman, with your life before you. You can earn your own living, you can live alone, you can do whatever you wish. But don't think about it until the morning.' Then he gently turned her chin towards him and Lili felt the firm pressure of his mouth on hers. She smelled the faint odour of starch and cigar and clean, warm flesh as she leaned against him, agreeably surprised at the strength of his arm.

Serge stormed into Senequier, drank a bottle of brandy, then drove wildly to Cap Camerat where he strangled the white cockatoo.

～ 47 ～

FROM the jasmine-scented terrace, the view across the valley looked like a Cézanne painting. Rows of silver olive trees climbed to the blue line where the mountains met the sky of southern France. Dark cyprus trees lined the road that wound up to Vence between terra-cotta villas surrounded by orange and lemon trees.

'It's unlike Jo to be so late without letting us know,' Lili apologized to Zimmer. 'His driver usually telephones from the car. Are you *sure* he said three-thirty, Constantine?'

'Yes, I'm sure Jo said three-thirty, but really it doesn't matter. The contracts don't have to be signed today, we can backdate them.' The big man smiled at her, but only with his mouth. His heavy-lidded, half-closed eyes never showed any expression. His fleshy beak of a nose hung over a luxuriant moustache and beard. Shoulder-length, silvery locks made Constantine Demetrios look oddly patriarchal, more like a Greek Orthodox priest than a lawyer.

Behind them, the villa stretched away, ornate as a wedding cake and large as a palace. The marble terrace where Lili sat was as wide as a ballroom and edged by a classical stone balustrade, upon which stood stone urns, planted with white geraniums and babies' breath.

'Well, I'll tell them to put off tea for another half an hour,' Lili said. 'Would either of you like to stroll around the garden?' Demetrios shook his head, but Zimmer stood up.

'It looks too perfect to be real, Lili, I'm going to check whether those yews are plastic.' He pointed beyond the marble statues which surrounded the splendid baroque fountain below, to the hedged walk which led towards the thirty-metre swimming pool.

Lili tucked her arm in his and they moved away, towards the curving marble steps. 'We grow our own vegetables and fruit here. Everything you ate at lunch came from the estate, it's brought in daily by the head gardener. We also produce our own chickens, turkeys and pigs; we press our own olive oil and make our own vin rosé; unlabelled but very good.'

Zimmer laughed. 'You make it sound so quaintly rural, but this must be one of the most splendid estates on the French Riviera. Very different from that dank villa I found you in three years ago.' As they passed one of the statues, he patted its marble fanny.

In fact, he didn't much care for the huge house, though he had to admit that the pictures were wonderful. No obligatory El Greco, no suspect Rembrandt, no second-rate Degas, no self-consciously slick Salvador Dali. With the exception of a little Constable river sketch, the pictures had mostly been painted after 1850 and had obviously been chosen by a connoisseur to please himself. Zimmer's favourite was a soft, mauve Seurat of a girl picking cabbages, but that Monet – the lily pool at Giverny – was breathtaking.

'Yes, very different from every place I've lived in,' said Lili, as they reached the yew walk. 'Everything about me is different from three years ago, thank God. We lead a very quiet life, and if I'm not filming I spend most of my time here.' She was silent for a moment as they strolled towards the aquamarine pool. 'The first thing that Jo did was to free me from my contract with Serge. Constantine handled it – he's Jo's chief lawyer and they're old friends, so we see a lot of him. If any loophole exists in an arrangement, then Con will find it. He never signs anything that he can't get out of.' They moved downhill to the left. In front of them, half-hidden by the trees, was a simple, white, rectangular building. The whole of the north wall was glass. 'Did I tell you that I'm studying history with a retired professor in Vence?' Lili asked. 'I generally paint in the afternoon. This is our studio.'

She pressed a button and the wooden door swung open on a twenty-foot-high room lit by overhead skylights. The interior smelled of turpentine, linseed oil, dust and Diorissimo, that lily-of-the-valley fragrance that Lili always wore. There were four big easels, a couple of donkey stools and two old wooden tables, all spattered with paint.

'I'm not very good yet, but I love painting. I have a teacher twice a week; Jo chose a tough one because he wants me to learn about structure, not just to pat paint on.'

'Jo's collection certainly is fantastic.'

Lili hesitated before she responded, 'It isn't *his* collection. All the pictures are mine. He gave them all to me on my last birthday.'

Zimmer's mouth fell open. '*All* of them? That Van Gogh cornfield and the Matisse goldfish bowl?'

'Yes, all of them, his whole collection. You haven't seen the ones upstairs yet.'

She remembered her birthday. Although it had been October, her bedroom had been filled with lilies and roses. Jo had led her to the big bay window. On a circular marble table stood a large antique box inlaid with ebony and a design of ivory cupids. She had opened the box expecting to see a piece of jewellery, but instead there had been a mass of legal documents. Jo had explained that the papers were proof of the authenticity of each painting and proof that she, Lili, was now the legal owner of each one. The gift was a relatively quick, discreet way for him to give her a fortune. The museums of the world would bid fiercely for most of these pictures. If she wanted a house in Paris or an apartment in New York, she need only sell one picture.

Zimmer whistled. 'And they say that diamonds are a girl's best friend!'

'Oh, I've got diamonds as well, and ropes and ropes of baroque pearls. Jo loves to see me in diamonds and pearls. He says I look best in white, with sparkling wrists and throat and hair.'

Zimmer whistled again. Stiarkoz was obviously still completely besotted. They left the studio and started back to the house up the grassy slope towards the long, low mansion.

'Is this what you want, Lili? This quiet life? Isn't it a bit staid for a girl of twenty-four?'

'What you really mean is how can I possibly be happy with a man who's nearly forty years older than me, isn't it? People are always asking me that indirectly. Of course Jo isn't *young*. He can't leap about and play tennis for hours and he'll probably die before I do. We've discussed all that. But that's his only disadvantage and it doesn't much affect me.' Lili bent and tugged a sprig from a rosemary bush. 'As a matter of fact *I* feel constantly at a disadvantage with him because I'm so ignorant.'

'Ah, that's exciting for an older man,' Zimmer said. 'To open a young girl's eyes, to awe her, to be a god to her ... Until she meets someone who says, "That's not a god, that's just an old man with money."'

Lili scowled. 'I find it odd that other men should assume that Jo has nothing to attract me *except* money.' She pointed a rosemary branch at him accusingly. 'Jo has plenty of advantages that a young man couldn't have. He's carved his own path through life, he's forged his own way; he's gutsy and that's always exciting in any man, whatever his age. Age doesn't matter so much to an intelligent man, because he doesn't rely only on his physical attributes to attract a woman.' She crushed a couple of rosemary spikes between her fingers and paused to inhale the fragrance. 'I love to hear Jo *talk*.' She sniffed again.

'Of course I'm not denying that Jo can provide what women have traditionally *always* looked for in a man – protection and security.' Lili's voice shook as she tucked the rosemary sprig down the front of her dress. Jo represented all the protective men she had lacked since losing Felix, and for that she loved Jo with passionate gratitude. 'As a matter of fact, I don't even consider Jo's age to be a drawback, because without his age, he wouldn't have that wisdom of experience. A relationship that's going to last isn't based on sheer sexual madness and nonstop sexual excitement but on ... understanding and tolerance.'

'And so there is no sexual madness?'

'Jo has never left me unfulfilled, Zimmer. Not once. And that's more than I can say about most of the men in my life.'

They had nearly reached the long pool, its immaculate surface unruffled by wind or leaf. 'Are you two getting married?'

'What's the point? I don't particularly want to marry Jo. You see, so many women have tried to force him to do that. I don't want marriage.' Zimmer turned to look at her and raised a quizzical eyebrow. 'No, Zimmer, I want Jo. I do not ask for marriage. This way he knows that I'm not ... what his children tell him I am ... a gold digger.'

They walked around the blue pool and the surface quivered in the breeze as Lili added, 'Anyway, Jo's never suggested marriage, although I'm sure he's thought about it. Zimmer, haven't you noticed that these very rich old men never marry their luscious young mistresses? They're afraid of making fools of themselves, especially if the marriage doesn't work out. And they never seem to.'

They moved up the worn, stone steps. A white-gloved footman was about to place a silver tea tray on a terrace table. Zimmer said, 'It's none of my business, Lili, but I can't see how this is going to last. Your life is just beginning, and you're tying yourself down to a man whose life is ending. And you're still not happy – don't deny it, I *work* with you and I *know* you! You're *still* being dominated, only in a different way. Pretending to enjoy this staid, matronly life in the sun! You're a brilliant actress and you're never going to get where you should be if you're semiretired. The public forgets unless it's constantly reminded.' He shrugged his shoulders. 'Your own personality is being swamped. Stiarkoz has to dominate everything in sight, even *you*, so you're in danger of losing sight of yourself again. If you abandon your real identity, you're going to lose your true self. When you live by somebody else's standards, you betray your own. You're turning into Jo's echo, Lili!'

Lili looked exasperated. 'I've never felt I had a real identity, so how could I lose it?'

Zimmer snatched at a honeysuckle branch as they passed it. 'I can see that Stiarkoz can buy you plenty of expensive toys, but haven't you noticed, Lili, that with all his wealth he hasn't attempted to give you what you really want?'

'*Shut up*, Zimmer! You can't know what Jo gives me. He makes me feel protected, he's given me dignity, he educates me and he – demands little in return.'

'But he hasn't tried to give you what you *really* want – because he knows the danger. He might be able to trace your parents for you! But if you found your true identity, he's afraid he'd lose his power over you. And he's very possessive, he likes your being dependent on him, because if you weren't – you might leave him!'

'How dare you say such things about Jo!' Lili said, glaring at him.

'Lili, I'm one of the few men who value you and don't want to

485

possess you. I've known for years that you won't feel what you call "real" until you feel real self-confidence. At the moment, you only have that when you can shed yourself and be an imaginary person.'

In the sunlight, Lili suddenly looked exhausted and forlorn. 'Zimmer, I think you'd better leave.'

'Darling, I was just about to go. Tell Jo I'm sorry to have missed him.'

Lili saw him to his scarlet Maserati parked halfway down the white gravel drive, then she wandered back towards the house.

Suddenly Demetrios appeared in the open front door. He came running towards her in an oddly slow way, a heavy man in a dark, expensive suit. She felt an odd foreboding.

Demetrios heaved towards her, crunching across the gravel in slow motion, his pink silk tie flapping over his jacket. It was so odd to see him running.

She knew immediately that something dreadful had happened to Jo.

～ 48 ～

'THERE'S been an accident, a car accident,' Demetrios panted. 'They've taken Jo and his driver to a hospital in Nice. That was the police on the telephone. They couldn't tell me anything except that the Rolls had been travelling back from Monte Carlo when it shot off the Nice motorway aqueduct. It simply went through the wall and plunged over the side into the valley below. They've taken Jo and the driver to the Princess Grace Hospital.'

He didn't tell her that the police had asked for someone to visit the hospital and identify Jo. Both he and his driver were dead – their bodies had had to be cut out of the mangled Rolls Royce.

Cold water was trickling down her neck and back. Lili opened her eyes. She must have fainted. Her maid, silent and frightened, was kneeling by the couch and sponging her face. The footman stood a few paces behind, looking helpless and apologetic, as if he'd just dropped the silver tea tray.

Demetrios reappeared and walked across the carpet towards the little group. He leaned over the back of the couch. 'Lili, my dear, don't move. The doctor is on his way.'

The doctor wasn't Doctor Jamais; he was a small, sallow man with rimless glasses whom she'd never seen before. 'Where's Doctor Jamais?' she murmured, but he took no notice. He merely pulled back her eyelid, felt her pulse, murmured something to the maid, and moved to a table where he undid his bag and turned his back to her. After a couple of minutes he turned towards Lili, and she saw a syringe in his hand. 'What's that for?'

'Shock, madame. You are in a slight state of shock. There's nothing to worry about.' He crouched by the couch and with a piece of cotton swabbed the inside of her left arm. Lili smelled hospitals. 'Just a *slight* prick. There, that's over. It didn't hurt, did it?'

'I don't understand, I'm not ill, I just felt dizzy. I fainted ... I don't understand.'

Her eyelids slowly closed and then her jaw fell.

Someone was holding her right hand. She was in bed in a small, gloomy room that she'd never seen before. Lili turned her head to the right and saw that Demetrios held her hand. She felt too weak to speak. Slow, silent tears trickled down her cheeks, her right ear felt damp. Demetrios patted her hand and replaced it gently on the blanket.

'How are you feeling, my dear?'

'Awful. I've got a splitting headache. But I've got to get to the hospital. I've got to see Jo. Where is this place?'

'It's a clinic outside Nice. Do you think you can get dressed? If so I'll call for a nurse to help you, then I can drive you to the hospital. But first there are a couple of formalities. Would you mind signing this, please.'

'I can't sign anything now. Surely it can wait, Con, whatever it is?'

'I'm afraid not, my dear. It's the authority for the hospital to release the ... er ... Jo. Oh, my dear child, I'm so sorry that you have to suffer this, but bureaucracy is always with us, so exhausting.'

Gently he pushed a pen into her hand and guided it to the page.

487

'And here also.' Shuffle of documents. 'And here, and here, and this is the last . . . Oh, no, there's one more.'

He patted her shoulder, quickly took the typed documents away from her, leaned to the floor for his briefcase, snapped it open on his knees and swiftly tucked the documents into it. 'Now I'll call the nurse to help you dress.' He pushed the bell knob.

'But, Con, you must tell me what *happened*.'

'It was the driver. He had a heart attack. Only thirty-five and looked as fit a man as ever I'd seen. The police think that he slumped over the wheel with the weight of his leg on the accelerator. The car was very heavy. It simply leaped forward and smashed through the retainer wall, then went over the side of the aqueduct.'

'But Con, you must tell me what happened to Jo.'

'Jo was cremated three days ago,' he said quietly.

Lili gave an anguished shriek and tried to sit up. The nurse swiftly restrained her and lifted the telephone for help. 'Tell the doctor that this patient needs another shot,' Demetrios whispered. 'She's hysterical.'

When Lili regained her senses, she waited for half an hour until her head felt clearer. Then she put her legs over the side of the bed. She felt very weak and seemed about ten pounds thinner. She hobbled to the armoire in the corner, tugged open the door and found her clothes inside. She carried them to the bed, then sat on it and slowly dressed. Then she moved to the washbasin and looked in the mirror. Her eyes were sunken, her face looked thin and her hair was flat and listless. She splashed cold water on her face and looked out of the window. The sun was almost overhead.

The door to her room opened and a starched little nurse appeared.

'My goodness, you shouldn't be up and about.'

Lili turned, the tooth glass in her hand, her only weapon. She was looking into the pleasant, surprised face of a girl of about her own age, who said, 'I'd better call Sister.'

'No, don't yet,' said Lili. 'How long have I been here?'

'Why, ten days.'

'But *why*?'

'You were brought in unconscious, you'd had a very bad

hysterical reaction to a shock and had to be treated with sedation. My, you were a difficult patient! The doctor insisted on looking after you himself.'

'Well, I want to leave now. Would you please call a cab?'

'Oh, my, you can't discharge yourself like that, madame.'

'Get me the doctor, please.'

'He's out at the moment. Sister is in charge.'

'Then get Sister, please.'

Lili settled into the back seat of the cab. It had taken her twenty minutes to talk her way past the head nurse, but in the end they had asked her to sign a paper and she had left. Of course, there must be some simple reason for her stay. Jo would explain . . . No, of course he wouldn't, couldn't. If only she hadn't fainted when she heard that Jo was dead!

Forty minutes later they reached the iron gates of the estate, but when the cab honked no one came running to open them. She got out and walked over to the small side door which was always open. There was nobody on duty at the lodge.

Lili walked up the white gravel drive to the house and rang the doorbell. She rang it again, sharply. Twice. What on earth were they all doing?

Then she heard footsteps cross the marble, a bolt was drawn back, the great door swung open and Lili found herself looking into the mournful, creased face of Socrates, Jo's bodyguard.

'Hello, Socrates,' Lili said, 'where is everybody?'

The burly sailor scratched the mole on his cheek. 'The whole staff was dismissed, Madame, the day after the funeral. There's only the housekeeper and me left up here now, and we have strict instructions from Mr Demetrios not to let anyone into the grounds. Of course I know he didn't mean you, Madame, but the photographers have been a bit of a nuisance. We all thought you were very wise to stay away until it was over.'

'Did Mr Demetrios tell you that was why I stayed away?'

'Why, yes, Madame.'

'D'you think you could ask the housekeeper to bring some coffee to my bedroom, please. I think I'd like to lie down for a bit, but first I want to talk to her.'

'But Madame, the furniture has all been moved, it's gone into a storage warehouse. The rooms are empty. Mr Demetrios told us. We assumed you *knew* that, Madame.'

Lili looked around the circular, domed hall and saw that it was indeed bare of furniture, curtains and carpets. As she climbed the circular staircase, her legs trembled. She still felt very weak, but her bedroom suite was just at the top of the stairs.

The room was empty. In fact, the only thing in it was her wall safe, which was normally covered by blue taffeta curtains. She moved closer. The door to the little grey safe was ajar.

But only she and Jo had the keys to the safe! Not that Lili's best jewellery was kept there, that was all in the bank vault.

She pulled the safe door open and peered inside. There was a small gleam of gold at the back. She fished it out with her forefinger – it was a charm from her bracelet, a miniature copy of the *Minerva*.

No, she wasn't dreaming.

Then she realized that all the pictures were missing. She looked around the room at the rectangular blank where her Rousseau bicyclist used to pedal in his red striped vest, at the pale patch where the pretty Dufy watercolour of Antibes had once hung.

She rushed into her dressing room and opened the doors. Even her clothes had disappeared. She ran to the window, threw it wide and looked out. The garden looked as usual in the low rays of the setting sun. She ran back to her bedroom, knelt by the ivory telephone on the floor and lifted the receiver. It was dead. Demetrios must have taken leave of his senses.

And then she remembered signing the papers.

For about an hour she remained motionless, kneeling by the telephone. Then she heard heavy footsteps climbing up the carpetless circular staircase and Demetrios appeared in the doorway.

'The clinic telephoned to tell me you had discharged yourself. Very foolish of you, Lili.'

Demetrios still looked the same, but now, instead of being reassuringly large and dependable, he seemed large and sinister. His dark clothes looked menacing, the heavy nose seemed predatory and the dull brown eyes were hard and cold as stones.

'Where are my clothes, Con?'

'They have been packed and are waiting for your instructions.'

'You got Jo's key to the safe, didn't you? Did the police just hand it over to you? Yes, I suppose they did, you're his lawyer after all. Where am I supposed to sleep tonight? I don't even have a change of underwear.'

'You have over fifty-three thousand francs in your current bank account.'

'How do you know what's in my bank account?'

'I know you have plenty of money, so you can stay at a hotel. And you've got your own car to drive to one.'

'And my pictures, Con? Where are my pictures?'

Demetrios looked straight into Lili's angry face and slowly stroked his beard. 'What pictures?' he asked softly.

Jo had been right. Con *was* fast and clever and had undoubtedly tied up every loose end, but Lili knew that Jo would have wanted her to try to regain her pictures and her jewellery, so she consulted a lawyer. He listened in silence to Lili's story, then regretfully he said that nothing could be done, and that under French law Lili had no claim to any part of the estate of Mr Stiarkoz. There was a silence, then he added, 'It sounds as if Mr Demetrios bribed a shady doctor to keep you sedated, then he probably offered a deal to the children of Mr Stiarkos. Possibly he offered to get your signature on all the necessary legal documents upon payment of – oh, perhaps ten million francs or more: that's a fraction of what such paintings might be worth.' It was well known that the art collection was the property of the late Mr Stiarkoz; it was *not* known to be the property of Mademoiselle Lili and she had no documentation to support her case.

Mr Demetrios had undoubtedly removed Mademoiselle Lili's strongbox from the bank, but he had her signed authority to do so, and nobody at the bank knew what was in the strongbox when it was removed or when it was returned. When Mademoiselle Lili eventually opened the strongbox herself, it only contained copies of Mademoiselle's old contracts and there was no jewellery and no documentation concerning the origin and authenticity of the paintings, and there was no deed of conveyance specifically assigning the ownership of each picture to Mademoiselle Lili. And as Mademoiselle did not know the whereabouts of the jewellery or of the art collection, from whom could she possibly claim them?

Lili sat silent, thinking that the jewellery and the pictures were not all that Jo had given her: he had given Lili something else of great value – her self-confidence. Instead of sheltering her completely, instead of allowing Lili to exchange one golden cage for another, Jo had encouraged her to find out what she was good at and to use her gifts. He had insisted that she make at least one film a year, so she hadn't dropped out of sight and she wasn't broke.

She would sell the Rolls Royce Corniche and buy an apartment in an inexpensive part of Paris.

Then she would ask Zimmer to recommend an agent and get back to work as fast as possible.

~ PART NINE ~

49

THROUGHOUT 1969, 'Life & Style', the newspaper section Kate edited, had continued to be what Kate called 'froth rather than beer'. After much argument, she was allowed to run a letters column and had hired a 'Dear Abby' who visited their new consultant psychiatrist once a week with the readers' more difficult problems.

After Kate's thirty-seventh birthday, she started a second book, *Danger! Women at Work*. Although it was based on her vast mailbag, she also interviewed many women on the difficulties of getting work, the difficulties of working, the special difficulties of working mothers and the difficulties of not working. To launch the book, her publisher and the *Globe* jointly sent her throughout England on a promotion tour. Once outside London, Kate became even more conscious that she was no longer really interested in the empty froth of 'Life & Style'. She was far more interested in real women, in real situations and problems. As this seemed to be what concerned the newly formed Women's Liberation Movement, Kate had looked it up. This was not easy, since no telephone number was listed and the directory personnel hadn't heard of the Women's Liberation Movement. Eventually, Kate got a telephone number that turned out to be a bookshop off Leicester Square, but the number had just been disconnected for nonpayment of account. Kate was to discover that one of the most depressing things about Women's Liberation was that everyone in it seemed to be broke.

Kate attended four meetings of the Women's Liberation group, but found them all disappointing. Every woman's experience was considered of utmost importance, however boring. There was much rapping and consciousness-raising, but not much seemed to get *done*. The sisters never seemed to talk about practical considerations; discussion was either directed to experience-sharing or else utopian theorizing. Kate was depressed by the muddled Marxist political thinking: '. . . The family is a basic unit of capitalism ... system of oppression ... We must destroy it ... Women are slaves whose function is to service the male workers ... Before the Industrial Revolution the home was the centre of productivity with husband and wife participating equally in work and child care ...'

Kate started to wonder what could be done for the women who wrote those sacks of letters to her every week. On the whole, her readers loved their men and depended on them. If they didn't have a man, they wished they did. Kate's consciousness had already been raised by the lawyers after her father's death and before her divorce. She knew society was unfair to women. However, it wasn't about to change overnight. Women would have to tackle injustice slowly, without hate or aggression, which could frighten other women away. Kate wondered what she could do to help the situation. She didn't think there was much point in attending any more meetings.

For two weeks Kate brooded over an idea before she phoned Judy. 'Judy, I want to launch my own monthly magazine for the new, emerging woman. Will you help?'

'Haven't you got enough problems?' Judy's voice barked back. '*What* new woman?'

'For heaven's sake, you're one of them!' Kate exclaimed. 'It's 1970 and the Sleeping Princess is waking up. She's got her own job, her own money, she can make her own rules and run her own life. At the moment she's tentatively groping her way, but she's alert at last and she's got a lot of power, because – collectively – she's first generation money.'

The line buzzed and faded. Kate yelled, 'I want to start a magazine that will pay special attention to the psychological needs of a woman, a magazine that will help her understand her own emotions. No magazine is doing that; there's a clear gap in the market.'

'What about *Cosmo*? What about *Ms*.?'

'We don't have them yet in Britain.'

'Describe your readers again.'

Kate repeated her idea. 'Obviously I can't give you an off-the-cuff answer,' Judy said. 'I'll talk to Tom about it and call you back.'

*

'We're interested,' Judy told Kate. 'Why don't you fly over for a couple of days. We want you to talk to a few people over here whom you already know. Griffin Lowe, my favourite publisher, and Pat Rogers, my former boss, who's now features editor of one of our top magazines. She feels pretty much the same way as you do – fed up with the frosted pap that's being put out for women. But we're not thinking of starting in Britain. We're thinking of starting over *here*.'

Kate booked a Thursday night flight and took a long weekend off. Those four days were spent in Judy's apartment with Judy and Pat, who did most of the talking, and Griffin and Tom, who didn't say much or do much except scribble the occasional note on their alligator memo pads. It was the first time that Kate had met both men. On her previous visit, Tom had been working with the LACE office on the West Coast.

Griffin grilled Pat and Kate until he knew everything about their reader except her pantyhose size. Then he and Tom sat at one end of the dining table and wore out a calculator, while the three women continued to talk, argue, guess, predict and hope.

The bulk of women's magazine advertising lies in the multibillion-dollar beauty business. After Kate had returned to London, Griffin and Judy took Mrs Lauder out to lunch at Orsini's to see what she thought of the idea. Mrs Lauder was small, quiet and extremely shrewd. Lunch for four cost three hundred and fifty dollars. Every dish had a special sauce, but nobody ate anything – they just pretended to.

Mrs Lauder thought the idea sounded plausible.

After a second meeting, Mrs Lauder agreed that *if* the magazine were to be as they described it, and *if* it hit the anticipated circulation, then she *might* take space. She agreed that there was a gap in the market. A definite maybe.

One by one they lunched the other beauty-business magnates. Eyeing the bills, Tom suggested maybe they ought to go into the restaurant business. Judy called Kate again. 'We're getting a market survey, and if that looks good we'll do it.'

But Judy didn't like the deal that Griffin offered. 'I can't agree to seventy per cent for Orbit, Griffin.'

'– Judy, I have to justify this to the shareholders. Our relationship isn't the world's best-kept secret.'

'– And I want the staff to have some kind of participation.'

'– A nice idea, but I've never known it to work. It's an incentive that stops working as soon as they get it. Stick to bonuses based on increased profit. Don't encourage equality on the editorial floor or you'll never get anything printed.'

Judy phoned Kate again.

'I'm phoning to offer you the job of joint managing editor and to say that we're willing to offer you two per cent of the action if you can raise $170,000. Tom can arrange a five-year, back-to-back loan for you in some way that's legal if you can put up collateral in Britain. It'll cost you one per cent extra interest, but it's the only way that you can buy in because apparently your idiotic exchange-control regulations won't let you take money out of Britain to invest elsewhere.'

Kate rushed off to Barclay's Bank. If she sold all her stock she would still be about five thousand pounds short, but her mother agreed to guarantee an overdraft to cover it. So after another quick trip to New York, she told Scotty that she wanted to leave.

'Agh, you bitch,' he said. 'How could you do this to me after eight years together? What d'ye expect me to say? Except congratulations. Now stay out of my way for a few days, I'm too angry to talk to you.'

Kate let Walton Street on a three-year lease to a General Motors executive, put her furniture in storage and flew to New York, where Tom had taken a short lease on an eleventh floor suite of offices on Fifty-third Street.

Countless evenings were spent in Judy's apartment, trying to decide on a name for the magazine. Eventually they decided to call it *Verve!* with an exclamation point. It has an exultant, glad-to-be-alive feeling (which is how they wanted their readers to feel), and it was short and easy to remember.

Verve! threw its first party at the Four Seasons.

Tom, looking like one of those suave, impeccably dressed fashion drawings in *The New Yorker*, made a brief speech of introduction. Then Judy introduced her team and stated their editorial policy. The presentation lasted almost forty minutes.

Kate felt oddly detached, as if she were watching her own performance from somewhere on the ceiling. 'The key to self-expression is style, and every woman should learn how to develop her own. Every reader is important, because she is an individual and we want to encourage her individuality. But every reader also forms part of an enormously powerful economic force. Who are the enormous spenders of this country? Not Jackie, not Zsa Zsa, not Liz. The collective mass of American women probably form the biggest money-spending force in the world. *Verve!* will not only show them *how* to spend it, we'll also show them how to make it, how to earn it and how to multiply it. It's time that women thought more about money – and had more of it for themselves. We intend to make this very clear.'

Judy hoped that the magazine would give its readers the support that she had found in Kate, Maxine and Pagan. Together, the four of them had certainly brought out the best in each other. Without the other three where would they be? Kate was the only one who had real talent, but she was a quiet mouse who worried too much. Without Judy to push her, she'd probably be an unhappy divorcée, spending too much at Harrods. Without Kate, Pagan would still be a misfit brought up in a privileged world in which she never felt at home – a perplexed, hopeless drunkard. Maxine had gone a long way with her determination and hard work but she would never have been world-famous without Judy to show her to the world, and although Judy was a tough go-getter, she would never have started her own business if Maxine hadn't pushed her into it. Alone, their frailties might have overwhelmed them. Together, they had strength and speed and style – which is what *Verve!* was going to push as hard as it could.

50

'Do you want to know what a woman finds attractive in a man?' Kate asked. 'I just got the survey results.' She looked at the alert faces around her desk at the eleven o'clock Monday conference. It was thirteen weeks after the party at the Four Seasons, three weeks before the first issue was due to be published. 'What women find attractive in a man and what men *think* women find attractive in a man turn out to be entirely different. Twenty-two per cent of males admitted that what they thought appealed most to a woman was a large, tight-trousered bulge, but only three per cent of the women thought so.'

They all giggled. *Verve!* had started with a shoestring full-time staff of fourteen plus freelancers and contributing editors. Most of the journalists were always working on at least three stories at once, in different stages of progress. The fashion editor was due to join them in two weeks – in her absence they were using high-powered fashion stylists at enormous expense.

'The men didn't think that slimness was important in a man, but most of the women thought it was vital,' Kate continued. 'Only two per cent of the men thought that the male buttocks were important, whereas this area easily was top attraction with women, at forty-two per cent.'

Kate had started that morning's conference by giving a run-down of the schedule for the next issue: sixteen weeks in advance of publication, they discussed the rough shape of the magazine; copy deadline day was ten weeks later, and the following six weeks to publication was a fast-moving battle between the editors, the assistants, the art department and the printers.

Life was fun, thought Kate after the conference, but it wasn't the sort of fun that their readers imagined. It wasn't a playgirl existence lived from champagne reception to dress show. *Verve!* was absorbing work. *That* was the best possible fun. Sitting with six snarling telephones in front of her and a couple of people leaning against the wall just inside her door, Kate reflected that most of their readers would probably hate her job, but as far as she was concerned, she would gladly have paid to do it. Launching *Verve!* was the most exciting thing she'd ever done and, however exhausted she was, she hated to stop in the evenings.

There was only one fly in the ointment. Kate didn't find Tom easy to work with. He had been brought up on the West Coast and before teaming up with Judy, he'd worked only in the motion picture industry, which inevitably coloured his attitude to women. He couldn't help categorizing women as mothers or hookers of one variety or another. Some of them were also properties, and these were liable to give trouble; you treated a property warily, as you would a baby cheetah. For Tom, Judy was a very valuable property. But Kate – well, she hadn't proved her value yet. Tom intended to produce a magazine packaged a bit like the Virginia Slims ads ... 'You've come a long way, baby ...' But Kate didn't fit the glossy, Virginia-Slims-Lib image any more than she did the heavy *Ms.* image. Tom couldn't place her. Sure, she wrote that book, she was a minor celebrity, but that didn't mean she was going to make money for him. So Tom and Kate kept clashing until Judy took it upon herself to soothe Kate down. 'Look, Kate, all backers are difficult. One of the reasons that Tom keeps our backers happy is because he thinks the same way as they do. We're taking a big, big gamble, which we certainly couldn't do without Tom. His personal disadvantages are business advantages. He can deal with all that shit and leave us to get on with the work.' Judy took Kate by the shoulders. 'Remember that *your* responsibility is to get the magazine out on *his* budget. It's *his* responsibility to make a profit and he's very, very good at that; but he might not be if he were the sort of liberated guy that you approve of.'

As they neared publication date, Tom's growls could be heard around the office. 'Do you *realize* what a bleed-off costs? ... Does anyone in the art department realize that the little rule around the picture on page ninety-two added fourteen per cent to the page cost? ... Does anyone in the art department *care*?'

Kate had always been terrified of violence – both physical and verbal. As a child she had never dared to show her own anger and always quailed before her father's rage. As an adult, she still always caved in when voices were raised. But Kate didn't forgive and she didn't forget. She capitulated and remembered. Instead of discharging her anger in a blazing row, she stored up her resentment, which always built into a bigger and bigger head of steam until the day that Kate exploded.

A messenger hurried down the office aisle. It was ten o'clock at night and the room was silent except for the occasional machine-gun burst of a typewriter. Only three people were still at their desks. Kate and the art editor were brooding over the page proofs as the messenger came up to them and handed over a big envelope.

Inside, fresh from the printing press, was a rough-cut copy of their first issue. Blazing confidence, Lauren Hutton grinned up at them.

Kate picked it up and ran to Judy's office. 'Look!' she yelled. 'We're in business.'

~ 51 ~

ALL the right people turned out for *Verve!*'s launch party. There were plenty of celebrities, some agency heads and a lot of big advertisers – about five hundred people in all. The top columnists were there, the dailies had turned up and a couple of reporters from *Time* and *Newsweek*, as well as the trade press. There was no television coverage, but it was probably just as well – cables and lights would upset the party atmosphere, and anyway Kate and Pat had already appeared earlier on the breakfast shows.

There was a murmur of voices, a clink of glasses, cigar smoke mingled with expensive perfume and the champagne flowed. Unexpectedly, however, the party to which Kate had looked forward to for months seemed to her a depressing anticlimax. She would have preferred to see this money spent on the magazine. She looked pinched and ill, so miserable and woebegone that Tom moved over to her.

'Cheer up,' he said, '*we've* just had a successful launch and *you're* having a normal, understandable reaction: you're experiencing the depression that sets in with exhaustion after some mighty exertion that results in achievement. That's how Shakespeare probably felt after he'd finished *Hamlet*.'

Kate didn't laugh. 'I know it all feels stale to you,' Tom added. 'You've been thinking about nothing else for the past three months. I know some of those guys out there looked bored, but when people are listening very carefully, their faces always look blank. It just means that they're concentrating on what's being said to them. Every single guest tonight was sounded out first, they're all good potentials and a great many of them have already agreed to support us. You, Kate, are now part owner of a real, live magazine.'

Kate's eyes brimmed. 'It's just that I'm feeling exhausted and homesick and I suddenly felt so lonely. I'm missing Walton Street and London and Scotty most of all.'

'Yes, well, it's tough being a big girl. I'd better take you home.'

They caught a cab back to Kate's apartment where Tom said, 'Going to help myself to a real drink, can't stand that fizzy stuff. You get into bed and when you're comfortable I'll get some food sent in.'

'I really couldn't eat a thing, thank you, Tom, but there's some cold stuff in the fridge.'

When she was wearily propped against the pillows, Tom appeared with a tray of coffee, some stale doughnuts, a stick of limp celery and a bowl of soup. 'I promise I'll do better next time,' he said, sipping whisky from the depths of the blue cotton-covered armchair. He wondered how to cheer her up as Kate picked at her food.

'Do you realize, Kate, that in the last three months we've spent more time together than the average married couple?' He leaned forward, elbows on his knees, and earnestly added, 'Another thing you probably don't realize is that you've made a lot of my old ideas look pretty stale. I'm not sure that this is the right time to say it, but I want to apologize. I underestimated you – your ideas, your originality and your experience. I thought you were just Judy's British buddy and I didn't see that we needed you. But now I've seen you in action and I am impressed. I'm sorry I've been so abrupt and offhand and, well, such a tough bastard.'

'I like tough bastards. That's one of my problems.'

'Well, one of my problems is that I can't get results *without* being a tough bastard. Now get some sleep and see you tomorrow.'

For one moment Kate had thought he was going to make a pass at her. Her love life had been nonexistent in the past few months, and it hadn't been so great before that; she'd almost given up hoping that one day she'd meet a man who would make her climax effortlessly with love and truth and abandon.

But none of them did.

*

The following day she woke feeling much better and was just getting out of bed when the intercom rang.

'There's a guy down here with some flowers.'

'Send him up,' Kate said, expecting a delivery boy. To her surprise, Tom appeared behind a foaming armful of yellow mimosa and a paper sack containing fresh coffee, bagels, lox and cream cheese.

'Hi. Breakfast. Back to bed,' he said, and handed her the morning papers. All the dailies had covered their launch, including a front-page splash in *WWD*. Kate immediately felt better.

'I feel ashamed about last night. I tend to cry when I'm tired.'

'Forget it,' said Tom. 'That's what intrigues me – you're such an odd combination of strength and vulnerability. You're tough without being masculine, you work as hard as Judy, and that's saying a lot, but you're very fragile in some areas. Although you won't admit it, you need looking after.'

'I'm *being* looked after,' said Kate, grinning at him. 'Lucky it's Saturday.'

'I'll have to go into the office pretty soon.'

'Me too.'

She looked pale but pleased with herself as she lay back against pink pillows in a white lace négligé. Tom, watching her against the pillows, suddenly realized that he was going to make love to her. The tray crashed to the floor and bagels flew across the room.

After one moment of astonishment, Kate was conscious of his hands on her skin, his hard mouth on hers, the smell of newly laundered cotton and a man's warm body. She didn't even have time to be self-conscious as she felt his hands exploring her body, sliding over the lace. 'I don't think this is a good idea,' she gasped.

'I think it's an *excellent* idea,' Tom murmured into her hair.

'I thought you were against fornication among the staff . . .'

'Yes, this is madness,' Tom cheerfully agreed, as he felt for her breasts. 'Now are you going to undo this or do I have to tear it off you?'

With one wriggle Kate was out of it, and then he was stroking her body with possessive tenderness. His mouth never left hers as he unbuttoned his shirt and pulled off his tie, and then she felt his hard chest against her soft breast and smelled the erotic, fresh-straw-smelling sweat of his armpits. She bent her head and nuzzled there, inhaling the soft down in the pit of his arm, the only soft hair on his body. Then they were both naked and lying together, each wondering at the warmth of the other's body, each touching and feeling, slowly exploring each bend of arm and leg.

Very slowly, Tom slid on top of her and she felt him warm inside her. He moved softly, then with more strength, his hard legs against her soft thighs, his mouth crushing hers, his broad hands cradling her breasts, feeling her small, beige nipples harden beneath his touch.

Kate felt excited and yet strangely peaceful. Of course her body had been made for Tom, this tender, tough man, her love. *Her love?*

Alarm bells rang. She gasped and suddenly stopped moving. 'What's up?' murmured Tom.

'Well, I don't want to get involved.'

'Of course not,' he murmured and softly stroked her breasts, as she quivered under him. Slowly she let him draw her down again into the soft, warm, erotic depths. As their passion mounted, she felt Tom's warm breath in her ear, his hard, insistent body on top of hers, then she was up on the ceiling, oddly dispassionate, looking down at herself and Tom in bed below, and for Kate the moment was lost as Tom climaxed with an animal growl.

They lay clinging to each other. A faint almond whiff of semen rose from the rumpled sheets.

'Mmmmmmmm, mmmmmm . . .' he murmured, hugging her, 'but I wish you had come.'

'I did.'

'No you didn't, darling. I don't mind if you don't have an orgasm, but I *do* mind if you fake. Where does it get you? What's the point?'

Gently he kissed her and stroked her shoulders. She felt his hands slowly slide over her body until, softly, he started to stroke the small, dark forest, started to feel her with a soft, steady touch, his hands moving lightly and with sensitive patience until Kate relaxed then suddenly arched towards him in ecstasy and fell back, melting into his muscular arms.

She woke to feel his lips on her small secret slit, his tongue gently caressing the pale pink seed pearl, his face against the delicate folds that surrounded it. Pink upon pink, soft, sucking flesh; swirling, exquisite oblivion, falling into a caressing sea.

'What a wonderful way to wake up,' murmured Kate, going to sleep again.

Afterwards they took the phone off the hook, had a shower together, started to make love under it and decided that it wasn't really all that comfortable in the slippery tub with the water raining down. They slid back into the crumpled bed. Like a bird's-eye view of the Alps, thought Kate for one moment, before all thought was wiped from her mind and sensation alone flooded her body.

Later, still naked, they pulled the bed straight, but as soon as they'd smoothed the antique patchwork spread Tom gently pushed her back on it and again reached for her breasts. Kate pulled him down, dodged his hands and instead slid down between his thighs; lying curled between his legs as she stroked him, feather-soft, cupped him in her hands. He felt her warmth, the soft stroking touch of her hand on his manhood, then her lips were sucking, soft as a sea anemone, then more insistently. He felt her tongue searching, reaching, sliding, slipping, sucking until Tom could think of nothing except the scratching fingernails on his inner thighs, that sure insistent mouth, the mounting, quickening pressure of her lips upon him until, with a groan, his pent-up force was spent.

Kate, who never knew whether to swallow, spit or dribble, tasted the oddly pungent, acrid almond odour. 'What do men like?' she timidly asked Tom later.

Silence, then he said, 'Naturally, I can't speak for the rest of my sex, but when borne on summits of delights such as I have just experienced, I neither know nor care.'

It was six o'clock in the pearly greyness of Monday morning. 'You're quite something,' Tom said. 'I don't want anyone or anything else. But let's keep this from the office, huh?'

Naturally, that was impossible. Monday, Kate was a different, sparkling creature, thought Judy, from wan, little Friday Kate. Tom hadn't been in all weekend and she'd left plenty of messages, getting crosser and crosser with his answering service. Both of them had been unavailable. Unavailable together all weekend, concluded Judy.

Before Monday was over, Kate had casually asked Judy what Tom's wife was like. 'She's just a simple all-American girl,' Judy said. 'Aged twenty-three, golden hair and a handspan waist, radiant as the dawn, that sort of thing ... No, I'm joking, she's really ninety-five and the poor woman's only got one eye, no teeth and these thirteen lovely children, all very hungry ...' She relented. 'In fact, they split up before Tom and I joined forces. His ex is all right, there's nothing wrong with her; she's just a spoiled Jewish princess who never stops yacking – heavily into macrobiotic nutrition and meaningful encounter groups. But the two boys are really neat. Tom doesn't talk about them, but he sees them as much as he can.'

When they were together, Kate felt an irresistible and seemingly irreversible love for Tom. This wasn't like her girlish wish to be married to Robert. This wasn't like the awed infatuation she'd felt for Toby, her ex-husband. This was a growing, tender lovingness. She didn't feel hemmed in, she didn't feel humble or in any way subservient, she didn't want to get on her knees and worship and she didn't feel that she was putting on an act or altering herself to please him. Not once did she feel the urge to scribble Kate Schwartz, Mrs Tom Schwartz or even Kate Ryan-Schwartz. She simply wanted to be with Tom, whenever she could, and to hell with the future. Suddenly Kate's neat navy suits were seen no more; instead she appeared in an amethyst linen suit from Yves Saint Laurent that she wore with no blouse underneath. This went down so well that she went back and bought another version in shocking pink. Shortly afterwards she turned up at the office wearing a Spanish orange jersey jumpsuit. Nobody in the office needed to be told that Kate was in love.

Tom also had suddenly changed. He became more affable and mellow, he was seen to smile during office hours and his sharp sarcasm softened. To Kate, he was surprisingly loving, gentle and generous. Aware of his office reputation as a tightwad, he consciously tried to overcorrect, and Kate loved him for it.

But she didn't want diamonds, she didn't need emeralds – all she wanted was Tom.

The first edition of *Verve!* had a good cover but it was not well printed. It was way over budget and the advertising was sparse. Nevertheless, they all had secret joyous moments when women on buses were seen to be reading *Verve!* or someone was spotted actually *buying* the thing from a newsstand.

The second issue contained better text, better pictures and marvellous beauty coverage, but again, it was badly printed. Again the ads were sparse, and it was a day late on the stands.

The third issue was always the test, after initial curiosity had died down. For the third issue they had to go bigger. Pat frantically tapped her secret network of moonlighters – journalists on the staff of other publications who were prepared to make extra money by unofficially and anonymously taking on extra work. The third edition was still thin on advertising, because the agencies weren't prepared to take space in the early issues of a magazine which had now lost its novelty value but wasn't firmly established. They were sitting back and waiting to see whether *Verve!* was going to be a fast folder.

But the third issue had an exclusive Jane Fonda cover, and a lead interview that they were able to tag 'How to Enjoy Your Man in Bed' and link with their sexual pleasure survey.

The ads came in for the fourth issue and *Verve!* took off.

Kate was frightened of her new happiness. Everything was going too well; she was frightened of allowing herself to be vulnerable again. She already knew that what triggered love for her was harsh rejection and an abject, humiliating need for approval. She knew that as soon as she fell for a man, she turned into a grovelling doormat and asked to be kicked in the teeth. She knew that the last thing she needed in a permanent mate was another man who would make her feel unlovable.

So she was terrified of admitting to herself that she was in love. She hesitated to commit herself. In order to test the strength of her feelings for Tom, she started going out with other men, rather as some women flirt in front of their husbands with men who don't interest them in the slightest. It wasn't difficult for Kate to find other men, because success is a powerful aphrodisiac. Besides, at thirty-nine, Kate's invisible, sexual glow was as much in evidence as it had been when she was seventeen. For the next few months, tough Burt Reynolds look-alikes waited for Kate in the small reception area of the *Verve!* office. Kate broke dates with Tom at the last minute, and other men's shirts and shaving gear were obtrusively obvious when he stayed overnight at Kate's apartment.

Tom scratched his head and decided to turn a blind eye to her odd behaviour. He seemed to be the first man (except maybe for Scotty) who was genuinely fond of Kate as opposed to being irresistibly attracted to her. He loved her for what she was, and he didn't demand what he realized she couldn't yet give him – her trust. So although he found it difficult, Tom ignored her exasperating behaviour, ignored the muscular hulks in the lobby and her other little tedious traps to test his love. Tom understood Kate's insecurity better than she did herself, and the reason was that he had suffered similarly.

One Saturday afternoon, after she had asked some question about his family, Tom clasped his hands behind his head as Kate snuggled up to his bare chest. 'To a certain extent, I can understand how you feel about your father,' he said, 'because what *I* resented in *my* life was my mother. She was a very domineering, typical Ukrainian boss-mother. If I asked my father for anything, he'd say, ask your mother. He was a huge, strong man – he'd been a professional fighter – so physically he would never lift a finger to his wife or to me, because he was afraid of really hurting us. And my mother knew this, so it gave her complete control of the household. *He* would decide whether Roosevelt was right to appoint Eisenhower supreme commander in Europe, but he wasn't allowed to decide whether I could have a new pair of shoes – because she made all the decisions. I resented her complete control and the way she threw it in his face. They had an argument or a fight every single day for thirty-seven years, after which she died. I still resent those arguments. I also resented the fact that she always criticized everything I did. *Nothing* was ever good enough for that woman. I felt guilty because I wasn't good enough for her and guilty because I felt resentful.'

'That's how I felt, too. What did you do about it?'

'Look, I'll show you.' He gently pushed her aside, jumped out of bed and padded back with his wallet in one hand. 'I look at that.' He pulled out a white business card upon which was scrawled in capital letters FUCK GUILT.

'I taught myself to accept guilt and then forget guilt. Sometimes I have to say I'm sorry, and sometimes I have to compensate for some revolting thing I've done. But then I simply go out and get on with my life, and somewhere up in the heavenly accounting department, I assume that an angel is adjusting my profit-and-loss sheet. I'm sure I'll end up showing a net profit.'

The other side of the card said FUCK 'EM ALL.

'It helps me keep cool,' Tom explained, 'stops me from paying too much attention to other people's opinions instead of relying on my own.'

Kate nestled closer to him.

'There's one further thing we have to discuss,' Tom said quietly. 'I'd appreciate it if you don't fake orgasm *ever* with me again. Keep it for these handsome hairy hulks that leave their shirts here.'

There was a pause, then she said sulkily, 'I don't always.'

'I know,' he said gently, pulling her to his chest, and stroked her hair softly, as he carefully said something that he'd been meaning to say for a long time. 'Kate, darling, sex is the closest possible communication between two people and faking is lying.' He gave an exasperated sigh. 'I can't think why women do it.'

'Out of politeness, sleepiness or feelings of inferiority,' Kate said defensively. 'I suppose I do it because I'm frightened that I'm not up to standard; I don't get there in ten point nine seconds or whatever the going rate is.'

'What's the point? Where is it going to get you? Why don't you *help* me to make you feel wonderful? Faking isn't helping, it's sabotaging yourself and our relationship because you're sometimes too damn prim to tell me what you want, you silly little prude.' Tom nibbled her left earlobe. 'You have as much right as a man to an orgasm and the way you reach it is your business. *You* know what's right for you and until ESP is with us, it's up to you to show me, otherwise how the hell am I to know?'

So Kate told him a bit. Then she told him a bit more.

Then Tom swung into action and pulled out his entire repertoire. First he went down on her, and then she went down on him and then they tried it on the kitchen table and knocked the milk jug over, so they moved to the living room floor and took up sixty-nine positions on the carpet and then Tom impaled Kate and staggered around the living room thus, and all the time they asked each other all the relevant questions, such as do you like it like this, harder, softer, faster, slower, and then Tom produced a little packet and said don't for God's sake sneeze and he laid out three lines each on the low glass table in the living room and offered Kate his hollow gold telephone dialler from Tiffany and she dutifully said it was wonderful, which was nothing less than the truth . . . except that it left Kate with a slight chemical tang at the back of her throat and in her heart. Compared with the dizzy excitement that Tom aroused in her, the coke didn't quite make it. Somehow the whole scene hadn't been about loving, but about scoring.

'How was it for you this time?' asked Tom tenderly, and she started to say wonderful, but then heard herself say, '. . . Darling, if we're telling the truth . . . I thought it was strung-out and artificial.'

A flash of blind panic crossed his face, followed by a defensively aggressive expression that meant he was about to hurt this person as hard as he could for attacking him when he had laid down his defences and offered her his all. He opened his mouth and was about to tear her to pieces so that she'd never be able to put herself together again, when he paused to consider. Then an expression of relief crossed his face and he said softly, 'I know what you mean.'

Kate said tentatively, 'I think I like you better than that.'

Tom said, 'I think we both like each other enough not to play games.'

Suddenly Kate was no longer afraid that he might despise her or leave her if she didn't perform satisfactorily. She no longer felt that she had to impress him or seek his approval.

'It's not that I don't like conformist sex, I just don't like it according to the self-improvement books,' she confessed. 'I'm conformist all right, but I can't perform if some dominant person in bed is determined to make me come, or if I feel that some invisible doctor is nodding wisely as he watches my efforts from the ceiling.'

She wriggled on to her bare stomach on the greengage carpet and propped her head on her hands. 'What I *really* like sexually,' she said thoughtfully, 'is corny rubbish. Candlelight and sheer chiffon and being pressed to his manly breast by his muscular arms and feeling the seas pounding relentlessly in my ears and fierce waves surging up the unresisting beach as I sink back and he murmurs thickly in my ear, God, darling, I never knew it could be like this.'

She turned to Tom, also lying naked on the green carpet, and added, 'Corny rubbish is what really makes me feel sexy.'

'If I suddenly started spouting purple prose, you'd only laugh,' said Tom with conviction, 'and what's more to the point, I'd feel like a fool. So I don't know how I'll handle the dialogue, but I promise you that next weekend is going to be in the land of corny rubbish . . .'

'. . . By the seaside?'

'Connecticut,' Tom promised. 'The complete experience. Sandy beaches, pounding spray, lobster dinner and galloping white horses. And there we will play at total corniness.'

The following Friday evening, they arrived at a seashore cottage that belonged to a friend of Tom. On Saturday, they ran along the beach, climbed grey rocks with the wind whipping their hair, licked the salt from each other's lips and ran along the lace-fringe of the grey ocean, barefoot, with their jeans rolled up. On Sunday Tom tried, and failed, to climb a pine tree, and then they went for a ride. (It had taken Tom over an hour on the phone from New York to arrange for the horses to be waiting for them after breakfast outside the cottage door.) Tom had been on a horse only once before, in his teens, when he'd spent a weekend on a dude ranch outside El Paso. Kate amused him with her prim English trot, and then she amazed him by making her bay hop, one foot at a time, over a fallen tree trunk. Tom couldn't get his stubborn chestnut mare to move – she took no notice of the human on her back, but kept putting her head down and cropping grass in a determined manner, as if she intended to shave the whole of Connecticut.

'Take up your reins and use your legs; squeeze firmly with your thighs,' Kate advised. Tom did, whereupon the mare took off as if someone had set fire to her tail. Somehow Tom stayed on, until Kate caught up and yelled, 'Sit back and gently tighten up with your hands,' whereupon the chestnut suddenly stopped as if she'd been switched off, and Tom tumbled over her head.

That evening, after sipping white wine in front of the flames and eating the regulation lobster dinner, Tom carried Kate up the open redwood stairs to their bedroom. They could see through the triangular window, beyond the dark pines to the starlit sea and the lighthouse, and they could hear the wind shrieking around the house and the rain slashing against the plate glass as they snuggled under the flowered quilt. Tom started to caress her. 'Too tired,' murmured Kate, 'too sleepy.' But holding her to him and stroking her softly, he slipped into her.

And suddenly, through the mist of sleepiness, Kate realized that it was going to happen. *It* felt exactly as she had read it felt like. Soft, intense waves rather than her excitingly violent, direct clitoral orgasm. *It* was unmistakably different and *it* was undoubtedly happening. Kate felt fecund, indescribably female, an earth mother. She felt happy, she felt at last a complete woman. For a never-ending moment she gloried in it, then flung her arms around Tom and clung to him, held him tight in her arms; she was never, never going to let him go.

'I did it, I did it!' she shouted.

'No, *I* did it.'

'Well, *we* did it.'

Tom said, with considerable satisfaction, 'I knew it would happen when you finally relaxed.'

～ 52 ～

KATE and Judy were waiting for Tom with growing irritation. They would now be too late for the first act of *La Bohème*, which contained most of the best arias. 'Dammit, why doesn't he call? After all, this *is* supposed to be a little party for your fortieth birthday, Kate ... and it's not as if La Scala popped over to the Met every other week,' grumbled Judy.

'He was looking forward to it as much as we were, but he didn't know how long the medical conference would continue, and you know he wanted to talk to some of the doctors afterwards. After all, you started this fuss, you're the one who wants him to sell the Hoffmann-La Roche shares.' Kate leaned back against the suede and stared at Judy through the haze of yellow flowers that stood on a low, smoked-mirror table.

They were sitting on the beige suede couch in Kate's huge, quiet living room. Leopard-skin and tiger-skin cushions were strewn on the couch, which ran thirty feet along the depth of the room. Above them hung a collection of paintings and engravings of tigers and leopards – some were primitive oil paintings, one was a charming child's drawing. An exquisite Stubbs engraving of tigers was so ominous that the hairs almost rose on the back of your neck.

The wall opposite consisted entirely of panels of smoked-mirror glass, each concealing liquor, games, TV, stereo, projector or other valuable clutter. One complete side of the huge room was a sheet of sliding glass that led on to a leafy terrace, beyond which stretched a sumptuous treetop vista of Central Park. Opposite the vast window was a fifty-foot run of floor-to-ceiling bookshelves lacquered Chinese red. Not all the shelves contained books; Kate's collection of antique snuff boxes stood on one; another held a small collection of terra-cotta ancient Greek votive statuettes and other shelves held small, charming objects – a seventeenth-century bronze of a man wrestling with a bull by Garnier, a tiny yellow Meissen patch-box that had once belonged to Madame de Pompadour.

The lights were turned low. Instead of lamps, Kate created atmosphere with an intricate system of ceiling spotlights – just a single moonbeam if she and Tom were listening to Sibelius; a series of pencil-slim beams for parties, to spotlight their Mexican art collection.

As they sat waiting for Tom, suddenly Judy felt a sharp, nasty feeling – a sort of yellow jab in her head – that, to her surprise, she immediately recognized as jealousy. Jealousy of Kate. Judy's apartment was just as luxurious as this one, Judy was just as successful, Judy was just as attractive as Kate, in a different way, and Judy loved her man as much as Kate – and was passionately loved in return. But Kate *lived* with Tom; they went to bed together and didn't always make love, they yawned together in the morning; Kate knew what Tom was like when he had influenza, and he knew how to look after her if she had a bad period. *Judy longed to share that same intimacy with Griffin.* Kate had her man,

Maxine was happily married and so was Pagan – now that the medical world had decided to encourage heart-attack patients to make love – but Judy didn't have what most women expected and took for granted, once they'd got it. Judy felt ashamed of herself for feeling this way towards Kate but couldn't stop.

'When Tom bought the Hoffmann-La Roche shares nobody realized the harm that tranquillizers could do,' Kate was saying. 'It seemed an ideal medicine for a world with plenty of harassment, plenty of tension, but not enough psychotherapists or mental hospitals.' She picked up a small, amber-inset, eighteenth-century pillbox and carefully examined the pattern without seeing it. 'You know Tom's view is there's nothing immoral about tranquillizers; his view is that they're not being prescribed or taken with enough caution.' She snapped the box shut. 'He bought twenty shares on fifty per cent margin at $16,000 a share and they're now worth $48,000 each. He said this morning that's a gross profit of $800,000, and apparently you've also benefited from an increase in the value of the Swiss franc during 1972, which makes it almost a million-dollar profit on one deal.' She looked straight at Judy. 'He feels you're ungrateful to complain. After all, he isn't *always* successful with his deals and he wants to hang on.'

'But it's not as though it's his *only* deal,' Judy said. 'We're deep into sophisticated engineering companies and computers as well as pharmaceuticals.' She sighed and looked at the low cedar table beside her. She picked up an enamelled Russian bear. 'You have such beautiful things, such a beautiful apartment, but Tom seems to see such an ugly future. Americans besieged on the energy front, deep into military muscle and popping tranquillizers as they work out their interest rates on their little pocket calculators.'

The door banged as Tom hurried in. He kissed both of them and ran for his dinner jacket. 'You know how sorry I am to be late,' he called. He appeared in the doorway. 'Kate, could you please fix this tie. Okay, Judy, I'm selling the Hoffmann-La Roche shares, not that I've changed my opinion, but we might as well take a profit and I think I'm going to leave it all in Swiss francs, I don't see why this upward trend should stop. Where are my cuff links, Kate? Where's Griffin?'

'He couldn't make it. His goddamn wife and her goddamn charity function.' Judy longed to hear Griffin call her to fix his shirt or find his cuff links. She yearned for this hurried intimacy as Kate stood behind Tom, pecked the back of his neck and then tied his black bow.

Griffin and Judy had now been together for four years. Twice during that time they had fought bitterly and split up. The first time was after their first year, when they had a blazing fight about Griffin's possessiveness. The second time had been after two years together, when Griffin's wife, Delia, finally made a stand and demanded that he give up Judy. She hadn't minded the models too much, but she felt humiliated and embittered by her husband's open liaison with a successful, well-known woman. For the sake of his family and their years together she wanted him to attempt a full-scale reconciliation and an exclusive relationship with her again. His children had been brought into the row. His elder son had been bitter and scornful; his elder daughter had been so understanding that he had broken down and cried.

Griffin and his wife both tried hard but they both knew they were trying to rekindle cold ashes. Griffin then asked Delia for a divorce on any terms she wanted. But although she finally agreed to their living separate lives, she asked him to continue to live in their home for the sake of their children; whatever happened she wanted to keep their family together. When Griffin pointed out that their youngest son was fifteen and would soon leave home, Delia had threatened suicide and hauled in her doctor. From then on, they had lived in a sexless truce under the same roof.

Or was it sexless? Judy sometimes wondered. Men always said they never made love to their wives, but they always did. What else could they say to you?

As the theatre curtain fell for the last time, Judy felt the same old sadness returning, those same pangs that she firmly called sentimentality, that longing to share Griffin's life as opposed to seeing a lot of him. As always when she was fighting misery, she turned a little truculent.

Tom was annoyed at not getting more reaction to his morning news that they were about a million dollars richer and his evening news that he'd done as Judy wanted. As they took their table in the Four Seasons, he shrugged his shoulders and said to nobody in particular, 'Naturally, I didn't expect to be thanked.'

'Thanks for some things and no thanks for others,' said Judy, staring hard at the chain draperies that shimmered like cascades of water. She wished they'd gone somewhere gayer; she really only liked the Four Seasons for lunch. 'Of course I'm glad I'm not poor anymore, but now we've been in business for nine years and you no longer have any interest in LACE or *Verve! You're* only interested in making more money. *I'm* interested in being paid up so I can sleep at night without counting all the money we owe.'

'For nine years I've been telling you that your old-fashioned virtues are a poverty trap.' Tom mimicked a mindless, singsong female voice. 'Save up for the purchase price before you buy something, never borrow money, don't buy real estate because it's better to rent and if you're going to save money, then stick it in government bonds. I am making you *rich*, and all you do is whine Where are your *guts?*'

'Never mind my guts. I know where your *heart* is. In that cluster of money boxes called Wall Street.'

'It's sad to see an insecure poor girl turn into an insecure rich one. Originally you aimed high, remember? Don't get frightened just because you passed your target.'

They ordered baked oysters followed by roast pheasant. Tom continued in a low, angry voice. 'If you really want to split, I'll sell you my shares in LACE and you can sell me your shares in *Verve!* or vice versa.'

'Judy doesn't want to give up anything and neither do you, Tom,' Kate interjected. 'Perhaps Judy would be a little happier if she were a bit less rich. And you, Tom – I love your speculative streak because I've got one myself, but you are turning into a walking, talking investment company.'

She stopped while they were served and then continued, 'You think Judy's ungrateful, but she's not, she's very grateful for what you've done for her, but there's a sort of tension that she loves and a sort of tension that she can't stand. Surely, with this latest gain you can sort out the LACE portfolio and separate the investment business from the rest of the company?' She paused and sighed, then said crossly, 'I don't know what's gone wrong with this evening, but I wish you could stop arguing about money and tell Judy our news.'

Tom fiddled with his wine glass, raised his eyebrows, opened his mouth, shut it again, then said, 'Uh, I don't know how to put this, but Kate and I are going to be married. The full commitment.'

Judy flung herself towards him and kissed his ear.

'Tom, you dear old-fashioned fellow! Why, that's wonderful.' She gave a Cheshire cat grin. 'I know exactly what I'm going to get you for a wedding present. Kate will love it and you'll loathe it because it's a conditional gift.' The happy couple both looked quizzical. 'On condition that you have it standing in your living room, I'm going to give you half of the T'ang horse.' Kate shrieked with surprise and joy. Tom looked uneasy.

'Well, that's wonderful, Judy, but . . .'

'We do still have that horse, don't we?'

'Yes, but it's really not feasible to have it in the apartment where it might get broken; it's a museum piece; it's too valuable to have out, Judy.'

'I don't think the guy that made that horse intended it to be stabled in a bank vault. I think he'd want Kate to have it.'

Tom looked at Kate's excited face. 'Yes,' he agreed, 'I guess he would.'

Over the breakfast grapefruit, one warm October morning in 1978, Griffin's wife suddenly freed her husband from the tentacles of guilt and duty that had bound him. They were eating at a walnut dining table that was big enough to seat forty, and as usual, Griffin was tearing through the morning papers as he ate.

Suddenly, triumphantly, Delia had said, 'Griffin, this is the last goddamn time I have to sit here and listen to you eat grapefruit.'

Griffin put down his spoon, mumbled sorry, read another inch of the *Wall Street Journal*, then did a double take and jerked his head up. 'What do you mean, the *last* time?'

'I'm leaving you, that's what I mean!' She looked exultant. 'That's what you *want*, isn't it? Well, that's what you're *getting* for Christmas. For two years now, Griffin, there's been another man and *you* haven't even noticed . . .'

Quickly he did a flashback in his mind; no, he had noticed no man . . . Except . . .

'That guy who fitted my contact lenses, Greenburg, Granheim, something like that ... The optician.'

'Greenheimer, right. Right as usual!'

Griffin said nothing, but over the top of the *Journal*, she had his complete attention for once.

'We're going to Israel together to start a new life on a kibbutz before it's too late.'

Griffin put down his paper and looked warily at his wife. He couldn't see Delia labouring in the fields and eating communal meals. He suspected a trick. 'What about the kids?'

'Fred's hardly a child. When he's home from school he's practically never here as it is – he's always out with that girl. I think he's going to move in with her. He'll need a little financial help from you of course, and so shall I. But I know I can rely on you to look after me. In fact, I've already had a word with Marvin about it.'

Griffin dashed down his paper, stood up and roared. 'You've already been to a lawyer without so much as mentioning to your husband the fact that you're leaving him?'

'Do you think I'm a fool?'

That evening Judy opened the door of her apartment to see Griffin leaning against the living room wall, swirling his usual predinner glass of ginger ale. He looked oddly taut and gauche. As soon as she untwisted her key from the lock he strode across the room, and without pausing to kiss her, he grabbed both her wrists. As if he could no longer keep it to himself, as if he couldn't believe that it was true, he burst out with the news.

Judy's mouth fell open. 'You mean *she* wants a divorce? *Really* wants one? Do you believe it? This isn't another of her cat-and-mouse games?'

'Yes, I believe it this time. She's never been like this before – gloating, exultant, almost vengeful.'

'Griffin, to be honest, I don't blame her.'

'None of that has anything to do with you, Judy. Delia and I had a relationship that didn't work and she didn't want a divorce. So we regrouped.' Gently he shook her wrists. 'Now look, I didn't come here to discuss that guilt-and-responsibility thing again.

I'm here to ask you, now that it's possible – will you marry me, darling?'

To her surprise, upon hearing the words for which she had waited ten years, Judy found that she couldn't say yes.

She simply didn't know.

~ PART TEN ~

～ 53 ～

BEYOND the orange trees and marigold beds at the end of the palace gardens, a scarlet Kiowa waited on the concrete helipad. The small, orange windsock hung limp. Two armed guards in khaki fatigues stood smartly to attention as the royal party approached.

Although in 1972, many educated Eastern women wore Western clothes in their home, Queen Serah always wore traditional robes in Sydon. Now she flicked up her long white *burka* as she was helped into the front of the helicopter. Squealing with pleasure at the prospect of the coming flight, ten-year-old Prince Mustapha and his white-uniformed servant climbed into the three back seats of the transparent bubble. A stickler for detail, Abdullah walked around the machine to see that all the doors were shut and handles latched. He completed his circuit at the right door, climbed in and settled himself in the right-hand seat of the opulent custom-built cabin. The trip from Dinada Palace to the hunting lodge in the eastern mountains, which would have taken nearly eight hours by car, was only twenty minutes in the five-seater jet turbine helicopter.

Heat shimmered on the sand as Abdullah strapped himself in. He went through the start sequence and a sudden wind whipped up the sand as the helicopter roared, shaking the bones and teeth of the passengers. Abdullah clapped on his earphones, turned on the ADF and dialled in the eastern mountains frequency; the needle on the instrument face immediately pointed in the direction that they were to take. As he rolled the twist-grip throttle away from him, the noise was deafening, as if their ears were being pierced by a pneumatic drill. The royal pilot flicked a last look at the dancing numbers on the control panel, checked that pressure and temperature were stabilized, then smoothly lifted the helicopter clear of the ground.

Once in the air, the noise wasn't so bad, more like the steady throb of a submarine. Peering down from the rear window, the small boy waved goodbye to the shrinking white Dinada Palace as their magic dragonfly rose, then turned east before settling on a straight course. On the perimeter of the helipad below, a small cluster of guards and courtiers still stood   the salute and would remain so until the machine had vanished over the horizon.

A sudden gust of turbulence distracted him momentarily, so Abdullah didn't notice the needle on the oil pressure gauge shudder for a moment, then draw towards zero. At 300 metres above the desert, Abdullah levelled off. He was looking forward to a few uninterrupted days with his son.

On the previous afternoon, a mechanic had suspected that an oil line running on the outside of the engine to the front engine bearing was cracked and he had replaced it. It was almost unbearably hot in the hangar, and just as he began to tighten the front end of the line, he felt a buzzing in his ears and his knees gave way. He grasped the side of the aircraft with suddenly weak hands, slid down from the ladder and took a swig from the water bottle at his waist. When he felt better, he climbed the ladder again, checked the connections and signed off the machine as airworthy for flight. But he forgot that the oil line connection was only finger-tight.

Suddenly, sound blared from the overhead panel. Every faculty alerted, Abdullah swiftly checked the instrument panel before him. Adrenaline flooded his blood and he tensed like a runner waiting for the starting gun. It was unlikely, the odds were against it, but it was happening!

Then the engine-failure horn sounded. All three engine indicators were fast unwinding to zero; the continuous loud screaming from the low rotor speed horn meant that the blades were slowing down. To Abdullah, everything that was happening so swiftly appeared to be in slow motion, but the long hours of pilot training rendered his movements fast and automatic.

He had no time to be frightened, and there was no need for fear. In the event of engine failure a helicopter doesn't drop like a stone, it glides to the ground like a glider. Abdullah lowered the pitch control on his left, which put the helicopter into a glide, and it entered the stabilized autorotation which Abdullah knew, after hours of practice, would safely land the aircraft.

The helicopter dropped and for a moment became weightless.

As toys hit the cabin roof and a teddy bear was flung violently against the Queen's head, all passengers were thrown against their safety belts and the servant in the rear began to scream with fright.

As the helicopter dropped, the Queen instinctively grabbed the front panel and cried, 'Stop playing tricks, you're frightening the child!' She turned to look at her husband. His face was tense and masklike as his hands and feet worked in perfect coordination, fighting to regain control of the aircraft.

The Queen had never seen him look like that and she panicked. 'You're not to let it crash, it will frighten Mustapha!' she screamed, pulling at his shoulder. 'Stop it, I say, Abdullah, stop it!'

Abdullah heard neither his wife nor the screaming servant. All his concentration and willpower were focused on the machine. He realized with relief that he had the autorotation under control, and that when he had gone into the glide, the machine had felt exactly as it had in practice long ago, when his instructor had been sitting on the seat beside him.

Confident once more, his mind ran swiftly through the emergency checklist. He could touch down almost anywhere ahead in the sand.

'Stop it! Stop this machine immediately!' the Queen shouted hysterically. It was the first time she had ever dared raise her voice to her husband. She started to pummel his left arm with her fists and then, screaming, she lunged for the black control stick between Abdullah's knees.

The helicopter shuddered and dipped.

Once more his wife lunged towards him. Abdullah hit her as hard as he could with the side of his left fist. It caught her on the cheekbone, split open the side of her mouth and knocked two teeth inward. She fell back, clapping both hands to her bleeding mouth, still screaming with fear and panic as Abdullah turned once more to the controls.

He was now down to twenty miles an hour and dropping, which was far too slow. He would have to regain a speed of at least sixty miles an hour if he was to avoid a crash. Abdullah shoved the stick forward to regain speed by diving. Suddenly he was frightened and sweat started to run into his eyes.

Again the helicopter dropped violently and correctly, but the needle didn't climb fast enough, and at fifty feet above the ground Abdullah knew that he would have to make a sloppy emergency landing. He flared the aircraft, easing the control stick back towards his body, in order to haul the machine out of the dive and bring it to a halt before touching ground.

Obediently the machine slowed up and started to sink. Abdullah realized that it would probably be a walkaway crash; it wouldn't be his first. He prepared to level the helicopter before touchdown, easing the stick forward.

It was at this moment, with touchdown imminent, that the Queen again threw herself against him, beating Abdullah's body with her fists and wildly shouting through her bleeding mouth, 'My child! My child! You don't care about my child!' She lunged towards him and with both hands, she yanked the control stick towards her, bent her body over it and clung to it with surprising strength. The aircraft obediently rolled to the left.

There was an enormous, bucking jolt as the travelling blade in the back struck the ground hard and dug deep into the sand, then stopped dead.

The braces that held the blades in position snapped cleanly, but the huge and very expensive pin that held the blades to the aircraft did not snap. The tip of the 150-pound blade was still travelling counter-clockwise and near the speed of sound when it smashed into the front of the cabin and crashed downwards, slicing through the overhead panel, silencing the screaming horns, and slashing the Queen's head roughly from her body.

The severed, bloody head was flung backwards on to her son's lap. Little Mustapha screamed and pushed the bloody horror away from his bare knees, down among the toys on the cabin floor, as, with one last tremendous jolt, the blade finally hit the ground and the aircraft jerked to a halt.

A gush of blood spurted up from the severed lump of crushed bone and tattered flesh that had been the Queen's body. The sticky scarlet fountain drenched Abdullah, the incarnadine, inescapable spray clung to his hands and soaked his clothes, his arms, his hair and his face. He tried to wipe the blood out of his eyes, but with fingers that were red, wet and dripping.

For a few seconds he was mentally and physically paralysed. After one look at the bloody lump of flesh on his left, Abdullah's conditioned pilot's mind registered that he wouldn't need to help her – his priority was to get the screaming servant and the child out of the wreckage as soon as possible, because apart from the stench of blood and vomit from the back, he noticed two distinct smells – the burning electrical wires in the smashed overhead panel, and the fumes from the seventy gallons of volatile jet fuel that was pouring into the back of the cabin from the tank beneath the back seats.

He jerked into action, tore off his safety belt and tipped off the headphones. He levered his body upright, neck and shoulders protruding from the smashed and buckled front window. Then, less than sixty seconds after the helicopter had touched ground, there was a sudden roar. Abdullah felt as if a huge hand had picked him up and flung him through the air and across the desert sand.

He landed on his stomach, winded, gulping and gasping for breath, with his leg twisted beneath him. He felt no panic or pain, although in fact he had suffered a concussion, a compound fracture of the leg and broken several ribs. For a moment he lay dazed, then, with enormous concentration and willpower, he lifted his head.

Slowly, steadily, sickeningly, the horizon tilted forty-five degrees to the left. Trembling with the strain, Abdullah hoisted his body on his arms, the jelling blood dripping, as he faced the helicopter. The machine had turned into a roaring ball of fire. Impotent, Abdullah gazed at the flaming mass of debris. Grimly he started to drag himself forwards on his hands towards the fireball before he collapsed unconscious on the sand. Apart from the searing, roaring flames, there was no sound in the impersonal silence of the desert.

It had been exactly seven minutes since takeoff.

 54

IN the late June sunshine, Lili's scarlet Jaguar dipped along the highway, heading east of Paris. Five kilometres after Epernay, she turned off the N51 towards Le Mesnil-sur-Oger. On the right, meadows of brilliant yellow mustard flowers alternated with stretches of golden corn, sprinkled with scarlet poppies, blue cornflowers and white marguerites. On the left the dark green, seven-foot box hedge bordered the de Chazalle estate.

Lili swung the car to the left through a pair of open, black, curlicued iron gates. The hedges and trees looked unusually neat, the grass was freshly cut. Half a mile away, at the end of a straight gravel drive, was the eighteenth-century French château, a perfectly proportioned stone building, with row upon row of tall windows that glistened in the sunshine.

Zimmer was right. It was time she started to go out by herself again. She had sheltered – or rather hidden – under his wing for eight months.

For all those months Lili had lived alone with her grief for Stiarkoz, refusing to discuss him even with Zimmer, with whom Lili would only talk about her work. Then one day Zimmer had entered the dressing room where Lili sat in a mauve flowered wrapper, wiping off her makeup in front of the brilliantly lit mirror. Without asking, Zimmer shoved past her dresser and locked the door. Then he stood behind Lili with his hands on her shoulders, looking at her in the mirror, and said, 'Lili, I've tried to hint, but you refuse to listen, so I'm telling you directly that to shut yourself off from the world and everyone in it is bad for your acting. My dear, Jo is dead and you are alive. You must make a conscious effort to interest yourself again in all the things that you pursued with Jo – and you must also make an effort to make new friends and have some fun. Fun is good medicine; moping is self-indulgence.'

In the mirror Lili had glared at Zimmer, but she knew that isolation *was* bad for her acting. Which was why she had accepted the invitation from Madame de Chazalle.

Lili stopped the red Jaguar in front of the imposing portico, climbed out and rang the bell.

Nothing happened.

She had expected at least two liveried footmen to swoop out and pick up her luggage. She peered through the glass panels of the door and saw an enormous stone-flagged hall flanked by pillars, between which hung gold-framed portraits. Still no sound.

Puzzled, Lili rang the bell again. A masculine voice behind her said, 'There must be another crisis in the kitchen. Let me carry your suitcase.' She turned to see a very tall young man wearing a turtle-neck navy sweater and jeans so tight that they might have been sprayed on to his long legs. Untidy, toffee-coloured hair fell over hazel eyes and a thin, tanned face. His overlarge mouth slowly widened in a welcoming grin.

'No need to ask who *you* are.' At the age of twenty-four, Lili was world-famous. He took her navy leather suitcases, kicked the door open, and stood aside to let Lili walk through. As they ascended the six-foot-wide, curving marble staircase, they met Maxine descending.

For ten seconds, Lili found her formidable, then Maxine smiled. 'So you've already met my youngest son, Alexandre. I'm delighted to see you again. It is not often that I meet anyone so charming on a charity bazaar platform. I was really only there for publicity, so to make a friend was a bonus.'

She led the way downstairs, still chattering. 'As I said in my letter, this weekend we celebrate our anniversary. It's been eighteen years since the château was opened to the public.'

'Where is everyone, Maman?'

'The entire staff is on the terrace preparing the fireworks display. *You* should be helping them, Alexandre.' She ruffled the toffee-coloured hair. But her son, who had no intention of leaving Lili, ran upstairs, dumped the suitcases at the top and then followed the two women into the salon.

Beyond the terrace was a silver rectangle of water into which fountains gently splashed. The sixty-foot-long, white-panelled room shimmered with reflected light from the lake outside and from the great antique mirrors that hung along one wall. Little glass tables held seventeenth- and eighteenth-century objects. They stood on soft lavender and grey Aubusson carpets. A sleek grey Weimaraner was trying to gnaw a hole in the arm of one of the brocade sofas.

'Sheba gives the place that lived-in look,' Maxine observed. 'I'm always being told that I am overneat. The whole place would look like a museum if it wasn't for my sons and my dogs.'

'The whole house *is* a museum,' Alexandre explained to Lili, 'but it isn't dull or dusty. Maman has made it most fascinating.

You'll see when you tour the public rooms. The lighting changes by remote control, the rooms are full of flowers and the room in which Diaghilev stayed is daily sprayed with Mitsouko because it was his favourite perfume.

Lili's suite overlooked the park. The bedroom walls were covered in pale yellow silk, as was the couch in front of the hand-carved, white marble fireplace. The huge bed was set back in an alcove of dark topaz velvet. On either side of it were a row of shelves, upon one of which lay a pile of the latest best-sellers and a history of the castle entitled 'Château de Chazalle – A Place to Make Friends.' There were also a candle in a brass holder, an ivory telephone, notebooks with little gilt pencils, a velvet box of tissues, an antique gold box containing biscuits, and several little china dishes of pink sugared almonds and peppermints. A silver nightcap tray offered different sorts of expensive bottled water and cut-glass decanters of whisky and brandy. Beside the telephone was a list of the guests, with room numbers as well as telephone extensions.

Lili picked up the thick cream card engraved in green with the de Chazalle crest – a rearing lion with a rose in its paw. Under the date – June 21, 1974 – her fellow guests were listed: two ambassadors; a producer and his ballet-star wife; a Hollywood film director; a Greek shipowner whom she had met with Stiarkoz; three other very rich men; a world auto-racing champion and his beautiful wife; a red-headed, jet-setting jeans designer from New York with her sixth husband, an Italian prince; a British duke and – aha – Andi Cherno from *Paris Match*. So there was going to be photo coverage of the party. No wonder the guest list was so ostentatious. Lili mentally ran through her clothes. They had already been unpacked by the Portuguese maid and were hanging in a dressing room lined with cupboards that lit up when opened. The maid had run her bath, told Lili to ring if she wished to be helped with her dress and hair and had disappeared.

On Friday evenings Maxine served an informal buffet dinner so that guests could move around and meet each other. Although there were sufficient footmen in green and gold livery, Charles de Chazalle circulated about the silver salon carrying a bottle of the estate champagne. Monsieur le Comte hadn't his wife's ability to slide into an animated conversation for ten minutes, then extricate herself and glide gracefully towards the next cluster of guests. Charles used the champagne bottle as an entry and exit device. He would wander up to a group of guests saying, 'Everybody got a drink?' and he would detach himself by saying, 'Well, I'd better move on,' slightly lifting the bottle in a farewell salute as he went about the duties of a host.

Very tall and thin, he stooped slightly as if a chill wind were blowing on the back of his neck. His fair hair was turning grey and had started to recede, but this only made him look more distinguished. His face reflected amiability and slight astonishment at the way his wife had altered his life. Personally, he preferred the place as it used to be, although it had been a bit shabby when he was a boy. But if it wasn't for all this razzmatazz, they wouldn't be able to live here at all, and he didn't know if he could bear that. So Charles viewed the glittering celebrity occasions, the crowds, the applause and the wall-to-wall photographers as a sort of penance that had to be endured in order that he might be able to vanish to the library.

As women always expected Lili to pounce on their husbands at parties, she always made a point of talking to the women first. Linda, the red-headed jeans designer, was surprisingly funny and charming as they talked about the universal difficulty of doing up the zip of a garment that women always bought one size too small. 'But then, jeans are the modern equivalent of corsets; you squeeze into them and they mould you into a predetermined shape,' the designer said. 'If Scarlett O'Hara were alive today, she wouldn't be lacing up her corsets. She'd be wriggling on the floor trying to zip up her jeans.'

Andi Cherno pointed his lens at them and the two women immediately stopped talking and posed as *if* they were talking. They were both used to being photographed and knew that if you really talked, then the picture would probably show you with your eyes shut and your mouth lolling open above three chins. '*Ecco belle!*' grinned Andi and asked them to stand by the window with the Hollywood director and the Greek shipowner, whose eyes brightened hopefully as Lili moved towards him.

'Hello, Steni. Last time I saw you was on the *Creole*.'

531

'Yes, it took two weeks for my nose to stop peeling and ten weeks for my liver to recover.'

Maxine worked hard to make her parties look effortless. She had been up since six o'clock that morning, consulting her lists and ticking off items or conferring with the head gardener, her chef or her butler. She had checked the fireworks display on the far side of the lake, as well as the one on the terrace, and then inspected the food, the wine, the ballroom, the cloakroom, the first-aid room and toilet arrangements for the band and disco. At nine in the morning she had been joined by Mademoiselle Janine, who had been busy removing all small valuable objects in the public rooms.

Maxine moved around the château, working steadily until eleven, when she went to her bathroom, satisfied that her home was ready for the four hundred guests who would be at the ball that evening. Maxine hated the formality of traditional country house parties. She always offered her guests plenty of amusements, but she also made it clear that if they wished to stay in their rooms, or if they wanted to wander alone over the wooded estate, that was fine, too. Today, Maxine had organized horseback riding, a miniature-golf party, and tennis for the Americans. But the men would probably laze around the swimming pool while the women rested or had their hair done by the two hairdressers sent from Paris.

Nobody appeared until lunch time. The meal was served on small tables on the terrace. The fountains were soft silver plumes in the sunlight, ice clinked in glasses and scrunched in buckets; the tinkle of silver cutlery and laughing conversation were the only sounds to accompany the meal.

Alexandre had got to the terrace before anyone else and changed the place names so that he was next to Lili. He could not take his eyes off her, as his mother noticed with exasperation. She had never allowed her sons to behave with familiarity towards her guests. They were not allowed to speak to the press, or be photographed with a celebrity or ask for anyone's autograph. She would call Alexandre to her dressing room that evening and remind him of his manners and his youth.

*

Lili's nipples were only just hidden by the white taffeta dress that Zandra Rhodes had given her as a twenty-fourth birthday present. The enormous puffed sleeves emphasized her tiny waist, pulled in by a tight cummerbund above swirling folds of taffeta skirt. She wore a pair of blazing diamond chandelier earrings, all that remained of her Stiarkoz collection. (On the day Jo died, they were being repaired by Van Cleef in Monte Carlo.)

Lili looked like a delicate, eighteenth-century Spanish princess as she slowly moved down the marble staircase. The scent of jasmine and warm grass from the countryside outside the windows mingled with the more sophisticated fragrances that rose from soft, bare shoulders. The gentle buzz of conversation sparkled with an occasional burst of laughter, and in the long, chandelier-hung ballroom the orchestra softly played 'I'll Be Seeing You'. Beyond the row of open glass doors that led to the terrace, a warm, hay-scented dusk hung over the lake.

An elegant buffet, *un repas rose*, had been laid out in a salon next to the ballroom. Everything was pink. Pink tablecloths were hung with swags of dark green laurel and crystal vases of palest pink rose-buds stood behind the food. White-hatted chefs carved slices of York ham and paper-thin slices of dark red prosciutto. There were piles of translucent rosy prawns, silver bowls of *sauce aurore*, great, dark-red mottled lobsters, brittle crayfish, delicate, pale-pink poached salmon and seafood salad of squid and octopus. One long table was banked with salads that still smelled of early morning gardens; another pink stretch of linen held four-foot-high pyramids of rose meringues Chantilly, silver dishes of straw-berries Romanoff and deep crystal bowls of raspberries and cream. And naturally there was pink champagne.

Maxine knew that Charles' sisters would think it all un-speakably vulgar, but the press would love it.

In contrast to the ballroom elegance, a couple of wine cellars on the other side of the château had been turned into a darkened, strobe-lit disco, where even the bottles at the bar pulsed to the exuberant thump, thump, thump and vibration of rock music.

Not until six in the morning did the last car vanish through the summer mist at the end of the gravel drive. Lili had been asleep for three hours. She had snuggled into her warm bed thinking that the evening could not have been more perfect. She had been on her best behaviour, had danced with all the men in the house party and had posed endlessly for photographers. As usual, she had been besieged by men and had flirted with a couple of them, but she carefully did not dance with anyone in particular. She still didn't feel Jo had gone.

Not a guest was seen before Sunday lunch, which was a very quiet, sleepy meal. After Alexandre had carried coffee over to Lili, he asked if he could show her the woods and the rock pool where he and his brothers swam. He had spent the last two days planning how to get Lili away from the other guests.

Lili was not unpleased by this youthful adoration. After drinking her coffee, they strolled over the spongy lawn, sprinkled with buttercups and daisies, and into the forest.

Alexandre couldn't believe his luck. If only his classmates could see him! He felt as lighthearted as one of the Weimaraners as he bounded along the path, occasionally leaping up to grab high overhead branches. Lili felt relaxed and curiously young as she followed him. His naturalness, his directness and his exuberant boyish energy were a contrast to her sophisticated, brittle fellow-houseguests.

When the path became overgrown, Alexandre held the beech branches back so that they didn't tear Lili's white voile dress.

The pool was a shallow, pebble-floored bulge in the river, edged by tall green reeds and bulrushes. Willows leaned over to caress the water and their branches trailed soft, grey leaves dappling in the sunlight. They pulled off their shoes and dangled their legs in the river, watching the clear water shiver and distort their pale feet.

Suddenly Alexandre could bear it no longer. He had to touch her. With gauche determination, he slowly lifted Lili's hand off the grass and kissed the little finger with grave ceremony. His lips pressed her pink nail, then quivered apart, and the end of her finger slid into his mouth, up to the first little joint, then farther to the second joint, then he sucked her whole finger in his mouth, between his wide, quivering lips. Panting, he held her finger gently between his teeth, rolled his wet tongue around it, pulled softly and insistently on her flesh, tasting the soft skin.

Lili had half expected something of the sort, but she certainly hadn't expected the violence of her reaction. She had thought she would gently push him away. He was too young. But at his touch her back arched, her stomach tightened, her nipples tingled and she felt as if they were connected to her groin by two invisible, tugging threads. She gasped, and for a few moments she didn't move, but her trembling body demanded that she respond. Unable to stop herself, she pushed her trembling fingers through his thick, strawlike hair, and stroked the sunburned nape of his young neck. Neither of them spoke as he raised his eyes to hers. Her lips slowly parted as she gazed at the golden down on his cheeks, the aristocratic nose.

His hazel eyes looked oddly dazed as he lunged towards Lili; his large mouth brushed her cheek, then his lips were on hers and she felt his insistent, silky lips.

Slowly, they fell back on the grass. Alexandre lay half on top of Lili and his eyes closed languorously as he sucked her mouth into his. At each pull, Lili's stomach contracted, and her body stiffened under Alexandre's smooth hands. Suddenly she remembered that the hands of Jo Stiarkoz had felt like wrinkled walnuts. She felt a sudden stab of disloyalty as she smelled Alexandre's musky odour, the erotic odour of fresh sweat on a young body. She sniffed the sweet fragrance of his hair, mingling with the green scent of the crushed grass beneath them.

Her slim arms wrapped around his body, then slipped up inside his T-shirt. She felt the rippling muscles on his back as with his eyes shut, he edged his way further on to her body until she was firmly imprisoned beneath him. As if possessed, her hands slipped down the back of his jeans, slid under the rough, tough fabric and over his silken, hard buttocks. Oh, God, she thought, young, *firm* flesh. For a fleeting second she again remembered, with guilt and against her wish, the tortoiselike, slightly pendulous pouches of Stiarkoz, the doughlike sinking of his flesh when touched.

Clinging to Alexandre, she felt his hardness through the bulging denim. Slowly he pushed his quivering hands inside her dress, slowly undid each pearl button, his lips still sucking at her mouth. Her tingling nipples were erect and waiting for his hands. Gently he squeezed the soft whiteness and felt her hard little rosebuds under his palms. Then his hands brushed farther down her body, as his lips ran clumsily over her breasts, sucking insistently first one pink nipple and then the other. Harder and harder he sucked, and with each gentle tug Lili felt a matching, yearning tug deep in her groin. With one hand he pulled up her skirt and felt beneath the fragile fabric. Lili felt the hard warmth of his hand pressed against her stomach, then slowly slide downwards beneath the scrap of white lace. Softly, hesitantly, he touched her and she arched towards him, helpless beneath his hand. With growing confidence he stroked her, laced his fingers in her dark silken hair and tugged it gently; then rhythmically, insistently, he stroked again until she arched her half-clad body to the sun and gave one sharp, high cry among the rustling trees.

For a few minutes she was oblivious as sun freckled through leaves from the blue sky beyond. Then she felt his trembling hands tearing at her belt, unhooking it. She helped him to pull her dress from her body. Together, they tugged off his jeans so that they both lay naked in the long grass. With a low moan, Alexandre flung himself on top of her, his eyes still closed. Again Lili felt that wonderful moth-mouth settling on hers, his hands on her breasts, his hardness on the naked flesh of her soft belly. Aroused again to the point of frenzy, she felt for him, and as she guided him, throbbing, into her body she could feel the heavy beating of her heart against his own. More than anything she wanted to feel him inside her, to feel joined to this wild, hard-muscled boy bucking on top of her, thrusting deep inside her body, groaning until he flung his head back to the sky, quivering as he called the name that had possessed his mind for the last three days. 'Lili, Lili, Lili!'

He clung to her, his eyes still closed, his downy lashes against the tanned face, and eventually he whispered into her ear, 'Was it . . . all right for you?'

Lili wrapped her slender, brown arms around him. 'It was wonderful,' she whispered.

So Alexandre made love to her again.

Afterwards he was still unable to keep his mouth off her. Lili snuggled against the golden body, purring into his armpits, sniffing the soft down. She felt alive again, excited, exalted. She bent her head so that her cloud of dark hair hung down, and then she trailed the black silken sheet over Alexandre's body until he flung himself at her again.

He couldn't stop touching her. Every soft stroke of his hand felt as if he were holding something fragile and precious.

They slithered naked down the bank and stood, waist-high, in the water. Lili felt her toes sink voluptuously into the soft mud as Alexandre pulled her, laughing, spluttering, into the clear water of the stream. For a few minutes they struggled playfully. Then gently Alexandre lifted her dripping, satin body and laid her on the river bank where he sat and looked at her. Slyly, as if it were forbidden, his gaze travelled down her wet brown body. He exulted. He gloated. Like a young wolf, he was unstoppable. He leaned forward and ran his mouth over her breasts again, tugging harder now at the nipples. Lili shuddered in ecstasy as she felt the warm tongue move down her ribs, the wet warm tip trickle across her stomach, dip lovingly into her navel, then trace its slithery route south. She felt his hot breath in her dark hair and his tongue flicker over her quivering flesh, gently insistent that she yield totally to the pleasure he was affording her.

Afterwards they waited in the wood until Alexandre reckoned that everybody was gathered in the drawing room for drinks. Quietly, they slipped from the trees at the side of the lawn to the door of the orangery. Alexandre looked like a tawny, sleepy beast. He was hugely pleased with himself and he still couldn't keep his hands off Lili, whose hair was a wild tangle and whose dress was grass-stained and ruined.

Inside the glass-walled orangery stood dark green tubs of fragrant white camellias and sour, sharp-scented scarlet geraniums. Orange and lemon trees stood between the carved stone benches that were placed every five metres.

On the end bench, sitting upright in tangerine satin, was Maxine.

Earlier that afternoon, Mademoiselle Janine had pressed her forehead to the window of the blue salon as Lili and Alexandre wandered across the lawn towards the wood. She was not the only person to have noticed their departure, but she was the only one who immediately moved over to the coffee table and murmured the news to Madame la Comtesse. Maxine was suddenly possessed by a violent jealousy that swept away all logic. Like everyone else, Maxine had noticed her son's infatuation, but she had hardly expected her star guest to take much notice of a fifteen-year-old boy, especially when there were so many more suitable men present. Try as she might, Maxine found that she couldn't ignore the situation. She was bursting with indignation and rage. She guessed that they would not be back before sunset, when (if Alexandre was anything like his brothers or his father) they would no doubt enter by the little hidden door to the orangery where the woods came nearest to the château.

As they changed for dinner, Maxine asked Charles to look after their guests for a few minutes. He gave her a swift, worried look; something was up when Maxine used that carefully casual voice, but he judged it better to say nothing and do as she wished.

Quietly the door to the orangery opened and they slipped inside. Alexandre immediately pulled Lili to him again and bent his head down to her throat, but she gently laughed. 'You must *never* touch me when anyone might see.'

'Then may I come to your room tonight?'

'You will go to *your* room *now*, Alexandre.' It was his mother's voice. Caught off guard, the tall boy suddenly looked like a guilty six-year-old who had been caught stealing candy.

He hesitated. Lili gave him a little push towards the corridor and he fled.

Maxine looked at Lili with loathing. 'Couldn't you leave my son alone? Did you *need* to seduce a fifteen-year-old boy? Can't you leave *any* man alone?'

'Don't be ridiculous. *He* seduced *me* . . . Is he *really* only fifteen? . . . I thought eighteen . . . or maybe seventeen.'

'I hate to think of his *touching* you.'

'But what is so dreadful? It was obviously not the first time.'

'He should love someone of his own age and his own kind.'

'I'm only twenty-four.'

'I don't care *how* old you are. You're no better than a whore.'

Maxine had gone too far. Lili was suddenly furious. 'You are *jealous* because I had him and *you can't.*'

Stepping forward, Maxine slapped the face of this creature who had bewitched her youngest and favourite son.

As fast as a fighting cock, Lili flew at Maxine and her hand flashed across the older woman's face. Blood flowed in three small trickles down Maxine's face.

Crying with indignation, Lili flung herself at Maxine, pounding at the older, bigger woman, arms flailing, engrossed in her rage and her need for revenge. Aghast, Maxine flung up both arms to protect herself from her attacker and kicked Lili with one tangerine satin toe. But Lili sprang back at her, eyes narrowed, lips drawn back.

Maxine was ashamed, mortified and alarmed. She had never hit anyone in her life, not even her sons when they were children. Yet she had now allowed herself to behave as badly as this slut. She broke away and fled to her room, her hair falling down on one side, her cheek bleeding and her dress torn.

She flung herself on the blue silk bed, grabbed the ivory house telephone and dialled the housekeeper. With difficulty she kept her voice calm. 'Please pack Mademoiselle Lili's clothes straightaway, and tell Antoine to bring her car to the front door. She will be leaving immediately.' Then she rang for the butler to come to her bedroom.

She changed quickly into her bathrobe, brushed and pinned her hair into place, bathed her scratched cheek, which had stopped bleeding, and dabbed Concealstik on the wounds. When the butler arrived she simply said, 'There has been a slight disturbance, Lamartine. Miss Lili is leaving. I want you to see that she is out of this house within half an hour. And Lamartine – the meal had better wait until she has gone. We do not want to disturb the other guests, and we don't want a scene. Serve more champagne, please.'

Lili was already flinging her clothes into her suitcases. She left the house with head held high, conscious of the expressionless, watchful Lamartine in his role of upper-class bouncer.

Shrouded in twilight, the beautiful château receded in the rearview mirror as the Jaguar sped down the drive. As soon as the car had nosed out of the gate, Lili pulled into the side of the road and collapsed in tears.

But the episode had not yet ended. In the following issue of *Paris Match* there was no photo coverage of Maxine's glamorous guests at her anniversary ball. Instead there was a single colour spread under a banner heading that read 'Château de Chazalle – A Place to Make Friends.'

It was the first of an idyllic series of photographs of a young couple lying in a forest clearing. *There*, unmistakably, lay Lili in the long grass and it was undoubtedly Alexandre who leaned over her. *There* was a close-up of Alexandre's mouth and his hand on her breast. *There* they were clasped together and laughing as they fell through the spray of river water.

It was fairly discreet as these things go – no nipples, no pubic hair, no sex organs, no navels – but it was unmistakably erotic.

Andi Cherno's telephoto lens had snapped another scoop.

When she saw it, Maxine sat up in bed and burst into tears of mortification.

So did Lili.

So did Alexandre. He had been painfully humiliated. Lili had left without a word, and he had been ferociously punished by his parents. Nevertheless, he could feel the wordless, amazed admiration of his father and brothers and the awed respect of every single boy in his class.

But he would rather have had Lili.

THE winter of 1975 was unusually cold in Paris, and the scarlet Jaguar skidded slightly as Lili drove – rather too fast – along the cobbled streets of Paris.

'Slower,' Zimmer suggested, as they slid sideways towards an ornate, dark green urinal. Lili steered into the skid, straightened and continued as fast as before. Zimmer said, 'I don't know what's got into you, Lili, but I know something's wrong. *What is it?* We've made nearly a dozen movies together, and in the last year or so you've had two wonderful parts. You're only twenty-five and you've won every European acting award there is. What's eating you?'

Lili was silent. After Stiarkoz's death, she had felt like an outsider among the rich. She buried her grief in the one distraction that had never failed to absorb her – her work. She started to work with a passion and discipline, as if her life depended on it. Which it did. Even Zimmer was surprised by her fierce concentration and tenacity. He'd always known she had star quality, but it had originally been hampered by lack of ambition, lack of self-discipline, lack of direction. Now, at twenty-five, Lili seemed to know what she wanted, where she wanted to go. There was no holding her.

And Zimmer was the perfect counterbalance for their relationship. He knew, with cynical self-awareness, that he wasn't egomanic enough ever to be a *great* director, he couldn't be tough enough with himself or anyone else, but with Lili his work was outstanding and so was hers. She trusted him completely, she seemed to know instinctively what he wanted and he always drew a first-class performance from her. Until now.

'Why are you finding this part such a problem?' Zimmer sounded puzzled, although he knew the answer perfectly well. 'You've got one of the best female roles ever written.' He twisted around to look at Lili's profile, the little jutting chin, the slightly predatory nose. 'Think of the women who have already played Sadie – Gloria Swanson, Joan Crawford, Rita Hayworth – it's a classic. But for the first time since I've worked with you, Lili – you're overacting. You're hamming it up. *What's the matter?*'

Lili snorted and drove a little faster.

'What you need is a man,' said Zimmer, with irritating conviction, knowing it was a remark that always annoys a woman, especially when it's true. He wanted to get a reaction from her.

'It may be the answer for you, but it isn't for me. So stop pushing Schenk at me!'

'You're not very sophisticated in your business, Lili,' Zimmer said, with a shrug. 'After all, Schenk is putting up forty per cent of the money for *Rain*. Why did you have to turn down such a powerful man so publicly?'

'Because he *asked* me so publicly! And he made it clear what I had to gain. Look where that sort of filth got me before I met Jo. I never want to go back to doing anything I'm ashamed of. Those pictures in *Paris Match* were bad enough!' The little red car screamed around a corner and Zimmer grabbed the dashboard.

'Oh, my dear, it's exasperatingly self-indulgent of you to ignore Schenk. You're like a self-willed little girl who's just been told not to step on a banana skin, but insists that she's got the right to break her own leg.'

'Oh, God! Does the whole world revolve around sex and money?'

'Yes.'

'I don't have to obey Schenk. It's not a royal command. What can he do, anyway? Ruin my career?' She snorted again.

'My dear, don't think he can't.' The light from the dashboard glowed green over Zimmer's tense face. 'Nobody gets a big role by screwing, but anybody can lose one by not screwing. Of course, it wouldn't be attributed directly to that, you'd be described as "uncooperative" or "neurotic".' Briefly Zimmer mentioned the name of a Hollywood studio chief and a once-famous star whose career had suddenly seemed to dissolve.

'I've heard your story dozens of times,' Lili said, 'and each time about a different actress. It's amazing how people will believe anything if it's nasty enough. Look at the rumours that fly around about me, although I haven't slept with a man for months.'

Zimmer said nothing. The humiliating episode at the Château de Chazalle had had the effect of making Lili retreat further into the shell of privacy that she had carefully constructed after the death of Stiarkoz. Now her reputation as a serious actress was suffering because those magazine pictures reminded everyone of the way in which she had originally become notorious. She slammed her foot on the accelerator and burst out, 'Oh, what's the point of working so hard when my every move is misinterpreted to fit their filthy image of me so that they can feel better about themselves! You *know* how hard I try, Zimmer.'

Zimmer nodded. He knew the tough, self-imposed routine she followed when not working. Exercise and dance classes, drama and voice lessons, early to bed and a careful diet.

At one point Zimmer had feared that he was in danger of becoming her substitute for Stiarkoz, but he realized quickly that Lili didn't want to lean on anybody, she wanted to stand on her own feet. She was determined to succeed, to carve her way like Jo.

Lili didn't like to think too much about Jo, for the sharp sting of her loss was still too painful. Instead, she found – just before she fell asleep – that her thoughts were turning childishly again to her unknown real mother. Increasingly, Lili saw that shadowy maternal figure as her invisible guardian angel. Yearning for such warmth, Lili had started to daydream again, to wonder who her real mother was, whether she was still alive.

The scarlet Jaguar swerved dangerously as Lili remembered that Sunday afternoon when Serge had telephoned her – speaking in his old masterful voice as if he'd last seen her only the day before. 'Lili, darling, it's like trying to get the fucking President's telephone number. I've missed you, you naughty little girl, and I wondered if you felt like having dinner tonight, for old time's sake . . .?'

Carefully, gently, Lili had placed the receiver on the table and walked away, leaving Serge talking to the air. At the memory, Lili felt so agitated that she braked too late and the Jaguar nearly hit a Renault in front of it. Impatiently, Lili waited for the light to change.

'Tell me what's wrong, Lili,' Zimmer urged again. 'Before you fucking kill us both.' She was silent, so he thought he'd better tell *her*. 'When an actor works on a part that's so close to him, he often can't see it objectively, so he feels frustrated and angry because he feels he has no control over his part. What such an actor finds difficult to realize is that what he has to do is – nothing.' The Jaguar passed dangerously close to a truck, which blasted its horn. Zimmer continued gently, 'You know what humiliation feels like, Lili, you know what it's like to feel worthless, *you* understand exactly how Sadie feels, so what you should do with this part is – just let it happen.'

'*Shut up, Zimmer!*' There was an explosion of wrath from Lili as the little scarlet car skidded again, swerved around 180 degrees and slid sideways into an ornate lamppost. Lili and Zimmer were flung forwards, then yanked backwards by their safety belts as the car stopped abruptly – the right front fender crumpled like a discarded tomato can.

'Now, look what you've made me do!' cried Lili. 'If you're going to analyse my acting and my character, you should have picked a better time!'

A small crowd started to gather around the sports car. Lili took no notice of them as she said angrily, '*Of course* I understand Sadie. She's basically a nice, cheerful tart who likes a good time because it makes her forget that her real life is such a mess and she hasn't enough imagination to see that things could be different. But that sanctimonious missionary rams home the fact that she's worthless until Sadie actually *believes* it. *Then* he promises her he can provide salvation, so Sadie starts to hope . . . But *then* the dirty bastard rapes her and that . . . destroys her hope, rapes her soul.'

A blue-cloaked gendarme was hurrying towards the car but still Lili took no notice. 'That's not going to happen to me, Zimmer. I'm *not* Sadie – and no man is going to do that to me! I'm an actress and my imagination is my soul – what makes me an actress. I *had* to develop it to survive those dreadful years. It's all I have to show for them. That's why I can think myself into someone else's head so easily.'

The gendarme had nearly reached the car. 'Oh, I know I'm calm and efficient on the set. That's because I know exactly what has to be done and how to do it. But off the set I have to be *me* and I don't know how to do that, I don't know my lines, I don't understand the plot and I don't know who I *can* trust.'

Zimmer nodded.

'On the set I'm a star, off the set I feel that everyone's sneering at me . . . and it's such a damn lonely feeling.' She hid her face in her hands and burst into tears.

Zimmer opened the car door to the gendarme. 'Officer, might I have a word with you? . . .'

As soon as Lili's name was mentioned, the officer's face lit up and the crowd doubled as if by magic. Within minutes six passers-by had tugged and lifted the crumpled car away from the lamppost and Lili, now smiling like an angel, had scribbled autographs for all of them. She then drove off slowly as snow began to fall, having given the policeman an extra autograph for his mother.

'Bloody lucky that cop recognized you or we'd still be at the police station,' Zimmer grumbled.

'I can live without such fame!' Lili said sourly.

The little red car limped through a pair of huge green doors and into the courtyard beyond. Zimmer and Lili dashed through the snowflakes to the door of the apartment building as lace curtains twitched at the concierge's window.

As they waited for the old-fashioned elevator cage, Lili shook the snowflakes from her silver fox cloak and Zimmer said, 'Maybe you think you don't like fame but you'd miss it if it disappeared. Those people weren't threatening, they only wanted to know what you're like, Lili.'

'*I* want to know what I'm like, Zimmer.' Lili shrugged off her fur cape and threw it on a chair. 'I want to know who I *really* am. I want to meet the real me!'

She kicked off a maroon-leather boot, hopping on one foot as she struggled with the other boot.

Zimmer chuckled. 'I've had to conceal the real me for years or I'd have been arrested. We all have to come to terms with what we are, as opposed to what we *wish* we were. In the end, we all have to settle for what we've got – and you've got so much, Lili!'

'Yes, except what everyone else has – a family. I *really* don't know who I am.'

'So what! Who *does* know who they are? Don't you think that perhaps you use your lack of a family as a convenient excuse for whatever's going wrong in your life?'

Lili didn't hear Zimmer's last remark as she padded on stockinged feet into the dining room, poured neat whisky into a cut-glass tumbler and brought it out to him. Zimmer, who was throwing more logs on the blazing fire, straightened up, took his drink, turned towards the mantelpiece and blinked in astonishment. 'What's *this*?'

He picked up a large white envelope covered with exotic stamps that had been propped against the gilt carriage clock. Turning it over, he peered at the ornate crest and started to laugh. 'Oh, my dear, *now* how do you feel about your fame?'

He handed her the envelope. Quickly, Lili tore it open, pulled out a large gilt-edged card and read, '"I am commanded by His Majesty, King Abdullah . . ." Why, it's an invitation to Sydon, to celebrate the anniversary of his reign. But I don't *know* the man!'

'Ah, but he knows *you*! *That's* fame!' cried Zimmer, already planning what to tell his publicity department. 'It will be wonderful publicity for you! *Now* you can't say you don't care about fame!'

Lili turned around to face him. 'Do you know how much this means to me?' She waved the invitation in his face. 'Nothing! One minute Serge is telling me to shake my tits at the camera, the next minute some king is inviting me halfway around the world. Who the hell do they think I am? I really would like to know. There's a part of me that's missing and I don't even know what part it is. I just know that I feel the emptiness inside me, and high-powered invitations aren't important compared to that feeling.'

'High-powered invitations are always important, Lili. Especially when you stop receiving them!' Zimmer put his drink on the mantelpiece and looked amused, which further enraged Lili.

'Do you know how much this means to me?' Lili waved the card at him again, then threw it into the burning logs.

'Oh, Lili,' exclaimed Zimmer, 'don't you know how much you mean to me?'

He thrust his bare hand into the flames and plucked the invitation out.

～ 56 ～

A THRILL of trumpets rang out as the double doors at the far end of the Grand Hall were thrown open. Men bowed and women curtsied as His Majesty King Abdullah I I I slowly strode over the crimson carpet towards the golden throne of state, pausing en route to greet his guests. Lili thought the King looked more alive than in his official photographs, which always showed him in combat clothes or ceremonial uniforms.

Tonight, knowing that many women would be wearing formal white dresses and diamond tiaras, Lili had picked a halter-neck, backless, sea-silver-green chiffon dress embroidered with art nouveau lilies. As Abdullah reached her, Lili bent her head – a permed, gypsy-like cloud of dark curls – and sank into a curtsy. She lifted her eyes and gazed up into his, and Abdullah's sensual, heavy-lidded stare met another of equal power. He forgot his formal few words of greeting and stopped as they both stood and stared at each other in silence, both feeling an electric tension between them.

During the three years since his family had been killed, Abdullah had rarely appeared in public. Racked with grief and guilt, he had been unable to discuss his feelings with anyone. For weeks after the helicopter crash, Abdullah had spoken to no one and nobody dared speak to him. Occasionally he rode alone into the desert, where the silence of the sand soothed his grief but could not eradicate his memories. In his heart, Abdullah knew he would have other sons, but no other child would ever replace Mustapha – the only person Abdullah had ever loved.

As his royal master grew increasingly irritable and morose, Suliman racked his brains for schemes to divert Abdullah and had his head bitten off for his trouble. Abdullah seemed unable to concentrate on his hitherto cherished irrigation schemes or the desert reclamation and reforestation projects that had been his main interest before the fatal crash. A scheme to drill for underground water lay on his desk for weeks. He was listless, unable to work, without his former concentration and energy. Abruptly he cancelled all plans for the 1973 festivities to celebrate the twentieth year of his reign. Instead of rising at dawn, he got up late, slumped through the day and spent his evenings watching old movies before retiring early and alone.

Then, one evening, he suddenly sat up, watched the movie with alert concentration and immediately commanded the projectionist to run it again. 'I feel I already know that woman,' he puzzled, 'although I'm sure we haven't met and I've never seen this film. Q – strange!' He leaned towards Suliman. 'Get her for me.'

'Oh, Sire, this actress is well known in Europe. For what reason should I invite her to our country? And for how long, Sire?'

'Invite her with a small group. No, a large group. Oh, I don't know. Just get her.'

Suliman saw his chance. 'A reception, Sire? As we had planned for the twentieth year?'

'Oh, I suppose so. Reduce the original fortnight of events to a couple of days, but make sure this woman comes.'

'It is done, Sire.'

Now, as Lili sank before him in a sea-green curtsy and her

black-fringed eyes stared at him, Abdullah took a deep breath and suddenly – at last – he felt alive again. He gave her a slow, unusually gentle smile and then regretfully moved on towards the next white satin curtsy.

Lili clutched her neighbour's arm. The long flight from Paris and the subsequent reception at the airport had been more tiring than she thought, and it had been followed by a motorcade to the palace on the hill. The excitement and the jet lag must have exhausted her.

Golden trumpets heralded two hundred guests into the dining room. White damask tables were set with silver and lit by candles. The meal had been supervised by a team of chefs flown from le Grand Véfour in Paris. Beluga caviar was served, then fresh sliced oranges vinaigrette, followed by roast duck stuffed with boned pigeon, stuffed with quail, stuffed with spiced rice and almonds. After salads, rose-leaf sorbets were served with pomegranates and grapes.

Abdullah, seated among the most important guests, was far from Lili. At the end of the meal he rose and made a speech of welcome, then announced that trifling mementos of their visit would now be handed to each of his honoured guests. White-robed servants placed small dark wood boxes in front of each place, each exquisitely inlaid with a geometric design of mother-of-pearl. Every man received a pair of cuff links made from ancient Roman gold coins, and every woman found a pair of earrings; each was different from the next, and each had been especially designed by Andrew Grima, the jeweller most favoured by the oil sheikhs. Lili's earrings were robin's-egg-size turquoises set with small diamonds and sapphires in roughly worked gold.

There was an instant buzz of delight. The speeches of extravagant congratulation from the diplomatic corps lasted until past midnight, when the guests returned to the throne room for dancing. As the band struck up 'Oh What a Beautiful Morning', His Majesty offered his arm to the wife of the American Ambassador. Lili found Suliman at her elbow and together they whirled under the chandeliers. At the end of the dance Suliman immediately steered Lili up to King Abdullah, who smoothly requested the next dance.

She felt the warm palm of his hand on her naked back as,

lightly, he pressed her to his white dinner jacket. She could feel Abdullah's chest rise and fall as he breathed. She raised her eyes to his. Neither of them said much as they moved together, each aware of the rhythmic breathing of the other.

As the music stopped, Abdullah murmured, 'Regrettably, I must now dance with the other ladies, but I should like to talk to you later. Shall we say in half an hour's time in the jasmine garden? Colonel Hakem will escort you.'

Lili felt the silky brush of his moustache on her hand, and as he moved away, she found Suliman bowing before her.

'I don't think I want to dance,' Lili said, her face pink, the blood still pounding through her temples.

'Perhaps you would care to sit in the jasmine garden?' He led her through long, white marble corridors and out into the star-sprinkled night. The creamy moon floated in the sky above a small, softly lit garden. Great sprays of star-white jasmine hung from the high walls, scenting the dark air with intoxicating perfume. Colonel Hakem patted his hands twice, and white-clad servants appeared with a silver tray of coffee and sorbets.

Lili turned to the Colonel, but he had melted away and in his place stood Abdullah, fiercely handsome in the moonlight. He lifted the tips of her fingers to his lips and she felt the touch of his teeth on her nails, the soft caress of black silky hair against her hand.

'I feel that I already know you, that I've always known you,' she whispered.

'That's exactly how I feel,' he murmured as his lips brushed against her throat, 'as if we belong together.'

After that Lili remembered nothing but kaleidoscopic flashes of moonlight, the velvet night, the jasmine, the fairytale unreality of the shadowy garden, and the yielding couch beneath her, as her white arms reached up to him.

It was almost midday when Lili opened her eyes and saw the unaccustomed cerulean-domed ceiling and a brilliant blue sky beyond double-arched white windows. Abruptly she sat up in bed and pulled the soft sheets to her naked body. She was alone.

But she hadn't been alone.

Slowly she lay back on the pillows, remembering the feel of his flesh. Her visual memory was blurred. It had been dark in the garden, and later, when he had guided her back to her suite, she could only remember a dim figure. But never would she forget what had happened among the jasmine flowers, and for the rest of her life the smell of that sweet, erotic odour would magically, instantly, transport her thousands of miles back through time to the silver and black silent garden where, for the first time in her life, Lili had felt passion.

A servant slid into the room and bowed, barefoot in a long, white robe. Silently he offered a silver tray upon which was fruit, tea and the little earring box that Lili had left in the jasmine garden. Then he bowed and disappeared again. Lili glanced at her wristwatch, then reached for the thick cream official folder that contained the programme of events. Thank goodness, there was still nearly an hour before the ladies' luncheon, after which the wife of the commander-in-chief was to escort the ladies on a tour of the bazaar while the gentlemen, who were lunching with His Majesty, would spend the afternoon inspecting the desert reclamation plans and models.

In the early evening the guests assembled in the outer courtyard, where a fleet of Land Rovers waited to drive them along the coast towards Dinada and into the desert for a moonlit feast. The men wore casual clothes, the women wore silk dresses, and each guest had been presented with a crimson wool *burka* in case the night turned cold.

The scarlet-robed guard presented arms; silver scimitars flashed through the air, to be held level with fierce dark eyes, as King Abdullah slowly descended the shallow, *bleu belge* marble steps of the palace. He moved slowly in public, his back ramrod-straight, his head thrown back, apart from other men, distanced from them by his rank. Never for one minute was anyone allowed to treat Abdullah as an equal in public, and very few were foolish enough to try it even in private.

Now, as his guests bowed and curtsied, Abdullah looked at Lili with no sign of recognition, but when all the guests had been ushered by the major-domo into the long line of Land Rovers, she found herself seated at his side. Lili felt a touch, light as a butterfly, brush her left arm, raising the soft down, making the hairs lift on the back of her neck, taking her breath away. Apart from that,

Abdullah behaved to her exactly as he did to his other guests – so much so that for one moment, she wondered whether she had imagined his hard, naked body against her soft white belly on that silken dark divan. But then her eyes caught his, that black, liquid stare met hers, lingered, and she felt a thrill of exultation, of passion and suspense.

As dusk fell, they bumped through a yellow haze and on to the rough desert track. Twenty minutes later, as they passed through a gully of blackened, blistered rocks, the moon slowly rose above the endless silver sand.

'How on earth can the driver see where he's going?' Lili exclaimed.

The King laughed. 'The desert only looks the same to Westerners. A Bedouin can find his way back to the same spot again and again, with no more trouble than you'd have in getting from the Place Vendôme to the rue de Rivoli.'

Suddenly, on the horizon, they saw the ancient ruins of an enormous Roman amphitheatre. Three crumbling, curving, rose-brown tiers of arches were open to the sky: cunningly spotlit, from the distance, each arc of blazing light looked magically perfect, as if the amphitheatre had been built yesterday. Silken rugs had been laid before the old arena, where gladiators had once fought for their lives, where runaway slaves had shivered before the glaring green eyes and open jaws of lions and leopards, where crowds had bayed for blood.

That night Lili again hurried along wide, marble corridors to the dark silent warmth of the jasmine garden. Abdullah moved forward from the leafy shadow and clasped her in his arms. She felt his lips on her dark hair, her slender neck, and then her mouth as effortlessly he swung her into his arms and strode towards the silken couches.

Before an hour had passed Lili realized that for the second time in her life she loved a man, but this time it was with a violent passion, a total abandon such as she had never experienced.

Much later she felt his velvety cheek nuzzling her. 'Will you stay here?' he asked.

Lili had no means of knowing that Abdullah had never before brought a European woman into the kingdom, that he was flinging caution to the winds, that his passion for her was politically dangerous.

She hesitated. Her heart and her body told her to say yes, but her reason and her memory reminded her that she lay in the arms of an international playboy. Lili definitely didn't want to appear to the world as merely the latest in Abdullah's string of women. Since finishing *Rain* she had felt a growing sense of self-esteem. The picture hadn't yet been premiered, but everyone in the business knew that Lili's Sadie Thompson was a superb performance – and a personal victory for Lili. She was determined that *nothing* was going to rob her of what she had worked so hard to achieve – respect as a serious actress. But life was for living, and never before had Lili felt so alive and yet so at peace.

The premiere was still five weeks away.

A week or two in Sydon could hardly matter, could it?

～ 57 ～

A YEAR later, Lili was still in Sydon. Those idyllic twelve months had seemed endless, and yet they had passed quickly. Abdullah was passionately devoted to Lili. When he was with her, his past unhappiness ceased to exist and he could think only of that moment. To her surprise, Lili found that her initial, dazzled fascination developed into an inexplicable happiness. She felt an extraordinary peace when she was with Abdullah, something that was totally different from the sedate calm that she had experienced with Stiarkoz and had thought was peace. Lili also experienced an unexpected respect for Abdullah as she saw how great his dedication was to his people, how awesome was his responsibility to them, how total was his power over them. One word from Abdullah could mean death to a man. Just a nod to Suliman and the servant who had been caught hiding in the Dinada royal garage, where he had no business to be, started to scream in horror as he realized his fate and was roughly dragged away.

'There was no proof, no poison, no bomb, no knife! That man

wasn't allowed to say a word in his own defence. How can you possibly know that he wanted to kill you? How can you be so cruel?' Lili burst out, as they sat upon the terrace that overlooked the sea.

Abdullah looked thoughtfully at her. 'You're wrong, I'm not cruel,' he said. 'Cruelty is finding pleasure in inflicting pain. I inflict pain only when it is necessary, and I don't find any pleasure in it.'

He looked up at the sky and added, 'However, I am certainly ruthless. If I weren't, I'd have been dead before I was sixteen. Some people find that after a shock their hair turns white overnight. After the first assassination attempt, when I was fourteen, I woke up next morning and found that I was ruthless. You see, the alternative was death.'

She had come to accept the harsh reality that lay behind this life of luxury. She loved living at Dinada Palace. Poised on the outer curve of a sheltered bay, the palace was built into the low cliff and descended in a series of white, arched spans, down into the rocky waters of the sea. Each of the five levels had its own terraced garden – below her Lili could see white-turbaned gardeners bending over rosebeds as they tended the honeysuckle and white-starred jasmine that quivered against the palace walls in the light sea breeze.

Surrounded by junipers, cypresses and silver-leafed olive trees, Dinada Palace was a quiet, informal retreat compared to the ceremonial formality of the imposing old palace at Semira. Semira was where Abdullah waded through all the paper work, where he conferred with his council and his commanders, where he gave audiences to foreign diplomats and tribal sheikhs. Dinada was where they relaxed, swam in the fishscale-silver sea or in the underground, heated swimming pool which had been carved from the rock. Dinada was where they rode horseback along the white sands of the bay, water-skied, fished and sometimes entertained their friends aboard the royal motor yacht.

Zimmer had visited them twice and was due to reappear shortly for a few days before he and Lili flew back to Paris. Lili had made no films during the previous year, but Zimmer had eventually tempted her with 'The Jewels', a classic story by de Maupassant. Lili was to play the modest, angelically virtuous wife of a government clerk who adores his wife, although he disapproves of her interest in the theatre and her passion for imitation jewellery. 'My dear, when a woman can't afford to buy real jewels,' the little clerk says sternly, 'she ought to appear adorned with her grace and beauty alone.'

'Not that anybody can afford just to be beautiful, darling,' Zimmer had murmured one evening, as he and Lili leaned over the terrace balustrade and watched the sun slowly fall into the sea. 'A girl needs status, especially if she isn't married and is involved with a very powerful man. Status is what they understand and respect.' He turned to look straight into Lili's eyes with a seriousness that belied his mocking voice. 'Status is what gets a girl mass admiration. A girl's status can occasionally remind such a man how fortunate he is to have her – and how many other men would like to. In other words, my darling, status is what keeps him toeing the line and stops his eye from wandering when he's bored.'

Lili had thrown back her head and glared at Zimmer, but he was determined to say what was on his mind. 'It might be as well for you to remember, my darling, that although you are as ravishing as ever, His Majesty is not exactly famous for his fidelity.'

Unwillingly, Lili thought of Zimmer's words as she moved slowly into her bedroom, a fifteen-metre-long room with three glass walls and a mirror-covered rear wall that overlooked and reflected the sea so that she felt suspended in azure space. Lili had already considered the possibility that Abdullah might tire of her, but she had shrugged it to one side. She would think about it only if it happened. In his strong brown arms, her face upturned to his kisses, entangled together in silken sheets, she could not believe that it ever *would* happen, that he would ever want such happiness to cease. But when, as now, she had been alone for several days, she sometimes felt a sudden dread, a twinge of panic.

Slowly she shrugged off the gauze gown that glimmered with gold and silver thread and was embroidered with real pearls. She wandered naked through her second bedroom, where she slept when the weather was hot. It was an arched room of similar size, painted the soft peach shade of her powder compact so that the room exactly matched her skin. This second bedroom had a three-metre-square sunken bed that was covered with cushions of apricot silk. The only other furniture in the room was a French

Empire chaise longue, upholstered in Abyssinian leopard skin, and a large marble writing table with a white Saarinen swivel chair behind it.

Lili threw herself on to the bed and forced herself to assess her situation. This carefree luxury was all too easy to accept without giving a thought to the future. But she was twenty-six and *had* to think of her future.

Lili had been flung from her protected childhood to the harsh regime of the Sardeau apartment in Paris. She had survived her first lover's betrayal. She had survived the world's contempt when she was a porno star. She had even survived the shock of Jo's death and his lawyer's corruption and theft. After a struggle, Lili had started to regain her self-confidence and had worked hard at her profession, hoping for reason to be proud of herself. She had tried to direct her own life, to follow her own path and not be dragged down somebody else's. And then she had flung all her endeavour aside for love.

She knew that Zimmer was right; she could not rashly abandon her career or her new, hard-won success. This sybaritic life of love and luxury could not continue indefinitely, and Lili wasn't even sure she *wanted* it to. Arab women couldn't understand Lili, they were as contemptuous of Lili as they were jealous of her. Their menfolk kept the women away from Lili, with her dangerous ideas of freedom. A woman's place was with the women, in the harem. Prudently, the men, too, stayed away from Lili; they wished no casual conversation with her to be misinterpreted by their King; few of them spoke good French or English. Abdullah's days were filled with official business; Lili never knew when she would see him, so although her nights were exciting, her days were lonely. She felt an itch to get back to work, to lead a life of her own rather than this soft, confined life as the mistress of the King.

The attraction that had lost none of its power to charm Lili was Abdullah. From time to time he would take her face in his hands and look into her eyes and then with one finger trace her eyebrows, her forehead, her nose, as if he were planning to sculpt her head or as if he were trying to imprint it upon his memory forever. When he did this he would smile at her gently with the same odd, infinite sweetness that she remembered from the first time she had looked into his eyes. Then Lili knew without a doubt he loved her. But at other times, when he was preoccupied by some political question, he treated her as if she were a tiresome puppy that exasperated him.

He had never spoken to her of his wife or child. Realizing the terrible loss he had suffered, how deeply it still pained him, and how private and agonizing were his thoughts about the tragedy, Lili never dared refer to it. But she knew there was no possibility that Abdullah would marry *her*. She was an infidel. It was his duty to his people to choose a pure-blooded Queen who would provide acceptable heirs to the throne.

The painful part was that Lili longed to *give* him a son, she longed to feel Abdullah's child stir in her body, feel it kicking, take Abdullah's hand and proudly place it on her swelling stomach, watch her breasts grow big and heavy, ready to suckle his child. More than ever, Lili longed for permanence in her life and the things that most women seemed to achieve without difficulty – to settle down, to be married, and to have a baby upon whom she could lavish all her stored-up love.

There was another reason why Lili could never marry Abdullah. In this land, where a girl risked having her throat slit by her father if she were suspected of being alone with a man, Lili was regarded as the concubine of the King, and she could sense the polite disregard in which she was held by the Court. She was the King's whore.

And there was still another reason why Abdullah could never share his life with her – a reason that was also uncontestable proof of his love for Lili. She was a Westerner and, as such, an enemy.

The previous week, when Arab guerrillas had launched a seaborne attack on Tel Aviv, Abdullah had been sullen and preoccupied before granting an emergency audience to the American Ambassador.

After an early breakfast, Lili, wearing jodhpurs and a white shirt, was crossing the turquoise tiled courtyard of the old Semira Palace, heading for the stables, when she heard her name called and turned to see a beaming face that she recognized. 'Why, Bill Sheridan, how wonderful to see you again! Is Linda with you?' she called.

The big Texas lawyer tumbled out of his official limousine, bounded over to Lili and enveloped her in a bear hug. Warmly, she kissed the old man's cheek. 'Of course Linda is with me – getting used to being an ambassadress and rearranging every stick of furniture in the Embassy. We heard you were here, but I didn't expect to run into you so quickly. Now when can you come and visit? D'you remember the barbecues Linda used to fix in that place we had in the rue Monsieur? That's nothing to what she has in mind for Sydon. They're gonna see real Texas hospitality!'

He pumped her hand. 'But *you* don't have to wait until we've got the carpets down! I'll bet it's been months since you had a good steak with all the trimmings! I've had them flown over from the ranch. When can I send a car over for you, honey?'

Lili considered. Abdullah was about to attend a *mansef* in southern Sydon and he'd be away for at least three days. 'How about next Thursday?'

'Fine, fine, Lili, around six o'clock? We'll sure look forward to it. Now I'd better get in there with my briefcase.' He nodded towards the arched main entrance of the palace and lumbered up the *bleu belge* steps, as Lili continued towards the stable.

When she returned from her ride, a white-clad servant was waiting for her. He bowed, then barked, 'The King wishes you to attend him immediately.'

Lili hurried into the palace, past a group of white-robed courtiers waiting outside Abdullah's chamber of state: they shot her sullen looks of hate and resentment. What had she done now? Lili wondered.

Abdullah was pacing the chamber like an enraged tiger.

'*What is this I hear about your consorting with the new American Ambassador?*'

'Why, Bill Sheridan is an old friend. I've known him and his wife for years!'

'He is an uncultured millionaire lawyer who happens to know just enough about the oil business and to have contributed enough cash to the Republicans to get this position! If he wasn't the U.S. Ambassador I wouldn't sit down to eat with him. You will most certainly *not* see him, or his wife.'

'I most certainly *will* see my friends, Abdi!'

'I cannot allow you to associate freely with the Embassy, no doubt to be casually questioned over the hamburgers by that dog of a C.I.A. agent who calls himself the cultural attaché! We know you never see or hear anything of strategic importance, but *they* don't! And they all saw you being – *embraced* – by that American pig!'

Lili suddenly realized the significance of what the infuriated Abdullah had said. 'You mean, *you* have me watched! You don't trust me, Abdullah?'

Abdullah turned away from her, folded his arms and glared at the orange trees outside the arched window. 'You must understand my position! My advisers resent my – consorting – with a Westerner, and they cannot *afford* to regard you as trustworthy!'

Lili gave him a silent look of fury, turned on her heel, stormed out of the chamber and through the disdainful group of white-robed men gathered outside the door. *Never* had she felt so humiliated! Suddenly she wondered what she was doing in this heap of sand where she wasn't allowed to drop into the American Embassy to meet an old acquaintance.

By evening Lili had calmed down and she listened in silence to Abdullah's heated attack on American policy towards Israel as they were driving to Dinada. But at sunset, as they walked bare-foot along the edge of the sea, their caftans soaked at the hem, she suddenly said, 'How long is this senseless fighting going to continue? Obviously not forever. Why *can't* the Arabs make peace with Israel?'

Abdullah swiftly turned and caught her wrist. 'For the last time, woman, I will tell you why war will continue in Palestine. In 1917, the infidel British decided that it would be a good idea to make Palestine a home for the Jews.' He snorted. 'But they didn't seem to realize that ninety-three per cent of the people of Palestine were Moslem or Christian.' In the dusk his face was bitter with rage as he took her by the shoulders and roughly shook her. 'So those Arabs found themselves homeless, they were thrown out of their homes and their country – for the benefit of seven per cent of the population and a lot of other Jews who had never *seen* Palestine, let alone lived in it.'

Suddenly Abdullah saw Lili only as a Westerner, his enemy. He wanted to dominate and possess her. For a long time he had refused to admit to himself that he had fallen helplessly in love with a European woman. Abdullah could only see this as a weakness in himself and a possible breach in his defences. He was alarmed by the intensity of his feelings and he was frightened of loving another human being as deeply as he had loved his little son, frightened that if he loved again, he might again lose that love. Exasperated by these mixed feelings, he again shook Lili's shoulders.

Sharply Lili looked at him, silhouetted against the blood-red sea. She stumbled, felt him roughly push her down, then she was lying half in shallow warm water, half upon the beach. She felt his weight pressing her into the sand as his wet hands quickly felt beneath her sodden caftan and with a grunt he thrust inside her – hard, rough, heavy, male, with not a sign of *imsak*.

Afterwards, drenched and covered with grit, Lili sat up on the sand and scowled at Abdullah, who had flung off his caftan and was about to plunge into the sea. It was too much! Too much like one of those stupid films she used to make – and just as humiliating. Suddenly Lili was tired of being the wrong race, the wrong creed and on the wrong side.

'This is never going to work, is it?' she cried. 'Constantly I am made aware of the reasons that I am *wrong* for you, Abdi, but do you realize that there is a major reason why *you* are wrong for me?'

She pounded the sand with her fists. 'No matter how passionately our bodies are united *you cannot give me* your unreserved love.' Her voice shook. 'We both knew your position makes that impossible – but I'm not sure that's the only reason.' She took a deep breath. 'The problem is, Abdi, that you can't *trust* anybody – not even me – and you can't love someone if you don't trust her.'

There was a pause. 'It's difficult to trust someone,' he said, his voice imperious and sulky, 'when you know that however well you do your job, there are many people who want to kill you simply because you have that job.'

'I could have killed you a thousand times if I'd wanted to!' Lili cried, wiping a strand of wet hair back from her face. 'You withhold the important part of yourself from me and I find that unbearably painful and humiliating.' Her voice trailed off, then she burst out again, 'I'm ashamed of this part of you – the part that makes you deny me. I'm ashamed that I'm not good enough for you for reasons that have nothing to do with me. It makes me hurt and angry that you deliberately withhold your love from me.'

'Your hurt and anger aren't because of me,' Abdullah said,

roughly pulling Lili to her feet and cunningly changing the point of the conversation, as men so often do when women get too close to the truth. 'Your hurt and anger, Lili, are because – as you've so often told me – you don't know who you are, and you're relying on love to make your life worthwhile, to give it meaning.'

She saw amused contempt in his eyes, as if he were listening to a child's outburst.

'You're right,' said Lili, 'I was.' She was astonished to find herself using the past tense.

Abdullah was disdainful. 'You Westerners, with your endless quest for identity, you never know who you are. If you really want to know, then why don't you try to find out, instead of simply talking about it?'

'All right,' said Lili, 'I will.' She pulled her wrists from his grasp and ran away from him, along the lace-fringed, darkening sea.

~ PART ELEVEN ~

As soon as the press realized that Lili had returned to Paris, her apartment was besieged by reporters, the building opposite her bedroom sprouted telephoto lenses at every window and her telephone had to be left permanently off the hook. She lived in a state of siege, grappling once again with her misery and humiliation, but this time Lili also felt the impetus of anger and indignation.

'I know I did the right thing,' she said to Zimmer, as they sat in front of a log fire and she repaired his vicuna overcoat, the lapel of which had been torn as Zimmer forced his way to Lili's front door. Lili bit the thread. 'There, you'd never know it had been torn ... I suddenly realized the country and the people were hostile to me so that a break with Abdullah was inevitable and that the longer I stayed, the more painful the break would be.' She threw back her head as she added, 'And I felt that for the first time, I was deciding what was going to happen in my life. Oh, Zimmer, you can't believe what despair I felt, how miserable I was – still am – to be without Abdullah. I felt as if part of my body had been torn away, and I swear that sometimes I feel physical pain.' She pressed her left hand to her breast and was silent for a moment. 'But the odd thing is that I've never *once* regretted what I did. I'm proud I had the strength to do it. For once I felt really *proud* of myself. I expected to feel a sense of psychic destruction – God knows I've felt it before – but instead I felt grimly determined never to be humiliated again.'

'Aren't you going to talk to the press? It's been six weeks since you left Abdullah, but they're still waiting outside –'

'– like a pack of wolves! For once, my private life is going to *stay* private – I'm not going to talk to anyone about it, Zimmer. What I want to do is get back to work as fast as possible. It's the one, never-fail anodyne for pain.'

Dripping with fake diamonds, Lili shivered in the skinny clerk's arms. She was wearing a tightly laced, burgundy satin evening gown with a bustle and had just caught a cold on her way home from the opera. She was about to die of pneumonia next week. The skinny clerk's pince-nez fell off his nose, and he said, 'Shit!'

'Cut!' Zimmer said, as the crew started to laugh and the skinny clerk bent to pick up his rimless eyeglasses.

'The spring needs tightening,' he announced, 'but I can probably fix it myself if you give me a couple of minutes and a pair of eyebrow tweezers.'

The actor's pointed chin was covered by a short beard, required for his part as a Victorian government clerk, but Lili had nevertheless recognized his long, lean figure and the steel-blue flash of his eyes.

'I've met you before, haven't I?' she said when they met. 'A long time ago on my first film – you explained what everyone did. You're . . . Simon . . . aren't you?'

Simon looked a little wary. 'Simon Pont,' he said. 'I didn't think you'd remember.' He'd already decided to keep his distance – to keep well away from Lili. He wanted no complications, no paparazzi, no P R-organized romance, just a nice, juicy, well-paid part in a quick film with Zimmer, and, please God, no trouble with Tiger-Lili.

However, during the next few weeks, Simon found to his surprise that Lili was not the spoiled prima donna the media said she was. She seemed surprisingly quiet, almost shy. She hardly ever ventured from her dressing room, but if the door was open she could be seen sitting behind a ridiculously large pair of tortoise-shell spectacles, reading a book and making notes as she did so. 'And it isn't a pose,' Zimmer told Simon over lunch in the cafeteria. 'That's what Lili's really like, only I didn't bother to tell you beforehand because I knew you wouldn't believe it.'

'But who's going to read her notes?'

'Oh, there's always some teacher or professor creeping in or out of her apartment,' Zimmer said. He added, 'You see she's relatively uneducated and very much aware of it. I think her little self-improvement programme is rather touching and charming.'

'She's very professional,' Simon reflected, 'and I haven't seen a sign of the famous temper.'

'As a matter of fact, she's not short-tempered,' Zimmer said.

'She's medium-tempered. But she does tend to overreact if she's attacked, which happens quite often. Basically, she wants a quiet life when she isn't working. She's still unhappy about Abdullah, and she's besieged by journalists trying to find out why they split up. That's why she's a bit remote – she's wary, she knows that her most casual sentence might be misinterpreted, repeated and sold to a gossip columnist.'

'What's Lili like when she's with her friends?' Simon asked.

'She doesn't have many friends,' Zimmer said. He wiped his plate with a bit of bread. 'Look, I didn't have lunch with you to discuss Lili. I want to go over tomorrow's scene, once more. When she's dead and you're starving and you try to sell the fake jewellery, because that's all you have left to sell, I want you to think what it means to you when the jeweller tells you that the stuff is all real. There are so many implications and I need to see them *all* on your face at that moment ...'

'What would hit first?' Simon asked. 'Incredulity ... hope ... relief ... Then the realization that the wife he adored must have had a rich lover for years ... Their relationship has been destroyed ... But it also means that he is rich, free ... After all, he celebrates in a brothel, doesn't he? Do you want them to laugh or cry, Zimmer?' Simon was an established comedy actor.

'Both,' said Zimmer firmly.

'Couldn't I *really* swing from a chandelier in the brothel scene?' Simon asked hopefully.

'We could give it a try.'

Simon was agile and athletic and insisted on doing all his stunts himself when he was filming, which wasn't often, for he preferred the legitimate stage and the reaction of a live audience to the impersonal tedious repetition of film work.

'He's doing this film strictly for the money,' Zimmer had told Lili, 'lump sum alimony. He was married for years to a spoiled little bitch who's really stinging him. He's still badly bruised.'

'Married for how long?'

'How should I know, Lili? Long enough to have a little girl, maybe seven years, something like that. Just avoid the subject, darling.'

'Don't worry, I'll avoid *every* subject. It's not difficult. He hardly ever says a word to me off the set.'

On the second week of shooting Lili caught her fragile gold link bracelet on a door handle and tore a link. 'I'll fix it,' Simon offered, picking it up as he pulled out his red Swiss penknife. Lili looked horrified, but five minutes later the bracelet was back on her wrist. 'Faster than Cartier's,' she said with approval.

'And cheaper.'

Two days later Lili turned up with a bandaged thumb. 'I nearly always burn the toast,' she explained. 'I'm a rotten cook.'

The following day a huge, shiny, beribboned box was delivered to her dressing room. Digging deep beneath the tissue paper, she found a small toaster and a loaf of bread. Laughing, Lili thanked Simon. 'He might not say much, but he certainly listens,' she told Zimmer later. 'Now, I'll have to buy a present for *him*.'

So the following weekend Simon accompanied Lili to the Paris flea market, where, unobtrusive in a mackintosh with a turned-up collar and an old scarf tied under her chin, Lili liked to browse among the curiosities, hoping to pick out an antique from the junk. She chose a teak chest inlaid with an elaborate mother-of-pearl design for Simon, then she saw a group of Noah's Ark miniature wooden animal carvings – pairs of giraffes, elephants, monkeys and lions. 'Oh, what a perfect present for a child,' she cried. 'Simon, would you prefer these? You could give them to your little girl!'

Simon scowled at her. 'I haven't got a little girl,' he said roughly, and turned away.

Afterwards, driving Lili home in his Range Rover, Simon broke the silence. 'Look, I'm sorry I was rude,' he said, with visible effort. 'I used to have a daughter, but she died two years ago. Meningitis. She was only four. There was no need for her to die, meningitis is rarely fatal now, they treat it with antibiotics. But we were filming in Egypt and there was a hospital fuck-up. It all happened so fast. She was so small in that hospital bed, shrieking with pain and we could do nothing about it. Jean and I just stood there, clutching each other, although we hadn't so much as held hands for years. Then they told us that she was going to recover but that night they phoned to say she'd had a relapse.

We rushed around and she was lying there, very still and a horrible pale colour. She died almost as soon as we arrived. She didn't move but we both *knew*. One moment she was lying there and the next moment she'd left us . . .'

Lili leaned across and pressed his hand in silent sympathy.

Next Sunday they went to the zoo. Laughing, Lili was feeding a white goat in the children's enclosure, when suddenly she heard an unmistakable click. Simon leaped over to the two men on the edge of the animal compound and said, 'Please don't photograph her. This is a private visit.'

'For me, it's business,' the photographer said. 'Piss off.'

He deliberately raised his camera at Simon. Angrily, Simon jumped forward and knocked the camera out of the man's hand, then suddenly the back of Simon's head hit the ground. 'Plenty more of that if you want it,' offered the second photographer, as an anxious zoo keeper hurried up.

Lili helped Simon to his feet. 'Let's get out of here,' she urged. 'You're going to have a nasty black eye. The faster we leave, the less there is to report.'

Back at Lili's apartment, she soaked a pad of cotton with witch hazel and the excess ran down his neck and soaked his shirt. 'Oh, how silly of me!' Lili cried. 'Look, take the shirt off, put on a bathrobe and I'll dry it and mend the tear. No, no, as a matter of fact I'm proud of my sewing – I guarantee you won't be able to spot the tear when I've finished. You're not the only one who can fix things.'

The maid brought a tray of coffee to the sofa, where Lili sat in front of the log fire, carefully stitching the shirt, while Simon, wrapped in a white terrycloth bathrobe, examined the books on the antique desk. He picked up a well-thumbed *Encyclopédie Larousse*.

'Zimmer said you were studying,' he said. 'Do you read any philosophy?'

'Good heavens, no,' Lili replied, laughing. 'I'm not at all intellectual.'

'Oh, philosophy isn't only for the intellectuals. Philosophers want to understand why the world exists as it does and what the best way is to live in it.'

'That certainly interests me.' Lili bent her head and cut the thread with her small white teeth. 'Here's your shirt and good as new.'

'I'll bring something amusing to the studio tomorrow. You're right! I can't see where the tear was.'

'I was taught to sew when I was very young,' Lili said, suddenly sad.

On Monday morning, Simon told Zimmer of the incident, adding, 'Who'd have thought that Tiger-Lili was a seamstress!'

Zimmer grunted. 'She's always yearning for the quiet domestic life. The child in Lili wants the nursery fireside – but that's only one side of her, the underdeveloped part. Lili is a born actress and she's stuck with it. That talent demands fulfilment; talent stifled is personality stifled. She'll never be happy if she isn't working in front of a camera, however well she stitches shirts.'

'She's amazing on camera,' Simon agreed. 'It's as if nobody else is on the set and she's having an intensely confidential relationship with the lens. I know *I* haven't got that magic.'

'You don't even *like* making movies, Simon.'

'Right, that's why I don't often make them. I was twenty-four years old when I had my first movie success nine years ago, but I knew there were dozens of better actors who hadn't achieved that instant fame.'

'You've never wanted fame,' Zimmer said. 'But of course you've always wanted *success*.'

'I'd rather call it achievement. I'm still learning, but you don't learn in front of a camera, you learn in front of an audience: you learn timing and boredom-tolerance. You get an instant brutal reaction to what you do, and you have to edit yourself instantly according to that reaction – and without any help. So I consciously decided that my first ambition was to be a good actor – it was more important to me than making a lot of money, and the place to learn wasn't in front of a camera, it was on the stage.'

Later that day, as they ate canteen hamburgers, Simon read aloud to Lili from *An Outline of Intellectual Rubbish*. Naturally, Zimmer noticed and smiled with quiet satisfaction. Perhaps what Lili needed after two larger-than-life, powerful, destructive men was a quiet, intelligent fellow who wasn't more interested in himself than he was in Lili – someone secure enough to handle her with firm indulgence and give her the reassurance she needed. Simon wouldn't be jealous of Lili's film career, and he would understand the strains and pressures of it, he would accept that as an actress she would be demanding and fiercely so, but not in her personal relationships. He would understand that she needed more protection and attention than most men are prepared to give a woman.

Simon presented Lili with an antique orange circular tin music box. As they listened to the crystal tinkle of '*Au clair de la lune, mon ami pierrot* ...' Simon stopped turning the handle when he noticed tears in Lili's eyes. 'What's the matter, don't you like it?'

'Oh, Simon, it's a lovely gift. It's just that it reminds me ...' She remembered Angelina rocking her to sleep as she sang the lullaby in the moonlight, while outside her little bedroom window, the pine trees rustled in the night.

Then Lili gasped with pain.

'What's the matter?' Simon asked, alarmed.

'It's nothing ... well, I hardly slept last night, it's my back tooth. But an aspirin will fix it, it always does.'

'Why don't you visit your dentist?'

'I hate dentists. It'll go away.'

'No, they don't go away, they get infected.' Simon picked up the telephone. 'I know an excellent dentist; he's my neighbour and he won't hurt you, I promise.'

It was late afternoon in the Place Saint Sulpice and the little Parisian square with its overpruned trees and the beautiful old church had the dusky purple tinge of a Monet street scene. Since the 1968 student riots, this charming, quiet little square was where the riot police parked their vans.

Astonished, Lili stood on the steps to the dentist's door. An hour beforehand the snow-covered square had been empty, but now it was a heaving mass of unruly students waving placards tacked on sticks. According to these, the students were protesting against the abrupt and forced resignation of a favourite left-wing professor, and they were all chanting 'We want Boulin!'

Nobody took the slightest notice of Lili, partly because she looked much as they did. When not in front of the camera, Lili rarely wore makeup and had the useful knack of being able to switch off her high-voltage glamour and walk down the street unrecognized, in a beige raincoat and a drab headscarf pulled well forward and knotted under her chin.

The novocaine injection from the dentist had left her face feeling swollen and numb. She felt groggy and her eyes started to water in the wind as she gingerly moved down the steps, hanging on to the rail. Suddenly she found herself pressed back against the stone building she had just left as a young man with a megaphone started shouting slogans and the students' chants swelled into a roar. Lili tried to push her way through to the street, but in the swaying crowd this was impossible and twice she was swept off her feet.

As the police started to spread out around the square, Lili pushed harder, surrounded by the student yells of '*A bas les flics! ... enfant de putain ... sale vache ... salope ... sale con*.' Lili dropped her purse and found it impossible to pick up. Helpless and suddenly frightened, she tried to push harder towards the front of the swaying shouting crowd.

She was jabbed hard in the chest by an elbow and then unexpectedly found herself in the front of the picket line, facing a dark blue line of cops who were removing their capes. The capes of the Paris police force are weighted in the hem with several pounds of lead; judiciously swung, such a cape can break every bone in a man's body and yet the agent cannot be said to be carrying a weapon.

Suddenly the crowd behind Lili swayed forward then sideways and she was thrown to the left against one of the banner poles; the rough edge of the wood caught her cheek, which started to bleed. Lili staggered and to prevent herself from falling she clutched at the banner, which read '*Reinstate Boulin!*'

It started to snow again, lightly.

The police charged.

The angry, shouting crowd fell back and Lili found herself struggling with a furious cop. She was suddenly more indignant than she was frightened. '*What* do you think you're doing? Stop hitting these kids!'

'Shut up!' said the cop, flinging Lili's banner aside as he roughly started to drag her towards one of the black windowless vans into which angry, noisy students were being pushed. Angrily, Lili fought back as a wail of sirens announced the arrival of the riot police, who tumbled out of their wired window buses wearing battledress, bullet-proof vests and gas masks. Carrying riot shields, cans of teargas and flexible rubber truncheons, they quickly formed a line and started to advance on the crowd to Lili's left as she continued to struggle with the cop. '*Vous faites une erreur,*' she gasped. '*Je ne suis pas une étudiante.*' As she flung her head back defiantly and glared at the man, her scarf fell back from her head.

'I don't care *who* you are! You're a pack of filthy scum,' he yelled, as Lili kicked him on the ankle.

'Take your dirty hands off me!' she cried.

'*Merde!* You little bitch,' he shouted, grabbing Lili by a handful of her thick black hair and reaching for his handcuffs.

As he unbuttoned his fur-lined overcoat, Simon watched the scuffle from the windows of his apartment. The students had deliberately provoked the police and the police had reacted in the way that French police always react. What else did the kids expect? . . . Wait a minute, he thought . . . That woman reminded him of . . .

As she tossed her head and glared at the cop, her headscarf fell back and he realized that it was indeed Lili.

Simon ran for the door, leaped downstairs and fought his way across the square to Lili. He managed to insert himself between her twisted body and that of the cop, who still had Lili by the hair. Above the noise of the crowd, Simon shouted, 'Wait . . . there's been a mistake, officer.'

'*Ah, non, alors!* Fuck off or I'll take you as well!'

Simon knew that French cops are generally accommodating if you treat them tactfully and are careful not to provoke them, so he spoke to the furious policeman as politely as if they were both in a duchess's drawing room.

'I hope you realize what you're doing, officer,' he said. 'You do understand that this is Lili, the actress.'

'Lili, my ass,' grunted the cop.

'No, officer, look again,' urged Simon. The cop looked sideways at Simon, calm in his fur-lined vicuna overcoat. Then he looked at Lili in her torn raincoat, her black dishevelled hair, her puffy face, swollen mouth and bleeding cheek, her nose and eyes red from the wind. She looked just like the rest of them, he thought. What the hell would a famous actress be doing in this mob? Nevertheless, he paused to consider, the handcuffs dangling from his right hand. He'd better make sure before he snapped the cuffs on her, because after that he wouldn't be able to change his mind.

Simon said, 'I would be happy to accompany this lady to the police station with you,' and he whipped off his coat, revealing his immaculately cut, pale grey Cerutti suit. He draped the coat, mink-side outwards, around Lili's shoulders. '*Smile*,' he managed to whisper as he did so. Reacting as if to Zimmer's direction, Lili somehow managed to draw herself up six inches and flash a gracious smile at the officer who had been trying to put the handcuffs on her. Simon, still behaving as if all three of them were in the foyer of the Ritz, pulled out his visiting card and presented it to the officer, who looked at him again more carefully. Yes, he thought, this guy certainly *looks* like Simon Pont – he'd often seen him on television – and his clothes were unmistakably expensive. He'd better not risk it.

He took his hands off Lili and muttered, 'Well, you'd better get her out of here!'

Left shoulder leading, Simon forced his way through the swaying crowd, protecting Lili with his body and leaving the puzzled-looking policeman standing with handcuffs in one hand and Simon's visiting card in the other.

Once inside his first floor apartment, Lili started to shake again from the tension. 'My God, Simon, it was terrifying when they charged!' She couldn't talk properly because her mouth was still swollen.

Simon gently lifted the coat from her shoulders. '*What* were you doing down there?'

'Leaving your dentist. I was in there for over an hour. Then before I knew what was happening, I found myself in the middle of that mob and ... I was helpless ... I couldn't understand what was happening. Then suddenly that cop attacked me.' Lili caught sight of herself in the cherub-encrusted hall mirror. 'No wonder he didn't recognize me! I look terrible.'

'You don't to me. To me, you look wonderful.'

Lili peered at herself. 'I think I've got a black eye. Zimmer will kill me on Monday ... I don't know how you can say I look wonderful, Simon!'

He gave a Gallic shrug of the shoulders. 'I like you without makeup. I like seeing the real you.' He added, 'You ought to have some tea; sweet tea is how to treat shock. Let's go to the kitchen.'

He took her hand and led her through his apartment. She noticed the rich, dark colours, the book-lined corridors, the antique horse portraits, the cosy, luxurious warmth.

The kitchen, gleaming with copper saucepans and smelling of herbs, was a country-style kitchen exquisitely executed by John Stefanidis for a price that no peasant could ever afford. Simon pulled a walnut rocking chair forward. 'Sit down and let me wash the blood off your cheek.'

Lili collapsed on to the chair. 'I feel awful,' she snuffled. The Charvet silk handkerchief was whipped out of Simon's breast pocket. A runny nose merely made Lili look more vulnerable and appealing. He liked the idea that very few people had seen her so defenceless, he thought, as he boiled the kettle and then served tea at one end of the long, pine harvest table.

'I don't take sugar.'

'You do today. Four lumps.'

Reluctantly, Lili reached forward for the sugar bowl at the same time as Simon reached forward to push it towards her, and for a moment their hands met. Lili almost gasped as she felt the light touch of his warm flesh, unexpected and thrilling. Incredulous, her swollen lips slightly apart, she stared up at him. Simon stared back at her in the same way, a blank look of surprise on both their faces. Then Lili's caution about men got the better of her and she jumped to her feet. She didn't want to get involved with anyone. Clumsily, she started to button up her raincoat. 'I really ought to get back home and go to ...'

Simon walked across to the window and stared out of it with his hands in his pockets and his back to her. 'Yes, of course, you must go,' he said.

Lili sat down again. Then she stood up again. He turned from the window and she took a step towards him, her hand automatically outstretched to say goodbye, as is the French custom.

573

Simon took her hand. But he didn't let it go.

As Lili nervously tried to pull her hand away, she said jokingly, 'I can't leave without my hand, Simon.'

'You can leave without it or stay with it.'

FROST had left a pattern of white lace that veiled the grey rooftops of Paris beyond the bedroom window. Snow started to fall, the scene grew paler and less distinct. Inside the bedroom Simon gently tickled Lili's toes, often a prelude to his lovemaking. For two years now they had lived together here in her flat in peace and relative quiet. Never in his life had Simon known such calm happiness. To his astonishment he found Lili undemanding. Apart from moments of sudden rage when she saw some lie printed about herself in the papers, Lili was quiet and liked a quiet life. They read a lot and listened to music, and Lili still painted on Sundays.

Simon wiggled Lili's left little toe. He started to stroke her thighs, to feel the little dark forest. On Sunday mornings he liked to wake her like that, and she loved to drift back to life, conscious of erotic sensations that slowly deepened into passion. Now, eyes still closed, she fumbled sleepily for him.

Much later he brought in a tray of coffee. Lili sat up, gazing as she did so at a small oil painting that hung between the two windows opposite the vast cream bed. It was a picture of a twisting mountain river that she had bought the week before from Paradis in the rue Jacob.

'I'm not sure I like that, hanging there,' she pondered. 'It's too small to see from this distance, but it's so pretty. It reminds me of the river when I was a child at home; you couldn't see it from our chalet because it was in a deep gorge and we weren't allowed to go there, but my brother Roger often took me. We used to catch trout there and splash in the shallows.'

Her voice softened as, holding her bowl of coffee in both hands, she gazed at the picture opposite the bed. 'There was a rickety old suspension bridge over it; the water was very deep in the middle, always ice-cold and very clear, always twisting and turning, always rushing and noisy, especially in the spring when the snow was melting on the mountains.' She took a sip of the café au lait, not taking her eyes from the picture. 'It was always prettiest in the early morning when the mountain slopes were covered with silver mist and the far hills just a smudge against the sky.' She shut her eyes and smiled. 'It used to be very quiet, except for the rushing water and the whine of the sawmill in the valley, cutting pine planks and stacking them, ready to metamorphize into another little chalet in no time at all.'

'I wonder if you realize how constantly you dwell on the past,' Simon said, with mild irritation. 'Why aren't you thinking of building a future with *me*? We could build our own chalet in Switzerland with the planks from that sawmill. And you could start your own family, instead of always harking back to the one you lost. We've been together nearly two years now, and I'm damned if I understand why you won't marry me.'

'Such an old-fashioned idea.'

'And a good one. I want a commitment, Lili. It's 1978, I'm thirty-five and I want children. What puzzles me is that I know *you* do as well. Yet time and again you've wriggled out of talking about this. Is it that you don't love me? That you don't believe I love you? That you don't want to commit yourself because you're afraid that if you do, I'll dominate you like Serge and Stiarkoz and that bastard Abdullah?'

'No, it's not that.' She was hesitant. 'It sounds so silly. I just don't feel *settled*. You know where *you* belong, but I don't.' She put the empty coffee bowl back on the tray. 'Most women long to have a baby by the man they love and I'm no exception, Simon.' She looked at him – a sad, long look. 'A baby would be a new life, my rebirth, a wiping-out of the pain of the past, a fresh start with a family of my own. *Don't think I don't want that. I long for it.* But how can I have a baby, how can I take on such a responsibility, when I'm so unsure of myself, when I don't know who I am? I want my baby to feel rooted, settled. So I want to wait until this restlessness of mine has passed.' Her voice shook, then hardened. 'But it hasn't and sometimes I'm afraid it won't. I don't think it will disappear until I know who my parents are. And although I

575

desperately long to know, at the same time I'm frightened of finding out. Because they might be – oh, unpleasant in some nasty way. After all, they abandoned me.' She sighed. 'Anyway, it's probably impossible to trace them. It's hopeless.'

Simon said thoughtfully, 'No, I'm sure I can fix it for you – or at any rate, I'll try ... At least if you found your real parents, you might stop looking for substitute parents in almost everyone you meet. That's why you're so vulnerable to these exploiters you inevitably attract.' He drained his own bowl of coffee, put it down and said, 'A man has only to say something in a reassuringly avuncular voice and you think he's Santa Claus; you'll sign any paper he puts before you. But Santa Claus doesn't exist, so stop looking for him, Lili.'

'I can't help this ... yearning.' She hugged her knees tighter, laid her cheek against her knees.

'Then for heaven's sake, let's try to trace your parents instead of vaguely hoping they'll pop up out of nowhere,' Simon urged. 'We'll hire detectives. Your lawyer can recommend a firm. I've been thinking about it for a long time. But you must realize that you might not like what you find.'

Lili moved her knees and the coffee tray lurched dangerously towards the edge of the bed. Simon stood up and stretched. 'I think your mother was probably a young, unmarried girl who worked in town but who came from a country peasant family. You know how practical the Swiss are – a middle-class family would probably have tried to arrange an abortion for the girl, even though it was illegal and possibly against their religion.'

He wandered over to stare at the little picture of the river. 'Another thing – your father may have been married to someone else. I can't help thinking that if your mother had stayed unmarried and if she were alive, then she would have claimed you, or at least visited you. So my theory is that there was a mountain village girl who came down to the valley to earn money for her dowry, had a baby by a married man, then went back to her village and married some peasant and never dared confess about the child.'

'Oh, I don't care, I just want to *know*,' Lili exclaimed.

The following afternoon a detective called Sartor visited Lili in her apartment. He had thin, grey hair, parted in the middle, and wore rimless spectacles that somehow rendered the rest of his face invisible. He was neat, dapper, polite and expressionless. Her lawyer had recommended the Sartor Agency because of its international connections. He had explained that Sartor had contacts with a well-known detective agency in each of the biggest cities in the world so he could simply subcontract any work in that country to the local agency.

Sartor sat in Lili's sitting room taking notes on a pad that fitted into his left hand. No, she knew nothing about her birth except that she was supposedly born in Gstaad or Château d'Oex, Switzerland, on 15 October 1949, and that she was not the natural daughter of her foster mother. Her foster mother had at that time been Angelina, widow of Albert Dassin, a guide who lived in the village of Château d'Oex, Switzerland. No, she had no proof that Madame Dassin was not her natural mother. Yes, that was a possibility, but she would have imagined that Madame Dassin, a widow, could not have disguised her own pregnancy in that small village. Lili's real mother was definitely a mystery to the village – she had been teased at school about that. That Madame Dassin was her foster mother was generally accepted, although Lili was called Elizabeth Dassin. Yes, Madame Dassin had remarried in 1955, a Hungarian waiter, Felix Kovago. Yes, it definitely had been established by the Swiss consulate that both the Kovagos and the child, Roger Dassin, had been shot and killed by Hungarian border guards in 1956. Certainly she would like Monsieur Sartor to check that. No, she could think of nothing to add to those details, except that Madame Kovago had arranged for her to take private lessons in English and French elocution, and Lili felt that it would have been out of character for her to have done this of her own accord. No, her son, Roger Dassin, had not been given such lessons, neither had any other child in the village school. No, Madame Kovago had not given her any photographs or jewellery that might have had any bearing on her birth.

'We'll check the birth certificate straightaway,' said Monsieur Sartor, pushing his tiny notebook into his inner breast pocket and standing up. Simon saw him to the front door and handed him his beige raincoat, still damp with melted snow.

Three days later he telephoned. Simon was away on a promotional tour for two weeks and Lili answered.

'Our Swiss contact has checked with the registry office. The Gstaad area is in the region of Saanen, which has a population of around 6,000. Two baby girls christened Elizabeth were born there on 15 October 1949. We have already traced and spoken to one of these young women, who is unmarried and still lives in Gerignoz with her widowed father. The other child was born in the hospital at Château d'Oex to a woman called Post – Emily Post. The Swiss birth certificate always gives the name of the obstetrician. In this case, it was Doctor Alphonse Geneste, who unfortunately for us died on November 4 last year, but our man in Switzerland has spoken on the telephone to his widow, who lives at Siedenstrasse 9, Gstaad, and they have arranged to visit her tomorrow.'

'Goodness,' said Lili, 'Emily Post. That sounds English, doesn't it? Not Swiss-French, not German or Italian – which is what you'd expect of a woman having a baby in Switzerland.'

'There is, of course, the possibility that it was a Swiss, French, German or Italian woman who assumed a false name – perhaps the name of a foreigner, perhaps the father of the child.' A dry cough. 'On the birth certificate the father is listed as "unknown".'

Another almost apologetic cough. 'But if the name is genuine, then certainly the mother might be English, Scottish, Welsh or Irish. Or she could be Canadian, American, South African or Australian. Or perhaps she came from some other part of the British Commonwealth – Kenya, for instance – or even from some of the smaller English settlements – Hong Kong, perhaps. I will telephone as soon as there is further news.'

'You're the policeman, aren't you?' The man nodded, untruthfully, to the shrivelled old woman who had opened the door of Siedenstrasse 9, Gstaad. Her thin, bouffant hair was dyed an unnatural shade of blue. She wore blotchy makeup with blue eyelids and uneven patches of heavy rouge on each cheek. Her sagging neck was encircled by a thin, scarlet velvet ribbon and she wore a bright red jersey trouser suit. She looked terrifyingly decrepit as, with bent back, she shuffled slowly into an over-heated, unfurnished living room.

'I don't know whether I can help you, young man, but from what you said on the telephone, one thing is lucky. As you know, under Swiss law, one must keep one's account books for ten years. My husband's go back to when he first started out here in his own practice in 1927. I kept the old books up in the attic and never bothered to move them.' Blue eyelids blinked before him. 'I was his bookkeeper, you know; that's how we met. I married the boss!' She gave a dry cackle and the agent smiled encouragingly. 'I can get them down from the attic if you want, officer, although not today, it's one of my bad days today. Now you say you want to trace a missing person . . . a baby that my husband delivered. You said on 15 October 1949? A baby girl, you say, and the baby was fostered by a woman in Château d'Oex, a Madame Dassin?'

Again, the wrinkled blue eyelids were lowered, then suddenly lifted to reveal surprisingly bright black eyes. 'Well, I don't need to refer to the books for that. I remember it very well because the girl was so very young – she was still at school – and because she didn't pay her bill.'

'She didn't pay her bill?'

'No, the bill was paid by four other girls. I think they were all at l'Hirondelle, a school that closed about ten years ago when the headmaster died. Anyway, you'll find all those details in the documents books. I seem to remember that one of the girls paid cash. Those girls were very good to the young mother, and my husband also helped her a great deal . . . too much. But he had a kind heart and an eye for a pretty girl.' She smiled. 'Anyway, the payments will all have been noted in the accounts book. No, we couldn't go up there today – and tomorrow is Sunday – but Monday morning, perhaps? I'm better in the mornings.'

On Monday morning the detective stood again on the snowy doorstep. The old lady let him in and, after a few moments of conversation, led him upstairs to the attic where the old records were stored in dusty piles.

At a snail's pace, the old lady moved up the stairs to the landing, where a steel ladder hung down from a ceiling trapdoor to the attic. 'I can't manage that thing, young man, but you go up with the flashlight. You'll find the account books in the thirteenth file from the left, right at the back. You'll want the ledger, it's a brown cloth book and the year slip is pasted on the spine. You said 1949, didn't you? Yes, well, up you go.'

Prepared for a difficult, dirty search, the agent gingerly clambered up into the cold, unheated attic and picked his way over the dust-laden ceiling beams to the back. To his surprise, he found the book he was looking for almost immediately, exactly where the old woman had said it would be. He blew the dust off the book, hopped back over the beams, carefully descended the wobbly ladder, then pushed it back to the ceiling.

The old lady turned the pages until she came to the right one. 'Here we are, young man. The first entry is in mid-June, you see, under Post. That was the girl's name. And here are the payments, you see. To start there were three cheques signed Trelawney and Ryan – and big cheques they were – then a small cash payment from Mademoiselle Pascale.'

A series of erratic payments were listed as being paid by J. Jordan, P. Trelawney, M. Pascale and K. Ryan but – according to the immaculate account book – never a sou was paid by Miss Post, the young mother.

Strange.

Madame Geneste couldn't remember what Miss Post looked like. She had never seen her.

On Tuesday the agent telephoned Monsieur Sartor in Paris, who immediately delegated to his chief assistant a search to check all Swiss finishing-school archives in the Gstaad area. He also wanted to locate the birth certificate of Maxine Pascale, probably born between 1928 and 1932, possibly in Switzerland, Belgium or France. Sartor then placed telephone calls to the detective agencies that he dealt with in London, Washington, Montreal, Canberra, Johannesburg and Auckland. That would do for a start. He wanted routine birth certificate checks on Emily Post, Pagan Trelawney, Kate or Catherine or Kathleen Ryan, Judith Jordan – probable dates of birth between 1930 and 1935.

On Wednesday morning an overnight cable from Washington lay on Sartor's varnished desk.

JUDITH JORDAN EASY   STOP   BORN ROSSVILLE
VIRGINIA 1933   STOP   RICH NEW YORK BUSINESS-
WOMAN DOSSIER FOLLOWS AIRMAIL   STOP   EMILY

POST ARE YOU KIDDING BORN BALTIMORE MARY-
LAND 1873 PARENTS BRUCE JOSEPHINE LEE PRICE
MARRIED EDWIN POST 1892 TWO SONS DIVORCED
1906 WROTE MAGAZINE ARTICLES THEN BOOK ON
ETIQUETTE PUBLISHED AUGUST 1922 IMMEDIATE
BESTSELLER REPRINTED 99 TIMES IN 47 YEARS
EMILY FAMOUS AMERICAN LEGEND DIED PNEUMONIA
1960 STOP PURSUING BIRTH CERTIFICATE DATES
GIVEN ACES

So Mrs Post was seventy-six years old in 1949 and unlikely to have been pregnant. But perhaps that was the first name that jumped into the mind of a frantic, pregnant girl who wished to conceal her identity? If you choose a fictitious name, you try to choose one that is in no way connected to yourself and yet is easy to remember.

By Friday, Maxine Pascale's birth certificate had been traced and by the following Tuesday he had a photocopy of her marriage certificate. Also on Tuesday afternoon, Monsieur Sartor had received a telephone call from London. Pagan Trelawney (chris-tened Jennifer) was born at St George's Hospital, London, in 1932. Married twice, presently Lady Swann, living in London, photocopies of birth certificate, second marriage certificate and current address upcoming. Her first marriage was thought to have been in the Middle East.

There were dozens of Catherine and Kathleen Ryans born in England and hundreds in Ireland. The agency was ploughing through them, narrowing them down by date. South Africa, Australia, New Zealand, Canada and America were also com-piling great lists of baby Ryans, but Washington cabled NEW YORK JOURNALIST KATE RYAN BORN BRITISH FITS DATE NO BIRTHCERT USA SHOULD PURSUE? ACES.

On Wednesday Sartor put through another call to Washington and asked for a check on whether Jordan or Ryan had been at school in Switzerland in 1949 and if so, where? He carefully didn't suggest a possible location – that would be his check on the accuracy of the information he received.

By Friday he had further information on Emily Post. It seemed that the etiquette writer had not only been heard of, but also admired, wherever English was spoken. One had to suspect that some of the Miss Posts had been deliberately named after her. There were seventeen in the United States, one in Canada, six in Britain and two in Australia, although none had been registered during that period in New Zealand or South Africa.

On the following Monday, three weeks after he had been assigned to the case, an overnight cable from Washington awaited him. JUDY JORDAN KATE RYAN NOW WORK TOGETHER STOP BOTH IN GSTAAD SWITZERLAND 1949 ACES. Sartor telephoned Lili and asked to see her as soon as possible.

At six that evening, the doorbell was answered by Simon and the three of them sat around the log fire as Monsieur Sartor reported to them.

'I am of the opinion that the mother was one of the four girls we have located, and that if we are successful in tracing the Emily Posts, they will be found to have no connection with this matter.'

Sartor gave his little dry cough. 'But there *is* another possibility. If our Emily Post exists, all four of the women we have tracked down will know about her. Do you wish my agents to attempt to interview them?'

'No!' Lili sprang to her feet. Her face was flushed from sitting by the flaming logs and her dark hair was dishevelled.

'No!' she repeated violently. She thought of the screaming row she had had with Judy Jordan; the article that Kate Ryan had written about her; that terrible scene in the orangery with Maxine. She didn't know about this Pagan woman, but she never wanted to have anything to do with the other three.

Simon gently took her shaking hands in his. 'My darling, you must realize that one of these women might be your mother.'

'No!' Lili's wistful yearnings for *vraie maman*, for the quiet, kindly and gentle madonna of her dreams had, in an instant, turned to rage. It looked as if Lili had not been abandoned for pathetic and forgivable reasons by a humble peasant woman. It looked as if Lili had been *dumped* by some rich little bitch who'd been unable to get an abortion. She choked back her fury.

'I know three of these women, and if they have anything to hide, then I don't believe for one minute that they will see one of your agents. And if they do, I very much doubt that they will give away any information they don't wish to divulge.' She thought for a moment. 'I would like you to let me have a dossier on all four of them.'

'No problem, madame. It would be easy, they'd all have c.v.'s.'

'I will decide what to do after I have seen the dossiers.'

Lili carefully read the dossiers that Monsieur Sartor provided on Pagan, Kate, Maxine and Judy. Her mother was almost certain to be one of those four women. She hoped it was Pagan, since she had never clashed with her. But regardless, Lili was determined to discover which one was her mother.

For some reason these four women had covered up Lili's birth, had kept it a secret. If one of them was approached, she would probably contact the others immediately and then they'd all clam up. None of them was a stupid woman; they were all brilliantly successful. Lili reasoned that the only chance she had of finding out the truth was to confront them together, to surprise or shock them into telling the truth. She would watch their faces, watch their eyes and their reactions. Surprise was her only chance of getting them to reveal something.

~ PART TWELVE ~

OUTSIDE, the trees of Central Park rustled in a warm, October breeze. Inside the hushed, creamy opulence of the Pierre suite, Lili harshly repeated her question.

'*Which one of you bitches is my mother?*'

Pagan, Judy and Maxine had regained their composure after the surprise of seeing each other. Kate, however, standing just inside the door that led from the hall to the suite, was still too astonished to understand what was happening. She couldn't connect the world-famous Lili standing before her in a white silk gown to that remote incident in Switzerland or that little girl who had been killed while trying to escape from Hungary in 1956.

Lili tried again. 'Which one of you bitches is *Emily Post?*'

This time Maxine flashed a quick look at Pagan. None of the three looked at Judy, Lili noticed.

'Unless you can really catch them off guard they'll either deny it completely or say it's Judy,' Simon had prophesied. 'She's the only one who isn't married. She's the only one who wouldn't have to explain anything to a husband. She's the only one whose life wouldn't be complicated by the sudden addition of an adult daughter who's a celebrity.'

Lili took two steps towards the apricot velvet couch, clenched her fists and hissed, 'Which one of you had a baby delivered by Doctor Geneste?' She spun around to Kate, still standing by the door in her smart mulberry suit. The memory of the vicious article that Kate had written about her flashed across her mind.

'Was it *you* who had the baby?'

Kate's eyes slid sideways as she looked towards the seated group. Thinking fast, she tried to counter Lili's verbal attack with an equally aggressive one. 'Why have you brought us here? What are you trying to do? What's your game? What makes you think that one of us is your mother?'

'Because I *know* that one of you is my mother. I know that one of you four had a baby on 15 October 1949.' Lili swiftly twisted around to Maxine. 'Was it *you*? Did you have a baby in the hospital at Château d'Oex? Did *you* farm me out to Angelina Dassin?'

The coffee cup rattled slightly in Maxine's hand and a few drops spilled on her pale blue silk dress, but her face remained impassive and she said nothing. She was not going to be bulldozed into blurting out whatever Lili wanted to hear. Besides, the whole thing was impossible. That poor child had been killed. There had been official proof of it, that letter from the Swiss consulate. How dare this fornicating bitch bully them. No, this infamous gold digger, this seducer of children could not possibly be that little waif whom they had left with Angelina.

'Is Lili your real name?' Pagan suddenly asked. After all, Lili had mentioned Emily Post. How could she possibly know about Emily Post? She'd got the correct date, the correct place and the foster mother's correct name.

'No, my real name is Elizabeth, but Felix always called me Lili. Felix was married to my foster mother and it was he who saved me from the soldiers in Hungary. He threw me over the barbed-wire fence and told me to run.'

'What happened to you then?' Pagan asked gently.

'I was taken to a refugee camp in Austria, then on a train to Paris where I was adopted. I don't really remember much about it, I was ill and only seven at the time.'

Lili did so hope it was Pagan! She desperately didn't want to discover that her mother was Maxine, Alexandre's mother. The possibility that she had committed incest was too painful to consider.

Lili moved swiftly towards Pagan and crouched down, grasping the arm of the apricot couch as, yearning, she looked up into Pagan's face and murmured in a voice that trembled with hope, 'Are *you* my real mother?'

Pagan looked desperately at the other three women in the room. Lili had a right to be told. Couldn't the others see that she probably *was* little Elizabeth? Pagan looked down into Lili's upturned face. All the sophistication and poise had vanished: Lili suddenly looked eager, trusting and very vulnerable.

Then suddenly Judy spoke. 'No, Pagan isn't your mother,' she said. 'I am.'

All heads turned towards Judy.

'I had a baby girl in Château d'Oex on that date. If you really are that baby, Lili, then I suppose – I am your mother.' Judy felt confused and exhausted. She had thought her daughter dead, she had almost pushed her baby out of her mind. Yet now this notorious little prima donna was claiming to be that daughter! But it was impossible to think of Lili as the gentle little girl whom Judy had cherished in her mind and read about in Angelina's letters, which she still kept hidden away.

Upon hearing the answer to the question that had tormented her ever since she could remember, the pent-up pain and accumulated fury of twenty-nine years exploded in Lili.

'*Why didn't you keep your child?*' Lili cried. She sprang up, beating her fists against her thighs in impotent rage. 'Why did you give me to somebody else? Why didn't you ever come and see me? *Why did you abandon me?*' She leaped towards Judy, and as she did so, Maxine threw down her cup and saucer and Kate ran forward with apprehension. But it was Pagan who thrust herself swiftly between Lili and Judy, who still sat slumped in her brown velvet suit on the edge of the apricot couch.

'My dear girl,' said Pagan, 'you *must* let us explain what happened, you mustn't jump to conclusions. We can all guess how you feel, but *please* listen to us because, you see, you were frightfully important to *all* of us. It could have happened to any of us.' She paused. 'Any one of us *might* have been your mother, and so we decided that we would *all* be responsible for you. In a way you had three godmothers, Kate, Maxine and me. We all wanted you, we all worried about you, we all hoped for you and we all loved you.'

'And we all paid for you,' said Maxine. 'In every way we felt that you were our joint responsibility.'

'Then why didn't you keep me with you?' Lili threw at Judy through clenched teeth.

'My dear,' Pagan tried to explain, 'you *can't* imagine what the moral climate was at that time. Things have changed so utterly in the last thirty years. Then, nobody *ever* even admitted that they had slept with a young man before marriage – even if they were engaged – and, in fact, very few girls did. You must realize that your mother was only fifteen years old, still a child herself. Please try to imagine how *we* felt. We were at our wits' end to know what to do. Certainly your mother couldn't take a baby back to America with her. She refused to abandon you, so we arranged for you to have a foster mother until Judy could get a home of her own for you to live in – and we all knew it would be years before she would be able to do that.'

Pagan put her hand on Lili's shoulder and her voice softened. 'But we didn't abandon you, we did what we thought was for the best. Don't you see, it was a frantic attempt of four schoolgirls to save one of us from disaster? We never, *never* intended to abandon you.'

Gently stroking Lili's shoulder, Pagan was mildly surprised to find that she felt so maternal towards this tempestuously glamorous creature. Pagan had felt a twinge of jealousy when the newspapers had started to report Abdi's love affair with Lili, when she saw photograph after photograph of them together. She had to admit to herself that one of the reasons she had wanted to meet Lili was to get a good look at the only European woman whom Abdi had ever taken to Sydon, the only white woman with whom he had lived openly.

'The alternative would have been adoption,' Kate broke in, 'and Judy wouldn't hear of it. She couldn't bear to give her own child to someone else. She loved you. We all did. You *must* believe that, Lili.'

Maxine said gently, 'If it had happened today things would be different. Your mother would probably have an abortion at an early stage, but such an alternative was rarely possible in those days. And if your mother *had* had an abortion, *you* would never have existed. You owe your life to her, you know. She carried you in her body for nine months, and she had to work hard all that time.'

Lili felt a sudden pang of guilt as she remembered that she too had been pregnant when still a child. But Lili had gone to an abortionist. The life had been scraped out of her body, and until that minute she hadn't felt a moment's guilt. In fact, what she had felt at the time was a flood of relief; Lili could still clearly remember sitting in that café, listening to the jukebox, sipping milky coffee and thinking that her troubles were over.

But Judy had not had an abortion. Judy had had a baby.

Pagan advanced her arm farther around Lili's shoulder. 'We *all* wanted you and we are all happy to meet you at last,' she said, still unaware of Lili's disastrous encounters with the other three women, all of whom were remembering those unhappy clashes.

There was a moment's silence and then Kate walked up to Lili and said earnestly, 'Lili, I'm really sorry I was so unkind just now. There's no excuse and I can't say anything except how deeply I regret it.' She took a deep breath. 'But Pagan is right, you *mustn't* condemn your mother. Couldn't you perhaps try to admire her decision, as we did? She was young and alone and we were proud of her. And we still are. She did the best she could. In fact, we all did.'

'In that case, why didn't you look for me after the revolution?' cried Lili. She was still resentful and agitated, though she felt less hurt. She was starting to understand what had happened, starting to lose her resentment.

'We did,' said Maxine. 'Why don't you sit down again, then I'll tell you.'

Lili sat with her back to the window, next to Kate, and Pagan sat beside Judy on the adjoining couch.

'Judy telephoned me as soon as she heard the news on the radio,' Maxine began. 'She knew you'd gone on holiday to Hungary, and she knew you should have been back at school, but she wanted to make sure. Angelina had no telephone so Judy phoned the manager of the Hotel Rosat, who told her that Felix had injured his leg in Hungary and hadn't yet returned. We were pretty sure you were on the other side of the Iron Curtain, so Judy caught the next plane to Paris and I met her at Orly. We went straight to Austria on the night train. When we eventually got to the border, we found that the situation was chaotic. Refugees were pouring out from Hungary – over a hundred and fifty thousand escaped, you know – and most of them were being sorted out in temporary camps. The weather was terrible, the camps were disorganized and everything was muddled.' She shuddered. 'We visited every single camp. We checked every single list, we talked to everyone we could and we checked every child we saw. But nobody had any news of Elizabeth Dassin.'

Every night during their search at the Austrian border, it had

591

been almost impossible for Maxine to drag Judy away to bed. Judy felt that if she left the frontier, she might miss some tiny clue, some pointer. Maxine remembered Judy's frenzy and self-accusation as they waited in the snow outside a hut, hoping to see yet another refugee committee official.

'If only I hadn't left her, Maxine.'

'You had nowhere to take her.'

'I should *never* have left her.'

'*You could do nothing else, Judy*. Stop blaming yourself. What's happened is terrible, but it's not your fault.'

Months afterwards, Judy had received a short formal letter from the Swiss consulate in answer to hers, informing her that a family of Swiss origin called Kovago, formerly Dassin, had been shot and killed by Hungarian border police while illegally attempting to cross the border near Sopron.

Heartbroken, Judy never ceased to blame herself for Elizabeth's death. She almost managed to control her mind, but in her heart Judy had often felt the sudden, chilling pain of bereavement, a silent sense of loss, endless yearning and constant regret for what might have been.

Hesitantly, Judy tried to explain this in the unnatural quiet of that luxurious hotel suite. She found it difficult to find the right words. Her habitual self-assurance had deserted her and she was unusually deflated.

Lili listened. What was important was not that she should be placated, but that at last she should know *the truth*.

Lili knew she had to double-check the answer that Judy had given her – and she knew exactly how she was going to do it. Whomever the women now looked at would be her *true* mother.

'In that case,' Lili said, 'who is my *father*?'

∼ 61 ∼

OUTSIDE it was still snowing hard. If it didn't stop, there wouldn't be much point in going with Nick to Saanenmoser tomorrow, thought Judy. The 1949 ski trials would probably be postponed, so they might as well stay in Gstaad. Midnight had just passed; it was officially 7 February, her mother's birthday. Judy had sent her a card and beautiful cream lace blouse. It must be awful to be thirty-five, she thought, thirty-five and stuck in Rossville forever! 'Happy Birthday,' Judy murmured as slowly she bent down outside the bedroom door, picked up a tray heaped with the debris of a meal, then hurried along the dim passage of the Hotel Imperial. In another hour and a half she could get to bed. She was almost asleep on her feet; she'd never felt so exhausted.

Eight months of too little sleep, tough physical work and the effort of concentrated study in a foreign language were starting to whittle away her youthful resilience. Longingly, she thought of her iron bed in the partitioned cubicle under the attic roof. She was lucky to have a room to herself. She drew a deep breath, puffed it out and straightened her back.

As she hurried along the corridor towards the back staircase, the metal door of the old-fashioned elevator was suddenly flung open.

Judy crashed straight into it.

Filthy half-filled ashtrays, semiempty coffee cups and sauce-smeared plates flew into the air and fell silently on the maroon carpet. Judy's elaborately embroidered blouse and scarlet skirt were splattered with dark brown stains.

'Goddammit,' she said, and burst into tears.

The man who had charged out of the elevator looked uncertainly at her in the dim light. 'I regret this deeply.'

Snivelling with exhaustion, Judy ignored him as she wearily bent to pick up the broken china.

'It was clumsy of me. I ask your forgiveness.' She turned a white, tear-streaked face towards the man and wobbled to her feet again, holding the tray.

'Don't drop it again,' he said, taking the tray from her. 'Let's clean you up a bit. My room is the second on the left.' Balancing the tray on one hand he unlocked a door and beckoned her in. Judy followed.

This was one of their best suites, Judy thought, looking around the sitting room. He must be an important guest. Side lights were already switched on, lazy flames flickered from the log fire on to a black bearskin rug; glasses and a jug of orange juice stood on the low table.

'Sit on the couch,' said the strange man. He put down the tray of shattered china and went into another room. When he returned he had a towel, a sponge and a glass of water. 'I really don't know how you do such things, I thought maybe these . . .'

Dazed and exhausted, the coffee-smeared blouse sticking to her breasts, Judy drooped in front of the fire, wishing she were in bed with no problems. She took the sponge from the man, and for the first time he saw her pale and fragile face. Then she bent her head and he could only see fair hair as she started to rub at her skirt.

Judy supposed he was very good-looking, if you liked dark foreigners. Then she jumped. He had sat on the couch beside her, stretched out one hand and gently touched the base of her neck.

The stranger drew her towards him, pulled her head against his chest and slowly stroked her hair. Judy let him do so, surprised by her lack of resistance. But it was very nice. This soothing stroking could easily send her to sleep. It was *very* nice.

She caught her breath as she felt a warm mouth brush her neck. Then the tip of his tongue touched her earlobe. Slowly and surely, Judy felt her body relax. Her exhaustion fell away to be replaced by a softly erotic trance. As the dark stranger murmured softly into her ear, she felt an odd, silken sensation that she had never felt before, as if each slow movement was somehow predestined and she could only respond to it. She gave a soft sigh of satisfaction as she felt his arms shelter her in the comforting warmth of his body. She felt safe, surrounded by the silence and quiet warmth of the room, as he gently lowered her on to the rich fur rug.

She could smell the crackling pine logs, the musky harsh prick of fur against her face, the disturbing scent of this man whose cheek was rubbing hers, whose firm mouth softly pressed upon hers. Judy no longer felt in charge of her suddenly languorous body as he tugged the drawstring of her blouse, and then she felt the flesh of his warm mouth. Her body twisted as desire fought shame and apprehension, then she yielded to that mouth.

Sometime later she was naked to the waist and clinging to him, mouth to mouth. She felt as if she were swimming in warm water, in a delightful dream. Then she felt his hand cup her knee, slide

594

snakelike up her leg until it reached the taut, black stocking top and hesitate for a moment at the black elastic garter. Roughly he thrust his hand up between the soft flesh of her thighs.

The spell broke. Judy jerked sharply back to reality. She couldn't believe this was happening to *her*. That she lay, half-naked, under a total stranger, had been eagerly responding to his hands, his mouth, his warmth as it melted into passion and passion pounded into frenzy.

She *had* to stop this. She tried to move away but his body pinned her to the fur rug. Still she struggled to push him from her body. But suddenly his breath was almost a snarl in her ear as he thrust his hand higher between her wriggling thighs, up her pantie leg. Then his thumb found the quivering point it sought, and at this new, sharp ecstasy, Judy again felt her body blot out her mind. She felt the strength of her passion crash against the barrier of her puritanical upbringing.

'Stop, stop,' she panted. 'Please. Please!' She struggled to get away. 'No, I mean please *stop*.'

He was far stronger than she and his body pinned her to the floor.

'Please, you don't know what you're doing.' She started to sob but he fastened his mouth to hers. She could not jerk her head away from his.

Fiercely he yanked at her skirt and Judy heard the fabric rip. Then he was pinning the top of her body to the floor with his chest and tearing at her panties with one hand. For one moment Judy didn't want him to get off her. Except for her black laced corselet and stockings, she was now naked, and nobody had seen her naked since she was ten years old.

She had to *stop* him!

She jerked her head away and gave a wild, strangled cry, but the stranger thrust his left hand over her mouth. She couldn't cry now. She couldn't breathe. He was stifling her. He was going to smother her. Maybe he was going *to kill her*.

Judy had been alarmed when she felt her body respond to the stranger. When he thrust his hand over her mouth and nose she was frightened. But she felt claustrophobic terror as he roughly forced his way inside her body, tearing her flesh, plunging into her, gasping, thrusting. No longer able to struggle, Judy could smell his animal lust, could feel salt tears run silently down her cheeks and into her mouth. She cried with no sound, eyes open, blindly staring upwards. Oh the pain, the splitting *pain*!

She felt her puny weakness, the hopelessness, the soundless panic, then desolate shame engulfed her as, with a wild cry, the dark stranger climaxed.

'Don't cry, little bird,' he murmured, 'why this weeping? The first time there is always pain, little bird.' Like many men he didn't regard rape as rape if it didn't happen in a back alley and there weren't any bruises. He rolled over on his back, stretched luxuriantly upon the rug, and the fire's shadow blackened the lower part of his face and his crumpled clothing. Thank God for that, she thought, because she couldn't bear to see his thing.

At first unable to believe that she was free, she lay there limp, spread-eagled on the rug, then she curled her body, ashamed that he should see her nakedness, her humiliation. Then slowly she got up and staggered to the door – clutching to her body what was left of the traditional Swiss costume – grabbed the handle with a hand that trembled, flung open the door and ran along the corridor, naked except for black stockings and corselet, her only thought to get to her room at the top of the servants' staircase.

She spent the rest of the night trying to scrub him off. She was disgusted by the physical evidence of his possession, his power over her, that relentless animal lust. She was disgusted by his slime and her blood. She washed it off fiercely, hating to touch it, hating it to touch her.

Nobody must ever know. No boy ever goes with a girl that's been raped. She would only be despised. She had to suffer this misery *by herself*.

Once in bed, she couldn't sleep, she felt humiliated, embarrassed and oddly vexed. What a stinking rotten way to lose your virginity. She didn't worry about catching a sexual disease because she didn't know that they existed, and oddly enough, it never once occurred to her that she might be pregnant. Not when it had happened only once. Not when the Lord knew that she hadn't really wanted it to happen, that she had been harshly violated, taken by force.

But one thing worried her very much. Across the valley, above the dawn mist, snowcaps slowly turned pink as Judy reluctantly faced her anxiety. Had it been ... that is, how *much* had it been ... in what way had that incident been her own fault?

Had she led him on? And, if so, to what extent was *she* guilty?

For two days Judy refused to leave her room. Listless and pale, she pretended to be ill. Knowing that she worked zealously, nobody disbelieved her. They thought she had either overtaxed her strength or was suffering from a bout of influenza. Nick hovered anxiously at her door, brought her hot milk, homemade beef broth, glasses of fresh orange juice and aspirin.

On the third morning, Judy watched the red winter sun scatter diamonds on the snow beneath her window. I must put this behind me, she thought. I mustn't let it ruin my life.

With determination she buried her shame and mortification, lifted her chin and went out to face the world.

On the night of St Valentine's, there was an excited bustle in the ballroom as pretty girls and muscular young men swarmed to foxtrot in aid of the Swiss ski team. Then the band slid into 'Mean to Me' and more couples moved to the dance floor. Judy had just started night work again. During the holiday season you worked without query or complaint until all the work was finished, and the Chesa staff often had to help out at the Imperial on gala nights.

Suddenly the music stopped. Everyone felt that expectant hush that precedes the entrance of royalty, and the band launched into a boombadoom national anthem.

Two figures appeared in the doorway. The girl was Pagan, wearing a spangled cloud of grey tulle as she stood in the doorway, her hand on Prince Abdullah's immaculately tailored arm.

Judy almost dropped another tray.

The man with Pagan was the one who had raped Judy the previous week. Her dark stranger was the Prince of Sydon.

With a half-smile, he turned to murmur fondly into Pagan's ear, and Judy realized something else, something that upset and bewildered her. The dark stranger was obviously in love with Pagan.

Judy felt a rush of indignation and pain. Suddenly she felt again the humiliation and anxiety that she had felt on that dreadful night. She felt unable to breathe, she needed air.

Carefully she put her tray on a table, pushed through the staff

597

swing doors, down the backstairs, out of the crowded noisy kitchen and into the starlit night. Shivering, she watched the black shadow of a dog lope along the silver walls of the street.

It didn't really matter who he was or why he had behaved as he had. If he was Pagan's man, she was going to stay silent. She wouldn't say a word and, by God, he'd better stay quiet too! Eventually, she rubbed her cold bare arms and turned back to the kitchen door.

She wasn't waiting on the top tables, and although Pagan twice winked at Judy as she passed them, Prince Abdullah never noticed her. It would not occur to him to notice the face of a waitress. He was accustomed to being surrounded by obsequious servants: they were there to give service, and he no more thought of paying attention to their feelings than he would to the feelings of a faucet or a chair.

On the evening when Abdullah had so unexpectedly bumped into Judy, he had just left Pagan, who had aroused his passion to an extent that he would never have believed possible. But she was maddeningly elusive. In spite of his rank, his royal wishes and the arts taught him by the *hakim*, she resisted him. One moment he thought that he held her, and then she would give a throaty laugh, he would hear that damned bathwater gurgle of hers, as physically and mentally she slipped away. He wanted to possess her, not only her body, but also her brain: he wanted all of Pagan with a power and an urgency that he knew he could convey to her if only she'd let him.

But he couldn't have her. She wouldn't allow it.

So he had left her, but his blood was pulsing with passion and frustrated desire as he crashed towards his rooms. Then there was a smash of china and that tiny blonde girl was weeping on the floor. What had happened afterwards would be considered an honour for a serving girl in his country. Abdullah had been mildly surprised that Judy had disappeared before he could press a benefice into her hand, but apart from that he never again thought about the incident.

By April Judy had missed two periods and woke up retching every morning. She felt even more tired than usual, and kept rushing to the lavatory.

She knew why, of course. Her main reaction was fear – not of giving birth, but fear of her father and mother. Nothing so shameful had ever happened in her family. Whatever happened, she couldn't go back to America before it was all over.

Apart from her family's reaction, Judy also panicked at the thought of being responsible for another life. Although she rarely admitted it, Judy knew that she was still only a schoolgirl herself.

She wished she didn't feel so alone.

It was *so unfair* that she should feel guilty. But she was guilty, wasn't she? After all, she had trotted after the stranger into his suite. She simply hadn't thought about it at the time, had felt no reason for alarm. It had never entered her head. He was a guest in the hotel and she hadn't entered his bedroom. But then, before the seductive warmth of that fire, she had to admit that, at that moment, she *had* been guilty, hadn't she? Oh, dear, it had all happened so fast there had been no time to think.

Eventually Judy decided she would ask the girls to help her, but she swore to herself that she would never say anything about the person who was responsible for her condition, the man that Pagan loved. But she needed advice, she needed money, she needed moral support, and the girls seemed her only source of help.

Over the red-checked tablecloth, three pairs of eyes widened with astonishment and awe, three mouths fell open, speechless. It was what every girl dreaded.

'Who *was* he?'

'Was it Nick?'

'Look. I'm not going to tell you who he was, so please don't ask me. There's a very good reason why I'm not going to tell you, but

I'm not even going to tell you what it is. All I can say is, there's no hope of any money from him or any help of any sort.'

'Does Nick know?'

'No, and you're not going to tell him. In fact I'll kill you if you tell anybody.'

'What are you going to do?'

'I want to get an abortion.'

There was another silence. Hot bath and gin, all four of them immediately thought, but Maxine was the one who suggested it. They decided that the following Saturday morning, Maxine would sit by Judy as she drank a bottle of gin in the hotel bath-tub.

Judy gasped and spluttered. With difficulty, she had eventually drunk the whole bottle of gin and now she was going to be sick.

'Please don't throw up,' pleaded Maxine, '*please* don't. That gin was so expensive, and we'll only have to buy another bottle. Please don't waste it. *Please* try not to vomit.'

Neither of them had expected Judy to throw up. Without mentioning it to each other, the girls had expected Judy suddenly to go berserk. She might start smashing things or run amok, naked, down the hotel corridor, hollering raucous soldiers' songs. It was Maxine's duty to prevent that sort of thing: in fact, she had an extra scarf in her handbag with which to gag Judy and stop the drunken singing.

Instead, Judy fell asleep in the bath. Maxine reluctantly prodded Judy's shoulder. She had never seen another woman entirely naked and certainly never touched one. This uncovered flesh was embarrassing for both of them. She prodded a bit harder, then shook the shoulder. Alarmed, she gripped both shoulders and shook hard.

Judy's head lolled sideways, she gave a little grunting snore and started to slip downwards into the water. Quickly Maxine pulled out the plug and kept Judy's head above the water until it had all been swirled around and sucked down by the drain.

'Judy, get out,' Maxine hissed in her ear, trying to heave the wet, floppy body out of the tub. *Mon Dieu*, how did murderers manage? She remembered that man who drowned six brides in turn, having thoughtfully insured their lives. Who would have thought little Judy could be so heavy? Maxine hoped she wouldn't have to call Nick. She'd sworn not to tell him.

Eventually Maxine removed her shoes, stockings and skirt, climbed into the tub herself, pushed Judy's head over the side, pushed each wet arm over the rim, then heaved Judy up around her middle so that her shoulders fell over the side of the tub, then heaved on her waist again until Judy slithered unconscious over the side of the bath and lay beaming on the wet green linoleum. Maxine wrapped her dressing gown around Judy's floppy body and half-carried, half-dragged her back to her room and on to the iron bedstead. Maxine covered her with a quilt, towelled her hair dry, sat with her until seven o'clock and then quietly left.

But nothing happened.

'I think there are some pills you can take,' Kate said. It was the first day of May. 'My cousin Tessa's a student nurse. She's a bloody smug prig and I'm not sure she'll help, but I'll write to her and say it's urgent.'

She wrote off to her cousin, who immediately assumed that Kate was pregnant and airmailed her a box of Black Magic chocolates. The second layer contained a phial of little pink capsules, stilbestrol, the cousin explained in her letter. She didn't know if they would work, but one should try taking them over two days.

That's what Judy did, but nothing happened – except that she felt sick for two whole days instead of only in the morning.

Pagan had privately decided that if nothing had happened by 1 June, then she would ask Paul for help. Surely he, the headmaster's driver, must have encountered this problem before? Naturally, he would think that it was *she* who had the difficulty. Pagan had the sinking feeling that if she asked Paul for a small favour, he would ask her for a big one in return. But she would try playing that card if all else failed.

In the meantime Maxine had suggested that they simply do the obvious thing and ask a pharmacist.

As the only fluent French speaker, Maxine hung around the doorway of the pharmacy for an hour before she dared enter. She gazed with feigned absorption at the window, lined with white-china, gold-lettered apothecary jars, until the shop was empty of customers. Then she went inside and, blushing so hard that she looked as if she were suffering from a bad case of sunburn, she asked the pharmacist if he could give her some medicine to bring on a period.

How long overdue?

'Four months.'

The pharmacist's face was immediately wiped of expression. It was like speaking to an automaton, thought Maxine. He said, 'You mustn't consult me, you must ask a doctor. Try Doctor Geneste, he's a gynaecologist. A very sympathetic man. I regret that I can sell you nothing.' He wrote down an address and handed it to Maxine, who couldn't get out of the shop fast enough.

Once outside and around the corner she leaned against a stone wall until she regained her self-possession. Then she asked the way to the gynaecologist.

It was an old-fashioned house in a quiet street. Maxine looked for a long time at the worn brass plate on the olive-green front door, then slowly lifted her hand to the doorbell.

A nurse with low-heeled white shoes, a white uniform and an empty face opened the door. Maxine asked to make an appointment with the doctor. 'Speak up,' said the nurse, 'I can't hear you. What's your name?'

But Maxine found it impossible to raise her voice above a whisper. 'It's not for me,' she said. 'It's for a friend.' Hurriedly, she gave the false name that Judy had suggested.

The following Saturday Judy stood outside the olive-green door accompanied by Maxine. The girls sat silently in the reception room until they were beckoned into the consulting room by the impassive nurse. The consulting room was a cream cubicle with two metal chairs in front of a pine desk. On the desk stood a telephone, an old-fashioned brass dinner bell, a large diary, a scribbling pad and a small green-glass jar of cornflowers. In one corner of the room stood a green cotton screen, and in another was a white porcelain sink over which the doctor bent, his back to them.

The girls could smell the faint, reassuring odour of antiseptic as he turned around to face them. He wasn't a cross, fat French doctor, as they had both feared. He was tall, thin, relatively young and handsome – rather like Gary Cooper, Maxine thought.

He treated them like adults. They agreed that the weather was wonderful. Then, in a kind voice, he asked, 'How long has it been since your last period?'

'I think the third week in January,' said Judy, 'I mean, I never took much notice.'

There was a silence. 'Better check whether or not there is real cause for alarm,' he said. 'I would like to examine you, so perhaps your friend won't mind waiting outside.'

Judy took her clothes off behind the screen and stood shivering, not wanting to leave its protection. Then she put on the sleeveless gown that was folded over the screen and sat with her legs dangling over the side of the high examination couch, at the end of which were fixed two unnerving stainless-steel stirrups.

'You must remember that I am here to help you. There is no need to be frightened. I have to make an examination. But I am a doctor and you must regard me as your confidant, not as a man, and my nurse will be here. Now, have I your permission to examine you?' Judy nodded. He rang the brass bell for the nurse. 'Now please just lie back and rest your legs on the stirrups.' Shutting her eyes and feeling unbearably humiliated, Judy lay on her back and allowed her legs to be pulled apart and propped into the impersonal steel stirrups. She felt a probing of rubber-gloved fingers. She heard sticky, greasy sounds. Then he helped her down. The nurse left the room and Judy went behind the screen again to dress. Maxine returned.

The doctor sat behind his desk looking gravely at the girls. 'Of course, I will do tests. But I don't need tests to know that this miss is almost certainly four months pregnant.'

Judy felt black despair. No hope. She was caught. Trapped. She wanted to scream and stamp. She would refuse. She would demand a replay. It could *not* happen. Not to *her*. Why, why, *why*?

The doctor said that abortions were illegal. In any case, miss might be twenty weeks pregnant, so it was too late. If they did not mind his saying so, the question was not whether miss was pregnant, not how to get rid of this baby, but rather to consider where and when it would be born. There was another silence, then casually the doctor asked if the father was likely to be supportive.

'No.'

'Ah.'

603

Another long silence. Then the doctor added that he understood Judy's situation and he would like to assure her that it was not nearly so rare as she supposed. He had attended other young ladies in similar situations and was used to exercising discretion in these matters. It would almost certainly be possible to keep the matter secret, but the problem was Judy's age, her parents would have to be told.

'That's not possible, both my parents are dead,' Judy heard herself say.

The gynaecologist looked sceptical. 'Then who are your guardians?'

'My elder sister, who's married,' she said. Then, with a flash of inspiration, 'My sister, Judy – Judy Jordan.' Innocent navy-blue eyes stared at him.

'Then I must write to your sister and inform her of these matters and ask her permission to care for you. There is also the matter of payment. Where you have your baby depends quite frankly on what you can afford.'

'There will be no problem about payment,' said Maxine swiftly. Judy opened her mouth, then shut it again. They were talking as if having a baby were no more of a problem than buying a pair of skis.

But already, sitting in this neat consulting room, and talking to an adult, she felt calmer. Perhaps it wouldn't be so terrible, provided her parents never found out. Perhaps, after all, it wasn't the end of the world. And she didn't know quite how to describe the sensation, but her feelings had altered in the last month in a very strange way. It was as if the rest of the world didn't really matter. What mattered was that under her rotund little stomach (now hard as a tennis ball) she had felt a sort of flutter, a butterfly-wing touch.

In fact she thought it *might* have moved.

Suddenly she had realized that *this was a real baby*. It was *her* baby. To Judy's surprise, she had dwelt on this private thought with catlike complacency, and after those first moments of panic, when she faced the doctor, this feeling of smug unreality had returned to her.

The gynaecologist was saying, 'After the baby is born you will have three choices. You can keep the baby; the baby can be adopted; or it can be cared for by foster parents until your life is more settled.'

He carefully rearranged the little blue flowers in the green jar. 'If you have the baby adopted, then you will have to say good-bye to your child forever, but the advantage would be that you will never have to pay anything. On the other hand, if you find foster parents for the baby, then you would have to pay for its keep, because the child would still be yours.'

He looked up at Judy gently and said, 'Naturally, you can't decide such things immediately. You will no doubt wish to consult your sister.'

'Look, I can tell you right away what I'd *like* to do,' said Judy. Suddenly she felt that her baby was not rubbish to be got rid of, not an unwanted pet to be handed over to somebody else. Her baby was lying there under her heart, curled up in her body. Already it had a little nose and mouth and minuscule fingers. It *was* her flesh and blood. She couldn't hand that to somebody else, like a parcel over a post office counter.

Without much logical thought, but with already developed maternal instincts, Judy suddenly heard herself say, 'I want to keep it. I don't want to give my baby away. I would like to find my baby foster parents until I'm old enough to have a home of my own for him.'

'Well, that is something to be thought over carefully,' Doctor Geneste said. 'We can discuss it on your next visit.'

Afterwards the two girls went to a quiet tearoom. 'Why did you say there would be no problem about money?' Judy wanted to know.

'Because there won't be. I'll talk to the others tonight. Between the three of us we should surely be able to raise the money for your medical bills.'

It was after midnight. The white lace curtains had not been drawn back from the window. In front of the silver rectangle, three dark figures sat whispering on Maxine's bed. 'Doctor Geneste said that the hospital fees would be about one thousand Swiss francs. Between us we can almost certainly raise that amount. He said that to put a child in a foster home costs five hundred francs a month. That's six thousand francs a year.'

Maxine summed up the financial situation on her fingers. 'That's fifteen hundred Swiss francs a year from each of us. Now the question is, can we afford it?'

'Only twice as much as stabling a horse in London,' Pagan offered. They all pondered.

The girls treated Judy's pregnancy with the awed respect and horror of those who had narrowly escaped such a dreadful fate, and were therefore prepared to make a financial sacrifice of thanksgiving. They also regarded the situation as if it were a school escapade in a girl's adventure book, desperate but not immoral. They, her friends, would stand staunchly by Judy. With the cheerful idealism of girls who have never had to face a truly serious situation, they all agreed that they wanted to help support the child.

'I'll have to tell some enormous lie,' said Kate thoughtfully. They all told lies and only regarded lying to each other as a sin. 'I'm sure that if I can think of a real whopper, I'll get money from my father. The only problem is that he might be very inquisitive.'

Maxine said, 'Aunt Hortense has promised me a dress allowance when I get back to Paris. It won't be much, but I'll also have an allowance from Papa. I'm sure that somehow I can scrape up thirty Swiss francs a week.'

After a great deal of arithmetical plotting, Kate wrote and asked her father if he would send a contribution to the Gstaad Athletic Fund. As Miss Gstaad, she wanted to make a truly magnificent contribution.

By return post came a letter from Kate's father saying that he'd asked the headmaster to advance her four hundred pounds, and was delighted that his girlie was featuring so prominently in local life.

The same evening Pagan clattered up the wooden stairs, burst into the bedroom and triumphantly flung a sheaf of francs on to Kate's bed. '*My* contribution! Three thousand six hundred francs.'

Maxine gaped at the notes. 'But how generous of your mother!'

'Oh, I didn't ask her! I wouldn't have got a sou from *her*. No, I took my pearl necklace to Cartier ... I've always hated the bloody thing! Every birthday I was given two extra pearls to add to it ... Cartier wouldn't buy it – they only buy back their own stuff – but they were terrifically kind and that little man with the pince-nez took me to another jeweller, who at first offered two thousand, but pince-nez beat him up to that.' She pointed gleefully to the money on the bed. 'The only other thing I had to sell was Grandfather's signet ring, and that really would have been painful, so I'm glad it wasn't necessary.'

Those two sums alone would take care of the first two years. They had plenty of time to plot where they'd get the next payments.

Maxine was only able to pay three hundred Swiss francs in cash from her allowance. She couldn't manage to squeeze another sou from her family, but she asked her papa if her stay at l'Hirondelle could be extended so that she could sit for the French Commercial Diploma in the autumn. She was taking the course anyway, and as the class proceeded at the snail's pace of the non-French-speaking girls, it would not require much work to pass the course. Thus she could stay in Gstaad until Christmas and look after Judy till the baby was born.

Judy's next visit to the gynaecologist was calm and reassuring. Nothing is really important except birth and death, and the people who sat in that small consulting room only thought hopefully and happily of birth. Other problems, such as money and danger, seemed distant and unreal. What was important to them and Doctor Geneste was that nothing should upset his mothers and their babies.

By Judy's third visit, Doctor Geneste had received a letter from Miss Post's sister. She thought that under the circumstances, the doctor was doing the right thing for her sister Emily. She herself had only recently married and didn't want to take on someone else's child at the moment, but Emily could rely on them for help when she returned to the United States.

'She isn't much of a letter-writer, but I knew I could count on her,' said Judy, whose parents had forwarded Doctor Geneste's letter to her. She had immediately written and thanked her mother for forwarding the letter – a dentist's bill mistakenly sent to her U.S. address instead of the hotel. She then wrote a reply from her 'sister' to Doctor Geneste, addressed the envelope to Monsieur Geneste rather than Doctor, and sent it to a girlfriend in Rossville. Judy asked her to post it to Switzerland, explaining that it was a brush-off letter to a boy and Judy wanted him to think she was back in the United States.

By her fourth visit, Doctor Geneste said he had heard of a suitable woman to be a foster mother. Farther along the valley in the village of Château d'Oex was a hospital where he worked as a consultant. One of their ward maids, a young widow with a baby, had applied to be a foster mother. She was strongly recommended by the hospital as quiet and reliable. Would Miss Post care to visit her?

The following Saturday, Maxine and Judy caught the little blue bus and travelled up the valley. It was a narrow valley, with low-lying fields and a few clusters of chalets around a grey church with a very thin spire. It was midsummer and the cows had been taken up to the mountain pastures. The bus passed through fields thickly sprinkled with wild flowers under a sky that was the same colour as the wild forget-me-nots at the side of the road.

Judy had felt miserable for months. She only felt calm in the doctor's consulting room. But suddenly she felt indescribably happy and contented as they bounced along that little country road. Furtively, she felt the hard curve under her coat. For the first time she longed for it to grow bigger.

Angelina Dassin was waiting for them by the fountain in the cobbled square. A young woman with dark hair drawn back in a bun, she had the rather gaunt, highly coloured face that is typical of that region. She was carrying a black-eyed, solemn baby boy whom she shifted on to her left hip in order to shake hands with them.

They all walked through the village to the dark wooden chalet with the fishscale-tiled roof. Madame Dassin had been told the situation and felt sorry for this small, forlorn blonde child. While Madame Dassin went for glasses of fresh milk, Maxine and Judy sat in the barely furnished living room and looked at the spectacular view across the valley to the snow-topped mountains.

Both Judy and Maxine thought this rustic scene ideal. The atmosphere was one of serenity, the little boy seemed a lively child and Madame Dassin seemed to live up to her hospital recommendation. So they arranged that Judy would move into the chalet for two weeks after she stopped work, before the baby was born. After the birth, she would then rest at the chalet for a month while she breast-fed the baby. Both girls earnestly stressed that, when Judy was older and had a home of her own, she would wish to take back her child. Madame Dassin nodded.

Maxine added that, at the suggestion of Doctor Geneste, Judy did not want the child told any details about Judy, other than that one day his mother would come and take him to his real home. There was to be no attempt to deceive the child by telling him that Madame Dassin was the natural mother.

Angelina Dassin agreed to this. 'What do you intend to call your baby?' she asked.

Hunched in a shabby armchair, Judy looked out of the window across to the sharp Alpine skyline and said, 'If it's a girl it will be Elizabeth after my mother. If it's a boy it will be Nicholas.'

Maxine wasn't surprised.

By the end of September, Judy's stomach seemed enormous. Her situation was apparent to the rest of the hotel staff, who sympathetically said nothing. She now walked with an odd sway, a stiff-backed lurch, and she found it hard to sleep the whole night through because of the baby's kicking. She would lie in the moonlight, thinking how wonderful it was to feel her own baby dancing under her heart.

On the seventh of October, two weeks before the baby was due, Judy said goodbye to the staff of the Imperial and caught the bus to Château d'Oex laden with gifts: a fine white knitted shawl and two boxes full of baby clothes from Maxine, Kate and Pagan, a bottle of kümmel, a jar of peaches pickled in brandy and a magnificent smoked ham from the head chef.

On the thirteenth of October Judy woke at five in the morning. 'Ouch!' She caught her breath. No, it wasn't the baby kicking, it was a pain in her back.

She sat up in bed, already feeling an excited thrill of achievement. She couldn't wait to tell Angelina. She heaved her unwieldy body out of bed, wrapped the white lace shawl around her shoulders and sat in the living room, twisting the twin coral rings, one for each middle finger, that Nick had given her just before he left Switzerland.

'I know you won't accept a ring for the finger I want to put it on,' he had said, as they sat among the brilliant yellow king-cups that grew in the damp soil on the river bank, 'but I want to give you a ring, because somehow a ring is connected with a promise, and with this ring I promise that I'll always love you.' He had slipped one rosebud on the middle finger of her right hand. Then he picked up her left hand.

'Just a minute,' Judy had said, 'what does *that* ring promise?'

'That I'll always be ready to help you.' He had kissed the fingertip and slid the second ring on it. 'You can always rely on me.'

Suddenly Angelina appeared in the living room and scolded Judy. 'Back to bed! You don't want a cold as well as a baby,' Angelina cried. She felt a proprietary interest in the impending birth.

The flutters in Judy's abdomen continued irregularly throughout the day. Doctor Geneste had been alerted and was quietly reassuring. 'Nothing is likely to happen yet,' he said.

Twenty-four hours later, Judy began to experience definite strong contractions.

By eight o'clock in the evening the contractions were coming at half-hour intervals and Angelina decided to take her to the hospital. They left Roger with the farmer's wife next door and two red lollipops, then together they walked down the main street in front of the arched town hall, where they waited for the bus.

Once inside the hospital, all romance was wiped from Judy's mind. Angelina was not allowed to be present. She would have to wait in the waiting room. Judy undressed, had a bath, was given an enema by an unfriendly nurse and then found herself lying in a small cubicle on an anonymous, iron-hard hospital bed, rather like her old one at the Hotel Imperial.

Nobody sat with her. Every half hour the nurse brisked in and bent to examine Judy. 'Hmm, not time yet,' she always said.

At eleven o'clock, the nurse said 'Hmmm, six centimetres dilated.' By then Judy's contractions were between two and five minutes apart. It was agonizing. 'Stop making a fuss,' warned the nurse. 'There's worse to come.'

Judy felt oddly irritable and sick. She felt cold, shaky, and was getting cramps in her left leg. The pain in her lower back was now severe and she felt increasing apprehension and fright. She wanted to stop this whole business. At eleven-forty-five p.m. Doctor Geneste was alerted, and at fifteen minutes past midnight Judy was wheeled into the labour ward. She was propped up in a semiseated position, against a mound of pillows and under a blanket, with the soles of her feet together and her knees lolling apart. Already she felt tired and shocked. It was so much more painful than she'd expected.

Again her body stiffened and arched, but this time with a different motion – it started to writhe in a compulsive manner, similar to that involuntary, expulsive feeling that meant you were undoubtedly about to throw up. Judy felt that something inside her had to be violently, immediately expelled from her body. She began to feel slightly – then with increasing urgency – the need to push downwards. The muscles of her abdomen were jerking to expel something, like machinery that hadn't been oiled or used for a long time.

Another spasm racked her body, arched it. Now her body was no longer controlled by her mind. Her gasps grew louder, then turned into screams. A second nurse appeared, held her hand encouragingly and wiped her streaming forehead. Judy started to whimper as her body went out of control again. Why hadn't anybody told her what would happen? Why hadn't anybody explained? Why hadn't they warned her?

Another great pain tore at her body.

'Don't push,' commanded the first nurse, '*don't* push.'

'But I want to push, I can't *not* push, my body is pushing, it's irresistible, I can't stop it, I can't control it, I'm frightened.'

'Your cervix isn't completely dilated, the aperture isn't yet ten centimetres, you *mustn't* push or you might hurt the baby's head, *stop pushing*.'

'Give her gas,' said the second nurse laconically, bending down to examine Judy. The first nurse wheeled over a trolley with six gas cylinders clipped on it and placed a rubber mouthpiece over Judy's nose. 'When the pain gets too bad, take a deep breath, but use it as little as possible.'

Judy took a great greedy gulp.

Eventually, she heard the nurse's voice again. 'Try to go along with the contraction, but don't force it.' It sounded as if the woman were speaking from the end of a cotton-lined tunnel. 'Right, now you're ten centimetres. You can push, but only during contractions; try to relax between them. No! Take your hands off your stomach, no use pushing there. You must let the perineum stretch naturally, otherwise your flesh will tear.'

By now she was very tired, and the area around her vagina felt as if someone was cauterizing it with a white-hot poker. She couldn't stand much more of this burning pain that seared her body. One nurse muttered to the other, 'It's about time the doctor arrived, I think this baby's going to be born any minute.'

Suddenly Judy saw Doctor Geneste's head above hers; over the surgical mask, his eyes were lined and looked exhausted. He had just come from his fourth birth of the day and hadn't had a proper meal since breakfast. Another scream was torn from Judy's mouth, but she felt a sort of weak relief. Her friend had arrived.

'Now you must be brave, because your baby's soon going to be here,' he soothed, 'and you're soon going to be a little mother. We're all here to help you,' he added, as another agonizing contraction shook her body.

She took another gulping breath of gas and felt the room swim slightly, mercifully. Her eyes were shut tight, her face was running with sweat, her hair was wet with sweat and behind her eyes all she could see was a mist of pain. She could hear the murmur of the doctor and the nurse at the opposite end of her body, which was being torn apart. Dear God, she had never, never thought it was going to be as awful as this.

'Steady, steady. Please try not to bear down. The baby mustn't be born too quickly.'

Judy tried to control herself.

'This might be the last contraction.' Somebody swabbed her forehead, someone was holding her hand. 'Pant again, now slow breathing please, now pant again.'

The red and green mist was turning black and she felt another searing pain as the doctor quickly bent to rotate and ease out the baby's head. The doctor and the nurse leaned over, absorbed in their task, as the little dark wet crown of the head grew larger, then the wrinkled little scarlet face slithered out. There was a pause, then Judy was told to give another gentle push as each shoulder was eased out into the rubber-gloved hands of the doctor. A perfectly formed baby slipped out of her body and, with a whimper, little Elizabeth was born.

～ 63 ～

IN the luxuriously hushed hotel suite overlooking Central Park, Lili looked with less resentment at the four women. As she listened to Pagan's explanation of the events surrounding her birth, Lili had started to thaw. She began to understand what had happened almost thirty years ago to those four girls, and her resentment started to melt.

In front of her, Pagan sprawled elegantly in pink wool across an apricot couch. Judy sat on the edge of it, an anxious little figure in brown velvet. On the other apricot sofa, Kate, in her mulberry suit, sat upright and alert at Lili's side. Opposite them, in the square beige armchair, Maxine fingered her blue silk collar.

Lili had just launched her second bombshell – the other question that she'd waited a lifetime to ask.

'In that case, who is my *father*?'

Immediately three heads turned to look at Judy, and Lili thought, It's true, she really is *vraie maman. She* is my mother, *this* is the one!

Judy had never thought so fast in her life. She had not yet recovered from the shock of finding that her long-mourned daughter was still alive, and that the little girl had metamorphosed into the spectacular Tiger-Lili. It left her almost speechless and uncertain of her feelings. She, too, had seen all the photographs of Lili and Abdullah's closely documented love affair. Without meaning or wanting to, Judy couldn't help noticing what the papers said about Abdullah, couldn't help being interested in anything she read about Sydon or about Arabs. She couldn't simply forget someone who had so drastically altered the course of her life, who had caused her such physical and mental pain.

But it was incest!

The word flashed so loudly in her head that Judy was almost

surprised the others couldn't hear it. She couldn't avoid Lili's question. But how could she *possibly* tell Lili who her father was?

In the last few minutes Judy had suddenly realized the secret of Lili's personality. That hot-headed, hasty, volatile temper, that proud rebelliousness, was obviously inherited from her father.

And so were her guts. In spite of her past, Lili had been an amazing success in the eyes of the world. She was undoubtedly a gutsy lady. Her natural gift for acting had reluctantly been acknowledged by the critics, and in the previous three years, Lili had steadily improved her performance. She had worked hard, she had turned down lucrative, showy parts and had accepted only those roles that would build up her reputation as a serious actress.

What effect, Judy wondered, would the truth have on Lili and her career if Lili were told that she was the illegitimate daughter of a king who had raped her mother? And would Lili not be equally horrified when she thought what her past relationship had been with her father? What psychological damage might such knowledge inflict on her? Certainly Lili was unlikely to shrug her shoulders and accept these unpleasant revelations as another of Fate's little quirks.

As these thoughts flashed through Judy's mind, she slowly twisted the coral rosebud ring on her left hand. Nick had said she could always count on him, that he would always help her.

Swiftly, Judy reached a decision. Her story should sound plausible – and loving.

She sat up, flicked a glance at her friends and then said slowly and carefully, 'Your father's name was Nicholas Cliffe and we loved each other very much. In fact, on one occasion – too much. It was on St Valentine's night. He wanted to get married before he did his National Service, but we couldn't because I was only fifteen and it would have been illegal, so we were going to wait. By the time I found out I was pregnant, he was in the army in Malaya, and then, just after you were born, he was killed.' She paused and gave a sigh, as she remembered Nick. 'But I shall never forget him,' she said firmly.

Lili suddenly looked happy enough to cry. Yes, she'd swallowed it. Her voice was catching as she leaned eagerly towards Judy and said, 'I have waited for this moment all my life. I have often imagined it, but now it comes to me as a complete surprise.'

In the reunion scene that Lili had imagined all her life, she had always flung herself into the arms of *vraie maman*. Now slowly she stood up and took a tentative step towards Judy. Her mother wasn't what she had expected, but nevertheless, Lili had found her. And to Lili's surprise she had already warmed to Judy. Judy had carried Lili in her body for nine months, had given birth to her and had then supported her. In fact, for seven years all four of these women had supported her, and it couldn't always have been easy for them. She felt their supportive warmth, their closeness to each other, and the invisible bond that certainly existed between them. They even seemed to communicate without speaking, just by a look or a glance.

Lili didn't realize how fast and fierce were the invisible messages flashing around the room as she took another hesitant step towards Judy and said, 'You know, I can't believe it's true.'

The other three women looking at Judy had immediately known she was lying. Lili couldn't see the incredulity, astonishment and disbelief in their eyes because she was looking at Judy. But Judy could. She held her breath, willing the others to keep silent. Did Pagan and Kate know? Or guess? Would any of them say anything? Why the hell had she said St Valentine's night? To make her story sound more romantic, more charming and acceptable to Lili than the ugly, brutal truth. Lili had to be protected, Judy thought, as she glared at Maxine, Pagan and Kate, whose mouth was open and whose green eyes were big with disbelief.

Kate was remembering the night of the St Valentine Ball, that night when she had stayed with Nick, when they had clung to each other on his creaky iron bedstead. Kate had told herself there was no need to feel guilty; she reminded herself that Judy didn't *want* Nick. Nevertheless, Kate wouldn't have wanted Judy to know that she and Nick – were – well, as a matter of fact they *weren't* ... Because try as she might, even with the most delicate strokes and kisses, with encouragement and affection, Nick was unable to make it. Embarrassed, neither of them referred to this, but there it was, limp, impossible.

Neither was it possible for Judy to have spent that night with Nick because Kate had been in his bed. So why was Judy lying? Why had she mentioned that particular date? *Could* Judy have slept with Nick on some subsequent night?

Kate didn't think so. Although he never so much as kissed her again, although Kate guessed that Nick also felt guilty and faithless, although they neither of them ever again mentioned that night together, from then on Kate had become Nick's confidante. He poured out to her the hopes and yearnings that Judy, more sensible, refused to take seriously.

Kate had no idea who Judy's lover had been, but she was sure it wasn't Nick.

Maxine's eyes had also widened in astonishment at Judy's news. She knew Judy had just lied and couldn't understand why she should do so on a matter of such importance. Maxine was remembering that summer afternoon in the yellow nursery at the Château de Chazalle, when Nick's mother had clearly said that after contracting mumps complicated by orchitis, Nick could never have children.

Oh, no, it certainly couldn't have been Nick, thought Maxine. However, Maxine wouldn't let Judy see that she had disbelieved her story. After all, Judy had been Maxine's friend for over a quarter of a century. It had been Judy's idea to open the château, and it was she who had organized Maxine's American lecture tours. It would be indiscreet and foolish, Maxine decided, to let Judy see she knew her story was a lie.

Maxine also knew that, try as she might, she could never be fond of Lili. She would never be able to forget that horrible scene in the orangery with her adored son. But for Judy's sake she was determined that nobody should ever know her true feelings, so, lying in her teeth, Maxine turned to smile at Lili. Gently she said, '*Ma chère*, you have not only found a mother, you have found a whole family. We are, of course, surprised. But we are also very, very happy to have found you again.'

Lili was also surprised. Suddenly she felt the warmth of total happiness. Amazingly, something had happened in twenty minutes that she would not have imagined could happen in twenty years. Suddenly Lili realized the deep truth of what Maxine was saying and she felt a part of this warm, tightly knit group of women. Whereas twenty minutes ago, Lili didn't have a mother, she felt now that for the first time in her life she had four firm friends.

Judy felt drained. In only twenty-four hours her life had

changed dramatically. She was still finding it hard to realize that her long-mourned child was not dead, that she really had a daughter. For years, Judy had been lucky enough to have success, fame, money and love, but until today, she lacked what most women hope for, and indeed expect – a husband and a child. And now she suddenly knew that she could have it all. Griffin was free to marry her, and he *wanted* to marry her – that was what mattered to Judy. To her surprise, however, a small voice at the back of her head kept insistently whispering, 'What have you to gain by marrying Griffin? Griffin consistently cheated on his wife: ignore the reasons and remember the fact; for years Griffin has followed a pattern of cheating on his wife. No matter whether he felt trapped, bored or resentful, or whether he felt he was missing something, *Griffin has developed the habit of cheating on his wife*. So why risk turning into Griffin's wife? Why not continue your present relationship, which has been rock-steady for so long?'

Yesterday Judy would perhaps have grabbed at the chance of a loving and supportive relationship that was underlined by the traditional laws of society. But today ... and so unexpectedly ... Judy had suddenly discovered that a firmer bond existed in her life: her child had been restored to her.

Judy stood up and moved towards her daughter, her face still tense but smiling.

'But ... but,' Pagan blurted out. 'It was impossible, *impossible* ...'

She stopped short in midsentence, as Lili looked astonished and Judy turned furious blue eyes on her. Pagan, remembering Nick's aquamarine eyes, turned her head and looked up – straight into Lili's big, slanting, velvet-brown eyes.

As she stared, Pagan was remembering what her husband had said, years ago, when she had first discovered she was pregnant. She had told Christopher she wanted a little girl with big brown eyes and her husband had said, 'Well, you're not going to get one, my darling.'

And then he explained that the colour of a child's eyes depends on the gene-grouping of its parents. Two blue-eyed individuals could not produce a brown-eyed baby. He had been definite about it.

Pagan turned her head again and looked at Judy's navy-blue

eyes and then at Lili. Why on earth was Judy lying? What *possible* reason could there be?

Pagan had only paused for two seconds as these thoughts flashed through her brain, but in that time Maxine had jerked upright and said sharply, 'Sick and sin, remember, Pagan.'

'But, but . . .' Pagan stuttered, realizing that she had just been reminded to support Judy now and always.

What the hell had she been saying? Oh yes.

Pagan beamed at Lili and carefully continued, '. . . It was *impossible* for anybody to forget your father, Lili.'

And that at least was the truth.

EPILOGUE

LACE: a delicate, decorative fabric woven in an open web of different patterns and figures: a cord or string drawn through holes: to lace: to fasten: to add a dash of spirit: to interlace: to join together (fingers, patterns): to intertwine: to mingle or blend in an intricate way: to intersperse, to diversify, to change the patterns.

ACKNOWLEDGEMENTS

I owe a great debt to my editor, Michael Korda, for teaching me so much and making the process so enjoyable. I also greatly appreciate John Herman's support, care and editorial involvement.

Without Morton Janklow's perception and judgement this book might never have been started, let alone finished, and I also owe a great deal to Betsy Nolan for her shrewd advice.

For reading my manuscript, I am most grateful to George Seddon, Celia Brayfield and Giorgio Sandulescu. For typing on and on ... and on, I would like to thank Bettina Culham, who somehow managed to decipher Linear C.

For helping to ensure that this book is technically accurate, I would like to express my gratitude to Professor T. W. Glenister, Dr Jonathan Gould, The Cancer Research Institute, Alexander Mosley, Victor Sassie, Richard Pearce, Patrick Forbes, William Frankel, Clive Carr, David O'Brien, Mike Ricketts, Peter Alexander, Michael Crawford, Lanham Titchener, Ian McAlley, Roger Wood, Alexander Weymouth, David Maroni, Patrick O'Higgins, Peter Boumphrey, Sebastian Conran, Jasper Conran, Rowland Castro, Anna Weymouth, Dee Wells Ayer, Lesley Blanch, Sandy Fawkes, Mary Quant, Tina Vanzyl-Lubner, Pat Miller, Shirley Lowe, Ruth Janner Morris, Deirdre McSharry, Anna Palmer, Myrna Shapiro, Jill Haas, and Ellie Boris.

My thanks also to Arthur Klebanoff, Jerry Traum, Anne Sibbald, Arnold Kinsman, Aimée Mikaelis, Rebecca Head, Deborah Gordis, Willow Morel, Mary Jo Valko, Joan Feeley, Anna Wintour, Nina Santizi and Mallory Andrews, who were kind enough to help me when I needed their expertise, and also to my assistant, Linda Sheridan, for what can only be described as everything.

Lace 2

For Peter
With Love

～ PROLOGUE ～

THEY are the most expensive breasts in the world, thought Lili as she soaped them. Lace rivulets of foam slipped over her rounded flesh and, as she touched one cinnamon-tinted nipple, Lili shivered with sensuous pleasure. She stretched one rose-tipped toe to push the old-fashioned, ivory-handled dial which released hot water; then she stroked her other nipple with the sea sponge, and again her body quivered in response. It was as if the tips of her breasts were part of an electrical circuit of sensation which connected directly with the sensual core of her body, Lili thought as she watched the two cinnamon buds grow hard, then break through the carnation-scented foam.

Everything was in perfect working order; Lili's body was fully practical, as technicians said when they checked props on the set. But the satin slopes that started to swell immediately below her collarbone were considerably more than practical; Lili's breasts had been her passport, her work permit, her meal ticket, and now they were her fortune. Currently, those two impertinently rounded breasts were insured for a seven-figure sum by Omnium Pictures, which had just negotiated a record fee for Lili to play Helen of Troy.

Nowadays my breasts are worth far more to other people than they are to me, Lili reflected wistfully; but for almost fifteen years, whatever power she had possessed over her destiny had been derived from these two pounds of flesh which, to Lili, were as familiar as her knees and hardly any more remarkable.

Lili sighed, threw the sponge aside, slowly rose from the over-full bath and carelessly splashed a lake of water over the pink marble floor. She wrapped herself in a buttercup-yellow towel and wandered into the sitting room. A bowl of figs stood on her breakfast tray, each fruit cut into quarters to expose the red flesh; Lili nibbled at a segment as she glanced at the newspaper:

1979 was not proving a good year for President Carter, she thought as she read about the siege of the American Embassy and the hostages held in Iran. Lili knew what it felt like to be suddenly confronted by violence.

Born in Switzerland, Lili had never known her mysterious mother, but when she was six years old she had been on holiday with her foster family in Hungary. They had been trapped by the 1956 Hungarian uprising against the Communists, and Lili had seen her beloved foster parents shot by border guards before she had managed to escape. From an Austrian refugee camp she had been sent to Paris where she had been adopted by an ageing, childless couple. By the age of seven she had virtually become the unpaid servant of Monsieur et Madame Sardeau, a skivvy who longed for the love, peace and happiness that she had once known and still hoped for.

It had been easy for the rich American playboy to seduce Lili, and easier still for him to abandon her when she found herself pregnant. Thrown out by the Sardeaus, Lili had paid for her abortion by posing naked for a truck drivers' calendar. Overnight she became famous as a lewd, baby pin-up. Terrified, helpless and dependent on her exploitative manager, Lili had eventually been rescued by Jo Stiarkoz, a Greek shipowner who had encouraged Lili's natural acting and painting talents, and who gradually changed her from a suspicious, wary child of the gutter, unable to equate sex with love, into a cultured, discerning beauty.

When Jo was killed in a car accident Lili sought oblivion in her film career, and then had flung herself into a notorious year-long affair with Abdullah, King of Sydon, a tiny oil-rich state on the Persian Gulf. But eventually Lili could no longer tolerate her position, described by some as an unofficial concubine and others as the Western Whore. Lili then returned to her home in Paris to search once more for dignity, love and peace. And so far she had not found them.

Sighing, Lili threw aside the *Herald Tribune* and slowly walked through the carved cedarwood shutters on to her balcony, which hung over the grape-green water of the Bosporus. Around the balcony the domes and sharp minarets of Istanbul sparkled in the hazy morning sunlight of August. The sounds of the city, muted and distorted, travelled over the waters of the Bosporus as shouting voices, bicycle bells and the occasional goat bleat blended with the roar of the traffic. Lili hugged the golden bath sheet around her as she absorbed the sights and sounds of Turkey. There were worse places to want love, peace and happiness.

Across the Straits, on the Asian side of the water, the sun also warmed the stubby grey barrel of a Smith & Wesson Magnum ·357, UZI 9mm, a Kalashnikov and two hand grenades. They lay on a rickety table in a small room that smelt of stale marijuana smoke.

He hadn't been able to risk bringing the hardware through customs, but when he'd arrived in Istanbul he'd obeyed instructions and everything had gone smoothly. He'd ordered two cups of coffee, simultaneously, in the small Bazaar café, then he'd sent them both back, complaining that the coffee wasn't strong enough. After a few minutes a dark-suited, dark-featured man had appeared before his table, and he had followed the dark stranger as they walked through a maze of narrow streets, then up a dirty staircase to a small dark room, where he had shown his passport. From the poor selection of guns that he had been offered he'd picked three, realizing that he had very little choice in the matter.

He'd hoped for a .44 Magnum because that stopped anyone close up; even a big man would be thrown, dead, on his back. The UZI sub-machine-gun was easy to get anywhere in the Near East because it was used by Israeli infantry. It weighed seven and a half pounds and was the shortest sub-machine-gun (twenty inches folded), which made it not impossible for you to strap it inside your trouser leg. It could fire 600 rounds a minute as well as single shots, and used 9mm ammunition, which was easy to get hold of because it was a common size for pistols as well as SMGs. He'd also chosen the Kalashnikov because it was handy and reliable. It was slower than the UZI but the longer barrel made it more accurate. God knows how it had ended up in Istanbul, because it was a Chinese '56 model with a wooden stock and a permanently attached folding bayonet, which might well be useful.

Beside the hardware lay an untidy heap of bullets, two

ammunition clips, a coil of nylon rope, 500 millilitres of clear solution in a glass bottle, a roll of three-inch-wide white surgical tape, two maps of the city, a water pipe with a few crumbs of half-burned resin in the bowl and a copy of *People* magazine.

The man moved to the rusting, metal-framed window and swept the opposite shore with high-powered, army field glasses. He saw low hills wooded with cypresses and pines; too high, he thought, and corrected. He saw a blurry mass of buildings pierced by the decorated spires of minarets; he was still too high. Then he was focused at the correct level, but the jumbled, dirty-brown houses were confusingly similar and only the larger shapes of a mosque, shrine or palace offered directions to the watcher. Impatiently the man picked up his tourist's map and peered at a photograph. Again he raked the distant shore with the field glasses, this time slowly tracking along the water's edge.

At the point at which Galata bridge spanned the Golden Horn the man fiddled with the focus until the image was so sharp that he could see the faces of the passengers on the ferry, which was pulling away from the landing. Carefully he watched the laden boat begin its journey towards him, then he swept the binoculars further to the right and saw the gleaming façade of a palace, a small park shaded by Judas trees, and the ruined shell of a fortified tower. Finally, with a grunt of satisfaction, he was focused on a large terracotta-coloured building directly on the edge of the water. Systematically he checked each window, beginning with the square casements of the top floor and working down to the tall French doors on the first floor, some of which opened on to small domed balconies, suspended over the water like white birdcages. While the man watched, a pair of shutters was pushed open and Lili, wearing her golden towel, walked out on the balcony.

The man dropped the field glasses and grabbed the copy of *People* magazine. Those tawny, almond-shaped eyes, the mass of black curls, the provocatively out-thrust breasts were unmistakable. He had found more than he had expected.

Lili wandered back into the sitting room of her suite, squashed another fig segment into her mouth and moved into the dressing room, where she stepped into a loose white linen shift, the only thing which offered her any hope of navigating the Grand Bazaar without being pinched black and blue by lecherous fingers. Yesterday she had spun round after a particularly insulting nip to find that the fingers had belonged to a ten-year-old boy. Lili slipped her feet into snakeskin sandals, pinned up her mass of dark hair with antique tortoiseshell combs and applied as little make-up as possible because, thank heaven, she wasn't the photographic target for today. Leaving clothes and cosmetics scattered all over her suite, she left it, then knocked on the next door.

'That you, Lili? Come on in, honey, I'm waiting for this to dry.' The preoccupied voice held a hint of Louisiana. Sandy Bayriver (born Flanagan) was finishing a delicate job of restoration. The area on which she was working had been cleaned and rubbed down, and she was draping a minute web of strengthening gauze over the fingernail crack. In Sandy's business, a girl could not afford to be seen without a perfect set of ten matched talons.

Lili wandered around the opulent, brocade-furnished drawing room, picked up a tawdry diamanté crown slung rakishly over the marble ear of a bust of Alexander the Great and held it on her head. 'How d'you keep this thing on, Sandy?'

'Bobby pins, honey. Once, when I was Lake Pontchartrain Oyster Queen, I clean forgot to pin it on and the damn thing fell off halfway across Churchill Plaza.' She looked up. 'It really suits you, Lili – maybe you should take over as Miss International Beauty and I'll just go shopping today.'

'You won it, you wear it,' Lili threw the coronet back on the statue's head. Sandy never missed an opportunity to say something sweet, the way some people never missed an opportunity to say something nasty. It was easy to forget that she was in the piranha pool of competition for these gaudy crowns, Lili thought, as Sandy wriggled her toes into scarlet sandals.

'Four-inch heels would cripple me,' said Lili.

'Hell, honey, I'm used to them.' Sandy tripped into the bathroom where she carefully removed the heated rollers from her wild tawny hair which curled naturally, but Sandy preferred a disciplined cascade of shiny ringlets. 'Let's go find your mamma.' Sandy giggled, ever conscious of the two notorious women with whom she was travelling.

At the top of the immense double staircase, which swept down to the foyer of the Harun-al-Rashid Hotel, Sandy hung on to Lili's arm as, carefully, she moved sideways down the slippery marble steps. Waiting at the bottom of the ornate staircase was a small, delicately boned woman in a red silk dress.

Judy Jordan, founder of *Verve!* magazine for working women, was not sure that she was enjoying her role as travelling companion to two of the most beautiful women in the world – one of whom happened to be her long-lost daughter.

The guide in baggy black trousers led them to the water gate of their elegant, rose-washed hotel, which had once been the summer palace of a queen, built at the water's edge for coolness. 'Where are we going today?' asked Lili as the three women settled into the canopied private launch.

Judy pointed. 'Over there. The Topkapi Palace, where the Ottoman kings lived. That enormous pile of buildings on the hill; you're both being photographed in the Palace Harem.'

'Surely not me, too?' exclaimed Lili. 'I'm not made-up.'

Judy looked at her, thinking now that patience was the outstanding quality required by any mother as she said, 'Lili, last night I told you that we needed shots of you, as well as Sandy. Anyway, you look fine.'

Of course Lili looked fine; Lili always looked fine, thought Judy wistfully. I always looked fine when I was her age. Now if I watch my diet and work out every day and only drink wine at Christmas, I can still look good, but not as good as I did when I was Lili's age. Judy knew that in her red Chloë dress, with its rippling bias-cut skirt, her figure was still girlishly slim; she still had the waif-like appeal of an exhausted Little Orphan Annie, in spite of her present problems. Judy thought, I wouldn't have to be involved in anything as tacky as a beauty queen competition if I wasn't so broke, and Lili hadn't been so indiscreet, and Tom hadn't taken one business risk too many.

And there was one other problem. After almost a year as Lili's mother, and a week travelling with eighteen-year-old Sandy, Judy was forced to acknowledge that she was of a different generation, and that made her feel uneasy. Not jealous, of course, just uneasy. If Judy felt uneasy, by now she knew that millions of her women readers felt the same way about the same things. Putting her life into her magazine, and knowing when to trust her gut instincts, had made Judy her first million dollars.

She found Lili the more disturbing of her two travelling companions because elegance, to Judy, meant neat hair and formal clothes, not expensive garments that were *intended* to look crumpled and hair that had been carefully dressed to look untidy. Nevertheless, since gaining a daughter Judy had stopped arguing with her fashion editor when spreads were proposed on street-chic or models swathed in knotted muslin.

Sitting with her back to the Bosporus, Lili dearly wished she had not forgotten about today's photographic session. Eventually she leaned towards her mother and said, 'I'm sorry I forgot. I'm so glad you persuaded me to come on this trip, Judy.'

Judy smiled politely, recognizing the peace offering. It was the politeness that came between them, thought Judy, but she didn't know how not to be polite. A real mother isn't polite; she yells at her kids, hollers when her daughter pinches her panty-hose, then goes without a new winter coat so that her daughter can have a really pretty first formal. A mother washes your clothes, and her time and her love are the ingredients that go into every stack of lunchtime sandwiches she cuts. A mother's always at you about your galoshes (putting them on, taking them off, putting them away) and you ignore her or groan theatrically, but her scolding is comforting because you know it means that she cares. Every day, between a daughter and the mother she's grown up with, there are a thousand unspoken reference points which add up to the feeling of comfortable, affectionate intimacy, the feeling that a puppy has for the blanket in its basket. Without discussion, a mother knows that you like goat's milk cheese and don't like Aunt Bertha. A mother knows your temper tantrums, and where they come from, and how to stop them before they start. Between Lili and Judy there was liking, respect and even the start of a touching friendship, but both of them were silently aware that there should have been love, and there was no love – yet. They both pinned their hopes on that 'yet'.

From the other side of the boat Lili watched her mother's short blonde hair ruffle in the breeze. Lili had always expected her unknown, mysterious mother to be a quiet, kindly madonna, an apron-covered, ample figure, always stirring something delicious on an old-fashioned kitchen range. But when, almost a year ago, Lili had finally tracked down her mother, she had found this glamorous, lonely public figure instead of the comforting creature of her daydreams.

Both Lili and Judy were alone in life and they both longed not to be; so they tried to behave as they imagined a mother and her daughter should behave. They made odd little stabs at what they thought was the appropriate way to act. But although she had made such a great effort to discover her real mother, Lili was suspicious of her own feelings. Lili was an instinctive actress; her fame was the result of having the raw talent, then slowly acquiring the craft, then polishing the talent. She had always had to play her life by ear, so her impulses were important, but she was suspicious of her facility to take on a mood when she wanted to act it. Lili did not want to act love. She wanted the real thing. She wanted what she had always felt she had been deprived of – mother love. Lili knew she was not getting the real thing, she felt it deep in her heart and her bones and her being, but she did not want to face it; so she continued hopefully to grope for it.

Lili also feared that something else might sabotage the relationship with her mother that she was trying so hard to establish. Lili knew from her acting work, and from watching other people's stage work, that when a coach or a director asks an actor to play affection, what sometimes unconsciously comes up is bitter rage, always followed by sudden tears and breakdown. This was another reason why Lili feared that she might unconsciously be acting the love of her mother that she so longed to establish with Judy. Lili did not want suddenly to cause an unforgivable but unforgettable resentment of her mother's abandonment.

The pink fringe of the canopy swayed in the breeze as their little launch darted over the grey-green water. Lili leaned over to Judy. 'After the photo session, can I go shopping? I want to buy a carpet in the Grand Bazaar.'

'I'll come with you, it's better to bargain with two people, you'll get a lower price if I stand behind you looking grim. Offer one third of what they ask and settle for half.'

'That's not really the way I hoped to do it. I want to buy you a present, Judy. I want to buy you the most beautiful carpet in the Bazaar.'

'That's sweet of you, Lili, but you know it's not necessary.'

Without realizing it, Lili had expected her real mother to be a duplicate of her beloved Swiss-peasant foster mother, Angelina, and Lili had expected her mother to be poor, like Angelina. Lili had expected to be able to show her love by helping her mother financially. She had had a little fantasy of taking her mother to the best store in town and buying her mother her first fur coat. But then her mother had turned out to be a millionaire. So Lili kept trying to buy Judy expensive presents, which embarrassed Judy. Any show of affection embarrassed Judy, especially touch. Her strict, Southern Baptist parents had never touched each other; they had not kissed or cuddled their children or each other and, consequently, there was a distance in all Judy's relationships, because, to her, touch was related to sex, not affection.

Lili sensed the loneliness that Judy would have fiercely denied. Judy had achieved everything that spells success – she was a Liz Smith regular, a Page Six standby, she had expensive designer clothes, maids, secretaries, an East Side apartment, a place on Long Island, plenty of men friends and three very special women friends. But nobody ... close. Perhaps that stemmed from her feelings of guilt.

Judy had spent many years feeling guilty about abandoning her child, feeling responsible for her child's death, feeling guilty that her life hadn't turned out as planned, and all because she hadn't been an instant success in the Big Apple.

However much she justified her actions, however tenderly her friends reassured her, there was no getting away from the fact that she had – as Lili felt it – abandoned her own daughter when she was three months old. There had been plenty of justification. Judy had been a sixteen-year-old waitress, working her way through the Language Laboratory in Gstaad, Switzerland, when she had been raped. Judy's three rich girlfriends at the nearby finishing school had all helped to pay for Lili's birth and then for her keep. But no matter how hard Judy had tried, business success always, at first, seemed just beyond her reach, and whatever way Judy turned, she came up against an impersonal blank wall at the end of a cul-de-sac. And all the time she knew that she had to succeed as fast as possible, because – her own ambition apart – she couldn't support her baby daughter until she was successful and made money. Judy's lack of early success had made her feel helpless and unloved, as well as a failure.

With the cheery arrogance of youth, Judy had expected quick success to be the result of brains and hard work. She didn't realize that you can put all your heart and energy into your work but the opportunities you deserve just aren't offered to people who are only moderately attractive; it can make you bitter when the other, less gifted people get the opportunities that should be yours.

Sure, Lili had suffered, but nevertheless Lili had all the things that Judy had never had at her age: beauty, sexuality, money and time. Time to play, time to go out in the evening without feeling exhausted, time for men. Judy remembered once wondering whether she would be successful while she was still attractive or whether she would ever be able to afford to wear a wonderful dress, to go to a wonderful place and perhaps meet a wonderful man there?

Perhaps it would all have been much easier if only she had been a little bit more beautiful. Judy was ashamed of the fact that she was jealous of Lili's beauty.

On the opposite side of the water, in the Asian part of the city, the man with binoculars still slung around his neck pushed his way through the boys selling chewing gum and evil-eye beads until he reached the Galata ferry. A few minutes later the wide wake of the flat-bottomed ferry crossed the wash of the pretty little launch that carried the three famous women as they sped towards the shore, where richly decorated palaces and mosques crowded together at the water's edge; the entire view rippled in the heat, so the buildings seemed to be part of the water itself.

'Problems, Judy, problems,' warned the photographer at Topkapi Palace. 'They say we can't shoot in the Harem. It's impossible.'

People with longer experience of Judy Jordan never used the word 'impossible'. If you told Judy that something was impossible she merely lifted her little nose an inch or so and said, 'Only impossible people use the word "impossible",' or simply, 'It *must* be done.' Now Judy said, 'We *must* shoot in the Harem; the copy has already been written, all the headlines are set and your film is going straight back to New York tonight to be developed and printed in time for Friday's deadline.' She turned to the guide from the Turkish Tourist Board, 'What's the problem?'

'The Harem quarters are enormous, Mrs Jordan . . .'

'Can't we use part of it for us to get a few shots? Everything was cleared with your office.'

'There must have been a misunderstanding. Photography is forbidden because of the restorations.'

'But isn't there even one room . . .'

'Please understand, Madame. The Topkapi Palace is a magnificent national treasure and the government would be most unhappy if it were not seen at its best. All the most beautiful rooms are in the part of the palace which is open to tourists. Let me show these to you.'

'OK, do that,' agreed Judy. She looked at her watch and thought, an hour to set up, another hour to get the shots. Yes, there would be time for a quick tour.

'Do you suppose they'll let us come back and have a proper look?' Sandy asked Lili as they hurried through a library lined with carved wooden bookshelves, inlaid with mother-of-pearl and tortoiseshell.

'No.' Lili was listening to the guide's heavily accented voice as he told a story about some favourite concubine.

'Is it always like this? Being on tour?' asked Sandy, still reluctant to learn that the glamorous life looked better than it lived.

'Yes,' said Lili. 'You never have enough time, except in airports; it doesn't matter where you are, all you really see is the inside of dressing rooms and studios; you can't go to the discotheques because you'll have bags under your eyes tomorrow; you can't sunbathe because you'll look browner in some pictures than others; you can't eat most of the food so you won't either get fat or sick; and everyone is always late and frantic. Isn't success wonderful?'

'Time to get ready, girls,' said Judy. 'We're going to shoot in

633

the king's dining room.' She led them to a tiny chamber with walls and ceilings covered in gold-embellished paintings of lilies and roses, pomegranates and peaches. The photographer looked doubtfully at his light meter. 'All this Interflora stuff might look like psychedelic oatmeal by the time the pictures are printed.'

'Then let's do a few more shots outside, by the Harem gate, where you'll get better light,' Judy suggested.

After the photo session was finished and the film had been dispatched to the airport, Sandy and the photographer stayed behind for a more leisurely look at the palace. 'After all, honey,' said Sandy, as they headed for the treasure chamber, 'how often does a girl get a look at rubies the size of pigeon's eggs?'

Judy and Lili climbed into their limousine, kicked off their shoes and asked the driver to take them to the Grand Bazaar.

As she got out of the car Lili's tiny snakeskin bag slipped off her shoulders and fell on to the cobbles, spilling coins, lip-gloss and letters. Quickly Lili snatched them up, but Judy had spotted the airmail letter.

'Not fast enough, Lili.' Judy couldn't stop herself saying it. 'He's still writing to you, isn't he?'

Lili opened her mouth and then shut it again; after all, whatever she said would be wrong.

Still Judy couldn't stop herself. 'Do you think I don't know my lover's handwriting after all these months?'

'Judy, *I* can't stop Mark writing to me. *I* don't want anything to do with him, I never did . . .'

'But he wants *you*, Lili, doesn't he? And he certainly doesn't want me any more.' Judy knew she was being destructive and knew that she should stop, but now that she had begun she could not stop; she had been suppressing this for weeks. 'Lili, don't tell me you didn't know that Mark was falling in love with you in New York, right under my nose. You can't pretend that you don't know what effect you have on men – Lili, the world's most famous sex symbol.' Judy knew Lili's most sensitive point.

'You're not being fair, Judy. What kind of a woman do you think I am?'

Suddenly Judy's self-control snapped as jealousy, unhappiness and fear controlled her. 'The kind of woman who might seduce her mother's lover. The kind of woman who could ruin her mother's business – that's the kind of woman you are!'

Lili burst into tears of rage. 'You're impossible! I wish I'd never found you. I wish I'd never met you. I never want to see you again.' Impulsively she turned, plunged into the jostling crowd, and vanished. Grimly Judy watched her go. Their raised voices, the faces twisted with anger and misery, had gone unremarked in the noisy crowd. But both women knew that their play-acting was over. Within two minutes the fragile relationship that both had tried so hard to establish had been wrecked.

The man with the binoculars watched them argue, then saw Lili burst into tears and disappear under the great stone gateway of the Bazaar. Quickly he followed her, elbowing his way through the heaving mass of people, determined to keep Lili in sight.

'Where the hell can Lili be? She should never have gone off alone like that.'

'Going off alone is her idea of luxury,' Sandy reminded Judy as she tipped back her chair, crossed her feet on the balcony rail and watched heavy black clouds gather behind the minarets. 'You know that Lili doesn't like the usual star entourage. The rest of them may not move an inch without PR people, bodyguards, a couple of studio executives, two gofers and a hairdresser, but that's exactly the part that Lili hates. Nobody can make an entrance better than Lili but, although she's not exactly Garbo, Lili doesn't care for all the fuss and glitter that I long for.'

'But she knows we're supposed to meet the agency people in ten minutes.'

'Maybe she doesn't want to meet the agency people. Why don't we just go ahead and eat?' Sandy stood up and pulled down the zipper of her gold lamé jumpsuit. 'Lili can follow us when she turns up.'

But when Judy tried to leave a message for Lili the clerk pointed out that Lili's key was still in its pigeonhole. 'Miss Lili went out many hours ago. No, not alone. With a man.'

'What sort of man?'

'Not a guest. Maybe Turkish. I don't remember his clothes. A dark suit, maybe.' In luxury hotels in Turkey the clerks speak impeccable English.

'That's odd; we don't know anyone Turkish, except the agency people,' Sandy said as they turned towards the dining room. Judy said nothing.

As the agency people made over-polite conversation, Judy picked her way through a series of dishes with suggestive names: Holy Man Fainted (stuffed eggplant with tomatoes, onions and garlic), King's Delight (sautéed lamb with onions and tomatoes), Ladies' Navels (fried pastries with pistachio nuts and whipped cream). Then the lights dimmed and six plump girls in neon-pink gauze undulated across the dance floor. After the belly dancers came the fire-eaters, then the snake-charmer. Not until two o'clock in the morning, when the last cobra had been re-coiled in its basket, could Judy stand up and leave.

Back at the hotel reception desk her anxiety increased as she stared at Lili's key, still in its pigeonhole. 'This is not the kind of town for a girl to be out with a strange man,' Judy said to Sandy. 'However angry Lili was, she would have sent us a message. After all, she wouldn't want the police looking for her if she was just romancing.'

Feeling increasing guilt, Judy turned to Sandy. 'We'd better not call the police. We don't want to upset the local people and we don't want to look foolish if Lili, if she only . . .' she paused.

'Exactly,' agreed Sandy.

As soon as Judy woke she telephoned Lili's suite. No answer. In her red silk dressing gown, Judy hurried down to the reception desk. The clerk, a nervous new boy on the daytime shift, refused to give her the key to Lili's rooms. Judy demanded to see the hotel manager and, together, they hurried up the marble stair-case. An anxious Sandy waited outside the double doors of Lili's suite.

They rushed across the empty drawing room and threw open the bedroom door. The billowing pink silk canopy of the elabor-ate antique bed was caught back with golden rope, but the plump velvet pillows in their lace coverings were undented and the ivory chiffon sheets were still as smooth as when the maid had turned them down the night before.

Sandy ran into the dressing room and opened the closets. 'Her clothes are still here.' She pulled open the bathroom door. The make-up was scattered on the marble counter as Lili had left it.

Sandy dashed back to the sitting room to see Judy on her knees, tearing at a cylindrical brown-paper parcel on the floor. She pulled out an exquisite silk rug. 'Lili must have bought that after she left me in the Bazaar.'

'Maybe the man she went out with was a rug merchant?' suggested Sandy.

'Maybe she met someone in the Grand Bazaar?' Judy worried aloud.

Sandy always told people what they wanted to hear. 'Lili might have taken up with some good-looking guy and decided to have a little fun,' she soothed.

The discreet tap at the door made both women jump, then hurry towards it. Judy was the first to reach the handle. 'Lili, thank God you're . . . oh!' Outside stood a hotel page boy, carrying a gigantic bouquet of red roses.

'Who would send us flowers when we're leaving tomorrow?' Sandy wondered as she unpinned the tiny envelope and handed it to Judy. She pulled out the card and read it, then gasped, 'Oh, no!' and dropped the card.

Sandy snatched up the card and read it aloud. 'Wait in your hotel suite to hear from Lili's father. He must pay the ransom.' Slowly she turned to Judy. 'So now we know. Lili's been kidnapped.'

∼ I ∼

STANDING, dazed, in her hotel room, gazing at the beautiful bunch of red roses which had accompanied the kidnap letter, Judy said nothing. But she thought, this is my fault. Once again I have been responsible for a disaster in my daughter's life. Why, oh why, doesn't God stick up red flags when you accidentally do some little thing that's going to lead to calamity? *I* persuaded Lili to come with me on this tacky trip because I never had enough *time* for her back home in New York; there I told myself that it wasn't my responsibility, I hadn't been expecting a long-lost daughter to drop in on me. I had a magazine to run and a business to run and my charity commitments, and my lover to look after. But that article on Lili in *Verve!* was my idea. I should have known that article was asking for trouble – and that we'd all get it in shovelfuls. I wish I could turn the clock back to a year ago, to that first meeting at the Pierre Hotel.

15 October 1978

It had been a warm October evening; nevertheless, a log fire had burned softly in the quiet, cream hotel suite, with the spectacular view across the purple dusk of Central Park. Firelight had flickered across the faces of the two women as they moved towards each other. Judy had felt the strange animal magnetism that emanated from Lili. Looking at Lili's black, soft curls, falling to the folds of her white Grecian tunic, Judy felt a new appreciation of that world-famous oval face with the high cheekbones that looked both innocent and predatory, the thickly lashed chestnut eyes that always glistened as if tears were about to fall. Judy found it hard to accept that her daughter, believed dead, was alive – let alone that she was Lili, the most famous professional waif since Marilyn Monroe. It was impossible to match this sensuous creature with the image that Judy had treasured of a well-behaved, six-year-old girl with braided hair.

Judy had always imagined that her long-lost daughter would look exactly like herself, but their only resemblance lay in the slim-boned frames of their bodies. The three other women in the room sat motionless – hypnotized by the drama of the moment – as Lili took a hesitant step towards Judy. Pagan, elegant in pink wool, suddenly noticed that Judy and Lili had the same doll-like hands. She leaned across to the green-eyed woman in the mulberry suit. 'Do you think we should leave?' she whispered to Kate, who was sitting next to her on the apricot silk sofa.

Kate Ryan shrugged her shoulders, unable to take her eyes off Lili. She found herself mentally taking notes, as if writing one of her articles, as Lili moved towards Judy, but Judy stood motionless and silent. Kate opened her mouth to say something but the third onlooker, an elegant blonde in blue silk, lifted her fingers to her lips as all three women watched the mother and daughter hold each other in a nervous embrace. Sharing a natural impulse to dissolve the pain and embarrassment of the moment by reaching towards physical contact, they were hugging each other, but not kissing each other, Kate noticed.

As she held her daughter Judy realized that this was the first time she had touched Lili since the sad moment when she had handed her three-month-old baby to her foster mother that morning years ago in the Swiss hospital where Judy's illegitimate child had been born. As she held Lili close to her heart Judy realized that, since that day, they had shared a physical need for each other that was close to hunger; their embrace was an expression of that need, rather than of warmth, of affection, even of liking; but both women realized that this was an expression of goodwill.

This is my daughter, thought Judy, as she felt the trembling warmth of Lili's body; this voluptuous woman once came out of my body; those wild brown eyes and slanting cheekbones – once they were a part of me, I made them. She looked down at Lili's gold-skinned forearms and thought, that is flesh of my flesh.

She does not *feel* like my mother, thought Lili, hugging the slender Judy in her brown velvet suit. A mixture of resentment and relief swirled in Lili's mind; she had built up her unknown mother's identity into a romantic mystery because the alternative was to face her mother's brusque rejection of her as a baby. When she finally met her mother Lili had expected to feel as protected as a child, but when she looked into Judy's eyes and saw pain, fear and guilt, Lili felt unexpectedly protective towards her mother.

Oblivious of the three seated women who watched, Lili was also near to tears as she remembered her deep-rooted restlessness, the profound anxiety and uncertainty that had shadowed her adult life. Now she instinctively recognized it as a sense of loss – sad and constant – even though it was for a woman that Lili had never known, her *vraie maman*, as Lili used to think of her mother, in the little Swiss village where she had been raised by the local seamstress. 'Mother?' Lili said the word softly, as if forming it for the first time, and then tried it again. 'Mother.'

The two women drew back, gave tearful laughs and simultaneously said, 'You're not what I expected!' Then Judy added, 'How did you find us?'

'It wasn't difficult,' said Lili. 'I hired a detective. He discovered that my mother had been one of four teenage girlfriends who had been students in Switzerland, and then he followed the trails until he identified you.' She turned to the green-eyed woman in the mulberry suit. 'You were the most difficult to track down, Kate, because the world is full of Katherine Ryans. But, once he did find you, my detective couldn't discover *which* of you four was that teenage mother, which is why I arranged this confrontation.' She hesitated, and nervously bit her lower lip. 'I hope you'll forgive me; I do so hope you'll understand why I had to know who my parents are, why I had to know *who I am.*'

The last thing Kate had expected to feel for this sex goddess was a sudden rush of affection and pity. Gently she said, 'We do so hope, Lili, that you will understand why Judy couldn't keep her baby. In 1949 a sixteen-year-old girl from a poor family, who had to earn her own living, couldn't also look after a baby.'

Anxiously Judy said, 'Did you . . . were you . . . did your foster mother look after you?' She added in a rush, 'I can never forgive her for taking you to Hungary after the Russians occupied it.'

Lili said, 'I shall always love Angelina. She loved me and she never lied to me; she always told me that one day my *vraie maman* would come for me.'

'She did come for you.' The elegant blonde in the blue silk dress spoke, for the first time, with an unmistakable French accent. 'We knew you were on holiday in Hungary and, when we heard there'd been a revolution, Judy flew over to Europe and we went straight to the Hungarian border. The situation was chaotic: a hundred and fifty thousand Hungarian refugees were pouring over the Austrian border into camps for displaced persons. We visited every one of them. But nobody could trace you.' Maxine remembered Judy's frenzy and self-accusation as they stood in the snow outside hut after hut, waiting to see yet another refugee committee official.

As Judy remembered her constant self-reproach for having abandoned Lili, for not having done enough to find her, she sat down heavily on the apricot silk sofa and buried her face in her hands; her little gulps, splutters and sniffs were the only sounds to break the silence.

Kate picked up the ivory telephone and said, 'Champagne is what you celebrate a new baby with, isn't it? D'you think they have any Krug '49?'

'I would prefer you to order our champagne,' said Maxine firmly. 'Ask for a magnum of Chazalle '74.'

After a great deal of emotion and champagne Pagan suddenly said, 'How is the press going to react to this news? Do you think we should keep it secret?'

'It's bound to get out somehow,' said Maxine. 'We're all public personalities as we all live our lives in the spotlight. Why, within a week, someone would have overheard a telephone conversation, stolen a letter and sold the story to the *National Enquirer* for a meagre fifty dollars.' She turned to Kate. 'You're a journalist, right?'

Judy remembered the cruel descriptions that she had quite enjoyed reading about Lili, as maliciously enjoyable as any tidbit about Elizabeth Taylor, Farrah Fawcett or Joan Collins. 'We'll be able to set the record straight, Lili. We'll print your *true* life story, as told by you.'

'No!' Lili looked frightened and anxious. 'You know the lies, the filth that's published about me. They'll all just dredge it up from their files again.'

'Don't worry, Lili,' said Kate. 'I'm the editor of *Verve!*

magazine, so you can control the story. We'll print whatever you want.' She turned to Judy for confirmation. 'If we get in first with an exclusive story and splash it big enough, we'll have scooped the rest of the world; nobody will want to run it after that.'

Lili said, 'It's quite a story.'

As Maxine poured champagne all four women listened to the quiet voice of Lili reciting the tale of her life since 1956, the success story of the Paris porn model who became an international movie star, the sad story of an exploited, lonely girl as incapable of controlling her own destiny as the autumn leaves that fluttered from the trees below them in darkened Central Park.

It was two o'clock in the morning before Kate let herself into her apartment. She stood in the doorway of her huge living room, rubbing her tired eyes as she looked across at the man who lay asleep on the thirty-foot-long, beige suede sofa that ran along one wall. Above the sofa hung a collection of antique paintings and engravings of tigers. On the floor below the man lay a pair of loafers, a pair of socks, a crumpled copy of the *Wall Street Journal*, and a silver salver upon which was a slice of cold, left-over pizza and a half-empty glass of beer. Tom would never be a gourmet, no matter how many elegant meals she served him, thought Kate as she tiptoed over to her husband and gently shook him awake. 'Bedtime, darling,' she whispered, as he leaned against her, blinking, then suddenly hugged her in a hard grip. 'How'd it go, darling? Did you reach an agreement with Tiger-Lili?'

'Tell you in the morning. Everything's fine, but right now I'm exhausted and I just want to be in bed. How I wish that someone would invent a machine with a button that you press and suddenly you find yourself undressed, showered and in bed with your teeth cleaned.'

'With me.'

'You'd be an optional accessory. Very expensive.'

In her softly lit bathroom at the Plaza Hotel Maxine carefully broke open three glass ampoules, mixed the clear liquids together, then patted the solution carefully around the delicate skin of her eye socket. She used a pink cream to remove her make-up, a clear solution to exfoliate her skin and a white preparation to stimulate cell renewal while she slept. Along the fine lines of her forehead, no more definite than the veins on a leaf since her face-lift, she traced a tiny paintbrush dipped in a solution of synthetic collagen. Finally, her generously rounded right buttock, smooth as a peach thanks to regular treatments to dispel *la cellulite*, received a slimming injection. Carefully she hung up her blue silk dress, then wrapped herself in an oyster silk peignoir edged with point-de-Chazalle lace. She brushed her hair with a hundred strokes, then climbed into bed, opened her maroon leather travelling office and dictated half a dozen memos to be telexed to her secretary on the following day. Then, in her large, loopy handwriting, she thanked Judy for making her so welcome in New York and wrote an encouraging note to Lili. She always wrote her thank-you notes at night, when she was still feeling grateful, no matter how late the hour. Maxine never considered it an excuse to neglect her body, her business, or her gift for expedient politeness.

Pagan sprawled across her old-fashioned brass bed in her room at the Algonquin and again tried to direct-dial her husband.

It was two in the morning in New York, which meant seven in the morning in London, so with luck she'd catch Christopher just before breakfast, she thought as she looked around the small pretty room. Her Jean Muir pink coat was thrown carelessly over the rose velvet armchair and her discarded underwear was scattered over the malachite-green carpet.

'Darling, that you? How are the dogs? Is Sophia doing her homework *directly* when she comes home from school? Are you helping her with geometry? ... Sorry, it doesn't seem like twenty-four hours, it seems weeks since I saw you last, darling ... Yes, I've met Lili, but I don't want to talk about it on the telephone ... No, we didn't discuss the possibility of a donation to your laboratory, darling, you're even more tactless than I am ... No, there simply wasn't a chance to discuss the importance of cancer research.' She pushed her heavy, wavy mahogany hair away from her face and wriggled her long-legged, lean, naked body into a more comfortable position on the lace blanket cover. '. . . Yes, I know I forgot to pack my nightclothes, but nobody's noticed, darling, I'll hide in the loo when they bring breakfast up . . . Oh, damn, did I really forget the grocer order again? Thank heaven for Harrods and Globe Car Service . . .' Eventually, in a carefully casual voice, Pagan said, 'How are you feeling, darling?' After his heart attack, she always worried when she was away from Christopher.

'. . . No, I hardly slept at all last night, you know I mustn't take sleeping pills or anything addictive. But tonight I'm prepared to enjoy a sleepless night. I've bought this absolutely gripping book called *Scruples* . . .'

Judy had also spent a sleepless night. Huddled under the red-fox spread of her big, luxurious, peaceful bedroom, she restlessly gazed at the peach-coloured walls and matching wild-silk curtains, at the pretty Victorian oil paintings of peaches and grapes, apples and apricots that hung from the walls. She was almost glad that Griffin wasn't here; he'd had to fly to the West Coast for a couple of days to launch a new decorating magazine, the first of his many publishing ventures to be based in San Francisco. Only the previous evening Griffin had asked Judy the question that she'd been waiting to hear from him for ten years. Although Griffin was a major shareholder of *Verve!*, and although they'd been lovers for over ten years, there had always been a subject that she was forbidden to discuss. That subject was Griffin's home life. Everyone in the media world knew that it had been clearly established years ago, before he'd met Judy, when that tough, clever bastard, Griffin Lowe, was still being seen around town with the best-looking models and young actresses in New York, that none of them stood a chance: Griffin would never leave his wife and three children because he'd fought too hard to climb his way up the ladder of success and he wanted all of it, the successful, respectable life that he'd established as well as his notorious, amorous adventures.

And then, a few days ago, Griffin's wife had left him for another man; they were going to Israel together, to start a new life on a kibbutz. The long-suffering Mrs Lowe had walked out on her handsome, rich, debonair, double-crossing husband.

What was equally surprising was that Griffin had immediately asked Judy to marry him. What was even more surprising was that, after hearing the words for which she'd waited ten years, Judy found that she didn't want to marry Griffin. Griffin had developed a habit of cheating on his wife and therefore she wasn't too sure that she wanted to become his wife. Old habits die hard.

Silhouetted against the russet shade of the bedside light, the slim, naked figure looked like an alabaster Praxiteles; slowly his fox-shaped face broke into an intimate smile. 'No, darling, it's absolutely safe; Lili's out there playing the biggest role of her life.' Softly he laughed into the ivory telephone. 'I'll be back on Saturday . . . promise, darling . . . you can save it for another couple of days . . . you'd better . . .' The man's head jerked up as the door was flung open and Lili stood there smiling. Hastily the man said to the telephone, 'Sorry, this is suite 1719. I think you've got the wrong number.' He replaced the telephone and held out both his arms to Lili, who hurled herself into them. 'You were right, Simon! It worked just as you said it would!' She threw her arms round his neck and kissed him full on the lips. 'At last I know who I really am, at last I know who my mother is!'

Simon Pont was an actor. A good stage actor who needed an audience to produce his best work, who hated movies and only occasionally made one, strictly for the money. He and Lili had lived together for two years and it was Simon who had originally persuaded Lili to search for her mother. A quiet, intelligent thirty-five-year-old, he seemed secure enough to handle Lili with firm indulgence, seemed to understand that she needed more protection and attention than most men are prepared to give a woman. It was Simon who had given Lili the reassurance she had needed, and it was he who had realized that Lili needed to trace her mother in order to firmly establish her own identity. Simon had pointed out that if Lili found her real parents, then she might stop looking for substitute parents to love in almost everyone with whom she became involved – which is why she was so vulnerable to the exploiters, the con men and the con women that the rich and the famous invariably attracted.

Now Simon held Lili to his handsome, naked body and licked her ear with his long, curly tongue. 'Tell me who your mother is, darling. Lady Swann?'

'No, not Pagan Swann; it's Judy Jordan. She admitted it almost at once, but I remembered what you'd said – that they'd be bound to pin it on the only woman who wasn't married and didn't have to explain me to a husband!'

He pushed the white silk from her shoulder, and nipped the golden flesh with his little wide-spaced teeth. Lili wriggled. 'So I suddenly asked Judy who my father was and – just as you said – the other three all snapped round to look at Judy, so I knew that she was telling the truth, that she really *is* my mother.'

Simon pushed Lili's dress from both shoulders, and gently flicked one sandalwood nipple with his finger and thumb. Lili wriggled again. 'Listen, Simon, she wasn't some rich bitch who'd just dumped me because she couldn't get an abortion.' Simon tugged at Lili's white belt as she continued. 'Judy was poor, from one of those grim Baptist families in West Virginia, a scholarship student in Switzerland, working her way through college by waiting on tables. And she was only fifteen when it happened.'

'And who helped it to happen?' Simon's voice was gentle. 'What about your father? Who's he?' He tugged again at Lili's belt, and the white Grecian tunic slithered to the floor. Simon pressed her naked body against his and stroked Lili's hair.

'That part's sad,' said Lili, sorrowfully. 'He's dead. He was an English student that she met in Switzerland, but he was drafted into the British army and died fighting the Communists in Malaya. He never even knew she was pregnant.'

'Do you believe that?' Simon put his arms round Lili and grasped her buttocks.

Lili thought for a moment. 'There was something odd about the way she told me. Pagan Swann started to say something, then thought better of it.'

'What about the rest of his family?'

'I haven't asked Judy yet. There was so much to talk about. It's a really strange story. Apparently all four girls paid Angelina for my keep. Judy didn't dare to tell her parents, you see. Judy intended to come to Switzerland for me as soon as she was able to support me by herself. But she was only a twenty-two-year-old secretary when I disappeared.'

'I'm glad she didn't get an abortion.' He rubbed himself against Lili's big, soft breasts.

'She couldn't have done that in Switzerland in 1949. It was illegal and dangerous.'

He trickled his finger up her spine. 'So now, can we start a family of our own?'

'What, right now?'

'Right now.' Gently he pushed her backwards on to the grey silk bedcover. She always felt safe with Simon, Lili thought as he began to kiss her. She trusted him. There was no need for him to dominate her, envy her or exploit her, because he was a successful actor in his own right. And she knew that he had her interests at heart. Why else should he have encouraged her search for her mother?

After her sleepless night Judy didn't feel tired. She felt contented and apprehensive. A fizz of anticipation coloured all the chores of planning future issues of her magazine, because the future was now the future for both Judy and her daughter. She picked up the telephone. 'Dick?' she said, unable to keep the excitement out of her voice as she spoke to New York's most famous portrait photographer, 'I want you to take a very special picture for me . . .'

Next she called her florist. 'Do you have tiger-lilies?' she asked, her voice quivering. 'Then please send every single one to Mademoiselle Lili at the Pierre, and put a card with it saying . . . "With all my love, Mother".' As she hung up she savoured that word. All her life she had thought of a mother as someone like her own mother – disappointed and inwardly desperate. The picture of that ineffectual woman setting out for chapel every Sunday flashed into Judy's mind. Sin and its avoidance were the only things in which her mother had seemed interested, and when Judy's father had plodded home from the grocery store to break the news that he had lost everything, all her mother had done was to kneel and pray; she had merely accepted the disaster, and hadn't tried to fight it. Motherhood, to Judy, meant drudgery, dependence and the sublimation of all the joy of living into faith in an unforgiving God. But now that Judy herself was a mother – truly a mother – with a living daughter to prove it, the notion of motherhood began to become exciting. Her morning rushed by in a froth of delight.

'D'you suppose there's a new man in Mrs Jordan's life?' wondered the junior secretary as, one after another, the magazine's senior staff came out of the pastel-painted office looking startled, but pleased, because for once their proposals had been received with uncritical enthusiasm. 'Did you know that Griffin Lowe's wife walked out on him last week?' the senior assistant whispered as she stood up to take in Judy's morning mail. 'I think that's why she's lit up. When your lover's wife finally concedes after ten years it must feel pretty good.'

Every Friday Kate the editor and Judy the publisher of *Verve!* had an editorial conference for all staff. It always took place over lunch in Judy's office. The ten men and women who created the magazine pulled up lucite chairs and hurled ideas at each other for an hour and a half over the long table, cold meats, cheese and sodas. Judy found the Friday conference an excellent way to channel the thoughts of her staff for the weekend, and Monday always produced a satisfying stack of memos which crystallized the ideas that had been thrown about during the Friday brainstorming session.

Today Kate's green eyes flicked over her agenda as she tried to work up the necessary enthusiasm to motivate her staff. Thank heaven, next week she'd be away from the highly polished, shallow world, where, at the end of the day, nothing could happen without the lipstick advertisements. It had been eleven years since her last bestseller, eleven years since she'd done something worthwhile on her own, and now she was itching for the end of the month, when she was to start her first sabbatical – a year on her own.

Suddenly Kate was startled to hear Judy ask, 'What do we think about working mothers?' She picked up a stick of celery and nipped off the end. 'I'm concerned that our feature coverage is getting too heavy on emotional and sexual issues; we didn't get two million readers by treating them as if they had nothing more important to think about than multiple orgasms.

649

I want some solid feature ideas about the basics of our readers lives.'

The team couldn't believe it. Family life was a no-no on the magazine. Few principles were written on tablets of stone in that office, but one of the unbreakable commandments was that children should never be mentioned between those assertive, glossy covers. Both Judy and Kate were childless.

The youngest assistant editor tentatively said, 'The last readership survey showed that the majority of *Verve!* readers planned on working again after they had started their families.' She picked up a celery stick with the same gesture as Judy; she was editing an article on body-language-in-the-workplace, which advised that mirroring a superior's movements was a good way to establish subliminal empathy.

'Let's have a breakdown of those figures.' Judy snapped the celery stick. 'I want to know everything we can find out about our readers' attitudes towards children, childcare, step-parents – that whole important area.'

There was an astounded silence as Judy continued, 'And I'd like to see us become a little less parochial, a little more international. How about a regular feature on successful European women? Starting, of course, with internationally known actresses.'

'Our readers don't relate to these European stars.' Judy's business partner, Tom Schwartz, raised his eyes from the hot dog he'd had sent up. He winked across the table at his wife, Kate, and Kate knew that the idea was about to get firmly kicked at as Tom continued, 'My instinct is that our readers are interested in the new identity that women are creating for themselves and these sexy actresses from over the ocean merely represent everything they want to reject. They aren't relevant to a girl who's focused on getting her qualifications and her business skills in shape.'

Judy was about to protest when she realized she was over-reacting. Twenty-four hours ago she, too, had considered Lili a glamorous, irrelevant, continental pain in the ass.

Kate wished that Tom hadn't taken a stand on European stars, since she was about to do as Judy asked and propose the feature on Lili without telling the magazine staff the full significance of the story. Now she was forced to override her husband's opinion in public and, despite Tom's unsinkable self-esteem, she felt ungracious as she announced, 'There's always an element of risk when we're trying a new idea. But I've decided that we're going to run a major interview with Lili in the December issue.'

The production editor looked as if she'd swallowed a toad instead of a caviare canapé. 'It's already too late. Unless we put it in the Hither and Yon section, it'll cost us a fortune. The printers will probably need to replate.'

'It'll be the cover story, so whatever it costs we're going to do it,' said Kate. 'I want it run over two spreads and we're getting a special cover picture from Avedon. Tomorrow.' Kate raised her eyebrows at Judy, who nodded behind her tortoiseshell spectacles. The rest of the staff, who respected Kate's sure judgement and professionalism, were irritated, but not surprised. Kate's background in newspapers had given her what the staff called a 'hold-the-front-page, I'm changing-the-comic-strip' mentality. Correctly, they felt that she rather enjoyed wrecking editorial plans at the last moment, for the sake of squeezing in the most up-to-the-minute material.

'We're going to tell Lili's story right from the beginning,' Kate went on. 'She's agreed to tell us everything about her early days, even that blue-movie stuff when she was thirteen. Things she's never talked about before.'

'Small wonder,' somebody muttered (but very quietly).

'Can we dig up one of those classic tyre-calendar shots of her?' the art director wondered from the far end of the table. 'Maybe that one with a sunflower in the navel?'

Judy shook her head. 'No early shots. Only the Avedon portrait.' Kate threw a warning glance at Judy, catching the protective, emotional tone of her voice.

'What about the men in Lili's life?' Tom reached for another prawn, wondering what his wife was up to. This morning over breakfast Kate had been oddly reticent about her meeting with Lili.

'All of them,' Kate explained. 'The photographer who put her in dirty movies and ripped her off until . . .'

'Until she had a nervous breakdown on the promotional tour I managed for her first straight film. I'll never forget that.' Judy found that the memory of that television tour – previously nominated as the worst fuck-up of Judy's career – now seemed less painful; but she tried to sound correctly resentful in front of the staff.

'We all know about her relationships. What we're dying to know is *more* about some of them. That Greek shipping millionaire, Jo Stiarkoz and then, after he died, King Abdullah. And what's it like with Simon Pont? And are they going to marry?'

Kate gave her tight smile. 'If they are, she'll tell us. Lili's promised to tell us the whole truth and I think you'll find it's quite a story.'

After lunch, as they all left Judy's pretty cream-and-green office, Kate felt a hand on her shoulder. 'Wait a minute, Kate,' said Judy, 'I want a word with you . . .'

Kate threw herself on to the cream art deco sofa. 'It's no use. You can't stop me. I'm off,' she said, her British accent still distinct in the clipped short 'o' sound. 'It's been terrific, Judy, but I feel smothered under equal opportunities programmes and contraceptive sponges. I want to get back to hard news.'

'Kate, for heaven's sake – the goddamn magazine was your idea in the first place.'

'You can run it with Pat Rogers for a year – she should have been promoted long ago. I'm going to Chittagong.'

'But Kate, who *needs* a book about settlement wars in the hill tracts of Chittagong? It won't sell two thousand copies.'

'That's not the point. And anyway, I've a feeling that the situation's going to escalate.'

'Where the hell is Chittagong anyway?' Judy's new maternal euphoria started to disperse. Sure, Judy and Kate's deputy could run the magazine while she took a sabbatical, but Judy's plans for 1979 had included launching a new magazine, aimed at the generation of readers who had grown up with *Verve!* and now had mature lifestyles, families and spending power to match. Unless she made a last-ditch attempt to stop Kate leaving, she'd have to postpone the new magazine.

'Bangladesh, east of the Ganges delta. It hasn't changed location since I told you about it last month, Judy. The Bengalis have been fighting the hill tribes there ever since the state of Bangladesh was created seven years ago, and it virtually amounts to jungle genocide. Thousands of people have died, but because the war area is so remote nobody knows what's going on.' Kate was becoming irritated. 'It's a terrific assignment, Judy. You bullied me into becoming a writer. I wouldn't have written my first book if you hadn't pushed me into it. Now be a pal and let me bug out.'

After leaving Judy's office Kate poked her head back around the door. 'There's an enormous Tarzan figure out here waiting to see you. Who's he?'

'Our new exercise instructor,' said Judy. 'I've decided we can all work out for an hour.'

Kate laughed. 'It's the mean Irish in you. You don't want the staff to even leave for lunch.'

Under their continental quilt Tom's elbow gently prodded Kate. 'Sure you want to go?'

'Sure. Judy won't really miss me, once I'm gone; she's more identified than I am with the magazine. That's one of the reasons I want to get out and do something on my own.' Kate turned on her back and watched a little wink of light from a passing 747 travel from one corner of the window to the other. 'I'll be on that shooting star next week.'

'How do you know I'll be here when you come back?'

Kate gently prodded Tom. 'You'd better be.' The reason she hadn't gone off earlier was that she couldn't bear to leave this wonderful man, who loved her without wanting to own her, encouraged her without patronizing her, and admired her talent without exploiting it. 'I'll miss you, too. Be careful.'

'Come over here, woman.'

'What's on your side of the bed that isn't on my side?'

'Me.'

Judy handed Griffin his vodka martini with olive on the rocks and sat down in her living room, which had just been restyled by David Laurance in soft turquoise, an excellent background colour for blondes. Judy drove her decorator crazy by decorating one room at a time instead of having the whole apartment done over.

Griffin said, 'So when are we doing it?'

'I'm not sure, Griffin.'

'Not sure about what?' He ate his olive. 'Tell me about it while you get dressed. We're due at the Sherry Netherland in twenty-five minutes.'

Judy hurried to her dressing room, not because she was late but because she wanted to put off the discussion. But, as she started to select her clothes, Griffin followed her and, leaning against the door, he repeated, 'Have you decided when you want to get married?'

'Not yet.' She turned away from him and selected a black sequinned jacket, then thought, better get it over with, and gently said, 'Maybe not ever, Griffin. I don't really want to share the whole of my life with you or anyone.' She carefully avoided looking at him. 'I think we should face the fact that we're both independent people – and that's why I suited you as a lover. I didn't pester you to get divorced and marry me . . .'

'But we've waited so long! I always thought . . .'

'*I've* waited so long, is what you mean, Griffin. I've waited too long. It's become a way of life with me. I've had to make too many excuses for you; I've had to spend too many Thanksgivings without you, too many Christmases, too many holidays and too many Sundays – *they're* the loneliest days of the week, Griffin.'

She looked at Griffin and a hundred tall, dark, astounded Griffins looked back. The entire dressing room, including the ceiling, was covered in mirror glass. Judy could stand in the middle of the room and see herself from every angle without craning her neck. She could also, in a playful mood, give a high kick and see herself reflected to infinity, like a one-woman Busby Berkeley chorus.

'Do you really mean you *don't* want to marry me?' Didn't all women want to get married? Was she really turning down one of the most successful publishers in the country, whose empire included some of the best magazines in America? Was she turning down the maroon Rolls-Royce, the money, the servants, the old-English manor house in Scarsdale, the social position, the sensational times in bed? Griffin's forehead wrinkled in perplexity. 'What's got into you tonight? Is it the wrong time of the month?'

'Griffin, it isn't premenstrual tension, it's common sense.'

Judy thought she'd better be firm or she'd duck out. 'After all, what do I really know about you except that you're in the habit of cheating on your wife? How do I know that when I'm your wife you won't want the same surreptitious excitement?'

Carefully Griffin put his drink on one of the glass shelves that lined a complete mirror wall but did not interrupt the reflected perspective into infinity. 'That's a cheap shot after all these years. You didn't complain when you were getting your share.'

Judy looked at him. He thinks he's a great lover and he's right, she thought. But, for him, the satisfaction is being seen to be a great lover, not simply enjoying himself with me. His constant craving for admiration will always make him flirt with other women, because his ego is insatiable.

Griffin rubbed the scar on his left hand, a sure sign of irritation. 'So where do we go from here?'

'How about the Sherry Netherland? What's wrong with business as usual, Griffin? Can't we continue as we are? You keep that mansion in Scarsdale, I'll stay here, and we'll be together three or four times a week. And maybe Sunday.'

What Judy really meant to say was, 'This relationship will stand or fall on how we feel for each other, moment by moment. I do not want you to take me for granted, Griffin. I do not want cosy warmth and domestic security. Or even domestic insecurity, which would be more likely.' Griffin wasn't used to earning a woman's affection. He wanted his mate dependent, tied, safe and always there – waiting. Workaholic Griffin needed a steady partner because his kind of insecurity meant that he needed to know that there was always someone waiting at home for him, no matter what he did or where he went.

Suddenly Judy realized that she didn't like having a man watch her while she got dressed. She opened the walk-in shoe closet, newly covered in jet-black moire to match the carpet. 'Griffin, I've got something really important to tell you.' She picked a pair of silver sandals. 'Yesterday my past caught up with me.'

'What happened?' Was that why she was acting so strangely tonight?

'You know I was a scholarship student in Switzerland. I got pregnant while I was there. The baby was adopted.'

'Well, that was a long time ago.' Now that Griffin understood,

he knew when to be magnanimous. 'That shouldn't come between us. Don't let it upset you.'

Suddenly the love affair, which had seemed overwhelmingly
important to Judy for ten years, looked very insignificant beside
the new fact that she had a daughter. 'Griffin, will you listen?
My child is alive and she's tracked me down.'

'Huh?' He was suddenly all attention. 'I'll get the lawyers on
to it first thing tomorrow. Boy, has she picked the wrong lady to
touch for a few bucks!'

'Griffin, she isn't short of a few bucks. She's Lili – the actress,
the Lili.'

'Tiger-Lili?' That was what she was called by the press.

'Yes.'

Griffin thought for a moment. 'There must be a reason for it.
She's after the publicity.'

'Griffin, she can get all the publicity she needs by simply
appearing in public.'

'Don't worry, I'll fix it. She's bound to be after something.'

Judy gave up.

Maxine leaned forward and sighed with pleasure as the navy-
blue Peugeot crested the gentle hill and she saw her vineyards
spread below her. She always enjoyed flying Concorde on a
Sunday, when it was never crowded. The car cruised quietly out
of the snow-speckled forest and began the gentle descent towards
the Château de Chazalle. Maxine's mind was already running
down the list of arrangements she needed to make for the
forthcoming week, when she and Charles were to meet a rider
from the French Olympic equestrian team, and Maxine's first
boyfriend, Pierre Boursal, now the trainer of an exciting young
skier who had already won the European women's slalom. Since
Maxine had decided that Chazalle was going into sponsorship
they had entertained more suitors than a fairy-tale princess, she
reflected with satisfaction.

The car scattered a flock of white doves on the crescent-shaped
gravel drive and the cooing birds bustled out of Maxine's way as
she walked happily up the wide stone steps to the imposing
doorway, where the butler waited with a footman behind him.

Eagerly Maxine ran upstairs to her bedroom. 'Honorine, have

all my bags put in the dressing room,' she called over her shoulder to her maid as she pulled off grey kid gloves. 'Send the jewel box to the strongroom and please run me a bath . . .'

She was fully inside the bedroom before she realized that the room was not as it should have been. Instead of being smooth and perfectly in place on the enormous boat-shaped Empire bed, the pale-blue silk bedcover was crumpled on the floor. On tousled sheets her husband Charles lay naked on his back, and astride him sat a big, dark woman wearing the shreds of a green silk camisole. Charles clutched her breasts so tightly that flesh bulged between his fingers as, with one arm, the woman held up her mass of dark hair; her other hand was busy between her legs, helping herself to climax.

Like a stunned animal in an abattoir, Maxine buckled at the knees. Her first instinct was to step back and swing the doors shut, to blot out the sight of her bed, her husband and his mistress. She leaned against the wall of the wide corridor, shaking with shock, but then her tactician's mind told her what to do.

Maxine pulled on her gloves, then she flung open the double doors of her bedroom and strode furiously up to the disordered bed. She grabbed the writhing woman by the hair and pulled her away from her husband's body. 'Charles, how dare you?' Maxine demanded in fury. 'In *our* bed! Why couldn't you keep this whore in Paris, with all your other *divertissements*?'

~ 2 ~

17 October 1978

UNHAPPILY for Maxine, the dark woman was no cheap *jupon*; after the hallucinatory flash of the first few seconds Maxine realized that the girl making love to her husband was Simone, his impressively qualified personal assistant.

'We thought you were coming back tomorrow.' His explanation was hardly an excuse, thought Charles, and his habitual expression of mild astonishment changed to frantic alarm. The girl in the shredded green slip shook herself free of Maxine, then calmly sat on the side of the bed, grabbed Charles's limp hand, and twitched the sheet over his long, thin, naked body with a gesture of possession.

'Charles has something to tell you, Madame la Comtesse.' Charles's assistant looked Maxine straight in the eyes. 'Go ahead, Charles, don't let your wife push you around.'

For an instant husband and wife looked silently at each other, then Charles cleared his throat and said, 'Maxine, I want a divorce.'

Maxine could not believe her ears. 'Never,' she said softly, sounding far more resolute than she felt. Then her voice rose. 'Get her out of this bed! Get her out of this room! Immediately!' Maxine's legs shook and she felt as if she were running in slow motion across the treacherous surface of the moon as she ran into her bathroom and slammed the door against those two naked bodies on the wrecked bed.

By the following morning Charles's assistant had disappeared and a frosty silence had settled on the Château de Chazalle. Maxine was still in a shocked trance, but she plunged into a frenzy of work to distract her mind from her grief and pain; she attacked her accumulated mail, demanded to check the china and linen lists, and sent servants scurrying on different errands all over the château. Maxine's secretary left her office with enough work for a month; without being told, Mademoiselle Janine, who had been with Maxine for twenty-two years, knew the reason for Maxine's frantic activity, and silently sympathized with her mistress for being faced, yet again, with one of the count's regrettable indiscretions.

By midday Maxine's competent mind had worked out that her charming, correct husband would never have acknowledged the existence of his mistress to her – let alone have asked for a divorce – had Maxine not surprised them together, had that bitch not forced Charles to speak. Too late Maxine realized that the cleverest action would have been quickly to close the bedroom door and walk away, then later to have tackled Charles on his own, when, Maxine knew, he would have agreed to whatever she demanded. But now it was too late.

It was not the first time Maxine had felt her marriage to be in danger. Traditionally, aristocratic French couples often lived discreetly separate sex lives, but they never allowed anything to threaten the sanctity of their family, their home and – most important – their inheritance. But Charles was too easily seduced, and Maxine too romantic, to follow this civilized way of life, and their friends considered the mixture of Charles's *déclassé* mistresses and Maxine's perfect fidelity to be an immature invitation to trouble.

After Charles's first serious affair, what had brought them together again had been Judy's intervention. A little of her Yankee common sense had made Charles realize what he stood to lose. So if she couldn't handle this situation by herself, Maxine thought, she'd send an S O S to Judy in New York.

Lili yawned as she answered the telephone. 'Who? Paul Kroll? For Simon?' Damned directors thought they could phone an actor at any time of the day or night. 'Paul, can't it wait until tomorrow? It's eleven o'clock in New York and Simon's in the shower.'

'Simon never minds what time I call him.'

'Well, I mind. Are you in London or Paris? I'll get him to call you tomorrow when we wake up.'

'Why not wake up now, Lili?' Paul's voice was slurred and backed by party noise.

'What do you mean? I am awake.'

'No, dear, you're in Dreamland.' The silky, bitter note in his voice reminded her that Kroll was gay.

'What the hell do you mean?'

'What I mean, lil ole Lili, is that you won't face what we all know.' Now his words were running into each other, but there was a triumphant note in Kroll's voice.

'What *do* you mean?'

'I mean that no matter how hard Simon tries to pretend he's straight . . . he's only pretending. We've been at it together for years, darling. We all know that any actor will do anything for a good part, but Simon does it because he likes it. He *loves* it, darling. He hates to admit it, but that long tongue gets in the strangest places, don't you find? When you were shooting *Chérie*,

Simon and I were in Marrakesh. When you were making *The Sun King*, Simon and I were in Tangiers. When you . . .'

Unable to speak, and unable to put down the telephone, hypnotized by Paul's disgusting, detailed story of lust and treachery, Lili listened with tears falling down her face until Simon's wet forearm reached over her shoulder and snatched the telephone from her. Without saying a word he, too, listened. Then he shouted, 'Shut up, Paul, you're drunk . . . because I can tell . . . you've wrecked everything, you stupid idiot.' Simon slammed the phone down and stared defiantly at Lili. 'Paul doesn't mean anything to me.'

Lili knew that Simon was lying.

The massed narcissi and pink rosebuds of La Grenouille defied the November mist outside; the cheery buzz of the lunchers – mostly elegant women – was a counterpoint to the white, strained face of Lili as she leaned across the restaurant table to Pagan and said, 'I never meant to tell you about Simon, but I'm so miserable that I haven't been able to think about anything else for the last few days. I didn't want to tell Judy because . . . it would just make our situation more complicated, when I want it to be simplified.'

'Lili, your reactions are understandable,' Pagan soothed her. 'That would have been a devastating experience for anyone. It was a rotten way to learn the news, and Simon did a rotten thing in walking out on you.'

'I suppose he was forced to choose. I suppose he was being honest with himself at last. We didn't have a row, you know. We both just sat on the bed crying. But after the things that Kroll had told me, I couldn't bear for Simon to touch me. And, as well as his homosexuality, there's his deception; the thought that I would have been used as camouflage; that we would have had children – just to make Simon look normal . . .'

'Be fair, Lili, he may really want children.'

'I can't be fair, I feel so . . . humiliated.'

There was a pause, then Pagan leaned across and pressed Lili's hand. 'There *is* life after humiliation, Lili, I promise you. As you get older, you'll find out. You have to learn to overcome humili-ation, to live through it. And although you never want anyone to know about it, it's always much easier for you if you tell some-body, because *everybody* has known the bitterness of humiliation at some time; everyone's experienced it, and that's why any sen-sitive person sympathizes with someone who's been humiliated.'

'I certainly know about humiliation, but I don't believe that any of you four rich, successful women really know the meaning of the word.'

After another pause, Pagan said, 'Yes, I do.' Even after all these years Pagan still felt a twinge of jealousy as she remembered the nineteen-year-old Prince Abdullah and the happy intimacy they had shared until he had contracted a political marriage at the command of his grandfather, then assumed the role of Sydon's ruler and embarked on his philandering career as the Playboy Prince of the Western World.

When his father died Abdullah's time was fully taken up with the political problems of his country and the gynaecological prob-lems of his wife, who had a series of miscarriages, a stillborn child and a son who died two weeks after birth. King Abdullah, as a Muslim, could have four wives. Four childless years later he was on the point of taking a second wife to provide him with heirs when his son Mustapha was born, and from the moment his father held the tiny body in his arms, Mustapha was the only person in the world that he loved.

In 1972 Abdullah, piloting his own helicopter, was flying his wife and ten-year-old Mustapha to their hunting lodge in the eastern mountains of Sydon. Because of faulty servicing, the engine failed, the helicopter had crashed, and the 150-pound propeller blade roughly slashed the Queen's head from her body; then the helicopter had exploded, throwing Abdullah through the air and across the desert sand, where, severely injured but not unconscious, he watched the helicopter turn into a roaring ball of fire that reduced his son, Mustapha, to a twisted black crisp.

During the following three years Abdullah, racked by grief and guilt, had rarely appeared in public until he met Lili. For the next year, Pagan remembered, Lili and Abdullah had been inseparable, until Lili had suddenly returned to Paris and her career.

Pagan looked across the narcissi and rosebuds on the restaurant table to Lili, the only white woman that Abdullah had ever openly taken to Sydon. Suddenly Pagan remembered Abdullah's arrogance and the commanding voice which masked his apprehension and, sometimes, fear. Lili had had what Pagan had never been allowed – and Lili had turned it down; she had walked out on Abdullah.

Pagan couldn't resist mentioning it. She said, 'If we're talking of humiliation, we must remember that you humiliated King Abdullah.'

'No, I didn't,' said Lili. 'He didn't feel humiliated when his Western Whore went back to the West.'

Again Pagan couldn't resist asking, 'Why did you leave him?'

'I was kept in a gilded cage, his courtiers spied on me, they didn't trust me. I was an infidel and there was no possibility of his marrying me, because Abdullah needs a wife – preferably a Muslim wife – to provide him with heirs, and my . . . shall we say my "exotic" past rendered me unsuitable wife material. In a word, Pagan, I was not respectable enough for the job.'

'But immediately after you left he adopted his only blood kin, his nephew Hassan, as his heir, so it doesn't look as if he intends to marry again. Haven't seen a word about him in the gossip columns lately.'

'He's too busy with his civil war.'

'No, Lili, it isn't a civil war. Abdullah's army is fighting the Communist-backed guerrillas in the eastern hills of Sydon.'

Lili gave Pagan a sharp look. 'I know that, but most people don't realize how complicated the political situation is in Sydon at the moment. You seem to know a lot about Abdullah.'

'We were all at school in the same little town in Switzerland. Abdullah and I used to be pretty good chums.' Pagan thought she needn't tell Lili more than that.

Lili threw a quick look of reassessment at Pagan; she noticed the Englishwoman's long legs, tucked awkwardly around the table legs, the mahogany-coloured hair that fell carelessly around her pale-blue eyes, and the beautifully cut tweed jacket with a man's cream silk handkerchief flopping out of the breast pocket. Lili asked, 'What happened to you after Switzerland, Pagan?'

'Something nasty happened to me. I married Mr Wrong and then found out that he didn't really love me, he was just after me for my money. Funny thing was, I didn't have any money. I'd inherited my grandfather's estate in Cornwall, but it was mortgaged to the hilt. Robert never forgave me for not being rich. I cheered myself up with vodka, which blotted out the reality of Robert, and eventually ended up a drunk most of the time.' She raised her glass of Perrier. 'You see before you a card-carrying member of Alcoholics Anonymous. I can assure you that I know about humiliation, because I was responsible for my own humiliation.' She took a sip of water. 'Kate saved me. Kate's always been my best friend since we were at school together. She took me over and wouldn't let me give up. I'll never forget what she did for me.'

Lili, who hadn't touched her avocado and salmon salad, said wistfully, 'There's something about the four of you that I can't put my finger on, something warm and protective. I could almost feel it when we were in the room together.'

Pagan finished her last forkful of mushrooms. 'That's friendship. Since we were in Switzerland together we've helped each other through thick and thin – or sick and sin as Maxine calls it. Like most French people, she pronounces "th" as "s".'

'Don't tell me that Maxine knows about sin!'

'Maxine may be a bit of a prig, but she certainly knows about sin – and humiliation. Her husband, Charles, finds other women . . . difficult to resist. Maxine felt humiliated for years until one day she couldn't take it any longer. Crunch point. Separation. Judy flew over to France and had a colossal stand-up fight with Charles, pointing out what he was going to lose if he was idiot enough to let Maxine walk out on him. Since then he seems to have toed the line. Judy can be a fierce little thing when she believes she's fighting for the right.'

'What was my mother like when she was young?'

'Brave, like a little drummer boy marching into war. Her father had gone bust in the depression and that made her determined to be successful. She always worked very hard. Unlike the rest of us, she had an iron discipline. The poor girl never even had time to learn to ski.'

'And my father? What was he like?' Lili's innocent question was the reason that she had invited Pagan to lunch. 'What did he look like?'

Damn, Pagan thought, I'm hopeless at fibbing, but I must make this sound good for Judy's sake. She said, 'He was – um – was very good-looking. He had black hair and aquamarine eyes and beautiful manners. He was terribly shy, like most English boys.

'Judy met him first because he was a waiter learning hotel management at the Imperial, where Judy worked. He was like a brother to us and we all adored him – but he had eyes for nobody but Judy.' Pagan didn't add that, although Judy liked him, she simply didn't feel sexually attracted to Nick. And if a girl doesn't, she doesn't. No matter how handsome, rich and eligible a boy was, if the chemistry wasn't present, there was no use trying to force it. Poor darling Nick had been potty about Judy – when he left he'd given her those two carved rosebud rings from Cartier, but, although Judy liked him, she had drawn away from a physical relationship.

'Judy said he was an orphan.'

I'll bet she did, thought Pagan. That meant that Judy would have no further questions from Lili to answer. 'He charmed us all,' Pagan said. 'Then he went to do his National Service as a soldier in Malaya, and the next thing we heard was that he'd been killed. We were heartbroken.'

Lili did not miss the hesitancy in Pagan's description, or the overcarefulness of her speech, so unlike Pagan's normal easy frankness. So there is something more to find out, Lili thought, mechanically brushing toast crumbs off her white leather trousers, 'Was Judy . . . er . . . popular with boys when she was a student?'

'Judy? She worked so hard that she hardly had time for dates. Why do you ask, Lili?' Attack is the best method of defence, Pagan thought, returning Lili's velvet-brown gaze.

She's challenged me, Lili thought, sensing the bond between the four women, so strong it was almost tangible, an invisible wall between her and the last shreds of the mystery of her identity.

'I suppose there was no doubt that Nick was my father?' There, I've said it, Lili congratulated herself.

'I should think not,' Pagan's tone was firm with a scandalized edge. Lili realized that she would get no further, as Pagan continued, 'What happened to Judy could have happened to any one of us. We were all experimenting with life, we all had our first love affairs in Switzerland and we shared everything, so it seemed natural to us to share the responsibility for you until Judy could afford to give you a home. But she was only earning a secretary's salary when you disappeared.'

'How did she start her business?'

'She worked in public relations, and then Maxine pushed her into starting her own business. In fact, Chazalle was Judy's first client. It was rough for Judy with no experience, no reputation and no money. She keeps quiet about it now, but she was twice evicted because she couldn't pay the rent. She was almost as broke as the Research Institute is today.' Pagan thought she might as well do what she'd come to New York to do. 'My husband was so excited when I told him you were considering a donation to the Anglo-American Cancer Research Institute. He desperately needs a new electron microscope.'

Lili wriggled, feeling guilty. She had certainly lured Pagan to that meeting at the Pierre with the promise of money for cancer research. 'I could ask my agent if we could open my new film with a benefit première in New York. Or a gala in London.'

'Or both?' Pagan had come a long way since, quivering with fear and shame, she had first asked for a charity donation.

'I'll do my best,' Lili said, then added, 'I wish that Maxine hadn't had to return to France. I wanted so much to get to know you all properly.'

'You will, in time. We don't see that much of each other these days, not that it matters.'

'Why doesn't it matter?' asked Lili as the waiter served their lobsters.

'A real friend is someone you don't have to be with. These days a friendship between two women can last longer than their marriages.' Pagan picked up her lobster crackers. 'If both women accept that there will be tough times as well as good ones' – she sucked the juicy flesh from the claw – 'and that sometimes you'll want to strangle your friend and sometimes she'll want to strangle you. A true friendship isn't static, it comes and goes.'

'Then what pulls friends back together?' Lili wondered.

'You just feel more comfortable, more at home, with certain people than with anyone else.'

'But why?' Lili persisted.

'Oh – shared experience, understanding, tolerance and trust, that sort of thing.' Pagan gestured with a red lobster claw. 'A good friendship is like a marriage is supposed to be, but very rarely is. Today the men seem to come and go in a woman's life, but our female friendships are often more enduring. In fact, as marriages crash and the generation gap widens, female friendship seems to be the only growth area in relationships.'

'What do you mean?' Lili was fascinated.

'Lots of relationships are now being questioned and rethought, because it's clear that the old relationships aren't working as we had been led to expect when we were young.'

'So what were you led to expect?' Lili licked a scrap of pink carcass.

'We were all taught that our purpose in life was to get a man,' said Pagan. 'So we all hung around, waiting for Prince Charming to turn up.' She separated shreds of flesh from shell. 'After I married I thought that I'd live in pink bliss for ever; I never imagined that my Prince Charming husband would be unkind or unfaithful. We've turned out to be pioneers, just as much as those women in covered wagons.' Pagan wiped her fingers on her pink napkin. 'But we are pioneers of the emotions, and one of our problems is that we don't realize this.' Lili had hardly touched her lobster, Pagan noticed as she continued. 'Those pioneers knew when they were travelling through hostile territory; they could hear the war whoops, see the Indians and feel the arrows. Today some of us are under fire, some of us are walking wounded and some of us on crutches; but our scars are invisible, and often you don't even realize that you've been in battle.' Pagan paused as they ordered coffee, then continued, 'The pioneers end up scalped, of course; it's the next generation that reaps the benefit and enjoys the promised land.'

'Where the hell is the promised land?' Lili demanded.

'A place where men and women can be honest with each other, and share their responsibilities, and base all relationships on truth, not inadequacies and fear.'

'What do you mean by fear?'

666

'Most relationships are based on fear to varying degrees; fear that your mother will be cross, fear that your teacher will be angry, fear that your boyfriend will leave you, fear that your boss will fire you, or fear that the Russians will kill you.'

'What do you mean by inadequacy?'

'An example of a relationship based on inadequacy is a marriage that a woman enters into because she's frightened that she's unattractive, or she's frightened that she'll never get married, or she's frightened that she can't support herself.'

Slowly Lili said, 'Then we are pioneers and explorers, and what we are discovering is a better way to live.'

'Hopefully, yes.'

Sand and rock spurted into the shell hole where the American war photographer and three Sydonite soldiers pressed themselves into the shuddering earth. Another shell burst at the far lip of the crater, half burying their legs. The next one will get us, thought Mark, his lean body cringing against the hot earth. I must not panic, I must not panic, I must not panic, he chanted silently to himself like a mantra; if the next one does not get you, you will have to run, and if you panic, your legs will turn to water, and you'll move so slowly, you'll get hit immediately. I must not panic, I must not panic. He brushed his dirty-brown hair off his forehead and knuckled the dust from heat-sore grey eyes.

At his side two soldiers leapt up as another shell whistled overhead; they struggled up the sliding sides of the crater, trying to run forward as the ground crumbled under their legs, and the shell ploughed into the sand behind the crater.

A burst of gunfire caught the men squarely in the neck and chest, and flung them back into the shell hole. Their blood splashed over the two remaining men crouched in the crater and Mark wiped some of the spattered drops off his camera. Mark's wide mouth was bleeding, his big lips were sun-cracked and his thin face was covered with sun blisters; his small, pugnacious nose was pink and raw because he always forgot his sunblock.

Another shell howled overhead, and bullets smacked into the sand around the crater. 'No way I'm going to get killed while being unprofessional,' Mark muttered as he reloaded his camera. 'When they roll my carcass over, the last shot will be fit to print.'

In the few seconds the distant mortar took to reload, two Sydonite soldiers and an officer hurled themselves forwards into the shell hole, falling over their dead comrades. They scrambled to their feet, pushed the bleeding bodies to one side and started to position a missile-launcher.

Mark noticed that the young officer was using an infra-red tracking device to aim the missiles. For once, thought Mark, King Abdullah's petrodollars have been well spent. The officer was calm and businesslike – they would have been proud of him back at Sandhurst. Did this quietly competent youth know that he was in charge of a suicide mission? Mark wondered. Major Khalid had tried to stop the photographer from coming out with this patrol. With hindsight, Mark realized that the major was *too* insistent that this was merely to be a routine reconnaissance mission, of no interest to the Western press. But because so much desert warfare was carried on at night, when it was impossible to take photographs, Mark had argued with the major. What the callous bastard had not chosen to spell out to Mark was that the platoon had been sent out as cannon-fodder, to draw the guerrillas' fire, and the major didn't want any half-baked heroics from an American journalist.

Again Mark wiped the lens of his Nikon, composed the shot in his mind's eye and carefully photographed the dead men, who were huddled together in the dirt like sleeping children; both were drenched in blood and the smaller soldier had a boot print clearly stencilled in carmine across his face. Concentration steadied Mark's hands and wiped the panic from his body as he cleared his mind to get the high definition which made his pictures look so vivid. A Mark Scott picture could be sent by wire around the world and not be reduced to a blur when it was printed.

Mark's panic surged back as soon as the shutter clicked, and he watched the other three men in the shell hole work to wipe out the enemy position, grimly aware that this was their only chance of getting out alive. One soldier loaded the first slim missile down the launcher's muzzle, and the officer watched his tracking device as it hurtled forward in a high arc.

From the hillside ahead another shell roared over the shell hole as the angle of the missile-launcher was lowered and again fired at the mortar emplacement ahead, which was tucked under a rocky overhang behind a wall of sandbags.

Mark focused carefully on the intent faces around the launcher. These men would have no chance of leaving this crater alive unless they could get a rocket into the eighteen-inch gap between the rocky overhang and the sandbags to blow out the gun and the men manning it.

Another adjustment to the weapon, another rocket down the spout, another retort as it was fired. This time no answering shell screamed back from the hillside ahead.

The Sydonite officer ordered another round and again there was no response.

The air was harsh with heat, smoke and the sweetly pungent stink of war. Now Mark fought relief with the same intensity that he had earlier fought panic. Cool it, cool it, for Chrissake stay cool, stay down, stay alive. Mark had often seen men jump up in elation, believing they had been snatched from the jaws of death, only to be mown down by an enemy who understood that his last chance would be the other side's carelessness.

The young officer ordered his two remaining men to crawl forward, one by one, taking advantage of every rock and every rise in the cracked earth as they snaked forward until they were below the rocky hill.

They started to scramble upwards. When they were closer to the enemy mortar emplacement a grenade was thrown into the gap from which the gun barrel still projected. Caution saved them. With a howl of pain, a man's body was catapulted out by the blast. Behind the billowing pall of dust and smoke Mark saw the machine-gun whipping to and fro on its tripod.

'Better use the back door,' said the officer. 'Grenades may have weakened the roof of that cave.'

They crawled out of the heat into another opening in the rock, part of an interconnected labyrinth across a limestone cavern, packed with stores which looked like the usual guerrillas' jumble of substandard or obsolete arms and explosives. Over a hundred crates, containing 1000-gram sticks of TNT were stacked by polythene bags, each containing twenty-four sticks of gelignite. Beyond was a box of safety fuses and a crate of No. 27 instantaneous aluminium detonators, half-hidden by a tangle of

Cordtex detonating cords. Further back in the cave were a few primer sticks of TNT and two boxes of TNT flakes. The hot desiccated air of Sydon had preserved the arms from rust, but nitroglycerine had soaked through the wax coating of some of the cartridges, so the pile was liable to explode at the slightest impact.

'Why did we bother?' The young officer was cheerful as he spoke to Mark in his correct, but guttural English. 'One cigarette would have done our job for us.' It was a weak joke, but to the four survivors of the fourteen-man platoon which had set out that morning it was hilarious.

Bright sunlight slid through slits in the rock and illuminated the interconnected caves as Mark wandered below the stack of old equipment. Seeing that some of the crates were marked in Cyrillic script as well as English, Mark used his Swiss army knife, the only weapon he ever carried, to lever out the nails. The crate was full of Russian MUV igniters for use in priming booby traps.

Further back in the cave Mark found crates of Kalashnikov rifles, Chinese grenades, 122mm BM 21 Katyusha rockets with twenty-kilo warheads and a Goryunova SG-43 machine-gun. The inner cavern was a treasure trove of Soviet arms and, unlike the elderly Western supplies near the entrance, they were clean and new.

Mark quickly moved to the devastated front of the cave, where the mortar still stood among the debris of fallen rock and torn flesh. The six bodies wore ragged US army surplus battle fatigues. One man was still alive, although his chest was a gaping hole filled with blood; his lips stretched wide in agony as he tried to speak. Realizing that the man might live long enough to give them useful information, the Sydonite officer reached for his water bottle and dribbled some liquid into the cracked mouth. As the dying man mumbled a few words, Mark realized that they were not Arabic. The man was dark haired and olive skinned but, as Mark looked at the dirt-caked face, he realized that those features were unmistakably Latin.

'Cubanos?' Mark asked.

The man hissed his last words. '*Si. Viva . . . re . . . revolución.*'

Four of the dead men were Cubans. One of the corpses wore a

neck medallion with Castro's head on it. The other two enemy corpses were unmistakably Arabs; one had a prayer written in Arabic script on a scrap of cloth tied around his right wrist. 'He asked the Prophet to guide his hand,' explained the officer, tossing away the rag.

'Mercenaries?' asked Mark.

'Sure,' the young officer answered. 'Intelligence warned us that the Fundamentalist guerrillas had Soviet equipment. It's not surprising that they also brought the men to use them.'

He ordered a soldier to carry the damaged explosives down the hillside; they then threw a grenade into the lethal pile and destroyed it.

The four survivors waited until starlight before approaching the nearest village. They entered the settlement with caution and were similarly greeted, then escorted to the headman's house. A young boy in white came forward and offered a brass bowl of dates. Wearily Mark pushed the food away.

'You will eat!' the young officer angrily told him. 'While you are with my men you are my responsibility, so you will eat and drink when I tell you.'

Mark apologized. He never remembered his physical needs while he was working; his goal was first to get his pictures, then to get back alive.

'And now we sleep,' the officer told him. Obediently, Mark stretched out with the three soldiers on the mud floor of the hut.

At dawn Major Khalid drove into the village and Mark shipped out on a truck that was crammed with wounded men. This was going to be a stinking, uncomfortable ride, Mark thought. Then, to his surprise, two black-veiled peasant women also climbed on to the truck. Between them they carried a seven-year-old girl, her abdomen greatly swollen above filthy swaddling bandages which bound her legs together like a mummy. The child was running a high fever, her eyes rolling upwards and her cheeks dry and flaking as she lay across the legs of the two peasant women.

When the truck reached the hospital Mark helped to carry the wounded into the building. Then he heaved his kit bag on to his back and set off for the gate. He was almost out of the hospital grounds when a male nurse ran up to him. 'Come,' said the nurse, 'come – take picture.' Mark followed him along the hospital corridor. Outside the casualty room stood a grey-haired, tired, skinny woman, with her hands thrust into the pockets of her white coat. 'You are a journalist?' she asked Mark.

'Sure.'

'To whom do you sell your photographs?'

'*Time*, *Newsweek*, all the European magazines; my agency sells worldwide.'

'Then I want you to photograph that girl. It must be done without her mother's knowledge or she will prevent it.'

Mark followed the white-coated woman to a small beige room where the girl lay on a stretcher, her stomach bloated as if she were pregnant. A female nurse was gently unwinding the bandages that held the child's legs together. Mark had asked no questions because the urgency in the doctor's voice had told him that whatever he was going to see might be important. In silence he prepared his cameras, while the nurse rigged a drip into the girl's thin arm; as she increased the volume of the liquid flowing into her vein, the girl slipped into unconsciousness. The smell of septicaemia pervaded the small room.

As the bandages were removed Mark saw a mass of pus and blood oozing between the little legs; her delicate young genitals were caked in a brown paste of what looked like chewed grass. As one nurse gently sponged water over the stinking mass, another held the small dusty feet together, then eased the girl's thighs apart, allowing the coltish knees slowly to fall outwards.

The lips of the girl's vulva were speared by a row of long acacia thorns lashed across with black twine. As the caked paste and scabs of blood were washed away from the cat's cradle of thorns and string, Mark saw cloudy green pus trickling from a tiny opening at the bottom of the closed slit. Quickly, he photographed as the nurse snipped the threads, picked each piece off with tweezers, then carefully, so as not to break them, pulled the thorns out, one by one. The last thing Mark saw was the child's mutilated genitals gaping bloody and rotten as the last thorn came out. Then he fainted.

Mark opened his eyes in an emergency room, reached for a kidney bowl and vomited the remains of the previous night's milk and dates into it. The woman doctor heard his retching and

672

came over to him. Mark said, 'What had they done to that girl? That's the most horrible thing I've ever seen.'

'They made her into good marriage material.' The doctor was unable to keep the fury out of her voice. 'A virgin bride and a docile wife. They do that in most of Africa and also some of the most primitive communities in the Arab states. They circumcised her, they deliberately mutilated her genitals. First, they cut out her clitoris and all of her labia minora; a wife that cannot fully enjoy sex is less likely to stray.'

'But who did it?'

'Probably the village midwife used the razor, while the girl's mother and her sisters held her down. Of course they have no anaesthetics. Then, earth or ashes would have been rubbed on the wound to stop the bleeding. Then they sewed her up, as you saw, with thorns and twine. They leave a minuscule opening for urine and menstrual blood. Then they bind her legs together to immobilize them.'

'Why is her stomach so swollen?'

'It is swollen with blackish, foul-smelling blood.'

'But what happens after she's married?'

'What do you think? Her husband cuts her open with a dagger, then runs around the village, waving the blood-stained blade so they can all see that the bride has just been deflowered. It goes without saying that mutilated women feel severe pain during intercourse, and sometimes the husband doesn't cut enough, so when the girl has her first child, she splits open like a melon.'

'Are they all . . . operated on at such a young age?'

'The earlier a child is mutilated, the greater is the damage, since infantile and adolescent masturbation teaches the orgasm.'

Mark heaved a further mouthful of bile into the bowl. 'What do you want me to do with the pictures?'

'Photographs may alert the Western World to what is happening here.' The doctor pulled off her heavy-framed spectacles and rubbed her tired eyes. 'I was one of the doctors who gave evidence to the United Nations Commission that investigated female circumcision in the Gulf States, but their report was ignored. However, as you know, a picture is worth a thousand words. I see cases like that girl every month; some are even worse.' She sighed. 'But the government of Sydon, which pretends that this practice no longer exists, would be unable to ignore a photograph in an American magazine. Western pressure would force the Sydonite government to take action.'

'Do you mean King Abdullah?' asked Mark.

'No, not the King. The Department of Health suppresses all information. I think they keep the facts from the King because many of his Western reforms are unpopular.'

Mark felt a quick sympathy for this doctor. Pity for the wretched peoples of the earth was the driving force in his life; however many corpses he photographed, however many of his friends disappeared in combat zones, Mark's compassion was as profound as it had been ten years earlier when, an idealistic teenager, he had run away to his first war. He said, 'Before I leave Sydon, I am to photograph King Abdullah. I will try to show him the pictures.' Behind the doctor's spectacles Mark saw gratitude and hope.

From his army helicopter Mark saw Semira on the skyline. The political capital of Sydon rose in tiers of white fortified walls from the green plain that lay below it, on the bank of the country's only river. As the helicopter flew over the white-domed rooftops Mark could see the royal standard flying from the castellated towers of the palace that crowned the ancient town. Even though he was stuck in the desert, Major Khalid had been able to pull the necessary strings to arrange Mark's audience with King Abdullah because the major wanted full credit for the discovery of the enemy arms dump, the existence of which had been proved by Mark's photographs.

Mark was conducted by two ADCs into the King's presence. The King rose from behind his elaborate antique French desk.

'*Salaam Alaikum.*'

'*Alaikum a Salaam.*' King Abdullah preferred the simple traditional greeting of peace to the elaborate extended courtesies which were his birthright, as the fourteenth hereditary ruler of his country. 'Intelligence tells me you have been in the eastern hill with Major Khalid, and that you are one of the survivors of the major's assault on the guerrillas in Wadi al Hasa. Let's look at your pictures.'

Mark knew better than to point out that Major Khalid had

nothing to do with the success of the operation, as he opened his folder of photographs and spread the still-damp prints on a mahogany table at the side of the room. Mark handed him a magnifying glass and, carefully, the King bent over the shots. 'These are really magnificent pictures of desert warfare.' He peered closer at the prints. 'You are obviously a brave man, Mr Scott.' He looked again at the shots of the Soviet arms cache. 'As every discontented man calls himself a Communist, we could not be sure of Soviet infiltration; we suspected it, but we had no proof. You have done my country a great service. Thank you.'

Mark saw his moment. 'Your Majesty, I have some other pictures I would like you to see.'

'By all means.' Swiftly Mark gathered up the pictures that proved Russian intervention in Sydon and replaced them with pictures of the circumcised child being tended by the nurses.

Abdullah looked in silence at the helpless, feverish face and mutilated young body, then softly he demanded, 'Who committed this atrocity? What kind of soldiers are guilty of this perversion?' Mark could see from the faces of the two ADCs that they knew what they were seeing, but that Abdullah's mistake was genuine.

'Your Majesty, this is not an atrocity committed by the guerrillas,' Mark explained, 'this is the result of an infibulation operation on a young girl. I was asked to take these pictures by a doctor at the Dinada hospital.'

Abdullah's calm was chilling as he walked slowly back to his polished leather wing chair and asked Mark to sit down and tell him about this barbaric practice. He scribbled the doctor's name on his note pad and ordered one of the ADCs to summon the Minister of Health immediately. The King then fixed the other young ADC with his black glare. 'Did you know of this custom?'

'Yes, Your Majesty.' The ADC stood stiffly at attention. 'But it is only practised by the most primitive peasant women . . .'

'Ninety-five per cent of our people are primitive peasants.' King Abdullah's voice was still quiet but his eyes were angry. 'Why was I never told of this? Is there any reason for it?'

'Nothing beyond superstition, Your Majesty,' the ADC answered, 'but the Muslim Fundamentalists approve it. There is no reference in the Holy Koran to such a practice, but some of the great learned men of the past regarded the tradition as commendable.'

'May Allah preserve us from the evil that is done in his name.' Abdullah turned back to Mark. 'What will you do with these pictures?'

'Offer them to *Time*,' said Mark at once. 'They'll certainly take the shots of the Russian armaments.'

'But what about these?' Abdullah asked, indicating the pictures of the suffering child.

'I'll also offer them to *Time*, but they may not take them; they're too shocking.'

Abdullah nodded, sharing Mark's opinion. 'Do you appreciate my difficulty? I can give the order for this practice to cease immediately, and the women will obey me. Thirty years ago no house in Sydon could be repaired, no man could even leave his village, without permission of the King, and the simple people will still obey royal commands without question. The simple people are not the problem. The problem is that if I make a dictatorial gesture, the fanatics will use it to foment revolt. If I am to succeed in stopping this disgusting custom, it must seem as if I am bowing to the will of the people, not trying to impose my will upon them.'

'So you need the Western press to shift the climate of popular opinion?'

'As well as Western politicians, scientists and diplomats ... Have you ever exhibited your photographs in a gallery, Mr Scott?'

'Yes, I'm with Anstruthers, in New York.'

'Then please arrange a gallery exhibition of these photographs. We will pay for it, of course. Our ambassador will see you when you get back to America.'

Quietly, a side door opened six inches. King Abdullah's head jerked round. Two nervous brown eyes looked round the door, then a twelve-year-old boy entered. He was wearing an elaborate miniature white military uniform. King Abdullah thought his heir should enter the room like a prince, not peer round the door like a servant.

'I'm sorry to bother you, Uncle. I thought you'd finished.' Prince Hassan had been waiting outside the door for two hours, torn between love and dread of his uncle, his guardian, and the King whose throne he would inherit.

3

November 1978

'Do you mind answering the door, Zimmer? That'll be the hotel maid with my dress.' Lili was, as usual, in the tub.

Zimmer stuck his head round the bathroom door. He had directed Lili in most of her best movies, including the scandalous *Q*, which had made her an international star. 'When you're ready, darling, a small jungle has just been delivered.'

'Check there isn't a small journalist swinging from the trees.' Since the news of her break-up with Simon Pont had flashed around the world, Lili had once again been besieged by photographers. Zimmer thought, thank heaven for Lili's sake that nobody had discovered the real reason for the break-up; but then, they never did.

Lili wandered out into the luxurious sitting room wearing a white bathrobe with her wet hair wrapped in a peach towel. With care, she approached the luxuriant orchid plant. From an arching spray of unnaturally perfect, succulent, pale-yellow flowers dangled a small emerald velvet pouch tied with silk cord. Lili opened the little bag and tipped out a small scarlet jeweller's box. Inside, a pair of dazzling blue-white diamond earrings sparkled in the weak November sunshine.

On the apricot couch by the fireside Zimmer clicked his tongue approvingly. 'That's the third packet this week – now you've got the complete set: Madame Pompadour's thirtieth birthday present, auctioned in Monte Carlo last month. No one can say Spyros doesn't try.'

'Shut up, darling.' Lili threw a kiss to the small, slender man on the couch and put the little scarlet box on the coffee table. 'You know Spyros Stiarkoz is only after me because I was his brother's girlfriend; I'm just another part of the old Stiarkoz empire to be annexed.' Lili tugged the white sash even more tightly round her slim waist. 'And, Zimmer, I'm not letting you bully me into a high-profile, low-satisfaction relationship just to make your next movie a little bit more bankable.'

'Not many women would turn down someone as rich and powerful as Spyros Stiarkoz.'

'I don't care about riches and his power. After Simon I want a bit of peace and quiet. I want to be left alone. Don't you understand?' Lili sat on the other end of the apricot sofa and started to towel her hair. 'Stiarkoz is *just another man* to me, another man chasing me because of something in his own imagination. Being pestered by Stiarkoz is just the same as being chased by photographers, or any of those sickies who write filthy letters to me. To them, I'm hardly human; I'm some sort of fabulous sex goddess. All that's important to them is how *they* feel! They never think of *my* feelings, of what *I* want.'

'Spyros knew as soon as Simon left for Paris. He's just trying his luck as fast as possible, before anyone else gets on the field.'

'Exactly, Zimmer.' Lili leaned forward and ruffled his greying blond curly hair. 'I am the hare, I am the quarry. This is the nightmare of my life, the obverse of the cost of success.'

'But basically it's flattering, Lili.' Zimmer waved his small, neat hands in the air, begging her to be reasonable. 'You're love-hungry, Lili, that's your problem and always has been. But you can't stand men being "in love" with you because you're more intelligent than the *average* sex goddess; you don't want to mesmerize them, you want communication, not lust. You want loving warmth instead of the heat of passion.'

'Exactly.' Lili stopped towelling and flung her still-wet hair backwards. 'I have had it up to *here* with sex.' She touched her nose. 'My allure, sex appeal, whatever the hell it is, brings me nothing but trouble, Zimmer.'

'At least you don't have to worry about that with me, darling.'

'No, but I come up against your naked-eyed, beer-swilling MCPs every time I set foot ouside the door. *You* can't imagine how it depresses me. *You* think it's a joke. But I sometimes wonder if anyone will ever love me just for myself, as Angelina did, instead of being mesmerized by the superstar, or loving because they really want something from you. There are so many star-fuckers, Zimmer, who just want to bed me and run out and tell all their friends, so many people who want me to endorse some body stocking or bicycle, so many people who want me to invest my money in their sure-thing project.' She turned to Zimmer and gently touched his hand, saying, 'That's why it's so important for me to establish a loving relationship with my mother.'

As he looked into the glowing dark eyes, although he wasn't the worrying sort, Zimmer thought, she can't really blame men for the effect she has on them.

'And that's why we can't persuade you to do this film? That's why you're wasting your career time hanging around New York, turning down all the parts that Swifty and I suggest?'

'That's why.'

'I don't want to press you, Lili, but please think again. Mistinguett is such a wonderful part; she was the Marilyn Monroe of the twenties, all Paris was in love with her, she was the girl who put the Ooh-la-la into the *Folies Bergère*, and her legs were the toast of Europe.'

And you, Lili, have the most wonderful legs, Zimmer thought but knew better than to mention it. '*The Best Legs in the Business* is going to be *the* biggest musical of the year. Glitter! Glamour! Fishnets! Showgirls! Sequins! Feathers! And we're after Richard Gere to play the young Maurice Chevalier.'

'Sounds over the budget before you start shooting.' Briskly, Lili tossed the diamond earrings back into the scarlet box and threw it to Zimmer, who caught it with one hand. 'In the hotel safe?'

'If we've now got the complete set I'll return them to Spyros tonight.'

'God, how I hate women who are too pure to accept jewellery. Why are you going out with him tonight if you want nothing to do with him?'

'I'm going to say no politely.'

Lili and Stiarkoz sat stiffly in their private box, hardly speaking to each other as, on the distant stage, Prince Albrecht danced with the vengeful spirits of maidens deserted at the altar.

'Why do you have to tell me here?' Stiarkoz hissed.

'Because,' Lili said steadily, 'I don't want to tell you in public but in private.' In fact, she wanted to be in a protective atmosphere. She didn't want to be taken out to sea, abducted by white Rolls to Greenwich, Connecticut, or flown to Spyros's private island in the Grenadines while he 'reasoned' with her for five days nonstop. 'Spyros, I'm flattered by your attention, but the answer is no. I'm sorry.' Lili's voice sounded suitably contrite. On stage the white net corps de ballet moved relentlessly towards Prince Albrecht, their pink slippers dancing lightly over the hallowed areas of the misty graveyard. 'You've been very generous to me, Spyros, but I cannot accept this beautiful jewellery from you.'

'Don't thank me, Lili. I want to give you everything you want.' He touched her soft hand with his wrinkled one, and Lili could not imagine anyone enjoying the touch of that claw.

Below them, fickle two-timer Prince Albrecht collapsed before the onslaught of ghostly brides. In the box an inch of cigar ash fell on the crimson carpet. 'I am a careful man, as you know, Lili, and I consider all my decisions. Is there nothing I can give you to persuade you?'

Prince Albrecht staggered on, but as far as Lili was concerned, the scene was over, and she hoped to escape. Lili whispered fiercely, 'How many times do I have to tell you, Spyros? All I want you to do is to leave me alone. So long as I'm dependent on a man, I'm frightened that I won't be able to cope on my own. That's why I want to start out again – by myself.'

'What rubbish! All women like to play hard to get. If you don't want to see me, then already there must be another man.'

Lili shook her head in frustration, and her pearl earrings shone as they caught the light. 'You men can't believe that when a woman says no, she means no.' She leaned forward. 'There isn't anyone else. The only other person in my life is *me*. Can't you understand that at the moment I don't know who I am or what I want, or what I can do? I have found my mother, I have the beginning of my new identity, and I want to be left in peace to discover the rest – that's all. That's why I want to be left alone.'

'Left alone? For twenty-four hours, perhaps.' Angrily, he ground out his cigar in the bank of white chrysanthemums that fronted the private box.

*

In the Stiarkoz white Rolls-Royce Lili thought, Spyros is a greedy old reptile. How surprising that two brothers could be so similar and yet so different. Spyros had Jo's twinkling black olive eyes and the rough, tough business acumen, but he lacked his dead brother's vitality and charm. Then, suddenly, in the hushed, padded interior of the car, Lili realized that Spyros was about to pounce, and that she was in a luxurious, pale pigskin prison. Lili panicked as she remembered being told that when a Greek shipowner meets a woman and likes her, he wants sex with her straight away.

Spyros was tough, coarse and muscular. He went straight for Lili's breasts, ripping the embroidered white chiffon gown. Seed pearls bounced over the carpet as his stubby hands reached for her. Lili cast a frantic look at the back view of the chauffeur. No hope there. She managed to shove Spyros away from her.

Spyros muttered, 'I don't need to rape you, you'll find you will belong to me. I will look after you better than Jo did. When he died my brother left you penniless, didn't he? But I will give you everything you want, Lili. Your place is on my yacht, *Persephone*, without a care in the world, except to go shopping.' Again he fumbled at her breasts and, this time, Lili let him. She realized that if she continued to resist, he might rape her. No, her only thought was how to get out of the Rolls.

'Spyros, you can either force me, or you can give me time. It's not . . . the right day of the month.'

His unblinking, tortoise-like stare searched her eyes. Lili held up her flower-like face to his lips and suffered his embrace until they arrived at the Pierre.

She was sweating with relief as she hurried down the long, cream corridor, pulling her chinchilla wrap around her wrecked chiffon dress. At the elevator she paused, then turned on her heel and approached the reception desk. She handed the night manager the scarlet jewel boxes. 'Would you please have security deliver these to Lady Swann at the Algonquin.'

Nothing would irritate Spyros more than giving his diamond bribes to charity.

Angrily Lili stood naked in the mirrored bathroom and looked at her breasts, where bruises were already starting to form. She remembered how her body had ripened early, at twelve; how embarrassed she had felt as her breasts had swelled. Young girls always worried about their growing breasts; they were either too big or too small or too low; but whatever they were like, they attracted attention. Lili remembered how she had hated the new interest of the unknown men who lounged on the street corners of the shabby Paris suburb where she had grown up; even her adoptive father, Monsieur Sardeau, from behind his prim, civil servant's pince-nez, had furtively swivelled his eyes over her body as Lili worked her way through the household chores each day after school.

From the age of six Lili's existence had been a vortex of catastrophe, a downward spiral of misery over which she had had no control. Lili had been one of life's victims – until she had learned how to use the power of her body, the power of those two upthrusting breasts.

Lili had once asked Jo Stiarkoz why men had this automatic, knee-jerk response. Why – even when they were talking to her – men would gaze helplessly at Lili's breasts, and not at her face; what was so compelling about those two pounds of flesh?

Jo had laughed and said, 'I've never thought about it.' Then he added thoughtfully, 'What's so good about breasts is that they *wobble*; when they bounce and they jiggle, a man just wants to grab them. I can't say why; it's an instinctive reaction, it's gut lust.'

'But *why*? When a woman sees a group of workmen in the distance, she knows that when she draws close, there'll be this glazed-eyed, following-the-tennis-ball-at-Wimbledon reaction as she passes them. *Why?*'

Jo had said, 'I really can't tell you. A man has no control over these feelings. But if a woman isn't wearing a bra, so that you can see her nipples and watch them bounce, or if she's wearing tight clothes that make her breasts look as if they are bursting to escape, then a man feels that there's a special conspiracy between himself and that woman because he's wanting to touch them and knows that he can't, and he knows that this unknown female knows just how the man feels.'

'What an impertinent assumption. So they wobble; so does Jello and men don't go glassy-eyed about that.'

682

'To a man, a woman's breasts are something hidden, mysterious, forbidden. And that soft lilting movement is both a hint and a promise of that woman's sexuality: those breasts convey a secret, sensual message from the female to the male.'

'Rubbish,' said Lili. 'That's the cause of all the trouble. No message is sent. When a woman's not making love, then her breasts just get in the way if she's doing anything athletic, or trying to look elegant, because clothes hang better on a flat body. *That's* what a woman thinks about her breasts; they're just *there*, like her knees. I'm not promising every man *anything*, simply by having breasts.'

'You may not be, but that's how it appears to the man.'

'That's just a man's excuse for bad behaviour,' Lili had sniffed. '*She was asking for it*, is what men say, conveniently shifting the responsibility for *their* attraction on to the woman. A woman likes to be admired by, and attracted to, men – but only the men of her choice.'

It was a typical New York small gallery opening. Clutching glasses of white wine, intellectual men wore jeans, and intellectual women wore Martha Graham robes or black dresses: standing with their backs to the dramatic photographs of Sydon battlefields, they bitched about the gallery owner, the other critics, and Beverly Sills. Mark Scott said even less than usual as Anstruther led him from the *Village Voice* critic to the *New York Times* critic, then turned to a small blonde woman who was actually inspecting the pictures through huge, tortoiseshell spectacles.

'These pictures of the little girl are shocking,' Judy said. 'I'd like to discuss what we could do about it in *Verve!* magazine. And I like your other work. We can't use war photography, but I'd like to see your portfolio. I'd like our art editor to see your work.'

Suddenly another man was at her elbow, a tall, muscular, swarthy man with coarse features and an expression that veered from anxious to menacing. 'Everything all right, Judy?'

'Yes, Tony, everything's fine. Would you mind getting my coat, please?'

Judy turned back to Mark. 'Tony is just being protective, he's

683

a little overzealous sometimes. He thinks I work too hard and I do too much and that people take advantage of me. I'm afraid he's especially protective when he sees me talking to a handsome young man.'

'Then let's talk where Tony can't see us. How about dinner?'

Tony's daily aerobics class at *Verve!* had been an instant success, and Judy fell into the habit of inviting her friends in to work out, instead of taking them out to lunch.

As Judy told Pagan about her new friend, the war photographer, Lili pulled on several pairs of dirty leg warmers, all full of holes. 'Zimmer calls these my refugee rags,' she laughed as she arranged the knitted layers over her black sweat trousers, then flopped over to tie her shoes with the well-trained suppleness of a Degas figure.

Pagan could admire with detachment the beauty of the slim young woman; Pagan had always been blithely unconcerned about her appearance until she met Christopher.

After forty minutes in the exercise class Pagan's face was flushed with effort and she was gasping for air. On either side of her, Judy and Lili seemed to be barely sweating. 'Thank God I'm going home at the end of the month – much more of this would kill me,' Pagan panted.

Tony's glistening muscles were set off by white satin shorts and a white T-shirt with rolled sleeves. His muscles bulged, knotted, quivered and twitched as he demonstrated the next exercise in front of a panel of mirrors that now lined one wall of the *Verve!* boardroom.

'This exercise increases flexibility.' He demonstrated. 'Feet apart, pointing forward. Now bend your knees, shoulders down and relaxed – don't stick your ribcage out, Pagan. Now move your hips forward right, back, left, swing your hips in a circle. Don't move any other part of your body.' Blank-faced with concentration, he rotated his pelvis.

Somebody snickered. 'Go to it, Tony.'

Tony stopped moving. 'This isn't funny. It's a basic jazz isolation exercise, also found in many other schools of dance.' He scowled. 'Even classic Eastern belly dancers perform this movement . . .'

Without thinking, Pagan interrupted him. 'No, they don't, Tony. Belly dancers don't bump and grind, that's far too crude a movement. They sort of . . . shimmy all over.'

Tony didn't like being contradicted. 'No girl gets to be the king's favourite unless she can shake her ass, and if she won't practise her exercises, she's whipped by the chief mistress of the harem.'

Stubbornly Pagan said, 'I don't know where you studied your Eastern philosophy, but you've got it wrong. There's no such person as a chief mistress; a proper harem is run by the king's mother and the chief eunuch and no wives would ever be beaten because royal blood must never be spilled. They used to strangle naughty wives with silken bowstrings.'

Judy didn't want Pagan to tease the not-overbright exercise instructor. 'OK, everybody, that's enough,' she ordered. 'Let's switch to inner thigh exercises and stop this nonsense.'

The girls groaned and started spreading out on the floor. As they stretched out on foam mats Judy muttered to Pagan, 'If they're not gay, they're health food nuts, or Harvard Business School robots, or Eastern philosophy freaks. I sometimes think that Mark Scott is the only normal, good-looking guy in New York. And that's not saying much!'

Later, in the changing room, Judy reprimanded Pagan. 'Listen, Tony hasn't had the benefit of your background and education, so it's unkind to tease him. He may be only an exercise instructor, but he's a damn good one and I don't want to lose him.'

'He *used* to be only an exercise instructor.' Pagan wriggled out of the black leotard which made her legs look four inches longer and her hips two inches smaller. 'Do you realize, Judy, that Tony's turning into your shadow?'

'Maybe he's a little over-devoted, but it's because he's been a garbage collector, a guard in a detention centre, a subway cleaner. He's merely grateful that he's now working in an attractive, clean office among a lot of attractive, clean women who all appreciate him.' Judy carefully smoothed on her coffee-coloured silk lace teddy. 'And Tony's very useful, very strong, very willing to do odd jobs for me that don't exactly fit into anyone else's job specifications. And he's touchingly devoted to me, simply because I gave him this chance. In fact, he's almost become . . .'

'. . . Your damned personal bodyguard,' snorted Pagan.

'Is that such a bad thing, considering the state of Manhattan today?' Judy checked herself in the mirror. 'As a matter of fact, if he's becoming anything, he's becoming my driver. I never realized how useful a driver could be until Tony came along.'

'They're useful, but drivers can also be a royal pain in the ass,' said Pagan, wriggling into her sheer black tights. 'They're never there when you really want them, which is late evenings and the weekends; you always have to see they're fed, and they're often sulky. The only way to have really efficient transport is to have three drivers, each working an eight-hour shift. I must say, that would be heaven.'

Pagan paused as she remembered what her grandfather had once told her, after reluctantly dismissing his driver for theft. Her grandfather had said that passengers often forget to close the sliding glass panel between the front seat and the back and, consequently, a driver gets to know everything about his employer's life, because the people riding in the back seat forget that the driver is a person, not an anonymous, automatic robot, not a piece of impersonal mechanism like a faucet. Pagan remembered her grandfather saying that a driver carried two dangerous weapons: his ears.

'Be careful,' Pagan said to Judy.

Judy looked up from her laden desk and jumped to her feet, beaming with surprise. 'Mark! I wasn't expecting you until this evening. I've got a meeting in ten minutes.'

He said nothing, looked at the four telephones on her desk, picked up the nearest one, and handed it to her. 'The meeting can go ahead without you, surely?'

Judy hesitated as he walked behind her, then she felt his right arm in the small of her back, pressing her against his frayed khaki sweater. She took the telephone from him. 'Tell Tom to start the meeting without me, Annette.

'Miss Jordan, I have Los Angeles on the line.'

Judy put her hand over the mouthpiece and looked at Mark firmly. 'Just give me ten minutes, O K?'

He sat down in her white leather desk chair, and Judy switched her attention to the telephone. 'Swifty? Hi, how are you? About the 1979 agreement, there are a few points I want to clear up with you before we finalize.' She dragged a heavy file towards her.

Exactly ten minutes later Judy was still discussing sub-clauses when she felt strong tapering fingers creep slowly up the inside of her thighs, stroking the petal-soft skin as the fingers moved upwards towards the neat globes of her buttocks in their covering of coffee-covered lace. Judy pressed her thighs together in discouragement. The fingers were not discouraged; instead they parted the thighs, pushing them apart so firmly that it felt almost painful; the fingers continued to stroke the pale skin, working relentlessly upwards, then two hard flat palms moulded themselves over Judy's rounded buttocks and squeezed gently, savouring the firmness of her flesh in silken covering.

Damn you, Mark, and damn your lovely hands, Judy cursed him to herself as she stood over her desk and tried to absorb the complicated point which the agent was explaining over the telephone. Right now, she had serious things on her mind – and again she wondered, a little cynically, if Mark's relish for making love in her office wasn't a way of expressing his resentment against the career which, as she had explained to this unexpected, thrilling man in her life, always would be her first love.

As she leaned forward to make another note an insinuating finger traced the crease of her buttocks and carried the movement down between her legs, transmitting a caress through the screen of silk and lace. His light butterfly touches felt like flames licking her legs. Most of Judy's consciousness was now confined to that small part of her body which he was stroking, but she struggled to keep her mind on the representation agreement. She felt Mark's fingertips carefully push aside the gauzy fabric and intrude between her moist lips. The he knelt down behind her and his warm, wet mouth kissed the inside of her thighs, light at first, and then more and more hungrily as his fingers reached deeper into her. He pushed her thighs further apart and she swayed in obedience to his touch, helpless to regain control of her trembling knees.

'Mark,' she whispered angrily, her hand over the mouthpiece, 'darling, this is important! I have to do it.' Judy tried to concentrate on the long-distance conversation as Mark took another nip at her thigh and said, 'I know you have to do it, darling Judy. You just go right ahead and do what you have to do, and I'll do what I have to do.' He stood up behind her, reached his hands around her, unbuttoned her dress and slid each arm out of it. The dress fell to the floor. Then Mark pressed his body against Judy's back and she realized that he was now naked and insistent. He ran his hands quickly up under the delicate brown silk and held her small breasts, slowly slipping into her as she tried to scrawl a note on the desk pad. He pulled her body back against his, rolling her small, hard nipples in his fingertips and with her thighs braced against her desk, she was trapped against him, the telephone still explaining into her left ear as Mark began to nibble the right ear. Damn it, she needed to hear Swifty's opinion.

Mark's pile of discarded khaki clothes on the floor reeked of stale sweat and cigarette smoke, but his body smelled hot and musky, and she could feel him moving gently as his hips pressed hard against her buttocks.

She could no longer concentrate and there was now an inquiring silence at the other end of the telephone line.

'Swifty, may I just look through the file again and call you back?' Judy asked weakly as Mark's left hand slid down from her breast over the small curve of her stomach to plunge between her legs once more.

'OK, you win.' She dropped the telephone, twisted round, reached up with both arms and claimed Mark's sun-blistered lips. Together they fell back into her chair. 'You bastard, you'll get me fired,' she giggled.

'You liar.' He was still hard and insistent in her body, his right hand still closed around her breast. 'The directors know you do your own research.' He kissed her hungrily, sucking her pink tongue into his mouth as he pushed a pile of papers off her desk, then the page proofs of the next issue cascaded to the floor, followed by Judy's in-tray.

Later, they shared the shower in her silver office bathroom, water sluicing down his knotted brown back and her pale body. In the outside office the secretaries grinned at each other. After ten years of that two-timing stuffed shirt, Griffin, the boss deserved a bit of fun.

4

2 December 1978

JUDY pinned up the December cover of *Verve!* on her office wall. The latest in a long series of glossy triumphs was the photograph of Lili and Judy. Judy wore a simple, high-necked, madonna-blue silk dress and Lili wore a crisp, white piqué dress with a low, square neckline, a tight bodice, huge puffed sleeves and a full skirt. Although they were holding hands, they looked different; there was an intimacy between them that was, simultaneously, natural but apart. How can a camera pick up something between us that we ourselves are hardly aware of, Judy wondered, stepping back to study the hypnotic double portrait of mother and daughter. Judy thought, I feel closer, more loving, towards Lili than I ever have to any other person. She is my only living blood relation and, at the same time, she's a stranger, almost alien.

Lili entered Judy's office, wearing the white piqué dress, in which she looked like a Spanish infanta; it was a ludicrous outfit for a Manhattan winter morning, but one that would show up splendidly on the monochrome page prints: *newspaper print*. If you want to jump out of a newspaper page, always wear white or black or stripes for maximum impact.

'Nervous, Lili?' Judy asked.

Lili shrugged. 'What's another press conference? Whatever we say will be taken down, twisted the wrong way and used in evidence against us.'

'I still think Kate's decision was correct.' Judy remembered Kate stuffing her underwear into a well-travelled Vuitton suitcase and advising, 'The best thing you can do, to take the heat out of the situation, is to hold a formal press conference just before the *Verve!* December cover goes on the stands. Give the papers a fair crack at the story and they won't want to buy anything from the paparazzi, who will then leave you alone.'

Lili came across the room and shyly kissed her mother on the cheek; they had never kissed on the mouth.

Judy said, 'There's something I want you to have.' She opened her desk drawer and produced a small, silver photograph frame; in it was a black-and-white, much-creased, blurry snapshot of a laughing young man, wearing a wool hat with a tassel, and brandishing a bamboo ski pole.

'That's Nick,' said Judy, 'your father.' She held out her little paw-like hands to Lili. On each central finger was a thick band of gold, mounted with a tiny, coral rosebud. 'Nick gave me these rings when we said goodbye, he said they were to remind me that I could always depend on him. I've worn them ever since. Now I'd like you to have one, Lili, so that you will feel you can always depend on me.'

'I already depend on you,' Lili said, as Judy slipped the ring on Lili's slim finger. 'Maxine was so kind to me. And Pagan and Kate were so supportive about Simon. It helped me get through the humiliation and the pain.' She hesitated, then shyly said, 'I've never really had a woman friend before, never felt this unconditional acceptance and silent affection.'

Someone yelled in the corridor, then Pagan stormed in. 'For God's sake, Judy, the security in this building is ridiculous! Some lout's just searched my purse!'

'Sit down, you stupid Limey. Lili's just telling me how warm and silent our relationship is.'

Pagan flung herself on to the cream art deco sofa as Lili said, 'I feel that I need female support to help me to learn to live on my own. After Simon, I've decided that I must live alone and learn to stand on my own two feet, or I'll never know what I'm capable of, I'll never get to know myself properly.' She looked at the endless, anonymous rows of windows in the opposite building. 'I still don't know who I really am, and I'm tired of relying on love to give my life some meaning.'

Judy looked across the room. 'A quest for identity is a journey that we all have to make.'

'Spare me the psychobabble.' Pagan propped her red leather boots on the sofa.

'Going through tough times is what forges your identity so fast that you don't have time to notice it.' Judy walked to the door.

Pagan said quietly, 'I don't think Lili and I would agree with you – tough times almost pushed us under. Friends are to keep you afloat.'

Jostling photographers filled the *Verve!* boardroom.

Journalists rapid-fired questions: 'How does it feel to be a mother, Judy?' 'Have you seen Lili's films?' 'What do you think of the tyre-calendar pictures?'

Suddenly, 'Who was Lili's father?' the girl from the *New York Post* asked.

'Lili's father was a British student whom I met in Switzerland,' said Judy smoothly.

Pagan looked carefully at the ceiling. No doubt there was an excellent reason for Judy's little fib, but this was not the right time to ask about it.

'Tits 'n' ass, that's all there is to Lili,' a balding photographer brayed over his shoulder as he jostled past Pagan on his way to the exit. 'None of these junior sex symbols turns me on – give me the mother. Fifty if she's a day and she still looks terrific.'

'Ms Jordan is forty-five,' the *Verve!* publicity girl said quickly.

'Oh sure, another child bride.'

Judy felt the first painful wrench of readjustment to the new status of motherhood as the press turned away from her and clustered around Lili. 'Is it really all over between you and Simon Pont?' 'Are you marrying Spyros Stiarkoz?' 'Is this true about Senator Ruskington?' 'Is it true that you're pregnant?' 'Is it true that you're dying of cancer of the breast?'

Lili smiled, looked sombre, turned left, turned right, crossed and uncrossed her legs because, after a basic clinch picture with Judy, each photographer wanted an exclusive shot of Lili.

'Can't think why I came,' Pagan laughed at Tom. 'Nobody's interested in me or the benefit for the Institute that Lili's promised.'

As Judy listened to them she suddenly caught sight of her reflection in the ornate mirror. Fifty if I'm a day, she thought bleakly. So that's it, is it? You become a mother and next thing you know your life is over – bang – just like that. Tomorrow I'll give away this boring dress; no one's going to write me off just because I've got a beautiful daughter.

*

The December issue of *Verve!* was a sellout.

The day after publication Tom Schwartz, Judy and the magazine's lawyer met in Griffin's grey, suede-panelled conference room.

Griffin rubbed the side of his nose with his left index finger. 'Is this true or not?' He tossed the writ back to the lawyer.

'Doesn't matter,' said the lawyer. 'Truth is no defence in a case like this. Senator Ruskington claims malicious libel.'

Judy leaned back in her grey suede swivel chair. 'Personally, I don't think we should lose sleep over this. We've had writs like this before. It happens all the time.'

Griffin looked over at the lawyer. 'What's the substance of the allegation?'

'In Lili's life story, as carried in *Verve!*, Lili states that Senator Ruskington tried to rape her when they were both staying in Spain at the seashore mansion of the Duchess of Santigosta.'

Griffin looked puzzled. Tom leaned towards him. 'Lili is quoted as saying that he looked like an ugly old tortoise and behaved like a billy goat on LSD.'

Judy grinned. 'He *does* look like a tortoise and every Washington call girl knows he's an old goat. Our readers love it when these sanctimonious jerks get their come-uppance.'

Griffin said, 'Aren't we covered by the first amendment?'

The lawyer cleared his throat. 'Not in this case, because the senator claims malice on the part of Miss Jordan. In essence, he's saying that *Verve!* magazine is repeatedly attacking him because he opposed Equal Rights legislation in his state.'

'He did,' said Judy, 'and certainly we wrote about it, and we have repeatedly criticized Senator Ruskington, with good cause.'

Griffin asked, 'How much is he claiming?'

Tom said, 'Sixty million bucks, which means about five, but that's enough to put the magazine out of business at this moment in time. Unfortunately, we're financially vulnerable right now.'

Griffin pulled out his alligator note pad and scribbled on it.

Judy burst out, 'I can't believe that a lecherous old senator can send us sliding into bankruptcy when *we're* telling the truth, just because *he* has a smart lawyer!'

'Judy, you know perfectly well that the law isn't about truth or justice.' Griffin was irritated by her naïveté. 'The law is about obeying a certain set of rules.'

Tom said, 'Maybe if we call his bluff, we won't hear about it any more.'

'Senator Ruskington has been my good friend in Washington,' Griffin said slowly. 'I assume that Lili will back her story?'

Judy looked at the serious faces around her. 'Of course she will!' But suddenly she wasn't sure.

Two days later Judy walked briskly up Fifty-seventh Street towards Griffin's office. It was odd that he wanted another office meeting when they would be having dinner together that evening. But Griffin's recent behaviour had been strange. Or had Griffin always been odd, but she'd viewed him through rose-coloured glasses, she wondered as she waited for the lights to change at Madison. Or was his behaviour simply a masculine reaction to rejection? After ten years of explaining to her – at least once a month – why he wouldn't marry her, Griffin had been amazed, angry, then sulky, when Judy had carefully explained why she didn't want to marry him.

From that moment Griffin had acted strangely, particularly about Lili, whose name he never mentioned, but to whom he always referred, with sarcasm, as 'your daughter', as in 'I see that your daughter's faggot boyfriend has left town.'

If it hadn't been for the new, and so far secret, excitement in her life, Judy realized that Griffin would have had her running in circles as usual, wondering what she'd done wrong. Instead of which, every time Mark suggested a date she minded less if Griffin broke one at the last minute; every time Mark laughed, Judy minded less when Griffin evaded giving an opinion; Judy sometimes wondered whether Griffin would commit himself to anything, even agreeing on the date, let alone promising to love and honour her for life. The only thing both men had in common was their concentration on their work, but, whereas Griffin never forgot his, Mark seemed willing, if not eager, when they were together, to concentrate on Judy. And what Judy most enjoyed was her increasing feeling of freedom, now that she wasn't bound to Griffin's routine of adulterous deception. So she didn't feel a bit guilty about these wonderful weeks with Mark. Well, not very guilty. Well, not guilty enough to stop seeing Mark, and feeling Mark, and feeling Mark feel her. Judy hugged her Burberry around her; the weather was almost cold enough for her new lynx, she thought, as she sniffed the tang of smoke from the hot-chestnut vendor's stand on the corner of Fifth.

To Judy's surprise, there were two lawyers in Griffin's office.

After a long preamble about the corporate image of his publishing empire, and the editorial policy of *Verve!*, Griffin avoided Judy's eye as one of the lawyers leaned towards her. 'Therefore, Judy, you will appreciate our reluctance for these two concerns to be further associated, and in view of Orbit Publishing's long-standing relationship with Senator Ruskington . . .'

'What long-standing relationship?' exploded Judy.

'Naturally, we do not care to publicize our Washington connections, but you should have known that the senator is aware of our position on the quotas related to imported wood pulp.'

Judy realized that, indeed, she should have made the connection, and she also realized that it would not have damaged the story impact, had she dropped those fatal paragraphs about Senator Ruskington.

'In view of Orbit's wish to distance itself from this issue, it has been decided to sell Orbit's fifty per cent shareholding to Creative Magazines.'

'At what price?' There was a steely glint behind Judy's tortoiseshell spectacles as she realized that this was Griffin's uptown, grey suede, bum's rush.

'Two ten. Ten above market price.'

'We might offer you two twenty.' Judy and Tom each held twenty-four per cent of the *Verve!* shares; Kate held the remaining two per cent.

'Judy, two thirty is a crazy price.' Tom was an experienced stock-market speculator. 'Don't make a fool of yourself for that rat fink's benefit.' Tom leaned back in his office chair. 'God, I wish Kate were here, she'd talk some sense into you. Sure, we made a wonderful profit last year, but it's not in a heap in a wheelbarrow. It's all tied up, and we're going to need all our cash to fight that scumbag, Ruskington.'

Judy had never seen Tom look so worried, and she also felt

694

that he was holding something back; gradually she realized what it was. 'I know what you're thinking, Tom. You're thinking that if it hadn't been for my asterisk asterisk daughter, Lili, we wouldn't be in this mess.'

Tom said nothing. Judy added gloomily, 'I suppose I think that as well. But I also suppose there's no parent alive who hasn't thought that at some time or other.'

Tom said, 'Kids! You hope that when they grow up the problems will stop . . . but that's when the big ones start.'

Tom leaned over and patted Judy's shoulder. 'It's pointless to worry about what's happened or whose fault it is. We should be concentrating our energy on how to get out of this mess. But this time I don't think we can, Judy. I don't think even you can wriggle out of this one.'

Judy thought, it's one of those rare occasions when we both need moral support from each other, and neither of us is strong enough to give it. She tried to sound cheerful as she said, 'Miracles sometimes happen.'

'Such as?'

'Oh, I don't know, Tom. Give me time to think. How about you kidnapping Lili for ten million dollars, then handing the money over to me?

Tom laughed. 'Sorry, I wouldn't know how to *start* to kidnap someone.'

'Weakling! If I can't rely on you, who *can* I rely on?'

As she lifted the telephone Tom asked, 'Who're you calling?'

'Curtis Halifax.'

'I could never understand why Curtis backed us in the first place. I know he's your old beau, but you can't expect the poor sap to be a perennial Santa Claus.'

Judy leaned back in her leather chair, grinned at Tom and started dialling.

'Get out of here!' Tony slammed his black-booted foot into the photographer's stomach to keep him out of the limousine. The man fell into the road, yelling obscenities at the back of the departing Rolls as it sped away from the airport. 'Those guys sure are persistent,' Tony said in amazement as the limousine cruised back to the *Verve!* office.

Lili ignored him, grabbed the radiophone and called the *Verve!* office. 'Judy, it's impossible,' she shouted. Limo telephones always sounded as if you were calling from outer space. 'We just couldn't move – if Tony hadn't been there I'd have been torn to pieces. I had to lock myself in the cloakroom and climb out of the window to get away.'

'Did Pagan get off all right?'

'Yes. You were right, it was crazy of me to see her off. These photographers really frighten me. I think I'll have to go back to Europe.'

'Don't worry, Lili.' Judy's voice crackled soothingly. 'I've arranged for you to hide out until this fuss dies down. You can stay at Mark's apartment in the Village for a couple of days. I'll send someone to the Pierre to get your things. Tony will see you safely into the apartment and I'll come down later.'

Mark's white loft in Greenwich Village had been transformed by Judy's staff with a speed and care which Lili found touching as she noticed huge vases of white lilies, the freshly made bed with lace-edged linen sheets, ample supplies of essences and scents in the bare little bathroom beside a complete range of cosmetics, courtesy of the *Verve!* beauty editor.

Tony ostentatiously checked the bedroom windows, enjoying his role as temporary bodyguard to an international celebrity. Logs of juniper wood blazed in the fireplace, and a light but steady fall of December snow began to drift against the wall of glass that overlooked the roof garden; the faint sounds of the city were blotted out. Lili felt that she was in a warm white nest, thousands of feet removed from any danger.

Snow swirled in spirals between the high buildings, as if a giant pillow had burst outside the glass wall. Lili felt safe. Fresh from a warm bath, wearing a white, lace-trimmed vest and shorts, she lay curled in front of the glowing fire, blinking into the heat like a comatose cat. For the first time in twenty-four hours her mind was blissfully relaxed, so she was nearly asleep, and she didn't hear the multiple soft clicks and rattles as the door locks slowly slid back.

Mark stopped abruptly in the doorway. His face was mottled

with cold, and melted snow was trickling down his neck. He could see the living room reflected in the wall of bronze mirror which ran from the front to the back of his loft, linking the different rooms and levels. In front of his fire he saw a topaz-tinted picture of some mythical creature – half woman and half cat, basking in the warmth. Then he realized that this must be Judy's daughter, his temporary houseguest – the notorious Lili.

For a few moments he was stunned by the force of his own appetite as he watched her. As Lili heard him dump his camera cases on the floor she jumped up with fear, then smiled. 'I hope you're Mark.' Mark felt as if his stomach had just dropped from the fifth floor to the basement.

'Is there anything to drink?' Abruptly, he headed for the kitchen, to get away from this exotic vision before he jumped on her. Judy's staff had filled the refrigerator with fruit, salad, cheese and several bottles of Chazalle champagne.

'Here.' Mark turned to Lili, who had hastily pulled on a sweater and jeans, and offered her a tumbler of champagne.

Lili smiled as she raised her glass. 'You've got ice on your eyelashes.'

Mark put a half-pound of Beluga and a loaf of rye bread on a tray, then carried it to the fireside.

'How did you meet my mother?' Lili wrenched off a caviar-laden corner of bread with her pointed little teeth. She liked the possessive ring of 'my mother'.

'It's hard for me to believe that I only met her a few weeks ago. I've never met anyone like her. I fell for her on the spot,' said Mark. 'We met when Judy came to an exhibition of my Sydon pictures. She looked like a fierce, inquisitive little terrier, dashing from one picture to the other with her eyes shining, while all the rest of the crowd was just drinking and yakking. I loved her enthusiasm. She's using some of my pictures for a feature on women as leaders.'

During the time it took to empty the caviare tin Mark talked increasingly about Judy and, if the conversation turned towards some other subject, Mark firmly steered it back to Lili's mother and the problems that might affect their relationship because of Mark's assignments in warring foreign countries.

'But maybe it'll be easier than if I was always around,' he said as he finished the caviare. 'It's lucky for me that Judy doesn't want the demands of a full-time relationship any more than I do; I'm pretty impossible when I'm not working; being inactive tends to make me edgy.'

'Why are you a war photographer?'

'Because I'm not a soldier.' He grinned at her in the firelight. 'I come from an army family; my father was an infantry colonel, and that's what they wanted me to be.'

'Then why aren't you in the army?' Lili poured herself another tumbler of champagne.

'If you'd grown up with my dad, you would have thought twice about the army as a profession. He was in Korea from the beginning, lost two toes on one of his feet from frostbite, but he was lucky – that was his only wound – until they were pulling out. Then a junior officer went crazy in the mess and shot seven people, including my dad. He came out of the coma with brain damage and, since then, he's been like a five-year-old child; I hardly remember him any other way.' Mark thought of the tall, stooped figure that floated like a ghost around the airy house in San Francisco, always shadowed by his mother's unspoken disappointment. 'The army ruined my father, and I disapprove of war. That's why I'm not in the army.'

'But surely what you're doing makes war glamorous?'

'No. There's nothing glamorous about killing people. I hope that my pictures show the horror of war.'

Silently they stared into the fire. 'I suppose this must be what it feels like to have a brother,' said Lili. 'Let's drink to brotherly love.'

Lili realized that, for the first time in her life, she had just enjoyed a couple of hours alone with an attractive man without feeling threatened by the man's sexual interest. But, as the snow piled higher and higher on the roof outside, the normally silent Mark found himself talking about anything to fill the silence, which would otherwise have been flooded with his growing carnal desire for Lili.

∽ 5 ∽

December 1978

TOM put his head round the door of Judy's office. 'First letter from Kate!' He waved the airmail flimsy. 'She says it's like the West Bank of the Jordan; it's a forced settlement operation. It's a way of invading without invading. Thousands of hill tribe people have been murdered, detained without trial or tortured. And Kate's got dysentery.'

Judy looked up and said, 'Just the holiday she needed,' then continued her telephone conversation. 'Maxine, of course I'll come. Invent an excuse for inviting me, let the situation cool for a few weeks and I'll fly over for a weekend in the New Year. Through thick and thin, remember?'

'You're crazy, Judy.' Tom looked disbelieving as she put the telephone down. 'You can't go to France now – we're up to our eyebrows in problems.'

Judy said, 'I'll only be gone over a weekend. Now, what do we have to tell the brilliant attorney who's going to wrestle Senator Ruskington to his knees?'

'Judy, I wish you wouldn't joke about this.' Tom was exasperated. 'The fees are piling up; you'd think those guys wrote to each other on solid gold notepaper. Financially, we're on the limit of our contingency fund, and if this should ever come to court – which I pray to God it won't – and Ruskington wins, we'll be completely ruined.'

'When the day comes, promise you'll hold my hand as we take a dive together from the fiftieth floor.' Judy briskly opened the file.

'OK, you've got a date!' Tom put his hand on her shoulder. 'Look, I want you to know that if this turns out to be real trouble, we'll be in it together. I'll be with you right to the end.'

'Thanks, Tom. Now, what do the lawyers need?'

'We have to demonstrate that you, personally, have no

699

malicious intentions towards the senator. We have to show that you are not prejudiced against him in any way. It's a tough one, Judy, because the old bird is a Bible-thumping Baptist, the biggest chauvinist pig in the pen, and your daughter claims that he tried to rape her. So he's pretty much everything you hate in a human being.'

'If the senator is a bigot and a rapist, surely hating him is a reasonable attitude?' Judy argued. 'He'll never take this to court, Tom. A scandal like this would finish him in Washington.'

'What's he got to lose? The scandal's blown up already and he wants whitewash. We're the ones who'll be in trouble, Judy – a mess like this won't do our circulation figures any good.'

Judy stood up, determined to rid Tom of his doubts and boost his confidence. 'What's got into you, Tom?' she asked. 'This loser talk isn't like you at all – you know that all publicity is good publicity. We won't lose any readers by fighting this case – they'll all be rooting for us.'

Tom left Judy's pastel office feeling that nothing would make her realize how serious the situation was. More anxious than when he entered, he took away the audited circulation figures for the past quarter without showing them to Judy, because they registered a definite fall. Could Judy's judgement – for years as deadly, fast and accurate as a cruise missile – be faltering at last? he wondered. As Tom passed the boardroom he noticed a few assistant editors limbering up for the daily exercise session. Judy had never been interested in sports, unwilling to walk if she could ride, and now the spectacle of her gallantly sweating through Tony's workout, whenever her schedule allowed, was surprising. Maybe Judy was starting to feel her age at last.

An hour later Judy put her head around Lili's bathroom door. 'I thought I'd find you here. Do you mind if I come in?'

Lili was up to her nose in pink bubbles. When Lili craved comfort and security she always headed for a warm tub.

'The whole world has already seen me in the tub, I don't see why my mother shouldn't,' said Lili. 'How are things with you?'

'The senator is really putting on the pressure.' Judy wondered if she should tell Lili the full scale of the battle that threatened *Verve!* magazine after her fatal interview.

Lili looked over the rim of the bath at her mother. 'I've been waiting for a good moment to say this, but I don't suppose there'll ever be one.'

'Say what?'

'I'm sorry that this lawsuit is all my fault.'

'You told the truth, Lili. We took the risk. Your life story in *Verve!* boosted the circulation. We miscalculated the senator's reaction and that's all there is to it. We're still hoping that the senator will settle out of court.'

'Oh, him . . .' Lili sniffed. 'He won't be any problem to you, Judy. I told you I'll stand by what I've said and what I printed. He won't want to face me in court' – Lili reached for the shampoo – 'because he won't want his voters to discover that the man they sent to Washington is a dirty old goat.' She submerged her head in the carnation-scented water and came up dripping, big-eyed and sleek-headed as a seal.

Judy hesitated, then asked, 'Was he really as unpleasant as you made him sound?'

Slowly Lili said, 'It depends on what you mean by unpleasant.' She remembered how, a few months after Jo's death, she had been a guest of the Duchess of Santigosta at her palatial Spanish beach house on the Malaga coast. Lili had still felt her loss after Jo Stiarkoz's death, but Zimmer had suggested that she try to get more fun out of life and accept a few of the stream of invitations that any celebrity receives.

The first two days had been delightful. The twenty-two other guests were mainly European business acquaintances of the duke, who was no longer rich and supplemented his income by acting as an entrepreneur, a go-between for his business partners when they wanted to establish contact with, and impress, someone with whom they hoped, later, to set up a deal.

They swam, they water-skied, and everyone else in the party water-parachuted, including the Italian jeweller's wife who was a grandmother and trying it for the first time. It was easy, she saw; so, obediently, Lili had been strapped into her parachute harness, taken a run off the end of the jetty, then found herself jerked into mid-air, fifty feet above the little speedboat that was towing her. Lili looked down, her stomach turned over, and she thought for one moment that she was going to be sick. She knew that she suffered from vertigo, so she never stood near the edge of balconies or bridges, but she had never felt vertiginous in an airplane, so it hadn't occurred to her that she would do so now. The ten-minute ride was purgatorial, but eventually the speedboat stopped back near the jetty and Lili floated down towards the blue waters of the Mediterranean where her harness was quickly unstrapped by the boatman's assistant, who then started to gather up the parachute that was drifting in the sea water. Gratefully, Lili floated on the water with her arms apart, feeling too ill to strike out for shore. It was at this moment that a nearby swimmer, a balding American senator with whom Lili had hardly spoken, swam up to her. 'Great sensation, isn't it?' he asked, then he noticed Lili's dazed expression. 'Are you all right, my dear?'

'Yes . . . no . . . I don't know . . . please . . .' A wave broke over Lili's head and she accidentally swallowed a lot of sea water. 'Please, could you h-h-h-help me back to the beach?'

'Put your arms around me, my dear.' Lili did so and felt her body drift against his, then the man was lying on top of her in the water as, dimly, Lili thought, surely this isn't the way that lifesavers do it? After what seemed an eternity the man panted, 'I think we'll make better progress if you let go, my dear, and I hold you from behind.'

A lifesaver swims backwards, kicking only with his feet, as both arms are needed – the left arm holds the drowning victim across the collarbone and the right hand cups the victim's chin above water. But this was not Senator Ruskington's lifesaving procedure. He had, indeed, swum backwards towards shore, kicking only with his feet, but he held Lili's body on top of his with both his hands firmly on her breasts.

Once ashore, Lili had lain in the shade and, within an hour, she had recovered, had thanked Senator Ruskington for helping her and had decided to go to bed early. And that, Lili thought, was the end of the incident.

Lili was awakened by a strange sensation. She opened her eyes and from her four-poster bed she could see the silver moonlight striping the room. Still half asleep, Lili shivered, then realized that the covers had been drawn back from her bed. Sleepily, she felt a flood of warmth in her body that she hadn't experienced since Jo's death, then slowly she awakened, realizing one thing at a time. Her nightgown no longer covered the lower part of her body. Between her legs she felt a warm, heavy, rough sensation, like having your hand licked by a calf. Lili realized that a man was crouched by her bed, parting her lower lips with his hands and steadily licking her clitoris. As she realized what was happening, a hand slid up her body and felt underneath the nightgown for the nipple of her breast, upthrusting and hardening in automatic response to this dark stranger's stimulation.

Lili gasped in horror and tried to sit up, but the hand that was on her breast pushed her hard, back against the pillows, and suddenly the man was on top of her. He was naked, she realized with growing horror, as she felt his hardness against her. She screamed, then his mouth was on hers.

I can't believe this . . . it's a nightmare . . . no, it isn't . . . he must be a burglar . . . And then he'd taken his mouth away from hers and, in the moonlight, she had recognized his face as he arched his back and tried to thrust into her, painfully holding her by her breasts against the pillows.

'You liked me touching you in the water, didn't you?' the man panted. 'You didn't stop me, you led me on, you little bitch.' It was that balding American senator who had helped her swim to shore that afternoon.

Lili screamed again and simultaneously reached down the bed and grasped for the balls behind his groping cock and twisted them as hard as she could. The man grunted, gasped, doubled up in pain and Lili felt thankful that she had remembered this old tart's trick from her past.

Lili managed to wriggle from beneath the gasping, fat body, then she shot across the floor to the door, flung it open and ran along the wide, silent corridors until she reached the servants' back stairs. She ran down three flights and threw open the door at the bottom. She found herself in the imposing entrance hall, silvered by moonlight. Lili raced for the guest bathroom and sat shivering on the cold seat for the rest of the night until she heard the bustle of servants starting to clean. Then Lili crept back to her bedroom.

It was hard to believe that horrible scene had really happened. The bed was in disarray but there was nothing to indicate . . . Lili ran forward as she saw a navy, red-dotted piece of silk protruding from beneath the bed. It was the tie of a man's dressing gown. Lili bolted the door and reached for the ivory bedside telephone and demanded to speak to the duchess ... well, as soon as Her Grace was awake, in that case. It was an urgent matter.

Two hours later the plump duchess floated into Lili's bedroom wearing an embroidered, pale-grey crêpe de Chine peignoir that must have taken months to stitch.

Lili poured out her story, showed the dressing-gown tie, and looked into the chubby face for sympathy. The duchess took the dressing-gown cord and held it in her hands. Then she said, 'My dear, Senator Ruskington is a very influential man with whom my husband hopes to arrange ... certain matters. This entire house party is being given to entertain him. I think perhaps you had a bad dream. And if you didn't, my dear, well, nothing has happened to you that hasn't happened to you before. A gentleman was *bouleversé* by your beauty; he had perhaps had a little too much to drink. I doubt if this morning he will remember what you say has happened. So any unpleasantness would be reduced to his word against yours. Or he might even say that you had invited him to your bedroom, in which case, what does a dressing-gown tie prove? The duchess stood up and, in a polite but distant voice, she said to an angry Lili, who could hardly believe what she heard, 'I feel it might be best for all of us, my dear, if you left immediately.'

Judy said, 'Rape is never pleasant.' She held out a terrycloth robe for Lili as she stepped out of the bath, 'Especially if anyone suggests you were asking for it.'

Nearly five and a half miles, thought Debra Halifax, relentlessly pedalling on. Although she was in her late thirties, her silhouette was that of a girl of twelve. Each rib was visible through the candy-pink leotard as she gazed with determination at the illuminated screen built into the bicycle's handlebar. The pre-programmed rides could be dialled on the control panel; they could increase the machine's resistance from an easy, five-minute trip to the toughest half-hour programme which, her husband complained, was like cycling over the Rocky Mountains.

Although the clock in her private gymnasium showed 8.30 a.m., Debra was halfway through the programme for the second time that day when her husband, Curtis, appeared at the door of the gym. He wore a handmade grey suit, a white silk shirt, and carried a well-polished black briefcase. There is something obscene about a woman who deliberately starves herself, Curtis thought as he saw bands of sweat spreading across the pink leotard below the areas where his wife's breasts used to be. Debra's whole appearance had become a macabre caricature of the delicate little sprite he had married; there was now a monkey-like appearance to her head, her face was deeply lined, and the outline of the skull was prominent at the temples. Curtis looked down at the bicycle dial and realized that she was pedalling the Rocky Mountain programme for the second time. 'Debra, please . . .'

'Don't say another word, I won't listen.'

'But you'll kill yourself.'

'I will do no such thing. I am promoting my health.'

'Surely it isn't necessary . . .'

'You know the way my metabolism is. I only have to look at a lettuce leaf to put on weight.'

Curtis gave up. 'I'll see you at the Peabody's tonight, dear.' He said goodbye with a dry kiss on the top of her head. She did not stop pedalling.

In his car Curtis leaned back and wondered what he could do to add some meaning to his wife's life. He reached for the window control, then remembered with irritation that he must always keep the windows closed. Each day Curtis left Chestnut Hill for the bank at a different hour. Hawkins, his driver, brought the car round to the front of the house only when the butler called him on the house telephone, and both Curtis and Hawkins wore coats with a layer of ballisticproof wadding in the lining – the least conspicuous substitute for a bulletproof vest. His staff were even more exasperated than Curtis by the new security procedures. He had been obliged to call them together and explain that the insurance people now insisted on a full executive-protection programme against kidnap or assassination, and that it was his responsibility, as the bank's chairman, to follow their request.

When he arrived at the bank, Curtis, who was no longer

allowed to take the mahogany-panelled private elevator to his suite, joined his employees in one of the regular cars. Alighting at the forty-eighth floor, he walked down the long corridor between two rows of early American primitive paintings to his office, where his large antique desk stood below portraits of his father and grandfather, so that anyone standing opposite Curtis looked at three generations of Halifaxes.

'Good morning, Miss Brady.' Curtis's secretary handed him the card on which she had listed his day's appointments. 'The usual reservation at the Philadelphia Club at twelve, but make it for two people, please. And no calls for an hour.'

In these impressive surroundings Curtis had very little work to do. No matter what kind of idiot Curtis Halifax III turned out to be, the basis of the family's wealth would always remain stable. The senior managers were all clever men from old, Anglo-Saxon, East Coast families. Their loyalty was to everything the Halifax family stood for – the best, historic traditions of American life: self-reliance, thrift, hard work and Republicanism.

Curtis's grandfather had been determined that the Halifax family would, one day, provide a president for America, a wise, dignified, cautious man who would lead the country back to the old-fashioned virtues and rigorous standards of their caste. He had married both his sons into similarly minded families, and had been disappointed that his two healthy boys, between them, had managed to produce only one son – Curtis, the sole heir to his grandfather's ambitions. Grandfather Halifax had insisted that Curtis's bride should also be chosen from an ideal background and, when she was nine years old, he had selected Debra for his grandson to marry. She had been born into one of the wealthiest Philadelphia families; her pedigree, her bloodline, her studbook entry were impeccable – in fact, too much so. Curtis had grown to suspect that Debra's inherent instability stemmed from over-breeding, and ironically, this would frustrate the ambition of Grandfather Halifax.

Curtis sighed as he settled into his leather wing chair beneath the portraits; he knew he had disappointed them. He had failed to fulfil his family's political hopes and because of Debra, he was becoming more of a liability than an asset to his political party. He settled his feet on the green leather-topped desk and picked up his appointment card for that day. The only name on it was Ms Judy Jordan.

Tony drove Judy to Philadelphia in her cream Mercedes 350SL convertible. He was a fast, neat driver and Judy always felt safe when he was at the wheel. During the entire two-hour journey Judy scribbled memos. She was only going to be in France over the weekend, but she wanted to leave nothing unfinished before she left. Tony never interrupted her train of thought. He now recognized Judy's moods, knew when she was feeling ebullient, knew when she wanted to work out an idea aloud, knew when she needed soothing, and he also recognized the rare occasions when she was thinking hard and didn't want to be interrupted.

When the Mercedes slid to a stop outside the Patriots Halifax Bank Tony jumped out of his seat and opened the door for Judy. Although her face looked strained Judy was very appealing in a violet suede Calvin Klein coat and dark-violet suede boots.

But her pretty appearance made no difference in her reception. After arguing, in the most charming way, for over an hour, Curtis Halifax leaned towards her over his huge, antique mahogany desk and clasped his narrow, nervous hands. Judy looked at the tall, well-built, fair-haired man and thought he'd probably never worn a store-bought suit in his entire life. 'I know we're . . . old friends . . . and because of our . . . special . . . relationship I've done as much as I could for you in the past, but this time I just can't swing it. The board won't wear it.'

'You might at least try once more.' With an effort, Judy kept calm reasonableness in her voice. 'If we show our projection figures for next year, your board will see that we only have a temporary problem.'

'Judy, don't be unreasonable. Last month I went to the limit for you so that you could buy Griffin out, and now you're asking for more.' Curtis looked uncomfortable as he fiddled with the new, automatic, gold Cartier calendar. He continued. 'No banker in his right mind would invest money in the outcome of a lawsuit. And, as I've already explained, my personal funds are committed, long term. This time the answer really has to be no, Judy.'

'No is not my favourite word, Curtis,' said Judy, a shimmer of a smile touching her lips as her dark-blue eyes looked into his pale-blue ones.

Curtis responded with a flash of exasperation. 'That's a low blow, Judy, and you know it. Stop trying to make me feel guilty.'

'I'm sorry, Curtis, but *Verve!* is my whole life and I'm desperately worried. Don't you know anyone in Washington who could lean on Senator Ruskington?'

'I'm afraid not.' Curtis started to feel resentful. 'I haven't got that sort of clout.' The door suddenly opened and Curtis and Judy looked up in surprise to see a fine-boned blonde woman with a beautiful but gaunt face, wearing a dark mink coat with a bunch of violets pinned to it. She said, 'Surprise, Curtis darling!' Then she realized that he was not alone and added, 'Oh, I hope I'm not interrupting anything important.'

Curtis stood up automatically. 'No, Debra. Of course not. I don't believe you know Judy Jordan. My wife, Debra Halifax.'

'So glad to meet you.' Debra flashed a faint smile at Judy, then ignored her. 'Curtis darling, I'm on my way to lunch with Aunt Emily, but I just dropped by to tell you that I've changed my mind. I don't want the emeralds tonight, after all, red looks better with white crêpe. So tell Perkins to get the rubies out of the vault, will you?' She blew a little-girl kiss towards her husband. 'Must go.' She flashed another brilliant smile at Judy and left the room. 'Bye-bye then.'

There was a short silence, then Judy said enviously, 'You can always tell old money It must be wonderful to have nothing to worry about.'

'Debra doesn't have such a carefree life as people think, and you know it, Judy

'What a pity that your folks were so wrong about her. Given a clever wife, you might be president by now.'

'Don't say that, Judy. Can't you ever forgive me? Can't you ever forget the past? You wouldn't really want to be in Debra's place.'

'Oh, wouldn't I!' Judy's light tone conveyed that she still felt rejected by this impeccable man with his duties, responsibilities, obligations – and money. 'I wouldn't mind Debra's wonderful clothes, Debra's marvellous parties and Debra's ability to wave a wand and have anything she likes. Just because she happened to have inherited a fortune. After that the rest just followed naturally – including you, Curtis.'

'Judy, don't be bitter. I really wish that I could help you, and you know that I would if I could. And money isn't everything; Debra has her own problems, as you know.'

His telephone buzzed. His car was waiting to take them to lunch. Curtis rose. 'Let's forget money and Debra for an hour, Judy,' he pleaded. 'We've got so many more important things to discuss, haven't we?'

Judy gave him her most bewitching smile.

It was after midnight, and the servants had gone to bed, when Judy arrived at the Château de Chazalle. Maxine, wearing a lace-edged, grey silk peignoir, kissed her warmly, then said, 'Let's go down to the kitchen and make a cup of hot chocolate, like we did when we were schoolgirls.'

In the cavernous kitchen of the castle Maxine selected a small, spotless copper pan, then pushed back the sleeves of her peignoir. She laughed. 'That reminds me of the evening before my wedding, when my mother gave me some advice.' She poured milk from an enamelled jug. 'She told me that if I cooked chocolate late at night after a party, I should always remove my fur coat, because otherwise I would singe the cuffs.' Maxine whisked the foaming chocolate, then poured it into porcelain cups. 'That was the only advice she gave me about married life – not much use, in these circumstances.' Suddenly Maxine put her head in her hands and her heavy blonde hair tumbled around her face as she began to cry. Judy put an arm round her heaving shoulders and waited for the shuddering sobs to stop.

'What am I going to do, Judy?' Maxine sobbed in despair. 'Charles has moved into his dressing room. He won't look at me and he doesn't speak to me. I feel so humiliated, so rejected.'

'What is she like?' Judy asked. 'Blonde? Beautiful? Slim?'

'No, no. She has no style, no delicacy. She's the sort of woman who wears a black bra under a white blouse,' Maxine sniffled.

'She must have something that Charles wants. And she sounds determined to have him, doesn't she?'

Maxine sat up and looked indignant. Good, thought Judy, she

won't be able to cope with the situation from a position of complete despair – she needs to be a little angry.

Maxine said, 'I'm sure that the bitch deliberately staged the whole thing. I sent a telex from the Plaza, giving Charles my flight time. She should have known that I was coming. I'm sure she never showed it to him. Charles can't stand rows, and he's always been absolutely discreet. I can't think how she managed to get him into bed in our home.'

'Maybe she bullied him into it,' Judy said softly. 'It's the classic mistress's move. Maybe Charles likes being bullied a bit?'

'But why would Charles . . .' Maxine began to protest, then she saw what Judy meant. Perhaps this awful woman appealed to Charles precisely because she was so domineering. She remembered that olive body writhing furiously on top of her husband, but Maxine could not recall the last time that she had climbed on top of Charles when they made love. She felt horribly exposed in such a position, showing the beginnings of a little double chin, looking fatter than she was to Charles below. Placid and easily contented, Maxine suddenly realized that she had lazily allowed Charles to assume all the responsibility for whatever had happened under the blue silk canopy; it was years since he had tumbled her wickedly in any other environment, as he had loved to do before they were married.

She pushed away her cup. 'I can't believe that he really wants to marry her – he can't possibly, she would destroy the business within a year. Please help me, Judy.'

'Maybe it's Charles who needs help,' said Judy, 'help to get out of a situation that he never wanted to be in. I've dealt with predatory women before.' She sipped her chocolate. 'Why on earth did you hire her?'

'We'd been asked to advise the Chinese government on the development of their own champagne industry – that bitch had a degree in Oriental studies.'

Maxine sat at her gold-columned dressing table, which had once belonged to the Empress Josephine. The light of the raw February morning, intensified by the crisp crust of snow on the grey parapet of the château, was harsh on her drawn face. The antique mirror reflected, with a dead grey radiance, the face of an opulently beautiful, but very anxious woman. She thought, I used to be a decorator, why ever did I design a grey bedroom? Why did I let good taste take the place of sensuality? What did my Aunt Hortense say? That no woman over thirty should wear grey.

A cheap office duplicate book was always near Maxine, so that she could immediately make notes and distribute them to her staff through Mademoiselle Janine, her secretary. Now she pulled a book from the dressing-table drawer and, by the time her maid came in, she had completed a new decoration scheme for the bedroom.

'Not sables this morning, Honorine, they're so heavy and dark,' she said as the elderly woman in black moved towards the fur closet. 'It's a long time since I wore the red fox. And for this evening, please lay out my pink Saint-Laurent with the red petticoat.'

With only ten guests to consider, Maxine had organized a simple programme; partridge-shooting on the estate, riding through the vineyards, cards and conversation for those who preferred to stay warm indoors and, on Sunday, a stag hunt on the neighbouring estate.

Charles was the first down to breakfast in the yellow Chinese morning room.

Diffident and modest, Charles was attractive in his sheer helplessness; it was the sweet, absent-minded Cary Grant bit that the girls fell for, Maxine had explained to Judy. Now, looking guilty, he stood in his favourite position, feet astride, back to the crackling logs in the fireplace.

Next to enter was Guy Saint-Simon, yawning in his navy foulard dressing gown. 'The Louis Quinze bed needs a new mattress, Maxine.'

Guy was getting chubby, Maxine thought, and his hemp-coloured hair was starting to recede from his forehead, but the slightly hooked Roman nose and the wide, sensual mouth were unchanged. She was still amazed that her childhood friend had metamorphosed into one of the top fashion designers of France, with his own chain of boutiques, 'Limited Editions'.

Guy pulled his square-framed black spectacles out of his breast pocket, stuck them on his nose, and picked up *Le Monde*. Slowly, all Maxine's guests entered, chose their food from the heated silver chafing dishes on the mahogany sideboard and sat down at the breakfast table.

A tall man beamed good morning at Maxine as he sat down next to her. 'Maxine, you defy time.'

'So do you, Pierre,' Maxine replied, thinking that it was indeed almost true. Living in the fierce Alpine climate had tanned her first lover's face a deep, leathery brown; the etched straight lines around his eyes were white against the tan, but his tightly curled blond hair was as thick as ever and his body looked hard and strong.

Judy was the last person to appear in the morning room. Her first reaction upon waking had been to telephone an old friend, now the head of *Time*'s Paris bureau. 'I can't tell you why I'm asking,' she began confidently, 'but I need to find a job for a girl with a degree in Oriental studies – something that involves a lot of travel, or even a posting abroad.'

That afternoon, while the other guests were shooting, Judy won four hands of piquet from Guy before he threw the cards at her, yelling, 'You haven't changed a bit in twenty years. A game is never a game with you. You Americans are obsessed by winning. You always want to be first. Here in France we know it's much more important to be first class.' In spite of his careless pose of witty decadence, Judy knew that the secret of Guy's success was an obsession with quality and the ability to work like a dog.

Judy picked up a purple paperweight and pretended to throw it at Guy, who laughingly held his hand up to ward it off, saying, 'I know you won't throw that hunk of amethyst at me. Kate gave it to Maxine as a wedding present.' Suddenly he stopped laughing. 'It was such a pretty wedding. I can't bear to see Maxine looking so unhappy today. I always know when Charles is fooling around because Maxine dresses so badly. Lugubrious colours and no jewellery. She really ought to give Charles a dose of his own medicine instead of letting him walk all over her.'

The butler appeared. 'A telephone call for Mademoiselle Jordan in the library.' Judy followed him to the panelled library where, in the rich atmosphere of hush, dust and old leather, she learned that Montpellier University had just acquired an important bequest of ancient Chinese jade and ceramics and was searching for a properly qualified curator to identify and catalogue the pieces, working in liaison with the People's Museum in Peking. Back home, a good networker can get to anyone in three moves, thought Judy, and asked Maxine if she knew anyone who knew anyone at Montpellier University. After a few minutes spent with her nose stuck in her maroon address book Maxine said, 'The best I can do is Ghislaine, my cousin, who is married to the Rector of Grenoble.'

It took four more contacts, six telephone calls and the rest of the afternoon to discover that Montpellier University had unsuccessfully advertised the curator's post for three months and were delighted by Maxine's recommendation.

At dinner Judy caught Maxine's eye between the silver trumpets of the flower-laden épergnes. Unobtrusively, she gave the thumbs-up sign.

'I can't thank you enough,' said Maxine later, as she slipped off her coral velvet dinner dress and reached into one of her closets for a pale-turquoise satin peignoir.

'Other people's problems are always easier to solve than your own.' Judy grinned at Maxine in the mirror. 'Especially their amorous problems. And we all have them.'

'Do you have them with this new young man of yours? Twenty-nine years old, isn't he?' Maxine tied her sash and looked up under her lashes. 'What is love like, Judy, with a much younger man?'

'Maxine, you sound like a soap opera. There *is* a difference and it *is* important, but not in the way you think. What's important isn't that women are starting to go to bed with younger men; what's important is that age no longer smacks of terror to a woman. Women often fail to develop a strong sense of personal identity until they're into their thirties or forties; it's then that they start to find out who they really are and what sort of man they really want.' There was a thoughtful pause, then Judy added, 'Anyhow, age doesn't come into our relationship; Mark and I suit each other because we're both independent and we respect each other's freedom. What he gets is a woman who admires his talent, respects his commitment, and doesn't want to cling to him for status or affection. And what I get out of it is a wonderful lover who doesn't demand hot dinners every night.'

'As I never cook, that would be no advantage.'

'A younger man's demands and expectations are different from those of men who can remember the Second World War as well as the sexual revolution.'

'In what way?' Maxine fluffed up her maribou collar.

'Older men don't like a woman to spread her wings in case that might get in the way of their wings. But a younger man is adventurous, and interested in having a woman who isn't only going to boost his ego but develop her own personality; that's what they like in an older woman and that's what they respect.'

'But aren't you afraid of the future, Judy, of looking an old hag, of being abandoned, of being humiliated?'

'There's the possibility of that at any age. With any relationship you can expect suffering when it ends, plus a kick in the pants to your pride.'

Maxine said, 'Men can get away with so much more than a woman.'

'The world has always known that a man can be fascinating at any age. Now we're finding out that a woman can be as well. Women have always been exterior-oriented, but we all know beautiful women who are dull. Fascination has nothing to do with the tortoise-like state of your neck, but the unwrinkled state of your mind.'

Maxine rushed to the mirror. 'You think my neck is like a tortoise's?'

Judy grinned. 'Maxine, I'm never sure whether you're into vanity or self-improvement.'

'Take care of Lili for me, Mark,' were Judy's parting words to her lover before she left New York. He had been dismayed. While Judy was present in his life and his bed, Mark could control the way that he was growing to feel about Lili but, without Judy, he was alone and at the mercy of the violent desire that Lili aroused in him. Hating to be out of control of himself, Mark found himself transferring the dislike of his own weakness on to the cause of it. Irritably, he complained to Lili that she was making his apartment untidy, and pointed to the make-up and magazines that were scattered over the living-room floor in front of the fire.

'I can't help it.' Lili looked surprised. 'I'm *stuck* here all day. I can't go outside because of the photographers.'

'Oh, don't be so dramatic; there's no reason not to go out. If you avoid the smart parts of town and stick to the places where nobody would expect to see a filmstar, you won't have any trouble.'

Lili looked sulkily defiant.

'Come on,' said Mark, 'I'll show you.'

He took her for lunch on Saturday to a tiny Oriental restaurant and listened patiently while Lili talked about the Mistinguett part that she had been offered. 'I'm not sure that I want to do it. I may be an international star but I think the part needs a brilliant dancer. There's more singing and dancing than I've ever done before, and I'm not sure I'm good enough. I'm afraid of making a fool of myself. Do you think I should do it?'

'I'm not the right person to ask, Lili. Surely your agent knows if you can do it. Why not talk to him?' As Mark passed Lili a bamboo steamer he thought that Judy never asked him to make her business decisions. He was desperately looking for traits to criticize in Lili and praise in Judy.

Later Mark took her to see the Rembrandts in the Metropolitan Museum and afterwards they walked through the dirty slush of Central Park. The snow howled down again in the evening, so they struggled no further than the Italian restaurant on the corner.

'Do you know,' Mark asked, 'how to get a free bottle of wine in an Italian restaurant? No? I thought not.' So he told the waiter that it was Lili's birthday, whereupon the rotund padrone rushed out of the kitchen, kissed her wetly on both cheeks and presented them with a bottle of Italian sparkling wine – on the house.

'Have you ever tried that with Judy?' Lili asked.

'No, I haven't done it since I was a kid.' Mark poured the wine. 'Don't worry. I'll pay for it in with the tip. Happy Birthday! Judy doesn't like Italian restaurants. She says the food's too tempting. She's very disciplined, as you know. It's one of the things I admire about her.'

'What are the others?' Lili crunched a slice of fennel.

'Lots of things, not just a couple. Apart from the fact that

Judy's clever and fun, I like her professionalism and her energy, her poise and her experience . . .'

'And her status, her position and her influential, interesting friends?' asked Lili cynically.

'Of course, why not? Like I said, lots of things. Some of the things I like about her are things that other people might not like. She can be sharp and tart. But that's part of being a straight-shooter. Women never understand that a man doesn't fall for this or that in a woman. He doesn't like the breasts but not the hips, like the eyes but not the nose. He doesn't like the wit but not the criticism. A man falls for the whole package, whatever it is. But women don't seem to view themselves that way. They're always worrying about the few things in themselves that they wish were different. But Judy doesn't waste time that way. And I like the way she's prepared to help me.'

'How?' Lili was astonished.

'She made me feel self-confident. A long time before I met Judy I lived with a model, but eventually I got tired of feeling like somebody else's supporting cast.' He refilled Lili's glass. 'However self-confident a young guy looks, he's probably uncertain of what he can do. It's good to get reassurance from someone whose opinion and experience he can respect – and who isn't his mother. He knows his mother thinks he's wonderful.' He laughed. 'Judy used to worry because she thought she had some sort of maternal attraction for me, but it isn't a bit like that. I already have a wonderful mother, so I don't need another one.'

'Isn't she lonely, though, when you're away?' Lili asked.

'I don't know.' It had never occurred to him that shiny, confident, poised Judy might ever feel lonely. In spite of himself, he again compared the two women. Lili ate lustily, Judy picked at food. Lili bored him with her indecision over the Mistinguett film, Judy never talked about her business when she was with him.

On Sunday morning Mark taught Lili to make popcorn, but it worried Mark to stand in the tiny kitchen right up against Lili and her animal magnetism. On Sunday afternoon they went to a scruffy little Chinese puppet theatre off Lower Broadway. The narrow benches were filled with noisy families. The owner welcomed Mark to his own bench and sat them between a moon-faced baby and his grandmother. In such surroundings, free from her crushing public image, Lili's natural grace flowered. Mark watched her take the baby on her knee to look at the dragons and the gods fight it out for the lily-footed maidens. The rest of the family chattered, smiled and nodded their approval as the baby threw handfuls of cookie crumbs on Lili's pink suede suit and tugged her hair over her face. So much, thought Mark, for the world's best-known sex symbol.

Maxine shivered on the high seat as the antique racing carriage followed the stag hunt through the forest. Cheeks stung scarlet with the bracing cold, she was feeling a little apprehensive. Shortly after they entered the humid forest three heavy, lumbering red deer had splashed across the muddy track ahead of the hunt. The tufters immediately leaped forward, baying with excitement. The mounted huntsmen, resplendent in gold-collared jackets, tore after the shaggy deerhounds, and the musical calls of their antique brass horns echoed plaintively through the forest.

Pierre, who was gently holding in the eager horses, turned to Maxine. As the high bench seat bounced on its curved black springs Maxine felt the stealthy pressure of his thigh against hers underneath the thick fur rug which was tucked around their knees.

'Is there a short cut? We don't want to get bogged down on this wet track.' Again Pierre pressed his hard thigh firmly against Maxine's soft leg. Message received and understood, thought Maxine as she pointed. 'If you take that track through the beeches, we can meet up with them at the bottom of the hill.'

The horses trotted swiftly as Pierre leaned closer to Maxine, and then suddenly turned and quickly brushed his lips against hers. Equally suddenly, Maxine thought, why *not*? He's been flirting with me for the whole weekend and I love it. It's especially flattering when your first lover makes it clear that he still wants to go to bed with you. I have been faithful to Charles for twenty years, and my reward was that bitch in my bed.

Maxine felt flattered, excited and a little nervous, which is the essence of flirtation. 'There's a barn a bit further on,' she suggested as they bounced past tall trees hung with tattered brown leaves.

'Perfect,' said Pierre. They both knew that an invitation had been issued and accepted.

Outside the high timbered barn Maxine now shivered with anticipation as Pierre put blankets on both horses and looped the long reins over the carriage hook. 'It's a hay barn,' said Maxine, so he brought out half a bale, grunting, 'This should keep them happy for hours.'

Then he turned and looked at her for a moment. As they faced each other he cupped her chin in his hands and quickly and firmly kissed her chilled lips. 'Let's climb to the top where it's warm.'

He caught her hand and they scrambled up the prickly steps of hay to the top. Pierre threw the fur carriage rug on the sweet-smelling hay, then leaned towards Maxine. At first she was taut and trembled, but then her tension dissolved and she felt soft and boneless as a pillow. He took her in his arms and, as he pressed her to his body, Maxine felt a long-forgotten lurch of pleasure. Warm, melting desire was heightened by the fact it was forbidden. She whispered, 'I can't stand up, my knees are shaking.'

'So are mine.'

Together they fell against the tightly baled hay. His fingers felt under the glossy red fox of her coat; her trembling fingers undid the fasteners, then he was pulling up her russet sweater and pulling down the lace cups of her bra. 'Maxine, your breasts haven't changed.' He teased her nipple with his tongue, then started to move from one breast to the other, nipping the little peaks with his teeth. Maxine purred with sensual pleasure, thinking that there must be a bit of inner, magic elastic tugging from the nipples to the groin.

This is it, Maxine told herself, this is the moment when all you want is to lie back and let this easy pleasure wash over you. But perhaps that had been what had gone wrong between her and Charles. She had always expected him to do it to her; she had always been passive and timid in a way that people who knew Maxine out of bed would never have believed possible. If only she hadn't been plump, if only she had been the perfect

718

shape, then she wouldn't have been so shy and self-conscious, wouldn't have minded bouncing around erotically all over the bed. But she was, so she didn't.

Pierre pressed her breasts together and ran his tongue down her cleavage. How can I do things to him while he's doing things to me? thought Maxine. I can't concentrate on two things at once; when he's kissing my breasts and driving me out of my skull with excitement, I can't think, I can't do, I can only feel.

'My turn now,' said Pierre, as if mind-reading. He rolled over on his side and unclasped the buckle of his belt, then Maxine reached for his hard, solid body.

Later Pierre gently pushed her head downwards and Maxine licked the pink tip of his penis, which swayed as she took it between her lips. She steadied it with her cold hand, hoping that she wouldn't shrivel him. She was terrified of biting him by accident. She tucked her lips over her teeth, making a hollow monkey mouth which slid easily over the penis. No way could she get all of this in her mouth, she worried.

Pierre wriggled. 'Move your hand and mouth up and down together at the same time with the same rhythm.' Sprawled happily on the fur rug, Pierre made small involuntary movements with his hips towards her mouth. I seem to be doing it right, thought Maxine. She could feel a bump under the ridge of his penis, so she swirled her tongue round it experimentally. Pierre whinnied with delight, and his hips jumped eagerly towards her mouth. Maxine lost the rhythm, panicked, and thought she was going to choke; then she felt Pierre's hands on her head, gently guiding her. Suddenly, she felt quite powerful and very pleased with herself.

Later Pierre pulled the red fox fur tenderly over her plump, white body then nuzzled underneath into her softness. 'I have dreamed of your breasts for twenty years. Did you ever think of me?'

Maxine thought this must be standard, French post-coital dialogue, so she did her best to reply in the same vein of syrup. 'Of course. Doesn't every woman always remember her first lover?' He raised the glossy fur and dropped a kiss of homage on her soft, honey-coloured pubic hair.

'What about your wife, Pierre?' she said curiously.

'Obviously you're not used to committing adultery, Maxine. Rule one is never to mention the wife but, since you ask, she is obsessed by the children and we do our duty every Saturday.'

Maxine thought, that sounds like Charles and me.

'You're not just after our sponsorship for your skier, are you?' Maxine asked, immediately wishing that she hadn't been so insensitive.

'No, I am after *you*. Seriously.' He kissed her. 'You can always find a sponsor if you're the best – and I think my pupil will prove to be the best. But I hope we sign up with Chazalle, because then it will be necessary to meet two or three times a year – at least.'

'At least,' agreed Maxine, carefully picking a wisp of dried grass from his hair.

'We wondered if you'd turned over,' called the huntsman as the antique racing carriage bounced across the glade.

'Took a short cut and got lost,' Pierre called back to him, his round blue eyes expressionless.

How can Maxine get lost on her own estate? wondered Judy and looked at Charles, scowling astride his slush-spattered grey as he wondered the same thing. In the circumstances he can hardly play the jealous husband to Maxine, Judy realized. But why did Maxine have to be so stupid and choose exactly the wrong moment to screw up Judy's pitch to Charles? If Judy ever got to make her pitch to Charles; in spite of her determined efforts to catch him alone, it was obvious to Judy that Charles had been avoiding her with equal determination.

So Judy was surprised when he offered to drive her to the airport to catch her Concorde flight. As they set off down the kilometre-long, gravel drive Charles surprised Judy by saying, 'I thought I might as well give you the opportunity to reason with me again, which is obviously why you hopped over the Atlantic for the weekend. How I hate women's plots!' He suddenly accelerated violently, tyres squealing round a corner, and Judy remembered what a bad driver Charles was as he continued, 'I fail to understand why Maxine expects me to behave with decorum when she fools around with her old boyfriend under my nose, as everybody saw yesterday.'

Maybe Maxine hadn't been so stupid to flirt openly with Pierre, thought Judy as she said, 'I'm sure Maxine wouldn't have looked at him twice, Charles, if you hadn't hurt her so. Why do you do it? Have you reached the age where you need to prove your virility?'

'You make adultery sound like arthritis. Why don't you mind your own business, Judy?'

'Maxine *is* my business, and she's your business as well, Charles. Surely you can see that this assistant of yours hasn't the sophistication or the style or the background to run the castle and handle all the business entertaining? The public associates Maxine's glamour with your champagne. She's starred in your TV commercials all over the world. You'll find you can't switch images as easily as you can switch wives.'

Charles turned on to the highway and increased speed. 'It's not that easy to switch wives – the lawyers have already made that clear. You needn't worry, Maxine will have plenty of money.'

'That's not what she wants. She wants you.'

'You expect me to believe that, after seeing her today with that attentive oaf?'

'I don't know anyone else who's been faithful to her husband for so long. But you know that Maxine loves you. And you love her. She makes you laugh. You've got used to her, like a baby to its blanket, and she's the mother of your children. Nobody's going to spell it out to you if I don't.'

They drove in silence through the sleet. Judy thought, I've got to give it one more try, and said softly, 'I think your hand was forced. I think that what you really want, Charles, is to have the clock put back a month.'

Another silence.

'So how would I get out of it?' Charles addressed the windscreen as they turned into the airport.

'You'll have to take a deep breath and tell this woman that you have no intention of altering your life. Maybe you'll have to pay her – call it severance, of course. A year's salary should do it. And fix a better job for her, with more prestige. Make it clear that she has a choice of the cash and the job – or nothing.'

'You American women are so tough.'

'Tough means being sensible and firm, refusing to be exploited. I hope you're tough, Charles.'

That evening Judy heard the whine of a police car hurtling down Fifth Avenue, far below. 'It seemed a long weekend without you,' Judy murmured sleepily as Mark snaked his arm around her thin waist and pulled her close to him under the cinnamon silk sheets. 'What did you get up to, Mark?'

'Nothing much, the weather was foul. Took Lili to a couple of restaurants.'

'Sounds a drag.' Judy wriggled hopefully against him.

'Yes.' Mark suddenly realized that those two days had been wonderful; that after spending forty-eight hours with Lili, his first reaction of purely physical lust had changed. He remembered her eagerness, her ebullience, her rages, her depression and her pathos. All now seemed violently appealing to him.

Mark felt the tip of Judy's tongue, and automatically slid his hand between her thighs. He remembered hearing her once say that when men feel guilty, they make love with especial care, because they don't want their women to guess what's happened, and because they want to reassure themselves that it really doesn't make any difference. Expertly, Mark began to caress Judy, determined that she should not realize that, instead of her neat firm buttocks he wanted Lili's ripe, rounded ass, and instead of Judy's little pink-nippled breasts he wanted Lili's golden, dark-tipped flesh, and instead of Judy's charming, button-nosed face, he wanted Lili's dark eyes, misty with ecstasy and her full lips whispering his name as he thrust inside her.

6

March 1979

PAGAN lay awake listening to the early-morning sounds of home: the click-whirr-click of a London milk cart, the chink of bottles, a blackbird piping with indignation in the mischievous March wind, a heavy thud on the doormat as *The Times* came through the letter box, a lighter thud as the *British Medical Journal* hit the doormat, soft swishes as the mail was pushed through the brass door flap. Downstairs her old sheepdog, Buster II, gave a token growl at each invasion of his territory by Fritz, the dachshund.

Sophia must be awake, thought Pagan as she listened to her daughter's rock music drift up from the basement. Seven o'clock in the morning and she's playing the drums already. Pagan then heard the noises she had been unconsciously waiting for, the sounds of her husband getting up. She heard footsteps on the polished boards of his dressing room, snatches of Mozart, whistled while he shaved, then stairs creaking as he thumped down to the kitchen.

With much whirring of weights and rattling of ancient brass chains, the grandfather clock struck seven. Then there was silence until Pagan again heard Christopher's feet on the stairs, then the rattle of her bedroom doorhandle – and there he was, grey hair still damp from the shower, deftly balancing her breakfast tray. 'We seem to have run out of marmalade.'

'Christopher darling, I'll never make a housewife, you must have noticed by now.' He rearranged the antique lace pillows behind her head, then took *The Times* from her tray and sat on the end of her bed, saying, 'I thought the lack of marmalade was part of a plot to force me to divorce you.'

Pagan began to pour their tea. 'Grabbing the newspaper first – *always* – is practically grounds for divorce in Britain.' Her primrose cotton nightdress slipped off her shoulder and her mahogany hair fell into her eyes as she leaned forward and handed him his cup.

'I once thought you might run off with a gigolo.' Christopher bit into his butterless toast. 'When the cardiologist said it might kill me to make love to you again, my first thought was, how long will Pagan stand it?'

'Thank heavens that medical opinion eventually changed its mind,' growled Pagan. 'But I've always loved you for your brilliant conversation.' She never told Christopher how much she loved him. She was superstitiously afraid of doing so. Christopher was the mainspring of her life, the focus of her days, the theme of her thoughts. Only her husband's care had transformed Pagan from a self-destructive, insecure, upper-class failure into a society figure famous for her outrageous glamour. Ironically, when Lady Swann, in some dazzling dress, swept into the room on the arm of her older, quieter husband, people naturally assumed that it was she who dominated the partnership, but the foundation of Pagan's cheerful flamboyance was Christopher's emotional stability.

For the first few weeks of their marriage Pagan and Christopher had continued their rich and, for Pagan, revelatory sex life. When his first heart attack had ended that phase of their relationship Pagan had been far more concerned about losing her husband than losing their good times in bed. 'Sex is like opera, darling,' she used to tell Christopher. 'Something that other people find fabulous, but which simply doesn't thrill me.' She hadn't really missed it that much.

'Are you ready for your joke of the day?' Christopher asked. Pagan crunched her toast and nodded.

'If you believe in the Virgin Mary's immaculate conception, then Jesus Christ must have been a woman, because the Virgin's baby could only have had X chromosomes!' He roared with laughter.

Pagan looked blank. 'Don't you remember my little lesson in genetics? Women have only X chromosomes, men have both X and Y. You can't give birth to a boy without Y chromosomes. You can't have Y chromosomes without spermatozoa. You can't have spermatozoa without a man.'

Pagan still looked blank. 'I can see you'll never win the Nobel Prize for genetics, darling. Don't you remember that I was able to predict when you were pregnant that Sophia's eyes would not be brown, because the colour of a child's eyes depends on the genes of its parents? Two clearly blue-eyed parents can't produce a brown-eyed child. More toast?'

'Tomorrow morning, darling, I'd like a joke that I can understand without a Ph.D.'

Pagan leaned back in bed, sipped her tea, then reached for her letters. She grabbed the one with the New York postmark and read it. 'Half a million dollars!' She sat upright, waved the letter at her husband, then threw it to him. 'See for yourself. That's from Stash, Lili's agent. That's the profit they expect from the première and it's all for the Foundation, as well as the money we'll get from Spyros's jewellery.'

'Tiger-Lili certainly wants to try out for the team.'

'I think she does; it's rather sweet. She seems to have had such a rotten life, in spite of all the fame.' Pagan leaned back against the lace pillows. 'She's always on her guard, always wary, very conscious that people try to use her – which they do all the time. It's perfectly disgusting. Lili can be a bit imperious but, basically, she's a perfect pet.'

'She's certainly a generous friend.' Christopher kissed the top of Pagan's head. 'I'm off. Cross your fingers for the new strain of hepatitis–B. It should either do the trick, or give us an epidemic.'

As he eased his elderly Rover into the flow of traffic heading south, Sir Christopher reflected that Pagan was probably the only woman he knew who would automatically feel nothing but sympathy for a voluptuous star like Lili. Perhaps Pagan understood her because both of them were a mixture of surface shockingness and underlying insecurity, he reflected as he waited in traffic between two container trucks.

A bread van cut into the line of vehicles ahead, then swerved violently out again. Sir Christopher checked a rush of anger. Traffic snarls were a classic stress-inducer; no sense in shortening his life over someone else's bad driving.

Morning mists lay in ethereal slabs over the grey river as the line of traffic started to move along the Thames embankment, then picked up speed down the clearway. He wouldn't be late, after all, thought Sir Christopher, still in convoy between the two massive trucks.

He never saw the bakery van shoot the lights, make an un-signalled right turn, then crash head-on into one of the graceful spherical street lights that stand on the stone balustrade of the river Thames.

But Sir Christopher heard the crump of metal, the thin crash of glass, then the louder impact as an oncoming automobile piled into the back of the bakery van. He slammed on his brakes at the same time as the orange truck ahead of him, which stopped abruptly, air hissing from the pneumatic breaking system.

The worn disc brakes of Sir Christopher's car were not so

effective, and he realized that he would not be able to avoid hitting the lurid orange truck ahead.

The driver of the green truck behind him reacted more slowly, and crashed into the back of Sir Christopher's old Rover. The momentum slammed the Rover into the truck ahead. As if made of paper, the Rover crumpled into the back of the truck. The steering column slammed against Sir Christopher's chest like a mallet hitting steak, smashing his ribs and heart to pulp.

He was rushed to St Stephen's Hospital and hurried into the intensive care unit.

Twenty minutes later Pagan, in her primrose nightdress, held her husband's limp hand.

'I'm afraid it's hopeless, Lady Swann.' The doctor felt that he could talk bluntly to a fellow doctor's wife. 'Even if we obtained a replacement organ, there's nothing left to attach it to – the thorax has been completely destroyed.'

In a daze, Pagan signed one form giving consent for the life-support system to be switched off, another giving permission for Christopher's remains to be used for medical purposes, and a third authorizing the undertakers to proceed. She felt very cold and, to her horror, very angry. 'How could he do it?' she thought. 'How dare he leave me now?' Then she thought, 'How can I even think such a dreadful thing?'

'A mother-and-daughter conspiracy suit? What the hell is that?' Judy demanded in the *Verve!* office, wondering if she had correctly heard what Tom had said.

'Just what it sounds like,' he told her. 'They allege that you and Lili hatched a malicious plot to ruin Senator Ruskington's political career.'

'But that's ridiculous,' Judy protested, her heels angrily kicking up the apricot kelim rug as she paced her office.

'Of course it is.' Tom was being patient. 'But conspiracy is a bitch, Judy. It's the vaguest, stickiest area in the whole legal code. Just talking to someone, even on the telephone, can amount to a legal conspiracy, if the circumstantial evidence stands up. The fact that Lili has now moved in with you could be disastrous if the judge decides that it's significant. Frankly, it's a pity that you've asked her to stay in your apartment.'

'Lili and I have a lot of catching up to do. God! This is all so stupid,' Judy raged. 'When Lili did this interview I hardly knew her.'

'Can you prove it?' Tom asked patiently. 'You'll have to go through all your papers tonight to see if there's anything that we can produce at the hearing on Friday which will substantiate what you say!'

So Judy cancelled her entire afternoon's programme, then read through an eighteen-inch-high pile of legal documents. After that she turned out her filing system, her desk drawers, her purse and her briefcase in search of anything at all to prove her point. She finished at eight that evening, exhausted by the effort of concentration. 'Damn that hypocritical old buzzard,' she said to Tom as she shrugged on her lynx jacket. 'Senator Ruskington has now lost me almost a day's work on top of every spare cent we have.'

Tom nodded. 'This case is wrecking our budget, Judy. We'll have to make fast compensation cuts, as many as possible, no matter how small.'

'What do you mean by small?'

'Do we really need an exercise instructor? Couldn't we let Tony go?'

'If we have to cut down, let's switch to a cheaper printer; that would be the easiest, quickest saving.'

'And cut the quality? You're only saying that because you're angry, Judy.'

'But it would be a really big economy and I would watch the quality like a hawk. We could make the contract conditional on quality. And what we pay Tony is a drop in the ocean compared to what we're paying the lawyers.' She jammed on her lynx hat. 'The exercise class is good for morale, and it means that I'm too tired to lie awake at night, worrying about that damned senator.'

'*You?* Lie awake?' he queried. 'What's happened to the unstoppable Judy Jordan self-confidence?'

'It was always more fragile than you thought.' Judy's voice was unusually low. For the first time Tom realized the depth of her anxiety, and immediately switched into reassurance. Playfully, he ruffled her hair. 'We've been in jams before, Judy, and you're still top of the heap.'

'So there's farther to fall. And you get no sympathy. You're supposed to be invulnerable. Did Henry Kissinger stay awake at night, crying?'

'At least you've got Mark,' he comforted her. 'I'm finding it tough without Kate.'

'I don't want to burden Mark with the troubles in my life.'

'Do you mean you're frightened of doing so? Frightened that he only loves the glamorous Judy Jordan that the world sees, not the real woman that I know?'

'Mark's a lot bigger on moral issues than he is on practical ones. I can't talk to him about business because he doesn't understand it. And he doesn't understand that a lawsuit is about a set of rules, not about justice.'

Fondly Tom put an arm around her fluffy fur shoulders. 'We'll struggle through somehow.'

'Talking of struggling, how's Kate?'

'She says the problem is much bigger than she had thought. It's not just a tribal war, it seems to be systematic genocide. The Bangladesh government has tried to settle the Chittagong hills with their own citizens, and drive out the peaceful Buddhist peasants who live there. They're trying to take away Kate's visa.'

'And to think I didn't even know where Chittagong was before Kate left.'

Judy said goodnight to Tom, then walked slowly down the dark corridor. She noticed a light shining under the boardroom door and opened it. Inside was Tony, sweating in his shorts and vest as he went through a sequence of fast turns and kicks in front of the mirror.

'Still here, Tony!'

'Yeah! Working out the new routine for tomorrow.' He leaped across the floor. 'D'ya think the girls will go for it! I think they're ready for this. I think they'll manage. What d'ya think?'

Anyone who put in longer hours than she did gained Judy's instant admiration. 'Hiring you was the best decision I ever made, Tony,' she called as he whirled past her, spinning drops of sweat from his forehead each time he turned. He finished in a dramatic pose, kneeling on the floor with arms outstretched, then slowly stood up, panting. 'Getting hired by you was the smartest thing I ever did. Did ya see my picture in *New York* magazine? My mom's shown it to everyone on the block.'

'That's great, Tony. I know they'll love it. And the girls all really appreciate the trouble you take.'

Tony began to towel his dripping face. 'Do you mean it? They really dig the routines?'

'Of course. And you, too, Tony. Why's that surprising?'

'All this female attention. Goes to a guy's head.'

'Oh, come on,' Judy laughed. 'With that body, you must have had hundreds of girls after you.'

'No, I was the original Charles Atlas weakling, that's why I started working out in the first place.'

'You've made up for it since, Tony.' Judy turned to leave the room. 'Don't work too late.'

'No chance, I'm taking my mom out tonight,' he answered.

'What a lovely thought, Tony. Enjoy yourselves.'

'Can't we turn the volume down?' Tony's mother scowled. Carefully dressed diners were shrieking with laughter, calling greetings and gossip from table to table, while waiters clattered with laden trays across the white tiled floor.

'The fashion crowd comes here, Momma.' Tony hoped she wasn't going to make a scene. 'I wanted to take you somewhere real nice.'

'Nice! This old-fashioned stuff!' A scornful laugh indicated her opinion of the fawn leather and chromium interior, all of which had been salvaged from the liner *Mauretania*, that floating *objet d'art* of the thirties.

'So now you've got the job, you got money to burn!' Tony's mother picked up the elegant menu. 'I could cook this stuff for a tenth of the price! Papa and I never wasted a penny. Now, there was a careful man.'

Tony didn't remember his father as being careful; his earliest memories were of his father fighting with his mother, while Tony cowered beneath the cracked, checked oilcloth that covered the kitchen table.

'What'll you have, Momma? I'm gonna try the crab salad.'

'Crab salad! What nourishment is that? You like chicken, Tony, remember?'

Tony remembered the different grease stains on the kitchen wallpaper, each of which marked a spot where his father had hurled a meal against it. Roast chicken had been the easiest dish to pick off the floor. Tony hated roast chicken. 'OK, I'll have the chicken, Momma. Now, what'll you have?'

Small black eyes peered at the menu, reading with difficulty. 'I'll have the hamburger. Why couldn't you let me fix something in your smart new apartment, Tony?'

She'd never stopped criticizing his apartment. Quickly he said, 'It's being decorated. Wet paint everywhere.' Tony wasn't clever enough to wonder why this small, scowling woman, who was in her forties but who looked twenty years older, should turn every pleasure offered by her son into an excuse to criticize him.

'Why aren't *you* doing the decorating?' She waved the menu at his face. Tony raised one arm and ducked as if to ward off a blow, then she continued, 'So now you're too high and mighty to paint your own apartment! You always were lazy; you always lay around doing nothing.'

They fell silent until their food was served, then Tony's mother suspiciously prodded her hamburger with her fork. 'This meat is raw!'

'It's continental style, Momma, underdone.' Tony felt an almost uncontrollable urge in his gut as his mother criticized on, on, on, and raised her voice until the other diners turned to look at her. This, too, had been the pattern of his childhood meals. She'd complain because Poppa was always late and, in return, he'd criticize the food. Then they were off, bickering about nothing. Voices would rise, fists would be raised, shouting would escalate into screaming, and then the food would hit the wall. Mealtimes were the only times that his family couldn't avoid being together, and they used these occasions to attack, undermine and casually wound, using their intimate knowledge of each other to destroy with the accuracy of heat-seeking missiles.

'Please keep your voice down, Momma,' Tony pleaded.

'That's a fine way to talk to your mother!'

'Momma, I'm only trying to give you a good time.' Once again Tony wondered whether he would ever earn adult status.

'Don't interrupt me, or I'll make you wish you'd never been

born!' Tony felt sick. Inside his magnificently developed body he felt again like a small boy, a small boy terrified of his mother's unpredictable, sadistic rages, a small boy overpowered by the unreasoned guilt of childhood. Every day the small Tony had heard that savage voice and moved about the apartment in terror, lest she should pick on some trifling fault – a peanut-butter stain on his shirt, unfinished schoolwork, chores skimped – as an excuse for a beating.

Tony unlocked his front door and crushed his mother's bag of homemade cookies into the overflowing garbage bag. Another treat for the roaches. He fed a tape of *Captain Blood* into the video, threw himself on the permanently converted, never-made Murphy bed, and turned to the night table, upon which stood a signed photograph of Judy in a silver frame. 'I don't take her out, I'm neglecting her; I do take her out, I'm wasting money!'

'Isn't Spyros ever going to give up?' Lili picked the plain diamond bracelet from the newly delivered basket of butterfly orchids and tossed it on Judy's blue and mauve silk sofa. 'If I had kept his bracelets, I'd have enough to reach my elbows.'

'Lucky girl, isn't she, Mark?' Judy picked up the brilliant stream of jewels and admired it over the back of her brown hand.

Mark shrugged his shoulders and gazed at the smouldering log fire. 'That bracelet would feed an African village for years.'

'Don't be so smug!' Lili reached forward, grabbed the diamond bracelet, and flung it at Mark. '*Give* it to the Africans, then,' she said. 'I don't want it, because I know it isn't a gift, it's a bribe.' Lili snorted. 'When one of Spyros's little gifts appears in a basket of flowers you're supposed to roll over on your back and be grateful. He orders these diamond bracelets, a dozen at a time, from Cartier. To him, they're trading stock.'

'Like beads and mirrors?' Judy suggested. 'As used by the conquistadores to buy Aztec gold?'

'Exactly.' Lili's expression was offset by her bizarre make-up; she had spent the afternoon trying to copy Mistinguett's make-up; her guide photograph lay among scattered cosmetics on the low, red marble table.

'You'd better get that stuff off your face or you'll be late for the concert.' Judy picked up the brass poker and prodded a falling log back into place.

'True.' Lili stood up, stretched and headed for the bathroom.

'Won't you need this make-up?' Judy called after her, meaning get this mess out of my sitting room.

Mark said, 'She likes being untidy, you should see the state she left my place in.'

'So what does a little mess matter? The reason Lili wanted to move in with me was so that our relationship could develop.' Softly, she touched Mark's long, tapering, brown fingers. Gently Mark pulled his hand away.

'Tom told me that having Lili living here with you, Judy, could be playing with fire; it might prejudice the lawsuit.'

Judy neatly replaced the poker on the poker stand. 'We're never going to get to know each other properly over restaurant tables and in hotels.' She turned as Lili appeared, glorious in dark-green shot silk and opal earrings. 'I'm off.'

Lili's carnation scent lingered in the sitting room as the front door slammed. Mark wished that he, too, could leave. It's a classic double bind, he thought miserably: if I leave, then Judy will take it as rejection, and if I stay, the whole thing will shortly explode in our faces. Here we sit, sipping Perrier on top of an emotional time bomb. Surreptitiously he sniffed the carnations and couldn't help imagining Lili's gold-skinned body as she emerged from the tub.

Lili let herself into the apartment and unclasped her green velvet cloak. They hadn't gone to bed yet – she could hear Judy's earnest voice saying, '. . . But why, Mark? Why have you tried for four hours, in various indirect ways, to get me to ask my daughter to leave this apartment?'

'For Chrissake, don't you understand, Judy?' Unseen, Lili heard Mark's weary pleading, and her hands halted on the gold clasp.

And, suddenly, Judy did understand. 'Of course! I must have been blind! You're in love with her, aren't you, Mark?' Her voice was hard. 'I must have been blind!'

'I don't want to hurt you, Judy.'

'Too bad, sweetheart, you just did,' she flashed back at him.

'Men always say they don't want to hurt you, when they've just dealt you a death blow.'

'I don't want to hurt Lili, either. She trusts me. I don't want to upset her life, or your life, or your life with Lili, or my life.' Mark tried not to raise his voice. 'To Lili, I'm the only man she knows who isn't trying to get into her pants.'

'Except that's what you want to do, isn't it?' Judy demanded.

There was a pause, then Mark said in a low voice, 'If you want the truth, I don't think any man could resist Lili's extraordinary sexuality.'

Lili caught sight of her reflection in the dim, silver depths of an elaborate Louis Quinze mirror. What is it, she thought, what is it that I have in me that casts this spell, this curse, on almost every man I meet? What is it? I can't see it. Why can't I switch it off?

As if echoing her thoughts, in the living room Judy shouted, 'I can't see it, and neither can any other woman. That's why it's so maddening to see you men all making fools of yourselves over Lili.'

Gazing at her reflection, Lili realized that she was tired of being a sex object, tired of being considered a male plaything, tired of being idolized by both sexes – unknown men because they desired her and unknown women because they desired to be like her. Lili realized that her fatal attraction was, above all, fatal to herself.

'Does Lili know you feel this way about her?' Judy was trying to control her voice, because she had to know the answer to her question.

'No,' Mark answered, 'and I don't want her to know.'

'What does she feel about you?'

'I think she trusts me.' He paused. 'I think she sees me as a brother.'

'Are you and I living in the same century?' Judy suddenly yelled. 'Brother, indeed!'

'I'm not going to threaten the only shred of family security that Lili's ever had.'

Judy interrupted him bitterly. 'Well, that just makes it perfect.' Her voice was vicious. 'I'm losing my magazine, my money, my job; then you try to fix things so that I'll lose my daughter and

733

my lover into the bargain. And to top it all, you're full of sympathy for *her*, not me.'

Mark shouted back, 'Look, I don't want Lili. I want *you*. But I want you like you used to be.'

Judy heard the pain behind his words and realized that Mark was telling the truth when he said that his passion for Lili was something that he didn't want.

'You're difficult to sympathize with, Judy.' Mark finally found an exterior focus for his anger. 'You've changed since I met you. You were such fun. Ambitious, hardworking, successful, and tough – sure. But fun. You were kind to people and strong. You gave me support and self-confidence.'

'Now I'm the one who needs support,' Judy wailed, suddenly out of control and frightened.

Suddenly Mark was able to crystallize his feelings and put them into words. 'You seem to have lost your own self-confidence.'

'What do you mean?'

'I don't recognize you any more. You taught me that real self-confidence isn't put on every morning like a silk shirt to impress the outside world. Self-confidence is something that's built on knowing what you can do and what you can't do. Now you seem to have forgotten that. What's got into you?'

'What's got into me?' Judy was suddenly quiet. 'I'm terrified that I'll end up like my mother, feeding the cat and watching the neighbours and waiting. I don't want to be powerless like she was, just sitting helplessly in the middle of her own life, waiting for it to end.'

'There's a lot to be said for that sort of life.' Now Mark was angry. 'At least that sort of woman isn't jealous of her own daughter.' He was unable to resist the urge to hurt the suddenly vulnerable Judy. 'You used to say that jealousy was the penalty of thinking only about externals. You used to say that there would always be younger, more beautiful women in the world. You used to say that jealousy never troubled a self-confident woman.'

'So now I know I was wrong!' Judy shouted. 'Do *you* want to know how it feels to become a mother when you're my age and then suddenly find that your baby is one of the most beautiful women in the world?'

In the hall Lili didn't want to hear any more but she didn't want to leave. Mesmerized, like a frog in car headlights, she felt unable to move.

'Do you *really* want to know what it feels like to be Lili's mother?' Judy continued. 'It feels as if I'm slowly becoming nobody! It feels as if I'm becoming the Invisible Woman! Little by little, I'm losing my identity! Very quickly, I'm losing the business that I spent twenty years building up. So I'm losing my job, my status, my money. I'm facing financial and professional disaster and disgrace. And I'm desperately afraid of failure – all because I'm Lili's mother.' Her voice cracked. 'Everything's slipping away and I'm frightened, Mark.' Too late she was finally telling her lover what was on her mind.

Lili stood up and tiptoed to her room, tears running down her face. She didn't want to listen any longer as the two people she cared for tore their relationship to pieces – because of her.

Judy perched in front of her breakfast counter sipping her high-energy drink – the juice of an orange, a teaspoonful of honey and a whole, raw egg; it was blended every morning for her breakfast, and tasted nicer than it sounded. Force of habit had compelled her to get up at her usual six o'clock, but this morning there had been no reason to linger because Mark had moved out the night before with his clothes stuffed into a khaki duffel bag. He had been exhausted and angry because Judy couldn't understand his predicament. As Mark saw it, he was being falsely accused of disloyalty, when he had tried to be truthful and faithful.

Gallant, confident Judy, the brave little drummer boy, had suddenly crumpled into a clutching, distraught female, and Mark simply didn't know how to cope with her; he wished he could help her but he couldn't. He could see that his presence upset her. So he had left. It seemed better than having an all-night row, which is what they had been obviously heading for. He had said, 'Take care of yourself, Judy,' then walked out of the door, leaving Judy bitterly to wonder why people always say, 'Take care of yourself,' when they mean that *they* don't intend to take care of you. She'd never needed a man in her life so badly before, and now, when she needed Mark, he was leaving her. He thought he'd be able to get an assignment in Nicaragua. It might as well be the moon.

As Judy finished her drink Tom called from the *Verve!* office. 'Not good news, Judy,' he warned.

'Hit me, I can take it,' she replied, dully, their joke formula for riding a crisis.

'Judy, I can't keep up this juggling act much longer. I've held the creditors off for as long as I can, but they won't take our-cheque-is-in-the-mail any longer. This is now more than a cash problem. We'll have to pull something out of the hat, fast, Judy.'

There's nothing left in the hat, Judy thought to herself as the other phone rang and she picked it up. It was Lili's agent, Stash. A phone clasped to either ear, Judy said, 'Morning, Stash, d'you want Lili? I think she's still asleep.'

'No, I want you.' His silky voice held a trace of middle Europe. Judy turned to the left telephone and said, 'I'll call you back, Tom,' then turned to the right and said, 'Why, Stash?'

'Would *Verve!* magazine like to be one of the sponsors of the International Beauty Pageant this year?' the world-weary voice inquired.

'Sounds interesting.' Judy's voice was guarded. 'What does it involve?'

'They want you to be one of the judges in Miami, and then you would chaperone the winner to Istanbul and Egypt on the start of her world tour.'

'Our policy on *Verve!* is to soft-pedal the beauty contests. We like to think that our readers have more on their minds than lipstick.' Judy's response was automatic. 'In any case, our sponsorship programme is allocated for this year.' Years of experience had taught Judy never to say no outright, even when people approached her for money.

'This isn't the normal deal; you won't have to put in a cent. They're offering you a big slice of equity in return for coverage in the magazine and identification with yourself. They want to reposition the beauty contests so that no woman would feel them degrading.'

'I appreciate your offer, Stash, but I couldn't leave New York.'

Stash said, 'These days New York is only twelve hours away

from anywhere, and your magazine works on a six-week schedule; it's not as if you were running a daily newspaper.'

Judy paused. Stash mentioned the money involved. Judy gasped. Carefully backpedalling, she said, 'We've always made a point of staying in touch with the average American woman and her ambitions, and there's no doubt that the beauty queen is one of the most fascinating figures of our age. Providing the terms are right, I think it would be in all our interests, but I may have to fly back if there are any . . . business problems.'

After discussing further details with Stash, Judy exuberantly called Tom. 'Hi, this time we really *are* about to mail the cheque.'

'She bought it right away, just like you said.' Wearing his usual vicuna coat and black leather gloves, Stash walked into Lili's bedroom without knocking. Judy had long since left her apartment and gone to the office. Stash knew that there was no chance of being overheard.

Lili gasped rhythmically as the Japanese masseur made delicate crisscross movements up and down her spine with his thumbs. 'Are the International Beauty people happy?' she asked as she was rolled over.

Stash's glance at her flesh was that of professional appraisal. Knowing how much Lili could eat, he vigilantly checked her weight and, when he did so, also made a covert inspection for needle tracks in her arms, crêpe skin that would indicate diuretic abuse, puffiness that might be due to drink. That was part of an agent's job. As usual, Lili was amused by the lizard-like, quick appraisal.

Stash said, 'Frankly, they took a lot of persuading. They said they didn't need a woman's magazine.'

Lili yawned, 'If they want me as a judge, then they've got to have *Verve!* as a sponsor.' The Japanese masseur started to attack Lili's left thigh as she continued, 'Oh, Stash, I've decided to do the Mistinguett film after all.'

Stash was surprised. 'I thought wild horses couldn't drag you away from your mother at the moment!' He looked serious. 'It's about time you got back to work again, Lili. We both know that I get no percentage if you don't work for six months. But you can't afford to be out of view for that long. *You* know how fast they forget, and how fickle the public can be.'

'Yes, but I thought that learning to love my mother was more important than money or fame; now I know that the best thing I can do for my mother is leave town.'

'OK, I'll set up meetings with Omnium.' He was delighted. Not only was it a great dramatic part, but it was the best vehicle yet for Lili's considerable singing and dancing talents. She'd have to get fit fast, but that was the only problem.

Lili sat up on the massage table and pulled out the tortoiseshell pin which held her silky hair clear of the massage oil. 'It'll be fun to spend the summer in Britain,' she said, without much conviction. 'Though I can't understand why they want to make a film about a French vaudeville star in Britain.'

Stash shrugged. 'Maybe they got a tax situation; maybe Omnium has some money blocked somewhere; maybe a reciprocal deal . . .'

March 1979

SIR Christopher's coffin was carried out of the chapel at Trelawney; on top of it was a single red rose from Pagan and a nosegay of white daisies from their fifteen-year-old daughter, Sophia.

In spite of the dreadful weather Pagan had insisted that the funeral party walk to the private chapel from the stone manor house. A fierce Cornish wind blew from the cliffs, thrashing the blooming thickets of rhododendrons, whipping at Pagan's black veil and threatening to blow the sodden, black umbrellas inside out.

Pagan had insisted on an old-fashioned burial, and there had been an explosive family row when Selma, her mother's partner, had remarked that, as most of Sir Christopher's organs were

738

now in the deep freeze waiting to be dissected by medical students, it hardly seemed worthwhile to bury what was left.

Pagan knew what had prompted her vicious remark. Selma had helped Pagan's mother to convert the debt-ridden manor house into a profitable health farm. Selma had almost succeeded in cheating Pagan of her inheritance, and Selma could never forgive the younger woman for the fact that one day the entire estate and the entire business would belong to Pagan.

'Darlings, don't come, I want to be alone,' Pagan had firmly told Judy and Maxine. So now Pagan stood alone at her husband's graveside, and the rain beat down on the big black umbrellas as the box that contained Christopher was lowered into the rich, red Cornish earth.

Pagan still couldn't believe that Christopher was gone and that, after her sixteen years of care because of his serious heart condition, her husband could have been wiped out by one careless driver's one careless moment. After long years of cancer research Christopher's team had been on the verge of a triumphant breakthrough, but now success had been snatched from him and he had been snatched from her.

Pagan felt far away, as if she were watching the entire scene from the top of the tiny seventeenth-century church. Everyone present, including herself, seemed doll-sized as they huddled in the graveyard. As the priest intoned 'ashes to ashes, dust to dust' in the teeth of the gale Pagan wondered if there was a sinister reason why the grass in graveyards was always so thick and green; she could hardly see the little yellow aconites which studded the turf.

Beside her, young Sophia cried silently into one of her father's enormous handkerchiefs. 'I'm sorry, Mummy, I can't stop crying.'

'It doesn't matter, my darling. Daddy won't mind you howling your eyes out.'

Why aren't I crying? Pagan wondered. She blinked her eyes to try to make tears come, but nothing happened. I *should* be crying, Pagan told herself, I've lost the only man who ever loved me. She tried thinking of all the tenderest moments that she had shared with Christopher, but still no tears came. Mortally wounded men on the battlefield often cannot feel pain. Similarly, some widows cannot cry, and although they often seem to be amazingly collected – almost unfeeling – they are anaesthetized by shock.

Suddenly a blast of wind blew Pagan's umbrella inside out and tore off her black velvet hat and veil. Blast God, she thought, for taking Christopher before his work was finished. How dare God do this to me! How *can* He? I did all I could. It's not fair. I can't be expected to put up with this. Why should I? I've done so much good. (Well, I haven't done much bad … Well, I've done less bad than most people.) What *more* does *He* want? Why did *He* have to pick on me?

After the mourners had left Pagan walked to her favourite cliff-top.

Her old sheepdog, Buster II, wheezed at her side through the dead bracken. Pagan sat on the weather-beaten wooden bench and recalled Christopher's black figure sitting here, hunched against the grey sky, when first they had met. Suddenly, Pagan no longer felt sheltered, like a big baby. She felt nothing: no misery, no pain, no grief. Her body felt numb. Inside her head there was chaos but no feeling; her thoughts bolted crazily in all directions, like a herd of panic-stricken animals. Unwelcome pictures slid into her mind, and she remembered, with distance, her husband's knobby feet, the way his bald head freckled in the sun, and his irritating habit of loudly crunching peppermints. Pagan thought, how dare Christopher leave me alone? She felt bewildered, disoriented and frightened by her own feelings. She felt as if she were in a never-ending black tunnel – the Valley of Despair.

During the following three weeks Pagan was unexpectedly calm as she held meetings with lawyers, trustees and accountants. Then she began to forget things. Christopher's secretary quietly took over the organization of his memorial service at St Bartholomew's Church in Smithfield after she discovered that Pagan had forgotten to invite most of her husband's closest friends.

Every morning Pagan heard the newspaper thump through the letterbox and waited hopefully. She always thought, it isn't true, it hasn't happened. God wouldn't let it happen to me. I haven't done anything to deserve it. It must have been a bad dream and Christopher is really shaving in the bathroom at this very minute.

'I wish that I wasn't so terribly tired all the time,' Pagan complained to Sophia, 'and I wish it wasn't so cold in this house.' She sat, swaddled in her old Persian lamb cloak, in front of a roaring log fire, and added, 'Christopher was so mean about the heating installation.' Sophia decided not to mention that, while the rest of London enjoyed an unusually balmy spring, Pagan's sitting-room thermostat registered 78 degrees.

Two days later Sophia came home from St Paul's school to find her mother pale but dry-eyed, briskly digging a hole at the bottom of the garden. Buster's dead body lay under the plane tree. 'I forgot his lead, and the stupid dog ran off after a cat – straight under a motorbike. God knows what we've done to deserve two road deaths in one month. But Buster's time was up, he was almost twenty.' To Pagan, life was unreal. It was a nightmare from which she hoped, shortly, to wake up. Actions were meaningless. People were meaningless. Nothing in life made sense. What *was* the point of life?

The following day Pagan's old MGB was stopped by the police, doing almost 100 mph down the crowded streets of Ladbroke Grove, and she could not remember the registration number of her car. 'I have all these huge, black holes in my memory, officer,' she explained, but he didn't seem to understand. Bloody man.

'I do think, darling,' Pagan told Sophia that night, 'that your father might have picked a better time to leave us. I've no idea how he wanted to allocate the money from the première, and there's nothing in any of his papers to tell us whom to appoint as the new director of the Foundation. Why on earth should I be expected to put up with all this? Just what am I supposed to do now?' She prowled around the pink, hydrangea-patterned drawing room, thinking, who can I talk to now? Who can I do things with? Who can I share things with? Who knows my past, my jokes, my fears? Who am I supposed to spend Christmas with? Aloud, she said, 'Just what am I supposed to do now?'

'You sound like Grandma,' said Sophia bluntly, hoping that this unforgivable insult would shock Pagan into becoming, once again, her erratically adoring mother instead of this whining automaton. Pagan took no notice. She switched on the television, picked up a box of chocolates and watched a raucous game show until Sophia burst into tears and rushed out of the room. Then a black pool of cold panic started to rise in Pagan's body as she heard that Mona, from Chipping Norton, had won a hostess trolley, a facial sauna and a giant Donald Duck. What's happening to me? Pagan wondered. Why can't I control what I'm thinking? As she watched Mona scream with unbelievable joy and hug her husband, Pagan thought, why can't I behave as I want to? Why can't I remember things? As Mona, who couldn't think of the name of a peanut farmer who lived in a white house, was ignominiously bundled off the stage, Pagan thought, perhaps I'm going mad. Perhaps I'll go to the doctor tomorrow. She did not know that she was suffering from the classic symptoms of bereavement, that she was groping her way through the tunnel of death.

But the next day she looked around her kitchen and decided not to visit the doctor. There's no point in saving a worthless person like me, thought Pagan, swinging from shock to depression. Doctors are for people who are really sick, not women who haven't enough self-discipline to pull themselves together. She looked around the cosy kitchen at the bunches of rosemary and thyme from Trelawney which hung from the ceiling, the well-used pans, the hand-thrown terracotta pots, the baskets of brown Cornish eggs and fresh vegetables. The delicate, pink-rimmed Minton dinner service she had inherited on her marriage was ranged along the ashwood shelves of the country dresser. Whatever is the point of trying to make a kitchen attractive? she wondered. It's just a food-processing plant, dolled up by pretty china. Plates always break in the end, however much you like them. Everything breaks in the end. Pagan took one of the Minton tea plates off the dresser, opened the window, threw the plate out and watched it smash in the basement area. That's what happened to me, she thought. My life is smashed like broken china.

Half an hour later Sophia stood in the kitchen looking at the empty shelves of the dresser. She had already noticed the pile of smashed china when she opened the front door. 'Mother, I'm going to stay in Tuscany with Jane for the holidays.' Defiantly she flicked spikes of auburn hair back from her face, silently daring her mother to care for her, daring her mother to say, 'Oh, no, you won't! You'll stay here with me.'

'Whatever you like, darling,' Pagan replied, absent-mindedly.

'Mummy, I can't stand seeing you like this any more. I'm leaving now,' Sophia shouted. Pagan took no notice as Sophia ran to her bedroom, stuffed two shirts and her tape-player into a tote bag, then rushed out, slamming the door.

Suddenly the house seemed quiet and empty. Pagan picked up the bottle of cooking brandy from the kitchen shelf and put it to her lips. She felt an emptiness within her. I am worth nothing, nobody cares about me, and nobody ever will again. I don't want to live. Life is my enemy and death is my friend. The future is black and pointless and threatening.

By midnight she had also drained the gin, whisky and vermouth in the drinks cabinet, followed by the Drambuie. She threw up in the kitchen sink.

Then she thought, I'm not going to let it happen to me again, and telephoned Alcoholics Anonymous to find out the date of the next meeting in the crypt of the church in Trafalgar Square.

'Now the openings – push against me, harder . . . harder . . . goddammit, will you take that away?' He poked a finger into Lili's stomach.

Lili shut her eyes and clenched her abdominal muscles with all her strength to pull her belly concave. 'It won't go any flatter,' she gasped between clenched teeth.

'Too much tension in your neck. Relax.' Again the Pilates trainer folded Lili's knees against her chest and leaned on them with all his weight. 'You'll have a back like Makarova by the time I'm finished with you. OK, that's enough. Now the weights.'

Lili moved across the studio to the fixed bed. Outside the rain lashed against the skylight; God, she was sick of this New York winter.

'Are you doing better in class, yet?'

'My ballet teacher's using me to demonstrate.' Lili strapped the black leather weight belts around her ankles.

The trainer believed her. Lili had been badly out of shape a month ago, and he had been surprised by her fierce concentration and tenacity. Accustomed to training professional dancers, he had seldom met with such a capacity for discipline in an actress. He knew that he could be tough with her, because she would fight back and try harder, whereas most actresses would burst into tears and he'd never see them again.

'You're not *Folies Bergère* standard yet, Lili.' He pushed her on to the exercise bed, where she lay on her right side, bending her right leg and extending her left leg straight in front of her.

'OK, up and down fifty times,' said the trainer. 'You still need more strength in that left leg.' He corrected her pelvis position and watched carefully as Lili slowly grunted to the fiftieth lift.

'Look – you're changing.' He pulled her upright, and in the mirror he pointed out to Lili the sleek, long muscles that were appearing on her thighs, the hollows in her buttocks, the flat, taut area below her breasts, where her stomach muscles were developing. It was OK. By May Lili would be in shape for *The Best Legs in the Business*.

The old London cinema had been especially decorated for the rock concert. It now looked like a giant scarlet parcel topped with a silver ribbon bow. The red plastic wrapping bellied in the wind, straining dangerously at the nylon ropes that held it together. Each time the wind gusted, the ropes slapped loudly against the giant yellow sign which announced: ANGELFACE HARRIS: GIFT-WRAPPED. BRITISH TOUR BEGINS TONITE. APRIL 5 SOLD OUT.

Eddie thought life had been a lot easier for a publicity agent back in the good old days of punk, when everybody was broke but believed in what they were doing and all you had to organize, publicity-wise, was getting one of the band arrested at the start of the tour, then the ballyhoo took care of itself.

As he approached the star's dressing room, the door was flung open, and a girl was thrown out into the corridor, blood streaming down her lower face.

'You fucking cow,' she yelled, shoving tufts of black hair back from her pallid face. She struggled upright against the grimy wall, pulling the black leather miniskirt over her chicken-skinny thighs. 'You fucking fat London tart!' One hand checked the silver chain that pierced her left nostril, looped across her left cheek and hung from her ear. 'Who the fuck d'you think you are?'

A cheap, orange plastic toolbox was flung out of the dressing room. As it crashed to the floor the box burst open, spilling greasepaint, wads of dirty cotton, glittering powders and gels in a dozen crude colours.

'I'm his wife, darling, and nobody better forget it!' A tiny woman, wearing a white fox, floorlength coat, appeared in the doorway. 'Now get your skinny arse out of here before I do you an injury.'

'Now would that be this week's wife or the one before?' spat back the girl in the miniskirt. 'Or is this one of Angelface's special relationships and you're going for a whole month of wedded bliss? Someone ought to organize a grand reunion for Angelface's old ladies – at Wembley Stadium.'

There was a moment of electric silence and then Maggie, the fourth Mrs Angelface Harris, stepped forward on her six-inch-heeled, silver cowboy boots, and raised her tiny hand to the other girl's face. But instead of slapping her Maggie hooked two fingers through the silver chain that ran from ear to nose and yanked it hard. The girl screamed as blood spurted from her nose and streamed down the length of her body, like rain down a windowpane.

Eddie, the publicity man, muttering 'For Chrissake' as he ran forward, pushed Maggie aside, then hurried the bleeding, screaming girl upstairs to the box-like room behind the stage where the two Red Cross volunteers were reading paperbacks.

Eddie reached for the radio in the back pocket of his jeans. 'Kev – the make-up girl's had an accident. Get a car round to the stage door and take her to the hospital. And there's a bit of a mess outside Angelface's dressing room. Get someone to clear it up.'

He walked into the dressing room and waved at Angelface Harris, who was standing at the counter, finishing his make-up. He wore only a dancer's support, the small black elastic pouch kept in place around his genitals by a G string running between his hollow-cheeked buttocks.

'Everything under control?' Angelface raised his cherubic eyebrows, widened his innocent blue eyes and put down the *Daily Mail*. Even with red greasepaint streaked down his cheeks, his face had an appealing urchin impertinence. Eddie looked at the white, sinewy body and wondered what was the secret of Angelface's legendary, evergreen youthfulness. Whatever he's on, I'd like some, too, Eddie thought to himself, as Angelface squirmed into a red-and-silver striped leotard and then clipped on a massive, winged silver collar, studded with rhinestones, which swept out beyond his narrow shoulders. Angelface now had a V-shaped silhouette of a body builder.

Of course, Angelface's musical secret was that he had always stuck, leech-like, to the spirit of rock 'n' roll, which was a mix of black American blues and American country music. Angelface had been one of the original rockers of the fifties; then in the sixties he'd re-invented himself, with a band, as a lead singer of the Dark Angels. Every time rock 'n' roll rushed up a blind alley, Angelface's career had wobbled. In 1967 he had been buried by psychedelic rock, but by 1977 Angelface was top of the heap again, and *Rolling Stone* magazine was wondering how many times this lovable old strummer could be recreated as Angelface relaunched himself in black leather and studs on the crest of the punk-rock wave.

It was simple, really, Eddie thought. Every time a new generation of fans rediscovered rock 'n' roll, they also discovered Angelface; two years older than Mick Jagger, he still looked as cute and skinny as the day he first stepped into the spotlight.

Maggie buttoned rhinestone-covered silver gauntlets around her husband's wrists, then fitted silver wings around her husband's Flash Gordon boots. Angelface peered into the dressing-room mirror and made a few, tentative passes at his eyebrows with the black greasepaint.

'I hate doing me own make-up, Maggie,' the singer grumbled to the bundle of white fox that covered his sulking wife. 'I wish to God you'd kept your hands off the make-up girl until she'd finished my face. You know I'd never touch a nasty scrubber like that.'

'Filthy bitch bled on me,' muttered his wife, sponging a spot of blood from the white fox. 'Right, I'm off to get me hair done for tonight.'

After she left Angelface sucked in his small beginnings of a belly and leaned towards the mirror again. Sometimes he wondered if Maggie wasn't a bit of a nutter. Chicks always got uptight when they thought it was expected of them, but Maggie sometimes went over the top with jealousy. Last week she'd set fire to that chick's hair, just because he'd touched her bum as he came off-stage; one click of Maggie's cigarette lighter and the girl was a hospital case. This week she tears the make-up girl's nose in half. What the hell was he in for next? Angelface wondered as he picked up the telephone and dialled a New York number. 'Judy? Yes, it's me again. Gotcha at last. Listen, don't hang up on me or I'll reach for me lawyer . . . I'll *tell* you why I'm phoning. Says in the *Daily Mail* that Lili's due to film in Britain next month . . . I've told you before, I don't believe you . . . You know bloody well that the reason I couldn't help you when the baby was born was because I was as broke as you were, but that ain't the case today, Judy. Today I'm worth eleven big Ms and I want to get to know me daughter. I want to meet Lili . . . what d'ya mean, I *can't*. I'm entitled to . . . don't you tell me I'm entitled to nothing . . . it's a bit late to tell me that I'm not her father, and I don't bloody well believe you, Judy . . . don't give me that line again about being irregular and getting your dates wrong. I gotta *memory*, Judy, and I remember you was crazy about me . . . Judy, I'd hoped that you'd be nice about this, but since you aren't, I'm *telling* you. First, I know I'm her father. She gets her looks from me, don't she? Second, I'm gonna meet her without telling her . . . because I'm gonna make sure she likes me for meself before springing the big surprise. And you can't stop me, Judy, so don't bitch it up from your end, or you'll be sorry. That's what I wanted to tell you!' Angelface slammed the phone back in its cradle.

In Manhattan Judy slammed the phone back in its cradle.

And somebody in the adjoining room quietly, carefully, replaced the extension telephone.

Lili stalked furiously across the café, ripped the lighted cigarette out of the man's mouth and slapped him across the face. Energized with fury at her insolence, he grabbed the cigarette back from her pouting lips. Again Lili snatched it from his mouth, so he flung her to the floor by the old, upright piano, then spat insults at her as she scrambled to her feet. Then he grabbed her arm and savagely whirled Lili into Mistinguett's famous apache routine. Lili kicked the man and he dealt her a brutal blow to the head. She fell to the floor again, and again he dragged her upright. She spat in his face as he ripped her skirt off, and so they danced on, portraying a lover's quarrel, at the end of which Lili grovelled at the man's feet in an ecstasy of masochistic passion.

'Cut!' Zimmer shouted. The technicians and the watching dancers softly applauded. Lili's magnetic animal sensuality effortlessly supplied the passion that was needed for the apache number.

'Zimmer!' Lili called, still on the floor of the French café set. 'Do I really have to hit him so hard?'

'But of course,' Zimmer shouted back. 'The apache number has to be savage and sadistic. It's about the eternal battle for supremacy between a man and a woman. You *must* hit him hard; you are hitting back for all the oppressed women of the world, remember! That's it for today, everyone.'

Zimmer nodded. 'Action!' The clapboard snapped.

Thirty-six showgirls in flesh-coloured fishnet tights, holding up their ten-foot-long, white ostrich-feather trains, paraded down the glittering staircase, their tall feather headdresses nodding as they walked.

At the top of the staircase Lili stepped forward. She was wearing a few square inches of spangled gauze, a spangled chastity belt and a huge, blue peacock tail.

'CUT!' bellowed Zimmer. 'What is this on your legs?'

'Tights,' Lili shouted back into the dark emptiness beyond the pool of bright light.

'Get them off – I want shiny legs!' the director hollered. 'Take five, everybody!'

Back in her dressing room Lili peeled off the fishnet tights and said, 'I should have listened to you, Guy.' Guy Saint-Simon was Lili's personal wardrobe designer for *The Best Legs*.

'He's edgy because he's so anxious,' Guy explained. 'This is the biggest budget picture that Zimmer's ever made. He merely wants your legs to have that smooth, shiny, twenties look. Let's get you into the silk tights.'

Carefully they eased three pairs of silk tights over Lili's legs. Lili replaced her spangled chastity belt, the designer fixed the huge blue peacock tail behind her, and they looked in the mirror. Lili wailed, 'My legs look like sausages!'

Guy nodded sorrowfully. 'Mistinguett must have had legs like sticks to get away with three pairs.'

Lili started down the staircase again.

'CUT!' yelled Zimmer. 'Your legs look like *saucissons*.'

'You wanted Mistinguett's authentic costume,' Lili shouted back. The technicians let out a mass sigh of ennui as another break was called. Lili released her cumbersome feather tail and ran down to the footlights, her breasts bouncing under their crust of glass jewels. 'Where are you, Guy?' She searched the darkness for the designer. 'Quick, I've had an idea.' The footlights flung dramatic black shadows over Lili's face and silken legs as she leaned over and peered into the dim stalls.

'Doesn't she look like an early Toulouse-Lautrec?' murmured Zimmer, who collected French music hall paintings, to his visitor.

'Yeah,' said Angelface Harris, 'that dwarf painter.'

Angelface had dropped his well-brought-up English accent. He no longer spoke correctly and enunciated clearly. Like so many pop stars, he dropped his h's and adopted a pseudo-working-class accent with a mid-Atlantic twang.

Angelface sat unusually still and silent as Lili pushed back her cloud of hair and called again for her costume designer. She was the most beautiful, amazing chick he'd ever laid eyes on. And she was the sexiest chick he'd ever seen, he thought as he watched it all spill out of the spangles.

'Anyone screwing her?' Angelface asked suddenly.

He can't wait to get in there, thought Zimmer as he shrugged his shoulders. 'No idea. You can't meet her today. She's not to be distracted.'

But Angelface had not felt lust; he had suddenly felt a burning desire to flatten whoever was screwing his daughter.

Twenty minutes later, plumes once more in place, Lili again started down the staircase, her legs gleaming under a thick application of oil.

'Perfect,' said Zimmer as Lili reached the front of the stage, the microphone swung over her head and she began to sing. '*C'est Paris* . . .' Lili's confident, throaty voice rang through the empty theatre as the chandelier twirled and the thirty-six showgirls twitched their feather tails and stepped forward.

'She can *sing*.' Angelface sat up in surprise. 'Her phrasing is great. She's got a sort of harsh quality in her voice that chicks can't usually get. It's a strong voice and a sexy voice, but not a sweet voice.' Angelface hadn't expected Lili to be able to sing. But he knew who she got her voice from.

'CUT!' Zimmer yelled. 'Mike in shot.'

And so it went on. Unlike the rest of the cast, Lili was in almost every scene and, when shooting finished at nine o'clock that night, she was too exhausted to absorb further criticism and her left eye had started to squint slightly, as it always did when she was tired. Nevertheless, Zimmer appeared in her dressing room with a sheaf of notes. 'About your singing, Lili.'

'I'm sorry I missed that top G,' she said quickly. 'I lose my range when I'm tired.'

'*All* your singing is wrong. Mistinguett, she had a voice like a cement mixer, you are singing too *well*. I want you to *rasp!*'

Three months with the Met's voice coach. Why did I bother? Lili snapped, 'If you want me to sing like Louis Armstrong, why not dub my voice with a cement mixer?'

A month later they were shooting in the countryside and Lili no longer had to try to roughen her voice because it was hoarse with overuse. A scarf was wound around her neck to protect it against the damp air of the May evening as Lili strolled by herself through the field.

Her calf muscles ached and her battered joints protested as she climbed over a five-barred gate.

Physically, Lili was exhausted, but mentally she was content. Halfway through the shooting, Mistinguett looked very promising, although Lili knew that you couldn't consider a film successful until you saw the final print. A film could be spoiled in the editing, badly dubbed or lost in a film industry vendetta, never to be screened. But the dailies were good and so was the atmosphere on set. There was a hopeful buzz about the whole production. Zimmer was no longer tense and had even grunted, '*Pas mal,*' today. He was rapidly turning back into the charming, supportive colleague who had been the first person to treat Lili as a serious actress, and who could coax a better performance from her than any other director.

Swallows cruised against the iridescent pink of the evening sky as Lili sauntered into a muddy lane. On either side of the road rainwater chuckled down the ditches, bluebells gleamed in the hedgebanks and raindrops dripped softly from fern fronds. England was very pretty when it stopped raining, Lili thought as she paused in the middle of the lane to re-tie her headscarf. Listening to the faint call of the swallows, Lili was hardly aware of a thin, insect-like whine in the distance, until suddenly the whine became a roar and a black shape leaped from the corner in front of her, mud and water spewing from under its wheels. Lili shrieked as she threw herself against the hedgebank.

The car howled past her, then screeched to a halt further up the lane. A man in dirty mechanic's overalls flung himself out of the car and raced back towards Lili, calling, 'Are you OK?'

'Of course not!' yelled Lili angrily as the man reached her. This reckless fool could have killed her.

'I'm most awfully sorry.' He helped her to stand upright. She winced with pain and started to pull the brambles from her hair as he continued, 'I never expected anyone on this road, because it's private. And this part of the country is always deserted in May – even in the holiday season it's only used by ramblers. Are you on holiday?'

'No, I'm working and I can't afford a broken leg. Why don't you look where you're going?' Lili took a few steps and winced again as pain shot through her left knee. She took another step, felt sick with pain and staggered. The man in dirty overalls steadied her arm. 'I'd better give you a lift back,' he offered.

'No, thanks, I can manage.' Lili set off, limping, down the road, hoping that this idiot hadn't blown the film for her.

He caught up with her, running his fingers through his sandy hair, streaking more grease on his already dirty face. 'I'm so very sorry. I promise you, I'm a safe driver. I was just seeing how fast I could corner her, because she still needs a couple of adjustments to the gears.'

He'd be quite good-looking if he washed, Lili thought, in spite of her pain. In fact, he might be *very* good-looking if he cleaned the grease and mud off his face.

'Please let me drive you home – it's the least I can do.' Nice grey eyes, long straight fair lashes, big freckled nose . . . Lili agreed. The low cockpit of the beetle-black car was little more than a shell of raw metal with wires taped in different directions across the interior.

He drove very fast. 'Doesn't this car do less than seventy mph?' Why had she agreed to be driven by this lunatic? Omnium's insurers would probably cancel on the spot if they could see her.

'She's not very good in the lower gears yet,' the gawky, good-looking Englishman apologized. 'This is the prototype. We're still working on it, and I shouldn't have taken it out of the garage. Would you mind not mentioning to anyone that you've seen it?'

As the car stopped in front of Lili's hotel (a famous eighteenth-century coaching inn) her driver asked, 'How long are you staying at the Rose and Crown?'

'Another four weeks. I've got a part in the film they're shooting at the manor house. What's your name?'

'Gregg Templeton. What's yours?'

'Um . . . Elizabeth Jordan.'

He made no move to help her out, and Lili made no move to open the door. It was that awkward moment when two people who have only just met are both reluctant to make the first move and invite rejection. Eventually Gregg offered, 'So shall I see you again, Elizabeth?'

'It's difficult, we never get any time off,' she said truthfully. 'Why not give me your number and I'll phone you when I'm next free. What garage do you work for, Gregg?'

'Eagle Motors in Whitechurch. I'll give you the workshop number.' He scribbled it on the back of an envelope, then helped her out of the car. She winced again. 'You need a shoehorn to get out of that thing.'

'Please forget you ever saw me in it.'

'OK, your boss will never know.'

Gregg looked faintly surprised, then grinned.

On Sunday afternoon Gregg collected Lili in a beat-up Jaguar XK 150 drop-head coupé, which was as grubby as if chickens were kept in the back. After another fast drive they swept over the brow of a hill and saw Lyme Regis lying below them, the distant cliffs glowing gold and white, the pretty circular harbour cluttered with fishing boats.

'Can we go out to sea?' Lili pointed to the small fleet of clinker-built craft at one end of the ancient, stone harbour wall.

'Why not? We'll take a motor boat.'

After an hour ker-chugging over sparkling water they walked back to the town and, in a bow-windowed Regency tearoom, ate fresh-baked scones with strawberry jam and clotted cream. When Gregg passed his cup to Lili for a refill he noticed her noticing his grimy fingernails. 'My mother's always complaining,' he grinned. 'Drink up, time to take you home.'

And, to Lili's disappointment, he drove her back to her hotel, then waved a cheery goodbye without making another date.

Lili gazed around the cream, oval reception room at the London Ritz. Elegant women drifted across the pink carpet, greeting each other among the small tables and large palm trees. Behind them a fountain trickled over a naked golden giantess with a strangely prim expression.

'I'm almost enjoying my Merry Widow act now that I've started the good works part.' Pagan's cheerfulness was brittle, Lili thought as the Englishwoman rattled on. 'Organizing your gala keeps me busy and stops me brooding. We can have Drury Lane Theatre on the last Sunday in July, if that suits you, Lili?'

'I'll have to check with Stash, my agent. He's coordinating with the choreographer, who's directing the show, and they'll check the date with the singers, the dancers and the musicians.' Lili poured out more tea; this weird British custom was habit-forming. 'Remember, Pagan, that we split up at the end of filming

The Best Legs in the Business, and it's a complicated job to get everyone together again just for a one-night live show for charity.'

'I've got a terrific committee together to organize the evening,' Pagan enthused, thinking that Lili looked preoccupied. Again Pagan felt that pain in her chest. The doctor had said that it was merely another manifestation of grief; he had reassured Pagan that her depression, memory loss and strange behaviour were not unusual after a bereavement. He'd also hinted at another delicate matter and asked her if she'd been, as he phrased it, 'missing her husband at night'.

'If you can't sleep,' he suggested tactfully, 'tune your radio to the BBC World Service.'

He thinks nice women don't wank, Pagan had thought. But the following night at 3 a.m. she had remembered his advice, twiddled the radio dial, found some pleasant Mozart, then settled back and let black night wash velvet over her. Suddenly a cheery, dynamic voice had urged her to buy tickets for a rock concert in Croydon. Crossly, Pagan had twiddled the dial, got what sounded like some soothing Sibelius, and recomposed herself just in time to hear the news in Dutch. As dawn blocked in the shape of her bedroom windows, feeling depressed and unsexy but wanting to sleep, Pagan had reached for Sheila Kitzinger's book on female sexuality, which fell open at the masturbation chapter.

In the Ritz tearoom Lili fidgeted in her gilt chair. 'What am I going to do about it?'

Pagan blinked. 'But we've already decided what you're going to do for the gala – a show based on some of the numbers in your Mistinguett film.'

'No, I don't mean that,' Lili waved aside the gala with one hand. 'I mean, what am I going to do about Gregg? Do you think I shouldn't have noticed his filthy hands? Do you think I embarrassed him? Do you think I came on too strong, Pagan? Do you think that tomorrow is too soon to telephone him?'

'Lili, you can't start an affair with some village mechanic, just because he's the only man you've met in the last five years who isn't dying to make love to you.' Pagan sipped her Earl Grey. 'Don't you think that perhaps you want this man so much simply because he doesn't want you?'

'I'm not sure what to think.' Lili sounded wistful. 'Except that Gregg behaves as if I'm normal.'

Pagan raised her mahogany eyebrows. 'Were you wearing that kit when you met him?' If so, Pagan couldn't imagine any man *not* wanting Lili, who was swathed in layers of pink-and-white knitting. All Lili's clothes seemed to be made in Paris by Japanese men who had never heard of skirts, blouses or frocks.

'No, I wasn't wearing this.' Lili was defensive. 'I was walking through the mud in an old raincoat without any make-up and with a scarf around my hair . . . Pagan, *how* can I see him again?'

'You have his number – telephone him.'

'Oh, I couldn't do that! I don't want to look too . . .'

If you don't care about someone, Pagan thought, it is perfectly easy to pick up the phone and dial his number; but if you care, then all you can do is sit and watch the telephone and silently *will* it to ring.

'If he's a mechanic, why don't you get yourself the sort of car that demands attention?' Pagan suggested.

'You mean something like a Porsche?'

'No, not at all like a Porsche.'

'Naturally, you can't expect everything that you would get in a new model, but our own guarantee accompanies every car we sell,' said the fat salesman in ginger tweed. 'How about this MGB GT – a collector's item now, Madam.'

'No,' said Lili, looking around the showroom at the array of battered agricultural vehicles, decrepit sports cars and ancient saloon cars that had been carefully maintained by old ladies. 'I want the cheapest car you've got.'

'That would be the Riley, then.' Just another lady customer; they never laid out on a car. 'Totally reliable model, this one, Madam.'

Lili shook her head.

'We're expecting a very fine Ford Granada in tomorrow.' The salesman sucked on his pipe to imply trustworthiness.

'No, this is my only morning off.' Lili's make-up call was at 5 a.m. 'How about that?' She pointed to a tiny Morris painted with pink and orange flowers, cabalistic signs and the words LOVE and PEACE, none of which disguised the rust on the doors.

'Frankly, Madam, you would be taking your life in your hands. That's a trade-in we accepted from the hippy commune in Uttoxeter and it's only fit for scrap.' No profit on that one, the salesman thought; he'd better scare her. 'We could not give it our guarantee, Madam.'

'Perfect,' said Lili. 'I'll take it.'

Ten miles out of town the little Morris gave a despairing clank, shuddered and stopped. Delighted, Lili walked another mile to the nearest telephone booth.

Within an hour Gregg was fiddling under the battered hood. 'We'd better give it a run.' He pulled a dirty rag out of his pocket and wiped his hands. 'But I don't think this clutch will last much longer.'

They jerked in silence along wet country lanes until Lili saw a painted sign swinging in the breeze at the roadside beside a white, thatched building. 'The Magpie and Stump! We don't have pubs in France.' Dropping a hint was a new experience for Lili.

Picking up a hint was a new experience for Gregg. 'Want to go on Sunday?'

Next Sunday, after visiting the pub, they sat in the tin-roofed country cinema and watched *Spartacus*. It was raining and there was nowhere else to go. On the following Sunday Gregg hired a fishing boat and they caught two evil-looking black lobsters. 'Let's take them back to my hotel and have them cooked for dinner,' said Lili. She found it uphill work. At this rate they would not be holding hands before Christmas. But she sensed that, surprisingly, this gawky Englishman did not know how to make the next move.

'Your leg OK now?' Gregg asked as they drove past high, honeysuckle-entwined hedges.

Lili pulled up her chamois skirt and thoughtfully felt her thigh. 'Almost.'

'Good.' He did not take his eyes off the road.

They crossed the hotel lawn and approached the kitchen door. As they reached it a shower of pink-tipped white petals fell around them. Lili stopped and looked up into the lichen-covered branches of the apple tree.

'Oh, the poor thing – it's trapped!' She pointed up to a terrified ginger kitten stuck on the tip of a fragile branch.

'Stupid moggy. Shouldn't have climbed up there in the first place.' Gregg, like most country people, was not sentimental about animals. 'Can we get into that room?' He pointed up at the mullioned window close to the struggling kitten.

'Yes, it's the staircase window. I pass it every morning,' said Lili.

They clattered up the uncarpeted oak staircase and Lili opened the window, but Gregg could not quite reach the kitten. Every time he leaned out of the window a little more the kitten retreated a little further back on the branch, then mewed more loudly. 'Cats always back off if you grab at them.' Gregg thought he was damned if he was going to risk his neck for such a dumb animal.

Slowly he twiddled his fingers as he withdrew his hand from the branch.

Slowly, the kitten followed the fingers.

Then Gregg grabbed.

'There, there, kitty, panic's over.' Holding it by the scruff of the neck, he handed the ginger scrap to Lili, who plonked down the eerily-moving bag of lobsters on the staircase and cuddled the kitten to her breasts, where it promptly hooked its claws into her white cotton sweater.

'Stroke it,' she said, pulling Gregg's hand to the kitten. His hand was much bigger than the little animal. Lili stood on tiptoe, shut her eyes, and kissed him full on the lips.

After a bit she said in a wobbly voice, 'My suite is just along the corridor.'

Lili's bedroom had an oak-beamed ceiling which sloped down towards the diamond panes of two small, stone-framed windows. The chintz curtains matched the yellow-flowered rug on the dark, polished floorboards; a copper warming pan hung on one side of the stone chimneypiece, while a row of hunting prints hung on the other. All this tourist-trap, Manderley kitsch was spoiled by the cheaply made, flimsy, standard British hotel bed, covered by a slippery, green satin quilt.

Gregg pushed Lili's lips apart with his tongue and explored her mouth. She felt the muscles move in his back as she slowly slid her hands down his spine, and an ache of desire tugged

757

between her legs. Gregg's soft dry lips brushed her throat, then Lili heard him murmur her name as his lips moved downwards.

Once in bed, Lili noticed, Gregg lost his awkwardness, but he wasn't very experienced, she thought, gasping as he nibbled a little too hard. I mustn't come on too strong, she thought. She felt the tremor in his fingers as he parted her pearl-pink lips and moved his fingers softly, cautiously inside her.

Ought I to be doing this with firm thrusts, or three fingers? Am I going to hurt her? Gregg wondered as, with small purrs she moved slowly against his hand. Where the hell is it? wondered Gregg, groping hopefully for the tiny seed-pearl lump. The tips of his fingers found a firm tip, like the point of a pencil under the soft, slippery skin. Lili arched like a leaping trout as he touched it. Got it, he thought with relief; no need to ask for directions.

After a bit Lili gasped, 'Now, now,' and he rolled carefully on top of her. With a sigh of joy, Lili welcomed him into her body and he began moving with slow, deep thrusts. The bed swayed and creaked with every thrust, releasing little clouds of dust from its chintz flounces.

Lili felt as if she were floating, falling, slipping unconscious, into a new incarnation as Gregg thrust steadily, his lips brushing the pale-blue veins of her neck. The erotic smell of his fresh sweat grew stronger as Lili pulled him into her at every stroke, clenching her muscles around his shaft to suck him into her body. The gasps and groans and odd little bird-like cries grew louder in the quiet room.

Then, suddenly, Gregg arched his back and shouted. 'That bloody cat!' he roared.

The frightened kitten had first hidden under the bed, then adventurously it had jumped on to the night table, where it had purred like a little sewing machine. Then, with bared claws, it had dived on to Gregg's naked back.

Gregg swatted at the kitten and half fell off the bed. The green satin quilt slid to the floor, and the kitten skittered under the carved oak linen-press.

Lili sat up and licked the tiny spots of blood on Gregg's back. 'Forget Ginger,' she murmured. Sensuous and eager, their bodies joined again. 'Lili, Lili, oh, Lili,' Gregg breathed as the rhythm of his body became urgent and inexorable. Lili realized that he was gone, he could not stop, he could not hear her, he was unaware of everything except that he was cresting that wave which . . .

With a crash, the bed fell apart.

'I think the earth just moved,' said Gregg from among the wreckage.

The sea was gunmetal, the sky was purple-grey, and black clouds collided overhead as they battled through the rain towards the end of the jetty. 'No chance of taking a boat out today,' shouted Gregg through the lashing rain and sea spray.

'Why is it that all the things Englishmen like to do make you cold and wet?' Lili yelled above the gale.

'Be fair, there are some things I'd rather do in the warm.' Gregg hugged her and their raincoat buttons tangled as he kissed her salty, wet lips.

'OK, I can take a hint. Let's get back.'

They turned and, heads down, battled against the shrieking wind towards the rocky beach.

There was a curse as the photographer slipped on the seaweed-covered rocks. 'Over here, Gregg,' he shouted. 'Just one shot – who's your ladyfriend?'

~ 8 ~

Early June 1979

LILI's face tensed as she looked at the photographer, but Gregg calmly turned to pose, his arm still around Lili's shoulders. 'Better make it just one shot, Eric,' he said pleasantly, 'I'm off duty today. This is Elizabeth Jordan.'

'How's the Spear coming along, Gregg?' The man reached inside his grubby duffel bag for an even grubbier notebook.

'Pretty good. We'll be racing at Silverstone next week.'

'I expect Sir Malcolm's over the moon, then. Are you going to run at Le Mans?'

'He's very pleased, yes,' said Gregg. 'But whether we qualify for Le Mans depends on how we run at Silverstone.'

To Lili's amazement, the man picked up his camera case, stowed his notebook and floundered back up the beach as Gregg said, 'Sorry, darling, I'm afraid I'm the only celebrity in town most of the time. That photographer was from the Dorset *Echo*.'

Then Lili remembered that on the hotel bed he had called her Lili.

'Gregg, you recognized me!' she said accusingly, her secure happiness starting to crumble like a child's sandcastle washed by the sea. He had been lying to her.

'Of course, Lili. You're a household face. Anyone would recognize you, in spite of the headscarf.'

Lili sighed. 'I thought we might have more chance of a relationship if you didn't know who I was. Any nice guy runs for cover when he sees me coming, and the creeps come out of the woodwork.'

'I guessed it was something like that, because in a minor way I have the same problem myself.' Gregg helped her scramble back to the beach over the slippery, seaweed-draped rocks. 'I lied to you as well, for the same reason. My name is really Eagleton, not Templeton.'

'Oh,' said Lili. 'So you own the garage?'

'Yes.'

'What did he mean by the Spear?'

'I nearly ran you over in it. I'm a racing driver and I also design cars.' They tramped up the pale, pebble-covered beach to the car park, where he helped her into his battered black XK 150. 'I took over Eagle Motors last year, when my father retired. The firm was headed sharply downhill, but we're managing to turn it around.' He drove out of the rain-grey town and headed into the open country. 'The Spear's the first new car that we've launched for a long time. We're producing a racing model first, in order to attract the maximum publicity. Then we'll go ahead with the road version; that was the car with which I nearly ran you over.'

'But that was just a tin can on wheels!' Lili remembered her first, bone-shattering ride with Gregg. A look of annoyance flashed over his face as she hastily continued, 'What's it going to be like when it's finished?'

'That "tin can" will perform better than a Porsche and have more prestige than a Mercedes.' They were driving through a gloomy, dripping beech wood. 'She's basically a four-litre, V8, turbo-charged engine which can produce 800 horsepower with four-wheel drive. She'll do about 210 mph.'

There was a pause. 'What colour is it going to be?' asked Lili.

'Black, because the sponsors like it.' Gregg swerved to overtake a cattle truck. 'When I appear on the track, I'm just a human advertising board. Sponsorship finances our entire operation.'

The car darted through heather-covered countryside. 'In the fifties Eagle Motors was one of the leading European specialist manufacturers.' They swooped round the bottom of a sugar-loaf hill. 'My dad was once the European Sports Car Champion, but you can't eat fame, Lili. I must have been about three years old when Pa went bankrupt. My first memory is of the bailiffs taking my tricycle away from me; they took everything we had.' Gregg slowed down behind a hay truck, then added, 'I'm determined to take us to the top again – only this time the accounting system will be as up-to-date as the maintenance log.'

They shot ahead of the hay truck. 'Once I've re-established our name on the racetrack, I'm going to launch our new sports car on the market. It looks as if we can get financial backing from the government. But first I've got to prove that I can deliver the goods.' The rain stopped as they turned into a gravel drive that wound between tall elms.

'Where are we going?'

'My home,' said Gregg. 'I live over the shop.'

The Eagle development workshop was a converted stable block at the rear of a large, ugly Edwardian house built of red brick. Inside the spacious workshop a number of black sports racing cars, in various stages of assembly, were lined up against the whitewashed brick walls. With careless pride, Gregg waved a hand towards a wedge-fronted, sinister machine. 'This one was sprayed yesterday.'

'It looks far more glamorous than the one you nearly killed me in,' said Lili as he opened the door of the glossy, panther-black car.

'It has a very special feature.' He patted the hood. 'It can manoeuvre sideways, crab-wise, for parking in town.' He ran his fingers lovingly over the black gloss gull-wing door and opened it for Lili. As she lowered herself into it Lili thought, cars are really sexy for men. Women don't understand this, because cars aren't sexy for women, they're just conveyors or status symbols.

'Not bad, is it?'

Lili recognized the Englishman's understatement. She also realized that she was falling in love with a man who was in love with a car.

They spent the next ten minutes growling round the laurel-edged drive and parking the Spear sideways. The car had a hydraulically operated fifth wheel and computer-controlled four-wheel drive. Gregg was as proud as a new father.

'Would you like a quick spin? We've got a practice track.' Like a big black panther, the car swooped, swerved and slid around the small circuit, spurting gravel and rainwater under the wheels. Eventually Gregg pulled the Spear up, neatly, in front of the workshop door.

Lili's knees were trembling, and again she felt sick as Gregg helped her out and said, as if to himself, 'The big question is, will the Spear be ready for the Silverstone Five Hundred Kilometre Race? If she performs well at Silverstone, it's been secretly agreed that we'll be allowed to race her at Le Mans next month. So keep your fingers crossed.'

'Why is Le Mans so important?' asked Lili, stretching her bruised legs.

'Because it is one of the toughest possible tests of a car. Le Mans is a twenty-four-hour endurance race, it goes on day and night. We'll need at least twelve pit stops to refuel and make minor adjustments,' Gregg explained. 'I have two co-drivers and we take turns at the wheel. The car hardly ever stops for more than two minutes and it's put under a fantastic strain. So you see' – he flicked a wisp of grass from the wing – 'if the Spear finishes well at Le Mans, it will immediately be taken seriously by the racing world – and by the government.'

Back in the workshop, mechanics in grubby, once-white over-alls were crawling around and under half-completed cars. Lili shook rain from her headscarf. 'Why are you working on Sunday?'

'They'll work around the clock if they have to; we're in this business to win,' Gregg said as they passed a mechanic who was bolting a power tool to the workbench. 'When I'm on the grid at Le Mans in the Spear, fifty people will have put us there, a lot of them volunteers.' They stepped over a pair of overalled legs sticking out from under a chassis. 'The support team does everything, from handmaking the parts here to buying my sandwiches at the track.' They passed a third pair of dirty overalls, bent over an engine. 'The team will drive through the night to get us to the race. There's never enough time, but they'll even work on the dockside at Boulogne if necessary.' Gregg stopped at the end of the workshop and looked fondly at a pimply lad in spectacles, who was filing down a bolt. 'And most of them do it for love, because I can't afford to pay them. Because they want to see Eagle on top again, just as it was when Pa was champion.' Gregg gently kicked a pair of overalled legs that stuck out from under yet another black chassis.

From beneath the chassis a voice said, 'Psychologically, the first race is the hardest, Gregg.' The legs wriggled out. They belonged to a small, stout man with an amiable red face and a beak-like, Mr Punch, nose. 'Gad, it's chilly under here, my feet are freezing. Let's go up to the house for a glass of sherry, and you can introduce me to this charming young lady.' Sir Malcolm held out his blackened hand to Lili.

Inside, the mansion was almost colder and clammier than outside, thought Lili as she reluctantly took off her white raincoat and enviously eyed the thick, shapeless, mauve knitted jacket worn by Gregg's mother. As they sipped sherry, conversation centred around the Silverstone race circuit. There were constant telephone interruptions from drivers, sponsors, volunteers and, finally, a London newspaper that wanted a quick quote for the diary page on what Gregg wore in bed. Lady Eagleton's serene grey eyes, a faded copy of her son's, did not register annoyance. 'In thirty years of marriage I've learned never to come between a man and his car,' Lady Eagleton said to Lili as Gregg was called back to the workshop, his father again called to the telephone.

'It's a pleasure to meet you, my dear. Gregg seemed to be keener on engines than girls. I sometimes think that motor racing is a disease, not a sport.'

'Don't you worry about him?' Lili tried to stop her teeth from chattering with cold. As it was June, the British considered it to be summer, no matter what the thermometer read.

'You learn to live with the worry. Eventually. My husband lived through a 180-mph crash.' Lady Eagleton shrugged. 'Gregg's chances of dying on the circuit are one in seven. But they improve each year. I simply don't allow myself to think about it.'

'WHAT DID YOU SAY?' Silverstone was the noisiest place ever, Lili thought as Gregg, in a baggy white fire-proof suit, climbed into the driving seat of the Spear. The Silverstone circuit looked like a cross between a filling station and a supermarket, set in a dusty, urban park. Behind the teeming crowds that streamed on both sides of the wide tarmac track, the dazzling billboards howled their messages like bright washing-powder packets. Every racing car, every racer, every mechanic, every ice-cream van was also plastered with advertising.

Lili could not imagine a more total assault on her senses than this riot of noise, colour, and stink, as Gregg shouted, 'I'LL SEE YOU IN THREE HOURS.' His lips poked through the balaclava which protected his face from fire. Then Gregg turned to his crew and Lili knew she was forgotten.

Two minutes later Gregg settled his helmet over his head, and the white-overalled team pushed the Spear towards the starting grid.

The Spear, with most of the cars, roared off behind the pace car, then belched flame at a corner. 'IS THAT NORMAL, JOHN?' Lili asked Gregg's psychological adviser, a lean, bearded man with a mid-Atlantic accent.

'YES. DON'T WORRY, IT'S GOING GREAT, EVEN BETTER THAN AT LAST WEEK'S TESTING.' He led her up to a glass box above the pits, where the noise level was lower. 'We shouldn't have any trouble this time.'

Lili did not understand why the car had previously given trouble. After all, it was an expensive car and, for the past few weeks, sixteen mechanics had crawled all over it, testing every nut and bolt, nurturing the car in every way short of breast-feeding it. She had not wanted to ask stupid questions of Gregg, but she didn't mind looking dumb in front of this kindly, ginger-headed Viking. So Lili asked, 'Why do so many things go wrong with these cars?'

John tried to explain in words of one syllable, such as could be understood even by a woman. 'A racing car is a sophisticated, complex mechanism. It always performs at the absolute limit of its capability. A lot of our problems are due to things like stress, high temperatures and fuel management microprocessors. Any human error is on top of that.' He turned as a Lancia limped into the pit next door with a plume of acrid, black smoke rising from its exhaust pipe. The mechanics scrambled to their posts like fighter pilots. John nodded. 'That Lancia went out on the track as perfect and precisely assembled as the team could manage, but it is being driven at speeds up to two hundred miles an hour for hundreds, perhaps thousands, of miles nonstop. Like a racehorse, the entire machine is designed for performance and nothing else. In order to get the speed that's necessary to win, the car has to be constantly pushed to its limit. So, inevitably, you get trouble.'

As the lead car passed the pits in a blur of green and orange Lili asked the last of the questions that she'd been dying to ask for weeks. 'What makes a good driver, John?'

He wiped his hands on a rag. 'Hair-trigger reactions, concentration and control. It's a young man's game; a driver starts to slow down when he's about thirty, but you also need an older man's mature judgement and steady nerves. While those guys are burning around the track, their minds are running like computers, and their bodies are sensing feedback through the car's level of performance and its speed. And, of course, they're violently competitive blokes, so they're always revising their own tactics to beat the rest of the field.'

'And does the biggest daredevil win?'

'There aren't any daredevils on that track. A good driver never takes an unnecessary risk. They aren't fool-hardy boy-racers, they're cool professionals with a deep respect for danger; they don't fool around.' He handed Lili a pair of black ear-protectors and they turned back to the pit where Lili sat for two and a half hours, deafened by the snapping exhaust roars as she inhaled the stink of hot rubber and fuel fumes. The howl of engines drowned the loudspeaker commentary as the cars spread out round the circuit. The noise was all enveloping, relentless and extremely exhausting, like a discothèque under gunfire.

'Gregg's just made the fastest lap speed ever recorded by a trial car in its first big race,' John yelled in Lili's ear. 'ONLY ANOTHER TEN LAPS TO GO.' Lili felt her headache lessen as the cars snarled into the last half-hour of the race.

Suddenly Gregg's team grabbed their tools and looked expectantly to the left.

The Spear appeared, cruised silently down the pit lane, then stopped.

Mechanics crowded round the back of the car as Gregg climbed out of the gull-wing door.

Ten minutes later Gregg noticed Lili. He stomped over to her, resigned exasperation on his face. 'Bloody gearbox blew up,' he yelled. Then Jack, the mechanic, who was doing calculations on a clipboard, held his thumb up. Slowly, Gregg grinned as a TV sports reporter shoved a microphone under his nose. 'So it's Le Mans next stop, Gregg, for the twenty-four-hour endurance race?'

'Yes, that's always been my ambition.'

'Are you going to celebrate this evening? Lili's giving a surprise party for you, isn't she?'

'If so, you've just spoiled the surprise, mate.'

'I don't understand why we had to come, Angelface, especially when no one invited us.' Maggie Harris looked round at the noisy party. The fresh-faced young racing crowd all wore Armani jeans and Cerruti silk shirts, with acquiescent Farrah Fawcett Major clones hanging on their arms. Nothing to worry about there, Maggie thought, as she dismissed her opposition with one flick of her eyelashes and glanced down at her white satin jumpsuit. From armpit to ankles, on either side, the suit had a two-inch gap, crisscrossed by white leather thongs over her naked flesh.

Maggie stamped one of her silver cowboy boots. 'I don't know any of these boy-racers, Angelface, and neither do you.' She turned on her silver heels. 'Let's go. I feel uncomfortable. It's not as if you were singing.'

As she started to elbow her way through the ebullient crowd Angelface grabbed her by the shoulder. 'Oh, no, you don't! I expect my old lady to stick beside me, even when I'm gate-crashing.' His face had the taut, sunken-cheek look of a sixties-generation rock star. Angelface Harris was tough, as only twenty years of rock 'n' roll tours can toughen you, thought Maggie as the famous blue eyes glared from the halo of wild black hair. His voice was a deceptively mild, throaty growl as he said, 'Shut up, darling, and have fun.'

'Take your hands off me!' Maggie gave a quick look around the room and decided not to cause a scene; it was too early and too crowded. Besides, even if he was a promiscuous bastard, even if he was getting a bit over the hill, Angelface was still the best-looking man in the room, and if she stormed out . . . well, she wouldn't want him to stay behind, not with all this spare talent, fresh from the hairdresser, and him in his best leathers. Angelface's studded, black leather suit was moulded to his body and wrinkled around the joints like an iguana skin.

'You stay here and behave yourself,' Angelface growled to Maggie. 'I'll get us a couple of drinks.'

He plunged into the crowd towards the bar, where Lili was greeting her guests. Angelface shoved his way past everyone until he stood in front of Lili.

He adopted his standard, lights-up pose – legs straddled, head on one side, hands clutching the neck of his leather jacket, which was unzipped to the waist. Lili blinked with the usual puzzled look of a hostess who can't recognize her friends when they're cleaned up. 'Er, hello.'

Angelface continued to give her the old, jean-creaming, lov-able, lopsided grin, the look that had launched forty albums.

'Why are you staring at me?' Lili stepped back, and her pink taffeta dress rustled. 'Did my teeth just fall out? What's wrong with my face?'

'Abs . . . olute . . . ly nothing.' Angelface pitched his sixties cockney-sparrow charm, then started to croon softly, in a camped-up voice. 'You must have been a beautiful baby . . .'

Everyone stopped pretending they were not looking, and the party turned into an audience. Again Angelface pitched the crooked smile at Lili.

> *When you were only startin'*
> *to go to kindergarten,*
> *I bet you drove the little boys wild . . .*

He put his arms around Lili's shoulders, crushing her taffeta ruffles, and together they faced the crowd, moving rhythmically together, Lili smiling, but still puzzled. She hadn't realized that Gregg knew this famous rock star.

At this point Maggie started to shove through the crowd, muttering, 'So that's the reason we came, he's got the hots for that stuck-up bitch.'

She reached her husband as Angelface finished the song to a spattering of laughter and applause. Angelface introduced her to Lili in a silky, amiable voice which Maggie correctly interpreted as a threat.

'Pleased to meet you, I'm sure, Lili.' She smiled brightly, then whispered in Angelface's ear. 'Let's get out of here – and I mean it. Now.'

Angelface ostentatiously kissed Lili goodbye and swaggered down the staircase, his tiny, blonde wife hanging grimly on to his black leather arm.

'If my wife acted like that, I'd send her back to the works for modifications,' Gregg whispered to Lili. 'If looks could kill, you'd be six feet under by now.' Lili shrugged her golden shoulders, and turned back to her guests.

'You're obviously doing well, Teresa.' Lili leaned across the Parisian restaurant table and flicked the pleated chiffon collar of the other woman's purple Saint-Laurent suit.

'Not too bad,' Teresa agreed complacently, 'and the work isn't as draughty as making porn movies used to be. D'you remember how cold it was in Serge's studio, Lili?'

'He did it on purpose, to make our nipples stand out.'

'Sssh!' The waiter served two silver plates of ice-bedded oysters to the glossy-haired, immaculately groomed women. Lili leaned forward conspiratorially.

'What's it really like, working for Madame George? Do you still go for the old guys, Teresa?' Lili was dying to catch up with the only female acquaintance she'd had in her youth. Teresa had been kind to Lili, and had taught her the rough, street wisdom of a high-class call girl.

Teresa said, 'It's a pity you can't stay overnight, Lili, and have a look at the office. Très chic, alors, to fly to Paris just for lunch.' She slid an oyster down her throat with a flourish. 'Working for Madame George is like working in a well-organized model agency. There are six girls in the office; they sit at desks, taking telephone appointments. We wait behind the office, in the pink salon, chatting, playing backgammon or watching television until we're booked out.' Another oyster vanished between her glossy lips. 'Madame George's drivers are all built like tanks, so you never get any trouble, and the accounts are computerized, so we always get paid on the seventeenth of the month. There's a fixed-fee scale for our services, and the girls are graded in categories.' Teresa carefully dripped Tabasco on the next oyster. 'Ever since that business with the minister, they all ask for me, so I'm in Category A – own chauffeur, own apartment, own maid and a Saint-Laurent credit card.'

'What are the men like?' She was genuinely curious.

Teresa gulped her last oyster, checked her lip-gloss, grinned and called for a second dozen. 'Madame George is a French institution, like the Louvre or the Crillon. Any cultivated man knows about Madame George, whether he's a filmstar, a politician, a general or a nuclear physicist. We see them all.'

'But are they any different from the johns off the street?'

'A john is a john. Some are clean, some are dirty, some are trouble, some are not, some are fast, some are slow.' Teresa shrugged. 'So long as they have the cash, they all get the same treatment – the best, and the most discreet – from Madame George's girls.'

'You weren't very discreet when the minister snuffed it. What exactly were you doing to him, you naughty girl?'

'Poor Maurice always needed a little . . . assistance.' Teresa gave an explicit gesture and Lili choked with unexpected laughter. 'Madame George said it served him right, he always paid late. If we hadn't all been at a hotel, she could have hushed it up. However, every cloud has a silver lining. Did you see my picture in *Le Figaro*?'

'Yes.' Lili leaned over the bowl of cream roses and lowered her voice. 'That was why I wanted to see you.'

Lili couldn't think why she had ever been frightened on the small Eagleton practice track, as Gregg drove round and round it in the commercial prototype Spear, muttering to himself nonstop. 'Bit of understeer there . . . still running a bit lumpy at 7300 on the straight . . . don't like the sound of third gear . . .' The high-pitched scream of the engine hurt Lili's ears, the oily stink of fumes clung to her hair and clothes and the bucket seat gave her cramp. Lili did not care for the life of a racing groupie and could not understand why Gregg seemed to prefer driving round and round this track to being in bed with her. There was always some excuse. He wouldn't do it for two days before a race, he was too exhausted the night after, and he seemed to spend every second night in the workshop, bent over some greasy hunk of malfunctioning machinery.

'Why can't I drive it?' Lili suddenly suggested.

Gregg laughed.

'No, I'm serious, Gregg. I can drive sports cars. I've got a Porsche in Paris.' She leaned across and lightly raked her fingernails down his inner thigh. 'I'll tickle you to death if you don't let me.'

Gregg wriggled and grinned. Lili added, 'After all, the commercial Spear is supposed to be driven by ordinary drivers like me!'

Eventually Gregg agreed. 'Go easy on the gas, the acceleration's pretty fierce.' He demonstrated the controls and then they changed seats. Gingerly Lili put the car in first gear. The machine leaped forward like a hunting leopard, then bounded down the drive and swooped into the green-fringed lane. At first Lili felt as if the machine were a savage, living thing that was running away with her, but once she became used to the power beneath her foot she felt exhilarated by the sense of danger and mastery that it gave her, as they hurtled between the pink-campion-sprinkled hedgebanks and wind tore through the prototype's glassless side windows. Ostentatiously Lili double-declutched as they plummeted down the sugar-loaf hill.

Gregg yelled, 'Go easy, this is a blind corner!' They were on it and round it before he had finished speaking; then, simultaneously, they saw that the road ahead was blocked with languid black-and-white cows.

Lili swung the wheel over and boldly headed for the open gateway through which the cows had just passed. She hit the brakes too hard. The car skidded on the muddy road surface, hit the bank with a sickening crunch, turned on its back, skidded along the slippery road, then slowed to a halt within inches of the terrified, stampeding cattle.

'Are you all right, Lili?' Gregg yelled as they hung upside down from their safety belts in the crumpled wreck of the Spear.

'Lili, you can't be serious!' Maxine protested. 'My butler tells me that you need another bedroom. Don't you and Gregg . . . er . . . I mean, aren't you . . .'

'Not for two days before a race.' Lili pulled a face, picked up a silver hairbrush and turned to the mirror. 'And as it's Le Mans, I'm to live like a nun all week. I had to promise not to seduce him, otherwise he seriously told me that he was going to share a trailer with the Spear team.' Gregg was affectionate, passionate, considerate and inexhaustible – but he spent almost every waking moment in that damn garage, passionately absorbed by those damn cars.

Men! thought Maxine, oddly comforted as she looked at Lili's beautiful, resigned face. Charles was just as bad. It had been weeks since that bitch Simone had left, but Maxine's husband still slept in his dressing room. Her bedroom had been redecorated in voluptuous shades of claret and a group of dishevelled Fragonard beauties hung provocatively on one wall. But Charles had not yet seen them, and Maxine did not know what to do next; she and her husband were on speaking terms – overpolite, in fact – but the air was still unfriendly.

'It's because of the Spear that I met him and because of the Spear that I hardly see him,' Lili gloomed. 'I just happened to turn up at the wrong moment in his life. Right now he needs every ounce of energy and concentration and effort for my rival, the Spear. And he's still got the big excuse.' Lili slowly started to brush her black hair. 'He's still bruised from our car crash, and he's supposed to rest his ankle. As the whole thing was my fault, I can hardly kick up a fuss, not when his whole future depends on this race at Le Mans.'

A distant engine snarled over gravel; from the terrace below rose a cloud of agitated doves. Lili jumped up and dropped her hairbrush. 'That must be Gregg!'

'What's their verdict on the fuel, Jack?' Gregg asked anxiously. Bleary-eyed from lack of sleep, the chief mechanic had just returned to the trailer after presenting the Spear in Le Mans town square for scrutinizing. He had been there for eight hours.

'Last thing they worried about, but there was a long wrangle over the driver's footwell measurements; bloody Frogs spent an hour crawling over her, taking measurements. In the end it came down to an interpretation of how the measurements were taken.'

'They're bastards about the regulations. Did you send in Johnnie Walker?' They didn't want to be disqualified on a technicality before the race started.

'Two cases. It did the trick.' Jack slapped him on the shoulder. The Eagle team's equipment included three crates of Scotch whisky with which to smooth the Spear's path through the maze of pettily enforced French regulations.

'Better not risk disqualification,' Gregg decided. 'We can reshape the footwell overnight.'

Lili drove back to the Château de Chazalle alone and Gregg worked through Wednesday night with his mechanics. By the following morning the Spear's wheel bearings and gearbox had been stripped down, checked and reassembled.

On Thursday panic threatened after lunch, when the clutch was discovered to be a millimetre off-centre, which was enough to lock the system. The men worked fast, but not fast enough. At dusk they wheeled the car out. 'Nothing to be done about it.' Gregg's freckled skin was pale. 'We'll have to do the qualifying laps as she is, then work on the clutch overnight.'

Lili managed to persuade Gregg that another broken night in the trailer with his team would leave him unfit to race, and reluctantly he agreed. So Maxine's chauffeur delivered him, white and tired, to the château steps just before midnight on Friday.

'We did it!' Gregg called triumphantly, plodding up the staircase towards Lili. 'Whatever happens now will be a bonus – we've qualified the Spear, we're in the race and that's the main thing.'

'What did you do about the clutch?' Lili asked as they both sat in the small yellow morning room. Gregg fell on the little pot of hot beef casserole and crusty French bread.

'Jack realigned it,' he said, between mouthfuls. 'He's a rare bird, works for sheer love of precision engineering. So much garage work nowadays is being a fitter, not a mechanic. They don't *make* anything and no real skill is needed. If something is wrong with a car, they simply take off one unit and put on another. But every nut and bolt on the Spear must be tightened to exactly the right torque. Do you know, I can take my hands off the steering wheel on the Mulsanne Straight at two hundred miles an hour and hardly feel it?'

Lili picked up one of his big, grease-stained hands and kissed it. 'Why would anyone want to take his hands off the steering wheel anywhere at two hundred miles an hour?'

The moon cast black, calm shadows over the undulating silver sand. Beyond the flames that leaped from the huge campfire King Abdullah could see the necks and swaying, supercilious heads of the camel herd, silhouetted against the sky. They had been couched for the night and their knees had been tied to prevent them straying. In spite of jeeps, helicopters and light planes, the most reliable desert transport was still the camel, Abdullah reflected. A camel ate very little, only needed a drink every five days, could survive twenty waterless days if it found grazing, and could carry 600 pounds of freight strapped to its back.

The Hakem tribe had spent much of the day racing camels in the desert and Abdullah had won the main race. The King's camel race win was now being celebrated by the poet of the tribe, a greybeard in black robes, who invented the verses as he declaimed them around the leaping yellow flames of dried camel dung and dead wood. Whenever Abdullah's name was mentioned, the men yelled and fired their rifles into the air in salute.

Opposite the King the firelight shone on the excited little face of twelve-year-old Prince Hassan, the King's nephew and his heir. Abdullah had brought Hassan to the Hakem mansef to present the boy to the tribe over whom, one day, he would rule. It was the fourteenth mansef that Prince Hassan had attended this month. Abdullah made these formal visits to only the most important sheikhs in his domain and it was on these trips that he recruited his soldiers. The freedom of his country depended on the loyalty of the army. Fighting was the price one had to pay for being a small, backward, oil-rich country that was strategically important to the Western powers.

The poet finished and harsh, guttural voices barked loudly in the night as the warriors started to reminisce of past fights, past camels, past hunts. The yellow flames cast shadows up into the men's lean faces, long shaggy black hair and black eyes that glittered like the star-spattered, black sky overhead. Tonight they would sleep on the sand around the campfire, protected only by their black cloaks from the chill night. Bedouins such as the Hakem tribe scorned comfort.

Thinking of his normal routine, the paperwork, the meetings with ambassadors, ministers, department heads and commanders, Abdullah felt a deep satisfaction at being among these tough, simple, courageous men who lived in the satisfying emptiness of the desert, where one day was pretty much the same as the next, and where time was not the master of men.

The feast was announced and the desert warriors followed their sovereign into the thirty-metre-long, black goatskin tent. At the entrance Prince Hassan stumbled and nearly fell. Abdullah glanced at the tired child as a white-robed bodyguard helped him to regain his balance. Inside the luxuriously carpeted tent young boys bowed and offered dishes of sticky dates and speckled figs. Bitter, black coffee, flavoured with cardamom seed, was poured from intricately worked brass pots into miniature cups with no handles. Gravely, King Abdullah allowed his cup to be refilled thrice, as was customary, and then they brought him the ceremonial bowl of camel milk, still warm from the udder and tasting slightly salty. When Abdullah had drained it, the sheikh of the Hakem tribe sprang to his feet and launched into the traditional welcome speech, spattered with overstated compliments, honey-flowered flattery and showy superlatives. He thanked Allah for the mighty Slave of God, which was the Arabic meaning of Abdullah, he praised all his deeds and wished him everlasting life. This took some time.

King Abdullah looked across the tent at Prince Hassan. The boy never complained and obediently performed all his royal duties, but obedience was not a useful virtue in a future king. Will Hassan have the spirit to control men such as these? Abdullah wondered as he glanced around him at the fierce, desert-hardened tribesmen.

Abdullah did not love his nephew. Since the death of his beloved son, Abdullah had loved no one and trusted no one. Abdullah had committed himself to no one and nothing except his country, the cause of his people, and his army. Abdullah's mother had died when he was born; he felt her death as a wistful lack. The murder of Abdullah's father provoked in his son only ice-cold anger. The knowledge that his own life was in constant danger left Abdullah feeling that deep involvement with any living person would render him too vulnerable to assassination.

Inside the tent richly-patterned carpets had been laid on the desert sand and heaped with tasselled cushions. Abdullah's watchful eyes moved warily from side to side, although he held his head still; arrogantly self-assured, with tawny skin stretched tight over the bone, his winged black eyebrows met above a nose that curved like a falcon's beak over the wide mouth.

Boys in white robes carried huge silver trays into the tent, each one piled with a bed of rice, surrounding a whole lamb which had been roasted over a wood fire and stuffed with a mixture of cinnamon rice, plump raisins, pine nuts and almonds. Eight men sat cross-legged around each tray, pulling off bits of lamb and dipping them in the silver bowls of yogurt, rolling the rice into small balls with their fingers, always only the right hand, because the left hand was used for sanitary purposes.

The boys served silver trays of kanafa, sweet cakes filled with white goat's cheese and served with hot syrup. The harsh wail of a primitive clarinet, the pipe of flutes, the insistent rhythm of the drums started; it was a prelude to the dancing and singing of traditional songs that were quavering ululations with no pauses, no rhythmic or harmonic variations, only repetitions of the wailing tune pattern.

Across the tent General Suliman Hakem caught Abdullah's eye, nodded and quietly moved behind Prince Hassan, ready to escort him forward for the presentation to the Hakem tribe. Gazing at Suliman's lean, hard face, Abdullah suddenly realized how extraordinary it was that Sheikh Hakem's son had accompanied Abdullah to the Royal Military Academy at Sandhurst. Together, he and Suliman had sat at those long, highly polished mahogany tables, sparkling with crystal, silver and candelabra, with everybody togged out in full mess kit and the strings of the regimental band sawing through a selection of *Oklahoma!* Suddenly Abdullah was sharply aware of the dichotomy between his Eastern life and his Western life as he remembered bicycling with Suliman from one classroom to the next and drilling endlessly on the parade ground in heavy, black boots. Together, he and Suliman had learned how to handle an infantry platoon. Fully dressed in combat clothes, they had together jumped into rivers, bumped in Land-Rovers over mountains at night and hurled themselves out of airplanes by day. Together, they had been acknowledged the best horsemen and the best shots at Sandhurst, which was hardly surprising as they had both been riding and hunting in the desert for as long as they could remember. Both, at full gallop, could shoot a partridge on the wing, as could most warriors sitting tonight in this sumptuous tent.

The music stopped abruptly when Abdullah stood up and made the ritual speech that asked the Hakem tribe to pledge their lifelong loyalty to his house and his heir. Abdullah then motioned Hassan to stand. As the boy got up his eyes lost their focus and he tumbled forwards on to the antique carpet.

There was an instant cry of alarm. General Suliman pulled the boy upright, but Prince Hassan lolled against him, unconscious and moon-pale. Abdullah's face was expressionless as he ordered General Suliman to accompany the prince to the women's tent.

Sheikh Hakem flung himself at the feet of Abdullah to protest his loyalty.

Nobody moved in the tent for ten minutes, until General Suliman hurried back to the King's side and whispered reassuring news in his ear. Prince Hassan had merely fainted, worn out by the incessant travelling and ceremony of the past month.

There was an immediate hubbub of relief.

As Abdullah washed his hands in the proffered silver bowl none of the tribesmen around him could have guessed how profoundly anxious the King felt. Prince Hassan had been constantly ill at Port Regis, his English school. Either the child was the victim of slow poisoning or else he was unfit to be a future king.

It was a blazing hot June day and the sun beat down on the concrete grandstand at Le Mans as gendarmes made periodic sweeps to control the crowds of hangers-on who swarmed over the track. The roars and snarls of the finely tuned engines could be heard far away, in the flat forests beyond the circuit, as the cars took their places on the grid. In the noisy, crowded grandstand an exuberant group waved Union Jacks and the black Eagle flag.

'Where's Gregg?' Maxine strained her eyes in the bright smoke-tinged air, but couldn't see the Spear in the line-up.

Lili wriggled out of the spectators' box and ran to the pit, where mechanics worked fast and silently on the Spear.

'Throttle's jammed. It's this bloody heat,' Gregg shouted over the roar of starting cars. 'We're going to lose a lap.'

Lili watched as the cars tore off, hugging the ground in formation behind the pace car for the pre-start lap. Then, with a howling crescendo, they began the race. Before the end of the first lap the Spear slipped on to the track.

By the end of the second hour the Spear was lying in tenth position. Triumphantly Gregg jumped out of the car, shouting, 'God, that car's so beautiful!'

'Who's leading?' Lili yelled, as Gregg's co-driver shot off in the Spear. The confusion of heat, the fumes, the cheering crowds and the distant cacophony on the fairgrounds made it impossible for her to keep track of the race.

'Nannini in the Lancia; he's really giving it stick,' Gregg bellowed as the Spear slip-streamed just behind the green BMW Sauber C7 and gradually nosed up to overtake it.

Five minutes later the Canon Porsche spun out of control, hitting Jacky Ickx's Rothman Porsche, which spun briefly on the grass, then rejoined the race, having lost a place.

By the end of the fourth hour the Spear was lying sixth. Lili watched the car shudder into the pit with damaged balance weights on the front right wheel; the mechanics worked frantically to replace the whole wheel in twenty-five seconds. 'See why we need so many spares?' Gregg prepared to take over from his co-driver. 'This race really puts a car through it.'

And it puts the drivers through it, thought Lili as, for the first time, she found herself desperately anxious about someone else's safety. Suddenly the race was not dull, it was not exciting; it was frightening. Lili felt only cold terror for Gregg as she saw a Mazda 717 briefly balk the Spear, then both cars veered apart as they tore under the Dunlop bridge.

At the end of the fifth hour a double pile-up on the Mulsanne Straight took both Aston Martin Nimrods out of the race and left Gregg lying second, behind the leading Porsche.

In the grandstand Lili heard the name Eagle Spear in the crackle of noise that was issuing from the commentary loudspeakers. 'WHAT'S HAPPENING?' she screamed to Charles.

'HE'S IN THE LEAD,' Charles yelled back excitedly. 'THE PORSCHE HAS GONE!'

Gregg knew that eight more Porsche 956s were snarling up behind him. Porsche always dominated all the endurance races, thanks to the excellent German engineering. At Le Mans a car could self-destruct under its driver; metal would shear, rubber would wear away, plastic would melt; in twenty-four hours' hard driving, a car could simply fall apart around and beneath its driver. Only the toughest survived Le Mans.

The third gear felt ominously sticky as Gregg changed down, anticipating the slow right-hand turn at the Tertre Rouge. Andretti, in the Kremer Porsche, was closing up behind him. Gregg's left ankle started to throb and, suddenly, he found it difficult to concentrate all his energy on the corner.

Then Gregg felt a stab of white pain, he heard a gnashing, mashing of metal, saw the world spin in front of him and fir trees rush towards him as the Spear shot off the road.

'Luck of the devil!' Charles threw his long, thin body into a velvet armchair. 'He crashes at two hundred and fifty kilometres and all he suffers is a sprained ankle.'

Outside the French windows of the château the bubbling

song of a nightingale and the tart scent of lime trees drifted into the library. Exhausted by the emotion, the excitement and the anxiety, Maxine shrugged off her voile jacket and collapsed on to the blue brocade sofa. 'Ouf, it's a hot night!'

They were silent for a moment. The servants had gone to bed and the library was dark except for a dim, brass reading lamp. Maxine sighed. 'Charles, I'm exhausted. D'you mind waiting up until Lili gets back from the hospital? She was making a lot of fuss, but her concern was genuine. I'm getting fond of her. Maybe she really will settle down with Gregg.'

'He seems like a nice enough fellow.'

'And very suitable for Lili.' Maxine yawned. 'If he becomes the European Sports Car Champion, he'll have nothing to gain from Lili's success. He doesn't need to hitch on to her fame and, as he's not in the same business, their ambitions won't clash.'

Charles nodded. 'He won't feel threatened by her.' Slowly he stretched his arms and legs.

'I can never understand why men find a successful woman a threat.' Maxine eased off her white sandals. 'Women don't find a successful man a threat.' She lifted her toes and wriggled them. 'Women think success is sexy.'

Maxine stretched her tired legs out and rotated her ankles. Even after twenty years of marriage, Charles couldn't take his eyes off Maxine's long, pale, rounded legs. Maxine knew this perfectly well, and so continued to twirl them slowly in the dim, amber light.

Eternally pragmatic, Maxine realized that seeing someone you know nearly die really sorts out your priorities fast. Charles had been nicer to her than he had been for months as they drove back from the hospital where Gregg had been taken. Delicately Maxine massaged her left calf, thinking: our situation won't be resolved until he says he's sorry, and he's never going to say he's sorry. But Charles will always *show* that he's sorry, if I give him the chance and don't rub his nose in it. She pulled back her voile skirt and started to massage her left knee. Softly she said, 'Charles, I'm sorry.' It was better to put yourself in the wrong and get your own way, than to stubbornly insist on being right and continue to be miserable.

'What are you sorry for, Maxine?'

'Everything.'

Charles pounced. 'Successful women are always overdressed,' he whispered in her ear as she squirmed happily beneath him. Charles plunged his hands inside the filmy fabric of Maxine's dress, ripped off her peach satin camisole, and started to flick his tongue, lizard-like, over his wife's creamy body.

Mid-June 1979

OUTSIDE the Sydonite Embassy the June sun sparkled on the distant Potomac. A picket line of dejected feminists in jumpsuits carried placards that read ARABS OPPRESS WOMEN, ISLAM EQUALS MUTILATION and CUT IT OUT!

Wearily the cops cleared a path for King Abdullah, who flashed out of the maroon Rolls, and through the imposing front door, followed by General Suliman.

'Mark Scott's exhibition is a great success.' His Majesty peeled off white gloves and thwacked them on to the silver salver proffered by a robed servant. 'And that leader in the *Washington Post* about the circumcised child was exactly what I'd hoped for.'

'If the World Health Organization really got behind us, such atrocities would be forgotten in ten years,' said General Suliman. 'Tomorrow Your Majesty will meet the Coptic woman doctor who led the campaign against female circumcision in Egypt. I have put the United Nations report on your desk.'

'What's the summary?'

'Only the Sydonite women themselves can stop this practice. A man may agree that a virgin bride need not be proven so by mutilation but the women do not believe that, when it comes to the point, a man will accept such a girl. Because of their fear, no progress can be made.'

Abdullah sighed, then asked, 'What's next?'

'The child specialist is waiting in the audience chamber, Your

Majesty; then this evening you will preside at a banquet which is being held here, in the embassy.' The general stood aside as Abdullah strode into the audience chamber. Two neat, grey-suited men were waiting for him. Abdullah looked surprised. 'I was expecting you alone, Doctor.'

'My colleague, Dr Margolies, specializes in the psychiatric problems of adolescents.'

The King raised his eyebrows. The doctor elaborated. 'After examining Prince Hassan, I find that there is nothing physically wrong with him, Your Majesty. He is a healthy boy.'

'Then why is he constantly ill at school? He's missed so many lessons that the headmaster's warned me that my nephew may not be accepted for Eton. Yet two years ago he was a perfect student.'

'Perhaps too perfect, Your Majesty,' the psychiatrist suggested. 'Prince Hassan seems to be a quiet, well-behaved and studious boy, but he is abnormally docile for a twelve-year-old, and shows little sign of aggression or curiosity. He is exhibiting the classic behaviour of a child reared in an overly authoritarian home environment.'

'What has that to do with his illness?'

'Prince Hassan seems to . . . prefer being ill to being healthy.'

'If my nephew is malingering because of idleness, then he must be disciplined.'

For nine months of the year Prince Hassan attended Port Regis, a British boys' boarding school in Dorset. During the holidays Prince Hassan was tutored in twentieth-century history, military strategy, tactics and modern statecraft. For one hour a day he was permitted to play. This meant training his falcons with the keeper of the Royal Mews. Prince Hassan was not encouraged to play with children of his own age, because it was thought that this would make him vulnerable to kidnap and assassination attempts.

Dr Margolies said, 'Prince Hassan is not malingering, Your Majesty. His bronchitis and sinus problems are genuine, the physical symptoms are unmistakable.'

'Then I don't understand what you're telling me. Is my nephew ill or is he not ill?'

'Psychosomatic illness is a physical illness in every respect, but the underlying cause is not physical. In Prince Hassan's case, his lengthy periods of sickness meant that he was confined to the school sanatorium, where he was cared for by the matron, who seems an exceptionally gentle, affectionate woman.' His Majesty looked perplexed as the psychiatrist continued, 'We suspect that your nephew's illnesses are merely nature's way of ensuring that he gets something he lacks, but which is vital to the well-being of a twelve-year-old. That is, the love and care of a woman.'

'Naturally, my nephew misses his mother.' Abdullah was puzzled. 'Sadly, my sister died five years ago, but there are women in the prince's household.'

'I don't mean female servants, Your Majesty,' Dr Margolies explained. 'Prince Hassan is lonely, and he is at the threshold of puberty. Normally, a mother encourages and supports her son as he grows to manhood. Ideally, an adolescent boy makes his first, inevitable mistakes in a non-judgemental environment of encouragement and shelter. Without this, a lonely child might well lack the urge towards curiosity and aggression, two qualities that are necessary to any adult male.'

And especially so to a king, thought Abdullah. No Bedouin tribe would be ruled by a weakling.

At midnight a depressed Abdullah, followed by General Suliman, strode from the banquet hall, through beautifully carpeted corridors, towards his bedroom. He had not been able to secure the help he needed to defeat the Fundamentalist guerrillas, who now controlled one quarter of Sydon. American diplomats were being held hostage in Iran, and the United States did not want another overt involvement in Middle Eastern politics at such a sensitive time.

This evening's banquet, designed to smooth the negotiations, had been a disaster. The old ambassador must be retired. Immediately. Clearly the wine had been ill-chosen, because the American guests had barely touched it; neither had they eaten the overelaborate nomad feast. In fact, Abdullah had heard one guest remark to another, 'Greasy rice and tough mutton is bad enough, but, by the end of those damn speeches, it was cold as well.'

The three American women guests had looked ill at ease among the many silent Sydonites, who were not used to making conversation with women. The atmosphere had not been one of all-male joviality, neither had it been one of graceful hospitality. Abdullah resolved that his next ambassador to Washington would have a cultivated, intelligent wife who could properly organize, entertain and administer the social side of his embassy, like the wives of the Western diplomats. He had heard that the wives of German diplomats received salaries for supporting their husband's work, and, after this evening, Abdullah understood why.

Earlier in the week Sheikh Yamani of Saudi Arabia had given a banquet in honour of Abdullah. Yamani's chef had been flown in from the Paris Crillon, the white truffles came from Italy and the string quartet from Vienna. Tonight, by comparison, the Sydonites had looked like prehistoric savages. Without being told, Suliman knew how Abdullah felt; he was the only person who understood why the carefree, promiscuous Abdullah had turned into this grim-faced ascetic. After years of bravery and patience, struggling to preserve his country from Communist infiltrators, after years of attempting to drag his reluctant subjects into the twentieth century, Abdullah was, quite simply, tired. He was also lonely and isolated, he trusted no men, and most women bored him.

Abdullah said goodnight to General Suliman, then lifted the red scrambler telephone. After arranging to replace his ambassador in Washington he opened the day's box of State Papers and began to work through them. At the bottom of the pile he found an engraved invitation with, attached to it, a three-line file update from Intelligence on Pagan, Lady Swann. Abdullah's black brows compressed in a puzzled frown as he recognized the handwriting on the invitation.

Behind her untidy desk, piled with brochures, gala programmes, opened envelopes, silver-framed pictures of her family, a moth-eaten rabbit's foot and old copies of *Horse and Hound*, Pagan looked puzzled as she worked her way through the morning mail. Again she read the thick, cream page, embossed with a crimson crest.

His Majesty, King Abdullah of Sydon, has asked me to reply to your invitation to the Royal Gala in aid of the Anglo-American Cancer

Research Institute on 31 July. His Majesty regrets that he is unable to be in Great Britain on that date, and will therefore be unable to attend.

His Majesty has further asked me to request the pleasure of your company at Ascot Racecourse on Ladies' Day to watch his filly, Reh al Leil, run in the Chesham Stakes.

It was signed with a squiggle, by an equerry.

But I didn't invite Abdullah to the gala, Pagan thought, checking the guest list again as the telephone rang. 'Yes, this is Lady Swann speaking . . . Oh, does he? . . . Hello? . . . Of course I'm surprised to hear from you . . . yes, I've just received it.' She turned over the letter. 'Of course I'd love to see you again, Your Majesty, but I'm afraid it's not possible . . . No, I'm no longer in mourning, but I can't go racing next week.' Pagan's automatic response to every invitation since Christopher's death had been to refuse it. '. . . not at all. I'm very busy, organizing a charity gala . . . A widow's life isn't as empty as you seem to think . . . it's just . . . it's just . . .' Flustered, she offered a final, weak excuse. 'Well, I haven't got the right clothes. You know how everyone dresses up for Royal Ascot . . . Oh, all right, Abdullah, I'd love to come.'

Pagan put down the telephone, thinking, that's the first time I've called myself a widow. It didn't sound so bad. She stood up and peered into the mirror over the mantelpiece. Anxiously Pagan counted her laugh lines.

Ever since she and Abdullah had first met, when they had been students in Switzerland, Pagan had possessed an almost magic power to make him discard his wary, formal attitude. Pagan could make Abdullah relax and laugh. In an odd way he had always regarded Pagan as a woman who belonged to him. She had been his first love and he had been her first love. He had never stopped trying to seduce her, even throughout her marriage to Sir Christopher, and Pagan had never stopped refusing him; although the relationship was only a friendship, Pagan never told her husband when she was meeting Abdullah; although it was only a friendship, she always dressed with uncharacteristic care before racing off to the Dorchester; although it was only a friendship, Pagan knew that Abdullah could only think of a woman in sexual terms, so their friendly meetings wafted along on an undercurrent of unmentioned eroticism. As she stared at her reflection in the mirror Pagan felt hopeful, flattered and afraid.

An hour later, the doorbell rang, and outside stood a messenger from Fortnum and Mason, carrying a tower of dress boxes. Beside him stood the deputy fashion buyer, ready to bring a further selection if nothing was to Lady Swann's liking.

Pagan dithered between a green-and-white flowered chiffon dress and a pale-primrose silk suit. Then the deputy fashion buyer opened the hatboxes. Secretly Pagan thought that she looked wonderfully romantic when she wore a hat but, invariably, as soon as she found herself wearing one on the street, she felt overdramatic or silly. So she picked the smallest hat. The buyer looked doubtful. Pagan snatched off the little white sailor beret. The buyer confidently handed her a large-brimmed floppy straw, which folded back like a fisherman's sou'wester. The rich ochre straw framed Pagan's pale skin and mahogany-coloured hair. The buyer nodded. Every woman looked good in the straw sou'wester.

'Isn't she getting overexcited?' Pagan asked Abdullah as Reh al Leil curvetted sideways round the paddock, her chestnut neck stained with sweat.

'Isn't it natural for a girl to get excited on her first outing?' Abdullah smiled. 'I seem to remember that when you were a débutante, you were sometimes quite hard to handle.'

Pagan laughed, then again looked doubtfully at the filly. 'Look at her, she's running the race in the paddock.' The filly was dancing in circles around her groom, a telltale white lather of perspiration building up around her girth.

'Aren't you going to bet on her?'

'Not if she carries on like that. She'll be exhausted before the race begins,' Pagan teased him. 'Young horses are pretty much the same over a short distance, so I always bet on the jockey, like the rest of the punters. I'm putting my fiver on Lester Piggott, on number seven.'

'Golden Gondola.' Abdullah checked the race programme. 'The favourite. So you want to play it safe, Pagan?' She became aware of his soft black stare and the warmth of his hand on her arm.

'You know I've always been a coward, Abdullah.'

He smiled at her and clicked his fingers. An equerry stepped forward. 'Lady Swann wishes to place a five-pound bet each way on the favourite.'

'Abdullah, don't be silly, I was only teasing. Of course I'll put my money on your horse.'

As soon as he had mounted, Reh al Leil pitched her jockey on to the velvet turf, and the odds lengthened to 100–7.

As the other horses cantered sedately down the course to the start Reh al Leil tore off at a gallop, her once-glossy flanks thickly plastered with white foam and her nostrils gaping wide and red. She reared in terror at the starting stalls, again unseated her jockey, and delayed the race a further ten minutes. When the starting gate finally flew open, Reh al Leil was twenty feet behind the other horses and heading in the opposite direction to the race.

'Wherever did you find that filly?' Pagan asked Abdullah as Golden Gondola set a businesslike pace in the lead.

'Kentucky,' he said pleasantly. At the first furlong Reh al Leil was the last horse in the race.

At the third furlong post she was halfway up the field of eight young horses, and showing extraordinary speed.

By the last furlong Golden Gondola had dropped back to third place and Reh al Leil, cheered on by the roar of the packed grandstands, was out in front, then triumphantly won by a neck.

'I'm glad I didn't bet on the favourite, she's lost a lot of money today,' laughed Pagan as they made their way to the winner's enclosure. 'She couldn't have gone slower if she'd been a real golden gondola.'

'Most modern gondolas are motorized.'

'How unromantic. Were there ever golden gondolas in Venice?' Pagan asked Abdullah as they watched Reh al Leil, draped in sweat rugs, being walked steadily up and down.

'Yes. In fact, there still are, Pagan. Haven't you ever been to Venice?'

'No,' said Pagan. 'What's your tip for the next race? Oh, watch out, here's the Queen Mother.' With difficulty, Pagan curtseyed in her tight primrose silk skirt.

Afterwards Abdullah and Pagan walked slowly past the

paddock to the sun-dappled half-circle of white rails at the end of the racecourse grounds. 'This is my favourite part of Ascot,' Pagan said dreamily as she watched the horses being prepared for the journey home. The farrier removed the light racing plates from Reh al Leil's oiled hoofs, and Abdullah rewarded the horse with a couple of peeled, scrubbed carrots.

'His Majesty is upstairs,' the ancient doorman told Pagan the next day, after directing her to the back staircase. Women – or lady guests, as they were known at Black's – could only enter certain parts of the club and they were forbidden to use the main staircase.

In the shabby dining room the walls were covered by gold-framed pictures of bloodstock. Elderly waitresses moved slowly from table to table. 'I see nothing's changed,' Pagan said to Abdullah.

'Nothing has changed.' Abdullah smiled back at her. 'The food is as bad as ever.' He nodded amiably at the Minister of Defence as he passed their table. The part of Abdullah that had been educated at Eton and Sandhurst, the lover of field sports and a respecter of tradition, was extremely comfortable in Black's. The part of Abdullah that was proudly Arab detested the claustrophobic atmosphere of privilege and prejudice in the dim panelled rooms, where judges, politicians, churchmen and diplomats drank fine champagne from silver tankards, snoozed in old leather chairs and, although polite, really wanted nothing to do with dirty wogs.

In the early days of their friendship, when lunch at Black's had been a frequent event, Pagan and Abdullah had realized that the only way to eat well in the club was to order food that had been purchased from the members' own estates, which meant river fish, game and esoteric vegetables such as salsify and samphire.

Abdullah watched Pagan as she dipped slim green asparagus spikes in melted butter, then ate plain salmon trout with new potatoes, fresh peas and cucumber salad.

When the raspberries arrived, Abdullah ate them with his fingers, picking up each small red fruit, one at a time. Why should such a harsh man have such a soft mouth? Pagan wondered, watching him; his lips look as soft as Reh al Leil's nose. Pagan felt the elation of flirtation. She realized that not once, since they had sat down, had Abdullah taken his dark eyes from her face.

When the waitress removed the silver raspberry dishes, their hands were half an inch apart on the white damask tablecloth. Abdullah slowly stretched his fingers and Pagan felt the warmth of his fingertips.

Speaking very slowly and pinching her fingertips very lightly between his, he said, 'I don't want to play games with you, Pagan, and I don't want us to mess it up this time. I want you. I want a real relationship.'

'I didn't realize that you have real relationships in Sydon,' Pagan babbled, speaking too fast in her nervousness. 'I thought you had political marriages.' She immediately regretted her words.

'Darling Pagan,' Abdullah said, thinking he'd like to thump her, 'we are not in Sydon now.'

'Will you be having coffee, sir?' the waitress interrupted.

'Why not have coffee in my suite at the Dorchester?' Abdullah suggested.

Pagan sat silent for a full thirty seconds, her lips parted, her legs trembling and her mind frozen with alarm.

Abdullah said a word he very rarely uttered, and he said it quickly, with force. 'Please, Pagan.'

'Why not?' Pagan heard herself agree.

What on earth am I doing? she asked herself as she glided down the back staircase, listening to the fears in her head. 'I'm a widow. I haven't made love for ages. I'm only used to Christopher. I must be out of my mind. I'm no longer the girl he remembers. He won't want me once he sees me with my clothes off. Arabs treat women like donkeys, and Abdullah's hurt me so much already. He's dangerous for me. If I get involved with him again, he'll hurt me again.' All her old feelings rushed back to frighten Pagan, the fear of private humiliation or, even worse, of public humiliation.

Internal red lights and warning sirens continued to blare at the back of Pagan's head as she reached the bottom of the threadbare staircase. Abdullah stepped forward, caught her in his arms, and pulled her out of sight behind a pillar. 'Don't you dare change your mind, you little coward,' he breathed, brushing her lips with his. She felt the tip of his tongue touch her lips, erotic and inviting. She melted, then clung to him. Abdullah said, 'Let's get out of here.'

At the doorway of the club they were stopped by a policeman. 'Sorry, sir, we can't let anyone leave the club. Another bomb scare. Please return indoors, and keep the lady as far as possible from the windows.'

Outside they could see that the road was crisscrossed by white tape; a police transporter was slowly towing away all cars except for a blue Ford on the right-hand side of the road. At the end of the empty street a small group of policemen chatted beside an ambulance, its door ominously open.

'What are we going to do?' Pagan asked Abdullah, almost crying with disappointment, but at the same time relieved. A group of club members, noisy with drink, was turned back at the door. Led by a rubicund bishop, they clattered up the staircase, back to the bar.

Abdullah led Pagan away from the door. He took her hand, quickly pressed the narrow, pale palm to his cheek, then kissed it and licked each finger with his warm tongue. 'I've wanted you for years, and I'm not going to be stopped by an I R A bomb.'

'Abdullah, stop starting, when we haven't anywhere to go. A bomb scare could trap us here for hours, you know.'

He kissed her palm harder, crushing his lips against it. 'Run up the ladies' staircase,' he whispered. 'I'll meet you on the top floor, in the billiard room.'

The billiard room on the top floor of Black's was as quiet as a cathedral. The windows were permanently covered by green velvet, so only a few motes of dust floated in the occasional ray of sunlight. In the green gloom stood two billiard tables. Larger than pool tables, they were made of smooth, heavy slate, covered by green cloth. Pagan eyed the polished boards of the floor, the narrow black leather bench that surrounded the room, and then the tables. 'Abdullah,' she whispered, 'we can't! Not on the table!'

'We can,' he said as he locked the door in the half-darkness and pulled her towards him. He kissed her slowly and gently.

Then he crushed Pagan's body against his, and she felt the side of the billiard table press against the back of her thighs.

Slowly Abdullah took off the green-and-white dress, kissing each exposed area of flesh as he did so. He looked at Pagan in her plain, white satin slip, picked her up in his arms and laid her long, white-satin-wrapped body on the green baize table. The slate felt cold and hard beneath the cloth. Soft, slow kisses traced Pagan's collarbone, then she felt his lips on the delicate skin below, where the faint shadowy outlines of her ribs appeared. As his warm lips touched her skin she thought dreamily, I'm lighting up, like the sun rising over the Swiss Alps, when the mountain peaks get that living pink glow that spreads slowly down to the valleys. Suddenly she realized that it had been years since her body had felt so alive.

Pagan's slip slithered off the table as Abdullah started to kiss her breasts, then moved downwards, beyond her ribs, his warm breath clinging like mist to the rise of her belly. Pagan suddenly thought of the dark velvet of a horse's nose, and the potential power of that animal's strength for danger and destruction. The tip of Abdullah's tongue traced round her navel and slowly trickled over her lower abdomen. Then, maddeningly, his lips returned to kiss her on the mouth, and Pagan felt the harsh fabric of his uniform, the hard metal of brass buttons against her bare flesh.

'But suppose we spoil the table?'

'Then the table will be spoiled.' He unbuckled his belt.

'Abdullah – please! What if somebody comes up?'

'They will find the door locked, that's all.' Slowly he undressed, and Pagan thought, why, he's treating me like a young horse. Act confident, make no sudden movements and never let them know you're scared. Having shed his clothes, Abdullah leaned over the table and kissed her body again until Pagan quivered, moaned and forgot about the table and the bishops and discovery as a warm arm encircled her long white waist. Abdullah's velvet-brown eyes looked into Pagan's pale-blue eyes, then his full lips moved forward as he bent to kiss her again. Then he pulled back, lips smiling, eyes dancing. Pagan tried to kiss him, but he ducked his head. Giggling, they struck at each other like snakes, then finally surrendered in a long erotic embrace as they both felt the strange hard chill of the slate that lay below the bright green baize covering the table.

As she became increasingly conscious of the lazy warmth and sympathy of their entwined bodies Pagan felt her self-consciousness evaporate. The comfortable friendship, which had endured since they were teenagers, now wrapped them in cosy intimacy as Abdullah's fingers slowly caressed her body as softly as his lips had done before. He kissed the arch of her mahogany eyebrows, the fine bridge of her nose, the long line of her jaw. He began to kiss her breasts, nuzzling her right nipple with his lips, sucking, first gently, then more insistently. He's taking the whole afternoon to get to know my body, thought Pagan, tingling with ardour.

As Abdullah slipped his hand inside the back of her white cotton panties Pagan wished with all her heart that they were apricot satin and lace from Keturah Brown, and didn't have a safety pin on the side. She felt another flash of vulnerability as light warm kisses fell on her soft mound, and the hot tip of his tongue wriggled into the opening under the curls. Then she felt nothing but yearning, crushing pleasure as his hands slid under her buttocks and pulled her to him, so that he drank from her, like a cat lapping cream.

Repeatedly Abdullah swept Pagan to the edge of orgasm, then moved up to kiss her mouth again. Then, slowly, he mounted her and began to enter her quivering flesh, pushing inside her a millimetre at a time. This deliberate, careful slowness made Pagan feel as if she were moving in a dream. When they had first met, Pagan had imagined what it would be like to let Abdullah make love to her. After her teenage decision not to let him Pagan had never allowed herself to regret it, or even to admit that there was anything to regret.

But she'd never imagined anything like this.

'Open your eyes, Pagan,' he breathed. As she looked at him, inhaling her own musky odour on his mouth, he pushed slowly on and Pagan felt as if she was being swept away on a foaming Hokusai wave. She gave a weak cry as her climax gathered, then broke over her. Abdullah held her body tightly to him, cherishing the communion of their flesh.

She did not cry, as he had expected, but lay quietly in his

791

arms, mouthing gentle kisses with her narrow lips. Abdullah considered taking her again to climax, but decided to wait until he knew the long, pale body better, as gently he returned her light kisses and began to satisfy himself. He knew that he could sensually dominate the timid Pagan, but he wanted her to love him and to come to his arms with confidence. Later he would show her how to caress him, teaching her, as he had been taught, the art of love.

Afterwards they lay together in the green quietness of the billiard room, her long pale body and his brown one side by side. Faint bursts of tipsy laughter wafted up from the bar on the floor below, where the bishop and his friends still quaffed champagne from silver tankards.

With his lips against the mahogany hair that spread over the green baize, Abdullah whispered, 'When I first met you, I tried to imagine you naked, but I never could. I think that's when I discovered that, for me, you were different from other women, because I couldn't do what I wanted with you. I couldn't even undress you in my own imagination.'

Pagan pulled him towards her and felt the room recede, together with her sadness and confusion and timidity, as she felt the flesh upon flesh of their lips.

Then the bomb went off.

The explosion shook the entire building, including the heavy, slate-bedded table on which they lay.

There was an instant of silence. It seemed to last for ever. Then, glass began to fall in deadly waterfalls from the windows.

Snake swift, Abdullah scooped up Pagan and pulled her naked body beneath the billiard table. A cacophony of voices rose from below them. 'We should perhaps get dressed,' Abdullah suggested.

The telephone call from a call box in Kilburn to the *Daily Mail* news desk was semicoherent. A voice announced that the bomb had been planted outside Black's Club, and that they hoped the Minister of Defence had enjoyed his last lunch.

When the anti-terrorist squad discovered King Abdullah playing billiards with Lady Swann, they realized how much more serious the terrorist attack might have been. This time, instead of the senseless, pulped-flesh carnage of the usual I R A bomb attack, there had been no casualties except for a superficial cut on the cheekbone of the uniformed doorman, who was reluctantly escorted to St Thomas's casualty ward, muttering that he didn't know what London was coming to, what with the Irish killing old women and children, the Iranians holding Americans hostage in their own embassy, the Lebanese machine-gunning each other, the Syrians hijacking airplanes and the Nigerians kidnapping their diplomats and crating them up for export. Sometimes he wished he was back in the trenches, he grumbled to the paramedic; at least on the Somme, you knew who your enemy was and where Fritz was hiding.

Abdullah turned to Pagan, who was huddled in the corner of his Rolls. 'Next time we must go somewhere quieter,' he suggested.

'Abdi, your driver will hear.'

'No, he won't. That's a permanent, bulletproof, glass partition.' He noticed that, for the first time, she had called him by his old pet name of Abdi.

'Will you spend the weekend with me? We could go where nobody knows you.' Abdullah's hand was insistent on her thigh.

Pagan gabbled, 'I couldn't do that. People would talk. It's only been five months since Christopher died and I was very fond of him, you know.'

'That is exactly why you need a few days away from life. A weekend in Venice. We could be there and back before anyone noticed.'

Pagan hesitated. 'What do you mean by a weekend?'

She felt his forefinger trace her calf, then her knee, then her thigh again. Pagan wished that she wasn't wearing chainstore pantyhose. She wished that she was wearing black, sheer silk stockings with black satin garters and lots and lots of lace. She'd better nip round to Keturah Brown before this trip to Venice.

Pagan walked slowly up the stairs. It seemed a very long climb to her bedroom. Once inside, the drawers of the Queen Anne tallboy were difficult to open. Where did I put my bathing suit? she wondered. Aimlessly she began to pull out clothes and throw them on the floor. Suddenly she felt something hard and knobbly in her hand. She looked at it for a few moments before realizing what it was. The old red dog collar was worn and curled at the end; a few of Buster's coarse hairs were still caught beneath the metal studs.

Suddenly Pagan saw Buster lying dead on the road, then this was replaced by a different mental picture. Pagan saw the hospital sheet draped over her husband's mangled body. She felt her mouth open in a distorted scream. At last she felt tears in her eyes. 'Christopher!' she shouted to the empty room as sobs tore at her chest. Why am I crying? she asked herself. I shouldn't be crying. Christopher died months ago. This is ridiculous. I must stop it.

One of Mark Scott's war photographs flashed into Pagan's mind. She saw a bombed building, exposed like an open doll's house to the outside elements. The flowered wallpaper was hanging in strips from the walls, the pictures were crooked, a chair and a smashed television set were piled on top of the rubble. Coats still hung from the hooks in the hall, but the end of the hall was missing. It wasn't meant to be like this, the building mutely said. That was how Pagan felt about herself and her altered life. One minute it was there, whole and complete, and the next minute it had been smashed. Half her life was missing, like half that building was missing.

Suddenly Pagan was able to accept that the life she had known was a thing of the past. It was gone for ever. She was able to accept that her situation had changed, that she had to make her own way in the world. She realized that she was not alone in the world, that she had known good times and bad times before Christopher died, and she would do so again. Life would never be the same again, but she would make a different life. Life would go on, and so would she.

Pagan could not stop crying. When Sophia returned home from school, she found her mother curled up on the bedroom carpet, still clutching Buster's collar in her hand and sobbing noisily.

'Mummy, what is it? Why are you crying?' Sophia stroked Pagan's head and wondered what to do, who to call.

'I don't know,' Pagan howled, 'but I can't s-s-s-s-s-stop.'

Sophia sat down beside her and also started to bawl.

At last, together, they were able to share their grief.

Late June 1979

'THEY'LL just have to wait for their money, my blood isn't bankable.' Judy wearily shoved a pile of bills off her knees; they slid down the fox-fur spread of her brown velvet bed with a menacing little shoosh to Tom, who was seated on the end of the bed. 'At least switching the printers paid off. We've saved a slice of this month's budget.' Noisily she blew her nose; her bout of summer flu just made everything that much worse.

Tom shook his head. 'I didn't want to discuss it until you were back in the office, but the colour reproduction of our July issue is way below standard.'

'The printers swear that they'll do a better job next month. Teething troubles, they said.'

Again Tom shook his head. 'Next month is too late. Lady Mirabelle Cosmetics has withdrawn the new fall campaign because they say our colour reproduction is no longer good enough.'

Judy's already pale face went white. 'When did that happen?'

'This afternoon. That's why I had to talk to you. A lot of advertisers have been griping; we've already lost a few of the smaller ones, but Lady Mirabelle's a body-blow.' Judy knew perfectly well that the Lady Mirabelle Christmas Gift campaign accounted for a big chunk of their revenue from September to Christmas. 'We can't replace that money,' Tom emphasized.

'Does anyone else know?' asked Judy.

'No.'

'Are you sure no one knows?' she persisted.

'No.' Tom gave a short laugh. 'Not even Tony knows about the Lady Mirabelle problem.'

Judy flopped back wearily on her cream silk pillows. Tom looked at her and thought, it's not like Judy to act so spoiled and sound so sorry for herself. And she hasn't got that much to be sorry about. Just because you were born poor doesn't mean that the world owes you a living at some later date. Parts of Judy's life had been hard, but they'd nearly all been interesting, and she'd had some really lucky breaks on her way to the top. Maybe she'd become over-ambitious, maybe they both had. Tom knew that was Kate's opinion. Trouble was, Judy wasn't used to losing. And they were both under great strain. Tom said, 'Judy, we took a gamble on the printing and we lost the gamble. But winners always take risks and sometimes they lose. Failing sometimes is a part of long-term winning. You can see their point, Judy. They aren't going to spend millions developing plum colours, then run ads for them in a magazine that prints them light purple. Switching printers was a false economy.' Tom's usually cheerful face was strained. 'And there's another thing that you may have forgotten. All our business loans are guaranteed against each other. The PR company is still doing fine, and so is the property company, but they guarantee the magazine, which, in turn, guarantees our stock market investments . . .'

'Losses, you mean!' snorted Judy.

'. . . which means that we can't liquidate one part of our business without the domino effect. They'll all start crashing.'

'Tom, this is like a nightmare. A crash is what I've always dreaded, and you've always told me my attitude was overcautious. You always said that we were borrowing in order not to miss business opportunities. Why, only nine months ago you told me that we were worth two million dollars *more* this year. What about the Hoffmann-La Roche profits that you stuck in Swiss francs?'

'That was before our copper futures problem.' Tom looked uncomfortable. Judy had always hated him playing the futures market.

Judy said, 'I wish we'd sorted out the *Verve!* portfolio and separated the investment business from the rest of the company, as Kate suggested.'

'We just never got around to it. I wish you'd never run that interview with Lili! Let's both stop wishing and think positive!' He handed her the box of Kleenex. 'Our financial situation is a house of cards; we've borrowed from Peter to pay Paul for months now and we can't go on much longer.'

'Sometimes,' Judy's voice was flat, 'I'd just like to take a plane and leave it all behind me.' She looked at the space on the wall where her treasured silk painting of a Manchu noble had hung until it had followed the jade collection to Sotheby's a few weeks earlier. Despite the warmth of the apartment and the thick fur spread, Judy felt cold and bone-tired. Why hadn't the *Verve!* lawyers picked up the danger in that fatal interview with Lili? Why didn't the First Amendment apply to magazines as it did to newspapers? How could one lousy paragraph of print have sabotaged her entire life's achievement? If I could wipe out five minutes of my life, Judy thought, I'd choose the time it took for Lili to tell me about Senator Ruskington.

Tom stood up, then picked up the heavy file box that contained their depositions for the hearing on the following day. 'I want you to read your statement once again before you sign it, Judy,' he said gently. 'We've got to get this absolutely right.'

Judy sighed, took the document from him and began to read it. 'At least after we win this hearing we'll wring a few thousand in damages out of the senator when we counter-sue for libel.'

'Nobody wins a lawsuit, Judy, you know that. Even if we win, we'll still be thousands of dollars in hock.'

'Not "if" Tom, "when",' Judy stressed, with weary stubbornness. She hadn't achieved what she had by giving up easily. Tom said nothing and looked at his scuffed Gucci loafers. To change the subject he asked, 'Want to hear what's happened to Kate?'

'Of course.' Judy brightened as Tom pulled from his pocket an airmail envelope covered with neat, small handwriting, with no loops or flourishes.

'"The hill-tribe guerrillas are getting stronger," she says. They've raided banks, attacked the Bengali settlements and the army garrison and she thinks they're secretly planning an assault on the oil companies. That will be Shell, I suppose. Her typewriter's been stolen, but she hopes to buy a new one on the black market, and she says she'll sleep with it chained to her wrist.'

'You don't seem very worried about her, Tom.'

'You know Kate. She hates a dull life, so I go along with what makes her happy. Of course I'm worried about her.'

'Hasn't anyone got any good news to cheer me up?' Judy picked up a second legal document from the pile.

'No news of Mark?'

'I've already told you, that's over. Mark and I were finished months ago.' She buried her head in her hands. 'I can't take it any more,' she whispered. 'Why is it that the minute you're off balance, the vultures close in, trying to bring you down? Mark's in Nicaragua, and he's in Nicaragua because he doesn't care to be around unsuccessful, old me.'

Tom silently offered her another tissue from the box on the rosewood table beside her bed. 'Judy, I can't imagine that anyone would leave you just because you're vulnerable or depressed or not sixteen any more. You're a complete woman, Judy, and an honest woman. I think you're the most honest woman I've ever met, and any man could love you for that alone.'

She shook her head and slowly wiped her reddened eyes. 'All that Mark really liked about me was the fact that I *didn't* need him. As soon as I needed him, *really* needed him, he ran away in the most destructive possible way.' Again the tears started trickling from the sides of her eyes. 'The crisp executive in me was irresistible so long as she was giving her attention to Mark's brilliant career and his home comforts. He was very pleased to live off my emotional strength when I had enough for two, but when I needed someone to take care of *me* for a change, he couldn't take it.' Judy's voice crackled with misery and she sobbed silently behind her hands.

Tom said, 'It's normal to suffer when a relationship ends. You get a few kicks in your pride, your dignity gets a bit dented, it's a diminishing experience for everybody,' he soothed. 'But Judy, you've only got to compare the divorce rate and the marriage statistics to know that people can split or hitch up any time, at any age. You're still attractive . . .'

'That's great, Tom, just great – that makes me feel like Methuselah's mother. "You're still attractive" means that when people look at me they can see the day coming when I won't be attractive any more. It means that time's running out.' She blew her nose again. 'This isn't the way I want to end up, Tom, alone in bed with my work. This wasn't the rosy vision I had in front of me when I first ran away from Rossville to make my fortune.'

She scraped her face with a tissue, leaving red weals on her cheeks.

'Don't be too hard on Mark,' Tom pleaded. 'I don't suppose either of us is the easiest person in the world to be with when we're under this sort of strain.'

'That's not it.' Judy pushed her fingers through her hair with a gesture of anguish. 'I'm not easy to be with because everybody's got the wrong idea about me. Mark's no different from any other man. To him, a woman in a top job is tough, self-possessed, independent – all the things he has to be to stay at the top of his profession. What he doesn't understand is that, just because I am those things at work, it doesn't follow that I want to be the same way at home. Like all you men, Mark thinks a successful career woman isn't interested in kindness, or caring and sharing, and he thinks I don't need it. But I *do*. I'm just as thirsty for love as any housewife running a couple of kids and a recipe club; the only difference is that I run a corporation.'

'Finish these papers, Judy, and then I'll take them all away,' Tom coaxed her. 'Crying won't get us out of the hole we're in.'

As Judy dried her tears and finished reading her statement, Tom turned on the TV in time to catch the late news. As he had anticipated, Senator Ruskington was interviewed with his loyal wife at his side. Her face was serious and indignant. The senator answered the interviewer. 'This is indeed a most unpleasant case, which is why my wife and I feel that it is my duty to the public to expose this situation for what it is.' Expertly Ruskington turned to face the camera head-on. 'An unpleasant attempt to sell an unpleasant magazine through salacious innuendo and un-Christian lies. Any money which comes to us through this lawsuit will be donated to a charity which will be chosen by my wife.' The senator was glibly pious.

'But you are claiming ten million dollars in damages,' the reporter reminded him.

'Whatever the court sees fit to award us will all be given to charity,' the senator confirmed. 'My wife and I wish it to be known that there is not a shred of evidence to support the vile accusations printed in *Verve!* magazine. We feel it is appropriate that the people who publish this dishonest magazine should see the rewards of their evildoing.'

Judy shook her fist at the TV screen and gathered up the scattered papers on her bed. 'I'm going to go through these once again, Tom,' she said.

The woman TV reporter suggested, 'Some people find it hard to understand why you are pushing this case against *Verve!* magazine with so much vigour.'

'Attagirl!' Judy cried, sitting up in bed. 'I bet she reads *Verve!*'

The senator again turned to the camera. 'My wife and I feel that, until some person in our situation makes a stand, any so-called actress can draw attention to herself by linking her name with that of a prominent public citizen.' The senator paused for breath. 'I want everyone to know that our family is united in fighting this attempt to blacken our good name and to brand me as a fornicator and an adulterer.'

'But, Senator, isn't this also an attempt on your part to obtain a great deal of money?' the reporter prodded him.

'My personal reputation is worth more to me than any sum of money,' said the senator. The interview ended and Tom switched off the TV.

Tom left her apartment shortly after midnight, saying, 'Take care of yourself, Judy.'

That's what I've been trying to do for the last thirty years, she thought.

Judy remembered how depressed she'd felt in Switzerland, where she'd worked all day at the language laboratory and every evening and weekend as a waitress at the Chesa. She'd never learned to ski, she'd never gone to dances and she'd never had pretty clothes like Maxine and Kate. She still remembered her sudden bitterness when the young Pagan had, without thinking twice, returned the diamond necklace that Prince Abdullah had tried to give her; that necklace would have paid for Judy's entire year in Europe.

Judy never permitted herself to remember what it felt like to be really poor, because she panicked when she recalled having only one pair of shoes and one repeatedly patched dress. But when she remembered her mother's hopeless face and the strained, tense atmosphere in their home for the two years during which her father was out of work, then Judy felt grim determination to succeed – at no matter what cost to herself.

Tom told me to take care of myself, she thought bitterly, picking up her ebony bedside mirror and looking at her face, which reflected the tension of the past few months.

Judy worked through the night on her deposition and finally finished it at six in the morning. She heard the maid's key in the lock, and called, 'Forget about breakfast, Francetta, and call me at eight o'clock. I'm off to Philadelphia again.' Then she drifted off to sleep.

'What time will you be home, Curtis?' Debra Halifax asked her husband.

He walked to the sideboard and lifted the silver entrée dish for a second helping of scrambled eggs. 'Usual time, I expect.' He wondered how it was possible to feel so worn and jaded at the beginning of a new day. 'What are you planning to do today, Debra?'

'I'm not planning to do anything.' Debra managed to make the statement sound like an accusation. At least, thought Curtis, she was eating again, although she did not seem to be gaining any weight. Dr Joseph thought that her infertility had been linked to her anorexia.

'Don't forget what Dr Joseph said. If you want to make a full recovery, you must start leading your own life and you begin by structuring your day. Why don't you go shopping with Jane?'

'You don't get over a nervous breakdown by going shopping. That's all I've ever done with my entire life. That's the trouble!'

'Now, Debra, Dr Joseph explained that it wasn't exactly a nervous . . .'

'Oh, yes it was!'

She's almost proud of it, Curtis thought wearily; it's her one achievement in life, the only thing she ever managed to do entirely on her own – have a nervous breakdown.

'Dr Joseph also said that what I needed was the love and support of my husband.'

'I do love you, Debra, and I try to support you,' Curtis said once again.

'Then why don't you spend more time with me?' she demanded. 'If you're not at the bank, you're at the Philadelphia Club or off playing golf or fishing with your friends.'

'Now that's not so. I spend a lot of time with you, Debra.'

'Not alone.' Her voice was vinegar. 'We give parties, and we go to parties; we meet the same people over and over.'

'But they're our friends,' Curtis protested.

'Would you say we have friends, Curtis? I wouldn't. We have your business people and your political people and our families, but we don't have any real friends, do we? And I never have a spare minute, but I lead an empty life.' Again her accusatory tone flicked at her husband as Debra started her weekly moan. Curtis never knew what to say or what to do or what to suggest. 'Look, I've got to leave, I'm late. Why not take Jane to a museum?'

'You know very well that museums depress me. A museum wouldn't solve *my* problem. Not now that I know what my problem is.' Debra's voice trembled. 'There's someone else, isn't there? You're in love with someone else, aren't you, Curtis? That woman I saw in your office. I know she lunched with you yesterday, I saw it in your appointment book. She's always coming down to see you. You're having an affair with the famous Judy Jordan, aren't you, Curtis?'

'No. I see her on business!' Curtis felt exhausted as his wife's persistent questions continued. Debra had started to stage jealous rages over his imagined infidelity almost immediately after they married. Dr Joseph had explained that Debra's jealousy was the classic result of paranoid delusions. Curtis had bowed his head under the onslaught of accusation. After all, he had a reason to feel guilty, although he was pretty sure that Debra didn't know about it.

Gradually Curtis recognized that Debra said little which was founded on reason, and then, slowly, he had come to realize that his wife was not entirely . . . well. Dr Joseph used the phrase 'borderline psychotic'. After twenty years of marriage Curtis Halifax knew that his wife's grasp on sanity was easily loosened; her family had always known of this and now the Halifax family knew of it, but the subject was never discussed. Debra was nervous, that was all.

Now she said, 'If Judy Jordan was only in your office to discuss business, then why was she crying?'

'I don't recall that she was crying.'

'Yes, she was. Or she had been. I saw her eyes.'

'I simply haven't got time to rerun this scene today. I promise you, there's nothing personal between us.' Curtis rose from the damask-covered breakfast table, gave his wife a quick, impersonal kiss on the forehead and left, late for his meeting.

Once her husband had left, Debra Halifax went up to her pink bedroom where, leaning over the hand basin painted with apple blossoms, she stuck two fingers down her throat and vomited up her breakfast. To disguise the telltale odour of her stomach juices on her breath, she swilled eau-de-Cologne around her mouth, then spat it out; the repellent taste was a punishment for having eaten two pieces of toast at breakfast. No wonder Curtis no longer loved her, she thought as she pinched her thigh. I'm fat, I'm self-indulgent, I've got no self-control.

Every time Debra looked up at her reflection in the mirror she really believed that she saw a lumpish, frowsy, fat woman, instead of a small, skeletal figure. She panted through her morning session on the exercise bicycle, dragging her body through the Rocky Mountain programme twice, then worked out with weights to punish what she believed were her too-plump thighs and well-cushioned stomach.

Afterwards, Debra aimlessly wandered through the quiet house. A lot of her day was passed in an uncoordinated mental state, in which she was never fully aware of the time, of where she was or what she was doing. She flicked through magazines, read a few sentences and left them. She picked up a piece of petit point which had lain on her worktable uncompleted for several months, sewed a few stitches and abandoned it. She watered a handsome Clivia plant, which the gardener watered each week in any case. Debra's luxuriant house plants often died because of their owner's erratic attentions.

For the fourth time that morning she picked up the telephone to call Jane, but the effort of talking was too much for her. Besides, Jane only liked being with her because Jane had no money. Perhaps Jane had her eye on Curtis. That would make sense from Jane's point of view. But Jane was a Catholic and she was married with two children. Always running through Debra's head, like the sound of a distant river, was the idea that Curtis was unfaithful to her with some woman. By midday, when the maid brought her lunch on a tray, Debra had formed the image of a faceless seductress who was stealing her husband away from her. By the middle of the afternoon, when the shadow of the magnolia tree was lengthening across the lawn outside, she hated this anonymous woman with murderous ferocity.

It was too hot in the garden. Debra drifted into the library and sat in her husband's chair behind the green leather-topped partner's desk. She imagined Curtis on the telephone to his faceless mistress, while she, Debra, slept innocently upstairs. She imagined her husband whispering hot words of love and saw his features soften with affection and sensuality, as she remembered them during the first few weeks of their marriage. By the end of the afternoon the vision of her husband's infidelity was far more real to Debra than any real experience she had encountered that day.

One by one she opened the drawers of the desk and rifled through the papers she found in them. There must be love letters, but where were they? Sure enough, the small top drawer was locked. Debra scattered the pens from the pen tray, found the silver paperknife and forced the little lock.

Inside the drawer were some black-and-white photographs of a small girl, a pile of press clippings and a curl of dark hair tied with a white ribbon. Debra's claw-thin hand pulled out a few recent clippings and turned them over. 'Lili to star as Mistinguett', she read. So Curtis was fooling around with an actress. Debra shivered with rage. You may be young, beautiful and famous, Lili, but let's see if money can hurt you.

The Spear flashed by, unmistakably black among the white, green and orange bodywork of the other competitors at Brand's Hatch. Inside the hot cockpit Gregg sat in a pool of sweat; a driver could lose over five pounds in a long race. Ahead of Gregg a white BMW went into Stirling's Bend too fast, lost adhesion, ploughed straight on to hit the bend hard and, as Gregg passed it, burst into flames.

Gregg suppressed the vision of his own body enveloped in flame as the Spear streaked past the grandstand for the fifth time. He listened to the high-pitched whine of the engine as he dropped two gears to set the car up for Druid's, the hairpin bend. Coming out of the bend, he saw the Dinetti-Mazda not far ahead. He's in trouble; I'll pass him on the Cooper Straight, Gregg thought.

By the end of the first hour of the 1,000-kilometre race Gregg was lying seventh, but the gaps were small and that meant nothing at this stage; a bit of bad luck could knock you right out of the race in a second.

He rounded Stirling's Bend, and accelerated away down to Clearways. He projected his mind ahead to Clark Curve, which always looked deceptively gentle, but which demanded extra concentration for a car with the power of the Spear. Gregg was now close enough to take the Aston Martin Nimrod on the top straight. He blinked sweat from his eyes as, three cars ahead of him, the green-and-white Jaguar shed a rear wheel with no warning, swerved into the barrier, then shot backwards on to the track amid a shower of sparks.

The Porsche behind it pulled out fast; the two cars touched but the Porsche managed to straighten up and hurtle on. The Nimrod driver miscalculated the Jaguar's continuing path across the track, and crashed into the spinning Jaguar. The two cars twisted together with a sickening crunch of metal, then the force of the impact hurled them both off the track, two seconds before Gregg would have hit them.

Now bathed in cold sweat, Gregg's legs involuntarily shook, and it took a fierce effort to turn his mind to the road ahead and away from the burning destruction behind him – of which he had so nearly been a part. Suddenly Gregg felt a thread of pain shoot up his left leg and his foot jumped on to the clutch. Must be that ankle. Thank God he got off the throttle in time. He'd hand over at the next pit stop.

Four hours later Gregg was lying close behind the leading Porsche, a position that, for the previous twenty-seven laps, he had grimly clung to, but had been unable to improve. Then the gap between the Spear and the car ahead began slowly to close as Gregg, sandwiched between two Porsches, crept closer to the lead car, and they braked for Paddock Bend.

Just ahead, Gregg calculated, a group of slower cars were bunched together. Gregg decided to make an immediate bid for the lead on the inside of Druid's, beyond which they would catch two of the slower cars. On Hailwood Hill he pulled out and left his braking to the last moment. The Spear shot past the Porsche as they entered the corner.

Gregg held the tight inside line, but slid out wide on the exit. The Porsche stayed behind; this was no place to retake. Then Gregg was weaving between the back markers in front of the South Bank stands, aware of a crescendo of spectator cheering as he roared past with sixteen laps to go.

His ankle ached but the pain was easily bearable. It was really just a bloody nuisance. Inside the noisy cockpit Gregg could not hear the mounting excitement of the PA commentator. '. . . and with three laps to go, it looks as if Gregg Eagleton in the Eagle Spear is increasing the lead over the Porsche . . .'

As he hurtled into Dingle Dell Corner for the hundred and fiftieth time that day Gregg struggled to keep his eyes on the track. The pain in his left leg was increasing. Suddenly his sight became misty and he thought, dear God, stop me blacking out before the race is over.

The turbo-charged engine belched flames as Gregg missed a gear before the grandstands. Suddenly each movement of his injured foot produced an excruciating wrench of agony. He heard the voice from the Eagle pit over the radio link that was built into his helmet. 'Stick with it, Gregg, you're well in the lead now.'

'How much lead have I got?' Gregg's stomach was beginning to churn with pain.

'Fourteen seconds.'

No chance of pulling into the pit and handing over to his co-driver for the last few laps. Nothing for it, he was in this race to the end.

The next time he left Paddock Bend Gregg again fumbled the gear change. His injured foot was now so swollen that he could barely move it.

'Porsche is creeping up, Gregg,' the voice warned in his ear.

The Spear flew on.

As he pushed the Spear out of Hawthorn Bend his left foot had only just enough pressure for the clutch pedal, and Gregg felt vomit in his mouth. For a moment he lost his concentration.

Passing the Aston Martin Nimrod, the Spear swerved frighteningly close to the other car, and got off line.

The Porsche slipped through at Dingle Dell.

Through a rising mist of pain Gregg registered the delighted howl of the crowd, then the Eagle flag, to signify the last lap, was flourished at the side of the track.

Another mouthful of bile and Gregg lost concentration for another fatal second. The radio voice registered no emotion. 'Stephenson in the BMW is creeping up as well. Will the foot hold out?'

'Yes.' Gregg's voice cracked with the effort of controlling the pain in his body. For the last time, and in a maze of pain, he took the car around the tree-lined circuit; he could feel an internal grating pain in his ankle at every movement. He barely noticed the BMW pass him.

'Yes, the Spear is definitely in trouble. This is going to be a great disappointment to the Eagle team,' gabbled the commentator as they turned into the Brabham Straight. 'And, as the flag drops, it's first place to Werner Hentzen in the Porsche,' announced the PA, 'followed by Stephenson in the BMW and Eagleton just manages to scrape third place in the Spear from Dinetti with . . . and something is happening to the Spear! . . .'

From the viewing area above the pits Lili saw Gregg flash past in third place, then the Spear lost speed dangerously fast and began to weave towards the side of the track. The drivers crossing the line swerved to avoid the black Spear. One did not.

Lili screamed in terror as the white-and-orange Lancia obliquely hit the back of the Spear. Both cars spun off the track and the Spear slammed into a barrier. Ignoring Jack's shout of warning, Lili set off, running behind the pit area towards the twisted wreckage of the Spear, from which a column of smoke was now billowing upwards.

'Get back, get back, you stupid bitch – she could blow at any second.' A paramedic picked Lili up and half threw her behind the barrier.

The other paramedic yanked open the door of the Spear and pulled out Gregg's inert body. Within minutes the medical helicopter, with Gregg aboard, lifted towards Sidcup and St Mary's Hospital.

The PA blared, 'Eagleton is definitely injured . . .'

'A stress fracture in these bones, that's the cause of the trouble.' The doctor waved his pen over the X-ray plate. 'As your first accident was several weeks ago, and the injury wasn't diagnosed at the time, I'm afraid it's possible that the associated swelling and distortion may have affected the other joints.'

'So how long before I can drive again?' Gregg's face was bleached and strained.

'Difficult to say. We'll give you painkillers, of course, and a series of injections to reduce the swelling, but healing the fracture itself is something that we can't do much about. Only time will put it right.'

'But how *much* time? I've got to race in France again in three weeks.'

'The best advice I can give you is to forget all about racing for at least two months.' The doctor slipped the X-ray back in the buff file. 'Complete bed rest for a minimum of six weeks, and no hard exercise of any kind until you are one hundred per cent fit. With this kind of injury, nature must take its course.'

After the doctor had left Gregg began to work through his letters with his secretary until Jack arrived with a detailed report on the Spear's condition. 'She's looking good, Gregg – the fuel pump was as clean as a whistle this time. What about you? Shall we get Pete to stand by for Richard?'

Lili waited patiently at the end of the line of visitors. Then, as she bent to kiss Gregg, a young blonde nurse popped her head around the door to say, 'Time's up for today, everyone. Doctor's orders. Mr Eagleton has to rest!'

As the others moved towards the door Lili said sadly, 'I've hardly had a chance to talk to you, Gregg.'

'Sorry, darling, but I'm trying to run my business from a hospital bed. I've got to see Jack, my secretary, the sponsors and Dad as well as you, and I'm only allowed visitors for an hour a day. I know you haven't seen much of me since you met me, but I don't want you to get the wrong idea. You've met the team, Lili, and you know what my responsibilities are.'

Lili looked down and sighed as Gregg said, 'I'm not in business on my own, darling. Everyone in Eagle Motors depends on me and I depend on them. I have to meet a pretty large payroll every month to feed families. There are men in the Eagle team working for me, for my father and for the idea of a British privateer outfit in saloon racing, who put in twenty-four-hour days on their vacations. I can't let them down, Lili.' He reached for her hand and pulled her to his side. 'I can't do what I want, or go where I want when I please, or step into that car at less than my best. It would be unfair and irresponsible. You've got to understand that the business comes first in my life, and I can't let anything divert me from it, not even you, darling.'

Silently Lili bent and kissed him. 'I can wait.'

Debra Halifax leaned back against white broderie-anglaise pillows and aimlessly turned the newspaper pages until she reached Liz Smith's column. Suddenly an item caught her attention and she read it aloud. 'Lili to star in charity benefit...' Debra looked up, instantly alive, and said softly, 'This is what I've been waiting for.'

～ II ～

Early July 1979

THE pink hydrangea wallpaper matched the heavy, chintz curtains, which were swagged back by tasselled gold ropes. A maple-framed portrait of Lord Byron hung above Pagan's desk. The back of the high satinwood desk was lined with tiny drawers and cupboards; silver-framed photographs, small bowls of potpourri, an antique silver calendar, jostled for space with a pile of letters that were weighed down by her long-dead grandfather's lucky hare's foot. It looked like a royal desk, the sort of desk upon which there was no space to work.

'Any other business?' Pagan looked around her drawing room at the eleven other members of the fund-raising committee that was planning Lili's gala for the Anglo-American Cancer Research Institute. They had discussed the rehearsal costs and the extra time demanded by the stagehands' union for working on Sunday; they had approved the programme design and the seating arrangements for the Royal Box. Pagan had joyfully announced that the theatre was sold out, and now her chewed yellow pencil was poised above the last item on the agenda.

'One final matter.' The organizing secretary passed her a letter on the blue writing paper of the Grosvenor House Hotel. 'Someone has offered to give a pre-theatre party for us.'

'How very thoughtful. Who is it?'

'Another anonymous benefactor, Lady Swann.'

Pagan skimmed the letter quickly, 'A champagne reception for two thousand guests! That's wonderful news.'

'Someone must think a lot of the Institute.'

'Or of Christopher,' said Pagan, momentarily sad.

'Or of Lili?' the wife of the chainstore millionaire suggested. 'Perhaps it's one of her admirers?'

'He must have a bob or two to lay on champagne for two thousand people,' said the grey-haired merchant banker, who was smoking a cigar.

'We'll send the invitation out with the tickets.' Pagan leafed through her file.

'But is there time to print invitations?' The Scottish duchess looked anxious.

'Yes,' said the secretary. 'I've already checked with the printer.'

Pagan, notorious for the tight financial control with which she organized her fund-raising events, flipped through her file. 'Have we got the cheque?'

'The Grosvenor House Hotel has been paid direct, by banker's draft.'

'How *very* thoughtful,' Pagan said. She stood up and opened a window, because she hated a room to smell of cigar smoke and it took at least two weeks to get rid of the smell. She walked back and leaned against the rather ugly, black marble fireplace, which was covered by a jumble of blue chinoiserie plates, a ginger jar, a Regency biscuit box and a small blue-enamel clock with a diamanté-encircled face that had been given to her grandmother by Queen Alexandra.

Pagan smiled at her committee. 'I'm sorry we've run a little over time, today, but this unexpectedly generous offer had to be discussed. Now, if you'll excuse me, I must dash or I'll miss my flight to Venice.'

The wind whipped at Pagan's hair as the high-powered speed-boat raced across the lagoon towards Venice. In the distance she could see the grey domes of the cathedral, the imposing belltower in St Mark's Square, the candy-striped mooring poles sticking at crazy angles out of the water, and clouds of pigeons fluttering in the hazy blue sky.

Abdullah's private jet had flown them to Marco Polo Airport, and they were now heading for the Cipriani Hotel. In the launch behind them travelled Abdullah's four bodyguards and a great deal of luggage, most of which belonged to Abdullah.

Pagan looked at the enticing city rising straight out of the water. She was excited. 'Oh, Abdi, it's so beautiful. It's floating in the sea like a shimmering, gold mirage!'

'Don't expect too much romance,' Abdullah warned her. 'A lot of people loathe Venice.'

'Why, for heaven's sake?'

'The smells, the crowds, the claustrophobia and that dreadful, vulgar glassware.'

Pagan laughed. 'In that case,' she said, 'I won't expect any golden gondolas!'

'The golden gondolas only come out once a year, for the gondoliers' festival races.'

The battered, green crocodile suitcase that had once be-longed to Pagan's grandmother was deposited on the pale-coral carpet of the suite. The walls looked hand-painted with an airy green forest, which blended with the green sofas and the green-and-silver Fortuny curtains. Pagan rushed through glass doors that led on to a terrace lined with miniature cypress trees; it overlooked the orange trees that surrounded the hotel swimming pool and, beyond that, the entire panorama of Venice.

'Do you like it?' She heard Abdullah's voice behind her.

Pagan looked embarrassed and uncomfortable. She didn't know whether Abdullah was planning to share her suite.

Abdullah grinned. 'I shall be in the next suite . . . if you need me. Sadly, there is no billiard room in this hotel. Space is at a premium in Venice.'

The following morning, as Pagan waited by the two black-and-white-striped mooring poles of the Cipriani jetty, she clutched at Abdullah's arm. 'Look! You were wrong!' A golden gondola bobbed towards them over the scummy green water.

Abdullah said, 'As a matter of fact, it's yours. I hope it's not too ostentatious for you.'

Under the golden, arched canopy, sitting on the faded, purple cushions, Pagan gazed up at the naked, golden backside of Neptune as he wielded his trident over the poop of the boat. To her disappointment, this glorious vessel was motorized, with a spluttering engine more appropriate to a fishing smack than a ceremonial barge.

The gondola chugged down the Grand Canal between boats delivering coal, Coca-Cola, Japanese tourists and gangs of workmen to their appropriate destinations. They passed pink-and-ochre baroque palaces, tidemarked by water, with ferns twisting their bricks apart and cobwebs veiling their patchy, peeling plaster.

'Don't ask the gondolier to sing Santa Lucia,' murmured Abdullah, 'because it is a Neapolitan song and he will grind his teeth.'

Pagan sniffed happily. 'I love everything about this place, even the smell.'

'The smell is decay and water rot, which smells fascinating so long as it is not in your home.'

Later they landed and explored a little of the town on foot, but as soon as they left the large, crowded streets for the narrow, winding alleys behind them, Pagan looked puzzled and stopped. 'All these alleys look the same. I'm confused.' One of the bodyguards stepped forward and muttered a few guttural words to His Majesty. They followed the man until they again found themselves at the small wrought-iron bridge where the golden gondola awaited them. Abdullah said, 'Although Venice is such a small town, it's very easy to get lost here. It's a well-known hazard. All the bridges and buildings look different according to whether the tide is in or not. The streets are a twisting maze, so you can't look back and get a sense of direction.'

Abdullah then insisted that Pagan do some shopping in the shops round St Mark's Square. She was measured for a pair of silver snakeskin shoes and then chose a classic shoe in red. Abdullah said, 'They're very elegant. Order them in every colour they have.' He waved his hand at the excited young shoemaker and strolled out of the shop as Pagan mused, 'What on earth will I do with twenty-seven pairs of pumps?'

By the time they were drinking their lunchtime Bellinis (the mixture of champagne and peach juice that was invented in Venice) the bodyguards were also guarding a second launch, laden with a complete set of calf luggage with golden clasps, twenty metres of handsome lace, which Pagan planned to keep for Sophia's wedding dress, and more clothes than Pagan had ever possessed in her life, including three antique Fortuny dresses, in coral, brown and dark green, and an opera cloak in canary-yellow silk.

They spent an unforgettable afternoon in bed.

'Your Majesty, this is the Sala del Maggior Consiglio, the very cradle of Western democracy, where the Great Council of Venice met to elect representatives to the governing committees.' Pagan and Abdullah obediently followed the curator's finger with their eyes as he pointed up to the painted ceiling, where the nacreous light from the lagoon outside played on the rich colours of the panels. 'Notice the frieze of the seventy-six Doges, the painting of Paradise by Tintoretto, and here the Apotheosis of Venice by Veronese.'

'Cradle of democracy!' muttered Abdullah, amused. 'How can they make such a claim when Renaissance Venice was a corrupt state, run by spies and assassins, with dungeons, daggers and poison.' He and Pagan were both tired after hours of pacing through the richly ornamented palace, followed at a respectful distance by Abdullah's two bodyguards. Pagan's neck ached from looking at the sumptuous stuccoed ceilings and her feet were sore from the hard marble floors.

'At least only the Venetians elected their rulers,' Pagan argued.

'They elected them from the aristocratic élite. That is not a free election in the democratic sense,' Abdullah corrected her.

Stung by his patronizing voice, Pagan retorted, 'Five hundred years ago Venice was still more democratic than Sydon is today. Your Council of Five isn't elected by a free ballot of all your citizens.'

'Pagan, don't be stupid. Democracy can only operate in a country with literacy, a good standard of living and no endemic corruption. The average citizen of my country would vote for anyone who promised him two goats and a bracelet for his wife.'

'Then why don't you do something about it?'

'You know that I'm trying.' Abdullah's voice was frosty.

'I think you're happy as a benevolent despot,' Pagan snorted.

'Democracy doesn't insure a healthy state. Good government does that.'

'In a democracy, wealth isn't in the hands of a few tribal clans as it is in Sydon.'

'That is a foolish remark.'

'Oh, don't be so bloody pompous!' Pagan snapped, turning crossly on her heel. She strode through a doorway into yet another immense room. Hearing footsteps behind her, she turned to see that one of the royal bodyguards was following her, while Abdullah, as if nothing had happened, was talking to the guide. Being a royal tourist was worse than being a schoolgirl, Pagan thought irritably; you were never allowed to walk alone. After only one day she found it oppressive. She started to walk faster. She was damned if she was going to be nannied.

As the Doge's Palace had been closed for their visit, Pagan moved with increasing speed through the empty rooms to the staircase which led down to the courtyard. But, as she dashed under the triumphal arch of the palace and out into the crowded Piazza San Marco, she could hear the bodyguard clattering down the steps behind her.

Damned if I'm going to let Abdullah's bloody sheepdog round me up, she thought angrily, darting through a small herd of German tourists.

Seeing the restaurant where, that morning, they had drunk Bellinis, she ran blindly into the back and opened the washroom door. But it turned out to be the kitchen door. Pagan hurried past astonished waiters and cooks, past crates of fruit and vegetables, to the exit at the end of the room. Outside, she found herself in a small, smelly alleyway where the rosy evening sunlight reached only the highest balconies that overhung the dustbins of the restaurant.

Pagan darted into a doorway and peered round it at the restaurant kitchen door until she was sure that the bodyguard had not followed her. Then, jauntily, she set off down the alley, intending to go back to their hotel.

But, although they had explored the city by gondola that morning, Pagan suddenly realized that she had no idea where she was or the address of her hotel. No problem. Venice is a small town. When she found a canal, she could walk until she saw a water-taxi, then ask him to take her to the Cipriani.

Getting lost had never worried Pagan. However far she wandered as a child, she had always been able to find her way across the Cornish moorland, back to Trelawney. In fact, she rather liked not knowing where she was, Pagan thought as she turned into another alleyway; life seemed full of delicious, unexpected possibilities when she was lost. I wonder why I like surprises and hate routine, Pagan mused as she considered whether to cross a carved stone bridge to her left or to plunge into the maze of alleys on her right.

At the top of the arched bridge Pagan stopped and watched the dirty grey canal below, crowded with boats of every kind. She could also see the landing place, where the little launches – taxis of the town – were taking on passengers. She moved towards it, but when she had nearly reached the landing, Pagan changed her mind. An hour of freedom in Venice was not something to be squandered, just because your feet hurt. She turned and strolled in the opposite direction.

Seeing an enormous wooden door ajar, Pagan walked inside, and found herself in an incense-scented church. Unlike the magnificent churches that she had visited with Abdullah, which were more like picture galleries than places of worship, this was a working church. Dressed in black, several old women were praying; the statue of the Saint, Anthony of Padua, was encircled by half-burned votive candles. An array of gold and silver tinfoil images were pinned to the wall, messages of thanks to the saint who had granted the prayers of worshippers. The tinfoil hands, feet, arms and legs, were for healed injuries; tinfoil babies were from once-childless couples; tinfoil hearts with crowns, roses or ribbons around them were from newlyweds. These people don't hide what they want, thought Pagan. That's one of the differences between the English and the Italians.

The huge door creaked as she squeezed through it into fading daylight. As Pagan turned around the corner she heard the door creak again, then light footsteps behind her. Pagan suddenly realized that those steps had been much too quick for the arthritic old ladies in the church. The pearly light of the Venice evening was fading fast as Pagan hurried back towards the canal. Only she hadn't been walking towards the canal, she discovered. She stood in front of a narrow waterway with houses rising straight out of the dark water. Suddenly she recognized a fall of asparagus fern from a first-floor balcony down the path on her left. Aha, she'd noticed that this morning; she was on the correct route.

Again she set off confidently. Again she heard the light, stealthy footsteps behind her.

She stopped and looked over her shoulder, her heart starting to thump as she realized that it was some time since she had passed anyone in these narrow alleys.

The footsteps also stopped. Pagan started to hurry between the high, crumbling walls.

She stopped again and listened. The light pitter-patter of footsteps behind her stopped again.

Pagan spun round. The road curved behind her and she could see no one, but she was certain that someone was following her and, suddenly, Pagan was frightened.

Darkness was falling and, as she began to run, Pagan thought, it's not Abdi's bodyguard, I'm sure I lost him. Perhaps it's a mugger? I'll go back to the church and ask one of the old women to help me. No one will mug me in a church. She ran faster.

As she scuttled down empty lane after empty lane, blindly turning corners at any faintly familiar sight, Pagan realized that she had no idea where she was. And, as she ran along the criss-crossing labyrinth of dank alleys, the footsteps behind her grew louder and closer. Pagan stopped helplessly at yet another crossroads.

Suddenly a powerful hand grabbed her by the shoulder and spun her around.

It was Abdullah.

With relief, she threw her arms around him. 'I thought you'd never catch up!'

'Why were you running?'

'I thought someone was following me,' she said, unwilling to admit that she had been frightened.

'Do you know where you are?'

'No. Where are we?'

'I haven't the faintest idea.' He put his arm around her. 'You know you're in the most confusing city in the world.'

'I think we're near the fish market.' Pagan wrinkled her nose.

'The whole of Venice smells of that watery, rotting smell,' Abdullah dismissed her suggestion.

Around the corner they found themselves in the deserted fish market.

'At least we know where we are.' Triumphantly Pagan pointed. 'There's the canal! Now, all we have to do is find a water-taxi!'

Abdullah looked at her tired face, drew her to him and kissed her.

'I've been hoping you would do that all day.' Pagan wound her arms around his lean body. 'It's so nice to be without your bodyguard chaperones.'

'You should be used to them by now.' Abdullah brushed her eyebrows with his lips.

'I don't think I'll ever get used to them; they make me feel claustrophobic. I'm so glad I managed to throw them off.'

Abdullah pulled back, alarmed. 'I sincerely hope you have not thrown them off.' He quickly looked around. 'If they aren't behind us, then we must return to the hotel immediately.'

They hurried on. As they crossed the wet market cobbles Pagan heard the stealthy noise of following feet. Again she felt a twinge of panic. 'Abdi, I think someone is following us. Maybe the bodyguards are catching up, after all?'

'Nonsense, Pagan, it's just the echo of our own footsteps. You always hear that in Venice, the sound ricochets around all the little alleyways.'

'Yes, of course.' Pagan's voice was doubtful. There were footsteps behind them, coming from the deserted market buildings.

Pagan and Abdullah had almost reached the canalside, when from a side street, two young men stepped out and blocked their path.

Abdullah pushed Pagan into a doorway with one hand and, with the other hand, he seized one of the men around the neck, grappling for the pressure point, through which he could make the man unconscious.

There was a dull glint of metal as the second youth opened a switchblade and circled the two struggling men, looking for his chance to attack.

'Run, Pagan! They've got knives!'

Abdullah slipped on the slimy stones and fell, losing his grip on his opponent, who fell with him.

Pagan was no longer frightened. She felt calm and almost elated as she whipped off her high-heeled shoes and flew at the attacker on the ground, when he tried to get up. With her metal-tipped stilettos, Pagan lashed at his head. As the second man lunged forward Abdullah seized his knife hand, and then, with an agile heave, he threw both the attacker and the weapon into the canal.

As Abdullah whirled to help Pagan the second youth managed to dodge her blows and started to run along the canalside, chased by Abdullah. The mugger ran fast, but he was unlucky. As he rounded the next corner he blundered straight against the broad chests of Abdullah's bodyguards.

'You're carrying a knife as well!' Pagan gasped to Abdullah. 'Goodness, you fight dirty.' She pushed her hair out of her eyes.

'All kings fight dirty,' Abdullah panted. 'When you are a king,' he added, adjusting his tie, 'you must always fight to win.'

That evening they had dinner on the terrace of their suite, looking at the blazing lights of the Piazza San Marco across the lagoon. Abdullah waited until the silver tray of coffee had been removed, then he leaned forward to Pagan, who was wearing her dark-green Fortuny.

Abdullah said, 'Shut your eyes.'

She heard his chair scrape against the stone flags as he rose, then she sensed that he was standing behind her. She felt his hands lift the hair from the back of her neck and place something warm and heavy on her collarbone as he murmured, 'I hope that by now you're old enough to accept a necklace from me.'

Pagan rushed to the huge Venetian glass mirror in the salon. A necklace of platinum links, scattered with emeralds, lay against her pale, freckled chest.

In the mirror she saw Abdullah approach and hold her shoulders. He started, 'We worked well as a team this afternoon . . .'

'You're not just a pretty face,' Pagan allowed.

'You aren't as tough as you think you are.' Abdullah grinned.

'You really were protective.'

'You really were aggressive,' Abdullah said. 'Can't we be together for longer than two days?'

Pagan suddenly felt nervous. 'I don't know.'

'Would you spend the rest of the summer at my place in Cannes?'

'I don't know,' she stalled.

'If I invited Maxine and Charles, would you come?'

'I've never thought of Maxine as a chaperone before.' Abdullah's insistent black gaze made Pagan feel as if her guts were dissolving. 'I think that would be . . .' She had intended to say impossible, but heard herself say, 'Wonderful!' As she said it, bursts of falling green and pink stars were reflected in the water from a firework display on the other side of the lagoon.

Abdullah held Pagan's bare shoulders and turned her towards him. She closed her eyes and turned her face up to him, expecting a kiss, but instead, Abdullah said earnestly, 'Listen to me, Pagan. I have to explain to you about Sydon. The Fundamentalists are getting help from the Communist bloc, and if I can't defeat their guerrillas soon, I'll have a full-scale war on my hands. I can't defeat them without American arms and aid, and at the moment I can't get help from the Americans.'

Pagan hadn't expected a political lecture. 'I know that modernization has brought you problems,' she said, hiding her disappointment.

'Another of my problems is the women of my country.'

'In what way?' Pagan asked, without much interest at that moment in the problems of other women.

'In every way. It has been far harder for the women than for the men of my country to become part of the modern world. In the old days, when they lived behind the veil, they were completely dependent on their men, but also completely protected. Independence frightens them, but they cannot cling to the old ways for ever.' A burst of golden sparks cascaded across the sky as he added, 'They pity Western women, struggling along without male protection . . .'

'But they don't!' exclaimed Pagan.

'Under Koranic law, a man is obliged to support all the women of his household. A Western man can discard his wife, with very little responsibility. So a Western woman does not always have the absolute security that she thinks she does.'

Thinking of her divorce from her first husband, Pagan could only nod as Abdullah continued, 'Nevertheless, the younger women of my country are starting to question some of our traditional ways.'

'Such as?'

'As you know, female infibulation is still practised. And a woman's body belongs to her father or her husband, like their goat's.'

'I know all that, Abdi, you've told me over and over again. Why are we discussing it now?' Pagan was puzzled.

'Because unless women play an active part in my country, we can never be part of the modern world.' A screaming green rocket flared briefly and fell into the sea. 'I need an experienced, diplomatic, sophisticated woman with organizational ability at my side. That is what my country needs.'

'You sound as if you're drafting a want ad,' Pagan told him. 'Gynaecological experience an advantage.'

Abdullah released her shoulders and walked across the terrace to the balustrade, then turned to face her. 'I need someone who understands Western ways, and Western women, and the need for our women to assert themselves.'

'Why not propose to Gloria Steinem?'

Abdullah's mouth twitched with anger. 'I swore to myself that I would not lose my temper. Pagan, I will *not* allow you to misunderstand me again.' He strode over to her and shook her by the shoulders. 'I realize that you're headstrong, impulsive and . . .'

'Self-conscious?' Pagan interrupted him. 'Mustn't forget that.

That's why we used to have so many rows when we were young. You were nervous and pompous and I was just nervous.'

Behind Abdullah's back the white filigree façade of the Doge's Palace gleamed in the floodlights at the far side of the lagoon. Abdullah said, 'We are no longer young.'

Pagan laughed. 'You're so tactful. But, Abdi, I still feel young and nervous and uncertain when I'm with you.'

'You would get used to me.'

Suddenly Pagan realized the reason for the political lecture.

Abdullah said, 'Yes, I want you to marry me!' Earnestly he said, 'Let's not mess it up again, Pagan.'

'I can't believe it.'

'I knew you'd say that.' He rose again and strode away to the edge of the terrace again, silhouetted against the gold flares of the fireworks as they whistled over the sea.

Pagan rustled across the terrace and laid her hand on his arm. 'You don't understand . . .' she began.

Abdullah interrupted her. 'Yes, I do understand, Pagan. You're afraid of being humiliated again, you're afraid that I'll reject you again, as I did when I was nineteen.' He sighed. 'Please remember that was a bloody long time ago!'

Pagan said, 'It's true, I don't want the pain of hoping again, Abdi. I don't want the uncertainty and then possibly . . . the realization that, at my age, I've allowed myself to hope for too much, that I've made a fool of myself again – but this time with the whole world watching.'

Abdullah took both her hands in his. 'But I *really* need you. *Especially* you, Pagan, because you have also been hurled from a life of ancient tradition into the modern world, so you will understand my people.'

Pagan still felt as if she were being recruited for a particularly unpopular diplomatic post, rather than being courted by a man who wanted to marry her. She thought, here we are in this beautiful romantic place, the moonlight is trembling on the waves and the gondoliers are poling around down there, singing love songs, and Abdi's talking to me as if he were hiring a Middle-East liaison executive.

'I can see why you need a queen,' said Pagan, 'but I'm not sure I understand why you need a wife.'

There was a pause. 'For the usual reasons.' He looked away from her.

'Abdi, in the centre of her heart every woman is always seventeen, and this seventeen-year-old wants to hear it.' I'll make him say it, if it kills him, Pagan promised herself. Every woman wants to hear it, and men never understand why.

Finally, Abdullah looked at the floor and muttered, 'I love you.'

Gently Pagan said, 'And I love you.'

'Can I assume then that your answer is yes?'

Again Pagan caught the odd, brisk note in his voice. Was this the notorious lover? The romantic playboy, the man who had spent a fortune on red roses? She said, 'There are a couple of subclauses that we really should discuss.'

Nuzzling her neck, he said, 'I don't want to hear that you're not young enough or unsuitable in any way. Let's brush these insecurities aside.'

'No, let's pull them all out in the open, *now*, Abdi. First of all, I think I'm too old for you.'

'Kindly let me be the judge of that.'

Pagan touched the green ribbons of the order of Semira, which hung over Abdullah's white dinner jacket. 'I know this isn't the traditional moment to bring this up, but it's very important to me. I must know. Do you intend to be a faithful husband, Abdullah?'

'Why must you Westerners confuse sex and love? Sexual fidelity has little to do with marriage.'

'*Do you intend to be faithful to me?*' Pagan felt as if she were walking on eggshells, but she was determined that Abdullah should answer her question. 'After all, in the East, sexual fidelity has a lot to do with marriage for the wife. Adulterous women are still occasionally beheaded, aren't they? So what are your intentions, Abdullah?'

'When one knows that one can have any number of nubile young women by snapping one's fingers, one feels less inclined to snap them.'

'Abdi, don't evade my question. Will you be faithful to me?'

'I cannot say.'

'We're being honest,' she reminded him.

He paused. 'Then I doubt it.'

'You might feel inclined to snap the fingers?'

'We're being honest.'

Pagan felt a dull ache. 'Then my answer must be no,' she said with dignity as her ache turned to pain. She pulled away from him, disappointed and angry. 'Why are you so impossibly arrogant?'

'You asked me to be truthful. But once again you put your pride before reality.' He looked at her, trying to control his anger. 'I swore that I wouldn't let you lose my temper again.'

'Me – lose *your* temper!' Pagan shouted.

Abdullah grabbed her hand. 'We must stop this, Pagan.' He controlled himself with difficulty. 'We're having a quarrel about something that happened thirty years ago.'

'Something that didn't happen, you mean.' Pagan's tone was bitter.

'Something that could happen now,' he insisted gently, pulling her towards the couch.

Pagan thought, he just demonstrated the perfect way not to propose to a woman. She said sadly, 'Abdullah, I don't think such a marriage would ever work. I couldn't bear it if you started being the Playboy of the Western World again.'

The last of the fireworks spluttered out and the sea seemed darker than before. Abdullah accepted temporary defeat. 'But you will still come to Cannes?' he asked quietly.

'Are you sure you want me to come?'

'I think we should both consider what we may be missing.'

Does he mean it or doesn't he? Pagan wondered. It was like listening to those pursuing feet earlier and trying to work out where the sound was coming from; every indication seemed deceptive.

But I'll never know if I don't dare to find out.

'I'll come to Cannes,' she promised him. 'After my Drury Lane gala.'

～ 12 ～

'WE'VE made a lot of extra money on the drinks fee and the raffle.' The Scottish duchess looked around the ballroom. Bare-shouldered women in bright taffeta gowns talked to men with pearl-studded shirt fronts, on their best behaviour.

Pagan, whose face ached with smiling at her guests, was hardly listening as she anxiously wondered whether the hotel had allocated enough waiters.

'It's a long time since I've seen so many real tiaras,' said the duchess. 'Hardly anyone wears their real jewels today. Nicole Birmingham said that the last time she wore her aquamarines, it cost five thousand dollars for the insurance and the body-guards, so the next morning she went straight round to Ken-neth Lane.'

Pagan anxiously eyed the clock set in the wedding-cake plaster moulding above the door. Another five minutes and she'd have to make her speech, then marshall the 2,000 guests to the Theatre Royal, Drury Lane.

Suddenly the banquet manager was at Pagan's side. 'May I have a word with you, milady?'

'What's wrong, Mr Gates?'

'I've just spoken to Mr Zimmer, who telephoned from the theatre. He told me to tell you that they've had a slight technical problem, something to do with the fire curtain. So Mr Zimmer asked if you would announce that the gala will take place an hour later than scheduled, at eight-thirty. He told me to tell you not to worry, everything is under control, the engineer just needs time.'

'What a nuisance, Mr Gates,' said Pagan, thinking *bloody* fire curtain. 'I'd better tell everyone straight away.'

She made her way to the podium, climbed up the steps and took the microphone. 'My lords, ladies and gentlemen . . .'

*

'The curtain should have gone up ten minutes ago, but there isn't one person out front.' There were tears in Lili's eyes as she peeped through the red velvet stage curtains. Beyond them were 2,000 empty theatre seats.

The stage manager, his bow tie askew, nodded tensely. 'There's still no sign of anyone in the theatre. Not one person.'

Behind her heavy stage make-up Lili's eyes looked scared. Nervously she pulled up the long black glove which covered her right arm. 'I can't believe it.' She shook her head, scattering spangles from the three white Prince-of-Wales ostrich feathers that hung from her skull-cap. 'What the hell has happened?' She bit her bottom lip to control her agitation, then nervously smoothed the skintight black velvet dress which left one shoulder and one leg bare.

'I don't know.' The stage manager ran his hands through his greased blond hair. 'They should have poured through the doors at least half an hour ago. The theatre is absolutely empty.'

Lili tapped her silver shoe, her leg elegant and taut as that of a polo pony in her gleaming silver tights. 'Please check the tickets again. Please check that they printed the correct date!'

'We've already checked. There's nothing wrong with the invitations.' The stage manager looked helpless. Charity benefits – run by amateurs – were always a nightmare.

Zimmer put his arm around Lili. 'Don't cry, darling, or you'll have to re-do your make-up. Best thing is to get back to your dressing room, like everyone else. Stash will find out what the hell's happening.'

Lili's agent nodded, patted her spangled shoulder, then hurried to the stage-door telephone.

Zimmer knew that this was not a run-of-the-mill theatrical disaster; there must have been some colossal street accident near the hotel, maybe a 707 had crashed in Piccadilly, but his job was to calm the leading lady, so he said, 'Toughen up, Lili. You're a professional remember? Worse things have happened in the theatre. Nobody's dropped dead on stage. Abraham Lincoln hasn't been assassinated out front. The Phantom of the Opera is still in Paris.'

Lili gave him a weak smile. Zimmer was at his best when

things were going wrong; the worse the crisis, the calmer he became.

Stash reappeared in Lili's dressing room. 'Mystery solved,' he said. 'They're all still at Grosvenor House because someone announced that we had backstage problems, and that the opening had been postponed for an hour. I managed to speak to Lady Swann and she's going to get everyone here within fifteen minutes. They're radioing for every cab in London.'

Zimmer said, 'It'll take fifteen minutes to seat everyone. So, Lili, you've got half an hour to calm down, to think yourself into your role and keep your legs warm.'

He was right. Lili reached for her grubby purple leg-warmers.

'And check your make-up, darling,' said Zimmer. Tears had smudged her thick black eyeliner. 'Then concentrate on your part, Lili. Forget everything else. Leave it to me.'

Zimmer knew that any actor is in a fragile state of mind before going on stage. Often the half-hour before curtain-up is spent quietly sitting in a chair and thinking himself into his part, concentrating only upon what lies ahead and blocking out any extraneous thoughts. During that time an actor hates to be spoken to, or interrupted. A good actor produces his performance from inside himself, which is an unconscious process; he's learned his lines, he's studied, he's rehearsed with the rest of the cast, and before curtain-up time is when the part takes over the actor. The conscious mind is suspended as the subconscious takes over, transferring all rehearsed input into a living performance.

Twenty minutes later there was a tap on the dressing-room door and a distraught Pagan appeared in a tulip-skirted cream satin dress, and Abdullah's emerald collar.

'I don't know what's happened, Lili, but I know that someone's tried to ruin our benefit and *we're not going to let them*. You'll have a full house in fifteen minutes.'

'It's all very well for you, Pagan,' said Lili, sounding exhausted. 'You don't have to go out there and smile and knock 'em dead, as if nothing had happened.'

'Lili needs to be alone, now,' Zimmer said firmly. He led Pagan out of the dingy dressing room and up to the backstage area, where the crowd of dancers were sweating in the hot July night. Zimmer tiptoed across the stage, peeped through the spyhole in the centre of the curtain, then tiptoed back to Pagan.

'They're coming!' he confirmed, then turned to the theatre manager. 'Please get your security men to search the entire theatre. Tip up every seat, check the flies and the scenery storeroom, empty the lavatory cisterns, clear the street outside.'

'We can't possibly do that; it'll delay the performance even longer!' The house manager promised himself that he'd never let the theatre owner give another charity event, so long as he still worked at that theatre.

'We know that someone out there doesn't like Lili,' Zimmer said. 'So we must insist on a full security check.' He turned back to Pagan. 'This is a terrible thing to happen to a performer. The opening is going to be very tough for Lili.'

'I know. That's why my opening speech is going to be different from what I'd planned.'

Pagan found that her legs were shaking as she walked out to the centre of the stage. A stagehand pulled the red velvet curtain aside for her. She took a deep breath and stepped through the opening. The spotlight temporarily blinded her. She held up her hand for silence and saw the upturned faces in the front-row seats. Beyond them was blackness, although Pagan knew that they had a full house, as she beamed at her audience and started.

'Many things can disturb a star's self-confidence, but the one nightmare that every performer knows about is that no one will come to watch the show. Because, without an audience, there can be no performance.' Pagan was aware of the hush in the theatre as she went on. 'Tonight, for almost an hour, it seemed as if that nightmare had become a reality, for Lili, our star . . .'

After Pagan ended her speech a few scattered handclaps quickly grew into a roar of applause. Pagan hurried into the wings as the curtains drew back and the lights dimmed, leaving the stage black. Then a single spotlight picked out the silhouette of Lili's small, silver-spangled figure at the top of the elaborate staircase.

The applause became a standing ovation as the audience clapped and shouted their approval for a full five minutes before Lili could start to sing. '*C'est Paris . . .*'

*

' ". . . can only praise her jaunty courage", that's the *Mail*.'
Lili's agent tossed the newspapers on to Lili's bed, pulled off his
black leather gloves and unbuttoned his vicuna coat. '*The Times*
says you're the natural successor to Piaf and Garland, and the
Sun's given you the front page – "Sex Goddess Lili Drama".
They've all run it as a news story. You've got great coverage.'

'And you still have no idea who planned this horrible joke.'

'All we know about him is that he must have plenty of money.
It was an expensive operation.'

'Talking of expenses, did you send the money to Teresa?'

On the nightstand lay a delicate pair of gold handcuffs from
Van Cleef in Cannes. An empty bottle of Bollinger and a lipstick-
smeared champagne glass stood beside a plastic bag of cotton
balls and a small pharmacist's box of amyl nitrate capsules. The
other glass lay smashed on the floor beside a purple satin, black-
fringed négligé.

Teresa was wearing an elaborate, black leather Barbarella
costume with four-inch spike heels on her black leather thigh
boots. She was lovingly cooing scatological insults into the ear of
the stout man who lay on the bed beside her.

'Please stop,' he begged. 'Don't be so cruel, I didn't mean it.'

'You mean you lie to me as well.' She shoved him away from
her and he fell over the side of the bed to the floor, yelping as his
body hit the broken champagne glass.

He crawled away from the bed on his hands and knees. Nimbly
Teresa jumped off the bed, kicked his wobbling, hairy backside
with her high heels, then, with a practised hand, she flourished
her thin black whip over her head, just missing the plastic
chandelier.

He whimpered, 'Don't kick me, don't kick me, please.'

'These boots are filthy,' she snarled, 'you haven't cleaned them
properly!' She took another neat jab at his rear, thinking, I'd
better be careful, I don't want to mark him.

As expertly as a rodeo cowboy, she lightly flicked his ear with
the whip. 'Turn around,' she commanded, thinking she'd better
get this over fast, she didn't want to be late for her tennis coach
this afternoon at Washington's prestigious Potomac Club. She
jabbed at the fat man's pendulous stomach. 'Now, lick my boots!'

As the man did so Teresa could see that at last his claret-coloured private parts were responding. Thoughtfully she tickled his spine with her whip, then threw it on the bed and leaned backwards towards the cotton balls and the capsules.

She kept up the litany of abuse and, from time to time, she gave him an encouraging whack with her hairbrush as she deftly wrapped the capsules in cotton, then twisted them in a handkerchief.

'Ah . . . ah . . . ah,' he groaned in ecstasy. Teresa looked down. The john was nearly ready for her. He wasn't a bad old boy and he was generous. She'd give him an extra kick or two, on the house. After all, she *was* getting paid twice over.

'You'll never learn to do it properly, you filthy pig.' She pulled her feet away from his tongue and reached for the whip. Briskly she kicked him flat, turned him over with an economical jab of her toe, and straddled the whimpering plump body. With her left hand she reached for his penis. Her right hand grabbed the empty champagne bottle, smashed it against the lumpy handkerchief, and then briskly held it under the fat man's nose. A purplish-red flush suffused his face and neck; Teresa heard inarticulate noises, gurgles, and groans as he turned purple and his pop-eyes looked up at her in ecstasy.

How much more can this old bastard take? wondered Teresa. By the time she got back to Paris, her backhand would be invincible.

'Would you please stick this in a red file before you leave for the night?' said Judy. In her personal office all productive work which had an end aim – and a deadline date – was put in a red, transparent plastic envelope. These red files had their own 'in', 'pending', and 'follow' tray. All 'in' red file work was always done first thing in the morning, before any other work was discussed, even before the telephone was lifted. This meant that priorities were painlessly sorted out and the achievement work was dealt with before the routine work.

The secretary left the office and Judy picked up the projected advertising figures for August. Next month looked as if it was going to be even more depressing than July; summer was always a thin period for advertising revenue.

There was a knock and Tony entered. 'You left this file in the car, Judy. Gee, I'm sorry we've lost Lady Mirabelle.' Judy looked up in surprise. Tom had said that nobody knew they'd lost that account. As Tony left the office he almost collided with Tom, who was entering. Tom waited until the door had closed, then he said, 'OK, Judy, we're ready to go belly up, if it has to be. I've prepared for everything except hocking our watches.'

Night after night, after the staff had gone home, Tom had secretly worked to prepare *Verve!* magazine for closure. Bit by bit, Tom had transferred every asset owned by *Verve!* magazine into the names of two holding companies which had been set up for the purpose. Now everything tangible, from the office lease to the messenger-boy's motorbike, might be saved from the wreck so that they might start again. Tom had checked through all the staff contracts and, without Judy's knowledge, quietly negotiated for two of the longest-employed editors to be offered good jobs on rival magazines, thus saving their compensation payments from his company. He had set these strategic savings against the disastrous projected loss. He no longer felt any regret for the years of business triumph, only the calm determination of self-preservation. Tom's clear head and inventive business brain would, he hoped, save the roof over both his families; Kate didn't know of the impending crisis, but now she owned their apartment and their country house. His ex-wife and two sons had a trust fund that could be touched by no one. Tom had always been more realistic than Judy. Although he took high risks in business, they were always carefully calculated. A good gambler always knows bad luck when he meets her, knows that when he's on a losing streak he has to toss the cards on the table, stand up and say goodbye.

'I'm afraid they'll have to be shot, Suliman, as quickly as possible. Give the orders at once.' General Suliman saluted and left the room. Abdullah leaned back and allowed his eyes to close for a few moments. He pinched the bridge of his sharp aquiline nose, where a knot of tension had formed between the winged black eyebrows. Then he rose, walked slowly to his London embassy, over the green grass of St James's Park and looked up the Mall towards the severe grey stone of Buckingham Palace.

He'd returned from Venice the day before to find a crisis waiting on his desk, of course.

His ancestors had not known the comfort or the complications of civilization. Their life was simple because there was very little to clutter it up; neither possessions nor sentimental attachments; but what his Bedouin ancestors possessed was the ultimate luxury of freedom; their lives were circumscribed by the cruel physical environment and pitiless discipline of the desert, but their spirit was free. Suddenly Abdullah felt the old, familiar urge for the harsh peace of the desert. He sighed and moved towards the drawing room.

'Well?' Pagan pushed her heavy mahogany hair back and looked at Abdullah with concern. He seemed to have grown ten years older in the two days that he'd spent anxiously considering the fate of those three terrorists.

'Execution.' Abdullah took the chair next to her, his sombre face and khaki uniform contrasting with the blue silk cushions. 'My father was right. Forget the smell of mercy when dealing with your enemy.'

You don't have to teach a cat to sit by the fire, Pagan thought, and you don't have to teach a Bedouin to be cruel. The desert is cruel, and so is anyone who survives in it. Desert life is so harsh that punishment has to be even harsher. Pagan could understand Abdullah's Bedouin nature, but she wondered if she could ever get used to it. 'Your father never had to deal with the Muslim Fundamentalists,' she said doubtfully, privately thinking that the old bugger had only had to deal with the traditional gang of power-crazed second cousins trying to stab each other in the back.

'No, but he had his own fanatics to put down,' said Abdullah.

'Will the priests find out?' Pagan knew that if the terrorists were executed, Abdullah risked making them martyrs.

'Not immediately. When they get no news of their men in prison, then they'll know, but too late. It's hard to make martyrs months after the event. And if these men had been popular in their own village, there would have been a greater outcry when they were arrested. The priests were unable to whip up much of a demonstration. I think their power is weakening, at last. The priests exploit the ignorance of the people. In Sydon we've had to achieve centuries of development in thirty years. It's the same for every nation on the Gulf; I don't want my country to go the way of Iran. I will not see Sydon hurled back into ignorance and superstition. My job is to guide my people into the twentieth century.'

He jumped up and prowled around the room, remembering his dusty country, neatly wedged between Oman and the United Arab Emirates on the Persian Gulf. He thought of the camels and Cadillacs side by side on the desert roads, the extremes of feudal poverty and half-assimilated modern sophistication.

'I've disposed of eleven revolutionary groups since I became King.' His voice was sombre. 'Each one of them was led by one of my own blood relations, and they were all executed.'

Pagan thought, no wonder Abdi has only one heir.

'They all want the same thing – power. The priests are no different, except that they use the sacred name of the Prophet to justify their betrayal. They confuse and frighten my people, who, like all people, hate change. It's difficult for them to change from our traditional ways to the modern way of life that's been developed in the West. They prefer to rush back to the Middle Ages.'

'It's the same choice for you, isn't it?' ventured Pagan.

'What do you mean?' Abdullah looked at her in surprise.

'You're also stuck between two worlds, aren't you? You can't be an absolute ruler like your father . . .'

Born in the East, Abdullah had been deliberately educated in the West so that he would be capable of dealing with the rulers of the West. Through his Western ego he had learned to criticize his own people; he had dropped one culture and not been accepted by another. So he felt an isolation in his life and Pagan had spotted this long ago.

Abdullah perched on the arm of Pagan's chair and kissed the tip of her freckled nose. 'My father's problem,' he said, 'was persuading the nomad to build a house. Then his problem was persuading the nomad to build a lavatory in the house. After that, when I became King, the problem was to teach the nomad to stand in front of the lavatory instead of climbing on the bowl. Now, if the priests are not controlled, the nomads will convert their cisterns into camel-troughs because the priests tell them it is not the way of Allah to piss indoors.'

Where other women felt an urge to rearrange the furniture, Maxine rearranged the now priceless treasures of the de Chazalle family. Years ago she had saved them from mildew and moth when she had saved the château by opening it to the public as a beautifully presented, historic showcase which also promoted the family champagne business.

When Pagan arrived at the Château de Chazalle she was shown to the wide, Chinese-yellow picture gallery on the first floor, known to the public as the History Walk, although the family called it Ancestor Alley.

Maxine, in her stockinged feet, was standing on a chair and hacking at a gold picture frame with a kitchen knife.

'Whatever are you doing, Maxi?' Pagan blew her a kiss. 'Why are you ruining that picture frame?'

'I'm not ruining it, I'm distressing it,' Maxine smiled down at her. 'I'm making it look old and worn, as if it has been hanging here for at least one hundred years, instead of three days.'

'What's the point of that?'

Maxine jumped off the chair and kissed Pagan on the cheek. 'It's the essence of shabby chic, the way that aristocratic houses should look. Anyone with money can have everything new, but it's far more difficult to achieve this slightly worn, not-perfectly-matched, artlessly charming look of a room in which a priceless painting hangs next to a watercolour of Sorrento by your grand-mother.'

'But what's chic about having a chipped picture frame?'

'Anyone with money can buy that glossy magazine look. You need generations of family history to feel comfortable with an Aubusson carpet that's worn on one corner, chintz curtains that are faded because they've been hanging at the same window for over one hundred years and Chinese hand-painted wallpaper that is, perhaps, a little dim because it was painted in the eighteenth century by Chinese artists whom your ancestors imported from China to do the job.'

'But what's the point?'

'Snobbery, darling Pagan. It's the new decorator look. The

point of shabby chic is that you can't achieve it unless it is authentic, or unless you have a very clever decorator.'

'Don't you ever stop working, Maxi?'

'If I enjoy work more than pleasure, then is it work or pleasure?'

'Crumbs, don't ask me. I hate decorating. If the shops have what I want in the right colour, then it's the wrong size. Always. Sophia wants her bedroom redone for her birthday, and I really can't face it. She wants stripped pine furniture and a Victorian brass bed.'

'I'll do it for you, if you like,' Maxine offered, 'but not in stripped pine and brass, that's too passé.' She took Pagan's arm. 'Now let me show you to your room, and then you can tell me why you have to see me so suddenly. What's so important that you can't talk about it on the telephone? What is it that can't wait until our holiday in Cannes?'

'I want to ask your advice. But first I want to talk to Charles.'

'Charles! What on earth do you want to discuss with Charles?'

'Politics. Eastern politics.'

After dinner Pagan steered Charles to a green leather sofa in the library. She knew that Charles had Middle East associates, and he had known Abdullah as an acquaintance since he had married Maxine.

'Charles, I want to talk about Abdullah,' she started, then felt embarrassed. 'You know – Abdi, Playboy of the Western World.'

Charles twirled the brandy in his glass. 'It's only in the West that people regard him as a playboy, Pagan. In his own country, and among the Gulf states, he's considered a brave, devoted leader.' He sniffed his brandy. 'Abdi is the most skilful of all the Gulf rulers at dragging his country into the twentieth century, although he's in such serious trouble at the moment.'

'What do you mean?' Pagan, accustomed to listening with only half an ear while Abdullah talked of his state affairs, suddenly wanted Charles to tell her more. Now that Abdullah and she were apart, Pagan managed to drag his name into every conversation, no matter how odd the context.

'Like every other oil-boom people, the Sydonites are bewildered by the modern world, and confused about their national identity.' Charles took a sip of his Napoleon brandy. 'You really want to know more?'

Pagan nodded.

'The Fundamentalist guerrilla army is getting help from the Communists, Pagan. If Abdullah can't handle that situation, not only will he lose his country, but the red flag will shortly be flying over one of the most strategic positions on the coast.'

'I had no idea . . . I didn't realize . . .'

'Combine that with the Iranian situation and the Ayatollah on the other side of the Persian Gulf and you might end up with Muslim fanatics controlling eighty per cent of the world's oil – and taking their orders from Moscow.'

'No wonder Abdullah's so grim about it all,' Pagan murmured.

'Sydon is a grim place and it's a crazy place. In fact, the whole Gulf area is crazy. I've done business with Saudi princes who wear silk shirts, drink whisky and speak better English than I do. But at their homes, their mothers and wives wear long black traditional robes. Then, underneath the robes they wear the latest Paris fashions, and the most wonderful jewellery, Christian Dior and Cartier. The women are never seen in public and only wear these beautiful clothes to drink tea with each other. And that's about all they're good for.'

'What do you mean?' Pagan asked, intrigued.

'Because they've always been excluded from public affairs, most Arab princesses have no sense of social responsibility. They don't do a thing to help the poor of their country.'

'How do *you* think a Gulf princess should behave?' Pagan tried to sound casual.

Aha, thought Charles, so that's it.

'She shouldn't be spending her time watching video tapes, gossiping and eating cakes. She should organize help for the young, the old and the poor. She should do the sort of work you do for the Research Institute, Pagan.'

'Do you think so?' Pagan didn't sound as casual as she had intended. She jumped up and fidgeted with a bowl of pink peonies. The library was filled with peonies and pink hydrangeas in blue chinoiserie bowls.

The following morning Maxine suggested a walk in the park. 'I want to get you on your own, Pagan,' she said as they strolled over the grass behind the bounding, pink-grey Weimaraners. 'Now, what's up?'

Pagan burst out, 'Maxine, why do men find it so difficult to say "I love you"?'

'Ma chère, they say it, but not in those words. They say, "I wouldn't be here if I didn't, would I?" or "But I married you, didn't I?"'

Pagan stomped across the grass in silence.

'Words don't matter,' Maxine encouraged. 'It's the actions that count. Any Latin con-man can say "I love you". You must judge men by what they do, not what they say.'

Pagan was silent until they reached a little arbour. They sat down under the lichen-covered statue of Apollo. Pagan said, in an off-hand voice, 'What do you think the world would say if I married Abdi?'

Maxine jerked her head around so suddenly that her sunglasses almost fell off. So Charles was right. 'You mean – he's asked you, Pagan?'

'Yes, but I haven't said yes. That's why I wanted to talk to you. You remember how he behaved . . . when we were young. That's why I haven't said yes.'

'Why not?' Maxine couldn't believe her ears.

'Because if I married Abdullah I'd also be marrying his country, his people, his oil fields, his seat at OPEC, his Communist guerrillas, his backward people and his oppressed women.' Pagan bit her bottom lip. 'I can't *cope* with all that, it scares me to death.'

'Rubbish! You coped with that audience at the Theatre Royal all right. You coped with Christopher's illness, you've raised thousands of dollars for the Cancer Institute. You have a positive genius for coping – except when you're in love.' Maxine took off her sunglasses and stared at Pagan's worried face.

'But suppose he dumps me, like he did before?'

'So few women realize that there *is* life after humiliation. And why should he dump you?'

Pagan jumped up nervously. 'Let's keep walking.'

They sauntered in silence along the seven-foot-high box hedge that bordered the estate. Eventually Pagan burst out, 'I asked him if he intended to be faithful. The rotter said . . . well, he indicated . . . Maxi, the silly bugger said, "I cannot promise you fidelity because I do not know if it is possible, I simply don't know."'

Maxine laughed at Pagan's imitation of Abdullah's most pompous manner. 'But that's very sensible of him. It doesn't mean that he's going to dump you. It means just the reverse. He's being very honest.'

Pagan looked anxiously at Maxine, as if asking a fortuneteller to read the future. 'But I don't think my pride would let me turn a blind eye to a crowd of young blondes with big tits. In theory, perhaps, but in fact, I'm pretty sure I couldn't.'

'Pride has always come between you and Abdullah. Abdullah's fierce pride and your stubborn pride. You'll learn that one of the good things about getting older is that one learns to compromise, to give and take.'

'So I've noticed with you and Charles. You give and Charles takes.'

Reaching the curlicued, wrought-iron gates, they turned to walk back on the grass at the side of the drive. 'Charles is very careful of my dignity,' Maxine said, with dignity. 'Well, nearly always. He has his little affairs, but he is very discreet, he never humiliates me. Well, hardly ever.'

'That's what *you* settle for – your dignity and a quiet life. What is the difference between your dignity and my pride, Maxine?'

'I have decided to settle for ninety per cent of the cake instead of fifty per cent of the alimony.' Maxine crossly removed her sunglasses.

'You see, here we are talking about divorce and I haven't even got married yet,' giggled Pagan. Maxine began to understand how Abdullah might sometimes be exasperated by Pagan's flippant charm.

'Oh, Pagan,' she sighed. 'Abdullah is what you've always wanted. I can't understand why you don't jump at the chance of marrying Abdi, when you've been in love with him for years.'

'Being in love is different from loving!' Pagan said. 'I can't imagine loving Abdi in the way I loved Christopher. Christopher really cared about all of me; we trusted each other, so we could expose our vulnerability. I wouldn't like to risk exposing my vulnerability to Abdi. And he'll never trust anyone.'

In the distance the eighteenth-century turrets of the château shone purple in the sun.

'But what about all the wonderful things that the hakim taught him when he was sixteen?' Maxine reminded Pagan.

Pagan hesitated. 'When we're in bed, it's physically wonderful, but Abdi's not emotionally involved. That love doctor in Cairo taught him everything about eroticism and nothing about love. I don't want only a sexual relationship. I want warm intimacy and mutual concern.'

'Perhaps you can change him?' Maxine made the female's fatal error of believing this to be possible.

'At least I'm not stupid enough to think that!'

'But if he's asked you to marry him and you're not certain, why not ask for a six-month engagement, a secret engagement that the world will never know about, to give you time to get used to the idea? You have nothing to lose with a secret engagement.'

On the distant stone building row upon row of windows glistened in the sunshine. Pagan turned the idea over in her mind. The most attractive aspect of Maxine's suggestion was that Pagan would now be able to put off her decision.

'Maxine, I think you've solved the problem,' she said, looking at the row of fountains in front of the château terrace, where the July sun formed rainbows in the dancing water.

~ 13 ~

August 1979

LAYER upon layer of swan-white lace swayed softly as Sandy moved her hips, and the half-hidden diamanté brilliants twinkled like the stars in a Walt Disney sky. Sandy crossed her wrists in front of her, which pushed her breasts together and upwards. The flounces helped as well, she thought, but she sure wished her tits were bigger.

'How much is it, Ken?'

The dress manufacturer's plump pink hand carefully smoothed the satin petals of the ice-pink rosebud between her breasts. 'Let's not talk about the price, Sandy. Just tell me what you think of it.'

Sandy knew that when a man said, 'Let's not talk about the price', the deal was going to be very expensive. However, the circuit gossip was that Ken liked it straight and came fast.

'Why it's just beautiful, Ken,' she cooed, right into her southern belle act. No girl got to be a beauty contest finalist in a dress run up by her mother, in spite of the rule that no evening gown could cost more than two hundred dollars. Which is why Ken Sherman loaned his dresses for publicity value, if he thought a girl had a good chance of winning the beauty pageant. And, of course, a girl had to be nice to Ken.

'I could not imagine a finer ante-bellum gown in the whole world.' Sandy smiled her gleaming, wholesome smile. In the gloom of the deserted showroom Ken twitched the pink satin sash into place, stood back from the spotlight and slowly nodded. No girl could lose in that dress. 'Right,' he said briskly. 'Care for a cocktail at my place?'

'Why Ken, I would be honoured,' Sandy breathed. The bullshit level had to be higher, the closer you got to the top.

The bedroom floor and walls were covered by white fur. The lamps were Lalique crystal seashells and the circular bed was covered with a white leather spread, upon which lay Ken with his legs apart while Sandy cheerfully sucked his stiff little cock. The girls were right about Ken, this was the cheapest dress she'd ever acquired. But Sandy was merely making her down payment; Ken wanted more for his money, and he knew that he wouldn't have another chance after tomorrow's contest.

'Let's take a look at you.' Ken pushed a white fur bolster behind her head and spreading out her waterfall of pale blonde curls, he felt for the zipper of her silver lamé boiler suit and yanked at it. 'Listen, baby, you got nothing to worry about, tomorrow.' He took a look and thought they'd hardly make a 34B as he ripped off the silver lamé. 'Like some music?' He pushed a couple of buttons on the bedhead console that looked capable of flying a 747. Dolly Parton started to wail 'Stand By Your Man' and, overhead, the remote control videocamera started to roll as Ken purred, 'Why, you're as bald as a baby down there,' and pushed Sandy on to her back.

Who did he think he was fooling with that mirrored ceiling, thought Sandy, as Ken squeezed gobs of body lotion over her breasts. Obediently, she massaged the translucent white goo over her breasts; no wonder the bedcover was easy-wipe white leather. 'Honey, you are amazing,' she breathed as she thrust one immaculately manicured finger inside her pink gauze panties, then stuck her rump in the air and pulled at the bows which held the pink gauze in place.

Half an hour later Sandy had been squeezed and shoved and pulled, pushed and arranged in a hundred different poses. She realized that the videotape must be running out, because Ken squeezed her breasts together, felt around her clitoris for a few moments, missed it, poured body lotion on his penis, shoved it inside her, gave ten very careful thrusts, gasped, rolled off, felt around for his cigarettes and said, 'What happened to the thatch, honey?'

'Electrolysis. Hurt like hell. Worse than having the teeth capped. They should give you an anaesthetic.'

Ken dragged on his cigarette. 'So do we have a deal?'

'What sort of deal?'

'If you win the Miss International Beauty Pageant tomorrow, you'll need more gowns, at three thousand dollars a throw.' He pushed his cigarette end into a built-in ashtray on the bedhead. 'You get the gowns from me for ten per cent of the prize money. And don't try to bargain, that's the going rate.'

'Why, honey, whatever you say. I have no head for business.'

Ken leered at Sandy. 'You don't need a head in this business.'

Sandy slid off the bed and smiled. 'Honey, I've got to take a shower and get home for my beauty sleep.' In the shower she ran through her plans. When Ken showered, she'd jump on that bed and push at the mirrored tiles until she found the one that concealed the camera. You certainly *did* need a head in this business: only last year the California Citrus Princess had been forced to resign when a boyfriend published split-beaver pictures of her in a stud magazine.

*

By the third day of the Miss International Beauty Pageant, the Clarence Plaza Hotel in Miami overflowed with females of every age and shape. Like grown-up children playing with their Barbie dolls, pudgy professional mothers, often obese, chaperoned their still-slim, professional-virgin daughters. Looking as wholesome as strawberry yogurt, these girls had learned to be as tough as infantry boots, but the rules insisted on one chaperone per entrant, and a mother added greatly to the clean-living, all-American apple-pie atmosphere. The unspoken, uncodified and unstated agreement was that this image should be preserved, unsullied. This was why, however jealous, desperate, cynical or vicious a competitor felt, she never let it show. The currency of conversation was always candy-coated. The myth was that all the girls were loving friends.

Sandy's mother, wearing a peach polyester pants suit, sat on the terrace overlooking the swimming pool. Ostentatiously she stitched the ice-pink rose on the front of Ken Sherman's extravagant gown; you scored extra points if your gown was homemade. Lying beside her, Sandy sunbathed in a swimsuit that was carefully cut to match her competition costume, so that her tan marks would match up. Sandy was certain of being one of the three finalists, and knew that she had a good chance of winning the title.

So did the other contestants. On the next lounger Miss Canada propped herself up on one elbow and asked, with honeyed friendliness, 'Are we going to see you use those wrenches today, Sandy?'

Sandy immediately dived into her tote bag and produced a pair of nickel-plated plumber's wrenches. 'Why, honey, I never go *anywhere* without them. Good conversation point. Good defence weapon. And you'll see me use them in the talent section.'

'How did you figure out your neat act?' marvelled Miss Canada, who was sick of seeing Sandy giving her frank, freckle-nosed, virginal grin as she brandished her gleaming wrenches in contest after contest, to the delighted surprise of the crowds.

Sandy allowed herself a moment of complacency. 'It's easy if you've got personality.' She put the wrenches back in her tote bag and reached for the suntan oil. They both knew that personality was the winning trick. It was what the judges were looking for, because they needed a girl who could speak up on a talk show or at an opening ceremony. Personality meant the ability to define your own chosen character in three words, and in Sandy's case it was SOUTHERN PLUMBER'S DAUGHTER.

'Sandy's always had personality.' Her mother bit off the cotton thread and held up the seafroth-white gown for inspection. 'Just as well, because she cracks the windows if she tries to sing, she can't dance worth a dime and the only thing she was ever any good at was baton.' Proudly she stroked the satin rose again. 'Sandy, honey, your dress is all finished.'

'That is the most adorable dress I have ever seen,' Miss Canada said, sitting up and curiously looking at the delicate lace. 'I can hardly believe it only cost two hundred dollars, honey.'

Sandy sauntered on stage in overlarge denim coveralls, with a red-and-white spotted handkerchief in the pocket, plumber's wrenches in each hand; she looked refreshingly wholesome. She began to twirl the wrenches as if they were batons, whirling them up in the air, then catching them with panache. As the banjo music slowed Sandy mopped her forehead with the red handkerchief, gave it a flourish and pulled a bunch of flowers from it. After her little conjuring trick, the tempo of the music quickened as Sandy produced three giant metal washers from the back pocket of her faded blue coveralls and deftly juggled the metal circles to a crescendo of applause. Sandy thought, fuck you, Miss Canada.

On the following evening Sandy dripped blue drops into her eyes to make them sparkle; she cleaned her teeth with red toothpaste to make them extra white; she checked the thick tan make-up on her shoulders; she looked at herself in the mirror.

Perfect.

Then she squeezed into the tight white satin corselette and hooped petticoat which went under Ken Sherman's gown. 'Hook me up, honey,' she murmured to Miss Canada, who was sticking on her left eyelashes. Carefully Sandy stepped into the middle of Ken's white lace masterpiece. Miss Canada felt for Sandy's zipper, then paused. 'Hey, Sandy, something's wrong with this zipper!'

Sandy instantly sensed disaster. She grabbed a hand mirror from the make-up counter, spun around and examined the rear view in the mirror. The zipper down the back of the gown had been slashed in a dozen places and, as she touched it, the zipper fell away from the dress.

What Sandy wanted to say was 'Holy fucking shit.' What she automatically said was 'Jeepers creepers.' Using unladylike language was a sure way to get thrown out of a beauty pageant on the spot.

Goddammit, I told Mama not to let the dress out of her sight, Sandy thought as she shrieked for the pageant supervisor. It was not abnormal for the best dress in the pageant to be sabotaged with a razor blade. It only took thirty seconds.

'OK, you're on last,' said the pageant supervisor, taking in the situation at a glance.

'Mama, go get the hotel maintenance man here with his toolbox,' Sandy ordered.

When the bemused janitor arrived outside the dressing-room door, Sandy dived into the toolbox for the roll of waterproof adhesive used to make temporary repairs in cracked water pipes. It was wide and strong and sticky on both sides. Swiftly Sandy cut twenty inches of the tape and ordered her mother to stick it down her back. Without a word, Sandy's mother spread a dust sheet on the floor, then held the dress as Sandy stepped into it. Clutching the white flounces to her breast, Sandy carefully lowered herself on to the dust sheet, face down. Then, while her mother held the edges of the dress in place, Miss Canada walked daintily on Sandy's spine, her bare feet pressing the dress firmly on to the double-sided strapping. Then both of them helped Sandy to stand up. She thought, thank Christ I really am a plumber's daughter as she said, 'Thanks. Guess I mustn't breathe too deeply, but I reckon every cloud has a silver lining, because now I've got the last number.' The last girl in the parade had the best chance of making a strong impression on the judges.

Sitting at the judges' table, Judy and Lili watched the endless stream of girls, glassy-eyed and stiff, walk down the catwalk towards the cameras, the host and microphone. Their smiles were peppermint-fresh, their faces were peach-perfect and their flesh was the colour of peanut butter.

'Can't think why they chose Miami in August,' muttered Lili to Judy.

'Politics, politics,' Judy murmured back to Lili, who had flown over from Europe for the judging. Both women had agreed not to stay in Miami for one minute longer than was necessary. The humid, tropical heat blasted them every time they left the over-elaborate lobby of their gaudy hotel, and within minutes their clothes would be soaked with perspiration, and the energy drained from their bodies.

The final parade, in formal gowns, was the first time that the audience had heard the girls speak. Each girl was inter-viewed to determine whether or not she had personality. Trans-lated, that meant whether she would be able to stand up for herself on talk shows in the appropriately charming, self-deprecatory manner.

Suddenly the hot, tired women in the theatre gasped as Sandy glided down the wide staircase. Sandy looked as if she had been sprayed with lace foam that was slowly slipping down from her shoulders and about to reveal her body.

'Tell us about yourself, Sandy,' encouraged the white-suited host as he handed the microphone to Sandy.

Sandy gave the judges her most brilliant smile. 'I am majoring in social science and then I plan to be a teacher because I just love children.' Pause at that point, thought Sandy.

'This is a beautiful dress you have on,' the host prompted, holding the microphone under the tip of her nose.

'I usually make all my own clothes,' Sandy confided, thinking, keeping the answers short, 'but my Mama helped me with this.' She blew a kiss to her mother in the audience.

'And what do you do in your spare time, Sandy?'

'I like to water ski, I go dancing, and I'm taking an evening course in domestic engineering.'

'*Domestic engineering?*' The host glanced briefly at his prompt card. 'What is that, Sandy?'

'I guess it's just a fancy name for plumbing,' Sandy repeated her confident laugh. 'My Daddy's a plumber and he taught me all I know. When I get married, I'll be able to fix the washing machine.' Roars of applause.

'May I ask if you are courting at this time?'

'Do you mean, do I have a boyfriend?' Sandy moved closer to the microphone so that her voice sounded breathy. 'Well no, I do not. Right now my life is just so full of opportunities that I want to get on and enjoy it to the full.'

'And now, Sandy, for the final question,' the host finished. 'Tell us why you are proud of your country.'

The beauty queens had all rehearsed their answers, but Sandy's reply sounded enthusiastically impromptu. 'Because America really *is* beautiful, America really *is* friendly, and America really *is* free! I believe that America is the land of opportunity and I am the living proof of that. My Mama was a dancer from Sweden and my father came over from Ireland, when he was just a kid. Why, if it hadn't been for America they would never have met up.' Sandy deliberately turned away from the host and waved to the close-up camera. 'Hi, Mama and Daddy, I am so glad *you chose America!*'

The theatre erupted in a storm of cheering and clapping. Many in the audience dabbed their eyes or wiped away tears as they stood and applauded. Sandy mentally evaluated her chances. Sudan was statuesque, almond-eyed, and the Third World girls always got sympathy votes. Sri Lanka might be an added threat because she had been a stunning sight in her national costume, ultramarine silk, with tinkling bracelets on her tiny, high-arched feet.

As the ten nervous girls clattered up the backstage stairs Sandy wondered why, for Chrissake, Canada had been selected. According to Sandy's research, Canada and the United States were never chosen together, since it was considered undiplomatic to pick neighbouring countries. Maybe Canada has something going for her that we don't know about, maybe someone down here owes someone up there one big favour, Sandy decided as, carefully, she pulled her full skirt clear of her high heels, and walked across the dirty backstage floor, crisscrossed with electrical leads.

While the audience was entertained by a team of dancers in azure chiffon and sequins, the judges withdrew to a side room and considered their decision. Judy unpinned the lurid purple orchid from her cream silk lapel and pondered the three nordic, three hispanic, three black and one oriental finalist; she realized that the colour mix for the final line-up was as predictable as the colours in an ice-cream sundae.

The international photographer offered first opinion. 'I want Sudan,' he said firmly. 'She's marvellously photogenic; she's got terrific presence and she's unattached.'

The Mirabelle man interrupted quickly. 'Sudan would be of limited value to us.' He meant that the Mirabelle range was not designed for a black skin. 'Our vote goes to United States; her microphone manner was professional.'

Lili asked, 'What about Sri Lanka?'

Several judges shook their heads. 'She'll never make it on talk shows.'

'My vote goes to Italy,' said the Hollywood agent.

'Italy is just a little bit adult for us.' The Mirabelle man meant that, at the age of twenty-three, Miss Italy's skin had already lost the childlike smoothness that made mass-produced cosmetics look good in a high-definition colour photograph. He added, 'And United States has the look that Mirabelle will promote next year.'

After another twenty minutes of argument the judges marked their prepared ballots and tossed them into the wire basket held by the organizer, who announced with satisfaction, 'United States it is, with Sudan second and Italy third.'

When the pre-recorded trumpet fanfare blasted and the host announced that Miss International Beauty of 1979 was Miss United States, Miss Sandy Bayriver from Louisiana, Sandy looked suitably astonished and elated, then wiped an imaginary teardrop from the corner of her eye, and allowed the host to lead her to the winner's throne. Gotcha, she thought, as yet another diamanté crown was placed upon her head.

Judy signed the hotel bill for two glasses of freshly squeezed lemon juice and turned over on her yellow sunbed to let the Florida sun toast her back. Lili sat up and poured both packets of sugar into her glass. Lili's sweet tooth and Judy's taste for bitter drinks were both satisfied if they ordered two freshly squeezed lemon juices and Lili used all the sugar before adding water to both glasses. In ten months, this was the nearest they had come to a family custom.

Lili wriggled on her sunbed. 'This heat! I'm going for another swim.' She jumped up and ran towards the blue sea.

After a bit Judy noticed that Lili's small red snakeskin purse lay between their two yellow sunbeds. The catch wasn't closed and the contents were spilling over the sand. Judy leaned forward and carefully shook sand from the lip gloss, the tissue and the unwritten postcards. Then she picked up the airmail envelope and froze as she noticed the Nicaragua stamp, Mark's familiar handwriting and his name on the back.

The envelope was still sealed, but it was badly sealed and only stuck down at the tip of the flap. Furtively Judy started to raise the side of the envelope. She couldn't help herself. Peering into the envelope, she could just make out the words 'love' and 'helpless', then she heard Lili's voice behind her. Quickly she stuffed the letter back in the purse.

'It's no use. You'd think they'd leave me alone when the place is stuffed with beauty queens. I'm going inside to the air conditioning.' Lili picked up the red snakeskin purse, stuck her sunglasses on and walked towards the hotel.

Judy turned on her stomach and buried her face in her beach towel to hide the tears which prickled her eyelids. Thank God Lili was flying back to Europe tomorrow.

Thank God this race was only 500 kilometres thought Lili as the Riviera sun blazed down upon the raw, white-painted concrete of the pits, and hurt Lili's eyes with its savage glare.

This sun was almost as fierce as Miami's had been, last week. The only difference between the Paul Ricard circuit and the British tracks seemed to be that the grandstands were flanked with dusty tubs of oleanders, the French spectators were not quite so badly dressed as the British ones and the car park was littered with empty wine bottles, rather than empty lager cans. Apart from these points, the tawdry souvenir booths sold the same tasteless B M W baseball caps, Ferrari bomber jackets and Lancia T-shirts as they did in Britain; the competitors were the same, they drove the same cars, the noise and the smell were exactly the same. Only the wording on the billboards was different – Michelin instead of Dunlop and Elf instead of Mobil.

Wistfully Lili looked at the purple-smudged hills in the distance and longed to be in the dappled shade of the pine forests instead of by this stinking, sunbaked racing circuit.

The low black Spear snarled past, hugging the ground like a sinister giant insect. Lili checked her stopwatch. Two seconds faster than his best practice time. With any luck, they'd be back in time to have a swim before dinner.

The PA droned on. 'And halfway through this five-hundred-kilometre race, it's Werner Hentzen's Porsche in the lead, followed by the Dinetti, then Gautier in the Lancia . . . and the Spear has just overtaken the Lancia and it's pulling ahead . . .'

Lili yawned, stuck her ear protectors back on and pulled the script for her next movie out of her leather hunting bag. It had arrived that morning from Omnium Pictures. She would have some terrific outfits as Helen of Troy and, after the Mistinguett role, she was in good shape for another musical.

A blue airmail letter fell from the leather hunting bag. Lili sighed. She'd stuffed it in there this morning before Gregg saw it. Mark knew and used the secret code that was used to bypass Lili's fan mail, so she always received his letters. And she always tore them up, unread. It was the least she could do, she thought sadly as she tore the pale blue envelope into strips, and threw it away. Then she turned her attention to the script.

By the time King Agamemnon had pitched his tent in sight of the walls of Troy the Spear was challenging the Porsche for the lead as the PA shrieked '. . . and, with only three laps to go, the Spear is lying behind the Porsche and Werner Hentzen is fighting off the challenge . . .'

By the time Paris wished that he had listened to Cassandra's prophecies the PA was ecstatically screaming, '. . . and now the Spear is neck and neck with the Porsche . . . and Eagleton has passed the Porsche! With only one lap to go, the Spear is in the lead . . .'

Insulated from the noise by her earmuffs, Lili did not know that Gregg had gained the lead. Neither did she know, as the triumphant Hector wearily unstrapped his gleaming breastplate, that Gregg had lost the lead and fallen back behind the Porsche.

But after the giant wooden horse, its belly full of soldiers, had crossed over the plain towards the walls of Troy, the other spectators started to jump up and down and this distracted Lili from the script.

Lilli pulled off her ear protectors, to hear the PA gabble '. . . and the Spear has taken the Porsche on the inside . . . now they're coming down the final straight towards the flag and it looks as if . . . yes . . . IT'S THE SPEAR . . . with the first win for Gregg Eagleton!'

Gregg was hauled out of the car, weighed down with a laurel wreath, soaked in champagne, kissed by half a dozen girls promoting a new cocktail mix, carried shoulder high to the grandstand, awarded a silver rose bowl, then more champagne, then photographed with his arm round Lili in a crush of champagne-drenched admirers.

Gregg posed for one last picture, then they stumbled away to the trailer park. The Spear, its wings coated with red dust, was being wheeled into its trailer by two mechanics. Gregg climbed into the driver's cab to change and shower in the tiny compartment behind the seat. The mechanics walked back to the pit to pack up their tools. Lili sat on the edge of the transporter, swinging her legs and waiting for Gregg.

Five minutes later he climbed into the back of the trailer, his hair still damp from the shower.

'Give her a rest, darling!' Lili jumped up and picked her way into the dark, petrol-smelling interior, knowing that Gregg could not pass the Spear without wanting to lift the engine housing and fiddle with something. She didn't notice the elated gleam in his eyes and the urgency in his manner as he pulled the lever that closed the back doors of the trailer.

'Gregg. Stop playing around! It's dark in here.' Lili crossly felt her way forwards in the dim, hot trailer and blundered into his arms. He kissed her hard, then pulled her up the ladder to the driver's bunk above the seats.

'Stop it, Gregg. And it's as hot as hell in here!'

'Can't stop, I want you now.' He kissed her harder as he pulled off her white linen shift, under which Lili was naked. The stink of oil and petrol normally made Lily feel faintly sick, but now it seemed erotic. Sweat poured from Gregg's body as their flesh met and Lili felt a hot rush of warm pleasure.

'What's got into you?' murmured Lili.

Gregg said, 'Winning. That's the real turn-on.'

'This is such a wonderful view!' Pagan jumped on to the parapet of Abdullah's turreted château, and waved her arm at the lavender hills of the French Riviera. Her loose, red cotton dress blew behind her like a flag in the breeze as she turned to Maxine and said, 'Aren't you glad you came? Who'd have thought, all those years ago in Gstaad, that we'd still be friends today.'

Maxine shrugged. 'Perhaps we wouldn't be such friends if we all lived next door in each other's pockets. As it is, we're not round each other enough to demand more closeness or support than we are able, or want, to give.'

'Maybe the secret of friendship is not being too friendly.'

They left the roof and started to walk down the elaborate wide staircase of the sumptuous château, passing richly coloured tapestries, suits of Moorish armour and crimson brocade curtains. What a pity, Maxine thought. The tapestries were nineteenth-century fakes, lacking the delicate colour, the rat-nibbled charm of the real thing.

Pagan wondered what the servants would think if she slid down the banister, then said, 'It was easy to be friends at school, when all our lives were pretty similar but, later on, friends travel down different roads, and some of them are marked "No Entry".' She lifted the elaborate metal visor of a medieval helmet, and said, 'Boo!'

'I don't know where Abdi got the decorator,' said Maxine, 'but he's gilded everything from the light switches to the banisters. All the furniture legs have claws, and look as if they're about to stagger across the floor.'

'I knew you'd hate it,' said Pagan as they passed a green malachite table edged with ormulu and supported by two overweight gold cherubs. 'It gets worse.'

For once, Maxine was speechless as they walked through the salon and out on to the terrace.

Abdullah waved from the side of the pool. How much older Abdullah looks, Maxine thought, noticing the frosting of grey hairs among his strong black curls, and the deeply etched lines in his forehead.

That evening, in the darkness, on the terrace, Abdullah pulled Pagan to him and kissed her. She could smell the vanilla-scented bougainvillaea bushes and the old-fashioned cologne Abdullah wore and the faint odour of his Turkish cigarettes and the starch of his shirt.

'Have you decided, Pagan?'

Nervously, she said, 'I need time to get used to the idea. I'm worried because it could be so difficult, not only for you and me, but for your country – if it didn't work out. I wondered, that is . . . would you mind if . . . we have a six-month secret engagement?'

He released her so abruptly that she almost fell over the parapet. 'Secret! Are you ashamed of me?'

Pagan's mellow happiness dissolved, leaving her with a stomachful of anxiety. 'No, I'm afraid of the future, Abdi.'

'You can't be ruled by fear in life. Who doesn't dare, doesn't win.' Abdullah was an angry silhouette against the blue-black sky. 'I'm sorry, Pagan, but you can't have me on approval.'

'But I want to be certain.' Pagan thumped her knee with her fist.

'Oh, Pagan, you can never be certain.' Abdullah sounded exasperated and sad. 'Life is a series of risks, Pagan. You either open the door marked "risk" or you stay in the cabbage patch for ever.'

'But, Abdi, you're asking for a lot. You're asking for my whole life.'

'Yes, Pagan, I am asking a lot. I am also offering a lot. I am sorry that you can't accept it.' He strode away, leaving Pagan alone on the empty terrace.

~ 14 ~

1 September 1979

IN his Philadelphia office Curtis Halifax watched his family attorney read the telegram. Telling Harry hadn't been as hard as he'd expected; in fact, Harry hadn't batted an eyelash as, haltingly, Curtis had told him of the long-kept secret; but attorneys were accustomed to hauling family skeletons out of the closet. Curtis leaned back in his winged leather desk chair, feeling relieved. At last he had told somebody.

'Dear Daddy, unless you pay them ten million dollars within fifteen days, they will kill me. Stand by for payment in Istanbul. Directions will be sent to Mommy at the hotel. Love – Lili,' Harry read and then raised his eyebrows. 'Curtis, this telegram reads like something from an Andy Hardy movie.' He read the telegram aloud. 'Are you sure this isn't some crazy joke?'

'No, I've already spoken to her mother.'

'And this Lili is the *movie star*?'

Curtis nodded.

'You're *sure* . . . that is . . . there's no doubt in your mind that you are the father?'

'No doubt at all, Harry.' Curtis shook his head. 'I've known about the child since she was born. She lived with foster parents in Switzerland, and her mother and I were told that she'd died at the age of six.'

Slowly Harry sipped his highball. It wasn't unlikely that a childless man of Curtis's age should be proud of fathering an illegitimate child, but the Halifaxes were an illustrious Philadelphia family and everyone knew what Debra was like; a scandal like this might push her over the edge.

'Curtis, are you sure you want to go to these lengths? You're really prepared to fly to Istanbul? How are you going to explain that to Debra?'

'No problem. I fly to Europe on business quite often. Debra won't mind, unless I'm not back in time for Ceezee's Thanksgiving party.'

Harry glanced up at the portraits of Curtis's father and grandfather hanging against the panelled walls. 'My advice would be to consider that other issues might come to light, as well as your paternity of an illegitimate child.'

Curtis knew that his attorney was hinting at the long series of loans the bank had made to Judy Jordan's group of companies, as Harry continued, 'Curtis, it all happened a long time ago. Why not just forget it?'

'It may have been a long time ago, Harry, but I've always regretted the way I treated her mother.' Curtis reached across his desk and held out his hand for the telegram. 'It's simple. My family raised me to be responsible, and I'm going to be responsible for my daughter, who's in danger.'

'But you say you've never even met this woman!'

'I wanted to meet Lili.' Curtis remembered the previous October and his meeting with Judy in the dim, discreet, New York restaurant. Angrily he had brandished a copy of *The New York Times* and pointed at the story of Lili's search for her mother. Wrathfully Curtis had asked Judy why she had invented the story that Lili's father was a dead soldier when he, Curtis Halifax, was the father of Lili. Reproachfully Judy whispered that she had lied to protect Curtis's marriage. How would Debra feel, if told that Curtis had an illegitimate child? How would an ex-porn star fit into Debra's social life in Philadelphia? How would such a beautiful stepdaughter affect Debra's anxiety about her external appearance; if she didn't starve herself to death, Debra would be in constant surgery having her body and face restructured and lifted.

'You must protect Debra.' As usual, Judy had gently played on his guilt. 'Leave Lili alone.'

Curtis had hesitated. 'But she's my . . .'

Judy had interrupted. 'After all, you once left me alone, didn't you? You made *your* choice twenty years ago. You didn't know that you were choosing loneliness when you married Debra, but I knew that loneliness was what you were choosing for *me*.'

Curtis's attorney looked at the silver-framed photograph on the banker's mahogany desk and, as if reading his client's thoughts, he said, 'Well, you know what'll happen to Debra, if any of this leaks out.'

'Look, Harry, I asked you to drop by to check my legal position, not to hand out marriage guidance.' Suddenly Curtis looked like the portrait of his grandfather.

'Curtis, if you admit paternity of this child, you could lay yourself open to . . .'

Curtis impatiently cut him short. 'Harry, I hear what you're saying, but I've made my decision. Now, can we get on with the logistics? How can I raise the money?'

'Even if we could raise that much fast, Curtis, there's no way you could pay kidnap ransom, because it is against government policy to pay kidnap ransom. So, for a start, remember that you'll be up against the law if you transfer the money out of the country.'

Again Curtis showed his grandfather's drive. 'What about our Bahamas operation, Harry, what can we raise there? And we've got the properties in Rio, as well as the Tokyo development. There's enough security there. You're not going to tell me that we can't raise a lousy ten million bucks outside the country!'

Harry looked doubtful. 'My advice is to play this one for time. Both Lili and her mother are influential people with influential friends. By the time you get to Istanbul you may find that the Turkish police have already found her.'

Curtis propped his neatly groomed grey head on one hand. 'I hope you're right, Harry, but in case you're wrong, I want you to raise as much as you can on those Brazilian leases and transfer it to Istanbul. Nothing you say is going to stop me flying out there tonight. I feel so fucking powerless, sitting behind this fucking desk when my daughter is in danger.'

In twenty years Harry had never heard Curtis swear. 'OK, Curtis.' The attorney stood up. 'But try to stay within the law. I don't want to be part of your defence team.'

2 September 1979

'Stop throwing plates, Maggie. I'll explain!' Angelface Harris ducked behind the closet door of the all-black kitchen as his wife hurled another handful of expensive, handmade pottery at him.

'I've had enough of your bloody lies,' Maggie screamed as she grabbed a yellow Italian soup tureen from the black worktop and threw it at her husband. A pile of ceramic shards was building up in front of his hiding place, and the gleaming black kitchen shelves were almost bare. 'You've lied to me every day of our marriage, why should I believe you now?' A scarlet meat plate followed the yellow tureen.

'It serves you bloody right for going through my pockets!'

'I was only looking for grass. And if I hadn't been, I wouldn't have found that telegram.' Maggie flung a Carol McNicholl teapot. 'Dear Daddy, unless you pay them ten million fucking dollars within fifteen days, they'll kill me.' Maggie picked up the food processor, then changed her mind and went for the coffeemaker. 'You ain't going to Istanbul, Angelface, and you ain't sending any money to that fucking porn queen.'

'Maggie, I told you, I've no idea what this is about.'

'I never knew you *had* ten million dollars,' Maggie shrieked, 'or I'd never have signed the fucking premarital agreement.' Maggie had now thrown everything she could lift and the kitchen shelves were bare.

'Maggie, be reasonable!' Angelface looked round the closet door. 'Of course I don't have ten million dollars! What's more, I intend to hang on to every penny I got.'

With difficulty, Maggie picked up the food processor and pitched it. The machine hit the door, scraped the paint off and flew apart as it crashed to the floor.

Angelface knew that Maggie had no ammunition left. Warily he stepped out. 'I got no intention of paying ransom for Lili *or* going to Turkey *or* getting involved with the fucking Turkish police.' He picked his way across the seventh set of crockery to be broken since their marriage. 'Now, will you swear not to tell about that telegram?'

Maggie scowled at him. 'I might and I might not.'

'You better not, you stupid bitch.' Angelface looked down at her and glared. She reached up and slapped his face. He grabbed her hand and pushed her back against the black worktop. Maggie was not intimidated, she was gasping with excitement, and Angelface's eyes were glittering as he tore her shirt open and lunged at her breasts. 'I'll teach you a lesson,' he panted, feeling his cock start to harden. Maggie tried to knee Angelface in the crotch, flailed frantically at him with her free hand, then she pulled a heavy cast-iron saucepan from the sink and smashed her husband over the head with it.

With a roar of rage, Angelface smacked her face.

Maggie's head cracked against the wall, and she collapsed into a screaming heap on the floor.

Angelface jumped to the far side of the black table, as if he wanted a solid barrier between himself and his wife.

'You shouldn't have bopped me with that iron pot, that wasn't playful,' he muttered.

Maggie continued to weep, blood streaming from her split lip. 'It wasn't funny, Mags.'

Piteously Maggie looked up; mascara, blood and lipstick streaked her face.

'Oh, shut yer face and come 'ere,' Angelface ordered out of the side of his mouth. He wasn't going to pick her up.

Maggie picked herself up and tottered towards his grudgingly opened arms. Angelface licked the blood from her split lip and whispered hoarsely, 'I'm sorry, baby, but you shouldn't provoke me that way.' He gently pulled off what remained of Maggie's silk shirt and used it to wipe the tears from her red-and-black streaked face. Cheekily he pinched one of her nipples and she gave a mollified sniff.

'For all I know, Maggie, I might have hundreds of kids around the world,' said Angelface reproachfully, 'but I'd be daft to own up to any of 'em.' He thought, I am tickled fucking pink to think that my kid's turned out to be one of the most beautiful chicks in the world, but I'd better not tell Maggie, or she might really try to hurt me.

Slowly Angelface pulled down the zipper of her jeans. 'You know how the chicks come after me, Maggie. Knickers off and legs up in rows outside me dressing-room door. It was before you come along, darling.' He slid his hands inside her jeans and comfortingly squeezed her ass. Maggie was so tiny that one of her buns was hardly a handful. 'You know I got me appetites, Maggie.' He grabbed her hand and thrust it down his pants, where she could feel his growing affection. 'And you know you love it, baby.'

Entwined, they tottered upstairs to the bedroom, then hurled themselves at each other on the unmade, black-sheeted bed.

Two hours later, when their Filipino houseman had cleaned up the kitchen and Angelface had locked himself in the recording studio with his band, Maggie leaned back against the black sheets, lit a joint, reached for the Mickey Mouse telephone and called her best friend. 'I dunno what I'm going to do, Joanie,' she moaned, with no preamble. 'He bust me lip again and I'm sure he's broken me wrist. D'you think I should leave him this time?'

Joanie asked what had started it, after which they discussed the ongoing tragedy, and the proper etiquette for an upgraded groupie when faced with an illegitimate stepdaughter who was far more beautiful than Maggie, and famous.

By eight o'clock the next morning, when Angelface crashed out on his bed, reeking of brandy, and Maggie was deep in barbiturate-assisted sleep, Joanie had called the rock column of London's evening newspaper. By eleven in the morning the editor had decided to splash the story and, by one o'clock, billboards all over the city screamed: LILI – KIDNAP SEN- SATION.

La Divina stretched her ripe, red mouth as wide as if she were projecting a perfect high C to the dome of La Scala, then firmly clamped her lips around the penis. Slowly she pushed her mouth over the smooth flesh. With satisfaction, La Divina thought that no younger woman, however beautiful, could do this as well as she. Twenty years of practice kept the rhythm steady and helped her to sense if she was going too slow, too fast or too gently (the most frequent male complaint) as Spyros rubbed against the roof of her mouth. Oops! Spyros twitched and La Divina nearly gagged as her uvula made an involuntary movement. That's what happened if you lost your concentration. It should feel, to the man, as sensuously satisfying as having a hand sucked by a newborn calf.

Suddenly the thought of calves and kittens and puppies came into her mind, and La Divina seemed to see a view of herself on the bed from a corner of the ceiling. Oh, Heavens, why was she doing this? It really wasn't an act of love, mouthing this bratwurst with such care. It was a well-practised, pathetic act of despera- tion, a sensual bribe, her last resort, inspired by despair at the thought of losing Spyros and all that he stood for. Her love was no longer love, it was fear; the fear of being abandoned, of public humiliation, of being alone. La Divina sucked harder. How much longer was he going to take? She would start counting the thrusts. Ten . . . twenty . . . forty . . . She started to get cramp in her jaw.

The fey young men who had formed La Divina's entourage when she was the world's most adored diva now sniggered that her mellifluous voice had failed because of the damage done to laryngeal tissues by her bedroom practices. But La Divina no longer cared about the gossip, which rustled through the opera houses of the world, about her affair with the Stiarkoz brothers. She was deathly tired of that demanding circus, the adoring audiences who would shout for blood as readily as for the thirtieth curtain call. Buenos Aires had been a nightmare. She had adequately performed the first half of the recital, then halfway through the aria from *Norma* she had failed to reach high C and an almost crow-like harshness had crept into her lower notes.

There had been catcalls, jeers and howls of laughter. On the following day, when she read her notices, La Divina had cancelled the rest of her tour and fled back to Europe and the sanctuary of the yacht *Persephone*, which was cruising the Greek Islands. Last night she had been reunited with Spyros. Now, all that she cared about was hiding from the world with this man in one of their private places – on his island or his yacht. She wanted to forget that she had ever been a *prima donna*, to forget the anxiety, the responsibility, as well as the honeyed applause. She wanted only to pass her days in sensual reverie and her evening hours feeling him move into her hungry body, thrusting a reason for living back into her immaculately maintained shell.

'I had forgotten how good it feels to be with you.' Spyros slowly drew his blunt fingertips down the fullness of her left breast until he reached the hard dark peak.

But I have forgotten nothing, thought La Divina. She remembered living in a mist of unhappiness after Jo Stiarkoz, as if hypnotized, had abandoned her for that bitch, Lili. It had happened overnight, and La Divina had at first felt numb with misery, then suspended in a miasma of pain and loss. For weeks that grew into months, La Divina lived in a trance of shock, sorrow and humiliation. Finally, she became apathetic; she couldn't be bothered to get out of bed, to get dressed, to go out or to see anyone. When Jo Stiarkoz had been killed in a car crash, La Divina did not (as everyone expected) become hysterical upon hearing the news, because she had been mourning Jo for years.

And then, one day, shortly after Jo's death, her maid had brought to her bedroom a willow basket planted with spring flowers. Twisted between the miniature cyclamen and wood anemones La Divina had found a delicate eighteenth-century diamond collar of rose-cut stones linked by fine bows of smaller brilliants. The card read 'Spyros Stiarkoz'. She smiled. This would only be the beginning, she knew. He would not expect her to thank him, but to wait for his next move.

The next morning she had unwrapped the warm croissant on her breakfast tray and a pair of matching diamond earrings fell from the pink napkin. As she held one, dangling to the light, her bedside telephone rang. 'I've just finished my calls to Hong Kong – may I see you?' asked Spyros Stiarkoz, without introducing himself. La Divina guessed what Spyros meant, because his older brother, Jo, had always preferred to make love in the early morning, after the Hong Kong trading had finished or late at night, after the American markets had closed.

Two hours after receiving the earrings La Divina had been standing on the deck of the *Persephone*. The tang of the sea had mingled with Spyros's faint odour of starch, cigar smoke and clean, warm flesh. That night, before she had a chance to undress, he had quietly appeared in her stateroom. Without a word, he had moved forward and silently held her against him for a long time.

Then, with care, he had softly pulled at the shoulder of her topaz satin gown. She had not moved as he pulled the dress down to her waist, then bent his lips to her large, dark nipples and kissed them lightly, feeling the buds grow hard. Then he had sucked hard at them, and fierce stabs of pleasure had shot, almost painfully, between her legs as he held the tips of her breasts softly between his teeth, then teased them with his tongue, and La Divina had shuddered as life washed into her body once more. Although she had scarcely begun to moisten, she had pulled Spyros close to her, hungering for his vital hardness, feeling the warmth of his erection through the thin silk of his navy dressing gown.

They had fallen back on the bed and she had felt his hand softly, slowly, stroking her inner thighs, higher and higher. Still he made no sound but, as he reached her mound of Venus and started to softly stroke it, she rose eagerly against the rhythm of his hand, feeling no anxiety, no necessity to hurry, just the certainty of her eventual orgasm. When she climaxed, her whole body arched in ecstasy, then she felt for the head of his penis and guided it into her; their mouths were together and their fingers entwined.

Later she had sobbed with gratitude as Spyros held her to his hairy damp chest.

Slowly La Divina's confidence, career and greedy appetite for life had revived and now, six years later, she knew the responses of Spyros Stiarkoz's body better than the power of her capricious voice.

Yes, I have forgotten nothing, La Divina thought, as she lay against the body of Spyros Stiarkoz. She would always remember what he had done for her. Why, when she had telephoned two days ago from Buenos Aires, after cancelling her tour, he had comforted her and told her to fly straight back to Athens.

She had only arrived this morning but his helicopter had been waiting to carry her to the *Persephone*, which was anchored off Aegina.

That afternoon they had made love for over an hour, until both were exhausted and sweating, but Spyros had been unable to have an erection. Afterwards La Divina had, silently, considered all the possible reasons. Of course, Spyros would never see sixty again. Perhaps he had a health problem; ten different sorts of tablets and capsules stood on the tray beside the gold dolphin faucets in his bathroom.

This evening La Divina was determined to arouse him. Now, as her throat accepted the flesh she loved so much, she ran her fingers lightly up his thighs, softly raked his buttocks with her fuchsia nails, then plunged her fingers into his dense pubic hair. But, as she massaged the sensitive area behind the base of his testicles, she felt his balls begin to slacken away from his body and realized that she was not getting the usual response.

La Divina hollowed her cheeks and sucked harder. But it was no good. Spyros's erection had faded.

Finally she pulled away, and looked at him, her eyes filling with anxious tears. Spyros seemed completely unconcerned as he said, 'It will be fine later, darling, I promise you.'

'No, no!' She broke into noisy sobs. 'It's different, isn't it? What have you done with that creature, that now you can't make love to *me*?'

Spyros did not reply, because there was no point in saying anything to her when she was determined to make a scene. And, in fact, he was extremely worried about his lack of response. Nothing like this had happened since he had started taking the serum.

'It's not enough for you to have Zeus Air! It's not enough for you to have more tankers and bigger tankers than Jo had in his fleet!'

La Divina started hitting the cream linen sheets with her clenched fists, and crying louder. 'It's not enough that the *Persephone* is ten metres longer than Jo's yacht! It's not enough that you have *me*!'

Spyros sighed. The first tantrum after twenty-four hours of peace. Ashtrays would be flying within five minutes.

'It's not enough that I love you, Spyros, more than I ever loved your brother! Don't you realize that *nothing* will ever be enough to make you feel you've beaten Jo?' La Divina started to hit his hard, grey-haired chest with her clenched fists. 'But now I know what you want. I didn't think it was true, but it is. *You want Lili as well.* Don't try to deny it. I saw that photograph of you two in the *New York Post*, last November, at the opera. *Dozens* of kind friends sent me the clipping. You remember, I was singing in Sydney. The press was on my neck the next day. Had I any comment, they wanted to know? I had to smile pleasantly, say no, no comment, *and then step out on that stage!*'

So she *had* known about Lili. And for ten months she had not mentioned it. Such emotional self-control was rare in La Divina.

'I promise you, darling, I haven't spoken to Lili for months.' No, Spyros thought, but Lili had been on his mind every day since he had touched her. La Divina's instinct was uncanny.

Spyros had wanted Lili's succulent body for added reasons that he did not care to acknowledge. Certainly, Lili had rejected him, but Spyros never gave up. When anyone opposed him in business, Spyros single-mindedly concentrated on destroying that person. When Spyros wanted something for his collection of Greek antiquities, he was prepared to wait for it – sometimes for years – and he was prepared to pay far, far above the market value for something he really desired. He was very rich and, because he was growing old, there was very little in life that he wanted.

But he wanted Lili.

Now, he briefly kissed the hand of La Divina and returned to his cabin, pausing to admire the purple silhouette of Aegina against the darkening Greek sky.

Back in his own suite Spyros telephoned for the ship's doctor and then showered. Afterwards, one millimetre of serum was injected into his muscular left buttock, which was then respectfully swabbed. The serum was provided by the Swiss clinic that Spyros attended every winter for a week. The precious drug was cultured from the gonadal tissue of embryo pigs; within an hour it would make the sixty-eight-year-old as virile as a fifteen-year-old, Spyros hoped as he dressed. By midnight La Divina would have dried her tears; she would be exhausted and contented and, he hoped, as his valet fastened his platinum cufflinks, she would also be quiet. Thank God she didn't know about the telegram, which had arrived that morning.

There was a knock at the door and a white-uniformed aide entered, holding a paper. 'Just came over the radio, sir. They've located Judy Jordan's hotel in Istanbul. Mr Menecik at the Turkish Foreign Ministry has radioed back to you, offering his services, and Mr Vlassos of Interpol will be available in twenty minutes.'

3 September 1979

Across the road from the Sydonite Embassy the ducks sailed serenely on the pond in St James's Park. Abdullah stared at them, then looked up in surprise as Pagan, wearing a blue Japanese kimono and no make-up, burst into his library, brandishing the *Daily Mail*.

'Abdi, this is terrible!'

Abdullah, who had already signed a thick folder of decrees and state instruments, used the peaceful morning hours to read the most important reports. Now he put down the précis of his Intelligence Department's Washington report.

'Look what it says in the *Daily Mail*!' Pagan read aloud, '"Angelface Harris and Lili, kidnap drama".' She looked up at

Abdullah. 'Lili's been snatched in Istanbul! Judy's still there. I must telephone her straight away.'

Abdullah waved his bodyguard out of the room. 'Does anyone know the identity of the kidnappers or what they want?'

'No idea who they are, but it says here that they've demanded ten million dollars from Angelface Harris. Judy will be frantic!' Pagan loped around the large library, her untidy hair unbrushed, her kimono flying out behind her. As she passed Abdullah's desk she caught her kimono sleeve on a silver tray and impatiently tugged at it. The filing tray fell to the floor, scattering a pile of papers and a telegram. Abdullah jumped up, picked up the telegram and stuffed it in his pocket, then started to shove the papers back on to the silver tray. Pagan was so distraught that she did not notice this strange action. Normally, Abdullah would have pressed a button on the floor beneath his desk, whereupon a black-robed secretary would have entered and picked up the papers.

'I'll get home and pack my bags straight away, Abdi. I'll have to go to Istanbul as soon as I can get on a plane. Judy will need friends around her at a time like this.' She flung a Burberry raincoat over her kimono as Abdi rang for the car.

An hour later Abdullah appeared at Pagan's front door. She had just hurled open a newly packed suitcase, hunting for her passport.

'I don't like the idea of your going to Istanbul alone,' Abdullah said. 'I think I'd better go with you. My people have never trusted the Turks, so we have a good intelligence system there. So we might be able to help in some way. We have a very pleasant little palace in the diplomatic quarter. My dispatch boxes can be sent there. Suliman has arranged everything, our plane will leave in two hours.'

Pagan jumped up and kissed him. 'Darling Abdi, you *are* so kind!' It did not occur to Pagan to wonder why Abdullah should be so willing to make this uncharacteristic gesture of support. 'Now, where the hell is my passport?'

Patiently Abdullah said, 'Your passport is of no consequence when you are travelling with me. I suggest, however, that you ask your maid to find you something more suitable to wear.' Pagan looked down and realized that she had been about to depart in her blue kimono.

*

'Miss Jordan is expecting me,' Pagan explained to the desk clerk for the fourth time, demonstrating the universal habit of raising the voice to uncomprehending foreigners. The next moment she was almost knocked off her feet as the plump and sweaty manager of the Harun-al-Rashid bustled forward with two assistants and bowed to the thin man in uniform, who was standing behind Pagan.

The marble lobby of the hotel was alive with journalists of every nationality. Television cables crisscrossed the rich rugs on the floor, tripping the flustered bellhops as they carried messages. The telephone switchboard was lit up like Las Vegas, and one of the operators was quietly weeping. Everyone was sweating, shouting to make themselves heard, and confused by the hysterical rumours which swept through the press corps every half-hour or so. Photographers jockeyed for position at the entrance on the side street; one intrepid lensman had climbed on to the roof of the hotel annexe and was hopefully fitting telephoto lenses to his cameras in order to pry inside Judy's suite.

Finally Pagan threw up her arms in despair and, having been told that Judy was on the first floor, she bolted up the staircase to the first floor, shouting, 'Judy, it's Pagan, tell them to let me through!'

Judy heard her, flung open the heavy cedar doors of her suite, and Pagan tumbled into the room, and the two friends hugged each other.

'It's like World War Three out there,' Pagan gasped when she got her breath.

'We're waiting for the police chief,' Judy explained. 'I hope he's got some news.' There was a knock at the door and she whirled towards it. 'That'll be him now!' But Gregg Eagleton, looking pale and crumpled, stood in the doorway. 'I couldn't get an earlier flight, Judy. What the hell is happening?'

Ten minutes later the hotel manager escorted into the room a small group of Turkish policemen, headed by the tall thin man who Pagan had seen in the lobby.

Colonel Aziz had round, heavy-lidded eyes and a melancholy expression. He wore the beige uniform of the Turkish police but spoke perfect English with a slight American accent, having done his basic training in Miami. He reassured Judy that everything possible was being done to find her daughter. 'We have involved Interpol, the Sûreté in Paris and the FBI; we have never had a case such as this. You, Miss Jordan, have informed the police of three ransom demands that sound like jokes, all beginning "Dear Daddy", sent to a Greek shipping magnate, an American banker, and a pop singer. But I understand from Miss Jordan,' he inclined his head to Judy, 'that Mademoiselle Lili's father died before she was born.' He spread his long, narrow hands in a gesture of surprise.

He thinks this is a publicity stunt, Judy realized as she handed over the telegram that Curtis had given her that morning, before disappearing to sleep off his journey. The British police had already sent out Angelface's telegram. And Stiarkoz, when he spoke to Judy via the ship's radio, had promised to deliver his cablegram when the *Persephone* docked in Istanbul.

Colonel Aziz examined the three pieces of paper. 'There is little we can discover from these, other than that the messages are identical. We found no sign of force or struggle in Mademoiselle Lili's suite, and our informants in the Grand Bazaar report no unusual disturbance yesterday.'

What would he describe as an unusual disturbance? Judy wondered, gazing up at the dusty chandelier as she remembered the noisy, sweaty crowds that jostled in the smelly booths of the Bazaar: you could have garrotted twenty people in that chaotic place and nobody would have noticed.

'So we are left with the possibility that whoever has abducted Mademoiselle Lili may be someone whom she knew, someone whom she would trust not to harm her.' The colonel sat back in his green velvet armchair and looked from one strained face to another in turn. Gently he asked, 'Who does Mademoiselle Lili know in Istanbul?'

'No one, as far as we know. She's never been here before.' Judy took off her tortoiseshell glasses and rubbed her tired eyes. 'Miss Bayriver, the Beauty Queen winner, and I are the only people that Lili knows in Turkey, apart from the hotel staff, our driver and the guides. I can't imagine any friend of Lili's being capable of this.'

Gregg was slouched in a corner of the sofa, one ankle resting casually on the other knee. 'Surely this is either a straightforward criminal case or a terrorist kidnapping?' Gregg had only ever before felt this anxiety fill his chest when his father was racing. He wished to God he hadn't treated Lili as an ordinary woman: that was what she wanted, so he had tried to hide his bedazzlement behind a façade of unconcern. But she couldn't be treated as an ordinary woman, because she wasn't one. If only he'd looked after her more carefully. He wanted to accompany her on this trip, but Lili had insisted that she wanted to travel in the smallest possible group in order to get to know her mother. Gregg couldn't stop accusing himself of neglecting Lili. If only, if only, if only, he thought.

'I'm inclined to rule out terrorism,' said Colonel Aziz. 'Certainly, in Turkey, we have our fair share of these groups – AMLA, the PLO, some Kurdish separatists. What modern capital city is free of these parasites?' Colonel Aziz shrugged. 'But when terrorists kidnap a person, they have two aims. They want a substantial sum of money to buy arms to use against people such as myself.' Colonel Aziz gave a tight smile. 'And they want the maximum publicity for their cause.' He coughed. 'Kidnapping an international celebrity is a highly effective way of ensuring worldwide maximum press coverage, but it's unusual for the terrorist group not to make themselves known immediately. Anonymous kidnapping is not terrorist style.'

Gregg said, 'Are there any other alternatives?'

'Regrettably, yes.' The colonel hesitated, looked at Judy, then continued. 'We cannot rule out the possibility that this is an elaborately disguised murder. It's not unknown for a murderer to lay a false trail, and the peculiar nature of the ransom notes suggests that this is not an authentic kidnap. Do you know whether Mademoiselle Lili had any enemies?'

'Why, I've just remembered something!' Pagan jumped up and knocked an engraved brass tray off its stand. 'Lili's just done a charity benefit in London and the performance was almost sabotaged. The man who did that is undoubtedly an enemy of Lili!'

Colonel Aziz made a note on his pad. 'Did you make any inquiries at the time?'

'Yes, of course. Someone threw a big party for the entire theatre audience at a smart hotel. That party was an expensive, well-planned, weird operation, like this kidnap.'

'Who paid for the party, Lady Swann?'

'The hotel staff were far too discreet to tell us who paid the bill. As nothing illegal had been done, they had to respect their client's wish to remain anonymous.'

'We have no proof that whoever paid for the party made the hoax telephone call,' Gregg reminded Pagan.

'Now that something illegal *has* been done, the hotel will have to tell us all they know, and so will the bank which paid the draft.' The colonel tore off a sheet of note pad and handed it to one of his assistants.

'I think it was a nutter,' said Gregg. 'Just another sicko, with a bit more loot than most of Lili's crazy fans. Lili gets a regular stack of hate mail. Any one of those creeps might have flipped his lid and decided to grab her.'

'I doubt that the person behind this operation is the sort of person who pesters filmstars.' Colonel Aziz looked from one face to another. 'The obsessive fan is usually an inadequate, pathetic personality who can't form relationships with real people, and so lives in a fantasy world. Any reality usually defeats such people.'

'But they still manage to assassinate the occasional rock star or head of state,' Judy observed sourly. Having seen Lili besieged by obsessive male admirers, none of whom appeared inadequate or pathetic, she was exasperated by the colonel's bland psychological explanation.

'Such acts are generally accidents, rather than carefully planned crimes.' The colonel dismissed Judy's point. 'But we are treating this as a carefully planned, clever crime. Whoever has kidnapped Mademoiselle Lili took great care to investigate your background, Miss Jordan. And he knew that Mademoiselle Lili would be in Turkey at this time.'

Gregg jumped up angrily, and started to pace around the room. 'Anyone who can read a newspaper knows that Lili was on tour in Istanbul with Miss International Beauty.'

Colonel Aziz ignored him. 'An obsessive man might want to possess Mademoiselle Lili as an art collector desires a painting.'

Gregg stood still. 'Do you mean that the point of kidnapping Lili might not be to get money, but to get Lili herself?'

Simultaneously Judy and Pagan thought of the same man.

Slowly the yacht *Persephone* sailed past the Leander Tower Lighthouse, then the vast white craft anchored in the middle of the shallow bay. Within a few minutes, the Harun-al-Rashid private launch, with one solitary passenger, was gliding across the blue-green water towards the yacht.

From the white linen cushions of the aft salon Spyros Stiarkoz rose to greet Judy. No wonder this man frightens Lili, she thought as she looked at the blunt hands, massive shoulders and acquisitive, Levantine eyes of her host.

'My lawyer says that it's unwise for me to be here.' Spyros waved Judy towards a white couch, and she sat down. A white-uniformed steward brought a brass pot of sweet Greek coffee as Spyros handed Judy the much-fingered sheet of buff paper. 'Here's the telegram.' Judy twisted her hands together in her lap, then pressed them against her thighs to steady the trembling. Wordlessly her face asked Spyros a question.

Spyros shook his head. 'I will not pay the ransom.'

'Then why invite me on your yacht?' Judy tried not to sound as hostile as she felt.

'Naturally, I'm concerned for Lili's safety or I wouldn't have sailed here. But my advisers have made it clear that if I accede to one single kidnap demand, I will be paving the way for every member of my family and every employee of my organization to be kidnapped. I cannot afford to be as soft as Getty, and see my grandchildren threatened by kidnappers for ever.'

Judy jumped to her feet. 'Then what exactly does your concern for Lili amount to, Spyros?' Her voice shook. 'Floating around on the Bosporus, wishing us well, while these bandits start cutting off Lili's fingers in order to motivate us?'

'I'm here to make sure that this affair is properly handled.' Spyros sipped his syrupy black coffee. 'Police are the same all over the world – incompetent, mediocre bureaucrats.'

'But . . .' Judy stopped as Spyros held his hand up.

'I wonder if you are aware, Miss Jordan, how easily a situation such as this can be mishandled?' He stressed the 'Miss' lightly, but with contempt. 'If the kidnappers' hiding place is found, the local police might be trigger happy and attempt to storm the building.' He put his cup down and motioned to the steward to refill it. 'If so, they would probably kill half the bandits, get killed themselves, and perhaps be responsible for the death of innocent onlookers. And by the time they found Lili, she would also be dead.'

Judy hated him for being right. 'Do you think the kidnappers are bandits?'

'Perhaps. My people are making inquiries, but we haven't had any firm news yet. It could be the Kemaiat – like your Mafia – or it might be AMLA, which is, as you know, a group called the Asia Minor Liberation Army. So far they've funded their activities only by robbing small-town banks and by hijacking lorries, but perhaps they're getting more ambitious.'

Half an hour later Judy had repeatedly, unsuccessfully, pleaded and begged Spyros to pay the ransom. She stood up, intending to leave, because there seemed no point in staying.

'I'd like to make it clear, Spyros, that I think the most useful thing you can do is pay the money. Somehow, between us, Lili and I will be able to pay you back.'

This damned yacht had cost far more than ten million dollars. The *Persephone*, for all its glittering white luxury, seemed sinister and claustrophobic to her, and Judy was afraid that if she stayed any longer, listening to Spyros's patronizing refusals, she might lose her temper and alienate a very powerful man. Judy was also afraid because Spyros Stiarkoz was a rich man, a careful, clever man, an obsessive art collector, and he was besotted by Lili. His other passion, as every gossip writer knew, was to acquire whatever and whoever had belonged to his dead brother.

Certainly, Stiarkoz had received a ransom demand, but wouldn't it be the move of a clever man to send one to himself in order to throw the police off the scent? With a heavy heart, Judy realized that if Stiarkoz had abducted Lili, then his presence there could only be for one of two reasons. Either he had the gall to openly check on police progress, or else he had arrived to gloat at their unsuccessful efforts to find Lili. Either possibility would mean that Stiarkoz could not be entirely sane. And either possibility meant that Judy was unlikely to see her daughter again.

*

Later that night, before dinner, Judy and Sandy waited for Pagan in the comforting darkness of the domed, carved balcony that hung over the Bosporus like an enormous birdcage.

'That Colonel Aziz shouldn't have questioned you for hours.' Sandy's voice was sympathetic, but she couldn't help wondering what was going to happen to Miss International Beauty's world tour. After all, they were now supposed to be in Egypt, but the Turkish police wouldn't allow Sandy to leave.

'He was only doing his job,' said Judy, 'and in very difficult circumstances.' The world's press had descended upon the hotel and Sandy's picture had been flashed around the world. The press couldn't believe their luck: one international beauty kidnapped, and another one available for photographs.

Sandy and Judy were now virtual prisoners in their hotel suite. All day one or other of them had been barked at by the police and eventually the telephone had been disconnected, because the Turkish operator could so easily be fooled by lying journalists, who assured her that they were returning Judy's calls.

'I could have spat in the eye and stamped on the foot of that colonel,' said Sandy. 'In fact, when I think of what he put you through, I felt like kicking him in the balls.'

Judy was astonished to hear Sandy drop her genteel speech. 'Why, Sandy, that's the only criticism I've ever heard you make.' Judy was eager to divert her mind by talking about anything rather than the kidnap.

'Honey, in my business, a girl learns to watch her mouth,' said Sandy.

Judy looked at Sandy; she was pretty, bright, shrewd and deftly practical, but all that cleverness and capacity for calculation was carefully used to give the impression that she was foolish and incompetent.

'Sandy, what made you decide to be a beauty queen?'

'Honey, that's only the first step up my ladder. In a few years I aim to be hostessing my own TV show.'

'But why start on the glamour circuit? No one will take you seriously after that.'

'What about Bess Myerson? She was Miss America and now she's in consumer affairs. Anyway, being a pretty girl is the only start you can get in a place like Baton Rouge.'

'Pretty is OK, Sandy, but what about your southern belle act? Sure, the guys love it, especially the old ones, but you'll have to stop being ... acquiescent ... if you want to host a talk show.'

'Honey, I guess I was brought up to be agreeable.'

'Sandy, it won't work when you get older, and it won't work when the going gets tough. There's nothing more gruesome than an ageing Blanche Dubois, simpering with girlish charm.'

Sandy was suddenly stung by the comparison to a Tennessee Williams version of a washed-up, neurotic southern belle.

Boldly she said what she'd been dying to say for days. 'Judy, what I can't understand is how Lili's father can pay the ransom, when Lili told me that her father died long ago?'

'I have no idea, Sandy, how this kidnapper could be so crazy or so cruel.'

Sandy remembered the ransom note that had been delivered in the bunch of red roses. It read: 'Wait in your hotel suite to hear from Lili's father. He must pay the ransom.'

Sandy said, 'I wonder how much longer we'll have to wait?'

Judy's nerves snapped. 'For heaven's sake, can't we talk about something else?'

Sandy said, 'Why, yes, Judy, there is something else I have been *longin'* to talk to you about, something I really want to ask you, Judy.' Sandy took a deep breath, then burst out, 'Just which one of those bastards *is* Lili's father?'

～ 15 ～

3 September 1979

'IT's none of your business!' Judy's voice echoed across the dark water and rang around the still room behind them. 'How dare you ask a question like that!'

'Honey! I'm not the only one who's asking,' said Sandy. 'Colonel Aziz gave me a really hard time in his office for two hours. After all, you told the world that Lili's father was dead, then suddenly all these guys got telegrams.'

'For all we know, Sandy, ten other rich men may have received that telegram. Next week the lunatic who's writing them is probably going to send one to John Travolta and President Carter!'

Sandy persisted. 'Who was it, Judy?'

'Lili's father was a British soldier who was killed by the Communists in Malaya.'

Sandy said, 'They'll check.'

Judy jumped up from her seat and leaned over the balcony, with her back to the other woman. Sandy added, 'Colonel Aziz said they'd do blood tests. He's spoken to Lili's doctor in Paris and he's getting Lili's medical records. A modern blood test can really narrow down the field, it's not like one of those old maybe-he-is tests.' Sandy's voice was soft but warning. 'They're going to find out, Judy.'

Judy turned around to face Sandy. Beyond the darkened balcony, just inside the sitting room, moths were dancing around the fringed, pink silk shade of a table lamp. As Judy watched, one of them swooped too close to the hot light bulb and fell, fluttering in agony, on the tabletop.

Sandy stood up and put an arm around Judy's shoulder. 'Honey, *I'm* rooting for you. We've got a lot in common, after all. *I'm* a small-town girl. *I* know what it's like to be no one from nowhere, and how tough it is to get started. I'm sure that there was a good reason for whatever you did or said.' She patted Judy's shoulder comfortingly. 'But I'm a card-carrying twister of the truth, and it takes one to know one. I'm sure it wasn't pleasant to hear Colonel Aziz ask if you'd slept with all these guys. But watch what you're saying, because I can see that the colonel doesn't believe *anything* you're telling him.'

In the cool, soothing darkness only the lapping of water under the elaborate balcony could be heard. Since Lili disappeared, Judy had been in a state of almost unbearable tension; she hadn't slept for two nights and, even before that, she had been exhausted by months of anxiety, due to her multiple business problems.

Suddenly Judy cracked under the strain, buried her face in her hands and started to cry.

Sandy stroked Judy's hair and softly reassured her. 'Don't fret, honey, you're not the first girl to screw more than one guy in a month.'

Through her sobs Judy snuffled. 'It wasn't the way you make it sound, Sandy. They weren't all in one month and besides, I've never been regular.' She gulped, snuffled again and blew her nose. 'The whole trouble started when I was a fifteen-year-old student in Switzerland and working as a waitress. For the first six months I had to work too hard to have any fun. One of the waiters, Nick, had a crush on me but, physically, the chemistry just wasn't there, for me. Then, one night, I was raped. It was on my mother's birthday, February the seventh. It's silly, the things you remember. He was one of the guests at the hotel.'

'Poor baby. What a stinking, rotten way to lose your virginity.'

'When I saw the bastard in the hotel afterwards, he didn't even recognize me. I meant nothing to him, but that experience changed my life. It made me feel degraded. So I never told anyone what had happened. It was my dirty secret.' She blew her nose again. 'Then I met Curtis Halifax, and he made me feel clean again.'

Like people who confide their secrets to a complete stranger on a train because of the unbearable urge to unburden themselves to someone, and because they feel that never again will they meet that stranger, the overwrought, despairing Judy told Sandy the story that she had never told anyone, the secret that only one person had guessed, the tale that had started so long ago in the small, Swiss luxury resort of Gstaad.

14 February 1949

Judy remembered the stars on the ballroom ceiling as the Swiss accordian band played 'La Vie en Rose' at the St Valentine's Day Ball. She had just carried a heavy tray of glasses at top speed up from the kitchens. Without a word, a hard-pressed barman grabbed the tray from her thin, childish hands, and crashed it on to a bench. '*Aidez-moi, paresseuse!*' he snapped.

Judy picked up two of the still-wet glasses. The barman quickly loaded glasses from the tray on to the rack above his head. '*Vite, vite!*' he shouted again. Judy stood on tiptoe as she tried to push the glasses on to the high wooden rack, but she couldn't reach it.

'*Mademoiselle n'est pas assez grande.*' It was the worst French accent Judy had ever heard. From the customer side of the bar a bow-tied American boy smiled at her.

Judy grinned. 'That sounds like an East Coast accent.'

'Philadelphia. I'm Curtis Halifax. Listen, I'm tall enough to put those glasses away for you, if you'll pour me a bourbon?'

Periwinkle-blue eyes crinkled, a bright, frank smile dimpled his cheeks. He looked the sort of tall, clean cut, wholesome guy you saw on Coca-Cola ads, thought Judy as she swiftly stacked the dirty glasses.

From their little table by the dance floor, Kate in cream moire and Maxine in pale-blue silk waved at Judy, who explained to Curtis, 'They're my friends.' Curtis turned and looked at them, gave a brief glance to the other rich, pretty girls sitting round the dance floor, then firmly turned his back on them, clearly fascinated by the tiny blonde American waitress behind the bar.

There was a sudden roll of drums. All heads turned to the glass ballroom doors, where the guest of honour, Prince Abdullah of Sydon, stood stiffly by the side of Pagan, in a sparkling, grey tulle ballgown. Curtis gave them a brief glance, then turned back to Judy. 'Do they ever let you out from behind that bar? How about skating on Sunday?'

Judy didn't have time to reply, as a waiter dashed forward with an order for the royal lemon juice.

'Nick, I can't read your bar slips,' Judy called. 'The head barman will have your head on a platter if you don't write more clearly, sweetheart.'

Curtis looked worried as Nick dashed off with his tray of *citrons pressés*. 'Sweetheart?'

'A figure of speech. We're just good friends.'

Curtis was no better at skating than he was at speaking French. While Judy whizzed around the crowded rink, Curtis struggled to stand upright but, every time he let go of the barrier, his long thin legs went gliding out from under him. Eventually he gave up, and sat with Judy on the terrace, sipping hot spiced punch.

Curtis said, 'Rumour has it that you have a fiancé back in West Virginia.'

Judy wasn't sure that she wanted Curtis to know about her nonexistent fiancé: she had invented Jim as a smokescreen, behind which she could escape from involvements she didn't want. Judy's goal was to learn fluent French and German in a year, then head for Paris to make her fortune. Her days were spent in the language laboratory and her evenings as a waitress at the Imperial Hotel, in order to pay for her year in Switzerland. There was no place in Judy's schedule for a man.

But Curtis took no notice of Judy's good resolutions. Every day, as soon as the sun left the valley and the shadows lengthened across the narrow, snow-packed streets, Curtis appeared in the hotel coffee-bar. Once, when her supervisor started to give Judy sharp looks because of the time she wasted talking to Curtis, he apologized to the man with Ivy-League charm, then tucked a big tip into the beer stein by the till, where the staff tips were pooled.

The following day, as Curtis slid into his usual seat with a bright-eyed smile that was simultaneously knowing and innocent, the supervisor winked at Judy and jerked his head. 'Here's your rich boyfriend again.'

Judy was thoroughly charmed. The boys she had known back home in Rossville were awkward and gauche; they preferred beer, football and fishing to girls. But Curtis had beautiful manners, which was why Judy felt completely at ease with him. Curtis treated Judy like a lady, and, shell-shocked by the peculiar, alien atmosphere of Europe, she enjoyed being with a fellow American who was as homesick as she was. They told each other what they missed about America: Hershey bars, thick milk shakes, steaks that were not leathery flat slices of *bifteck* which stuck in your teeth. 'And what I wouldn't give to go to an undubbed American movie,' said Curtis wistfully. 'I can't understand films in French.'

Curtis first kissed her after they'd been moonlight skating, and were watching a torchlit display on the ice. As Judy felt the rough, male touch of Curtis's fur-lined, camel-hair coat, she felt no longer homesick, but safe, warm and happy in his arms. She also felt a delicious melting-inside sensation. 'It's too cold to kiss outside,' said Curtis. 'Let's go to my place.'

*

Three weeks later Curtis sat on the edge of her bed, pulling on his white socks. 'Of course I love you, Judy. Ever since St Valentine's Day, remember?'

Judy sat up in bed, pulling the quilt round her shoulders. 'Then why are you going back to Philadelphia to marry someone else?'

'I've explained it over and over. This was all planned a long time ago. Debra and I were pinned on her seventeenth birthday and everyone expects us to get married, especially Debra. My father, and my grandfather before him, built up the business with the aim that one day a Halifax would become President of the United States. That's what they both live for, and I'm the only heir, so I have to try for them. It's my responsibility.'

And I'm not your responsibility, thought Judy sadly as Curtis earnestly continued. 'To get a crack at the presidency, I need money; politics is an expensive business. And I need the right wife.' Curtis looked uncomfortable as he reached for his snowboots.

'You mean a rich wife.'

'I've grown up with Debra. I'm very fond of her and I couldn't possibly hurt her. The whole of Philadelphia has known for a year that we planned to marry at the end of her débutante season.'

'But why didn't you tell me?'

'When I first saw you being bullied by that Swiss barman, something happened to me. I just wanted to put my arms around you, take you away, and look after you for ever.' Curtis couldn't look her in the eye, but he was trying to be honest. 'I can't figure out how a guy can love two women at once, but one minute I was drinking bourbon and the next minute I couldn't think about anything but you. You're so different from the girls I know back home, you've got so much pep and go, you're so full of life. I guess I just fell for you.'

'But how can you love me and marry someone else?' Judy scrubbed away her tears with the corner of the quilt.

'I can because I must,' Curtis said reasonably. 'Anyway, you're going to marry that guy in Rossville.'

Judy said nothing. Once again she wished that she hadn't invented that goddamn Jim in West Virginia.

*

The little scarlet cable car swung in eerie silence, suspended from one taut metal rope, high above the sparkling white valley. Doll-sized skiers swooped soundlessly over the ski *piste* below as Maxine listened to her Aunt Hortense's scurrilous Paris gossip and hoped that the two smart Italian women and the boy in the black ski suit couldn't understand English. The two Italian women were middle-aged, pear-shaped, and wore mink-lined parkas. They were immaculately made-up and coiffured and, despite their pristine pairs of Head skis, they obviously had no intention of skiing when they arrived at the top of the mountain.

In her gravelly voice Aunt Hortense confided to Judy, 'Of course, everybody likes to think that Roland is *tapette* and so when Zizi found him in the . . .' She stopped abruptly as the cable car gave a frightening lurch, halted, then started shaking from side to side as the couplings up above ground noisily.

There was a moment's sickening silence. Judy felt helpless and trapped, as if the walls of the car were closing in on her and growing smaller; she wondered how long the air supply would last, and whether they'd freeze to death before help arrived as claustrophobia started to set in.

'*Dio mio!*' cried one of the Italian women, and she lunged to the end of the car. Her shifting weight made the cable car bounce, as if it were about to uncouple itself from the cable and plunge on to the rocks far below.

'Don't move!' Aunt Hortense said sharply in Italian, but the woman ran back to her original place.

'*Santa Mamma Mia!*' Pink mink parka started to beat her breasts. 'My children! My husband! What will they do?' She threw herself into the arms of her friend. The cable car, which was the size of a small elevator, lurched under the sudden movement, then swayed sickeningly.

Aunt Hortense's craggy face looked mildly regretful as she briskly cracked the back of her ski mitt across the woman's face. 'Your husband and children would not want you to get hysterical, Signora.' Aunt Hortense's wide purple mouth softened. 'There's no danger, so long as we don't move. We should all sit down on the floor very carefully. Down there, they know what's happened to us, and the mechanics are working on it. What we must do is think about something else. I suggest a game of poker.'

Mauve parka whispered to pink parka, who was blazing with rage as she watched Aunt Hortense flip up the back of her white fox coat, then carefully arrange herself, cross-legged, on the floor of the cable car. She opened her large, crocodile Gladstone bag, groped inside and produced a silver hip flask of cherry brandy, which she handed round to the five other passengers as they carefully sat on the floor.

'I know there's a pack of cards in here somewhere.' Aunt Hortense searched in her bag. Her emerald eye shadow matched her Pucci après-ski outfit and, in spite of her shaggy white fox hat, her beaky nose was red with cold as she searched for the cards. She pulled out a Swiss army penknife ('So useful for the corkscrew'), a menu from Maxim's ('Bébé Bérard drew this picture of me the night before I left Paris'), and a battered hand-rolled cigarette, which she hastily put back; then she discovered the cards and turned her wide, enchanting smile on the boy in the black ski suit as he held out his hand to take the cards and shuffle them; obviously, he was the only other person present who could play poker.

Half an hour later, by the time the cable car shuddered into life again, the cherry brandy flask was empty, the Italians had lost all their money, and Aunt Hortense was kicking herself for not having called this English boy, Bobby Harris, on a pair of twos.

The restaurant was perched on top of the mountain. Maxine bit into a meringue as she leaned over the wooden rail of the sundeck and looked around at the shadowed peaks, jagged against the sapphire sky. 'Maman wrote that you've chosen me some lovely summer clothes from Christian Dior,' she said. Aunt Hortense blotted her purple lipstick and smiled indulgently. 'What are godmothers for?'

Judy felt angry and rejected, humiliated and crushed as she looked at Maxine. Thank heaven she'd never told the others just how involved she had been with Curtis. Curtis would never have dared dump a girl like Maxine, Judy thought. Dumb girls from poor families in small towns are always going to get screwed by hypocritical rich bastards with fancy manners, because they had all the power and all the know-how, they could use plain folks like Kleenex, then throw them away when they'd served their purpose. Feeling like a depressed sparrow, huddled in her old navy pea jacket, Judy momentarily envied Maxine more than her wealth and social position; unlike her, Maxine was happily in love and the sight of her complacent, sensual satisfaction made Judy feel that twinge of envy. 'That's your third meringue, Maxine,' she said. 'Pierre won't love you if you get fat.'

'But I'm still starving,' Maxine objected. For a moment Judy felt violent resentment. Judy's reluctant memory of the painful poverty that she had endured as a child was triggered when she heard anyone cheerfully say, 'I'm starving!' Suddenly Judy's knees would tremble, her guts would shrivel and she would feel as if she wanted to pee.

She felt a gust of rage as she thought, Maxine has no idea what she's talking about. Until she left home, at the age of fifteen, Judy had been gnawed by hunger almost every day. Her family in West Virginia had been painfully poor, and the shame had been almost worse than the hunger. Judy remembered the sniggers of the kids at school, because they knew that she would be forced to refuse anything that cost money; Judy also remembered the giggles as she appeared in the same threadbare winter coat, year after year. At first the kids sniggered because her brown coat was far too large for her, an obvious hand-me-down; eventually they sniggered because, when she outgrew the coat, her mother had sewn on cuffs and a false hem, cut from an old grey blanket. 'Listen to Judy's coat!' the kids would shriek with the cruelty of youth; her coat rustled because her mother had sewn newspapers behind the lining, to make the threadbare coat warmer for winter.

What Judy most remembered about poverty was the humiliation.

'And how do you intend to avoid starving? Or do you intend to play poker as a profession?' Aunt Hortense waved her gold bracelets towards Bobby, who was standing next to Maxine and shading his big blue eyes from the sun.

'My father wants me to be a stockbroker and join his firm.' Something in Bobby's voice made it sound unlikely. 'That's why I'm a student at the business school.'

'But what do you really want to do?'

'I want to be a singer.' He gave Aunt Hortense a crooked grin

'A singer? Like Frank Sinatra?' asked Aunt Hortense as Maxine licked her fingertips, stretched her arms to the glittering sun and then unzipped her jacket, thinking that nice boys from good families do not go into show business.

'Not like Frank Sinatra; not like anybody you know!' Bobby threw her an impertinent, urchin grin.

'Then do you play the piano, like Cole Porter?' Aunt Hortense persisted.

Bobby gave Aunt Hortense a cherubic smile. 'I play the piano, but not like Cole Porter.' Still modest at eighteen, Bobby could also play the guitar, the flute and the organ; if they intended to take music scholarships to Oxford or Cambridge, the most gifted music students at Westminster school were allowed to practise on the massive, seven-keyboarded organ in Westminster Abbey. Bobby Harris's stockbroker father had firmly told him that any kind of career in music was out of the question, but Bobby wouldn't and couldn't stop playing, any more than he could stop breathing.

'Where do you sing, Bobby?' Aunt Hortense demanded.

'I don't sing in public, I just sing.' Bobby scratched his curly dark hair and felt uncomfortable; he didn't want to make polite conversation about music to someone's aunt.

'So what are you going to do about your future?'

'I don't know.'

Aunt Hortense had no children, but was still, at heart, a child herself. She enjoyed doing whatever it was that young people were doing that week and (unlike them) she had all the adult goodies – the cars, the cash, the credit cards and the credibility – to make fact of the fantasies of the young. Now Aunt Hortense leaned forward and said, 'No one will throw you into jail if you don't become a stockbroker, Bobby. And if you don't like it, you'll probably be a bad stockbroker. People generally perform best at what they like doing best. So what do you like doing?'

'I write songs. I play a bit.' Bobby shrugged and lifted his high-arched eyebrows even higher.

'So why don't we go this evening to a nightclub, and ask the band if you can sing with them for a few numbers?'

'*We* can't,' said Maxine, crossly, 'because Monsieur Chardin, the headmaster, would never allow us out of school for the evening.'

'I can't.' Bobby was obviously embarrassed. 'Because my allowance has run out, and I've just paid for our lunch with my poker winnings.'

'Aunts are for when your allowance has run out. Would you like another meringue, Maxine?' Aunt Hortense waved her purple-nailed hand at a waiter. 'Myself, I have not much money, but I have enough for serious frivolity. I will ask Monsieur Chardin to make an exception for you tonight, Maxine, and I will beg your supervisor to free you for one evening, Judy. Then we will all dance all night together.'

'She will, too, she's as strong as an ox,' Maxine said to Bobby.

Unfortunately, Bobby did not sing the kind of songs that provided good rhythm for dancing, and he was embarrassed by Aunt Hortense's insistence that he perform in the small, dark, pine-panelled nightclub. Reluctantly he went into a huddle with the band – four middle-aged men, wearing lederhosen and green felt jackets. There was much head-scratching and explaining, then Bobby said, 'Forget it, fellows, just forget it. Give me the guitar and I'll get this over with.' He dragged a stool up to the microphone and started to play.

Judy was surprised to hear this diffident English boy open his mouth and holler two blues numbers as, under his agile, skinny fingers, the tired old dance-band guitar produced tortured wails and hot rhythms. Then Bobby jumped off the stool and replaced the guitar on its stand as the audience, sitting at candle-lit tables, gave a cheerful round of applause. But Aunt Hortense sent him back to the microphone saying, 'The band has taken a half-hour break, so it's your job to entertain us.'

Judy soon found out that Bobby only liked black American music. Under the bed in his chilly bed-sitting room he kept a heavy portable record-player and a suitcase full of American records. All the records seemed to be by blues singers with three names: Blind Lemon Jefferson, T-Bone Walker, Sunny Boy Williamson. Bobby treated his 78s as if they were made of spun glass; he dusted the records every time he played them, and he changed the steel needles in his record player almost every day, to make sure that the discs weren't damaged.

'I suppose you couldn't write home to one of your friends, Judy, to get me some records?' Bobby threw her his angelic smile. 'It's terribly difficult to get blues records, even in London, and it's downright impossible in Switzerland.'

So that's why he's being so cute, thought Judy, who now found it hard to believe that any boy could be nice to her simply because he liked her. But Judy soon found out that she was wrong about Bobby Harris. He genuinely liked Judy because she was nothing like the twinset-and-pearls, protected, fluttery girls of whom his parents approved. Bobby liked Judy because she was brash, independent and – above all – because she was American. Anything American was magic to Bobby. Little blonde Judy, in her pedal pushers and navy pea jacket, seemed as glamorous and alluring as his new pin-up, Marilyn Monroe.

Judy liked Bobby because he made her laugh, and because she was flattered by Bobby's comparing her to the blonde in the potato sack who was pinned up on his wall. Bobby's friendly attention helped to rebuild Judy's demolished self-esteem and, with the puppy-like resilience of youth, she quickly started again to look forward, hopefully, instead of backward, regretfully.

Bobby's courtship strategy was to play his most sexy, suggestive songs late into the night. However late Judy finished work at the Chesa, Bobby would always be awake and waiting for her, ready to throw open the big, double windows of his room and help her scramble up from the street below. His fat, sulky landlady would not have allowed it but, luckily, she was a sound sleeper. One night, as Bobby played to her, Judy went to sleep, sitting on the floor with her back against the wall, and didn't wake up until morning. Soon, Judy couldn't see the point of crunching back to the Imperial through the starlit streets at four in the morning, when she would have to be up again at six. Somehow, she managed to survive on hardly any sleep, muttering that if Napoleon only needed two hours a night, then she had better cultivate his habit.

One evening, when Judy was sitting cross-legged on the threadbare rug in Bobby's room, she said, 'Maxine's boyfriend,

Pierre, says you're going to get thrown out of the business school, Bobby, unless you start working. He says you're rude to the lecturers and never write any essays.'

'At least I'm not so dumb as that ski-bum, Pierre.' Bobby fixed a capo on the neck of his guitar to alter the pitch. 'The head had me in for a wigging but, as a matter of fact, I hope that they do chuck me out.' He readjusted the capo. 'Anyway, if I get expelled I'll be unemployable, and then I'll be *free!*'

'But you'll never get a good job,' Judy worried. 'You can't waste all your time playing these songs. You ought to be studying in the evenings.'

'I wish you'd stop telling me what to do.' Bobby was annoyed.

'It's for your own good, Bobby. I'm only thinking of you.'

'I wish you wouldn't.'

'What do you mean?' Judy thought, not another one, getting ready to walk out on me. She said anxiously, 'Why shouldn't I think of you? You love me ... don't you? You've told me so often enough.'

Bobby said nothing.

'Telephone, Monsieur Harris, from Paris!' He could hear the disapproval in his landlady's voice as she shrieked up the stairs after breakfast.

It was Aunt Hortense, with a surprising suggestion.

'You're a frivolous, irresponsible old woman,' he happily shouted into the black receiver.

'And I miss you, too.' Aunt Hortense's mellifluous voice floated out of the trumpet-shaped ear-piece.

'You have told them I like to sing the blues, not le hot jazz?' Anxiously Bobby raised his high-arched eyebrows even higher. This was too good to be true.

'They are delighted, delighted. It's a very *louche* little club, they love the idea. And, when they see that angel face of yours, they'll love you on sight.'

Bobby scrawled Judy a note, then caught the next train to Paris.

'Two men in two months – that doesn't make you a fallen woman,' said Maxine, comfortingly. 'It's not your fault.' She passed Judy her handkerchief, looked around Judy's narrow servant's bedroom and thought, growing up seemed to need a lot of handkerchiefs. Again Maxine read Bobby's crumpled note: '. . . I didn't tell you I was going because I knew we'd have a row . . . know you don't really like my songs or my music, but I'm determined to give myself a chance . . . hope you'll understand . . . hope you'll come and see me at the Hep Cat Club when you come to Paris. Don't be mad. Lots of love. Take care of yourself. Bobby.'

'But what did I do wrong?' Judy threw herself on her bed, lay on her stomach and buried her face in the big square pillow. Her muffled voice demanded, 'Why do they all leave me, Maxine?'

'Maybe you're a bit too . . . bossy?' Maxine suggested. She was not sorry to see the collapse of this unsuitable liaison, but she was sad to see Judy's misery. 'A boy does not like to be told what to do, he gets all that from his mother.'

'I'm not bossy, I'm decisive,' wailed Judy. 'Why can't I be how I am? All I want is a direct, honest relationship with a boy. I want to be loved and trusted. I want to be his friend as well as his girlfriend. I can't be a flattering, calculating, clinging vine.'

'Then you're in for a hard time, Judy, because most boys do not want an independent girl.' Maxine shrugged. 'Why not be clever, Judy, and pretend to be a little helpless sometimes?'

'I don't think it's possible for me to play a part. I want to be an honest person.' Judy sat up. 'But if that's how things are between men and women, I guess I'll just have to try being devious.'

In the darkness Sandy was only a curly-haired shape against the Istanbul skyline, but Judy could hear the warm sympathy in her voice as she said, 'So that's why you never knew which one was the father of your baby.'

'Bobby left for Paris in early April. By the end of April I thought I might have missed two periods, but then I've never been regular, so I didn't worry much. And somehow, I never thought that God would let it happen to me. After that I wasn't really interested in men for years.'

'Why didn't you get an abortion?'

'You're young, Sandy, you've no idea what it was like for a woman only a few years ago. We were only schoolgirls, we had no idea how to get an illegal abortion, and the doctor was Catholic, in Switzerland.'

'Did any of those guys help you, when the baby was born?' Sandy would never have got pregnant in the first place and, had she done so, she would have gotten rid of it, in the second place. And, on the way, she would have milked any man for any money she could derive from the situation.

Reluctantly Judy said, 'At first I didn't want to ask either of them, but then I remembered what Maxine had said. Why didn't I try a little female manipulation? Kate, Pagan and Maxine had been so supportive – they had each agreed to help pay for the baby – but I was the only one who couldn't manage to scrape the money together – although Lili was *my* baby.'

The Turkish balcony lit up briefly as the beam of the Leander Tower Lighthouse swept over it. Judy added, 'It was easy for Maxine, because she had an allowance from Aunt Hortense. It was easy for Pagan, because she had an allowance from a family trust fund. It was easy for Kate, because her father was rich, but I was a fifteen-year-old waitress.' Judy remembered that long-ago day, when Dr Geneste, her gynaecologist, had let her use his telephone to place the international call. She remembered Curtis's reaction. Even at this distance, his voice had sounded frightened as he said, 'But, Judy, why didn't you tell me earlier?'

'How could I?' she had hollered down the receiver. 'You'd just been married, Curtis. You were somewhere in the Virgin Islands, on a yacht.'

There was a pause. 'Don't worry, Judy. Let me have the details and I'll send you money for the baby's care. But promise me that Debra will never know about this.'

'Of course,' Judy shouted gratefully. 'I promise that she'll never find out.'

In the empty Hep Cat Club, just off the Champs-Elysées, the silver-foil fringe around the stage looked tawdry with the lights up. The smell of cigarette smoke and old cooking fat lingered in the air as Judy said, 'Look, Bobby, do you want to see your daughter?' She looked straight into his innocent blue eyes as she handed him the photographs. Bobby flipped through them once, then more slowly, then he stopped at the close-up of the pudgy

little face with blackcurrant eyes. Slowly Angelface grinne
'Yeah, she looks like me! Cute smile, isn't it?' He pulled out h
notecase and carefully tucked the photographs away. 'Just on
thing, Judy, we must keep quiet about this, and there's n
question of marriage, understand? There never was, and I tol
you that all along. So let's keep this just between you and m
and I'll let you have as much cash as I can.'

Judy felt weak with relief. She didn't care who was the fathe
or how she got the money, so long as her baby was properl
looked after. It looked as if things were fine for the moment, bu
you never knew what would happen next. She'd save any extr
money for a rainy day, in case the baby was ill or something. Sh
felt guilty because she hadn't told Curtis about Bobby, or Bobb
about Curtis, but then, had she done so, probably they woul
both have refused to help her.

The moon came out from behind a cloud and lit up the distan
domes of the Topkapi Palace. On the balcony Sandy turned t
Judy and said, 'You did the right thing, honey. Life is tough fo
a small-town girl, once she's left home. We have to do whateve
we can, to get wherever we can.'

Judy decided not to continue. Even Sandy might not under
stand the full story.

~ 16 ~

4 September 1979

THE building which Abdullah had described to Pagan as 'a
pleasant little palace' was an eighteenth-century, imposing, pale
building with an Arab garden, through which Pagan and Abdullah were walking in the early morning sunlight, along an avenue
of lofty palms, towards an elaborate fountain. The palace gardens, scented with rosemary, roses and jasmine, were purple
with falls of bougainvillaea. The soft splashing of water came

from the interlinked streams, fountains and pools among the verdant foliage and bright flowers.

At the end of the avenue was an octagonal, white-marble pool with fountains jetting into it. Pagan sat on the edge of the pool and trailed her hand in the water.

Abdullah sat beside her and gently caught her hand underwater. He said, 'Pagan, I know I'm a difficult man and I have a difficult job to do. I have been involved with many women but you were my first love, and it seems that you have always stayed in my heart.' He looked at her, in her lavender gauze, loose, long robe, with her hair streaming down her back. 'Let's not waste any more of our lives, Pagan. I love you and I need you, and I'm only going to ask you once, and I must request a positive answer. Will you marry me?'

Pagan looked at him and, slowly, she nodded. Abdullah took her in his arms and held her against his heart. Together they laughed with relief.

They felt that they shared a secret that the world did not yet know. Abdullah seemed to drop his worries, and, gleeful as a schoolboy, excitedly started to plan their future.

Much, much later, Pagan said, 'We can't announce it now. We'll have to wait until this business of Lili is . . . resolved.' She added, 'I can't bear to see Judy so distraught.' Hesitantly she looked at Abdullah. 'Are you sure that it's not possible to help her raise the money, Abdi?' Privately Pagan was thinking that ten million dollars wouldn't amount to more than one day's output from Sydon's oil fields.

Pagan, now sitting on the low surround of the marble fountain, said, 'Couldn't you possibly . . . help Judy directly, Abdullah?'

Abdullah thought, I shouldn't have come here. When first he had read that weird telegram, he had thought it some drunkard's joke. He had once loved Lili, but she had walked out on him and it was no affair of his. He had intended to stay uninvolved, to ignore the telegram. Then Pagan had read the newspaper report, and Abdullah realized that Lili's disappearance was genuine. They had arrived in Istanbul to discover that identical telegrams had been sent to other rich men in Lili's life. Abdullah had decided to keep silent about his telegram, rather than attract undesirable publicity. That wouldn't help the situation.

Pagan trailed her hand in the fountain pool. '*Please* help Abdi.'

'Pagan, I've already explained that one should never give in to kidnappers; many more lives might be in danger if ransom is paid to terrorists, because they'd use the money to kill innocent people.'

He seems so detached, thought Pagan. She was uneasy about the objectivity with which Arabs view women, particularly Western women. Suppose I had been kidnapped, Pagan wondered. Would Abdi talk like this? Maybe women are expendable to him.

Abdullah added, 'Paying the money wouldn't guarantee Lili's safe return. Once she'd served her purpose, as soon as they got their money, the kidnappers might kill her; it would be safer for them.'

A red-uniformed servant approached the fountain to announce Abdullah's next appointment, so Pagan went into the conservatory. Pagan had always loved conservatories. Waiting among the scented orange trees and the dripping fern fronds calmed her anxiety. She was feeling her usual optimistic self by the time she saw the grey Mercedes slowly drive from the palace entrance and pass the conservatory. In the back of the limousine was a small, slim figure who seemed familiar but, although Pagan strained her shortsighted eyes in the bright sunlight, she could not see the face of the passenger.

Mark Scott, wearing his usual crumpled khaki shirt and trousers, carried his battered, silver camera case into the lobby of the Harun-al-Rashid and asked for Miss Jordan. The clerk at the check-in desk was unhelpful; Miss Jordan and her party had left the hotel. Mark asked for a room, and was told the hotel was full.

Mark tucked a fifty-dollar bill in his passport, handed it to the desk clerk, said he was sure that there was a free closet somewhere and which suite did Miss Jordan occupy? The clerk said he would try to find a room, kept the money, handed back the passport and delicately rested his hand on the pigeonhole numbered 104. Mark dumped his bags and ran up the marble staircase to the first floor.

Somehow, Mark had expected to find Judy alone, not sitting with a group of people that included Gregg, Sandy and two policemen. His rehearsal speech forgotten, he simply looked at Judy and said, 'I came as soon as I could.' Judy seemed smaller, sadder and older than he had ever seen her look, thought Mark, longing to take her in his arms. 'Can I help in any way?' Mark asked.

'No, there's nothing you can do, Mark,' Judy said quietly, 'the police are handling the problem. Would you please go.'

Mark looked at the group. 'Judy, can't we speak alone? I want to tell you why I've come here.'

She longed to touch him, to smell him, to hold him. But she knew that she dared not invite humiliation. 'Mark, I know why you've come, but I want you to go. Please.'

Mark said, 'In case you change your mind, I'll let you know where I'm staying, as soon as I know.'

Back in the lobby Mark sat down and checked his cameras. After thirty minutes the desk clerk discovered that two German tourists were leaving, because they couldn't stand the pandemonium of police and photographers. So Mark had a room. Again he climbed up the marble staircase (no elevator), but Gregg, who had been watching him from the floor above, stepped out and barred his way. 'No you don't, chum. Find somewhere else to stay. Judy doesn't want you here.'

Angrily Mark shoved Gregg aside, saying, 'What's it to you?'

Gregg shoved Mark. Mark lost his footing and grabbed Gregg's arms, then slipped on the smooth marble staircase. Together the two men tumbled down the stairs, shouting accusations as they fell, and then continued their fight in the hotel lobby. As Mark struggled to rise Gregg grabbed Mark's foot, and again he lost his balance.

The two men were strangers. Gregg only knew from Lili that Mark fancied her. Mark didn't know who the hell Gregg was, but knew that he was frustrating Mark's attempts to see Judy. Had it not been for the tension they both felt because of the kidnapping, they would not have been fighting, but the fight enabled them to externalize their feelings.

As the two men kicked and punched, grappled and yelled, the pressmen who were hanging around the lobby formed a noisy circle, then started taking pictures, shouting, cheering on their buddy, Mark, and betting on the result of the fight.

Suddenly there was silence as Colonel Aziz and his escort entered the lobby.

'Who is Mr Eagleton fighting?' the police chief demanded of the nearest cameraman.

'Mark Scott – a freelancer who works mostly for *Time* magazine,' the man replied. Colonel Aziz immediately remembered that Mark's name had been included in the long list of men who were, according to Judy, obsessed by Lili.

Colonel Aziz pointed to Mark. 'Get that man off the floor and arrest him,' he ordered his men.

Accustomed to being jailed by hostile police officials, Mark knew that he had only to bide his time until his fellow journalists, who had seen the arrest, were able to telephone his editor at *Time* magazine. His editor would then telephone their man in Washington, who would have a word with the appropriate government department on Capitol Hill; he would send a note, via the US Ambassador in Turkey, to the Turkish Foreign Ministry and, at that point, some Turkish civil servant would lean on the Police Department and secure Mark's release. It would take less than twenty-four hours in a trivial case such as this.

Mark still thought he had been arrested for brawling, and not as a kidnapping suspect.

At about 3 a.m. Colonel Aziz decided to interrogate Mark. He was brought from his cell and told to sit in front of the police chief's table.

Colonel Aziz said, 'You have been arrested for causing a disturbance at the Harun-al-Rashid Hotel, and I am holding you to help us with our inquiries into the kidnapping of the French actress, Lili. Tomorrow a lawyer will be appointed for you by the court. You are not obliged to say anything but I strongly advise you to cooperate.'

'How long am I being held here?' asked the astonished Mark. 'I want to telephone my embassy. You have my passport, you can see that I only entered the country yesterday. Surely that's enough evidence? I can hardly have arranged a kidnap from Nicaragua.'

'Passports can be falsified. Nobody has accused you of being a

kidnapper, but it's interesting that you should jump to that conclusion. How long have you known Mademoiselle Lili?'

'None of your business.'

'Oh, but it is. Be careful, Mr Scott. You are perfectly qualified
to have committed this crime. You are accustomed to procuring
illegal services in foreign countries, and you are accustomed to
conducting clever, lengthy research investigations. And I am
informed by Miss Jordan that you were involved with the
victim.'

'And I'm probably the only suspect you've got?'

'Be careful. You are a long way from home, Mr Scott. You are
clearly capable of being involved with this crime, and you have a
motive.'

'A motive? Why would I do it?' Mark laughed and put his
hands behind his head.

A policeman stepped forward and prodded Mark painfully in
the ribs with a truncheon. Sharply Mark brought his arms
down.

'Your motive might be vengeance. You might have kidnapped
Mademoiselle Lili because she would have nothing to do with
you.'

'What a crazy idea! There was never anything between us.'
Mark wasn't worried, but he was irritated and knew he had to
hide his irritation. The best thing to do was not to refuse to talk
to Old Bootface here, but to say as little as possible, and just put
up with the situation for a couple of days.

'But perhaps you *wish* there was something between you, Mr
Scott. You are under suspicion because you know Mademoiselle
Lili. We have reason to believe that she was abducted by someone
she knew. If you had told her a plausible story, she might have
left the hotel, accompanied by you, without struggle.'

'If you look at my passport, Colonel, you'll see it would be
very difficult to fake.' Mark looked at his thick, much-stamped,
many-visaed, often-confiscated, dog-eared passport, which was
now lying on the colonel's table. 'You'll soon receive news of
me from your superiors, Colonel. As you also confiscated my
accreditation, you're aware of my connections.'

Colonel Aziz jerked his head and said to the policeman
standing behind Mark, 'Take him back to his cell.'

The next morning Mark was released and his property was returned. With resignation, he signed for it, knowing in advance that it was unlikely to include most of his cash and his most expensive camera.

In a small park by the edge of the Bosporus Curtis Halifax was walking with Judy, who wore large dark glasses. Judy said, 'So now you know as much as I do about these weird telegrams, and I've told you as much as I'm prepared to tell you about my affair with Angelface Harris, but remember that I only became involved with Angelface because you left me.'

After so many years of guilt, believing Judy's child to be his, Curtis had been stunned by the news of Angelface's ransom telegram, which he had read about in the *International Herald Tribune* as soon as he stepped into the Istanbul Hilton.

Honest himself, Curtis found Judy's deception difficult to understand. Now he said, 'But you let me think that Lili was my daughter. You asked me to pay for her care as a child.'

'Curtis, I'm sorry. I can't bear to hear myself say this but at the time I didn't know which of you was Lili's father. You paid twenty-five per cent of the cost of her care, and there was more than a twenty-five per cent possibility that Lili was your child.'

'She still might be my child.'

'No.' Judy was sorrowful but firm. 'The grown-up Lili resembles her father, in temperament more than looks. I'm truly sorry that I involved you, but at the time I thought I was doing the best thing for my daughter. You and Angelface both helped to pay for her care until she was six, when I was told she was dead. There was some surplus money, but not by the time I'd finished searching for Lili in the refugee camps. That trip cost a small fortune and left me in debt.'

'Nevertheless, I've paid for someone else's child. And why did you lie on TV? Why did you say that Lili's father was a British soldier?'

Judy spun round and faced the angry Curtis. 'Just be grateful that I didn't say it was you, Curtis.' Suddenly Judy was equally angry as she demanded, 'Do you understand what desperation is, Curtis? You've never been poor, you've never been desperate.

You've never been tempted, you've never had to survive by yourself!'

Judy remembered that bleak winter day in 1956, after the Hungarian uprising, when she had returned to New York from Europe after her unsuccessful search for Lili in those chaotic refugee camps on the Austrian border.

Returning after a fourteen-hour, overnight flight, Judy had staggered into the hallway of her apartment house on East Eleventh and dumped her shabby suitcase in the hall. She felt desolate and alone. After Lili's birth, after breast-feeding her for three months, Judy had been forced by poverty to hand her baby daughter to somebody else, and Judy had never seen her again. Now her daughter was dead; Judy would never know her. Judy felt as if the world had turned against her. Everything seemed pointless. She would never achieve anything. Life was going to be one endless struggle, and there was no reason to continue it. Everyone wanted to take, take, take. No matter what talent she had, however hard she worked, Judy was never going to get her head above water in this tough jungle called New York City.

She checked her mailbox. Bills, bills, bills. And on top of those, she owed Pat Rogers the plane fare. Pat Rogers was the department head of Judy's office. Pat knew that Judy hated to borrow money, because it made her feel humiliated, but Pat also understood that Judy couldn't exist in New York City on only stamina, ambition and one hot-dog a day, cut into three pieces.

Standing beside the dark waters of the Bosporus, Judy could still remember what it felt like to be hungry, not to be able to afford bus fares, not to be able to afford shoe repairs. Even though she lived and worked in luxury, Judy would always be that young girl who had lived on a hot-dog a day and, at heart, her sympathies would always lie with hopeful young girls who had not yet been kicked in the teeth by fate, or dumped by rich boys with no problems.

Judy looked at Curtis and suddenly didn't mind giving him her next bit of information. She said, 'I think I ought to warn you that the Turkish police think that your wife may be involved with this kidnapping.'

Curtis stood still and gaped at Judy. 'Debra?'

Judy nodded. 'You know that party I told you about, before

Lili's gala in London. It turns out the anonymous benefactor was Debra. We were only told this morning.'

Curtis's neat-featured face seldom registered emotion, but now he looked horrified. Somehow he knew that this time Judy was telling the truth. She said, 'The Turkish police got Scotland Yard on to the London hotel; they opened up their books and found that the money for the party had been anonymously paid, but it was traced through the paying bank. It came from Debra's account in Philadelphia.'

'My God!' Not for the first time in his life, Curtis wished that he had stayed in Switzerland with Judy, instead of bowing to the family ambition and marrying that bundle of trouble. He said, 'But Debra doesn't need ten million dollars! She's worth far more.'

'The Turkish police think that Debra might have arranged to have Lili killed, and that all these mad ransom notes are just a cover-up for the murder.' Judy's voice cracked. 'I've already been told that if Lili's body is found, Debra will be a murder suspect. I'm sorry to distress you, Curtis. It's obviously untrue and I don't believe it. Only a crazy person would do a thing like that.'

Curtis said, 'I'll have to get back home immediately.' He thought, I'll telephone Harry and Dr Joseph from the Hilton before I catch the plane. He dared not think further than that.

'Kidnapping insurance?' Hopeful ecstasy was on Judy's face. 'You mean, Omnium took out kidnapping insurance? The insurance company can pay the ransom? Wonderful!' She beamed at the three men who had been waiting for her when she returned from her meeting with Curtis.

Oscar Sholto was head of the legal department at Omnium Pictures. He was accompanied by a chubby man called Steve Wood, who was from Special Risk, Inc., Omnium's Paris-based insurance consultants. A weary, pale Colonel Aziz had joined the group and now they sat around the table in a private dining room, which Colonel Aziz had commandeered for his investigations. Around the room spindly gilt chairs were stacked in fours. The bedraggled decorations from a party were fading and curling.

Oscar Sholto had been darkly handsome, but it had all dropped a little. He cleared his throat. 'As you know, Miss Jordan, it's not unusual for the star of a major picture to be insured by the backers. Omnium has millions tied up in *Helen of Troy*.'

Smiling, Judy sat back in her chair. 'I'm thrilled to hear this! I know it's tough for the insurers but if I get my daughter back . . .'

'I must warn you, Miss Jordan,' said Oscar, 'that Omnium cannot act in any way against Turkish police policy. And the police don't want the ransom paid, because it's against their national policy. No payment for kidnapping, because it only encourages other kidnappers. The main aim of the police is to *find* the kidnappers, and that will probably take time.' He folded his plump hands on the dust sheet which covered the round table and said, 'But the Turkish police have to decide between two alternatives. They don't want an international kidnapping to take place in their country, but neither do they want to transgress their own laws by turning a blind eye to ransom payment.'

'Of course they've got to allow payment!' Judy's smile had disappeared.

Oscar said, 'What we're telling you is that the Turkish government may not allow us to pay the ransom *here*.'

Judy broke in, 'What are you going to do, as it's illegal to pay ransom in Turkey?'

'We have to work out how to get around the law. Maybe pay it over at sea, outside territorial waters,' said Oscar.

'All we can do for the moment,' said Steve, the insurer, 'is to wait for contact. The kidnappers will probably ask us to set up a safe, untapped telephone, so we can talk to them. Just give us time.'

'Time!' exclaimed Judy. 'How much time? Months? Years?'

'Two weeks,' said Oscar. 'Special Risk also covers Omnium for any other delay in shooting *Helen of Troy*. We're due to start shooting in a couple of weeks.'

'That should be ample time,' Steve confirmed. 'But, as you know, we first have to establish contact with the kidnappers, then establish that they really are holding Lili, then establish how we're going to get her back, then establish the price, then . . .'

'But we know the price!' Judy interrupted. 'They've already asked for ten million dollars.'

'At Special Risk we always try to bargain down,' Steve said evenly. 'If we draw out negotiations, it gives the police more time to discover where the kidnappers are holding their victim.'

'And your company saves its cash, of course. So what happens after that?' Judy had heard enough tactfully understated explanation; she wanted the bottom line on getting her daughter back. She had worked out the insurance company's old, familiar angle, which was always the same whether you'd had your bicycle or your Lear Jet stolen. Steve was only offering advance justifications for not paying the insurance in full. Judy was unimpressed; she'd used more ingenuity to string along the landlord of her East Eleventh Street studio, in the bad old days when she was starting out in business.

Smoothly Steve said, 'As soon as we are in communication with the kidnappers, we start stalling. We'll say that the payment has to be okayed by a lot of people in America, and then paid over discreetly, so we'll ask for five days' extension. Then we'll go back to them and say that we can only raise five million in cash, so we ask for more time. When they see five big ones within their greedy grasp, they'll give us more time. And then, in the end, we settle for six million.' Steve looked around the table, then added, 'And we take as long as we can over the whole business, so that the police and our special contacts can try to find Lili and perhaps obviate the necessity . . .'

'Of paying over your money,' Judy angrily interrupted. She turned to Oscar Sholto. 'Lili's made a fortune for Omnium. She won't be able to make any more money for you if she's dead, will she?'

'Miss Jordan, both you and Omnium want the ransom paid fast,' said Oscar. 'That's why Omnium paid enormous insurance premiums to Special Risk.'

Steve said, 'I'm here to pay the ransom to the right people, provided we get the right results. Of course, we'll do everything we can to get Lili released as fast as possible.' He saw the panic on Judy's face. He had encountered parent hostility before, so he emphasized, 'Remember, Miss Jordan, as soon as we start to bargain with the kidnappers. Lili's life is much safer.'

Judy threw him a flinty stare. 'I'm Lili's mother and the way I see it is that the longer we wait, the more dangerous it is for Lili. I can't bear to think of her in the hands of those thugs.'

'They won't be thugs if this is a terrorist operation.' Steve tried to smooth out the hostile atmosphere. 'If we're dealing with terrorists, they're not likely to be disadvantaged peasants striking back at society, they're far more likely to be clever, well-educated, middle-class idealists, and they won't treat your daughter badly, Miss Jordan. They'll be in the whole business as much for the sake of their public image as for the money.'

Colonel Aziz said, 'Whoever they are, I don't understand why the kidnappers haven't been in touch, to instruct us where to pay the money.'

'The delay makes me think it's likely that the kidnappers *are* terrorists,' offered Steve, 'because terrorists don't always want the money, they want the maximum publicity over the maximum time. Terrorists fight dirty because there aren't many of them, and they haven't got the money to run the sort of war they want. A kidnap is sometimes a really cheap publicity stunt. You don't need many people, or much equipment, and you get a nice financial bonus at the end. Their weapon is intimidation – kill one and frighten a million.'

'This is terrifying.' Judy looked at Oscar and Steve who had started to put their files back in their briefcases.

Oscar got up and extended a hand to Judy. 'Try not to worry, Miss Jordan. Lili will be in less danger as soon as we are communicating with the terrorists, and they see they're getting newspaper space for their message. It just takes time to set up the communication.'

Steve added, 'We're also concerned about your safety, Miss Jordan. We'd like to fly you out of here. There'll shortly be dozens coming forward with reports and information. All of it will be false, and every time another witness comes forward with another story, your hopes will be raised and then dashed to the ground.' For several reasons, Steve always tried to remove close relations of the victim. First, if any real communication was conveyed, then a distraught relative had only to tell *one* friend (and they always did), and the secret was general news within twenty-four hours. Second, you never knew what distraught

897

relatives might do. They might refuse to cooperate with the police, or agree to cooperate with the police and then change their mind without informing anyone, thus screwing up a carefully prepared police ambush.

'I'm not going anywhere!' Judy almost shouted at Steve. 'I've a right to be here! I'm not leaving my daughter and you've no right to make me leave. I also have the right to know everything that's going on – and I insist that you tell me everything!'

As he and Oscar climbed back in their car Steve muttered, 'Tough lady.'

'Are we going to keep her informed?' Oscar asked.

Steve looked at the rabble of photographers who still kept a disorderly vigil at the hotel. 'Of course not. We'd be crazy to pass on any information. She's emotional, and she might become hysterical, so she's a bad security risk. We're going to tell Miss Jordan as little as possible.'

Half an hour later Judy and Pagan sat together in Judy's hotel sitting room. In silence they sipped iced water. Judy had just finished telling Pagan of the conference with the Omnium lawyer and his security consultants.

Judy said, 'I can't stand this inaction. Just sitting around and talking is driving me crazy.'

Hoping to distract her thoughts, Pagan said, 'By the way, I got a letter from Kate today, sent on from London. She's bought a typewriter, a 1952 Remington which cost seven hundred dollars. The secondhand ribbon was fifty dollars extra. She says that the major powers – China, as well as Russia and America – are getting involved in Chittagong and it isn't just the little jungle war that it appears to be. It could be as expensive and senseless and unwinnable as Vietnam, she reckons.'

'Any more good news?'

Pagan turned over the crumpled blue paper. 'They interrogated Kate for two hours, and she's afraid that the Bengalis are going to throw her out. Apart from that, she's well and happy. Isn't it odd that Kate's never happy unless she's uncomfortable?'

Judy didn't answer.

The only sounds in the room were the faint roar of the city and the insistent lapping of the water below.

A knock at the door brought Judy to her feet. Pagan watched expectantly as she opened the double doors; beyond them, a page boy held a cellophane-wrapped bouquet of roses, identical to the one that had concealed the original kidnap note. Judy snatched the flowers and ripped open the plastic to get at the envelope that accompanied them. 'Thank God, they've made contact at last!'

Pagan peered over Judy's shoulder as she ripped open the miniature envelope and pulled out a garish florist's card.

Judy gave a moan and dropped the card as if it had burned her, then fell into a brocade armchair and began sobbing. Pagan picked up the florist's pink and yellow card. Below the good-luck messages printed in Turkish were a few typewritten lines.

Put one million ten-dollar bills into a briefcase. At six o'clock tomorrow evening, let a man with a red armband take it on the Guzelhisar ferry that crosses the Bosporus. Further instructions will follow. Tell no one. Lili will be strangled with silken cords unless I am obeyed.

It was almost midnight and Abdullah was working at his desk in a soft green study scattered with rich rugs and hung with cream gauze curtains.

As the breathless Pagan burst in he looked up, and his frown of concentration changed to a smile as he grabbed a newspaper and said, 'Look what's in the *Tribune*.' He gestured to a two-inch front-page story which announced the death of Senator Ruskington in the Washington apartment of a French call girl. 'So now, Pagan, Lili is vindicated, and it looks as if Judy's money problems can be resolved.'

Pagan paused for breath after running along three corridors and up a flight of stairs. 'That's wonderful news, darling. I mean, I'm sorry he died, but the old bugger was asking for trouble.'

'Why are you out of breath, Pagan? What's happened?'

Pagan held out a bit of paper. 'I wanted you to see this as fast as possible. Judy's received a second note from the kidnappers. Here's a copy.'

Abdullah skimmed it. 'I still can't decide whether these people are cunning or crazy. This sounds like an eighteenth-century king's threat. If they wanted to get rid of one of the royal concubines at Topkapi Palace, the woman was strangled with a silken cord.' He paused, then added, 'Common concubines were sewn up in sacks, weighted with rocks and thrown into the Bosporus. One king got rid of two hundred and eighty concubines like that. A few years later a diver found all those ghastly sacks, still upright on the sea bed, swaying in the invisible current, as if they were dancing to music.'

'I know, darling, you've told me before. A long time ago. But what do you make of the rest of the note?'

'Obviously, the police will lay an ambush on the ferry and at both landings, but often, with bandits, the first rendezvous is never kept, it's merely a test to check police reaction. However, this last sentence is strange. Why not just say that Lili will be killed?'

Pagan burst into tears. 'I can't bear to think of it.'

'My darling, it's late and we're both tired. Let's go to bed and I'll see what my people can deduce from this note tomorrow morning.'

~ 17 ~

5 September 1979

BUT Pagan could not sleep and turned restlessly on her bed in the hot night. Eventually, at three o'clock in the morning, she decided to take a soothing walk in the moonlit garden. It would be perfectly safe, because the grounds were guarded by sentries and also an electrical alarm system.

Pagan knew that someone would be watching her as she walked between the low clipped hedges of rosemary to the circular pool, where a family of terrapins were kept. It was impossible to be truly alone, wherever Abdullah slept. His bodyguards kept an endless watch outside his room, and in the corridors there were always silent servants waiting for commands or simply sleeping in corners.

As Pagan sat on the stone coping around the pool she disturbed a skinny, grey cat, which spat at her as it ran away in the half-darkness. Something in her head was prompting her; she felt that something important was lying half-hidden at the back of her mind, like an unanswered letter on her desk.

Suddenly Pagan jumped up, and nearly fell into the terrace pool. As the moonlight painted the beautiful garden in strange shades of grey she abruptly remembered the exercise class in the *Verve!* office, when that exercise instructor had started to make strange jokes about his harem; that is, his grave remarks had been interpreted by the class as jokes, but Tony had obviously been nettled when the girls had laughed at him. And Pagan had told Tony that royal concubines were strangled with silken cords. It could not be a coincidence. Tony must be the person whom Lili knew and trusted, the person who had been able to lure her away from the hotel. Tony must be one of the kidnappers!

Pagan hurried back to the palace, losing a slipper as she ran along the tiled pathway, still slippery with dew. The palm trees stood out as dark silhouettes against the pre-dawn sky as Pagan ordered a limousine from the sleepy-eyed attendant at the main door, after failing to get Judy on the telephone. The switchboard staff of her hotel were obviously still asleep.

Speeding through the pale-grey streets, Pagan sniffed the spray of jasmine that she'd pulled from the garden's ancient, high walls, and thought how cruel this twice-over loss of her daughter was for Judy. Pagan remembered the *Verve!* cover photograph of Judy and Lili, and the way it highlighted their similarities: the tiny, doll-like build and the little, paw-like hands –as well as the differences between mother and daughter. Judy looked so blonde, blue-eyed and Nordic whereas Lili was so dark and exotic. The cover photograph had also emphasized their odd apartness. However hard they tried, and however much they longed for intimacy, Pagan didn't reckon they'd achieve it; their relationship seemed almost a casual juxtaposition of two completely un-alike people. There was so much they had shared, but so much they couldn't seem to share. However much a mother might want closeness, however much a daughter might want closeness, often it isn't truthfully possible because they have so little in common; hence those dutiful birthday cards, Pinteresque monosyllabic Christmas dinners and uneasy outings to the theatre or the movies: anywhere where they could avoid conversation.

Pagan thought of the intimacy that Judy and Lili had struggled to achieve, the intimacy of love. I wonder if it will be like that with Abdi and me, Pagan mused. Sometimes, when they made love, Pagan looked at her pale English skin next to his tawny flesh and felt curiously apart from Abdullah, no matter how sensitive his caresses, or how strongly her body responded.

In some ways, I suppose Lili's like Abdullah, thought Pagan, as she crushed the sprig of jasmine and sniffed the cloying perfume of the dying sprig. Lili and Abdullah are both aggressively defensive; they both have that quick temper; they both have that greedy, sweet tooth. And sometimes, when Lili throws back her head and glares, she has that same angry-falcon look as Abdullah.

Abruptly the kaleidoscopic jumble of Pagan's random thoughts fell into a sinister shape. Then, reluctantly, the corroborating evidence flooded into Pagan's mind. At first the conclusion that she reached was so unpleasant that she tried to push the whole idea out of her head and look out of the window at the leaden waters of the Bosporus, but the unwelcome notion pushed back into her mind with a force of its own. Could Judy have slept with Abdullah? Could he be Lili's father? Pagan remembered Judy's expedient lies, from the desperate deceptions of her early, poverty-stricken years to that odd white lie she had told Lili about her father. Why, she'd even repeated on television that Lili's father was poor Nick, who'd been shot in a jungle war, when Judy's friends knew that, although Nick had had a crush on Judy, she would have nothing to do with him. So certainly Nick could not have fathered Judy's child. Then Pagan remembered her dead husband Christopher's last joke. He had said that two clearly blue-eyed parents could not produce a brown-eyed baby; he had been definite about it. Curtis and Angelface both had blue eyes. Spyros Stiarkoz wasn't around when they were all in Gstaad, so it couldn't have been him. Maybe I won't win the Nobel Prize for genetics, Pagan told herself bleakly as the car drew up in front of Judy's hotel, but I can't ignore the facts.

*

'I'll bet Tony wrote that ransom note,' Pagan insisted to a puffy-eyed Judy, who was sitting up in bed. 'Don't you remember that silly argument about harems we had in the exercise class in New York?'

'I vaguely remember.'

'But you were present when I told Tony about strangling disobedient concubines with silken cords,' Pagan insisted. 'The second ransom note is too much of a coincidence.'

'I should imagine that half Istanbul knows that tourist-guide story. Pagan, are you telling me that some guy who's only capable of pumping iron on Fifth Avenue could fix a kidnapping in Turkey?' Judy was still only half-awake.

'No, I don't believe that dumb ox could work this out by himself,' said Pagan. 'He must be working with somebody else.'

'That's certainly a possibility!' Judy jumped out of bed and pulled on an ivory-cream négligé. 'But that still doesn't tell us where Lili's being held.'

'I'm not so sure.' Pagan walked to the window and looked out. In spite of her tenseness, she appreciated the glittering sweep of water on which the Sancta Sophia Mosque and the Blue Mosque seemed to float. She said, 'The link between Tony and the second ransom note is the royal concubines. Where were they kept?'

Pagan looked at the rounded domes and soaring minarets of the Topkapi Palace and, suddenly, she had an idea where Tony might hide out. A place that would never be searched, because it was guarded: a place that nobody was allowed to enter.

Together Pagan and Judy tumbled into their limousine. As it drew away from the kerb another battered Mercedes pulled out from the side street and followed them.

In the limousine a reluctant Judy finally admitted to Pagan that Abdullah was Lili's father. So then she had to explain to Pagan how the conception occurred. In the nasty silence that followed, a grim Pagan finally asked, 'But why didn't you tell me at the time?'

'How could I?' pleaded Judy. 'You were my friend and you were in love with him. How could I tell you that your beau had raped me? And what good would it have done? I know that it probably didn't seem a rape to Abdullah. To him, it was merely a prince having his way with a servant. I'm sure he doesn't remember it, and I'm sure he wouldn't do it now. All our values have changed so much in the years since we were sixteen.'

Pagan was silent. Judy put her hands on her shoulders and turned Pagan to face her. Earnestly Judy said, 'Please don't wreck *your* future because of something horrible that happened years ago in *my* past.'

Pagan looked mutinous. Judy said, 'And you mustn't say anything to Abdullah about it, for the same reason I can't tell Lili who her real father is. Because the whole world knew that they had a passionate affair. Because, unknowingly, they committed incest. Why lay that burden of guilt on two human beings we care about, when it's unnecessary and will achieve nothing?'

Eventually Pagan asked, 'Does anyone else know about it?'

'Only one person. Maxine guessed, as soon as she saw Lili at the Pierre. She didn't say anything at the time, but she asked about it later, one Sunday when Tony was driving us up to Westchester to have lunch with Griffin. Maxine said that the resemblance isn't so strong today, but that as soon as she saw Lili she was reminded of Abdullah as a youth. Lili had his colouring, his features, his mannerisms . . . and his abrupt temper.'

Judy remembered that she didn't even have to admit it. Maxine had seen from her face that she'd guessed correctly. What's more, Maxine had immediately understood why Judy had found it difficult to establish a warm, loving relationship with Lili. Because Lili's beauty had come from a man who had raped Judy. She had always tried to push the thought to the back of her mind, but Judy couldn't help feeling forlorn because Lili was not a child of love. Lili didn't know it, but she was a child born from violence and hatred.

'We'd like to go into the other part of the Harem quarters, the part that isn't normally shown to tourists.' Pagan folded a 500-lire note and tried to tuck it into the shirt pocket of one of the palace guides. Accustomed to curious tourists with more money than sense, the guide said, 'I'm sorry, it is forbidden. There is nothing I can do.' He swept Pagan and Judy out of the entrance.

'Damn.' In the bright morning sun Pagan stamped on the ancient stone courtyard. 'I suppose I should have offered him more.'

Judy wasn't listening because she was peering across the court-yard. She jammed her tortoiseshell glasses on her nose, and again stared at the colonnade across the courtyard. 'Pagan, I know this sounds crazy,' she said, 'but I think I just saw Mark.'

Slowly they walked down the path to the entrance gate, then Judy spun around, almost tripping up two German tourists behind them. 'It is him! I'm sure I saw him. Mark! Mark!'

She ran towards the colonnade, still calling Mark's name, and the familiar khaki-clad figure appeared between two columns. Judy, breathless, stopped in front of him. 'What are you doing here, Mark? We thought you were in jail, number one suspect.'

'They let me out when my editor pulled rank, long distance, on Colonel Aziz. I've been following you, on the fire engine principle – follow the fire engine and you'll find a story at the end of it. So where's the fire engine, Judy? Why are you rushing off on this mad sightseeing tour with Pagan?'

Slowly Judy smiled. 'We think we've found out where the kidnappers have hidden Lili.' Judy wasn't ready to confess to Mark, but she needed help to get into the Harem. 'We think they're in the old part of the Palace Harem, but we can't get in because it's closed. D'you think you can help us to get in?'

Mark said, 'Should be easy. Come on, let's fall in with the next guided tour. It starts at ten o'clock.' He thought, first chance I get I'm going to grab her. I'm no good at explaining how I feel with words.

Again Judy and Pagan, now joined by Mark, were conducted through the labyrinthine palace. They inspected the Armoury, the Treasury, and the King's Robes. Some of the rooms were carved, some were gilded, some were tiled, and some were elaborately painted. They peered through pierced screens at the Valide King's apartments, and shuffled with the other tourists along the pillared façade of the Black Eunuchs' barracks.

The self-important guide reformed his group near the Harem entrance and, as he launched into another singsong speech, Pagan nipped to the far side of the group.

Suddenly Pagan clutched at the shoulder of a Japanese tourist, who buckled under her weight. Groaning, Pagan slid to the floor. The tourist party crowded around her lanky, prostrate body. The guide said, 'Get back, get back, everybody!'

As soon as Pagan's prearranged diversion had attracted the attention of the group, Mark and Judy slid unnoticed into the wide, dark doorway to the Harem. Above one of the doorways they had noticed a decorated grille. Between the top of the grille and the bottom of the stone arch of the gateway was a very small gap. Judy pulled off her shoes and climbed on Mark's shoulders. She could just reach the grille.

Quickly she scrambled up to the gap and wriggled through, then dropped into the open alley on the other side.

Mark followed her. They landed on a pile of builder's rubble and trash, and lay quiet, listening, as Pagan was carried to the first-aid room. In the hot sun Mark and Judy lay on the stinking heap of rubble until the noisy band of tourists had moved on, behind the guide.

Then Mark took Judy in his arms and held her tightly against him as slowly he kissed her mouth with his sun-blistered lips. And, lying in the rubble, Judy felt that, for the time being, nothing else mattered.

Eventually Mark said, 'Do I make myself clear? It's you I love, not Lili. It's you I want and nobody else. On a scale of one to a hundred, I shall probably feel something for every beautiful woman I see. So would any other man. But you're the woman I want to spend my life with.'

A bit later he said, 'Why didn't you ever write back?'

'I never opened your letters. It would have hurt too much.'

'That's what I guessed. That's why I wrote to Lili. I asked her to explain things to you, I asked her to tell you how I felt about you. But she never once replied.'

'I expect your letters met with the same fate as the rest of her fan mail, darling. We can find out later. But right now, we should be looking for Lili.'

Judy opened her purse and pulled out her expensive guidebook, which included a map of the palace. Mark took it from her and pulled out a pen. 'This place is on a hill. We won't get lost, so long as we remember which way is up.'

'Famous last words. There are supposed to be over three hundred rooms in this place.' Cautiously Judy set off down a dirty, stone-flagged corridor, dimly lit by an overhead skylight. Rusting iron bars braced apart the crumbling walls of the passage.

Gloomy corridors twisted through a maze of small rooms, linked by staircases and dark passages and tiny courtyards, where the sun scarcely fell. Sometimes a wall shone with blue or sea-green tiles, patterned with flowers. Through barred windows Judy noticed dusty, unlit lanterns hanging over the tiny rooms of long-dead concubines. She peered into the ornate, gilt, crumbling mirrors that still hung on the walls, dimly visible streaks of silver against the grey gloom. In some of the rooms they explored, the shutters of the windows were falling off, in others there were cobwebs, rotting sheets of rose velvet and tattered canopies.

As they peered into each debris-strewn room Mark methodically crossed it off their plan, but after half an hour he slowly realized that the tourist plan wasn't accurate. He checked his bearings, the corridor they were in, the rooms leading off it. Then he rechecked, and after that he was certain the map was inaccurate. But he didn't tell Judy that the map was wrong. He merely walked beside her in silence, noticing the frantic, mounting anxiety with which she searched each room.

Some corridors led down half-broken flights of steps to yet more rooms on lower levels of the palace. Some rooms smelled damp, others of urine or rotting hangings. One room was alive with rats, which swarmed over the carcass of a dead cat.

As the sunlight turned golden in the late morning Judy said, puzzled, 'I'm sure we've searched this room before. I remember those tiles with cypress trees on them.'

They were standing in the middle of a small, open courtyard. On all four sides the walls were pierced by small, screened windows. Below the windows were two iron-studded closed doors, and two doors that gaped open.

Mark said, 'I'm sorry, Judy, but the map's inaccurate. I hoped we might stumble on a way out, before I had to tell you. We're going to have a problem getting back, Judy. And we've nearly run out of matches.'

'Mark, this is hopeless, we'll never find her.'

'Yes, we will.' Mark took her in his arms and pressed her trembling body against his. She felt protected and consoled. Then, suddenly, she sniffed a scent that was familiar. There was nothing stale, mouldy, or rotten about it; it was a fresh, rich, delicious smell; it was Lili's carnation bath oil.

Judy pulled away from Mark, then raised her hand and put a finger to his lips. She sniffed, then so did he. He nodded, understanding. They looked around them. Nothing moved in the silence. Mark shook his head; they must have imagined it.

Then, suddenly, they smelled carnations again.

Outside, Pagan waited anxiously in the shade of the courtyard. Judy and Mark had been gone for ages. Pagan had just telephoned Colonel Aziz about her suspicions, but, as Judy had said, the colonel obviously regarded them as a pair of interfering, 'hysterical' women. Judy had been right to try to get proof before speaking to Aziz.

Pagan decided that she'd try to get inside the Harem to look for Judy. She'd just look around for ten minutes and, if she found nothing, then she'd come outside again and telephone Abdullah. He would fix Colonel Aziz.

She'd had a brilliant idea for gaining entrance to the Harem. The official tour of the palace included a brief visit to the roof. She'd wait for the start of the next tour and then hide on the roof. Then, when the rest of the party had gone on, she'd find her way across the roof to the Harem quarters, and try to gain access from above.

Making sure that it was a different guide from the one she'd fainted in front of, Pagan carried out her plan and, when the party was shown that part of the upper palace which overlooked the Divan Council Chamber of the Imperial Ministers, Pagan hid in an adjoining room until the party had moved on, then she climbed out of the window and on to the wide parapet.

The roof of the Topkapi Palace, a forest of little gold-topped turrets and rounded domes, looks like a small, enchanted, deserted city. Pagan was easily able to get her bearings because she could see landmarks that she recognized in the city and the water around the palace.

Without much difficulty, Pagan picked her way around the domes and turrets until she judged that she was above the Harem quarters. This part of the building had been uninhabited since 1909. Some of the windows that led on to the roof were rotting, some were only just hanging on their hinges.

Pagan picked the most decrepit window she could find,

smashed the glass with the heel of her shoe, then carefully put her arm through the smashed pane, undid the latch and pushed the window open.

It led on to a small staircase. Pagan followed it down until it ended in a foul-smelling, dusty passage, littered with mouse droppings. Pagan picked her way along it, and turned the corner.

From behind, an iron grip grabbed her arms and pulled her to a panting male body.

Pagan screamed. Her arms were mercilessly twisted.

Half an hour later Mark and Judy had still seen no trace of Lili. 'Let's just look in that last passage, then we'll give up and grope our way to the entrance,' Judy suggested.

'It's no use, Judy,' Mark said reluctantly. 'We've run out of matches, and we may have a problem just getting back. Let's concentrate on that, huh?'

As they moved on, at the foot of the passage that Judy had wanted to explore, a heavy iron door opened a crack, and a dark eye looked out at the departing couple.

'Thank God he's taken our gags off,' Pagan hissed to Lili. Both women were lying on a dirty, green-striped mattress in the corner of a bare room. Light came from two window apertures on the far wall; the window frames had long since rotted away.

'He knows no one could hear us, even if we yelled for help,' Lili whispered back. 'Any idea where we are?'

'In the Harem quarters of the Topkapi Palace.' Pagan wriggled into a new position. Her hands and feet were tightly bound with rope; Lili's wrists were handcuffed and her feet were also tied. The room was filled with rotting furniture that stank of cats' piss, rat-nibbled brocade bolsters, stained mattresses and semi-decayed hangings which had been arranged in a bizarre, conversational group around a brass table-tray.

Lili listened for sounds of Tony's return. In her four days of captivity she had grown acutely aware of his whereabouts, and since he had left the room five minutes ago she had tracked him mentally, listening to his fading footsteps. Now she could hear nothing.

'Lili, how did he got hold of you?' Pagan wriggled until she was sitting more or less comfortably against the cobweb-covered wall.

'It was ridiculously easy. I went to the Bazaar, bought a carpet, then took a cab back to the hotel. Tony was waiting in the vestibule. He carried my carpet up to my suite. He said that Judy had sent for him to look after the baggage. I wasn't surprised, because it had already been lost twice. Then Tony said Judy had asked him to tell me that she wanted me to meet her at the Saguchi Tea Room. He said she was seeing a diamond merchant there. He said she wanted to buy me a present. As we'd had that row, I thought Judy was trying to say that she was sorry.' Lili gave an exasperated sigh. 'I'm so used to Tony acting as Judy's hired muscle I never suspected there was anything wrong until he laid me out in the taxi. With chloroform, I think. Anyway, some chemical on a pad that he shoved over my nose. And I woke up here.' She shivered. 'He's got guns, hand grenades and God knows what in the next room. So, act obedient, Pagan, don't give him anything to worry about. Who knows, maybe he'll untie us.'

Suddenly Lili jerked her head up and listened. She could hear Tony's footsteps in the corridor outside. 'I think something's gone wrong with his plan, because he seems to be panicking and he's reacting aggressively, like a cornered man.'

The rusting, iron-bound door crashed open and Tony glared at them. Gently Lili smiled at him, in a way that she hoped was friendly without being seductive. 'Won't you please free our feet, Tony. I can't feel my toes, the circulation has gone.'

'Maybe I'll untie you later.' Tony walked towards the window, turning golden rose in the late afternoon sun. As soon as it was dark, they'd have to leave this place.

Pagan tried her luck. 'Could we please have water, Tony?'

Tony grabbed a brass jug from the tray-table and walked over to Pagan. He drank from the jug himself, then held it roughly to her mouth and carelessly jerked her head back, as if she were a rag doll. Pagan spluttered as the water ran down her face and stained her now grubby, black-and-white striped suit.

'Maybe you want something to eat, as well, Lady Know-It-All Swann?'

Tony moved to the low circular brass table, where a box of Turkish delight lay unopened. He ripped off the wrapper and took a piece of green, sugar-covered jelly out, walked back to Pagan and held it out.

Pagan said, 'But I hate Turkish delight, Tony.'

'Open your mouth!'

'No, Tony, it's OK, Pagan doesn't want any . . .'

'I said, open your mouth, Pagan.'

Reluctantly Pagan parted her lips and Tony jammed a piece of candy into her mouth. Before she had time to chew and swallow the sickly sweetmeat, Tony rammed another piece into her mouth, then another, then another. Pagan gagged but he roughly held her mouth shut until she swallowed the Turkish delight.

'And now, some pastry.' Tony picked up a honey-soaked baklava cake off the dirty brass tray-table and stuffed it whole into Pagan's mouth. She widened her eyes in helpless terror as he stuffed it down her throat, leaving her face smeared with honey and covered with flakes of pastry. Tears of anger began to dribble out of Pagan's blue eyes.

Suddenly Tony jumped up and listened. He grabbed the sub-machine-gun from the corner of the room and ran to the glassless window.

As Mark and Judy dejectedly left the Topkapi Palace they saw Gregg, Colonel Aziz and four minibuses packed with Turkish police, followed by armoured cars.

'Thank God Pagan has called the police,' said Mark as they moved forward to meet Colonel Aziz.

Colonel Aziz clearly believed himself to be on a wild goose chase but, as he had been summoned by the friend of the King of Sydon, he knew he would have to give a perfunctory search.

The small group marched briskly through the gardens surrounding the palace buildings, until Mark pointed to the corner of the building behind which, according to their map, the courtyard lay.

'I thought we'd never get out of there alive,' Judy muttered to Mark as she looked up at the ancient stone walls. Above, she could see the amazing roof of the palace: dozens of breast-shaped domes were crowned by gilt spires, while, between them, needle-like red-and-white turrets stabbed the sky. As she looked up, for one instant, Judy saw a face she recognized. 'There he is! Look! Tony's at that window!'

5 September 1979

'I CAN'T see anyone.' Using a pair of police binoculars, Mark scanned the windows, one by one. Judy followed his line of vision. 'Look to your left.'

'My God! Yes! That does look like Tony.'

With the binoculars, there could be no doubt. Colonel Aziz snatched up his own pair, then turned and issued a stream of commands into his hand-held radio.

Unaware that he had been seen, Tony spied on the small group in the tree-dotted park below. Aware that his attention had been distracted, Lili leaned over and, with her sharp little teeth, tugged at the ropes around Pagan's wrists. The thin nylon cord was harsh and slippery, but once Lili had succeeded in getting a grip on it, she pulled with all her strength, and the slippery knot unravelled with surprising ease. Pagan kept an anxious eye on the bulky back of her captor, who was trying to peer out of the window without being seen. With quiet, stealthy movements, Pagan freed her hands; then, with cramped and shaking fingers, she picked at the ropes around her feet, all the time aware that Tony might turn around at any moment.

Quickly Pagan wriggled down the bed and untied the knot that bound Lili's feet, but she could do nothing about Lili's handcuffs. Holding her breath, Pagan slid soundlessly off the bed. Barefoot, she tiptoed to the iron-studded door and gently touched the rusty bolt. Carefully she drew back the ancient catch, but a faint scrape of metal alerted her captor.

Tony whipped round, shouted, and bounded across the room, forgetting the central low brass tray-table, which tripped him. As he crashed to the floor Pagan slammed back the bolt, and fled from the room before he could reach her.

Outside the door was the square courtyard, overlooked by

high barred windows, where, unknown to the captives, Mark and Judy had so recently searched for them. Wildly Pagan ran across the courtyard, hesitated, then bolted at top speed under the nearest arch. She found herself running along a dark corridor, with a massive green-tiled fireplace at the end of it. Ahead and to her left, a narrow spiral staircase of stone wound upwards.

She heard the sounds of Tony thumping across the courtyard in pursuit as she started to scramble up the spiral staircase.

Tony sprinted along the dim corridor, then he stopped, uncertain of the direction that Pagan had taken. He ran to the fireplace that blocked the end of the corridor and looked up the chimney; he saw a magpie nest and the soot of centuries, but no Pagan. Then, from behind him to his left, he heard her scrambling up the spiral stone staircase.

Tony spun around, dashed back, then leaped in pursuit up the narrow stone steps. As he charged upwards he nearly tripped over his U Z I machine-gun. Cursing, he propped it carefully in an alcove, then once more bounded upwards.

The staircase gave on to the leaded roof of the palace. As Pagan scrambled out of the opening at the top of the staircase she found herself in a shimmering hot landscape of ten-foot-diameter domes and small towers with catwalks between them. As she heard Tony's angry shout the panic-stricken Pagan tore along a catwalk between two rows of gold-spiked domes until, breathless and sobbing, she reached a parapet, beyond which was a sheer drop.

In desperation, Pagan jumped on to the parapet and ran along the narrow wall. At the corner she stopped and turned. Tony was nowhere to be seen. Pagan realized that she was an easy target and made a split-second decision to hide in the deep shadow behind one of the red towers. Quickly she fled to the nearest small tower and dashed behind it – straight into the arms of Tony.

Triumphantly Tony grabbed her, but Pagan ducked and managed to evade his grip. Terrified, she jumped back on to the parapet and ran from Tony along the narrow edge. Tony's long athletic strides quickly lessened the distance between them, which grew shorter and shorter until Pagan could hear the rasping breath behind her. Sensing that he could almost touch her, Pagan panicked, screamed and almost lost her balance on the parapet.

Suddenly, down below, among the trees, Mark heard the scream, looked up, caught sight of the chase along the parapet, and started to run forwards.

Again Pagan screamed in terror, her arms flailing wildly as she tried to regain her balance. Somehow she succeeded and took a breathless step backwards to safety, but the enraged Tony was right behind her and, with one hand, he shoved her forwards, off the roof and into the sheer drop below the parapet.

Screaming, Pagan managed to spin round and clutch at Tony, her weight pulling him towards the vertical drop. For a moment they swayed together on the parapet, and it looked as if both the figures, silhouetted against the blazing late-afternoon sky, were going to plummet to the ground.

Then Tony managed to shake himself free of Pagan and violently shoved her forwards. Screaming, she fell over the parapet and plunged towards the earth below.

Transfixed with horror, Judy watched Tony recover his balance, scramble off the parapet and disappear from sight.

Down below, among the dusty foliage, police paramedics ran towards the copse of small trees where Pagan had fallen. A whistle blew and orders were barked. Colonel Aziz's men immediately scattered around the Harem area of the palace and, as Judy watched, police marksmen appeared on the domed roof and took up their positions behind the slender turrets.

Tony had again disappeared into the depths of the Harem.

Still handcuffed, her feet numb, Lili stumbled along yet another dark corridor. Her heart was pumping wildly and she was panting with fear but as she half ran over the uneven stones of the passage, her fright was nothing compared to the terror she had previously felt, lying handcuffed and helpless, as again and again Tony had loaded and unloaded his machine-gun, taken random aim at the wine jug, the window or the woman tied on the bed, then pretended to squeeze the trigger.

Suddenly Lili saw a faint glimmer of light and, hopefully, started to run towards it. Dimly she could make out a wide stone doorway.

Thankfully she reached it, then stopped in surprise. Beyond the doorway brilliant sunlight shone down like spotlights from the high arched windows of a big room; the far half was covered by a low platform surrounded by a golden balustrade. The ceiling was fretted and latticed in gold and the walls were edged with elaborate scrolls of gilt leaves and ribbons. The entire, sumptuous golden room was spotted with mould, and hung with cobwebs. Tiny, even rows of claw-marks on the floor showed where birds had hopped in the thick carpet of dust.

Opposite Lili, at the far end of the gorgeous room, was another elaborate doorway. Joyfully Lili dashed towards it, to find herself in another equally sumptuous, sunlit room with high, unreachable windows, and another elaborate doorway facing her. Each room led into another room and, as if in an eerie nightmare, Lili ran through salon after over-decorated salon, each one smothered with dusty, golden swags of fruit, and *trompe-l'oeil* paintings of formal gardens that seemed to offer fresh air and freedom, but then cruelly denied it.

Finally Lili reached the end room. It was a square, tiled chamber with no windows and no further door. The walls were covered in an ogee medallion pattern of neat blue flowers, and eight feet above the floor was a gilt frieze of inlaid Arabic script.

Frantic, Lili looked about her for a way out of this lavish, silent, cul-de-sac. But there was no way out, she realized. Despondently she started to stumble back along the way she had come, through all the golden rooms, following her own bare footsteps in the dust.

When she reached the last golden room, the dark corridor lay in front of her. Regretfully she turned her back on the treacherous sunlight. In the distance, echoing and distorted through the many passages, Lili could hear Tony's faraway voice, although at first she couldn't hear what he was yelling. Then, faintly, she heard him cry, 'I know you're there, Lili! I'm not going to let you get away!'

Lili firmly told herself that there was no need to be frightened. All she had to do was to hide in a dark place until she heard the sound of a search party. Lili's heart thumped with fear as she plunged again into the gloomy labyrinth before her, looking for somewhere to hide. As she half stumbled, half ran along she noticed, in an alcove, a horseshoe-shaped trap door, raised and lying at a drunken angle against the wall. Below it gaped an opening, down which led stone steps, hollowed by the passage of many feet. Lili hesitated, then she heard a door crash open near at hand, and Tony's voice again threatened. Quickly Lili lowered herself into the darkness, taking care to make no sound.

Once below the level of the floor, Lili's eyes quickly adjusted to the darkness. At the bottom of the stone steps an underground passage beckoned and, in the faint light, Lili could see a low, half-open door to her left. She would hide behind that door, she decided, and pushed it.

The door was stuck. Lili leaned against it and shoved as hard as she could. As the door flew open Lili felt a rush of unearthly, fast, frightening terror. She seemed to be surrounded by flying demons as, with a flapping of leathery wings, she felt sharp little claws, furry talons, skinny limbs and blinding little creatures beat against her head and body.

In the darkness Lili screamed and screamed and screamed.

She heard Tony cursing as he crashed down the steps behind her and grabbed her by the hair.

'Is Pagan dead?' Judy anxiously asked Mark, as he crouched down beside her in the juniper brush.

'No, but she's badly hurt. It looks like two broken ribs, and a broken leg, shock and concussion. Luckily, the trees broke her fall. They've taken her to the French hospital behind the Divan Hotel. I saw her into the ambulance, then came back here to look after you. Colonel Aziz is informing the King.'

'Nothing's happened here for the last thirty minutes,' said Judy. They were both silent for a moment, listening to the interminable police megaphone as it ordered Tony to come out with his hands up.

'The police always string out a siege as long as they can,' Mark comforted Judy. 'The longer it goes on, the jumpier the kidnapper gets, and the more likely he is to make a mistake, or lose his nerve and surrender.'

A burst of machine-gun fire came from the window overhead as Tony opened fire on the policemen below. Everyone scattered to take cover.

Mark pulled Judy behind some juniper bushes, out of the line of fire, then he snaked forward towards the shooting.

Judy jumped as she felt a hand on her shoulder. It was Gregg, who had crawled up behind her, through the juniper bushes.

'How did you get here, Gregg?'

'Came up with the *Tribune* reporter. The hotel bar emptied as soon as they heard about this siege. Is Lili still in there?'

'Yes, Pagan said he'd got her handcuffed in one of those rooms. Then Pagan passed out, so that's all we know.' Judy nodded upwards. 'He's up there, where the shots are coming from.'

There was a burst of fire from Tony's Kalashnikov. Again Colonel Aziz turned on his megaphone and ordered Tony to surrender. Crouching low, a junior police officer ran up to the juniper thicket and ordered the three Europeans to vacate their inadequate cover and get behind one of the armoured cars, positioned below the palace walls.

As they cowered behind the hot metal vehicle Judy, her face sunken and pale, leaned against Mark's chest for comfort. 'Mark, what's going to happen?'

'I don't know.' He stroked her fine blonde hair. 'I've seen gunmen behave this way before. They get carried away by the excitement of it all, and by what appears to be their power. Then, as soon as they've fired the first shot, it's too late for them to get out, so, whether they know it or not, they're in it to the death.'

'And Lili's up there with that lunatic?' Gregg anxiously watched the window where Tony had appeared. 'Are the police inside as well?'

'Crawling all over the Harem by now, but there's not much they can do while he has Lili as a hostage!'

On either side of them young, eager Turkish policemen crouched with their weapons. Judy remembered Spyros Stiarkoz's warning about trigger-happy police. She said, 'Colonel Aziz won't let us go into the building. But I'm terrified that if the police storm that room from the outside, someone will accidentally shoot Lili.'

'Judy's right. These boy cops are longing for a shoot-out; look at their faces!' said Gregg, picking up Mark's binoculars and scanning the palace walls. 'There are a lot of handholds on that building; it shouldn't be difficult to climb down it, from the roof, by rope.'

'What would be the point of that?' Mark asked.

'If somebody distracted Tony at one window, I could toss a smoke bomb in the second window and then jump in after it.'

'Smoke bomb?' queried Judy. 'Where do we get a smoke bomb?'

Gregg said, 'The police are sure to have some. If not, they'll have tear gas, which will be nastier, but even more effective.'

Mark said, 'I suppose you want me to steal a smoke bomb.'

'I'll offer the guard a cigarette while you sneak into the minibus.'

Ten minutes later Mark had a rope, two smoke flares, an axe and a distress rocket. Twenty minutes later he and Gregg were among the breast-shaped cupolas of the Harem roof.

Leaning over the parapet, Gregg pointed with one finger as he sketched his idea to Mark. 'This wall is at right angles to the wall with the windows in it. If you let me down on the rope to the little ledge, I can shuffle along it, swing round the corner, get my foot on the ledge again, edge along until I reach the window, toss the smoke bomb through, swing in after it, and grab Tony from the rear.'

'Why not drop down from the parapet, straight above the window?' Mark asked.

'Because my legs would appear in the window; there'd be no element of surprise. And I wouldn't be able to manoeuvre into the window with the correct momentum. I'm going to have to dive into that window.'

Mark thought, the guy's got guts. 'O K, let's go. Tell me what you want me to do.'

Gregg showed Mark how to slip the rope around the nearest turret and take the strain, as Gregg tied the other end of the rope around his waist, then threw a leg over the parapet.

Hanging on to the rope, Gregg planted his sneakers on the ancient stone wall, leaned out and started to walk down. As he descended, Mark played out the rope. Gregg could not be seen by Tony because the corner of the building lay between them.

Gregg passed two ornamental ledges, then stopped at the third one. Inch by inch, with arms outstretched, Gregg slowly shuffled sideways along the ornamental ledge towards the corner on his right. Trying to feel as if the wall were sucking him into it, he clutched at handholds in the rough stonework until his right fingertips eventually touched the corner.

Gregg silently looked up at Mark and nodded, then swiftly he pushed the upper part of his body out from the wall and swung himself around the corner, feeling with his right foot for the continuation of the ledge he was standing on. He had checked from below, before he started, that the ornamental ledge continued round the building.

Gregg was sweating as he put his right foot round the corner. This was partly because of the blazing heat and partly because he knew that, as soon as he turned the corner, he would be within gunshot range of Tony. Dangling from the rope, Gregg felt naked and vulnerable. Firmly he told himself that Tony couldn't see him, and wouldn't see him, because Tony wouldn't risk putting his head out of the window, or the Turkish police would shoot it off.

Then, to his horror, Gregg realized that the continuation of the ledge on the far side of the corner was not the same depth as the ledge upon which he had been standing. It had not been possible to see this, either from below the palace or from the roof.

Gregg kept feeling for the ledge with his right toe, but the ledge was only about an inch wide – too narrow to stand on – and, as soon as Gregg put any weight on it, his foot slipped off.

He tried again, but the ledge crumbled, and again his foot slipped as soon as he put his weight on it.

Gregg turned his sweaty face up to Mark and shook his head. Slowly he began to inch back along the ledge. He was almost directly below Mark when his left handhold, a piece of decorative leadwork, came away from the wall. Gregg stumbled, swayed, then fell off the ledge, dangling on the end of the rope like a spider on the end of a string.

Mark braced his feet against the parapet and took the strain.

Very slowly Gregg swung his legs, searching with his sneakered toes for a foothold on the pitted wall. Eventually one groping toe found the ledge. Gregg leaned out, pulled on the rope, and began to slowly climb to the top of the parapet.

'Shit!' he grunted as he swung himself over and on to the roof.

Mark nodded.

Once again inside that gruesome room, her feet tied more tightly than before, Lili lay on the green-striped mattress, quivering with terror. 'Tony, for God's sake, let's give ourselves up!' she begged. 'Otherwise the police are going to kill us both.'

Sheltering behind the window embrasure, Tony said nothing, but fired a burst of machine-gun fire into the dusk.

Lili closed her eyes and linked her handcuffed fingers in an unconscious gesture of supplication. As she did so she felt – on her centre finger – the coral rosebud of the ring that her mother had given her. It comforted Lili.

'I'm pretty certain that if he lets me in, I can talk him out.' Judy stood in front of Colonel Aziz, a resolute expression on her face. 'He knows me, he trusts me and, when he's in his right mind, he's devoted to me. If anyone can get through to Tony, I can.'

Covered with grey dust, Gregg added, 'There's only one guy in there; I don't see what we have to lose.'

Eventually Colonel Aziz said, 'As you say, it is worth a try. Very well. You will go in with six of my men. You will try to persuade him to open the door. You will stand aside as six of my men throw themselves into the room. If two men take the gunman, two throw themselves to the left, and two to the right, and shoot, we will have the best chance of getting Mademoiselle Lili out alive.'

'No!' Judy spoke quietly and firmly. 'I want to go in and persuade Tony to come out. I know exactly how to do it. If I fail, you can storm the room with smoke bombs, tear gas and bullets. But I won't have such unnecessary risks taken with my daughter's life until I've tried to get Tony to come out peacefully.'

Outside the studded wooden door Judy shouted 'Tony! Thank God I've found you. I'm alone. Please let me in.'

'What do you want?'

'To get you out of this alive. Please let me in.'

There was a long, nerve-racking pause.

'No.'

'Tony, I don't want you to come out, *I* want to come *in*.' Judy pleaded, 'I'm your friend, Tony. This is *Judy* out here.'

'Things ain't goin' as I hoped, Judy.'

'That's why I'm here, Tony, so that together we can work out what to do next.'

Nothing happened.

'You're sure you're alone, Judy?'

'I'm alone.'

Another long pause.

'OK, I'll undo the bolt and cover the door,' shouted Tony. 'Come in, then bolt the door behind you. If there's anyone behind you, I'll shoot.'

They heard the sound of the bolt slowly being pulled back.

Judy gestured frantically, and the men behind her took cover in the doorways.

Judy stepped forwards and pushed the massive door open.

'Bolt the door,' said Tony. 'Gee, I'm glad to see you, Judy.'

'Judy!' gasped Lili, struggling on the green-striped mattress. Judy looked at her with dismay, but fought back her natural inclination to run to her daughter. She ignored Lili and beamed at Tony.

'I've missed you, Tony.' Judy tried to behave as if they were still in the *Verve!* office. 'And I sure could do with a workout. I'm out of shape.'

'Yeah, well . . .'

'May I sit down, Tony?' Judy knew that she should move slowly and deliberately and, at any cost, avoid startling the gunman.

'Sure, go ahead.'

Judy sat on a stained, rose brocade mattress. 'May I eat a peach, Tony?'

'Sure, go ahead.'

From the central, low brass circular table Judy picked up a half-rotten peach, around which a few flies had been hopefully buzzing. She knew that the table was really a brass tray on a plinth, and she considered flinging it at Tony, then leaping to

921

unbolt the door. But not yet. She was supposed to try to get him out peacefully.

Outside there was total silence.

Inside, Tony stood, sub-machine-gun in his hand, with his back to the wall by the window. Lili lay on the green-striped mattress, not moving.

'What was the plan, Tony?' Judy asked.

'I never meant it to get outta hand like this, Judy. I only wanted to help you.'

'You've always been wonderful to me, Tony. But why did you think I needed help?'

'I knew that the magazine was gonna fold. I heard Tom talking to the Lady Mirabelle people. Then, late one night, when I was waiting to take you home, I heard you tell Tom that you wanted someone to kidnap Lili.'

'*What?*'

'It was after Tom had said something about kids giving you more trouble when they was grown up than when they was small.' Tony shifted his weight from one foot to the other. 'Judy, you said you wanted a miracle to happen. You asked Tom to kidnap Lili for a ten-million dollar ransom, then give the money to you. But the putz said he didn't know how to handle a kidnap. You called him a weakling, Judy. You said you couldn't rely on him.'

'But I *can* rely on you, Tony,' beamed Judy as, with horror, she vaguely recalled her joking conversation with Tom. She took another bite of the disgusting peach and leaned back against the pink brocade.

'Yeah, so I thought, I'll do Judy a favour and make a bit for myself as well, then hide out in Europe, change my appearance a bit, that stuff. I never had such a great life in the States until you appeared, Judy, and I knew that if the magazine closed, I'd lose my glamour job. But, like it says in the *Verve!* self-help articles, nobody has to put up with what they think they're stuck with.'

'The clever thing,' said Judy, hoping that she wouldn't retch, 'was those ransom telegrams. They got *front page coverage*, Tony! How did you think of that?'

Tony looked pleased. 'The Greek guy was easy. He wanted to be Lili's sugar daddy. That's what gave me the idea. Originally, that is. I sorta kept this idea hangin' in my mind, then bits got added.'

'Like?'

'Like I hear the pop star yellin' at you on the phone. I think the guy's got no manners, the guy's rich, and the guy seems to think he's Lili's father.'

'Then?'

'Then I'm waitin' for you outside Mr Halifax's office and the door's open a crack . . . I can hear you cryin' . . . well, I guess I opened the door. His secretary's got her own office, so she doesn't sit outside the boss's door. I reckon that's a big mistake. So, anyway, I hear that Mr Halifax has got the same idea as the pop star and I think, little Miss Jordan, she sure kept them guessin', even when she was a kid.'

'But how did you get here, Tony?'

'Simple. I flew to Britain, caught a ferry across the Channel, then got here by train and bus. Don't worry, Judy, I didn't leave a clear trail.'

'Then what did you do?'

'I had a copy of your travel itinerary, the one you left for the office. So I knew where you'd be staying, and I knew you'd have one of the fancy suites, facing the water, so I rented a room on the Asian side of the Bosporus and bought some hardware in the Bazaar. I followed you pretty well as soon as you arrived. I know Lili likes to go around by herself sometimes, so I just waited for a chance. It came sooner than I expected.'

'And what did you plan to do after you'd got the money?'

'My contact at the Bazaar, the guy I'd bought the guns from, put me in touch with a seaman who was going to hire a speedboat. After the man with the red armband got on to the Guzelhisar ferry, I was goin' to wait until the boat was in the middle of the water, then grab the suitcase from him and jump over the side. Then the speedboat was going to pick me up.'

'But wouldn't that have been very risky, Tony?'

'Judy, you know I'm a first-rate swimmer and the whole thing took less than thirty seconds in our trial. You see, the ferry can't stop suddenly. I knew there would be police on board, but they probably wouldn't be able to shoot straight, not from a moving boat on choppy water, at a speedboat on an erratic course.'

Judy thought with horror, I wonder if he realizes that kidnapping is a crime punishable by death in some American states. Gently she asked, 'And then what were you going to do?'

'I was going to send another bunch of roses to tell you where to find Lili.'

'Such a *clever idea*, Tony.'

'Yeah, then I was going to fly to Egypt, meet you there, and give you half the cash.' He frowned. 'Maybe *lend* you half the cash. Until your business was straightened out.' Suddenly he raised his machine-gun as something outside the window distracted his attention.

But it was only a bird.

Neither Judy nor Lili moved. They were both terrified. Suddenly Tony relaxed and grinned. 'I also reckoned you musta bin quite a goer, when you was a girl, Miss Jordan.'

Judy gave a tight smile as Tony continued. 'Then the fourth telegram I sent to your friend, the King, after I heard you and Maxine talkin' on your way up to Westchester last fall. She said she guessed . . .'

Judy looked astonished when Tony mentioned the fourth telegram, then she quickly interrupted him, 'Maxine was right, Tony, and so were you, to send those telegrams to men with plenty of money. But what we have to do now is figure out how to get out of here.'

'Yeah. I could do with a few ideas on that subject. Like I said, it ain't worked out as I intended.'

'How to get out of here *fast*, Tony. I've got a limo outside with smoked-glass windows. If we can make it into that, we've got a chance.'

'What about *her*?' Tony jerked his head to Lili, who was lying gagged and handcuffed on the green-striped mattress.

'What matters is *you* and *me*, Tony. All they want is her, so they can have her,' said Judy in a firm, reasonable voice. 'But you and I have to get to the limo.'

'How about we distract their attention by droppin' Lili outta the window?'

Judy's stomach turned over. She'd hoped to get Tony out and leave Lili in the room. 'Better if we use her as a hostage. Take her with us.'

Tony looked at her with an unnerving, cunning expression. 'How do I know there ain't an ambush out there?'

Judy swallowed hard. Dammit, she'd gone too far too fast, as usual. In a quiet, soothing voice, she reassured him. 'I'll walk in front and you follow, with the gun.' In a reasonable voice, she added, 'I'll hardly be likely to put myself right in the line of fire, would I? Anyway, the police don't know I'm in here.'

'You were in here before. With that guy.'

'Well, then you know I wasn't with the police. And I've shaken off Mark. You know, I haven't wanted anything to do with him for months, after I caught him in bed with *her*!' She threw a contemptuous glance at Lili.

Tony thought about this for a few moments, then grunted in agreement.

'So how do you want this played, Tony?'

Tony thought again. 'Untie her legs.'

Judy slowly got up, walked over to the green-striped mattress and, without looking at Lili, she untied the nylon rope around her ankles, then helped Lili stand up.

Lili felt painful pins and needles in her legs, because the rope had been tight around her ankles. She looked at the floor, avoiding eye contact with Tony.

'Now what, Tony?' Judy asked, then realized that she had made another mistake, as Tony looked harassed. He had no idea what to do.

Judy said, 'Would you like me to unbolt the door? Then you can follow me, with the gun, and that trouble-making little bitch can walk behind you until we're safe. Then we can dump her.'

Tony moved away from the window to the wall behind the door. 'OK, Judy, open it.'

Slowly Judy opened the door and walked out. As she appeared Colonel Aziz's marksmen drew back into the shadowed doorways of the courtyard, out of sight. They couldn't jump Tony because he had his gun in Judy's back. If anyone shot Tony, Tony would probably shoot Judy as he died.

Judy stumbled along the corridor. Although fully dressed, she felt so naked and exposed, totally vulnerable as they moved into the courtyard. Tony walked behind her. His right hand held his

SMG trained on her back and, with his left hand, he dragged Lili by her handcuffs.

They reached the courtyard beyond the room. Judy thought fast. She screamed, 'My God, Tony, the police are on the roof!'

Tony looked up.

Judy threw herself to the ground, covering her face with her arms. Lili twisted herself from Tony's grasp and flung herself to the ground. Tony was momentarily thrown off balance, and staggered.

There was a burst of gunfire, bullets ricocheted around the small stone-enclosed space and then there was silence.

Judy uncovered her head and slowly looked up. First, she saw a pair of large, cheap black boots that belonged to a police gunman. Beyond them she saw a rivulet of blood trickling into the centre of the courtyard.

Tony lay dead on the stained stone flags in front of her. Suddenly the courtyard was full of activity.

Judy picked herself up and ran to Lili. 'Are you all right? Are you hurt?'

Lili shook her head. Crying, Judy beckoned to a policeman, who produced a knife and cut off Lili's gag.

'Where are the keys to your handcuffs?'

'In Tony's shirt pocket.'

Judy ran to the slumped figure of Tony and, with shaking hands, felt in his shirt pocket. She returned to Lili with the key, but her hands were shaking too severely to unlock the handcuffs. Colonel Aziz stepped forward, took the key from Judy and unlocked the handcuffs.

As soon as Lili's hands were free, she flung her arms around Judy. 'You did come for me,' Lili said as she fought back tears of relief and happiness. 'My real mother did come for me, in the end.'